# ANNA LETITIA BARBAULD

# ANNA LETITIA BARBAULD

## SELECTED POETRY AND PROSE

*edited by*

*William McCarthy & Elizabeth Kraft*

broadview literary texts

**Canadian Cataloguing in Publication Data**

Barbauld, Mrs. (Anna Letitia), 1743-1825
    Anna Letitia Barbauld: selected poetry and prose

(Broadview literary texts)
Includes bibliographical references.
ISBN 1-55111-241-8

I. McCarthy, William, 1942- .     II. Kraft, Elizabeth.     III. Title.
IV. Series.

PR4057.B7A6 2001    821'.6    C00-932553-0

Broadview Press Ltd. is an independent, international publishing house, incorporated in 1985.

North America:
P.O. Box 1243, Peterborough, Ontario, Canada K9J 7H5
3576 California Road, Orchard Park, NY 14127
TEL: (705) 743-8990; FAX: (705) 743-8353;
E-MAIL: customerservice@broadviewpress.com

United Kingdom:
Thomas Lyster Ltd.
Unit 9, Ormskirk Industrial Park
Old Boundary Way, Burscough Road
Ormskirk, Lancashire L39 2YW
TEL: (01695) 575112; FAX: (01695) 570120; E-mail: books@tlyster.co.uk

Australia:
St. Clair Press, P.O. Box 287, Rozelle, NSW 2039
TEL: (02) 818-1942; FAX: (02) 418-1923

www.broadviewpress.com

Broadview Press gratefully acknowledges the financial support of the Book Publishing Industry Development Program, Ministry of Canadian Heritage, Government of Canada.

Broadview Press is grateful to Professor Eugene Benson for advice on editorial matters for the Broadview Literary Texts series.

Text design and composition by George Kirkpatrick

PRINTED IN CANADA

# Contents

# Acknowledgments

We are grateful to the holders of manuscripts for permission to quote or cite them: D. H. Weinglass and M. Carbonell; the Bodleian Library, Oxford University; the British Library; the Archives and Special Collections Department, Waidner-Spahr Library, Dickinson College, Carlisle, PA; the Director and Trustees of Dr. Williams's Library, London; the Hornel Library, The National Trust for Scotland; the Hyde Collection, Somerville, NJ; the Liverpool Record Office, Liverpool Libraries and Information Services; the Council of Trustees, National Library of Ireland; the City Librarian, Sheffield, England; the Suffolk Record Office, Ipswich, England; University College London, Library. For permission to reprint poems previously published in our edition of *The Poems of Anna Letitia Barbauld* (© 1994 by The University of Georgia Press), we thank the University of Georgia Press.

We are grateful also to the many archivists and librarians whose generous help, over the years, made the research embodied in this volume pleasant as well as fruitful. Most of them were named in the Acknowledgments to our edition of Barbauld's poems. Since then we have also incurred debts to Andrea Immel, Curator of the Cotsen Collection of Children's Books at Princeton University, and Sandra Stelts, of the Pattee Library, Pennsylvania State University.

For material support, McCarthy thanks the National Endowment for the Humanities, the American Philosophical Society, and Iowa State University.

For information, assistance, and advice of various sorts we are grateful to Francis Assaf, Julie Barfield, John Bloomberg-Rissman, Mark Boren, Martine Watson Brownley, Doug Canfield, Jeanine Casler, Brian Corman, Christy Desmet, Charles Doyle, Simon Gatrell, Elissa Henken, Nelson Hilton, Paul Hunter, Ann Kelly, Thomas Keymer, Kasee Laster, William Provost, Hugh Ruppersburg, Judith Shaw, Greg Timmons, Lisa Vargo, Anne Williams, A. J. Wright, and David Zuck. Four people to whom we are most especially indebted for their longstanding interest in our work are Paula Feldman, Mitzi Myers, Dr. P. O'Brien, and the late Conant Brodribb; our heartfelt thanks to them all.

McCarthy dedicates his portions of this volume—once again—to his dearest friend and colleague, Rosanne Potter.

# Introduction

If we could travel back to the year 1800 and ask who were the leading British writers of the day, the answer would not be William Wordsworth or Samuel Taylor Coleridge or William Blake. The answer instead would include, on anybody's short list, Anna Letitia Barbauld. Her début book, *Poems* (1773), had been greeted as an important event in the world of letters. "We congratulate the public on so great an accession to the literary world, as the genius and talents of Miss Aikin," wrote the *Monthly Review*. "We very seldom have an opportunity of bestowing praise with so much justice, and so much pleasure" ([Woodfall], p. 137). Mary Scott and David Garrick paid her tributes in verse; Elizabeth Montagu, "Queen of the Bluestockings," sought her acquaintance; and younger women, such as the future poet Mary Robinson, read her enthusiastically. The young Coleridge walked forty miles in order to meet Barbauld; the young Wordsworth imitated her in his early poems. In 1798 *The Lady's Monthly Museum* asserted Barbauld's poetic pre-eminence without reserve: her poems "are now in the possession of every person who has any pretensions to taste, and every library in the kingdom; and public suffrage has amply ratified their claim to distinction" (p. 173).

As a poet, Barbauld can claim to be considered a founder of British Romanticism. She was no less important—and, if anything, she exerted still greater influence—as an innovating writer for children. This part of her work originated in experimental teaching at the school she and her husband ran at Palgrave, in Suffolk, from 1774 to 1785. Her *Lessons for Children* and *Hymns in Prose for Children* profoundly affected infant pedagogy and the culture of childhood for a full century at least, both in England and the United States. *Lessons*, a reading primer, directly influenced the theories and practices of Maria Edgeworth and her father, and its impact on nineteenth-century readers is suggested by the fact that the poet Elizabeth Barrett Browning remembered *Lessons* so well that she could still quote its opening page at the age of thirty-nine (McCarthy,

"Mother of All Discourses," p. 196). Our headnote to *Hymns in Prose* attempts to sketch the even greater impact of *Hymns* on its readers. *Lessons* and *Hymns* were reprinted often during the nineteenth century.

Barbauld was also an admired essayist, regarded by her contemporaries as superior to Joseph Addison and nearly the equal of Samuel Johnson. In her essays she addressed leading issues of her time—ethics, esthetics, education, even political economy—on equal terms with writers such as David Hume and Edmund Burke. Both in verse and prose, she dared to engage in political debate, urging major concerns of her social group, middle-class Protestant Dissent. She stirred and shocked her contemporaries by her intense polemics in favor of religious liberty (*An Address to the Opposers of the Repeal of the Corporation and Test Acts*) and against the British government's entry into war with the French Republic (*Sins of Government, Sins of the Nation*). She vigorously condemned British participation in the international slave trade (*An Epistle to William Wilberforce*), and her last publication, the poem *Eighteen Hundred and Eleven*, incurred obloquy and political defamation for protesting against the apparently unending and catastrophic war with France.

As if these achievements were not enough, Barbauld also performed with distinction as a literary critic. She wrote the first biography of the novelist Samuel Richardson and edited the first collection of his letters; she produced a major body of commentary on the English novel and, like Samuel Johnson before her, lent her name and pen to a large-scale canon-making enterprise, *The British Novelists*, twenty-eight novelists gathered in fifty volumes.

Taken altogether, Barbauld's career can be described as that of a typical "person of letters"; she belongs to the first generation of professional women writers in England whose work was received with unqualified admiration. *The Lady's Monthly Museum* was one of many witnesses to Barbauld's leading rank among her peers: "This lady has been recognised for many years by the public ... as one of its best benefactors, for contributing ... very liberally both to instruct and reform the community. And we fondly trust, she will yet long continue to delight and cultivate the national taste, in the direction and improvement of which her labours have already been so singularly useful" (p. 170).

But Barbauld can also be characterized, in the phrase coined by Antonio Gramsci, as an "organic intellectual," an intellectual who articulates the issues of her own social class at a time when that class is asserting its claims to power and respect. Barbauld's class was the middle class, and she became an outstanding spokeswoman for it at its insurgent, liberal best. In what she liked to call the "middle station of life," she saw opportunities to create better, happier, and freer human beings than existing society allowed. To create a new kind of human being was the main conscious project of the Enlightenment; Jean-Jacques Rousseau's Émile, brought up to be ignorant of everything he has not personally experienced and to dismiss with contempt the "prejudices" of society, is the classic, but also the most extreme, product of that ambition. Barbauld, less ostentatious than Rousseau, and with a much more grounded sense of what can actually be done, never proclaimed herself an innovator. Nonetheless, as the Victorian feminist Clara Balfour perceived, Barbauld in her quiet way undertook nothing less than the re-education of her society (*Working Women*, p. 6).

**Dissent**

Of defining importance for Barbauld's outlook and project was the fact that she was the daughter and grand-daughter of Presbyterian schoolmasters. Doctrinally, Presbyterianism originated as a Scottish version of Calvinism. As formulated in the Westminster Confession (1647), its creed declared the total sinfulness of human nature and the consequent impossibility of good thoughts or deeds without direct intervention by God. Human beings having, in Adam's disobedience, sinned against God, they deserved nothing but divine wrath and punishment; only free grace (not earned—earning it would be impossible—but given by God for His mysterious purposes) could save humans from damnation. It was believed that rather few would be saved, and they only by throwing themselves on the mercy of Jesus Christ (Mautner, "Introduction," p. 10).

During the eighteenth century many Presbyterians receded from these doctrines ("gloomy" doctrines, as the receders were apt to call them). Under the guidance of the Scottish ethical philosopher Francis Hutcheson (1694-1746), two or three generations of recovering Calvinists—among whom were Barbauld's parents and grandparents—learned to regard human beings as the fundamentally good creatures of a beneficent Creator, and to believe that humans could achieve salvation by loving God and (in practice, much the same thing) acting benevolently towards their fellow beings. Barbauld built this revised, optimistic faith into *Hymns in Prose for Children*, making it the first influential religious primer for children that offered a kindly and loving religion. In 1792 she summed up this benevolent faith in the eloquent closing pages of a pamphlet, *Remarks on Mr. Gilbert Wakefield's Enquiry into the Expediency and Propriety of Public or Social Worship*:

> When a good man ... is about to resign his soul into the hands of his Maker, he ought to do it, not only with a reliance on his mercy, but his justice; a generous confidence and pious resignation should be blended in his deportment. It does not become him to pay the blasphemous homage of deprecating the wrath of God, when he ought to throw himself into the arms of his love.... The age which has demolished dungeons, rejected torture, and given so fair a prospect of abolishing the iniquity of the slave trade, cannot long retain among its articles of belief the gloomy perplexities of Calvinism, and the heart-withering perspective of cruel and never-ending punishments. (pp. 71-72, 75-76)

In the face of advancing Methodism, with its re-emphasis on Original Sin and human worthlessness, these sentiments were not just retrospective; they were again timely.[1] Doctrinally, Barbauld became—and remains today—an inspiring voice in behalf of the ideal of human self-respect.

Barbauld's co-religionists also adopted various opinions regarding the composition of the deity; instead of the orthodox Trinity (Father, Son—Jesus Christ—and Holy Ghost), they were inclined to regard God as a single being and Jesus as a created figure, perhaps divine or perhaps only an inspired human. There is little evidence that this particular issue mattered much to Barbauld; she wrote that "unity of *character* in what we adore, is much more essential than unity of person" (*Remarks*, pp. 70–71; our italics). She cared more about what she almost called God's personality than about the number of aspects to attribute to him. One of the leading arguments in her 1775 essay "on the Devotional Taste" is that theological disputation about the nature of God chills religious emotion and withers the believer's sense of relation to God as to a person. Although by no means anti-intellectual (she despised the "noise and nonsense" of popular evangelicalism), Barbauld had more than sufficient exposure to theological discussion during the years when her father was tutor in Divinity at Warrington Academy, and she wanted a large counterbalance of devotional feeling and imagination.

Socially, the consequences of being Presbyterian depended on where in Britain one lived. Barbauld's Aikin ancestors, as long as they lived in Scotland, were members of the established (i.e. legally supported) Presbyterian Kirk. As soon as her grandfather emigrated to England, however, his Presbyterianism condemned him to minority status as a second-class citizen, a Dissenter from the Church of England. There was a long tradition, fading but not dead—and galvanized into disturbing life in the 1790s—of regarding Dissenters collectively as threats to the state because some of their sectarian ancestors in the mid-seventeenth century had led a revolution against Church and

---

1 For the creed of the Methodist Countess of Huntingdon's "Connection" and a Methodist death-bed scene rather different from the scene Barbauld imagines, see *The Life and Times of Selina Countess of Huntingdon* (London, 1839), 2:440–43, 499.

King. Hence, laws restricting their liberties and acting to their prejudice remained on the books. Dissenters could not serve in the military, accept an appointive office under the Crown, or hold elective municipal office unless they "conformed" to the Church of England by taking the sacrament there. They could not take degrees at Oxford or Cambridge without "subscribing" to—that is, swearing that they believed—the creed of the English Church, embodied in its Thirty-Nine Articles. They were obliged to pay tithes to support the Established Church even though they did not attend it. If they took positions as schoolmasters they were obliged (until 1779) to subscribe to parts of the Thirty-Nine Articles. Their churches—or chapels, as they were called—received no regular public support (unlike the Church of England, which owned a great deal of property and was publicly funded as well); Dissenting clergy had to live on the salaries voted them by their congregations. Many became schoolteachers in order to eke out their incomes.

The line of work most open to Dissenters was commerce; "we are a mercantile people," Barbauld remarked accurately in *An Address to the Opposers* (p. 270 below). Whether they were shopkeepers, brewers, bankers, rich factory-owners or merchants who could afford to buy country houses, Dissenters regarded themselves as middle-class. They liked to think of the "middle station" (as the philosopher David Hume called it [*Selected Essays*, p. 6]) as especially favorable to virtue, both personal and political. Like other groups experienced in political subjection, they were sensitive to questions of political equity and personal rights. Joseph Priestley stated the connection succinctly in a 1774 *Address to Protestant Dissenters of all Denominations*: "*Religious liberty*, indeed, is the immediate ground on which you stand, but this cannot be maintained except upon the basis of *civil liberty*" (p. [3]). Thus, while the first demand of nearly all English Dissenters was an end to the laws that discriminated against them, many also sympathized with the American colonists in their complaints about being taxed without being represented in Parliament; most supported domestic efforts to reform Parliamentary representation by redistricting Britain; most supported abolition of the slave trade, and many became enthusiasts for the French Revolution and agitated against war with France. Political liberalism could be an act of Hutchesonian benevolence, too; one Dissenter in 1795 traced his partiality to the French Revolution directly back to his experience of hearing Francis Hutcheson's weekly lectures on Christianity. Hutcheson, he recalled, taught that Christianity was "the religion of Truth & Reason: wch can have no other enemies, but the irrational & the wicked. From this the transition to me seems natural & easy to the enlarged principles on wch the French Revolution was first founded" (Kenrick, Letter). Anna Barbauld's political liberalism was that of her group. Her expressions of it, in *An Address to the Opposers of the Repeal of the Corporation and Test Acts* and *Sins of Government, Sins of the Nation*, were hers alone, matched in eloquence perhaps only by the very different writings of Tom Paine.

## Education

Barbauld grew up surrounded by the boys at her father's school at Kibworth. At three and a half she acquired a brother, John, over whom she early attained to lifelong influence, and who encouraged her invaluably in her literary career. Her youthful surroundings accustomed her to dealing with boys; when she and Rochemont Barbauld opened Palgrave School in 1774, she must have felt quite at home.

Educating boys was attractive not only because it was familiar. It offered scope for Barbauld's "large ambitious wish" (to quote a phrase she used in writing of the Corsican patriot, Pascal Paoli ["Corsica," l. 124]) to intervene in the making of her nation's political and ethical culture. She and her husband regarded education as a patriotic act, and an act of benevolence: "the true patriot," Rochemont wrote, "... will gladly undertake a task whereby he may so essentially contribute to the welfare of his country." At the same time, "a prominent feature of his character is love towards the rising generation."[1] In a

---

1   Quoted in McCarthy, "Celebrated Academy," p. 295. A fine exposition of Barbauld's project for mediated intervention in her culture is Sarah Robbins, "'Women's Studies' Debates in Eighteenth-Century England: Mrs. Barbauld's Program for Feminine Learning and Maternal Pedagogy," *Michigan Feminist Studies*, 7 (1992-93):53-81.

patriarchy like eighteenth-century England, the best way to form (or reform) the culture would be to form the citizen, who by definition was male. At Palgrave School, Barbauld set herself to disseminating the culture of benevolence by forming boys into liberal citizens.

One way to describe Barbauld's project is to put it in terms of a text she almost certainly knew well, Francis Hutcheson's outline of "Our Duties toward Mankind" in his *Short Introduction to Moral Philosophy* (1747).[1] Hutcheson's starting-point, the epicenter of human relationships, is the nuclear family. From there, "benevolent affections" spread outward in an ever-widening circle of concern: to all who "are ... bound by an intercourse of mutual offices," to "acquaintance and neighbours," to "all our Countrymen"; and further, "in men of reflection there is a more extensive good-will embracing all mankind, or all intelligent natures" (*Short Introduction*, p. 67). Barbauld illustrates Hutcheson's widening circle in Hymn VIII of *Hymns in Prose*, where she begins with a family of father, mother, and children, moves thence to their neighbors, then to the village in which they live, then to the kingdom, then to the world itself, and a vision of inclusiveness which we today would call "multi-cultural": "All are God's family ... they pray to him in different languages, but he understandeth them all; he heareth them all; he taketh care of all." The next wave in Hutcheson's expanding circle is "a tender compassion toward any that are in distress, with a desire of succouring them" (p. 67); and in Hymn VIII there follows the address to the enslaved African, "Negro woman, who sittest pining in captivity ...."

Barbauld's two children's books, *Lessons for Children* and *Hymns in Prose for Children*, between them track Hutcheson's circle on a larger scale. The opening scene of *Lessons* presents Mother with her two-year-old son on her lap; she is about to induct him into the world of things and the symbols by which humans relate themselves to things and to other creatures. *Lessons* itself, through its four little volumes, performs that induction, leading the child to ever-widening horizons (infor-

---

1   She mentions "Hutcheson's Ethics" approvingly in *Remarks on ... Social Worship*, p. 70.

national and ethical horizons, and even geographical ones). Then *Hymns in Prose* leads the child reader, a bit older now, to the horizon of the divine. The mediator between child and world in *Lessons* is always Mother; in *Hymns* the mediator is not specifically identified, but the child who had just finished *Lessons* would probably assume the continuity of Mother into *Hymns*. Thus the two books themselves move outward, staging the family (in which, textually, Mother presides) as the place from which the world, and even the universe, is conceptually grasped.

It is even possible to conceive Barbauld's writing career itself in terms of Hutcheson's circle. She begins by constructing a self, an identity or range of possible identities which will embody a disposition capable of diffusing benevolent affection to friends and neighbors—and, not least, to herself. Her early poems may be seen as experiments in the making of such an identity—whether it be the carefree hedonist of "The Invitation," the chastened stoic of "Hymn to Content," or the severely powerful goddess Liberty in "Corsica." Publishing these explorations of potential selves, Barbauld incidentally became a model to her women readers, who, in the words of one of them, "feel thy feelings, glow with all thy fires, / Adopt thy thoughts, and pant with thy desires."[1]

Barbauld needed an identity which would be socially allowed to a woman and therefore realizable in action, but which would also make the most of what was socially allowed to woman: an identity which could be not merely realized, but made a stage from which to intervene in her culture. She could not be a doctor like her brother, but she could achieve comparable—indeed, greater—authority in a role to which women were increasingly being summoned: the role of Mother.[2] For Barbauld, motherhood was not a biological role (she never gave

---

1 Mary Scott, *The Female Advocate* (1774), quoted in McCarthy, "'We Hoped the *Woman* Was Going to Appear,'" p. 114. McCarthy surveys the range of female identities explored by Barbauld in her early poems.

2 For a detailed, if somewhat negative, reading of roles associated with motherhood in eighteenth-century literature, see Toni Bowers, *The Politics of Motherhood: British Writing and Culture, 1680-1760* (Cambridge: Cambridge University Press, 1996). On Barbauld's interest in medicine, see below.

birth) but a social one: at Palgrave School she was surrogate mother to some 130 boys besides her adopted son (and actual nephew) Charles. In *Lessons* and *Hymns*, "Mrs. Barbauld" became surrogate mother to thousands of English, American, and even (via translations) European children for a full century.

From Mother through Teacher lay the road to Reformer. Barbauld's first abolitionist statement was the address to "Negro woman" in Hymn VIII of *Hymns in Prose*. When, after a nine-year hiatus, she reappeared in 1790 as a political writer (to the delight of her co-religionists and the dismay of Establishment people who had accepted her as a poet), Barbauld was simply diffusing her benevolence to, as it were, the next circle out. Her great pamphlets of the 1790s and her two great poems, *An Epistle to William Wilberforce* and *Eighteen Hundred and Eleven*, extend the horizon of Mother's concern to the ends—and the end—of the British Empire.

In the latter poem, Mother might be said to appear as Niobe weeping over her dead children. For, indeed, in some important respects Barbauld's project came to a tragic end. The pupils at her school, who were to be the "rising generation" of a politically reformed nation, were mostly kept out of power by a government which, by 1792, had dug in its heels against reform of any kind and, in 1793, entered upon a twenty-year-long world war against France, the war which *Eighteen Hundred and Eleven* deplores. The liberal values espoused by Barbauld and her group increasingly became suspect; she found herself disliked and even ridiculed by the younger generation whom we now know as "the Romantic Poets." One member of that generation, John Wilson Croker, has often been credited—if that is the right word—with single-handedly ending her literary career; so abusive was his review of *Eighteen Hundred and Eleven* that it is said to have discouraged her from further efforts to publish.

In the longer run, however, liberal reform did achieve at least some success. The laws against Dissenters were repealed at last in 1828 and 1829. In 1807 Parliament consented to make illegal British participation in the slave trade; in 1834 it emancipated the slaves in the British colonies. Sadly, Barbauld did not live to see most of these achievements. But it is fitting, and she would have rejoiced to know, that the man who drafted the Reform Act of 1832—the act which, after fifty years' agitation for it, redistricted Great Britain to more truly represent the electorate in Parliament—was a man who, when a child, had been her pupil at Palgrave School, and who still, as an adult, remembered her maternal teaching with respect and affection.[1]

### "Ingenuous"

The leading project conceived and attempted by the Enlightenment was nothing less than the reinvention of the human being. Hence, from John Locke through Jean-Jacques Rousseau and Maria Edgeworth (and a host of lesser figures), theorizing education stands among the foremost intellectual efforts of the century. Although, as we have remarked, Barbauld was more modest and much less rash than Rousseau, like him she envisions a human being uncorrupted by various social malpractices. Her favorite adjective to describe that person is "ingenuous."

Synonyms for "ingenuous" in Barbauld's sense of the word are "unadulterated," "fresh," "authentic." She seeks, both in herself and in others, to cultivate the disposition (which she assumes exists) to respond "naturally" to experience. The "natural" response is the response that has not been dulled by repetition, smothered by false cleverness, tutored into mere intellectuality, or perverted by self-interest. The ingenuous person responds to experience directly, without equivocation, evasion, self-doubt, or self-consciousness. The emotion is appropriate to the event and is uncluttered by second-guessing. And—in line with Hutchesonian ideas of human goodness—it is a generous, outgoing, sympathetic emotion. If an emotion of joy, it wants to communicate itself to other people, to be shared: "joy," she writes in *Remarks on … Social Worship*, "is too brilliant a thing to be confined within our own bosoms" (p. 19). If it is an emotion of sorrow, it wants at once to relieve the suffering to which

---

1 The man was Thomas Denman; see her poem, "Lines to be spoken by Thomas Denman," below, and its headnote.

it responds; it takes the form of Pity, which in Barbauld's allego-
ry (pp. 207-09 below) is represented as the offspring of Sorrow
and Love.

Ingenuousness is easily spoiled, however, by social practices
which tend to produce shame. In "Thoughts on the Devotion-
al Taste," Barbauld invites us to "observe an ingenuous youth at
a well-wrought tragedy. If all around him are moved, he suffers
his tears to flow freely; but if a single eye meets him with a
glance of contemptuous indifference, he can no longer enjoy
his sorrow, he blushes at having wept, and in a moment his
heart is shut up to every impression of tenderness" (p. 219
below). Barbauld, we may gather from this telling passage, was
deeply sensitive to ridicule (no doubt because she was very
good at ridicule herself) and understood its power to shrivel
authentic emotion.

Ingenuousness is equally vulnerable to being deadened by
habit. A close student of associationist psychology, Barbauld
understood that habit has a contradictory character: on one
hand, it builds lifelong patterns of response (and that is what she
aims to do in *Hymns in Prose*), but on the other, it tends to
enervate response by making stimuli overfamiliar. Thus she says
to her co-religionists that devotional feeling is vitiated by their
habit of theological discussion, which renders the terminology
of religion so commonplace that religion loses its emotional
force. Among her many reasons for hating war is the effect of
war on human sensibility: it hardens human beings by inuring
them to atrocities. Emotions themselves can be exhausted by
repetition, especially if they have no outlet in action. Hence
Barbauld's cool remarks about fictions which inspire pity; read-
ers wear out their capacity for pity on imaginary figures instead
of actively helping real-life unfortunates. (She was of course a
great reader of novels herself, these views notwithstanding; and
in 1810, introducing *The British Novelists*, she asserted with a
challenging straightforwardness that she read them for pleasure.
In 1810, owning up to *enjoying* novels—instead of pretending to
read them for moral lessons—could also be an act of ingenu-
ousness.)

Ingenuousness, as this example may suggest, is not a matter *purely* of emotion; to have social impact, it must inform the moral and intellectual person also. An honest heart sheds tears at the horrific narratives of slave-trading presented in Parliament by William Wilberforce and his allies (*Epistle to William Wilberforce*, l. 31); had there been more such hearts in Parliament, Barbauld implies, the British slave trade would have been ended in 1791. In its intellectual aspect, ingenuousness is simply intellectual honesty. Barbauld appeals to the ingenuousness (in this sense) of her Church-of-England readers when she tells them that unless they can accept the Thirty-Nine Articles in their *purest and simplest sense*, unsophisticated by clever interpretations designed to accommodate heterodox beliefs, they are deluding themselves about their allegiance (*Address to the Opposers*, p. 275 below). The intellectual and ethical aspects of ingenuousness coalesce in what Barbauld calls "the delicacy of conscience" (*Sins of Government*, p. 306 below) or, much the same thing, "the genuine, unperverted moral sense of mankind" (*Remarks on ... Social Worship*, p. 73). A delicate (innocent, unequivocating—in short, *honest*) conscience is hurt by laws which require swearing solemn oaths on trivial occasions. An honest conscience cannot reconcile trafficking in human beings with claiming to be a Christian nation—or, indeed, implore the assistance of God in an effort to slaughter one's fellow humans. When invited to participate in such acts of ethical incoherence, an honest conscience responds, appropriately, with indignation.

In her writing Barbauld aims, among other things, to *model* the "natural" response to a stimulus. In her poetry, this will be better perceived if the poem is read aloud with attention to what she would have called "just" intonation: doing that, one finds oneself speaking "appropriately" in tones of affection, prayer, grief, or whatever. She grounds the "natural" response to stimuli in our physical makeup (the devotional taste, for example, is seated in the passions and "is in a great degree constitutional" [p. 211 ]); thus the physical action of uttering her poems puts us in touch with the "natural" responses which they encode. The greatest moments, perhaps, in Barbauld's political tracts are moments in which her rhetoric models for the reader the sound—indeed, the very rhythm—of moral indignation. To read such passages is to experience what moral indignation feels like, and to receive in that experience a lesson in political morality. In her writing Barbauld is thus always a teacher, always urging or modelling the appropriate response to events.

She was not just a "feeler," however. On the contrary, she values Enlightenment reason equally with feeling. (Contemporaries perceived this when they credited Barbauld, in gendered terms, with a "masculine" head and a "feminine" heart.[1]) In her early essays Barbauld uses reason to peel away false, confused responses to stimuli; to achieve clarity of understanding, which (she assumes) leads at once to honesty of feeling and thence to honesty of action. She hates false feeling and irrational displays of feeling (such as the "noise and nonsense" of evangelical religious meetings) and resents efforts to jerk her chain. The term to which she appeals here is "taste"; "taste" functions for her as the mediator between the reason which clarifies and the honest response which results from clarity. The fact that she values both reason and feeling equally will help to explain what might otherwise seem like a tendency in her writing to turn up on both sides of every issue: she is often trying to redress some imbalance between reason and feeling.

## Gender

When Barbauld's contemporaries praised her "masculine" head and "feminine" heart, they were acknowledging, in the only terms they seem to have had available, that her writings appeared to them to transcend—or better, to unite—qualities

---

1    Thus the anonymous author of *Jack and Martin: a Poetical Dialogue, on the Proposed Repeal of the Test-Act* (Hereford, 1790) credits Barbauld with "female Softness,— manly Sense" (p. 12). In 1826 the *Monthly Review* appreciated her "masculine understanding" and "truly feminine heart" (3rd series, 1:73). Henry Holland (1788-1873), who met Barbauld in his youth, admired her "masculine understanding and gentle feminine character" (Holland, *Recollections of Past Life* [London, 1872], p. 12).

which they were accustomed to assigning exclusively to one or
the other sex. They were saying that, contrary to custom, the
fact of her being a woman did not seem to bear upon her per-
formance as a writer—that her writings manifested, rather,
something like a completed humanity.

The situation is really more complicated than that, both for
her in her life and for us in our reading of her. Barbauld was
brought up by a mother with very strict notions of gender pro-
priety, and she chafed under the restraints imposed by her gen-
der: being "feminine" was always difficult for her, at every level
from the etiquette of body movement up to exclusion from the
male professions.[1] (Her poem "To Dr. Aikin on his Complain-
ing that she neglected him" evinces serious interest in medi-
cine, and medical metaphors are rather common in her writ-
ing; perhaps she would have liked to be a doctor.) Reading her
today, it is easy to see gender issues in her texts—especially her
early poems, in which, as we have remarked, she explores or
"tries on" a variety of possible female roles. Then too, modern
readers of Barbauld have always had to deal with Mary Woll-
stonecraft's accusation, apropos Barbauld's poem "To a Lady,
with some painted Flowers," that she denigrated women by
speaking of them in "the language of men"; and with Bar-
bauld's reply to Wollstonecraft, "The Rights of Woman," which
has usually been taken—erroneously, we think—as a repudia-
tion of Wollstonecraft's ideal of sexual equality.

That said, there is nevertheless value in trying to understand
Barbauld as a "trans-gendered" writer. In her own life, she had
no particular investment in being socially female; indeed, her
essay on "Fashion" displays a deep aversion to some aspects of
that social condition—to the encumbrances of late-eighteenth-
century female dress, and to the rituals by which active and
agile girls are transformed into constricted, "marriageable"
young ladies. Her early achievement of a lifelong authority
over her brother gave her mediated access to the public sphere
and confidence in managing younger men and boys, and thus,
as we have seen, opportunity to intervene in public culture.

---

1   On Barbauld's discomfort with her social femininity, see the letter published by
    Lucy Aikin in 1825 ("Memoir," pp. xvii–xxiv); on Barbauld's strict upbringing, see
    LeBreton, *Memoir*, pp. 24–25.

Important as the social role of Mother was to her educational project, it was not her sole writing guise: when she intervened directly in politics, she did so as an apparently ungendered "Dissenter" and "Volunteer." In her capacity as a middle-class spokesperson she behaves simply as a "citizen" in the 1790s Revolutionary sense, and her contemporaries do not always perceive her as female. (One of them, William Keate, was horrified to learn that the *Address to the Opposers* was the work of a "female pen" [p. 262 below].)

Barbauld even found some advantage in women's exclusion from the technical knowledge necessary to the male professions. She had seen enough of the male display of technical learning in theology discussions at Warrington Academy to perceive how professional knowledge can deaden sensibility. Women, she believed—and in this she was Victorian ahead of her time—surpassed men in the capacity to feel, and in sensitivity to imaginative constructs like literature. They did so in part from "nature," but also for the very reason that they were "excused from all professional knowledge" ("On Female Studies," p. 475 below) and thus preserved from the narrowing influence of specialization. As amateurs in literature and science, women would be better humanists than men.

To be sure, in her letters "On Female Studies" Barbauld works both sides of this street, asserting both that women have no profession and that their profession is motherhood and the management of the family. Since Barbauld herself was never a biological mother, and was by profession a writer, she has been accused by some latter-day feminists of imposing on other women a standard to which she did not hold herself.[1] But on this issue she is actually much closer to Wollstonecraft than has commonly been believed. (Wollstonecraft has sometimes been used, unjustly, as a stick to beat Barbauld with.) Both conceived of motherhood as a civic, or citizenly, role; as the role, par excellence, from which society would be reformed. Motherhood was a profession, but it also trumped all the mere professions because it was responsible for the fashioning not of doc-

---

1   See, for example, Marilyn Williamson, "Who's Afraid of Mrs. Barbauld? The Blue Stockings and Feminism," *International Journal of Women's Studies* 3 (1980):89-102.

tors or theologians or politicians but of entire human beings. Motherhood was the matrix of any future society; a fully humanized mother—which is to say, an educated woman— would be what Barbauld, as we have seen, sought to be in her role as civic mother, a reformer. That is the role for which Victorian feminists such as Clara Balfour valued Barbauld.

Logically, the role would not even have to be filled by a biological woman: a person of either sex could act as a civic "mother" to the next generation, so long as that person's own humanity was fully realized. Barbauld herself seems never to have drawn this inference, although it is implicit in her actual performance as a (non-biological) mother and as a teacher, and in the fact that she and her husband conceived themselves to be engaged equally, at Palgrave School, in the same enterprise. (To a degree, their provinces within the school even overlapped: she taught reading and religion to the small children, but also geography and history to older pupils; her husband taught Latin and Greek of course, but she reports that he "delighted to entertain" young children ["Memoir of the Rev. R. Barbauld," p. 708].) Barbauld always preferred an ideal of partnership between men and women to the thought of contention between them; that is part of the burden of her much-misunderstood poem, "The Rights of Woman." In the vocabulary of her time—a vocabulary which, we have seen, was applied to her by her admirers—she appears to have believed that "masculine" and "feminine" were two parts of a human whole.[1]

### "Mrs. Barbauld"

Today Barbauld is regaining what we believe to be her rightful place in literature, but her recovery is a recent event. Thirty years ago, "Mrs. Barbauld" was known, when at all, only as an historical appendage to "more important" writers, a background figure in the contexts literary studies had created for her canonized contemporaries.

---

1  A close reading of Barbauld's poem "Corsica" by Karen Hadley in a paper delivered at the Sixth Annual Conference on 18th- and 19th-Century British Women Writers (Davis, CA, 28 March 1997) argued persuasively that Barbauld's figure Liberty represents an androgynous ideal, neither merely feminine nor merely masculine.

One of those contemporaries we have already noticed: Mary Wollstonecraft. In the books and articles of those few (but increasingly prominent) scholars who were working at that time in early women's writing, Barbauld appeared as a socially conservative foil for Wollstonecraft and other radical feminists.[1] We have suggested already that this representation was more caricature than portrait, that Barbauld's stance on questions about gender was more complicated than such a polemical depiction could acknowledge. But being painted an "anti-feminist" was probably not as damaging to Barbauld's literary reputation as another distortion was. It was her treatment as an aesthetically conservative foil for Samuel Taylor Coleridge that firmly relegated Barbauld to small print, as it were; as his canonical stature rose, her claim to serious attention fell.

Anecdotes associated with Coleridge are largely responsible for keeping Barbauld's presence alive in our cultural memory, but they do so by creating "Mrs. Barbauld"—a somewhat prissy representative of the "last age" with a ludicrous surname. The story associated with Coleridge's most popular poem provides a clear example of the way Barbauld was caricatured by literary history. Students introduced to the English literary canon in the 1960s and 1970s by the standard anthologies were likely to read in a prominent and lengthy footnote Barbauld's objection to *The Rime of the Ancient Mariner* on the grounds that it has no moral. They also read there Coleridge's zinger of a response: "I told her that in my own judgment the poem had too much."[2] Twentieth-century instructors drew on that exchange to illustrate the difference between "neo-classical didacticism" and "Romantic imaginative freedom,"

---

1   In her introduction to the 1975 edition of Wollstonecraft's *Vindication of the Rights of Woman*, for example, Miriam Kramnick names Elizabeth Carter, Hester Thrale, Frances Burney, Hannah More, and Anna Barbauld as women who not only failed to "embrace [Wollstonecraft's] principles" but who were also "scrupulously careful to avoid any contamination by feminism" (p. 37). Kramnick finds Barbauld's refusal to support a plan for a "woman's college" particularly damning (pp. 37-38). On that issue, see McCarthy, "Why Anna Letitia Barbauld Refused to Head a Women's College: New Facts, New Story," forthcoming in *Nineteenth-Century Contexts*.

2   In the Oxford anthology, published in 1973, the footnote references the title of the poem; the Norton anthologies include the story in a note toward the end of the poem, referencing the mariner's summation of the meaning of his tale. The Norton retains the note in the 7th edition of the anthology, published in 2000.

generally for the purpose of valorizing Romantic sensibility at the expense of eighteenth-century aesthetic standards (real or presumed). Rhetorically, Coleridge "wins" the exchange; and, historically, overt didacticism fell out of favor with poets and critics alike. The anecdote does not redound to Barbauld's credit.

Barbauld's actual historical impact on Blake, Wordsworth and Coleridge received no documentation in mid-twentieth-century anthologies; even as late as 1996 the *Norton Anthology of English Literature* situated her as a "minor" poet following the "Major Romantics."[1] Until then, she survived only in Coleridge's pithy refutation of her critical judgment. Seeing Barbauld through Coleridge's eyes in this way, however, actually inverts the power dynamic as it would have been experienced by the writers themselves. For, from Barbauld's perspective, Coleridge was a member of the "younger generation"; from his perspective, she was a member of the literary "establishment."

Aspects of Barbauld's anecdotal status in the annals of literary history are directly related to a generational struggle we have insufficiently imagined. We have convinced ourselves of the powerlessness of women in the "patriarchal past" to the degree that we sometimes fail to perceive the actual influence exerted by women writers of Barbauld's generation upon their contemporaries. By the time Wordsworth and Coleridge came on the literary scene, Barbauld occupied significant cultural space. The Coleridge anecdotes—both positive and negative—might be said to arise from a young man's effort to position himself in a world where she represented literary authority. The story of Coleridge's long walk to meet Barbauld confesses her preeminence; Coleridge's claim to have bested her on *The Rime of the Ancient Mariner* is an attempt to subvert her power. Other antagonistic efforts took the form of jokes about Barbauld's strange (i.e., "un-English") name, a name no one was

---

1  Pamela Plimpton discusses the implications and distortions of this placement and selection in "Anna Letitia Barbauld: Editorial Agency and the Ideology of the Feminine." The latest edition of the anthology places Barbauld first in the volume and includes four poems: "To a Little Invisible Being," "A Summer Evening's Meditation," "Washing-Day," and "Life."

sure—then or since—how to pronounce. (The consensus today seems to be that Anglicized "Barbold" was favored by her contemporaries, although her husband's family would have pronounced it, in French, "Barbo.") Thus Charles Lamb, the essayist, joked about her kinship to the "other bald lady," the novelist and dramatist Elizabeth Inchbald. These jokes survived the moment that occasioned them, and "Mrs. Barbauld" survived along with them, at least in name—or something like her name. But the quips, like the anecdotes, had the effect of positioning her outside the literary mainstream. These attempts to "kill the mother" did just that—metaphorically, anyway. For, although "Mrs. Barbauld" became part of our literary heritage, she did so by associations that discredited her even as they kept her name alive.

Of course, Barbauld's fate was not unique. In 1970, few women writers from the period 1660-1830 could claim canonical status. Aphra Behn had yet to enjoy the attention she now receives, though by 1973 her tale *Oroonoko* was available in a Norton paperback edition, and critical essays on her had begun to appear in learned journals. Frances (then "Fanny") Burney enjoyed similar quasi-canonical status. Still, neither Behn nor Burney could claim equality with Jane Austen, whose novels, with their formal and linguistic precision, responded well to New Critical readings. Austen's excellence was demonstrable by twentieth-century aesthetic standards; the achievements of Behn and Burney somewhat less so. As for the host of female writers whose works seemed inextricably bound to the times in which they were produced, they remained the subjects of what we might term antiquarian or specialist interest. If they were anthologized, it was under the heading "minor poets" or "other writers," and most did not appear even there.

When the recovery of women writers of the past began in earnest in the 1980s, expressions of surprise at Barbauld's talent and achievement in light of her obscurity were common. Barbara Brandon Schnorrenberg called her "one of the most neglected writers of her day"—a judgment emphatically reiterated by Terry Castle in a review of Roger Lonsdale's collection of *Eighteenth-Century Women Poets*. Lonsdale himself articulated a more precise amazement: "[T]here is a striking confidence and authority in the *Poems* (1773) of Anna Aikin Barbauld.... There was no female precedent for the accomplishment of the blank verse in her 'Corsica'" (p. xxxiii).

As these comments suggest, it is a cause for wonder that Anna Barbauld suffered such an eclipse. The reasons are matter for speculation. Did Coleridge and Lamb indeed write the script for Barbauld's reception by generations of readers and critics to come? Or were the jokes and anecdotes merely the symptoms of deeper ideological biases? Barbauld's gender was surely one reason she was relegated to the margins for so long. And perhaps she was less interesting to critics and literary historians than she might otherwise have been because she did not write novels or plays—both genres associated with women writers and readerships. It is possible too that her Dissenting background was also a factor—perhaps even the primary factor—in the diminishing of her literary reputation.

Whatever the reasons, as we begin to look anew at Barbauld's achievement, to replace "Mrs. Barbauld" with Anna Letitia Barbauld, we must make an effort to do so without the assumptions about gender, class and genre that have prejudiced judgment in the past. And we should also remember that Barbauld is neither the first nor the last writer to be reassessed in terms of cultural or aesthetic significance. The recovery of the Metaphysical Poets by T. S. Eliot and others springs to mind as an available example. But there is another, closer to home. It is not so long ago that Defoe scholars had to fight both aesthetic (formalist) and ideological (Anglican) prejudice as they argued for the foundational role of that author not only in the development of the novel as a genre but also in the articulation of modern values and habits of mind.[1] That battle is largely won,

---

1   Defoe, like Barbauld, was a Protestant Dissenter, and he met with some of the same resistance she has encountered in terms of literary assessment. While he enjoyed a place in the canon of the English novel throughout the twentieth century, it was not until the 1960s that Defoe received attention as a serious artist as opposed to "intuitive genius" or "instinctive story-teller." During that decade, studies by Maximillian Novak, G.A. Starr, and J. Paul Hunter changed the conventional perception of Defoe.

but as we try to understand the importance of Anna Letitia Barbauld to our thought, culture and literature, it is instructive to remember that the case had to be made for other writers, male as well as female, whom we now regard as essential to our understanding of the field of literary studies, without whom we would consider ourselves and our discipline diminished. Barbauld's poems, essays and editorial achievements enriched the literary world of the late eighteenth and early nineteenth centuries. Her concerns remain pertinent at the juncture of the twentieth and the twenty-first centuries as we continue to fight oppression globally, as we struggle to maintain a sense of aesthetic pleasure in an increasingly technological world, as we confront the things that never change: birth, death, love, hope, loss, despair and faith. The following selections provide a glimpse into Barbauld's world, her historical moment; in doing so, they speak to us and future generations as well.

1743 Born 20 June, at Kibworth Harcourt, Leicestershire, first
child of the Reverend John Aikin, master of Kibworth
School, and Jane Jennings Aikin, both Presbyterian Dis-
senters.

1747 Birth (15 January) of her brother, John. Her early edu-
cation is conducted by her mother. Later she persuades
her father to teach her Latin and some Greek, and she
reads widely in his library.

1758 Father is appointed tutor in languages and belles lettres,
and subsequently in divinity, at the Dissenting academy
at Warrington, Lancashire. The Aikins move to War-
rington (July).

1761 Father's successor in languages and belles lettres, Joseph
Priestley (1733-1804), arrives at Warrington (Septem-
ber). She becomes close friends with Priestley and his
wife, Mary.

1763 Peace of Paris (March) concludes the Seven Years' War.

1767 Priestley resigns his Warrington tutorship (June) and
moves to Leeds. The Priestleys' departure is the occa-
sion of her earliest documented poem. Rochemont
Barbauld (b. 1749) is admitted to Warrington Academy
(September).

1769 Prompted by appeals on behalf of the independence
movement in Corsica, she writes "Corsica" (circulating
privately by June).

1771 John Aikin (brother) returns to Warrington from med-
ical study and engages her in his first literary publica-
tion (below).

1772 Songs I-VI published in John Aikin's *Essays on Song-
Writing* (February). Hymns I-V published in William
Enfield's *Hymns for Public Worship*. *Poems* published
(December).

---

1 This chronology corrects and revises the chronology in our *Poems of Anna Letitia
Barbauld* (University of Georgia Press, 1994).

1773 *Miscellaneous Pieces in Prose* (with John Aikin, September).

1774 Marries Rochemont Barbauld (26 May). Settles in Palgrave, Suffolk, and assumes co-management of newly-opened Palgrave School (25 July).

1775 Beginning of war with American colonies (April). *Devotional Pieces* (?October).

1777 Adopts Charles Rochemont Aikin (1775–1847), her brother's third son, to raise as her own.

1778 *Lessons for Children from Two to Three Years Old* (May); *Lessons for Children of Three Years Old* (June).

1779 *Lessons for Children from Three to Four Years Old* (April).

1780 Father dies (December).

1781 *Hymns in Prose for Children* (August).

1783 Treaty of peace with America (March).

1785 Mother dies (January). The Barbaulds resign from Palgrave School and depart for a tour of France (September).

1786 The Barbaulds return to England (June), taking lodgings in London.

1787 The Barbaulds settle in Hampstead (April). Rochemont ministers to Rosslyn Hill congregation; she takes female pupils. In subsequent years they make regular visits to friends in Norwich (the Taylor and Martineau families) and Bristol (the family of John Estlin, a graduate of Warrington Academy).

1789 Capture and demolition of the Bastille by the people of Paris (14 July).

1790 Aroused by Parliament's failure to repeal the Corporation and Test Acts and by Edmund Burke's speeches against the French Revolution, she publishes *An Address to the Opposers of the Repeal* (March).

1791 Responding to Parliament's refusal to abolish the slave trade, she publishes *An Epistle to William Wilberforce* (June). Joseph Priestley's house in Birmingham is sacked by a "Church-and-King" mob (14 July).

1792 *Remarks on Mr. Gilbert Wakefield's Enquiry into … Public or Social Worship* (April). Royal Proclamation against Seditious Writings and Publications (May).

1793 Contributes to John Aikin's *Evenings at Home* (January). Responding to England's entry into war with the French Republic (February), she publishes *Sins of Government, Sins of the Nation* (May).

1794 To escape political persecution, Priestley emigrates to America (April). She visits Scotland (September–October) and electrifies Edinburgh literary people by her reading of William Taylor's translation of Gottfried Bürger's *Lenore*.

1796 Commencement of *The Monthly Magazine*, edited by John Aikin (March). She contributes poems and essays.

1797 Meets Samuel Taylor Coleridge (August).

1799 Meets Maria and Richard Lovell Edgeworth (May).

1801 Peace of Amiens (October) temporarily ends the war with France.

1802 The Barbaulds remove to the village of Stoke Newington, north of London (March).

1803 Resumption of war against France (May). Commencement of *The Annual Review* (to 1809), edited by her nephew Arthur Aikin (1773–1854). She is known to have contributed, but few of her contributions are identified.

1804 Edits Samuel Richardson's *Correspondence*, with a biography of Richardson (June).

1805 Edits *Selections from the Spectator, Tatler, Guardian, and Freeholder, with a Preliminary Essay* (February).

1806 John Aikin leaves *The Monthly Magazine* (June) and starts *The Athenaeum* (1807–09). She contributes essays to it.

1807 Engages to write prefaces for a collection of British novels (November).

1808 Rochemont Barbauld succumbs to a mental disorder which takes the form of violent assault on her (January); the Barbaulds are obliged to separate (March). Rochemont drowns himself in the New River, Stoke Newington (11 November).

1809 Begins to write for *The Monthly Review* (July, to at least October 1815).

1810 *The British Novelists* (September).

1811 Edits *The Female Speaker* (February). Moved by the prolongation of England's war against France and by economic deterioration resulting from it, she writes *Eighteen Hundred and Eleven* (completed by December).

1812 *Eighteen Hundred and Eleven* (January) hostilely reviewed during the course of the year. It is her last separate publication.

1819 Death of Elizabeth Belsham Kenrick (January), her oldest friend.

1822 Eyesight begins to deteriorate. Death of John Aikin (7 December).

1825 Dies at Stoke Newington, 9 March. *Works* and *A Legacy for Young Ladies*, both edited by her niece Lucy Aikin (1781-1864), published (June and December respectively).

# Abbreviations of Titles Cited in the Notes

*P 1773*, ed. 1, 2, 3, 4, 5: *Poems* (1773), eds. 1-5
*P 1792*: *Poems*, 1792 edition
*MPP*, ed. 1, 2, 3: *Miscellaneous Pieces in Prose* (1773), eds. 1-3
*Works*: *Works of Anna Letitia Barbauld*, ed. Lucy Aikin (1825)
*MM*: *Monthly Magazine*
*OED*: *Oxford English Dictionary*
   For full details, see Sources of the Texts, pp. 505-06 below.

# A Note on the Text

Disliking abridgements, we print all but two of Barbauld's texts complete. The two exceptions are the "Life of Samuel Richardson" and the preface to Fielding in *The British Novelists*, which are represented by excerpts.

With one exception, the poems in this volume are reprinted from *The Poems of Anna Letitia Barbauld*, ed. William McCarthy and Elizabeth Kraft (University of Georgia Press, 1994). The exception is "[Lines for Anne Wakefield ...]," reprinted here for the first time. We have rewritten the headnotes to the poems reprinted from our edition.

In choosing copytexts for the prose works, we have preferred the earliest printings and incorporated into them those changes in later printings which we believe were made by Barbauld herself. Although in general we avoid the texts published by Lucy Aikin in 1825–26 when we have alternatives, we adopt 1825–26 variant readings when our copytexts show apparent error or defect, or when we suspect that 1825–26 variants represent Barbauld's revision. (For our reasons to believe they sometimes may, see *Poems* [1994], pages xxxviii–ix.) Because limitations of space require keeping textual notes to the minimum necessary, we seldom report these occasions. Significant textual variants are given in the footnotes to the texts.

We modernize quotation marks, digraph vowels, and the long *s*, and ignore most typeface variations. Otherwise we reproduce the spelling and punctuation of our texts exactly as we find them.

Silhouette portrait of Anna Letitia Barbauld in later life, said by her family to
be the work of Mrs. [Sarah] Hoare of Hampstead (Ellis, *Memoir*, 1:335).
Lithograph by Allan & Ferguson, Glasgow.
Private collection.

# AN ADDRESS TO THE DEITY

[According to Joseph Priestley, Barbauld wrote this poem after hearing him preach a sermon "On Habitual Devotion" in 1767 (Priestley, *Two Discourses*, p. v). "On Habitual Devotion" urged its hearers to think always with reference to God: a "truly and perfectly good man ... sees God in every thing, and he sees every thing in God" (Priestley, *Works*, 15:105). To develop this visionary power, one must cultivate a habit of associating God with every experience. While the poem does echo Priestley (we cite some passages in our notes), it has affinities as well with other writers: Edmund Burke, whose *Philosophical Enquiry into the Origin of our Ideas of the Sublime and Beautiful* (1757) it also echoes at times, and Francis Hutcheson (1694-1746), a Scottish philosopher whose re-imagining of God as a loving parent (instead of the wrathful punisher envisaged in traditional Calvinism) was a major source of Enlightened Dissenting faith. Moreover, the poem's affinities with a much older tradition of female mysticism must not be overlooked.

First published in *Poems* (1773), "An Address to the Deity" became one of Barbauld's most famous and most reprinted poems. Mary Wollstonecraft included it in her anthology, *The Female Reader* (1789). It was also recast as a hymn.]

> *Deus est quodcunque vides, quocunque moveris.*
> Lucan.[1]

    God of my life! and author of my days!
Permit my feeble voice to lisp thy praise;
And trembling, take upon a mortal tongue
That hallow'd name to harps of Seraphs sung.
Yet here the brightest Seraphs could no more         .     5
Than veil their faces, tremble, and adore.
Worms, angels, men, in every different sphere
Are equal all, for all are nothing here.
All nature faints beneath the mighty name,

---

1   Lucan, *Pharsalia*, 9:580, substituting "Deus" for Lucan's "Iupiter." All that we see is God; every motion we make is God also (Loeb translation).

10    Which nature's works, thro' all their parts proclaim.
I feel that name my inmost thoughts controul,
And breathe an awful stillness thro' my soul;
As by a charm, the waves of grief subside;[1]
Impetuous passion stops her headlong tide;
15    At thy felt presence all emotions cease,
And my hush'd spirit finds a sudden peace,
Till every worldly thought within me dies,
And earth's gay pageants vanish from my eyes;
Till all my sense is lost in infinite,
20    And one vast object fills my aching sight.[2]
    But soon, alas! this holy calm is broke;
My soul submits to wear her wonted yoke;[3]
With shackled pinions strives to soar in vain,
And mingles with the dross of earth again.
25    But he, our gracious Master, kind, as just,
Knowing our frame, remembers man is dust:[4]
His spirit, ever brooding o'er our mind,
Sees the first wish to better hopes inclin'd;
Marks the young dawn of every virtuous aim,
30    And fans the smoaking flax into a flame:
His ears are open to the softest cry,
His grace descends to meet the lifted eye;
He reads the language of a silent tear,
And sighs are incense from a heart sincere.
35    Such are the vows, the sacrifice I give;

---

1   "When your mind is labouring under distressing doubts and great anxiety ... fly to God, as your friend and father.... Your perturbation of mind will subside, as by a charm, and the storm will become a settled calm" (Priestley, *Works*, 15:115-16).

2   Cf. Burke: When experiencing the Sublime, "the mind is so entirely filled with its object, that it cannot entertain any other, nor by consequence reason on that object which employs it" (*Sublime and Beautiful*, p. 53).

3   "These fervours, however, will of course remit, and other objects will necessarily resume some part ... of their influence; but if a sense of God and of religion have once taken firm hold of the mind ... there will be reason to hope that an express regard to them will return with greater force" (Priestley, *Works*, 15:106-07).

4   "But ... we must learn to acquiesce in the sense of our manifold imperfections, and the unavoidable consequences of them: and to take refuge in the goodness and compassion of God, who *considers our frame, and remembers that we are but dust*" (Priestley, *Works*, 15:118, quoting Genesis 3:19).

Accept the vow, and bid the suppliant live:
From each terrestrial bondage set me free;
Still every wish that centers not in thee;
Bid my fond hopes, my vain disquiets cease,
And point my path to everlasting peace.                    40
     If the soft hand of winning pleasure leads
By living waters,[1] and thro' flow'ry meads,
When all is smiling, tranquil, and serene,
And vernal beauty paints the flattering scene,
Oh! teach me to elude each latent snare,                   45
And whisper to my sliding heart—Beware!
With caution let me hear the Syren's[2] voice,
And doubtful, with a trembling heart, rejoice.
     If friendless, in a vale of tears I stray,
Where briars wound, and thorns perplex my way,             50
Still let my steady soul thy goodness see,
And with strong confidence lay hold on thee;
With equal eye my various lot receive,
Resign'd to die, or resolute to live;
Prepar'd to kiss the sceptre, or the rod,[3]               55
While GOD is seen in all, and all in GOD.
     I read his awful name, emblazon'd high
With golden letters on th' illumin'd sky;
Nor less the mystic characters I see
Wrought in each flower, inscrib'd in every tree;[4]        60
In every leaf that trembles to the breeze
I hear the voice of GOD among the trees;

---

1   Jeremiah 17:13 describes the Lord as "the fountain of living waters," and Revela-
    tions 7:17 prophesies that "the Lamb ... shall lead them unto living fountains of
    waters."
2   One of the mythological sea nymphs whose song lured sailors to destruction; see
    Homer, *Odyssey*, Book 12.
3   To kiss the rod means to be grateful for correction or punishment.
4   "If he understand any thing of the principles of vegetation, and ... what we call *the
    laws of nature*; these laws he knows to be the express appointment of God; and he
    cannot help perceiving the wisdom and goodness of God in the appointment; so
    that the objects about which he is daily conversant, are, in their nature, a lesson of
    gratitude and praise" (Priestley, *Works*, 15:112-13). The idea that nature is the "writ-
    ing" of God was traditional, and the belief that science is a means to the worship of
    God was popular with Dissenters.

With thee in shady solitudes I walk,
With thee in busy crowded cities talk,
65 In every creature own thy forming power,
In each event thy providence adore.
Thy hopes shall animate my drooping soul,
Thy precepts guide me, and thy fear controul.
Thus shall I rest, unmov'd by all alarms,
70 Secure within the temple of thine arms,
From anxious cares, from gloomy terrors free,
And feel myself omnipotent in thee.
    Then when the last, the closing hour draws nigh,
And earth recedes before my swimming eye;
75 When trembling on the doubtful edge of fate
I stand and stretch my view to either state;
Teach me to quit this transitory scene
With decent triumph and a look serene;
Teach me to fix my ardent hopes on high,
And having liv'd to thee, in thee to die.

## TO MRS. P[RIESTLEY], WITH SOME DRAWINGS OF BIRDS AND INSECTS

[This poem, written perhaps during a visit to the Priestleys at Leeds in autumn 1767, was more than just a presentation piece to her beloved "Amanda," Mrs. Priestley. In it Barbauld takes up a patriotic challenge issued by British naturalist (and her brother's friend) Thomas Pennant, in his *British Zoology* (1766). Pennant urged British writers to take native fauna as subjects of poetry, and to base descriptive poems on careful observation of nature. Barbauld drew at least some of her bird lore from Pennant. She may have derived her insect descriptions from a splendid work by the Dutch naturalist Maria Merians (1647–1717), *Metamorphosis Insectorum Surinamensium* ("The Metamorphoses of the Insects of Surinam," 1705) or perhaps from Merians's original colored drawings on exhibit at the British Museum. ("I have seen some rich descriptions of West Indian flowers and plants," she wrote some years later, although she does

not say whose they were [*Works*, 2:16].) The poem was pub-
lished in *Poems*, 1773.]

> *The kindred arts to please thee shall conspire,*
> *One dip the pencil, and one string the lyre.*
>
> Pope.[1]

Amanda bids; at her command again
I seize the pencil,[2] or resume the pen;
No other call my willing hand requires,
And friendship, better than a Muse inspires.
    Painting and poetry are near allied;        5
The kindred arts two sister Muses guide;[3]
This charms the eye, that steals upon the ear;
There sounds are tun'd; and colours blended here:
This with a silent touch enchants our eyes,
And bids a gayer brighter world arise:        10
That, less allied to sense, with deeper art
Can pierce the close recesses of the heart;
By well set syllables, and potent sound,
Can rouse, can chill the breast, can sooth, can wound;
To life adds motion, and to beauty soul,        15
And breathes a spirit through the finish'd whole:
Each perfects each, in friendly union join'd;
This gives Amanda's form, and that her mind.
    But humbler themes my artless hand requires,
Nor higher than the feather'd tribe aspires.        20
Yet who the various nations can declare
That plow with busy wing the peopled air?
These cleave the crumbling bark for insect food;
Those dip their crooked beak in kindred blood:
Some haunt the rushy moor, the lonely woods;        25
Some bathe their silver plumage in the floods;
Some fly to man, his houshold gods implore,

---

1   Slightly misquoted from Alexander Pope, "Epistle to Mr. Jervas, with Dryden's Translation of Fresnoy's Art of Painting," ll. 69–70.

2   I.e., paint brush.

3   That painting and poetry are sister arts was a commonplace of neoclassical esthetics.

And gather round his hospitable door;
Wait the known call, and find protection there
30    From all the lesser tyrants of the air.
          The tawny EAGLE[1] seats his callow brood
High on the cliff, and feasts his young with blood.
On Snowden's rocks, or Orkney's wide domain,
Whose beetling cliffs o'erhang the western main,
35    The royal bird his lonely kingdom forms
Amidst the gathering clouds, and sullen storms;
Thro' the wide waste of air he darts his sight
And holds his sounding pinions pois'd for flight;
With cruel eye premeditates the war,
40    And marks his destin'd victim from afar:[2]
Descending in a whirlwind to the ground,
His pinions like the rush of waters sound;
The fairest of the fold he bears away,
And to his nest compels the struggling prey.
45    He scorns the game by meaner hunters tore,
And dips his talons in no vulgar gore.
          With lovelier pomp along the grassy plain
The silver PHEASANT draws his shining train.
On Asia's myrtle shores, by Phasis' stream,[3]
50    He spreads[4] his plumage to the sunny gleam:
But where[5] the wiry net his flight confines,
He lowers his purple crest, and inly[6] pines;
The beauteous captive hangs his ruffled wing,
Oppress'd by bondage, and our chilly spring.[7]

---

1   Probably the golden eagle. Pennant notes its presence in the Orkney Islands and
    occasional appearances "in *Snowdon* hills" (Wales), as well as its preference for
    breeding "in the loftiest cliffs" (*British Zoology*, 1:121-23).
2   Pennant notes of the eagle that "the sight and sense of smelling are very acute: *her
    eyes behold afar off*" (1:122, quoting Job 39:29).
3   On Asia's ... Phasis': In *P 1773* eds. 1-2, "On India's painted shore, by Ganges'"; in *P
    1773* eds. 3-5, "Once on the painted banks of Ganges'." The revision (in *P 1792*)
    accords with Pennant: "*Pheasants* were first brought into *Europe* from the banks of
    the *Phasis*, a river of *Colchis*" (1:212).
4   spreads: in *P 1773* eds. 3-5, "spread."
5   where: in *P 1773* eds. 3-5, "now."
6   Inwardly.
7   In *P 1773* eds. 3-5, lines 53-54 are absent.

To claim the verse, unnumber'd tribes[1] appear                55
That swell the music of the vernal year:
Seiz'd with the spirit of the kindly May
They sleek the glossy wing, and tune the lay:
With emulative strife the notes prolong
And pour out all their little souls in song.                   60
When winter bites upon the naked plain,
Nor food nor shelter in the groves remain;
By instinct led, a firm united band,
As marshall'd by some skilful general's hand,
The congregated nations wing their way                         65
In dusky columns o'er the trackless sea;
In clouds unnumber'd annual hover o'er
The craggy Bass, or Kilda's utmost shore:[2]
Thence spread their sails to meet the southern wind,
And leave the gathering tempest far behind;                    70
Pursue the circling sun's indulgent ray,
Course the swift seasons, and o'ertake the day.
        Not so the Insect race, ordain'd to keep
The lazy sabbath of a half-year's sleep.
Entomb'd, beneath the filmy web they lie,                      75
And wait the influence of a kinder sky;
When vernal sun-beams pierce their dark retreat,
The heaving tomb distends with vital heat;
The full-form'd brood impatient of their cell
Start from their trance, and burst their silken shell;         80
Trembling a-while they stand, and scarcely dare
To launch at once upon the untried air:
At length assur'd, they catch the favouring gale,
And leave their sordid spoils, and high in Ether[3] sail.
So when Rinaldo struck the conscious rind,                     85
He found a nymph in every trunk confin'd;
. The forest labours with convulsive throes,
The bursting trees the lovely births disclose,
And a gay troop of damsels round him stood,

---

1   Species.
2   Pennant mentions both the Bass isle (in the Firth of Forth) and St. Kilda (west of
    the Hebrides) as sites where auks breed (*British Zoology*, 2:517).
3   The upper atmosphere.

90    Where late was rugged bark and lifeless wood.[1]
      Lo! the bright train their radiant wings unfold,
      With silver fring'd and freckl'd o'er with gold:
      On the gay bosom of some fragrant flower
      They idly fluttering live their little hour;
95    Their life all pleasure, and their task all play,
      All spring their age, and sunshine all their day.
      Not so the child of sorrow, wretched *man*,
      His course with toil concludes, with pain began:
      That his high destiny he might discern,
100   And in misfortune's school this lesson learn,[2]
      Pleasure's the portion of th' inferior kind;
      But glory, virtue, Heaven for Man design'd.
            What atom forms of insect life appear!
      And who can follow nature's pencil here?
105   Their wings with azure, green, and purple gloss'd,[3]
      Studded with colour'd eyes, with gems emboss'd,
      Inlaid with pearl, and mark'd with various stains
      Of lively crimson thro' their dusky veins.
      Some shoot like living stars, athwart the night,
110   And scatter from their wings a vivid light,
      To guide the Indian to his tawny loves,
      As thro' the woods with cautious step he moves.
            See the proud giant of the beetle race;
      What shining arms his polish'd limbs enchase!
115   Like some stern warrior formidably bright
      His steely sides reflect a gleaming light;
      On his large forehead spreading horns he wears,
      And high in air the branching antlers bears;[4]

---

1   In ll. 85-90 Barbauld conflates two scenes from Torquato Tasso's *Gerusalemme Liber-ata* (1581). In one, the hero Tancred stabs a tree only to discover that he has stabbed his beloved Clorinda, imprisoned in it (13.xli-iii). In the other, the hero Rinaldo witnesses the "marvel" of trees giving birth to young women (17.xxvi-vii).
2   Lines 99-100 were added in *P 1773* ed. 3.
3   Maria Merians describes a butterfly "of burnished silver, across which shine green, blue [azure], and purple" (*Dissertatio*, p. 53; our translation).
4   Merians describes a beetle "completely black, polished like a mirror, and bearing two horns between which appears a trunk like that of an elephant" (p. 72; our translation).

O'er many an inch extends his wide domain,
And his rich treasury swells with hoarded grain.           120
    Thy friend thus strives to cheat the lonely hour,
With song, or paint, an insect, or a flower:
Yet if Amanda praise the flowing line,
And bend delighted o'er the gay design,
I envy not, nor emulate the fame                           125
Or of the painter's, or the poet's name:
Could I to both with equal claim pretend,
Yet far, far dearer were the name of FRIEND.


## THE INVITATION:
## TO MISS B★★★★★.

["Miss B★★★★★" is Elizabeth Belsham (1743-1819), Barbauld's
second cousin and closest lifelong friend, who paid a number
of visits to Warrington; we speculate that this poem was origi-
nally composed in letters inviting her to visit at different times
in the 1760s. In its present form (published in *Poems*, 1773) it is
a topographical poem celebrating a place, in the manner of
Alexander Pope's *Windsor Forest* (1713). Miss Belsham is invited
not only to share the pleasures of female friendship but also to
admire the achievements of liberal progress in the forms of
futuristic technology (the Duke of Bridgewater's spectacular
canal) and Dissenting education (Warrington Academy).]

> *Hic gelidi fontes, hic mollia prata, Lycori,*
> *Hic nemus: hic ipso tecum consumerer aevo.*
>
> Virgil.[1]


Health to my friend, and long unbroken years,
By storms unruffled and unstain'd by tears:
Wing'd by new joys may each white[2] minute fly;
Spring on her cheek, and sunshine in her eye:

---

1  *Eclogues*, X.42-43. Here are cold springs, Lycoris, here soft meadows, here wood-
land; / Here, with thee, time alone would wear me away. (Loeb translation)
2  Fortunate, happy.

5     O'er that dear breast, where love and pity springs,
     May peace eternal spread her downy wings:
     Sweet beaming hope her path illumine still,
     And fair ideas all her fancy fill.
     From glittering scenes which strike the dazzled sight
10    With mimic grandeur and illusive light,
     From idle hurry, and tumultuous noise,
     From hollow friendships, and from sickly joys,
     Will DELIA,[1] at the muse's call retire
     To the pure pleasures rural scenes inspire?
15    Will she from crowds and busy cities fly,
     Where wreaths of curling smoke involve the sky,
     To taste the grateful shade of spreading trees,
     And drink the spirit of the mountain breeze?
         When winter's hand the rough'ning year deforms,
20    And hollow winds foretel approaching storms,
     Then Pleasure, like a bird of passage, flies
     To brighter climes, and more indulgent skies;
     Cities and courts allure her sprightly train,
     From the bleak mountain and the naked plain;
25    And gold and gems with artificial blaze,
     Supply the sickly sun's declining rays:
     But soon returning on the western gale,
     She seeks the bosom of the grassy vale;
     There, wrapt in careless ease, attunes her lyre
30    To the wild warblings of the woodland quire;
     The daisied turf her humble throne supplies,
     And early primroses around her rise.
     We'll follow where the smiling goddess leads,
     Thro' tangled forests or enamel'd meads;
35    O'er pathless hills her airy form we'll chase,
     In silent glades her fairy footsteps trace:
     Small pains there needs her footsteps to pursue,
     She cannot fly from friendship, and from you.
     Now the glad earth her frozen zone[2] unbinds,

---

1  Barbauld's pastoralizing name for Belsham, taken from the elegies of the Roman
   poet Tibullus.
2  Girdle, belt.

And o'er her bosom breathe the western winds:                    40
Already now the snow-drop[1] dares appear,
The first pale blossom of th' unripen'd year;
As FLORA's breath, by some transforming power,
Had chang'd an icicle into a flower:
Its name, and hue, the scentless plant retains,                  45
And winter lingers in its icy veins.
To these succeed the violet's dusky blue,
And each inferior flower of fainter hue;
Till riper months the perfect year disclose,
And FLORA cries exulting, See my Rose!                           50
        The Muse invites, my DELIA haste away,
And let us sweetly waste the careless day.[2]
Here gentle summits lift their airy brow;
Down the green slope here winds the labouring plow;
Here bath'd by frequent show'rs cool vales are seen,             55
Cloath'd with fresh verdure, and eternal green;
Here smooth canals,[3] across th' extended plain,
Stretch their long arms, to join the distant main:
The sons of toil with many a weary stroke
Scoop the hard bosom of the solid rock;                          60
Resistless thro' the stiff opposing clay
With steady patience work their gradual way;

---

1   A late winter flower frequently mentioned in eighteenth-century poems. One
    commentator associates it especially with the poems of women writers ("with
    whom it appears to have been a deserved favourite"), citing Hannah More, Mary
    Tighe, and Felicia Hemans, and quoting "The Invitation" (Warwick, *The Poet's
    Pleasaunce*, p. 83).
2   Lines 51-52 recall the *carpe diem* (seize the day) theme favored by seventeenth-cen-
    tury poets of hedonism such as Robert Herrick.
3   "The Duke of Bridgewater's canal, which in many places crosses the road, and in
    one is carried by an aqueduct over the river Irwell. Its head is at Worsley, where it is
    conveyed by deep tunnels under the coal pits, for the purpose of loading the boats"
    (Barbauld's note, *P 1792*). Built between 1758 and 1767, the canal carried coal from
    the Duke's mines to the river Mersey and thence to Liverpool. It was admired as a
    triumph of engineering technology. "The most striking" of its aqueducts, thought
    John Aikin, was the bridge which carried it across the river Irwell "thirty-eight feet
    above the surface of the water, admitting the largest barges navigating the Irwell, to
    go through with masts and sails standing"; hence "the extraordinary sight, never
    before beheld in this country, of one vessel sailing over the top of another" (*A
    Description of the Country*, pp. 113-14).

Compel the genius of th' unwilling flood
Thro' the brown horrors of the aged wood;
'Cross the lone waste the silver urn they pour,
And chear the barren heath or sullen moor:
The traveller with pleasing wonder sees
The white sail gleaming thro' the dusky trees;
And views the alter'd landscape with surprise,
And doubts the magic scenes which round him rise.
Now, like a flock of swans, above his head
Their woven wings the flying vessels spread;
Now meeting streams in artful mazes glide,
While each unmingled pours a separate tide;
Now through the hidden veins of earth they flow,
And visit sulphurous mines and caves below;
The ductile streams obey the guiding hand,
And social plenty circles round the land.
    But nobler praise awaits our green retreats;
The Muses here have fixt their sacred seats.
Mark where its simple front yon mansion rears,[1]
The nursery of men for future years!
Here callow chiefs and embryo statesmen lie,
And unfledg'd poets short excursions try:
While Mersey's gentle current, which too long
By fame neglected, and unknown to song,
Between his rushy banks, (no poet's theme)
Had crept inglorious, like a vulgar stream,
Reflects th' ascending seats with conscious pride,
And dares to emulate a classic tide.
Soft music breathes along each op'ning shade,
And sooths the dashing of his rough cascade.
With mystic lines his sands are figur'd o'er,[2]
And circles trac'd upon the letter'd shore.

---

1   Warrington Academy, founded in 1757 and housed until 1762 in a plain building
    on the bank of the Mersey. ("Th' ascending seats" [line 89] are its new buildings,
    under construction.) The Academy prepared young men for careers in divinity,
    commerce, and the secular professions. Its faculty was intellectually "modern" and
    politically liberal, with a strong leaning towards the sciences.
2   Lines 93-94 imply that Warrington students wrote on the river bank. Perhaps, like
    Archimedes, they worked math problems in the sand.

Beneath his willows rove th' inquiring youth                    95
~~And court the fair majestic form of truth.~~
Here nature opens all her secret springs,
And heav'n-born science plumes her eagle wings:
Too long had bigot rage, with malice swell'd,
Crush'd her strong pinions, and her flight witheld;[1]          100
Too long to check her ardent progress strove:
So writhes the serpent round the bird of Jove;
Hangs on her flight, restrains her tow'ring wing,
Twists its dark folds, and points its venom'd sting.
Yet still (if aught aright the Muse divine)                     105
Her rising pride shall mock the vain design;
On sounding pinions yet aloft shall soar,
And thro' the azure deep untravel'd paths explore.
Where science smiles, the Muses join the train;
And gentlest arts and purest manners reign.                     110
Ye generous youth who love this studious shade,
How rich a field is to your hopes display'd!
Knowledge to you unlocks the classic page;
And virtue blossoms for a better age.
Oh golden days! oh bright unvalued hours!                       115
What bliss (did ye but know that bliss) were yours?
With richest stores your glowing bosoms fraught,
Perception quick, and luxury of thought;
The high designs that heave the labouring soul,
Panting for fame, impatient of controul;                        120
And fond enthusiastic thought, that feeds
On pictur'd tales of vast heroic deeds;
And quick affections, kindling into flame
At virtue's, or their country's honour'd name;
And spirits light, to every joy in tune;                        125
And friendship ardent as a summer's noon;
And generous scorn of vice's venal tribe;
And proud disdain of interest's sordid bribe;
And conscious honour's quick instinctive sense;

---

1   Students at the Universities of Oxford and Cambridge were required to subscribe
    to the Thirty-Nine Articles of the Church of England, and thus Dissenters were
    effectually excluded from taking degrees there.

130 And smiles unforc'd; and easy confidence;
And vivid fancy; and clear simple truth;
And all the mental bloom of vernal youth.
How bright the scene to fancy's eye appears,
Thro' the long perspective of distant years,
135 When this, this little group their country calls
From academic shades and learned halls,
To fix her laws, her spirit to sustain,
And light up glory thro' her wide domain!
Their various tastes in different arts display'd,
140 Like temper'd harmony of light and shade,
With friendly union in one mass shall blend,
And this adorn the state, and that defend.
These the sequester'd shade shall cheaply please,
With learned labour, and inglorious ease:
145 While those, impell'd by some resistless force,
O'er seas and rocks shall urge their vent'rous course;
Rich fruits matur'd by glowing suns behold,
And China's groves of vegetable gold;
From every land the various harvest spoil,
150 And bear the tribute to their native soil:
But tell each land (while every toil they share,
Firm to sustain, and resolute to dare,)
MAN is the nobler growth our realms supply,
And SOULS are ripen'd in our northern sky.
155 Some pensive creep along the shelly shore;
Unfold the silky texture of a flower;
With sharpen'd eyes[1] inspect an hornet's sting,
And all the wonders of an insect's wing.
Some trace with curious search the hidden cause
160 Of nature's changes, and her various laws;
Untwist her beauteous web, disrobe her charms,
And hunt her to her elemental forms:
Or prove what hidden powers in herbs are found
To quench disease and cool the burning wound;
165 With cordial drops the fainting head sustain,

---

1   I.e., using microscopes.

Call back the flitting soul, and still the throbs of pain.
　　　The patriot passion this shall strongly feel,
Ardent, and glowing with undaunted zeal;
With lips of fire shall plead his country's cause,
And vindicate the majesty of laws.　　　　　　　　　　　170
This, cloath'd with Britain's thunder, spread alarms
Thro' the wide earth, and shake the pole with arms.
That, to the sounding lyre his deeds rehearse,
Enshrine his name in some immortal verse,
To long posterity his praise consign,　　　　　　　　　175
And pay a life of hardships by a line.
While others, consecrate to higher aims,
Whose hallow'd bosoms glow with purer flames,
Love in their heart, persuasion in their tongue,
With words of peace shall charm the list'ning throng,　　180
Draw the dread veil that wraps th' eternal throne,
And launch our souls into the bright unknown.
　　　Here cease my song. Such arduous themes require
A master's pencil, and a poet's fire:
Unequal far such bright designs to paint,　　　　　　185
Too weak her colours, and her lines too faint,
My drooping Muse folds up her fluttering wing,
And hides her head in the green lap of spring.

## TO DR. AIKIN ON HIS COMPLAINING THAT SHE NEGLECTED HIM, OCTOBER 20th 1768

[In 1768 John Aikin was at Manchester studying surgery. He
and his sister, still at Warrington, corresponded regularly. This
poem excusing her neglect of his last letters circulated in man-
uscript but was not published until 1994. In our notes we
include a passage from an alternative manuscript copy.]

Will my dear Brother, and indulgent friend
Forgive a fault I strive not to defend;
For oft remorse has touch'd my conscious breast,

My careless hand so ill my heart express'd,
And, idly busy as the moments flew,
I thought, and only thought alas! of you.
But what, if now your penitent confess
Your kind upbraidings made her sorrow less;
And own, that when she shed the tender tear,
The grief that caus'd it was not half sincere.
What if she half enjoy'd the anxious care,
And almost triumph'd in the jealous fear,
Those fond misgivings, which thy bosom prove
As much alive to friendship as to love.
Not that our friendship needs such feeble aid,
Or draws its lustre from the fleeting shade;
In life's young dawn the impulse first begun,
And gather'd strength from ev'ry circling sun:
The first warm impulse which our breasts did move,
'Twas sympathy, before we knew to love.
As hand in hand with innocence we stray'd
Embosom'd deep in Kibworth's¹ tufted shade;
Where both encircled in one household band,
And both obedient to one mild command,
Life's first fair dawn with transport we beheld,
And simple pleasures, hardly since excell'd.²
How like two scions on one stem we grew,
And how from the same lips one precept drew:
"Let love for ever join your hearts," they said,
And well our hearts the gentle law obey'd.
Beyond the law, the fair example mov'd,
What had we been, if then we had not lov'd?
By stronger ties endear'd, what were we now,

5

10

15

20

25

30

---

1  Their childhood home until 1758.
2  Between lines 26 and 27, a different MS reads:

> Blest be that blameless roof, that spotless hearth
> Where dwells soft peace, and kind domestic worth
> Friends, parents, kindred every houshold name
> Which fond regard and sacred reverence claim
> A dearer name than these there cannot be
> Or if a dearer, 'tis not known to me.

Could dark suspicion sit upon our brow;
Could angry thoughts arise, or envy stain,           35
Or selfish passions in our bosoms reign?
They never did——Oh! trust the muse who vows
By all the sacred springs whence friendship flows,
By all the holy bands of brotherhood,
And ev'ry social tye that binds the good;           40
By the long train of mutual gentle deeds,
Whence faith confirm'd, and dearer love proceeds,
Sweet fruits of love on which affection feeds;
By all the soft endearing hours of youth,
By riper converse, and maturer truth,           45
Our hearts shall ne'er such gloomy tyrants own,
But friendship triumph on her steady throne.
Those hours are now no more which smiling flew
And the same studies saw us both pursue;
Our path divides—to thee fair fate assign'd           50
The nobler labours of a manly mind:
While mine, more humble works, and lower cares,
Less shining toils, and meaner praises shares.
Yet sure in different moulds they were not cast
Nor stampt with separate sentiments and taste.           55
But hush my heart! nor strive to soar too high,
Nor for the tree of knowledge vainly sigh;
Check the fond love of science and of fame,
A bright, but ah! a too devouring flame.
Content remain within thy bounded sphere,           60
For fancy blooms, the virtues flourish there.
To thee,[1] fair fate the pleasing task decrees,
To bring the sick man health, the tortured ease;
With potent drugs the spring of life renew,
And bid the drooping roses bloom anew:           65
To bid the half clos'd eye its fire resume,
And of its prey defraud the greedy tomb.
The hardy soldier, who, with conquest crown'd
Pours the warm blood thro' many an honest wound,

---

1   John Aikin, who after graduating from Warrington in 1761 had been apprenticed
to an apothecary.

70  By thee restor'd shall only shew the scar,
The seal of glory which he boasts to wear.
O'er the wan cheek where death's pale flag display'd
With dreadful omen, chill'd the languid maid,
Shall love once more his rosy banners wave,
75  And beauty triumph in the charms you gave.
Nor be thy skilful care to this confin'd,
But soothe the fears and anguish of the mind;
Join to the sage advice, the tender sigh;
And to the healing hand the pitying eye.
80  Beyond thy art thy friendship shall prevail
And cordial looks shall cure, when drugs would fail:
Thy words of balm shall cure the wounds of strife,
And med'cine all the sharper ills of life.
So on thy cheek may health unbroken glow,
85  May'st thou ne'er want relief but still bestow;
So shall thy name be grac'd with fairer praise
Than waits the laurel or the greenest bays:
Yet shall the bays around thy temples twine,
And make thine own Apollo[1] doubly thine;
90  For both our breasts at once the Muses fir'd,
With equal love, but not alike inspir'd.
To thee, the flute and sounding lyre decreed,[2]
Mine, the low murmurs of the tuneful reed;
Yet when fair friendship shall unloose my tongue,
95  My trembling voice shall ne'er refuse the song;
Yet will I smile to see thy partial praise,
With lovely error crown my worthless lays.

---

1  Patron god of poetry and medicine; Aikin was practising both.
2  The flute is associated with dramatic writing, the lyre with lyric poetry. The *reed* (l. 93) signifies rustic, pastoral verse.

# CORSICA

[The struggle of Corsica, under the generalship of Pasquale Paoli (1725-1807), for independence from the Italian state of Genoa took a new turn in 1768, when Genoa sold the island to France and France prepared to conquer it. In England, the Corsican cause was championed by James Boswell (biographer-to-be of Samuel Johnson) in *An Account of Corsica, the Journal of a Tour to that Island, and Memoirs of Pascal Paoli* (1768). Boswell aroused pro-Corsican sentiment among British liberals, who linked the issue of Corsica with perceived threats to "public liberty" at home: the refusal of the House of Commons to seat John Wilkes, three times elected by his constituents but detested by the government for his radicalism; and the government's efforts to impose new taxes on the American colonies. On 10 December 1768 a private subscription for the Corsicans was opened, and the money it raised was delivered to Paoli in March 1769. To no avail: on 8 May 1769 Paoli's army was overwhelmed by the invading French.

These issues reverberated at Warrington. Among the Academy students was a son of Samuel Vaughan, a London merchant who supported Wilkes and acted as trustee for the Corsican subscription; and the Academy's rector, John Seddon, acted as Vaughan's regional agent. Barbauld wrote "Corsica" presumably in support of the subscription; in June 1769, Joseph Priestley urged her to send it to Boswell and Catherine Macaulay "with permission to publish it for the benefit of those noble islanders" (LeBreton, *Memoir*, pp. 34-35). Apparently she did not send it, for the poem was published only in *Poems* 1773.]

> ———————————————*A manly race*
> *Of unsubmitting spirit, wise and brave;*
> *Who still thro' bleeding ages struggled hard*
> *To hold a generous undiminish'd state;*
> *Too much in vain!*          Thomson.[1]

---

1   James Thomson, *The Seasons:* "Autumn," ll. 897-99, 902-03.

Hail generous CORSICA![1] unconquer'd isle!
The fort of freedom; that amidst the waves
Stands like a rock of adamant, and dares
The wildest fury of the beating storm.
5      And are there yet, in this late sickly age
(Unkindly to the tow'ring growths of virtue)
Such bold exalted spirits? Men whose deeds,
To the bright annals of old GREECE oppos'd,
Would throw in shades her yet unrival'd name,
10 And dim the lustre of her fairest page!
And glows the flame of LIBERTY so strong
In this lone speck of earth![2] this spot obscure,
Shaggy with woods, and crusted o'er with rock,
By slaves surrounded and by slaves oppress'd!
15 What then should BRITONS feel? should they not catch
The warm contagion of heroic ardour,
And kindle at a fire so like their own?
      Such were the working thoughts which swell'd the breast
Of generous BOSWEL; when with nobler aim
20 And views beyond the narrow beaten track[3]
By trivial fancy trod, he turn'd his course
From polish'd Gallia's[4] soft delicious vales,
From the grey reliques of imperial Rome,
From her long galleries of laurel'd stone,
25 Her chisel'd heroes, and her marble gods,
Whose dumb majestic pomp yet awes the world,
To animated forms of patriot zeal,
Warm in the living majesty of virtue,

---

1  Boswell quotes an anonymous poem, *Pride*, beginning "Hail Corsica!" (*Account*, pp. 250–51).

2  "[A] most distinguished example of [the flourishing of liberty in modern times] actually exists in the island of Corsica. There, a brave and resolute nation, has now for upwards of six and thirty years, maintained a constant struggle against the oppression of the republick of Genoa" (Boswell, *Account*, p. 38).

3  "I wished for something more than just the common course of what is called the tour of Europe; and Corsica occurred to me as a place which no body else had seen, and where I should find what was to be seen no where else, a people actually fighting for liberty, and forming themselves from a poor inconsiderable oppressed nation, into a flourishing and independent state" (Boswell, *Account*, p. 287).

4  France.

Elate with fearless spirit, firm, resolv'd,
By fortune nor subdu'd, nor aw'd by power.                    30
      How raptur'd fancy burns, while warm in thought
I trace the pictur'd landscape; while I kiss
With pilgrim lips devout the sacred soil
Stain'd with the blood of heroes. CYRNUS,[1] hail!
Hail to thy rocky, deep indented shores,                     35
And pointed cliffs, which hear the chafing deep
Incessant foaming round their shaggy sides:
Hail to thy winding bays, thy shelt'ring ports
And ample harbours, which inviting stretch
Their hospitable arms to every sail:                         40
Thy numerous streams, that bursting from the cliffs
Down the steep channel'd rock impetuous pour
With grateful murmur: on the fearful edge
Of the rude precipice, thy hamlets brown
And straw-roof'd cots, which from the level vale             45
Scarce seen, amongst the craggy hanging cliffs
Seem like an eagle's nest aerial built:[2]
Thy swelling mountains, brown with solemn shade
Of various trees, that wave their giant arms
O'er the rough sons of freedom;[3] lofty pines,              50
And hardy fir, and ilex ever green,
And spreading chesnut, with each humbler plant,
And shrub of fragrant leaf, that clothes their sides
With living verdure; whence the clust'ring bee
Extracts her golden dews: the shining box,                   55
And sweet-leav'd myrtle, aromatic thyme,
The prickly juniper, and the green leaf

---

1  Corsica. Barbauld's description in ll. 35ff derives from Boswell's account of Cor-
   sica's harbors.
2  "The Corsican villages are frequently built upon the very summits of their moun-
   tains, on craggy cliffs of so stupendous a height, that the houses can hardly be dis-
   tinguished" (Boswell, *Account*, p. 61).
3  "Trees grow remarkably well in Corsica. There is here almost every sort of forest
   trees, but it is principally adorned with pines of different kinds, oaks, and chestnut
   trees. All these are to be found of great size; some of the pines in particular, are
   exceedingly lofty" (Boswell, p. 75). Boswell also names "the ilex, or ever-green
   oak," the arbutus "or strawberry-tree, which gives a rich glowing appearance as far
   as the eye can reach," the box, and the laurel (pp. 76, 77, 62).

Which feeds the spinning worm;[1] while glowing bright
Beneath the various foliage, wildly spreads
60 The arbutus, and rears his scarlet fruit
Luxuriant, mantling o'er the craggy steeps;
And thy own native laurel crowns the scene.
Hail to thy savage forests, awful, deep:
Thy tangled thickets, and thy crowded woods,
65 The haunt of herds untam'd; which sullen bound
From rock to rock with fierce unsocial air
And wilder gaze, as conscious of the power
That loves to reign amid the lonely scenes
Of unquelled nature: precipices huge,
70 And tumbling torrents; trackless desarts, plains
Fenc'd in with guardian rocks, whose quarries teem
With shining steel, that to the cultur'd fields
And sunny hills which wave with bearded grain
Defends their homely produce. LIBERTY,
75 The mountain goddess,[2] loves to range at large
Amid such scenes, and on the iron soil
Prints her majestic step. For these she scorns
The green enamel'd vales, the velvet lap
Of smooth savannahs, where the pillow'd head
80 Of luxury reposes; balmy gales,
And bowers that breathe of bliss.[3] For these, when first
This isle emerging like a beauteous gem
From the dark bosom of the Tyrrhene main[4]
Rear'd its fair front, she mark'd it for her own,
85 And with her spirit warm'd. Her genuine sons,
A broken remnant, from the generous stock
Of ancient Greece, from Sparta's sad remains,
True to their high descent, preserv'd unquench'd
The sacred fire thro' many a barbarous age:

---

1  The mulberry tree, which feeds silk worms.
2  Lines 74-75 allude to Milton, "L'Allegro," l. 36: "The Mountain Nymph, sweet Liberty." Thomson's poem, *Liberty* (1735-38), has as its narrator the goddess Liberty.
3  Alluding to Spenser, *The Faerie Queene*, II.xii, the Bower of Bliss, or earthly paradise that tempts heroes away from their duty.
4  The Tyrrhenian Sea, the region of the Mediterranean in which Corsica is located.

Whom, nor the iron rod of cruel Carthage,                        90
Nor the dread sceptre of imperial Rome,
Nor bloody Goth, nor grisly Saracen,
Nor the long galling yoke of proud Liguria,
Could crush into subjection.[1] Still unquell'd
They rose superior, bursting from their chains,                  95
And claim'd man's dearest birthright, LIBERTY:
And long, thro' many a hard unequal strife
Maintain'd the glorious conflict; long withstood
With single arm, the whole collected force
Of haughty Genoa, and ambitious Gaul:                            100
And shall withstand it, trust the faithful Muse!
It is not in the force of mortal arm,
Scarcely in fate, to bind the struggling soul
That gall'd by wanton power, indignant swells
Against oppression; breathing great revenge,                     105
Careless of life, determin'd to be free.
And fav'ring heaven approves: for see the Man,[2]
Born to exalt his own, and give mankind
A glimpse of higher natures: just, as great;
The soul of counsel, and the nerve of war;                       110
Of high unshaken spirit, temper'd sweet
With soft urbanity, and polish'd grace,
And attic[3] wit, and gay unstudied smiles:
Whom heaven in some propitious hour endow'd
With every purer virtue: gave him all                            115
That lifts the hero, or adorns the man.
Gave him the eye sublime; the searching glance
Keen, scanning deep, that smites the guilty soul
As with a beam from heaven;[4] on his brow
Serene, and spacious front, set the broad seal                   120
Of dignity and rule; then smil'd benign

---

1 Barbauld's sketch of Corsican history in lines 85–94 is based on Boswell's "Concise View of the Revolutions which Corsica has undergone from the earliest times" (*Account*, Ch. 2).
2 Paoli.
3 Pure, refined.
4 Boswell describes Paoli's "stedfast, keen and penetrating eye, as if he searched my very soul" (*Account*, p. 316).

On this fair pattern of a God below,
High wrought, and breath'd into his swelling breast
The large ambitious wish to save his country.[1]
125 Oh beauteous title to immortal fame!
The man devoted to the public, stands
In the bright records of superior worth
A step below the skies: if he succeed,
The first fair lot which earth affords, is his;
130 And if he falls, he falls above a throne.
When such their leader can the brave despair?
Freedom the cause and PAOLI the chief!
Success to your fair hopes! a British muse,
Tho' weak and powerless, lifts her fervent voice,
135 And breathes a prayer for your success. Oh could
She scatter blessings as the morn sheds dews,
To drop upon your heads! but patient hope
Must wait the appointed hour; secure of this,
That never with the indolent and weak
140 Will freedom deign to dwell; she must be seiz'd
By that bold arm that wrestles for the blessing:
'Tis heaven's best prize, and must be bought with blood.
When the storm thickens, when the combat burns,
And pain and death in every horrid shape
145 That can appall the feeble, prowl around,
Then virtue triumphs; then her tow'ring form
Dilates with kindling majesty; her mien
Breathes a diviner spirit, and enlarg'd
Each spreading feature, with an ampler port
150 And bolder tone, exulting, rides the storm,
And joys amidst the tempest. Then she reaps
Her golden harvest; fruits of nobler growth
And higher relish than meridian suns
Can ever ripen; fair, heroic deeds,
155 And godlike action. 'Tis not meats, and drinks,
And balmy airs, and vernal suns, and showers

---

1 Line 124 quotes Thomson's "Autumn": "The large ambitious wish / To make them
blest" (ll. 1021-22).

That feed and ripen minds; 'tis toil and danger;
And wrestling with the stubborn gripe[1] of fate;
And war, and sharp distress, and paths obscure
And dubious. The bold swimmer joys not so                        160
To feel the proud waves under him, and beat
With strong repelling arm the billowy surge;
The generous courser does not so exult
To toss his floating mane against the wind,
And neigh amidst the thunder of the war,                          165
As virtue to oppose her swelling breast
Like a firm shield against the darts of fate.
And when her sons in that rough school have learn'd
To smile at danger, then the hand that rais'd
Shall hush the storm, and lead the shining train                 170
Of peaceful years in bright procession on.
Then shall the shepherd's pipe, the muse's lyre,
On CYRNUS' shores be heard: her grateful sons
With loud acclaim and hymns of cordial praise
Shall hail their high deliverers; every name                     175
To virtue dear be from oblivion snatch'd,
And plac'd among the stars: but chiefly thine,
Thine, PAOLI, with sweetest sound shall dwell
On their applauding lips; thy sacred name,
Endear'd to long posterity, some muse,                           180
More worthy of the theme, shall consecrate
To after ages, and applauding worlds
Shall bless the godlike man who sav'd his country.

✻ ✻ ✻ ✻ ✻ ✻ ✻ ✻ ✻ ✻ ✻ ✻ ✻ ✻ ✻ ✻ ✻ ✻ ✻

    So vainly wish'd, so fondly hop'd the Muse:[2]
Too fondly hop'd: The iron fates prevail,                        185
And CYRNUS is no more. Her generous sons,
Less vanquish'd than o'erwhelm'd, by numbers crush'd,
Admir'd, unaided, fell. So strives the moon

---

1   Grip.
2   Lines 184-201 must have been written after news of Paoli's defeat reached Warring-
    ton.

In dubious battle[1] with the gathering clouds,
190 And strikes a splendour thro' them; till at length
Storms roll'd on storms involve the face of heaven
And quench her struggling fires. Forgive the zeal
That, too presumptuous, whisper'd better things
And read the book of destiny amiss.
195 Not with the purple colouring of success
Is virtue best adorn'd: th' attempt is praise.
There yet remains a freedom, nobler far
Than kings or senates can destroy or give;
Beyond the proud oppressor's cruel grasp
200 Seated secure; uninjur'd; undestroy'd;
Worthy of Gods: The freedom of the mind.


## ON THE DEATH OF MRS. JENNINGS

["The Author's Grandmother" (Barbauld's note to the title in
*Poems*, 1773, its first printing). Anna Letitia Wingate Jennings,
her mother's mother, died 15 October 1770, age 83.]

*Est tamen quieté, & puré, & eleganter actae aetatis, placida ac lenis
senectus.*

Cicero de Senect.[2]

'Tis past: dear venerable shade, farewel!
Thy blameless life thy peaceful death shall tell.
Clear to the last thy setting orb has run;
Pure, bright, and healthy like a frosty sun:
5 And late old age with hand indulgent shed
Its mildest winter on thy favour'd head.
For Heaven prolong'd her life to spread its praise,
And blest her with a Patriarch's length of days.[3]

---

1  In dubious battle: Milton, *Paradise Lost*, 1:104.
2  Cicero, *De Senectute*, V.13. But there is also the tranquil and serene old age of a life
spent quietly amid pure and refining pursuits (Loeb translation).
3  Old-Testament patriarchs such as Methuselah were credited with lifespans of hun-
dreds of years.

The truest praise was hers, a chearful heart,
~~Prone to enjoy, and ready to impart.~~ 10
An Israelite[1] indeed, and free from guile,
She show'd that piety and age could smile.
Religion had her heart, her cares, her voice;
'Twas her last refuge, as her earliest choice.
To holy Anna's[2] spirit not more dear 15
The church of Israel, and the house of prayer.
Her spreading offspring of the fourth degree[3]
Fill'd her fond arms, and clasp'd her trembling knee.
Matur'd at length for some more perfect scene,
Her hopes all bright, her prospects all serene, 20
Each part of life sustain'd with equal worth,
And not a wish left unfulfill'd on earth,
Like a tir'd traveller with sleep opprest,
Within her children's arms she dropt to rest.
Farewel! thy cherish'd image, ever dear, 25
Shall many a heart with pious love revere:
Long, long shall mine her honour'd memory bless,
Who gave the dearest blessing I possess.

---

1 "The elect are called the Israel of God, and the true servants of God Israelites indeed" (St. Jerome, quoted in *OED*).

2 Anna was "a widow of about fourscore and four years, which departed not from the temple, but served God with fastings and prayers night and day" (Luke 2:37).

3 Great-grandchildren.

# ON THE BACKWARDNESS OF THE SPRING 1771

[The spring of 1771 was unusually cold and gloomy. One observer recorded "weather excessively cold … with wind, hail, snow etc." on 17 April (Neville, *Diary*, p. 99). This poem was first published in *Poems*, 1773.]

> *Estatem increpitans seram, zephyrosque morantes.*
>
> Virgil.[1]

In vain the sprightly sun renews his course,
Climbs up th' ascending signs[2] and leads the day,
While long embattled clouds repel his force,
And lazy vapours choak the golden ray.

5    In vain the spring proclaims the new-born year;
No flowers beneath her lingering footsteps spring,
No rosy garland binds her flowing hair,
And in her train no feather'd warblers sing.

Her opening breast is stain'd with frequent showers,
10   Her streaming tresses bath'd in chilling dews,
And sad before her move the pensive hours,
Whose flagging wings no breathing sweets diffuse.

Like some lone pilgrim, clad in mournful weed,
Whose wounded bosom drinks her falling tears,
15   On whose pale cheek relentless sorrows feed,
Whose dreary way no sprightly carol chears.

Not thus she breath'd on Arno's[3] purple shore,
And call'd the Tuscan Muses to her bowers;

---

1   *Georgics*, iv.138. Chiding laggard summer and the loitering zephyrs (Loeb translation).
2   Of the Zodiac, through which the sun moves.
3   The principal river in Tuscany, associated poetically with Virgil's *Pastorals* ("the Tuscan Muses" in l. 18).

Not this the robe in Enna's vale she wore,
~~When Ceres' daughter fill'd her lap with flowers.~~[1]

Clouds behind clouds in long succession rise,
And heavy snows oppress the springing green;
The dazzling waste fatigues the aching eyes,
And fancy droops beneath th' unvaried scene.

Indulgent nature, loose this frozen zone;[2]
Thro' opening skies let genial sun-beams play;
Dissolving snows shall their glad impulse own,
And melt upon the bosom of the May.

## THE MOUSE'S PETITION[3]

[When Barbauld visited Joseph Priestley at Leeds in the sum-
mer of 1771 he was experimenting with noxious gases, using
live mice for the purpose. According to anecdote, one night a
mouse "was brought in after supper, too late for any experi-
ment to be made with it that night, and the servant was desired
to set it by till next morning. Next morning it was brought in
after breakfast, with its petition twisted among the wires of its
cage" (Turner, "Mrs. Barbauld," p. 184)—the petition being this
poem. When the poem was published in *Poems* (1773), review-
ers berated Priestley for inhumanity to animals. Barbauld
responded by inserting a footnote in ed. 3 of *Poems*: "The
Author is concerned to find, that what was intended as the
petition of mercy against justice, has been construed as the plea
of humanity against cruelty. She is certain that cruelty could
never be apprehended from the Gentleman to whom this is
addressed; and the poor animal would have suffered more as the
victim of domestic economy [i.e., in a mouse trap], than of
philosophical [scientific] curiosity."

---

1  Lines 19-20 allude to the story of Prosperpina, daughter of Ceres (a fertility goddess
   in Classical myth), who gathered flowers in the Sicilian valley of Enna.
2  Belt or girdle.
3  Found in the trap where he had been confined all night by Dr. Priestley, for the
   sake of making experiments with different kinds of air [Barbauld's note, *P 1792*].

However intended, the poem has indeed been read as a plea of humanity against cruelty, and also as a political statement. "Petition," as Marlon Ross has noticed, signifies "the most radical version of a political letter, which targets the heart of established power by directly addressing the monarch and parliament" (Ross, "Configurations," p. 98)—as the electors of the County of Middlesex had lately been doing on behalf of John Wilkes. Barbauld's full awareness of its meaning and use is manifest in her whimsical "Epitaph on a Goldfinch": "Though born with the most ... unbounded love of freedom, he was closely confined in a grated prison, and scarcely permitted to view those fields, to the possession of which he had a natural and undoubted charter. Deeply sensible of this infringement of his native and inalienable rights, he was often heard to petition for redress" (*Legacy*, p. 183). Moreover, Mitzi Myers has argued that the poem encodes feminist concerns within its humanitarian ones: "The animal victim was widely deployed by humanitarian writers for the young, ... but it was especially adaptable to women's concerns and their critique of masculine values. The gender-coded animal is everywhere in Georgian female writing, for adults as well as for children" ("Of Mice and Mothers," p. 275).

"The Mouse's Petition" became one of Barbauld's most popular poems. Mary Wollstonecraft reprinted it in her *Female Reader* (1789), and its many imitations include Mary Robinson's "The Linnet's Petition" (1775). And perhaps Samuel Taylor Coleridge's dislike of trapping mice, noted by his biographer Richard Holmes (*Early Visions*, pp. 138-39), may be traced to this poem's influence.]

*Parcere subjectis, & debellare superbos.*

Virgil.[1]


Oh! hear a pensive prisoner's prayer,
For liberty that sighs;

---

1  *Aeneid*, 6:853. To spare the humbled, and to tame in war the proud! (Loeb translation).

And never let thine heart be shut
Against the wretch's cries.

For here forlorn and sad I sit,                                    5
Within the wiry grate;
And tremble at th' approaching morn,
Which brings impending fate.

If e'er thy breast with freedom glow'd,
And spurn'd a tyrant's chain,[1]                                  10
Let not thy strong oppressive force
A free-born mouse[2] detain.

Oh! do not stain with guiltless blood
Thy hospitable hearth;
Nor triumph that thy wiles betray'd                               15
A prize so little worth.

The scatter'd gleanings of a feast
My frugal meals supply;
But if thine unrelenting heart
That slender boon deny,                                           20

The chearful light, the vital air,
Are blessings widely given;
Let nature's commoners enjoy
The common gifts of heaven.

The well taught philosophic mind                                 25
To all compassion gives;
Casts round the world an equal eye,
And feels for all that lives.

---

1   In *The Present State of Liberty in Great Britain and her Colonies* (1769), Priestley had
    argued for "a just idea of natural and civil rights" and denounced the government
    for attempting to "enslave" the American colonists (Schofield, *Enlightenment of
    Joseph Priestley*, pp. 212-13).
2   Alluding to a cant phrase, "free-born Englishman," used by political liberals, as in
    poet James Thomson's indignant line, "The free-born Briton to the dungeon
    chain'd" (*The Seasons:* "Winter," l. 371).

If mind, as ancient sages taught,
A never dying flame,
Still shifts thro' matter's varying forms,
In every form the same,[1]

Beware, lest in the worm you crush
A brother's soul you find;
And tremble lest thy luckless hand
Dislodge a kindred mind.

Or, if this transient gleam of day
Be *all* of life we share,
Let pity plead within thy breast
That little *all* to spare.

So may thy hospitable board
With health and peace be crown'd;
And every charm of heartfelt ease
Beneath thy roof be found.

So, when destruction lurks unseen,
Which men, like mice, may share,
May some kind angel clear thy path,
And break the hidden snare.

---

1   If mind ... same: Alluding probably to James Thomson's plea for "animal rights" in *Liberty* (1735), 3:63-68: "He [Pythagoras] taught that Life's indissoluble Flame, / From Brute to Man, and Man to Brute again, / For ever shifting, runs th' eternal round; / Thence try'd against the blood-polluted Meal ... To turn the human Heart." But Priestley did not believe the doctrine of transmigration of souls; he had just cited it as a reason for rejecting the idea that Christ's soul was created before his body (Schofield, *Enlightenment*, pp. 199-200).

# AN INVENTORY OF THE FURNITURE IN
## DR. PRIESTLEY'S STUDY

[Written perhaps during the same visit to Leeds (1771) that produced "The Mouse's Petition," but not published in Barbauld's lifetime. The inventory poem is a comic genre practised by Jonathan Swift, among others: see his "True and Faithful Inventory of the Goods belonging to Dr. Swift ... upon lending his House to the Bishop of Meath" (1726).]

A map of every country known,[1]
With not a foot of land his own.
A list of folks that kicked a dust
On this poor globe, from Ptol. the First;[2]
He hopes,—indeed it is but fair,—                    5
Some day to get a corner there.
A group of all the British kings,
Fair emblem! on a packthread swings.[3]
The Fathers,[4] ranged in goodly row,
A decent, venerable show,                            10
Writ a great while ago, they tell us,
And many an inch o'ertop their fellows.
A Juvenal[5] to hunt for mottos;
And Ovid's tales of nymphs and grottos.[6]
The meek-robed lawyers, all in white;[7]             15
Pure as the lamb,—at least, to sight.
A shelf of bottles, jar and phial,[8]

---

1 Priestley's *New Chart of History* (1769) shows "the rise, progress, extent, and duration of every considerable empire or state" (Crook, *Bibliography of Joseph Priestley*, p. 137).
2 Priestley's *Chart of Biography* (1765) lists important historical figures, including Ptolemy I, ruler of Egypt (d. 283 BC).
3 Perhaps another chart, showing the English monarchs. It hangs on the wall, and Barbauld seems to insinuate that Priestley is for hanging the monarchy.
4 The works of the Church Fathers (St. Augustine, St. Jerome, and so forth), in large folio volumes.
5 Roman poet Decimus Junius Juvenalis (c. AD 55-127), from whose works Priestley takes quotations (mottos).
6 Ovid's *Metamorphoses*, light reading for a man of Priestley's seriousness.
7 Classic works of legal theory, bound in vellum.
8 Probably the Leyden jar, in which Priestley stored electricity. Upon being discharged, the electricity sparked like lightning (line 19).

By which the rogues he can defy all,—[1]
All filled with lightning keen and genuine,
And many a little imp he'll pen you in[2]
Which, like Le Sage's sprite, let out,
Among the neighbours makes a rout;[3]
Brings down the lightning on their houses,
And kills their geese, and frights their spouses.
A rare thermometer,[4] by which
He settles, to the nicest pitch,
The just degrees of heat, to raise
Sermons, or politics, or plays.[5]
Papers and books, a strange mixed olio,[6]
From shilling touch to pompous folio;[7]
Answer, remark, reply, rejoinder,[8]
Fresh from the mint, all stamped and coined here;
Like new-made glass, set by to cool,
Before it bears the workman's tool.
A blotted proof-sheet, wet from Bowling.[9]
—"How can a man his anger hold in ?"—[10]
Forgotten rimes, and college themes,

20

25

30

35

---

1 Seems to imply in Priestley an eagerness for scientific controversy which his published work had not yet displayed. Perhaps Barbauld mimics his speech?

2 The phrase is hard to construe. Perhaps an allusion to one of the "entertaining experiments" described in Vol. 2 of Priestley's *History of Electricity* (1767)?

3 In *Le Diable Boiteux* (1707) by René LeSage, a student releases from a laboratory a spirit, Asmodeus, who causes havoc in the neighborhood by lifting the roofs of houses and revealing people's private lives. Line 23 below may refer to Priestley's *History*, which reports one experimenter's using "a metallic rod, to bring lightning into his house" (1:426-27).

4 Thermometer jokes based on the accurate sensitivity of the instrument were common in the 18th century: See Terry Castle, *The Female Thermometer*, Ch. 2.

5 Priestley wrote sermons and politics, but not plays. In ll. 38-40, "embryo," "mass," and "chaos" recall Pope's *Dunciad* (1728), 1:53-60.

6 A miscellaneous collection.

7 A shilling touch is a topical pamphlet. Priestley wrote no folios; these must be books in his library.

8 Works of controversy often bore titles like "An Answer to" and "Remarks upon." In 1771 Priestley was editing a periodical devoted to theological argument, and papers with such titles might be lying around his study.

9 blotted: spoiled by over-inking; Bowling: presumably, a printer.

10 Priestley was noted for his good temper, but this line seems to imply that the blotted proof has infuriated him.

Worm-eaten plans, and embryo schemes;—
A mass of heterogeneous matter,
A chaos dark, nor land nor water;—                          40
New books, like new-born infants, stand,
Waiting the printer's clothing hand;—
Others, a motley ragged brood,
Their limbs unfashioned all, and rude,
Like Cadmus' half-formed men appear;[1]                    45
One rears a helm, one lifts a spear,
And feet were lopped and fingers torn
Before their fellow limbs were born;
A leg began to kick and sprawl
Before the head was seen at all,                           50
Which quiet as a mushroom lay
Till crumbling hillocks gave it way;
And all, like controversial writing,
Were born with teeth, and sprung up fighting.
    "But what is this," I hear you cry,                     55
"Which saucily provokes my eye?"—
A thing unknown, without a name,
Born of the air and doomed to flame.[2]

# SONG I

[Barbauld's earliest known publications are the six "songs" she
allowed her brother to include, without her name, in his first
literary work, *Essays on Song-Writing* (1772). She wrote them
probably in the course of corresponding about songs and song-
writing with him while he was at Manchester studying surgery
(1766-69). "Song," here, does not mean "words set to music,"
but rather an amorous poem of the kind written by the seven-
teenth-century "Cavalier" poets or (more intensely) by one of

---

1  In Ovid's *Metamorphoses*, 3:88-123, Cadmus sows a dragon's teeth. They immediate-
   ly spring up in the shape of armed men who are barely formed before they kill one
   another. The passage was widely construed as a symbol of discord.
2  Barbauld seems to be witnessing a moment of discovery in one of Priestley's exper-
   iments—perhaps the discovery of hydrogen ("inflammable air").

Barbauld's favorites, Elizabeth Singer Rowe. "Song I," below,
became popular under the title, "The Symptoms of Love." The
songs were reprinted in *Poems* (1773).]

Come here fond youth, whoe'er thou be
That boasts to love as well as me,
And if thy breast have felt so wide a wound,
Come hither and thy flame approve;[1]
I'll teach thee what it is to love,
And by what marks true passion may be found.

It is to be all bath'd in tears,
To live upon a smile for years,
To lie whole ages at a beauty's feet;
To kneel, to languish and implore,
And still tho' she disdain, adore;
It is to do all this and think thy sufferings sweet.

It is to gaze upon her eyes
With eager joy and fond surprize,
Yet temper'd with such chaste and awful fear
As wretches feel who wait their doom;
Nor must one ruder thought presume
Tho' but in whispers breath'd, to meet her ear.

It is to hope, tho' hope were lost,
Tho' heaven and earth thy passion crost;
Tho' she were bright as sainted queens above,
And thou the least and meanest swain
That folds his flock upon the plain,
Yet if thou dar'st not hope, thou dost not love.

It is to quench thy joy in tears,
To nurse strange doubts and groundless fears;
If pangs of jealousy thou hast not prov'd,[2]

---

1  Prove.
2  Experienced.

Tho' she were fonder and more true
Than any nymph old poets drew,
Oh never dream again that thou hast lov'd.                30

If when the darling maid is gone,
Thou dost not seek to be alone,
Wrapt in a pleasing trance of tender woe;
    And muse, and fold thy languid arms,
    Feeding thy fancy on her charms,                      35
Thou dost not love, for love is nourish'd so.

If any hopes thy bosom share
But those which love has planted there,
Or any cares but his thy breast enthrall,
    Thou never yet his power hast known;                  40
    Love sits on a despotic throne,
And reigns a tyrant, if he reigns at all.

Now if thou art so lost a thing,
Here all thy tender sorrows bring,
And prove whose patience longest can endure;             45
    We'll strive whose fancy shall be lost
    In dreams of fondest passion most,
For if thou thus hast lov'd, oh! never hope a cure.


## SONG V

As near a weeping spring reclin'd
The beauteous ARAMINTA pin'd,
And mourn'd a false ungrateful youth;
While dying echoes caught the sound,
And spread the soft complaints around                     5
Of broken vows and alter'd truth;

An aged shepherd heard her moan,
And thus in pity's kindest tone
Address'd the lost despairing maid;

Cease, cease unhappy fair to grieve,
For sounds, tho' sweet, can ne'er relieve
A breaking heart by love betray'd.

Why shouldst thou waste such precious showers,
That fall like dew on wither'd flowers,
But dying passion ne'er restor'd;
In beauty's empire is no mean,
And woman, either slave or queen,
Is quickly scorn'd when not ador'd.[1]

Those liquid pearls from either eye,
Which might an eastern empire buy,
Unvalued here and fruitless fall;
No art the season can renew
When love was young, and DAMON[2] true,
No tears a wandering heart recall.

Cease, cease to grieve, thy tears are vain,
Should those fair orbs in drops of rain
Vie with a weeping southern sky;
For hearts o'ercome with love and grief
All nature yields but one relief;
Die, hapless ARAMINTA, die.

---

1 Lines 16-18 are quoted by Mary Wollstonecraft in *A Vindication of the Rights of Woman*, Ch. 4, "Observations on the State of Degradation to which Woman is Reduced by Various Causes": "The passions of men have thus placed women on thrones.... They will smile ... though told that [quotation]. But the adoration comes first, and the scorn is not anticipated" (p. 146).
2 In pastoral poetry, a name for a young man.

[Lucy Aikin tells a family anecdote about the occasion that prompted Barbauld to write this poem: "Somebody [at Warrington Academy] was bold enough to talk of getting up private theatricals. This was a dreadful business! All the wise and grave, the whole tutorhood, cried out, it must not be! The students ... and, I must add, my aunt, took the prohibition very sulkily; and my aunt's Ode to Wisdom was the result" (quoted in Bright, *Historical Sketch*, p. 14). The Puritan ancestors of late eighteenth-century Dissent had disapproved intensely of stage plays; the tutors at Warrington, more relaxed in their views, enjoyed reading plays but may have frowned on staged performance by the students. "To Wisdom" was published in *Poems* (1773).]

*Dona praesentis rape laetus horae, ac*
*Linque severa.*

Horat.[1]

O WISDOM! if thy soft controul
Can sooth the sickness of the soul,
Can bid the warring passions cease,
And breathe the calm of tender peace,
WISDOM! I bless thy gentle sway,     5
And ever, ever will obey.
    But if thou com'st with frown austere
To nurse the brood of care and fear;
To bid our sweetest passions die,
And leave us in their room a sigh;    10
Or if thine aspect stern have power
To wither each poor transient flower,
That cheers this pilgrimage of woe,
And dry the springs whence hope should flow;
WISDOM, thine empire I disclaim,    15

---

1  Horace, *Odes*, III.viii.27-28. Gladly take the gifts of the present hour and abandon serious things! (Loeb translation)

Thou empty boast of pompous name!
In gloomy shade of cloisters dwell,
But never haunt my chearful cell.
Hail to pleasure's frolic train!
20     Hail to fancy's golden reign!
Festive mirth, and laughter wild,
Free and sportful as the child!
Hope with eager sparkling eyes,
And easy faith, and fond surprise!
25     Let these, in fairy colours drest,
Forever share my careless breast;
Then, tho' wise I may not be,
The wise themselves shall envy me.

## HYMN II

[In 1772 William Enfield, rector of Warrington Academy, induced Barbauld to contribute five hymns anonymously to his collection, *Hymns for Public Worship*. When she wrote them is not known. They became very popular and were reprinted (usually in shortened versions) long into the nineteenth century.]

Praise to GOD, immortal praise,[1]
For the love that crowns our days;
Bounteous source of every joy,
Let thy praise our tongues employ.

5     For the blessings of the field,
For the stores the gardens yield,
For the vine's exalted juice,
For the generous olive's use:

---

1 "Although the fig tree shall not blossom, neither shall fruit be in the vines, the labour of the olive shall fail, and the fields shall yield no meat, the flock shall be cut off from the fold, and there shall be no herd in the stalls; yet I will rejoice in the LORD, I will joy in the GOD of my salvation. Habakkuk, iii.17, 18" (Barbauld's note).

Flocks that whiten all the plain,
~~Yellow sheaves of ripen'd grain;~~                          10
Clouds that drop their fatt'ning dews,
Suns that temperate warmth diffuse:

All that spring with bounteous hand
Scatters o'er the smiling land:
All that liberal autumn pours                                15
From her rich o'erflowing stores:

These to thee, my GOD, we owe;
Source whence all our blessings flow;
And for these, my soul shall raise
Grateful vows and solemn praise.                             20

Yet should rising whirlwinds tear
From its stem the ripening ear;
Should the fig-tree's blasted shoot
Drop her green untimely fruit;

Should the vine put forth no more,                           25
Nor the olive yield her store;
Though the sick'ning flocks should fall,
And the herds desert the stall;

Should thine alter'd hand restrain
The early and the latter rain;[1]                            30
Blast each opening bud of joy,
And the rising year destroy;

Yet to thee my soul should raise
Grateful vows, and solemn praise;
And when every blessing's flown,                             35
Love thee—for thyself alone.

---

1   The … rain: Deuteronomy 11:14.

# HYMN V

Awake, my soul! lift up thine eyes;
See where thy foes against thee rise,
In long array, a numerous host;
Awake, my soul, or thou art lost.

5     Here giant danger threat'ning stands
Mustering his pale terrific bands;
There pleasure's silken banners spread,
And willing souls are captive led.

See where rebellious passions rage,
10     And fierce desires and lusts engage;
The meanest foe of all the train
Has thousands and ten thousands slain.

Thou tread'st upon enchanted ground,[1]
Perils and snares beset thee round;
15     Beware of all, guard every part,
But most, the traitor in thy heart.

Come then, my soul, now learn to wield
The weight of thine immortal shield;
Put on the armour from above
20     Of heavenly truth and heavenly love.

The terror and the charm repel,
And powers of earth, and powers of hell;
The man of Calvary[2] triumph'd here;
Why should his faithful followers fear?

---

1  In John Bunyan's *Pilgrim's Progress* (1678), Christian must cross an "Enchanted Ground" where he is threatened with falling asleep and not reaching Heaven.
2  Jesus was crucified on Mt. Calvary.

# THE GROANS OF THE TANKARD

[The "hint" for this poem, according to Warrington legend, "was this; a large old family-tankard used to stand on her father's sideboard, filled with water, his only beverage. A gentleman dining with the Dr. observed on the degradation to which this noble vessel was subjected, after having been accustomed to pass round the festal board as the vehicle of so much more generous liquors" (Turner, "Mrs. Barbauld," p. 230). Published in *Poems* (1773), the poem was criticized by one reviewer for complimenting Dissenters "on their abstemiousness, in opposition to the sons of the church, who are supposed to indulge themselves in sacerdotal luxury" (*Critical Review*, p. 193).]

*Dulci digne mero!*

Horat.[1]

Of strange events I sing, and portents dire;
The wond'rous themes a reverent[2] ear require;
Tho' strange the tale, the faithful Muse believe,
And what she says with pious awe receive.
    'Twas at the solemn, silent, noon-tide hour,[3]      5
When hunger rages with despotic power,
When the lean student quits his Hebrew roots[4]
For the gross nourishment of English fruits,
And throws unfinish'd airy systems by
For solid pudding[5] and substantial pye,      10
When hungry poets the glad summons own,
And leave spare fast to dine with Gods alone;[6]

---

1 Horace, *Odes*, III.xiii.2. Worthy of sweet wine (Loeb translation).
2 reverent: in *P 1773* ed. 1, "reverend" (by error).
3 Line 5 parodies the first line of "William and Margaret" (1723), a ballad by David Mallet: "'Twas at the silent, solemn hour, / When night and morning meet; / In glided Margaret's grimly ghost, / And stood at William's feet" (Mallet, *Works*, 1:3). William, reproached by her ghost for abandoning her, dies on Margaret's grave.
4 Linguistic roots, but also the supposed diet of abstinent scholars.
5 solid pudding: quoted from Pope, *The Dunciad* (1728), 1:52.
6 Line 12 mocks Milton, "Il Penseroso" (1645), l. 46: "Spare Fast, that oft with gods doth diet" (*Complete Poetry*, p. 112).

Our sober meal dispatch'd with silent haste,
The decent grace concludes the short repast:
15  Then urg'd by thirst we cast impatient eyes
Where deep, capacious, vast, of ample size,
The tankard stood, replenish'd to the brink
With the cold beverage blue-ey'd Naiads[1] drink.
But lo! a sudden prodigy appears,
20  And our chill'd hearts recoil with startling fears;
Its yawning mouth disclos'd the deep profound,
And in low murmurs breath'd a sullen sound;
Cold drops of dew did on the sides appear;
No finger touch'd it, and no hand was near;
25  At length th' indignant vase its silence broke,
First heav'd deep hollow groans, and then distinctly spoke.
      "How chang'd the scene![2] for what unpardon'd crimes
Have I surviv'd to these degenerate times?
I, who was wont the festal board to grace,
30  And midst the circle lift my honest face,
White o'er with froth, like Etna[3] crown'd with snow,
Which mantled o'er the brown abyss below,
Where Ceres[4] mingled with her golden store
The richer spoils of either India's shore,
35  The dulcet reed the Western islands boast,
And spicy fruit from Banda's fragrant coast.
At solemn feasts the nectar'd draught I pour'd,
And often journey'd round the ample board:
The portly Alderman, the stately Mayor,
40  And all the furry[5] tribe my worth declare;
And the keen Sportsman oft, his labours done,

---

1  Water-nymphs in Classical myth.
2  How ... scene!: Ann Messenger notes that the words are quoted from James Thomson's *The Seasons*: "Summer," l. 784, and also that they echo fallen Satan's address to his comrade Beelzebub in *Paradise Lost*, 1:84 (Messenger, *His and Hers*, pp. 177-78).
3  A volcano in Sicily.
4  Roman goddess of agriculture. Her "golden store" is grain, which, combined with West Indian sugar ("the dulcet reed," below) and nutmeg ("the spicy fruit") from the Banda Islands of the East Indies, produces ale.
5  Alluding to the ermine robes worn by high public officers.

To me retreating with the setting sun,
Deep draughts imbib'd, and conquer'd land and sea,
And overthrew the pride of France—by me.[1]
    "Let meaner clay contain the limpid wave,         45
The clay for such an office nature gave;
Let China's earth,[2] enrich'd with colour'd stains,
Pencil'd with gold, and streak'd with azure veins,
The grateful flavour of the Indian leaf,[3]
Or Mocho's sunburnt berry glad receive;         50
The nobler metal claims more generous use,
And mine should flow with more exalted juice.
Did I for this my native bed resign,[4]
In the dark bowels of Potosi's mine?[5]
Was I for this with violence torn away,         55
And drag'd to regions of the upper day?
For this the rage of torturing furnace bore,
From foreign dross to purge the bright'ning ore?
For this have I endur'd the fiery test,
And was I stamp'd for this with Britain's lofty crest?[6]     60
    "Unblest the day, and luckless was the hour
Which doom'd me to a Presbyterian's power;
Fated to serve the Puritanick race,
Whose slender meal is shorter than their grace;
Whose moping sons no jovial orgies keep;         65
Where evening brings no summons—but to sleep;
No Carnival is even Christmas here,
And one long Lent involves the meagre year.
Bear me, ye pow'rs! to some more genial scene,[7]

---

1   Line 44 may allude to patriotic claims for the superiority of English ale, or it may indicate drunken anti-French boasting by the sportsman.

2   China's earth: chinaware (quoted from Pope, *The Rape of the Lock*, 3:110).

3   Tea. "Mocho's sunburnt berry" (below) is coffee.

4   Lines 53–60 echo Pope, *The Rape of the Lock*, 4:97–102, in which Thalestris demands of Belinda after the loss of her hair, "Was it for this you took such constant Care" to cultivate the lock?

5   The richest silver mine in Bolivia.

6   Stamped with the image of Britannia, the female figure symbolizing Britain, the tankard is thereby declared to contain the legal standard of silver per pound.

7   Bear me ... scene: An echo of Thomson, *Winter* (1726), l. 74: "Oh! bear me then to high, embowering shades...."

70 Where on soft cushions lolls the gouty Dean,
Or rosy Prebend, with cherubic face,
With double chin, and paunch of portly grace,[1]
Who lull'd in downy slumbers shall agree
To own no inspiration but from me.
75 Or to some spacious mansion, Gothic, old,
Where Comus'[2] sprightly train their vigils hold;
There oft exhausted, and replenish'd oft,
Oh! let me still supply th' eternal draught;
Till care within the deep abyss be drown'd,
80 And thought grows giddy at the vast profound."
  More had the goblet spoke, but lo! appears
An ancient Sybil furrow'd o'er with years;
Her aspect sour, and stern ungracious look
With sudden damp the conscious[3] vessel struck;
85 Chill'd at her touch its mouth it slowly clos'd,
And in long silence all its griefs repos'd:
Yet still low murmurs creep along the ground,
And the air vibrates with the silver sound.

---

1 The Dean and his fellow Church officer, the Prebend, suffer from overindulgence
 in food and drink.
2 A god invented by Milton for his *Maske presented at Ludlow Castle* (1634); the son of
 Circe and Bacchus, he preys on travelers and makes them drink a magic liquor
 which changes their faces to those of wild animals.
3 Self-conscious, as if feeling guilty.

[According to Warrington legend, the "alcove" in which Bar-
bauld wrote these verses was a summer-house in the garden of
the first Academy building. If so, the poem would be her earli-
est surviving work, written when she was not older than 19. It
was published in *Poems*, 1773.]

*Jam Cytherea choros ducit Venus imminente Luna.*

Horat.[1]

Now the moon-beam's trembling lustre
    Silvers o'er the dewy green,
And in soft and shadowy colours
    Sweetly paints the checquer'd scene.

Here between the opening branches          5
    Streams a flood of soften'd light,
There the thick and twisted foliage
    Spreads the browner gloom of night.

This is sure the haunt of fairies,
    In yon cool Alcove they play;         10
Care can never cross the threshold,
    Care was only made for day.

Far from hence be noisy clamour,
    Sick disgust and anxious fear;
Pining grief and wasting anguish         15
    Never keep their vigils here.

Tell no tales of sheeted spectres
    Rising from the quiet tomb;[2]

---

1   Horace, *Odes*, I.iv.5. Already Cytherean Venus leads her dancing bands beneath the
o'erhanging moon (Loeb translation).
2   As in Thomas Parnell's "Night-Piece on Death" (1721): "The bursting earth unveils
the shades! / All slow, and wan, and wrapped with shrouds, / They rise in visionary
crowds" (ll. 48–50).

Fairer forms this cell shall visit,
    Brighter visions gild the gloom.

Choral songs and sprightly voices
    Echo from her cell shall call;
Sweeter, sweeter than the murmur
    Of the distant water fall.

Every ruder gust of passion
    Lull'd with music dies away,
Till within the charmed bosom
    None but soft affections play:

Soft, as when the evening breezes
    Gently stir the poplar grove;
Brighter than the smile of summer,
    Sweeter than the breath of love.

Thee, th' inchanted Muse shall follow,
    LISSY![1] to the rustic cell,
And each careless note repeating
    Tune them to her charming shell.

Not the Muse who wreath'd with laurel,
    Solemn stalks with tragic gait,
And in clear and lofty vision
    Sees the future births of fate;[2]

Not the maid who crown'd with cypress
    Sweeps along in scepter'd pall,
And in sad and solemn accents
    Mourns the crested heroe's fall;[3]

---

1  Elizabeth Rigby, a local girl with whom Barbauld was close friends.
2  The Muse of epic poetry.
3  In Milton's "Il Penseroso," Melancholy wears "a *Cipres* stole" (l. 35) and Tragedy "In Scepter'd Pall com[es] sweeping by" (l. 98).

But that other smiling sister,[1]                                   45
    With the blue and laughing eye,
Singing, in a lighter measure,
    Strains of woodland harmony:

All unknown to fame and glory,
    Easy, blith and debonair,[2]                            50
Crown'd with flowers, her careless tresses
    Loosely floating on the air.

Then, when next the star of evening[3]
    Softly sheds the silent dew,
Let me in this rustic temple,                                       55
    Lissy! meet the Muse and you.


## HYMN TO CONTENT

[We do not know when Barbauld wrote this plea for inner peace; it was published in *Poems* (1773). In stanza six the poem glances at Elizabeth Carter's translation (1758) of the Greek Stoic philosopher Epictetus (see headnote to "Against Inconsistency in our Expectations"). Many years later stanza seven drew the fire of William Wordsworth and Samuel Taylor Coleridge: see notes below.]

> ————————————*natura beatis*
> *Omnibus esse dedit, si quis cognoverit uti.*
>
>                  Claudian.[4]

O Thou, the Nymph with placid eye!
O seldom found, yet ever nigh!
    Receive my temperate vow:

---

1   Mirth, in Milton's "L'Allegro."
2   The line quotes "L'Allegro," l. 24.
3   The planet Venus, which appears like a star in the western sky after sunset.
4   Claudian, *In Rufinum*, 1:215-16. Nature has given the opportunity of happiness to all, knew they but how to use it (Loeb translation).

Not all the storms that shake the pole
Can e'er disturb thy halcyon soul,
    And smooth unalter'd brow.

O come, in simple vest[1] array'd,
With all thy sober cheer display'd,
    To bless my longing sight;
Thy mien compos'd, thy even pace,
Thy meek regard, thy matron grace,
    And chaste subdued delight.

No more by varying passions beat,
O gently guide my pilgrim feet
    To find thy hermit cell;
Where in some pure and equal sky
Beneath thy soft indulgent eye
    The modest virtues dwell.

Simplicity in Attic[2] vest,
And Innocence with candid breast,
    And clear undaunted eye;
And Hope, who points to distant years,
Fair opening thro' this vale of tears
    A vista to the sky.

There Health, thro' whose calm bosom glide
The temperate joys in even tide,
    That rarely ebb or flow;
And Patience there, thy sister meek,
Presents her mild, unvarying cheek
    To meet the offer'd blow.[3]

---

1  Clothing.
2  Athenian; hence, elegantly simple.
3  As Jesus counsels in Matthew 5:39 ("resist not evil: but whosoever shall smite thee
    on thy right cheek, turn to him the other also").

Her influence taught the Phrygian sage[1]
A tyrant master's wanton rage
    With settled smiles to meet;
Inur'd to toil and bitter bread
He bow'd his meek submitted head,            35
    And kiss'd thy sainted feet.

But thou, oh Nymph retir'd and coy!
In what brown hamlet[2] dost thou joy
    To tell thy tender tale;
The lowliest children of the ground,       40
Moss rose, and violet, blossom round,
    And lily of the vale.

O say what soft propitious hour
I best may chuse to hail thy power,
    And court thy gentle sway?        45
When Autumn, friendly to the Muse,
Shall thy own modest tints diffuse,
    And shed thy milder day.

When Eve, her dewy star beneath,
Thy balmy spirit loves to breathe,        50
    And every storm is laid;
If such an hour was e'er thy choice,
Oft let me hear thy soothing voice
    Low whispering thro' the shade.

---

1  Epictetus (c. AD 55-135), from Phrygia, who endured enslavement by practising a philosophy of controlled desire and conformity to the laws of nature.

2  brown hamlet: In 1808 Wordsworth criticized this phrase for lacking "genuine feeling" and for imitating William Collins's "Ode to Evening." Henry Crabb Robinson, who reported Wordsworth's censure, justified the phrase: "Evening harmonises with Content. And the brown hamlet [village] is the evening hamlet" ("Reminiscences," 1:389). In 1812 Coleridge ridiculed the line in a public lecture on Milton (Robinson, *On Books*, p. 62).

# ODE TO SPRING

[Date of composition unknown; published in *Poems*, 1773. Richard Lovell Edgeworth wrote a commentary on this poem around 1806, for an unfinished sequel to his *Poetry Explained for the Use of Young People* (1802). "This elegant and harmonious ode," he remarks, "is written obviously in imitation of [William] Collins' ode to evening; the metre ... [is] the same and the same tone of description is observed in the whole structure of the poem." Edgeworth prefers Barbauld's ode to Collins's, finding "less inversion and less harshness of construction" in it. We quote some of his other observations in our notes.]

> *Hope waits upon the flowery prime.*
>
> WALLER.[1]

Sweet daughter of a rough and stormy sire,
Hoar Winter's blooming child; delightful Spring!
    Whose unshorn locks with leaves
    And swelling buds are crown'd;

5 From the green islands of eternal youth,[2]
(Crown'd with fresh blooms, and ever springing shade,)
    Turn, hither turn thy step,
    O thou, whose powerful voice[3]

More sweet than softest touch of Doric reed,
10 Or Lydian flute,[4] can sooth the madding winds,

---

1  "To my young Lady Lucy Sidney," l. 13.
2  "The islands here alluded to were called by the ancients the Fortunate islands ... by the moderns the Canary Islands ... they are situate in the Atlantic ocean & are beautiful and fruitful and fragrant" (Edgeworth).
3  "Here the word powerful does not mean strong[,] an epithet which would suit neither the age nor the sex of Spring[;] it relates to the power which Spring has in calming the storms of winter" (Edgeworth).
4  "The Doric mood or mode was a grave species of music though sometimes mixed with the cheerful[.] The Lydian soft and tender ... [and] sometimes used at funerals" (Edgeworth).

And thro' the stormy deep
Breathe thy own tender calm.

Thee, best belov'd! the virgin train await
With songs and festal rites, and joy to rove
    Thy blooming wilds among,                    15
    And vales and dewy lawns,

With untir'd feet; and cull thy earliest sweets
To weave fresh garlands for the glowing brow
    Of him, the favour'd youth
    That prompts their whisper'd sigh.           20

Unlock thy copious stores; those tender showers
That drop their sweetness on the infant buds,
    And silent dews that swell
    The milky ear's[1] green stem,

And feed the flowering osier's early shoots;          25
And call those winds which thro' the whispering boughs
    With warm and pleasant breath
    Salute the blowing flowers.

Now let me sit beneath the whitening thorn,[2]
And mark thy spreading tints steal o'er the dale;        30
    And watch with patient eye
    Thy fair unfolding charms.

O nymph approach! while yet the temperate sun[3]
With bashful forehead, thro' the cool moist air

---

1    "Ears of corn before their grain comes to maturity contain a milky fluid" (Edgeworth).

2    A flowering bush. "This is a beautiful passage—In a fine soft sunshiny day in spring the change of colours in the fields & hedges and gardens may be traced by an attentive and accurate observer" (Edgeworth, on the whole stanza).

3    "There is some thing indistinct in this [stanza]. The sun is made bashful in his youth while at the same time the veil of frequent clouds is requisite to protect approaching spring from his severer blaze" (Edgeworth).

35    Throws his young maiden beams,
      And with chaste kisses wooes

      The earth's fair bosom; while the streaming veil
      Of lucid clouds with kind and frequent shade
          Protects thy modest blooms
40        From his severer blaze.

      Sweet is thy reign, but short; The red dog-star[1]
      Shall scorch thy tresses, and the mower's scythe
          Thy greens, thy flow'rets all,
          Remorseless shall destroy.

45    Reluctant shall I bid thee then farewel;
      For O, not all that Autumn's lap contains,
          Nor Summer's ruddiest fruits,
          Can aught for thee atone,

      Fair Spring! whose simplest promise more delights
50    Than all their largest wealth, and thro' the heart
          Each joy and new-born hope
          With softest influence breathes.[2]

## TO A LADY,
## WITH SOME PAINTED FLOWERS

[Neither the lady's identity nor the date of composition is known; the poem was published in *Poems*, 1773. Flowers, as Mary Wollstonecraft complained in 1792, citing this poem in evidence, have always been gender signs for woman: an "error … which robs the whole sex of its dignity, and classes the

---

1   Sirius, in ascendance from July to September. Edgeworth calls this passage "highly poetic."

2   "This ode is not too long—a fault common to compositions of this sort. The mind tires of the repetition of similar images & allegorical personages—but here we are carried forward by the progressive subject of the poem—Upon the whole this ode and that of Collins are excellent specimens of poetry without rhyme" (Edgeworth).

brown and fair with the smiling flowers that only adorn the land. This has ever been the language of men, and the fear of departing from a supposed sexual character, has made even women of superior sense adopt the same sentiments" (*Vindication of the Rights of Woman*, p. 143). But when Barbauld wrote, she could not have been conscious of Wollstonecraft's critique. She might have recalled, rather, a passage from Frances Brooke's novel, *The History of Emily Montague* (1769): "Emily ... has a passion for flowers, with which I am extremely pleased, as it will be to her a continual source of pleasure" (p. 313). When young women began taking a serious, botanical interest in flowers in the 1790s, the potential for sexual suggestiveness made conservative men nervous.]

————————————*tibi lilia plenis*
*Ecce ferunt nymphae calathis.*

Virgil[1]

Flowers to the fair: To you these flowers I bring,
And strive to greet you with an earlier spring.
Flowers sweet, and gay, and delicate like you;
Emblems of innocence, and beauty too.
With flowers the Graces bind their yellow hair,    5
And flowery wreaths consenting lovers wear.
Flowers, the sole luxury which nature knew,
In Eden's pure and guiltless garden grew.
To loftier forms are rougher tasks assign'd;
The sheltering oak resists the stormy wind,    10
The tougher yew repels invading foes,
And the tall pine for future navies grows;
But this soft family, to cares unknown,
Were born for pleasure and delight alone.
Gay without toil, and lovely without art,    15
They spring to cheer the sense, and glad the heart.
Nor blush, my fair, to own you copy these;
Your best, your sweetest empire is—to please.

---

1  *Eclogues*, II.45-46. See, for you the Nymphs bring lilies in heaped-up baskets (Loeb translation).

# VERSES ON MRS. ROWE

[Date of composition not known; published in *Poems*, 1773. Elizabeth Singer Rowe (1674-1737), a Dissenter like Barbauld, wrote pastoral poetry which she published under the name Philomela; after the early death of her husband Thomas ("Alexis" in l. 14 below) she turned to the writing of religious verse and prose. Her hymns and love songs are notable for their intensity. She was admired by Anne Finch and Elizabeth Carter before Barbauld. "The Life of Mrs. Elizabeth Rowe" by Theophilus Rowe (in Rowe's *Miscellaneous Works in Prose and Verse*, 1739) probably provided the biographical information for Barbauld's poem.]

> *How from the summit of the grove she fell,*
> *And left it unharmonious———*
>
> Young[1]

Such were the notes our chaster SAPPHO[2] sung,
And every muse dropt honey on her tongue.[3]
Blest shade! how pure a breath of praise was thine,
Whose spotless life was faultless as thy line:
In whom each worth and every grace conspire,       5
The Christian's meekness and the Poet's fire.
Learn'd without pride, a woman without art;
The sweetest manners and the gentlest heart.
Smooth like her verse her passions learn'd to move,
And her whole soul was harmony and love.          10
Virtue that breast without a conflict gain'd,
And easy like a native monarch reign'd.
On earth still favour'd as by heaven approv'd,
The world applauded, and ALEXIS lov'd.

---

1   Edward Young, *Night Thoughts* (1742), 3:88-89.
2   Ancient Greek poetess (fl. c. 610-c. 580 BC) known both as the archetype of a woman poet and also as the author of sexually frank verse.
3   Lines 1-2 recall Pope's "Epistle to Robert Earl of Oxford," ll. 1-2: "Such were the Notes, thy once-lov'd Poet sung, / 'Till Death untimely stop'd his tuneful Tongue" (*Poems*, p. 313).

With love, with health, with fame, and friendship blest,                    15
And of a chearful heart the constant feast,
What more of bliss sincere could earth bestow?
What purer heaven could angels taste below?
But bliss from earth's vain scenes too quickly flies;
The golden cord is broke, ALEXIS dies.                                      20
Now in the leafy shade, and widow'd grove,
Sad PHILOMELA mourns her absent love.
Now deep retir'd in FROME's enchanting vale,[1]
She pours her tuneful sorrows on the gale;
Without one fond reserve the world disclaims,                               25
And gives up all her soul to heavenly flames.
Yet in no useless gloom she wore her days;
She lov'd the work, and only shun'd the praise.
Her pious hand the poor, the mourner blest;
Her image liv'd in every kindred breast.                                    30
THYNN, CARTERET, BLACKMORE, ORRERY approv'd,
And PRIOR prais'd, and noble HERTFORD lov'd;
Seraphic KENN, and tuneful WATTS were thine,[2]
And virtue's noblest champions fill'd the line.
Blest in thy friendships! in thy death too blest!                          35
Receiv'd without a pang to endless rest.
Heaven call'd the Saint matur'd by length of days,
And her pure spirit was exhal'd in praise.[3]
Bright pattern of thy sex, be thou my muse;
Thy gentle sweetness thro' my soul diffuse:                                 40
Let me thy palm, tho' not thy laurel share,
And copy thee in charity and prayer.
Tho' for the bard my lines are far[4] too faint,
Yet in my life let me transcribe the saint.

---

1   After the death of her husband, Rowe retired to Frome in Somerset.
2   "She was favoured with the esteem and acquaintance of ... the Lady *Carteret*, ...
    the honourable Mrs. [Frances] *Thynne*, the Earl of *Orrery*, Dr. [Thomas] *Kenne*,
    Lord Bishop of *Bath* and *Wells*, [the poet] Sir Richard *Blackmore*, Dr. [Isaac] *Watts*,
    Mr. [Matthew] *Prior*.... But above all she possessed the highest degree of friendship
    with another illustrious ornament of the age ... the Countess of HERTFORD"
    (Rowe, "Life," xcvi-xcvii).
3   Rowe died in the act of devotion.
4   far: in *P 1773* eds. 1-2, "yet."

# A SUMMER EVENING'S MEDITATION

[When this great poem was written we do not know; it was published in *Poems*, 1773. "A deservedly admired writer," remarked a commentator in 1813, "… has represented the vast extent of creation in some of the most majestic strains and harmonious numbers of poetry…. [Lines 90–97 are] true sublimity: our conceptions are elevated, our imagination is affected, our fancy and our expectations are still kept on the stretch by the description" (N., "Essay on the Infinity of Creation").

Women were urged to study astronomy by Hester Mulso Chapone in *Letters on the Improvement of the Mind* (1773): astronomy would "enlarge [the] mind and … excite in it the most … profound adoration" (2:140–41). If she had not yet read Chapone, Barbauld probably knew the earl of Shaftesbury's paean to the planets in *The Moralists* (1709): "But, O thou who art the author and modifier of these various motions! O sovereign and sole mover, by whose high art the rolling spheres are governed, and these stupendous bodies of our world hold their unrelenting courses!" (*Characteristics*, 2:113).]

*One sun by day, by night ten thousand shine.*

Young.[1]

'Tis past! The sultry tyrant of the south
Has spent his short–liv'd rage; more grateful hours
Move silent on; the skies no more repel
The dazzled sight, but with mild maiden beams
5     Of temper'd lustre, court the cherish'd eye
To wander o'er their sphere; where hung aloft
DIAN's[2] bright crescent, like a silver bow
New strung in heaven, lifts high its beamy horns
Impatient for the night, and seems to push
10    Her brother down the sky. Fair VENUS[3] shines

---

1  Edward Young, *Night Thoughts* (1742), 9:748.
2  Diana, the Roman goddess of the moon and of hunting; here signifying the moon.
3  The Evening Star, first seen just after sunset.

E'en in the eye of day; with sweetest beam
Propitious shines, and shakes a trembling flood
Of soften'd radiance from her dewy locks.
The shadows spread apace; while meeken'd[1] Eve,
Her cheek yet warm with blushes, slow retires                    15
Thro' the Hesperian gardens of the west,[2]
And shuts the gates of day. 'Tis now the hour
When Contemplation, from her sunless haunts,
The cool damp grotto, or the lonely depth
Of unpierc'd woods, where wrapt in solid shade                   20
She mused away the gaudy hours of noon,
And fed on thoughts unripen'd by the sun,
Moves forward; and with radiant finger points
To yon blue concave swell'd by breath divine,
Where, one by one, the living eyes of heaven                     25
Awake, quick kindling o'er the face of ether[3]
One boundless blaze; ten thousand trembling fires,
And dancing lustres, where th' unsteady eye
Restless and dazzled, wanders unconfin'd
O'er all this field of glories: spacious field!                 30
And worthy of the master: he, whose hand
With hieroglyphics elder than the Nile,
Inscrib'd the mystic tablet; hung on high
To public gaze, and said, adore, O man!
The finger of thy GOD. From what pure wells                     35
Of milky light, what soft o'erflowing urn,
Are all these lamps so fill'd? these friendly lamps,
For ever streaming o'er the azure deep
To point our path, and light us to our home.
How soft they slide along their lucid spheres!                  40
And silent as the foot of time, fulfil
Their destin'd courses: Nature's self is hush'd,
And, but a scatter'd leaf, which rustles thro'
The thick-wove foliage, not a sound is heard

---

1    Moderated.
2    The Hesperides, legendary gardens at the western edge of the world where golden
     apples grew.
3    The upper sky.

To break the midnight air; tho' the rais'd ear,
Intensely listening, drinks in every breath.
How deep the silence, yet how loud the praise!
But are they silent all? or is there not
A tongue in every star[1] that talks with man,
50  And wooes him to be wise; nor wooes in vain:
This dead of midnight is the noon of thought,
And wisdom mounts her zenith with the stars.
At this still hour the self-collected soul
Turns inward, and beholds a stranger there
55  Of high descent, and more than mortal rank;
An embryo GOD; a spark of fire divine,
Which must burn on for ages, when the sun,
(Fair transitory creature of a day!)
Has clos'd his golden eye, and wrapt in shades
60  Forgets his wonted journey thro' the east.
        Ye citadels of light, and seats of GODS!
Perhaps my future home, from whence the soul
Revolving periods past, may oft look back
With recollected tenderness, on all
65  The various busy scenes she left below,
Its deep laid projects and its strange events,
As on some fond and doating tale that sooth'd
Her infant hours; O be it lawful now
To tread the hallow'd circle of your courts,
70  And with mute wonder and delighted awe
Approach your burning confines. Seiz'd in thought,[2]
On fancy's wild and roving wing I sail,
From the green borders of the peopled earth,
And the pale moon, her duteous fair attendant;
75  From solitary Mars; from the vast orb

---

1   are they silent … every star: Wordsworth responded to this passage in two poems
    written in 1798, "A Night-Piece" and an untitled poem not published until 1992
    (Chandler, "Wordsworth's 'A Night-Piece'"; Davies, "'A Tongue in Every Star'").
2   Lines 71-98 appear to enact a sentence from David Hume's *Enquiry concerning
    Human Understanding* (1748): "the thought can in an instant transport us into the
    most distant regions of the universe; or even beyond the universe, into the
    unbounded chaos, where nature is supposed to lie in total confusion" (*Enquiries*, p.
    18).

Of Jupiter, whose huge gigantic bulk
Dances in ether like the lightest leaf;
To the dim verge, the suburbs of the system,
Where chearless Saturn 'midst his wat'ry moons
Girt with a lucid zone, in gloomy pomp,                          80
Sits like an exil'd monarch:[1] fearless thence
I launch into the trackless deeps of space,
Where, burning round, ten thousand suns appear,
Of elder beam; which ask no leave to shine
Of our terrestrial star, nor borrow light        ·              85
From the proud regent of our scanty day;
Sons of the morning, first-born of creation,
And only less than him who marks their track,
And guides their fiery wheels. Here must I stop,
Or is there aught beyond? What hand unseen                       90
Impels me onward thro' the glowing orbs
Of habitable nature; far remote,
To the dread confines of eternal night,
To solitudes of vast unpeopled space,
The desarts of creation, wide and wild;                          95
Where embryo systems and unkindled suns
Sleep in the womb of chaos; fancy droops,
And thought astonish'd stops her bold career.
But oh thou mighty mind! whose powerful word
Said, thus let all things be, and thus they were,               100
Where shall I seek thy presence? how unblam'd
Invoke thy dread perfection?[2]
Have the broad eye-lids of the morn beheld thee?[3]

---

1  In *P 1773* eds. 1-2, ll. 79-81 read, "Saturn 'midst her wat'ry moons / Girt with a
   lucid zone, majestic sits / In gloomy grandeur; like an exil'd queen / Amongst her
   weeping handmaids." Reviewing *Poems*, William Woodfall complained that Bar-
   bauld "speaks of Saturn in the feminine," an "offence against ancient mythology"
   (Review of *Poems*, p. 136n). In ed. 3, Barbauld changed the lines to their present
   text.

2  unblam'd ... perfection: Barbauld recalls Milton, *Paradise Lost*, 3:3 ("May I express
   thee unblam'd?").

3  "Eyelids of the morning" occurs several times in the Old Testament, e.g., in Job
   41:18 ("his eyes are like the eyelids of the morning"). Lines 103-05 recall the Lord's
   mocking questions to Job in Chs. 38-39.

Or does the beamy shoulder of Orion
105    Support thy throne? O look with pity down
On erring guilty man; not in thy names
Of terrour clad; not with those thunders arm'd
That conscious Sinai felt, when fear appall'd
The scatter'd tribes;[1] thou hast a gentler voice,
110    That whispers comfort to the swelling heart,
Abash'd, yet longing to behold her Maker.
      But now my soul unus'd to stretch her powers
In flight so daring, drops her weary wing,
And seeks again the known accustom'd spot,
115    Drest up with sun, and shade, and lawns, and streams,
A mansion fair and spacious for its guest,
And full replete with wonders. Let me here
Content and grateful, wait th' appointed time
And ripen for the skies: the hour will come
120    When all these splendours bursting on my sight
Shall stand unveil'd, and to my ravish'd sense
Unlock the glories of the world unknown.

## HYMN VI
### PIOUS FRIENDSHIP

[Barbauld wrote this hymn for the wedding of her Warrington friend Sarah Rigby to Caleb Parry, at Palgrave on 24 September 1778 (Roscoe, fol. 81). She published it in the 1792 edition of *Poems.*]

How blest the sacred tie that binds
In union sweet according minds!
How swift the heavenly course they run
Whose hearts, whose faith, whose hopes are one!

5    To each, the soul of each how dear,
What jealous love, what holy fear!

---

1   Lines 107-09 allude to Exodus 19, in which the Lord descends to the Israelites in a cloud of "thunders and lightnings ... so that all the people ... trembled."

How doth the generous flame within
Refine from earth and cleanse from sin!

Their streaming tears together flow
For human guilt and mortal woe;                    10
Their ardent prayers together rise,
Like mingling flames in sacrifice.

Together both they seek the place
Where GOD reveals his awful face;
How high, how strong, their raptures swell,          15
There's none but kindred souls can tell.

Nor shall the glowing flame expire
When nature droops her sickening fire;[1]
Then shall they meet in realms above
A heaven of joy—because of love.                    20

## TO MR. BARBAULD,
## NOVEMBER 14, 1778

[We do not know the significance to the Barbaulds of November 14. To Anna Letitia, November was a "dark dismal" month in which one had to look for indoor, imaginative amusements (*Lessons for Children of Three Years Old*, i.37-38); in the poem, however, Rochemont is the one who feels depressed. It was first published in *Works* (1825).]

Come, clear thy studious looks awhile,
 'T is arrant treason now
 To wear that moping brow,
When I, thy empress, bid thee smile.

 What though the fading year                    5
 One wreath will not afford

---

1 A reference to the end of the world at the Apocalypse.

To grace the poet's hair,
Or deck the festal board;

A thousand pretty ways we'll find
10     To mock old Winter's starving reign;
We'll bid the violets spring again,
Bid rich poetic roses blow,
Peeping above his heaps of snow;
We'll dress his withered cheeks in flowers,
15        And on his smooth bald head
       Fantastic garlands bind:
       Garlands, which we will get
From the gay blooms of that immortal year,
       Above the turning seasons set,
20   Where young ideas shoot in Fancy's sunny bowers.

A thousand pleasant arts we'll have
To add new feathers to the wings of Time,
       And make him smoothly haste away:
       We'll use him as our slave,
25        And when we please we'll bid him stay,
And clip his wings, and make him stop to view
       Our studies, and our follies too;
How sweet our follies are, how high our fancies climb.

We'll little care what others do,
30        And where they go, and what they say;
       Our bliss, all inward and our own,
Would only tarnished be, by being shown.
       The talking restless world shall see,
       Spite of the world we'll happy be;
35          But none shall know
         How much we're so,
         Save only Love, and we.

# LOVE AND TIME

## TO MRS. MULSO

[Mary Prescott Mulso was "the sister of General [Robert] Prescott" and the wife of Thomas Mulso (1721-99). Barbauld described her as "a lady as eminently calculated to inspire, as her husband was to feel, the delicacy and tenderness of that attachment which was only interrupted by his death" (Barbauld, "[Obituary of Thomas Mulso]"). Mrs. Mulso's sister-in-law and close friend was Hester Mulso Chapone, the writer, who addressed her in a poem "To Stella" (1775), the same name that Barbauld uses for her. By the mid-1790s Mrs. Mulso's health was poor (Pepys, 1:414), but this poem was written not later than the mid-1780s. It circulated in manuscript but was first published in *Works* (1825).]

On Stella's brow as lately envious Time
His crooked lines with iron pencil traced,
That brow, erewhile like ivory tablets smooth,
With Love's high trophies hung, and victories graced,
Digging him little caves in every cell,                    5
And every dimple, once where Love was wont to dwell;

He spied the God: and wondered still to spy,
Who higher held his torch in Time's despite;
Nor seemed to care for aught that he could do.
Then sternly thus he sought him thence to' affright:       10
The sovereign boy entrenched in a smile,
At his sour crabbed speech sat mocking all the while.

"What dost thou here, fond boy? Away, for shame!
Mine is this field, by conquest fairly won;
Love cannot reap his joys where Time has ploughed,        15
Thou and thy light-winged troop should now begone.
Go revel with fresh Youth in scenes of folly,
Sage Thought I bring, and Care, and pale-eyed Melancholy.

"Thy streams are froze, that once so briskly ran,
    Thy bough is shaken by the mellow year;
    Boreas and Zephyr[1] dwell not in one cave,
    And swallows spread their wings when winter's near;
    See where Florella's[2] cheeks soft bloom disclose,
Go seek the springing bud, and leave the faded rose."

    Thus spake old Time, of Love the deadliest foe,—
    Ah me, that gentle Love such foes should meet!
    But nothing daunted he returned again,
    Tempering with looks austere his native sweet;
    And, "Fool!" said he, "to think I e'er shall fly
From that rich palace where my choicest treasures lie.

    "Dost thou not see,—or art thou blind with age,—
    How many Graces on her eyelids sit,
    Linking those viewless chains that bind the soul,
    And sharpening smooth discourse with pointed wit;
    How many where she moves attendant wait,
The slow smooth step inspire, or high commanding gait?

    "Each one a several charm around her throws,
    Some to attract, some powerful to repell,
    Some mix the honeyed speech with winning smiles,
    Or call wild Laughter from his antic cell;
    Severer some, to strike with awful fear
Each rude licentious tongue that wounds the virtuous ear.

    "Not one of them is of thy scythe in dread,
    Or for thy cankered malice careth aught,
    Thy shaking fingers never can untwist
    The magic caestus[3] by their cunning wrought;
    And I, their knight, their bidding must obey,
For where the Graces are, will Love for ever stay.

---

1   The north and west winds, respectively.
2   A generic name for a young woman.
3   A belt or girdle.

"In my rich fields now boast the ravage done,
Those lesser spoils,—her brow, her cheek, her hair,      50
All that the touches of decay can feel,—
Take these, she has enough besides to spare;
I cannot thee dislodge, nor shalt thou me,
So thou and I, old Time, perforce must once agree.

"Nor is the boasted ravage all thine own,                55
Nor was the field by conquest fairly gained;
For leagued with Sickness, Life and Nature's foe,
That fiend accurst thy savage wars maintained;
His hand the furrows sunk where thou didst plough,
He undermined the tree, where thou didst shake the bough.    60

"But both unite, for both I here defy;
Spoil ye have made, but have no triumphs won;
And though the daffodil more freshly blooms,
Spreading her gay leaves to the morning sun,
Yet never will I leave the faded rose,                   65
Whilst the pale lovely flower such sweetness still bestows."

This said, exulting Cupid clapped his wings.
The sullen power, who found his rage restrained,
And felt the strong controul of higher charms,
Shaking his glass, vowed while the sands would run       70
For many a year the strife should be maintained:
But Jove decreed no force should Love destroy,
Nor time should quell the might of that immortal boy.

# LINES TO BE SPOKEN BY
# THOMAS DENMAN, ON THE CHRISTMAS
# BEFORE HIS BIRTHDAY,
# WHEN HE WAS FOUR YEARS OLD

[At Palgrave School Barbauld wrote many pieces for recitation by pupils at the annual examinations before Christmas and the theatrical evenings in May. These verses are among the very few known to survive. Thomas Denman (1779-1854), who was two months short of four when he recited them in December 1782, was her pupil for no more than two and a half years, but he remembered her affectionately for the rest of his life. He went on to be Lord Chief Justice of England and an author of the Reform Act of 1832 (see McCarthy, "The Celebrated Academy at Palgrave," pp. 318-19, 351-52). These lines were first published in 1994.]

> Nay, nay, I'll not be held, let me come by,
> The boys all spout, so pray why should not I?
> I won't be called a baby any more,
> Next February I'm completely four.——
> And now what pretty story shall I tell,
> Among the boys to bear away the belle.[1]
> Of Cinderella, or of Robin Hood,
> Or the poor babes that wander'd in the wood.
> Poor babes, their lips with blackberries were dyed,
> And when night came they sat them down and cried.[2]
> I'll shew you how St. George attacked the dragon,[3]
> There was a wonderful exploit to brag on!
> What are your Rodneys and your Howes to him,

5

10

---

1 Correctly, "bell": to win the prize.

2 Lines 9-10 quote the ballad, "The Children in the Wood": "Their prettye lippes with black-berries, / Were all besmear'd and dyed, / And when they sawe the dark-some night, / They sat them downe and cryed" (Percy, *Reliques of Ancient English Poetry*, 3:176).

3 St. George, patron saint of England, was depicted in plays, paintings and the insignia of the Knights of the Garter as a dragon-slayer.

Or tall De Grasse against an ogre grim?[1]
~~With seven league boots upon his giant legs,[2]~~ 15
Who swallows little children like poached eggs,
And fiercely stares—But soft, I would not fright ye,
So Ladies for this time I bid good night to ye.
Smile on me now, and in another year
I'll strut and fret my part[3] with any here. 20


## WRITTEN ON A MARBLE

[This brief reflection on world history was probably written for
Barbauld's pupils at Palgrave School, where she taught history,
and was perhaps first "published" in the school's "weekly
chronicle," which seems to have been mostly composed by
Barbauld (McCarthy, "The Celebrated Academy at Palgrave," p.
306). The poem first saw print in *Works* (1825).]

>     The world's something bigger,
>       But just of this figure
>     And speckled with mountains and seas;
>     Your heroes are overgrown schoolboys
>     Who scuffle for empires and toys, 5
>     And kick the poor ball as they please.
>     Now Caesar, now Pompey, gives law;[4]
>       And Pharsalia's plain,
>       Though heaped with the slain,
>     Was only a game at *taw*.[5] 10

---

1  Admiral George Rodney (1719-92) commanded the English fleet that defeated a
   French fleet under Admiral de Grasse in the West Indies in 1782; Admiral Richard
   Howe (1726-99) defended Gibraltar from Spanish attack in October 1782.
2  In the fairy tale "Hop o' My Thumb," a man-eating giant wearing boots that allow
   him to cover seven leagues at a step menaces a boy and his brothers.
3  Shakespeare, *Macbeth*, V.v.25.
4  Julius Caesar (100-44 BC) and Gnaeus Pompey (106-48 BC) vied for power in
   Rome; at the battle of Pharsalia (48 BC) Caesar's army prevailed.
5  A large variegated marble; a "game at taw" is a game of marbles.

# A SCHOOL ECLOGUE

[Barbauld wrote this parody of Virgilian pastoral at Palgrave School, probably for the school's "weekly chronicle." The three boys in the poem bear the names of actual pupils—several Williams, more than one Edward, and at least one Harry attended Palgrave (McCarthy, "Celebrated Academy," Appendix III)—and thus the joke may have been improved for the poem's first readers by their knowing the speakers. The poem was first published, unsigned and with line 91's reference to Palgrave removed, in *The Monthly Magazine*, 8 (August 1799); it was included in *Works* (1825).]

### Edward

Hist, William! hist! what means that air so gay?
Thy looks, thy dress, bespeak some holiday;
Thy hat is brush'd; thy hands, with wond'rous pains,
Are cleans'd from garden mould and inky stains;
5    Thy glossy shoes confess the lacquey's care;
And recent from the comb shines thy sleek hair.
What god, what saint, this prodigy has wrought?[1]
Declare the cause; and ease my lab'ring thought?

### William

John, faithful John, is with the horses come,
10    Mamma prevails, and I am sent for home.[2]

### Harry

Thrice happy whom such welcome tidings greet![3]
Thrice happy who reviews his native seat!
For him the matron spreads her candy'd hoard,
And early strawberries crown the smiling board;
15    For him crush'd gooseberries with rich cream combine,

---

1  "Sed tamen, ille Deus qui sit, da Tityre nobis" (Barbauld's note; Virgil, *Eclogues* I.18: But still tell me, Tityrus, who is this god of yours?). This and subsequent translations are from the Loeb edition.

2  Called home. Many Palgrave School pupils lived at the school, going home for holidays or family occasions.

3  "Fortunate senex, hi[n]c inter flumina nota" (Barbauld's note; *Eclogues*, I.51: Happy old man! Here, among familiar streams).

And bending boughs their fragrant fruit resign:
Custards and sillabubs[1] his taste invite;
Sports fill the day, and feasts prolong the night.
Think not I envy, I admire thy fate;[2]
Yet, ah! what different tasks thy comrades wait!     20
Some in the grammar's thorny maze to toil,
Some with rude strokes the snowy paper soil,
Some o'er barbaric climes in maps to roam,
Far from their mother-tongue, and dear loved home.[3]
Harsh names, of uncouth sound, their memories load,     25
And oft their shoulders feel th' unpleasant goad.[4]

### Edward

Doubt not our turn will come some future time.
Now, William, hear us twain contend in rhyme,
For yet thy horses have not eat their hay,
And unconsum'd as yet th' allotted hour of play.     30

### William

Then spout alternate,[5] I consent to hear,
Let no false rhyme offend my critic[6] ear;
But say, what prizes shall the victor hold?
I guess your pockets are not lin'd with gold!

### Harry

A ship these hands have built, in ev'ry part     35
Carv'd, rigg'd, and painted, with the nicest art;
The ridgy sides are black with pitchy store,
From stem to stern 'tis twice ten inches o'er.
The lofty mast, a straight, smooth hazel fram'd,
The tackling silk, the Charming Sally nam'd;     40
And—but take heed lest thou divulge the tale,

---

1   Drink or custard of milk sweetened with wine.
2   "Non equidem invideo, miror magis" (Barbauld's note; *Eclogues* I.11: Well, I grudge
you not—rather, I marvel).
3   "At nos hinc alii sitientes ibimus Afros, / Pars Scythiam, et rapidum Cretae
veniemus Oaxem [Oaxen]" (Barbauld's note; *Eclogues* I.64-65: But we must go
hence—some to the thirsty Africans, some to reach Scythia and Crete's swift
Oaxes).
4   A pointed stick used to prod drowsy or lazy pupils.
5   "Alternis dicetis" (Barbauld's note; *Eclogues*, III.59, translated in her text).
6   Critical, discriminating.

The lappet of my shirt supply'd the sail;
An azure ribband for a pendant[1] flies:
Now, if thy verse excel, be this the prize.

Edward

45  For me at home the careful houswives make,
With plums and almonds rich, an ample cake.
Smooth is the top, a plain of shining ice,
The West its sweetness gives, the East its spice;
From soft Ionian isles,[2] well known to fame,
50  Ulysses' once, the luscious currant came.
The green transparent citron Spain bestows,
And from her golden groves the orange glows.
So vast the heaving mass, it scarce has room
Within the oven's dark capacious womb;
55  'T will be consign'd to the next carrier's care,
I cannot yield it all—be half thy share.

Harry

Well does the gift thy liquorish[3] palate suit,
I know who robb'd the orchard of its fruit.[4]
When all were wrapt in sleep, one early morn,
60  While yet the dew-drop trembled on the thorn,
I mark'd when o'er the quickset hedge you leapt,
And, sly, beneath the gooseberry bushes crept;[5]
Then shook the trees, a show'r of apples fell,
And, where the hoard you kept, I know full well;
65  The mellow gooseberries did themselves produce,
For thro' thy pocket oozed the viscous juice.

Edward

I scorn a tell-tale, or I cou'd declare
How, leave unask'd, you sought the neighbouring fair;

---

1   A small flag.
2   Ionian isles: Greek islands including Zante (source of currants) and Ithaca, home of
    Ulysses or Odysseus in Homer.
3   Lickerish (greedy).
4   "Non ego, te vidi, Damonis—" (Barbauld's note; *Eclogues*, III.17, in which the line
    continues, "pessime, caprum excipere": Did I not see you, rascal, snaring Damon's
    goat?
5   "—Tu post carecta latebas" (Barbauld's note; *Eclogues*, III.20: You were skulking
    beyond the sedge).

Then home by moon-light spurred your jaded steed,
And scarce returned before the hour of bed.                    70
Think how thy trembling heart had felt affright,
Had not our master supped abroad that night.

### Harry

On the smooth, white-washed ceiling near thy bed,
Mixed with thine own, is Anna's[1] cypher read;
From wreaths of dusky smoke the letters flow;                  75
Whose hand the waving candle held, I know.
Fines and jobations[2] shall thy soul appall,
Whene'er our mistress spies the sully'd wall.

### Edward

Uncon'd[3] her lesson once, in idle mood,
Trembling before the master, Anna stood;                       80
I marked what prompter near her took his place,
And, whispering, sav'd the virgin from disgrace;
Much is the youth bely'd, and much the maid,
Or more than words the whisper soft convey'd.

### Harry

Think not I blush to own so bright a flame,                    85
Even boys for her assume the lover's name;—
As far as alleys beyond taws[4] we prize,[5]
Or venison pasty ranks above school pies;
As much as peaches beyond apples please,
Or Parmesan excels a Suffolk cheese;                           90
Or Palgrave donkeys lag behind a steed,
So far do Anna's charms all other charms exceed.

### Edward

Tell, if thou canst, where is that creature bred,
Whose wide-stretch'd mouth is larger than its head;

---

1  Anna seems to be a classmate (see ll. 79-80), although no girls are known to have
   attended Palgrave School.
2  "Long and tiresome rebukes" (*OED*). Progressive schools like Palgrave favored
   rebukes and monetary fines over physical punishment for offenses by pupils.
3  Unconned, not learned.
4  Alleys and taws are different kinds of marbles.
5  "Lenta salix quantum pallenti cedit olivae" (Barbauld's note; *Eclogues*, V.16: As far as
   the lithe willow yields to the pale olive).

95    Guess, and my great Apollo thou shalt be,[1]
      And cake and ship shall both remain with thee.

                        Harry
      Explain thou first, what portent late was seen,
      With strides impetuous, posting o'er the green;
      Three heads, like Cerberus,[2] the monster bore,
100   And one was sidelong fix'd, and two before;
      Eight legs, depending from his ample sides,
      Each well-built flank unequally divides;
      For five on this, on that side three are found,
      Four swiftly move, and four not touch the ground.
105   Long time the moving prodigy I view'd,
      By gazing men, and barking dogs pursu'd.

                        William
      Cease! cease your carols both! for lo the bell
      With jarring notes, has rung out pleasure's knell.
      Your startled comrades, ere the game be done,
110   Quit their unfinish'd sports, and trembling run.
      Haste to your forms before the master call!
      With thoughtful step he paces o'er the hall,
      Does with stern looks each playful loiterer greet,
      Counts with his eye, and marks each vacant seat;
115   Intense, the buzzing murmur grows around,
      Loud, thro' the dome, the usher's strokes resound.
      Sneak off, and to your places slily steal,
      Before the prowess of his arm you feel.[3]

---

1  "Dic quibus in terris, et eris mihi magnus Apollo" (Barbauld's note; *Eclogues*,
   III.104: Tell me in what land—and you shall be my great Apollo). The "creature"
   whose mouth is larger than its head (ll. 93-94) is a river.

2  In Greek mythology, the three-headed dog that guards the entrance to Hades. We
   have not solved the riddle presented in ll. 97-104.

3  The usher (i.e., assistant teacher) at Palgrave was Simon Westby. S. W. Rix, his pupil
   at another school, recalled him as a very punitive master ("Scenes of our Child-
   hood," p. 152).

# AUTUMN
## A FRAGMENT

[Written perhaps around 1780, and first published in *Works* (1825).]

Farewell the softer hours, Spring's opening blush
And Summer's deeper glow, the shepherd's pipe
Tuned to the murmurs of a weeping spring,
And song of birds, and gay enameled fields,—
Farewell! 'T is now the sickness of the year,                    5
Not to be medicined by the skillful hand.
Pale suns arise that like weak kings behold
Their predecessor's empire moulder from them;
While swift-increasing spreads the black domain
Of melancholy Night;—no more content                            10
With equal sway, her stretching shadows gain
On the bright morn, and cloud the evening sky.
Farewell the careless lingering walk at eve,
Sweet with the breath of kine and new-spread hay;
And slumber on a bank, where the lulled youth,                  15
His head on flowers, delicious languor feels
Creep in the blood. A different season now
Invites a different song. The naked trees
Admit the tempest; rent is Nature's robe;
Fast, fast, the blush of Summer fades away                      20
From her wan cheek, and scarce a flower remains
To deck her bosom; Winter follows close,
Pressing impatient on, and with rude breath
Fans her discoloured tresses. Yet not all
Of grace and beauty from the falling year                       25
Is torn ungenial. Still the taper fir
Lifts its green spire, and the dark holly edged
With gold, and many a strong perennial plant,
Yet cheer the waste: nor does yon knot of oaks
Resign its honours to the infant blast.                         30
This is the time, and these the solemn walks,
When inspiration rushes o'er the soul
Sudden, as through the grove the rustling breeze.

# TO THE BARON DE STONNE,
## WHO HAD WISHED AT THE NEXT TRAN-
## SIT OF MERCURY TO FIND HIMSELF
## AGAIN BETWEEN MRS. LABORDE AND
## MRS. B[ARBAULD]

[Visiting Paris in the spring of 1786, the Barbaulds met a charming, literary-minded, Anglophile nobleman, Alexandre-César-Annibal Frémin, baron de Stonne (1745-1821), who showed them around and exchanged verses and letters with Anna Letitia. On Thursday, 4 May, the baron took them to the Royal Observatory to watch the planet Mercury ("Hermes" in line 2) transit the sun—a periodic phenomenon whose recurrences had been calculated for the next hundred years. (See *Journal de Paris*, 3 May 1786, s.v. "Astronomie.") The fourth member of the party, Madame LaBorde, has not been identified; she may have been a relation of the baron. Barbauld wrote this poem a few days later; it was first published in *Works* (1825).]

> In twice five winters more and one,
> Hermes again will cross the Sun;
> Again a dusky spot appear,
> Slow-journeying o'er his splendid sphere:
> 5    The stars shall slide into their places,
> Exhibiting the self-same faces,
> And in the like position fix
> As Thursday morning, eighty-six.
> But changing mortals hope in vain
> 10   Their lost position more to gain;—
> Once more between La Borde and me!—
> Ah, wish not what will never be!
> For wandering planets have their rules,
> Well known in astronomic schools;
> 15   But life's swift wheels will ne'er turn back,
> When once they've measured o'er their track.
> Eleven years,—twice five and one,—
> Is a long hour in Beauty's sun:

Those years will pilfer many a grace
Which decks La Borde's enchanting face;
The little Loves which round her fly,
Will moult the wing, and droop, and die:
And I, grown dull, my lyre unstrung
In some old chimney corner hung,
Gay scenes of Paris all forgot,
Shall rust within my silent cot:[1]
Life's summer ended, and life's spring,
Nor she shall charm, nor I shall sing.
Even Cook,[2] upon whose blooming brow
The youthful graces open now,
Eleven years may vastly change:
No more the Provinces he'll range;
No more with humid eyes entreat,
And wait his doom at Beauty's feet;
Married and grave, he'll spend his time
Far from the idleness of rime;
Forgetting oranges and myrtle,
Will drink his port and eat his turtle;
Perhaps with country justice sit,
And turn his back on thee and Wit.
     For thee, my friend, whose copious vein
Pours forth at will the polished strain,
With every talent formed to please,
Each fair idea quick to seize;—
Who knows within so long a space
What scenes the present may efface,
What course thy stream of life may take,
What winds may curl, what storms may shake,
What varying colours, gay or grave,
Shall tinge by turns the passing wave;
Of objects on its banks what swarms—
The loftier or the fairer forms—
Shall glide before the liquid glass,
And print their image as they pass?

---

1   Cottage.
2   A young English friend of the baron who had been touring France.

Let Fancy then and Friendship stray
In Pleasure's flowery walks today,
Today improve the social hours,
And build today the Muse's bowers;
And when life's pageant on will go,
Try not to stop the passing show;
But give to scenes that once were dear,
A sigh, a farewell, and a tear.

## EPISTLE TO DR. ENFIELD, ON HIS REVISITING WARRINGTON IN 1789

[William Enfield (1741-97), tutor and rector at Warrington Academy from 1770 until it shut its doors, remained a close friend of Barbauld and her brother. He returned to Warrington for a visit in the summer of 1789 (*Poems*, p. 348). Barbauld herself had last visited in 1783. Dissenters were deeply saddened by the Academy's closing: "I know not how to think without poignant regret," wrote one, "on the approaching desecration of those buildings, so long the seat of learning and the muses, and which the venerable names of [John] Taylor [one of the first tutors] and Aikin [Barbauld's father] will render dear to every friend of science and virtue as long as the Dissenting interest shall last" (Williams, *Memoirs of Thomas Belsham*, p. 315). The poem was first published in *Works* (1825).]

Friend of those years which from Youth's sparkling fount
With silent lapse down Time's swift gulf have run!
Friend of the years, whate'er be their amount,
Which yet remain beneath life's evening sun!

5 O when thy feet retrace that western shore
Where Mersey[1] winds his waters to the main,

---

1   The river on which Warrington is situated.

When thy fond eyes familiar haunts explore,
~~And paths well-nigh effaced are tracked again;~~

Will not thy heart with mixed emotions thrill,
As scenes succeeding scenes arise to view?                    10
While joy or sorrow past alike shall fill
Thy glistening eyes with Feeling's tender dew.

Shades of light transient Loves shall pass thee by,
And glowing Hopes, and Sports of youthful vein;
And each shall claim one short, half pleasing sigh,          15
A farewell sigh to Love's and Fancy's reign.

Lo there the seats where Science loved to dwell,
Where Liberty her ardent spirit breathed;
While each glad Naiad[1] from her secret cell
Her native sedge with classic honours wreathed.              20

O seats beloved in vain! Your rising dome
With what fond joy my youthful eyes surveyed;[2]
Pleased by your sacred springs to find my home,
And tune my lyre beneath your growing shade!

Does Desolation spread his gloomy veil                       25
Your grass-grown courts and silent halls along?
Or busy hands there pile the cumbrous sail,
And Trade's harsh din succeed the Muse's song?[3]

Yet still, perhaps, in some sequestered walk
Thine ear shall catch the tales of other times;             30
Still in faint sounds the learned echoes talk,
Where unprofaned as yet by vulgar chimes.

---

1   A water-spirit.
2   rising dome ... surveyed: "the newer buildings in Academy Place, which she well
    remembers appearing one by one" (O'Brien, *Warrington Academy*, p. 101).
3   For a time after its close, the Academy's buildings were used as warehouses for sail-
    cloth and cotton goods.

Do not the deeply-wounded trees still bear
The dear memorial of some infant flame?
35  And murmuring sounds yet fill the hallowed air,
Once vocal to the youthful poet's fame?

For where her sacred step impressed the Muse,
She left a long perfume through all the bowers;
Still mayst thou gather thence Castalian[1] dews
40  In honeyed sweetness clinging to the flowers.

Shrowded in stolen glance, here timorous Love
The grave rebuke of careful Wisdom[2] drew,
With wholesome frown austere who vainly strove
To shield the sliding heart from Beauty's view.[3]

45  Go fling this garland in fair Mersey's stream,
From the true lovers that have trod his banks;
Say, Thames to Avon still repeats his theme;
Say, Hymen's captives[4] send their votive thanks.

Visit each shade and trace each weeping rill
50  To holy Friendship or to Fancy known,
And climb with zealous step the fir-crowned hill,[5]
Where purple foxgloves fringe the rugged stone:

And if thou seest on some neglected spray
The lyre which soothed my careless hours so much;
55  The shattered relic to my hands convey,—
The murmuring strings shall answer to thy touch.

---

1  Poetic (from Castalia, a spring on Mount Parnassus sacred to the Muses).
2  Barbauld's name for the Academy's authorities; cf. "To Wisdom."
3  shield ... view: Perhaps an allusion to an incident involving a student and one of the Rigby sisters, which ended with the authorities ordering their father to send them away.
4  Probably the Barbaulds themselves, who married at Warrington.
5  The fir-crowned hill: Hill-Cliffe in Appleton, near Warrington. "Even today it unfolds a marvellous panorama; across the Mersey valley to the North, with glimpses as far as the outskirts of Manchester to the East, and Liverpool to the West; then to the foothills of the Pennines ... conveying overtones of magic and witchcraft" (O'Brien, *Warrington Academy*, p. 102).

Were it, like thine, my lot once more to tread
Plains now but seen in distant perspective,
With that soft hue, that dubious gloom o'erspread,
That tender tint which only time can give;                    60

How would it open every secret cell
Where cherished thought and fond remembrance sleep!
How many a tale each conscious step would tell!
How many a parted friend these eyes would weep!

But O the chief!—If in thy feeling breast                      65
The tender charities of life reside,
If there domestic love have built her nest,
And thy fond heart a parent's cares[1] divide;

Go seek the turf where worth, where wisdom lies,
Wisdom and worth, ah, never to return!                         70
There, kneeling, weep my tears, and breathe my sighs,
A daughter's sorrows o'er her father's urn![2]

# EPISTLE TO WILLIAM WILBERFORCE, ESQ. ON THE REJECTION OF THE BILL FOR ABOLISHING THE SLAVE TRADE

[In 1787 Thomas Clarkson and other Quakers formed the
Society for Effecting the Abolition of the Slave Trade. Their
purpose was to lobby Parliament to prohibit British participa-
tion in the international trade in enslaved Africans. In 1789
William Wilberforce (1759-1833), M.P. for Hull and an Evan-
gelical conservative, undertook to speak for the Society in the
House of Commons. On 18 April 1791 he offered a formal
motion on abolition. In a powerful speech he chronicled the
horrors of the trade, leading to the pointed question, "Whilst
... we were ignorant of all these things, our suffering them to

---

1   Enfield had five children.
2   Barbauld's father, the Rev. John Aikin, died at Warrington in 1780 and is buried
    there. She had not been present at his death or burial.

continue, might ... be pardoned; but now, when our eyes are opened, can we tolerate them for a moment, much less sanction them, unless we are ready at once to determine, that gain shall be our god, and, like the heathens of old, are prepared to offer up human victims at the shrine of our idolatry?" (*Debate on a Motion for the Abolition of the Slave-Trade*, p. 40)

Although seconded by William Smith, Charles James Fox, and William Pitt, the Prime Minister, Wilberforce's motion failed by a vote of 163 to 88. Nevertheless, the abolitionist movement enjoyed strong literary support in the 1780s and 90s, particularly from women poets such as Hannah More (*Slavery*, 1788), Ann Yearsley (*A Poem on the Inhumanity of the Slave Trade*, 1788), and Helen Maria Williams (*A Poem on the Slave Bill*, 1788); Moira Ferguson has studied the connections between feminism and abolitionism in this literature (*Subject to Others*).

Barbauld wrote her poem soon after the debate, to which she alludes; its publication was advertised in *The Morning Chronicle* on 11 June. She sent a copy to Hannah More, one of the leading abolitionist writers, who thanked her warmly (LeBreton, *Memoir*, pp. 67-69). The novelist Frances Burney thought *Wilberforce* by far the finest of Barbauld's poems (*Journals and Letters*, 4:188); *The Monthly Review* likened it to the "vigorous and manly strains" of the Roman satirist, Juvenal (p. 227).]

> Cease, Wilberforce, to urge thy generous aim!
> Thy Country knows the sin, and stands the shame!
> The Preacher, Poet, Senator in vain
> Has rattled in her sight the Negro's chain;[1]
> With his deep groans assail'd her startled ear,
> And rent the veil that hid his constant tear;
> Forc'd her averted eyes his stripes[2] to scan,
> Beneath the bloody scourge laid bare the man,
> Claim'd Pity's tear, urg'd Conscience' strong controul,

5

---

1 Lines 3-4 allude to the outburst of antislavery discourse in poems, sermons, and pamphlets in the later 1780s, along with (and in response to) testimony in Parliament on the conditions of the trade.
2 Bloody welts made by whipping.

And flash'd conviction on her shrinking soul.                                        10
~~The Muse too, soon awak'd, with ready tongue~~
At Mercy's shrine applausive[1] peans rung;
And Freedom's eager sons, in vain foretold
A new Astrean[2] reign, an age of gold:
She knows and she persists—Still Afric bleeds,                                      15
Uncheck'd, the human traffic still proceeds;
She stamps her infamy to future time,
And on her harden'd forehead seals the crime.

   In vain, to thy white[3] standard gathering round,
Wit, Worth, and Parts and Eloquence are found:                                      20
In vain, to push to birth thy great design,
Contending chiefs, and hostile virtues join;[4]
All, from conflicting ranks, of power possest
To rouse, to melt, or to inform the breast.
Where seasoned tools of Avarice prevail,[5]                                          25
A Nation's eloquence, combined, must fail:
Each flimsy sophistry by turns they try;
The plausive[6] argument, the daring lye,
The artful gloss,[7] that moral sense confounds,
Th' acknowledged thirst of gain that honour wounds:                                 30
Bane of ingenuous minds, th' unfeeling sneer,
Which, sudden, turns to stone the falling tear:
They search assiduous, with inverted skill,
For forms of wrong, and precedents of ill;

---

1 Applauding.
2 Astrea was the goddess of Justice in the Golden Age. When human behavior became intolerably unjust she left earth for heaven; she would return if humans would reform.
3 Virtuous.
4 Wilberforce's motion received what would be called today "bipartisan support." Rivals Pitt and Fox supported the bill; Edmund Burke, regarded by liberals as a traitor for his early denunciation of the French Revolution, voted here on the liberal side. Wilberforce himself, a conservative, on other issues opposed the liberal positions.
5 Opponents of the motion defended the slave trade as, in the words of one speaker, "highly beneficial to the country, being one material branch of its commerce" (*Debate*, p. 104).
6 Plausible but false.
7 Interpretation.

35　With impious mockery wrest the sacred page,[1]
　　And glean up crimes from each remoter age:
　　Wrung Nature's tortures, shuddering, while you tell,
　　From scoffing fiends bursts forth the laugh of hell;
　　In Britain's senate, Misery's pangs give birth
40　To jests unseemly, and to horrid mirth—[2]
　　Forbear!—thy virtues but provoke our doom,
　　And swell th' account of vengeance yet to come;
　　For, not unmark'd in Heaven's impartial plan,
　　Shall man, proud worm, contemn his fellow-man?
45　And injur'd Afric, by herself redrest,
　　Darts her own serpents at her Tyrant's breast.
　　Each vice, to minds deprav'd by bondage known,
　　With sure contagion fastens on his own;
　　In sickly languors melts his nerveless frame,
50　And blows to rage impetuous Passion's flame:
　　Fermenting swift, the fiery venom gains
　　The milky innocence of infant veins;
　　There swells the stubborn will, damps learning's fire,
　　The whirlwind wakes of uncontroul'd desire,
55　Sears the young heart to images of woe,
　　And blasts the buds of Virtue as they blow.[3]
　　　　Lo! where reclin'd, pale Beauty courts the breeze,
　　Diffus'd on sofas of voluptuous ease;
　　With anxious awe, her menial train around,
60　Catch her faint whispers of half-utter'd sound;
　　See her, in monstrous fellowship, unite
　　At once the Scythian, and the Sybarite;[4]

---

1　One opponent of the motion argued that slavery was divinely ordained. "The Christian Religion itself showed no more repugnance to [slavery] than any other; and, in proof of this, he cited ... a passage in St. Paul's Epistle to the Corinthians" (*Debate*, pp. 68-69).

2　During the Commons debate, when William Smith recounted an incident of an African mother's being compelled to throw the body of her child from a ship, some members laughed (*Debate*, p. 89).

3　The moral degradation suffered by Britons as a result of participating in the slave trade was a theme in Thomas Clarkson's polemics and can be aligned with the representation, in ll. 86-105 below, of a Britain poisoned by its own empire.

4　Scythian and Sybarite: associated with savagery and voluptuousness, respectively.

Blending repugnant vices, misally'd,
~~Which *frugal* nature purpos'd to divide;~~
See her, with indolence to fierceness join'd,                65
Of body delicate, infirm of mind,
With languid tones imperious mandates urge;
With arm recumbent wield the household scourge;
And with unruffled mien, and placid sounds,
Contriving torture, and inflicting wounds.[1]              70
 Nor, in their palmy walks and spicy groves,
The form benign of rural Pleasure roves;
No milk-maid's song, or hum of village talk,
Sooths the lone Poet in his evening walk:
No willing arm the flail unweary'd plies,                 75
Where the mix'd sounds of cheerful labour rise;
No blooming maids, and frolic swains are seen
To pay gay homage to their harvest queen:
No heart-expanding scenes their eyes must prove
Of thriving industry, and faithful love:[2]               80
But shrieks and yells disturb the balmy air,
Dumb sullen looks of woe announce despair,
And angry eyes thro' dusky features glare.[3]
Far from the sounding lash the Muses fly,
And sensual riot drowns each finer joy.                   85
 Nor less from the gay East,[4] on essenc'd wings,
Breathing unnam'd perfumes, Contagion springs;

---

1 Lines 57-70 evoked comment by two contemporary readers. Hannah More wrote to Barbauld, "I could not forbear repeating to [Wilberforce] part of the animated description of the union of barbarity and voluptuousness in the West Indian woman, and he did full justice to this striking picture" (LeBreton, *Memoir*, p. 68). William Turner remarked in later years, "This picture, highly wrought as it is, is abundantly borne out by the ... evidence on the treatment of slaves, delivered before the committee of the house of commons" ("Mrs. Barbauld," p. 231). No mention of this behavior occurs in the published *Debate*, however.

2 Lines 71-80 retail traditional themes of poems in praise of the rural working life.

3 Moira Ferguson has noted the near absence in antislavery literature of "rebellious, voiced Africans" (*Subject to Others*, p. 26); Barbauld is unusual in imagining sullen, angry slaves.

4 East Indies, i.e., India. The behavior of Britain towards the people of India was also under Parliamentary scrutiny in 1791, for the governor of Bengal, Warren Hastings, had been impeached for abuses of power.

The soft luxurious plague alike pervades
The marble palaces, and rural shades;
90    Hence, throng'd Augusta[1] builds her rosy bowers,
And decks in summer wreaths her smoky towers;
And hence, in summer bow'rs, Art's costly hand
Pours courtly splendours o'er the dazzled land:
The manners melt—One undistinguish'd blaze
95    O'erwhelms the sober pomp of elder days;
Corruption follows with gigantic stride,
And scarce vouchsafes his shameless front to hide:
The spreading leprosy taints ev'ry part,
Infects each limb, and sickens at the heart.
100   Simplicity! most dear of rural maids,
Weeping resigns her violated shades:
Stern Independance from his glebe retires,
And anxious Freedom eyes her drooping fires;
By foreign wealth are British morals chang'd,
105   And Afric's sons, and India's, smile aveng'd.[2]
          For you, whose temper'd ardour long has borne
Untir'd the labour, and unmov'd the scorn;
In Virtue's fasti[3] be inscrib'd your fame,
And utter'd your's with Howard's[4] honour'd name,
110   Friends of the friendless—Hail, ye generous band!
Whose efforts yet arrest Heav'n's lifted hand,
Around whose steady brows, in union bright,
The civic wreath, and Christian's palm unite:
Your merit stands, no greater and no less,
115   Without, or with the varnish of success;
But seek no more to break a Nation's fall,
For ye have sav'd yourselves—and that is all.
Succeeding times your struggles, and their fate,

---

1   London.
2   Contamination by "Asiatic manners" was a theme of British imperial anxiety after
    the Seven Years' War. "The riches of Asia have been poured in upon us, and have
    brought with them not only Asiatic luxury, but I fear Asiatic principles of govern-
    ment" (a comment from 1770, quoted in Colley, *Britons*, pp. 102-03).
3   Register.
4   John Howard (1726-90), philanthropist and prison reformer.

With mingled shame and triumph shall relate,
~~While faithful History, in her various page,~~ 120
Marking the features of this motley age,
To shed a glory, and to fix a stain,
Tells how you strove, and that you strove in vain.


## THE APOLOGY OF THE BISHOPS,
## IN ANSWER TO "BONNER'S GHOST"

[When Barbauld sent her *Epistle to William Wilberforce* to Han-
nah More, More replied (4 July 1791) by sending a copy of her
poem, "Bishop Bonner's Ghost." In that poem, More flatters
the modern Church of England by having the ghost of
Edmund Bonner (1500?-1569), a Catholic bishop under Queen
Mary and notorious persecutor of Protestants, rebuke modern
bishops for tolerating religious diversity. Barbauld's reply to
More must have been written almost immediately, for only ten
days later a "Church-and-King" mob in Birmingham destroyed
Joseph Priestley's house and goods; lines 15-16 of the poem
would hardly be thinkable after 14 July 1791. The poem was
first printed in 1869 and 1874.]

> Right Revd. Brother[1] and so forth
> The Bishops send you greeting,
> They honour much the zeal and worth
> In you so highly meeting.
>
> But your abuse of us, good Sir                                        5
> Is very little founded!
> We blush that you should make a stir
> With notions so ill grounded.
>
> 'Tis not to us should be addrest
> Your ghostly exhortation,                                             10

---

1   A conventional greeting beween bishops.

If heresy still lifts her crest
The fault is in the nation.

The State, in spite of all our pains,
Has left us in the lurch,
The spirit of the times restrains
The spirit of the Church.[1]

To this day down from famed Sacheverel[2]
Our zeal has never cooled,
We mean to Truth and Freedom ever ill,
But we are over ruled.

Still damning Creeds framed long ago,
Help us to vent our spite;
And penal laws[3] our teeth to shew
Although we cannot bite.

Our spleen against reforming cries
Is now as ever shewn;
Though we can't blind the nation's eyes
We still can shut our own.

Well warned from what abroad befalls,[4]
We keep all tight at home;
Nor brush one cobweb from St. Paul's,[5]
Lest it should shake the dome.

15

20

25

30

---

1   The efforts of Dissenters to obtain repeal of the Test and Corporation Acts seemed on the verge of success in 1789, but failed again in 1790 (see headnote to *An Address to the Opposers*). Still, up to 14 July 1791 it would have been possible for liberals to feel optimistic about "the spirit of the times."

2   Henry Sacheverel (1674?-1724), notorious for his vehement pulpit abuse of Dissenters in 1709; the Church-of-England clergy generally supported him.

3   See the headnote to Appendix B.

4   A reference, probably, to the disestablishment of the monasteries in revolutionary France.

5   St. Paul's cathedral, of the city of London, masterpiece of architect Christopher Wren (1632-1723) who redesigned the building after the original was destroyed by the great fire of 1666.

Once in an age a Louth may chance
To wield the pastoral staff,
And Fortune for a whim advance                    35
A [Hoadly] or [Llandaff].[1]

Yet do not thou by fears misled
To rash conclusions jump,
So little leaven scarce appears,
And leaveneth *not* the lump.[2]                  40

What though the arm of flesh be dead
And lost the power it gives,
The spirit quickeneth, it is said,
And sure the spirit lives.[3]

Would it but please the civil weal                45
To lift again the Crosier,[4]
We soon would make those yokes of steel
Which now are bands of osier.

The Birmingham Apostle then,
And Essex Street Apostate,[5]                      50
Debarred from paper and from pen
Should both lament their lost state.

Church maxims do not greatly vary,
Take it upon my honour,

---

1  The 1874 text of line 36 (the only text known) prints "A —— or ——," with a
   footnote suggesting these names. Benjamin Hoadly (1676-1761) and Richard Wat-
   son, Bishop of Llandaff (1737-1816) supported efforts to repeal the Test and Cor-
   poration Acts. Robert Louth or Lowth (1710-87), archdeacon of Westminster, like
   them was generous towards Dissent.
2  "Know ye not that a little leaven leaveneth the whole lump?" (I Corinthians 5:6).
3  "It is the spirit that quickeneth; the flesh profiteth nothing" (John 6:63).
4  A staff carried by bishops as an emblem of office.
5  The "Birmingham Apostle" is Joseph Priestley, currently embroiled in pamphlet
   defenses of Unitarianism against Church-of-England clergy; the "Essex Street
   Apostate" is Theophilus Lindsey (1723-1808), a former Anglican cleric who left the
   Church and opened the first Unitarian chapel in Essex Street, London, in 1774.

55 Place on the throne another Mary,
We'll find her soon a Bonner.


## THE RIGHTS OF WOMAN

[The title and first two lines of this poem associate it with Mary
Wollstonecraft's *Vindication of the Rights of Woman*, published in
January 1792. The poem has been read as an attack on Woll-
stonecraft's feminism; the present editors themselves have sug-
gested that Barbauld wrote the poem in a fit of anger at Woll-
stonecraft's having criticized her earlier poem, "To a Lady, with
some Painted Flowers" (*Poems of Anna Letitia Barbauld*, p. 289).
Tonally the poem is complicated, and it is not easy to decide
where it is ironic. If it does criticize Wollstonecraft, it badly
misreads her: Wollstonecraft nowhere argues that women
should dominate men, she rejects at length the ideology of
"angel pureness," "soft melting tones," and "blushes and
fears"—and she certainly did not shun "discussion" of women's
rights! These are positions taken by Jean-Jacques Rousseau in
his *Émile* (1762), and they are attacked at length by Woll-
stonecraft. The question of this poem's relation to the *Vindica-
tion* needs to be re-opened; a promising start was made by
Leslie Ritchie in a 1997 paper, "'The Rights of Woman':
Nature and Reason in Wollstonecraft, Rousseau and Barbauld."
The poem was first published in *Works* (1825).]

Yes, injured Woman! rise, assert thy right!
Woman! too long degraded, scorned, opprest;
O born to rule in partial Law's despite,
Resume thy native empire o'er the breast!

5 Go forth arrayed in panoply divine;
That angel pureness which admits no stain;
Go, bid[1] proud Man his boasted rule resign,
And kiss the golden sceptre of thy reign.

---

1 An echo of Alexander Pope's ironic exhortations to humans in *An Essay on Man*,
2:19-30.

Go, gird thyself with grace; collect thy store
Of bright artillery glancing from afar;
Soft melting tones thy thundering cannon's roar,
Blushes and fears thy magazine of war.

Thy rights are empire: urge no meaner claim,—
Felt, not defined, and if debated, lost;
Like sacred mysteries, which withheld from fame,
Shunning discussion, are revered the most.

Try all that wit and art suggest to bend
Of thy imperial foe the stubborn knee;
Make treacherous Man thy subject, not thy friend;
Thou mayst command, but never canst be free. ·

Awe the licentious, and restrain the rude;
Soften the sullen, clear the cloudy brow:
Be, more than princes' gifts, thy favours sued;—
She hazards all, who will the least allow.

But hope not, courted idol of mankind,
On this proud eminence secure to stay;
Subduing and subdued, thou soon shalt find
Thy coldness soften, and thy pride give way.

Then, then, abandon each ambitious thought,
Conquest or rule thy heart shall feebly move,
In Nature's school, by her soft maxims taught,
That separate rights are lost in mutual love.[1]

---

1   The poem ends on a note of reconciliation, just as does "To a Great Nation."

# HYMN VII

[We do not know when Barbauld wrote this hymn; she published it in the 1792 edition of *Poems*. A text printed in *A Selection of Psalms and Hymns, for Unitarian Worship* (1810), compiled by Robert Aspland, bears revisions which seem likely to be hers.]

Come unto me all ye that are weary and heavy laden, and I
will give you rest.[1]

Come, said JESUS' sacred voice,
Come and make my paths your choice:
I will guide you to your home;
Weary pilgrim, hither come!

5      Thou, who houseless, sole, forlorn,
Long hast borne the proud world's scorn,
Long hast roamed the barren waste,
Weary pilgrim, hither haste!

Ye who, tossed on beds of pain,
10     Seek for ease, but seek in vain,
Ye whose swollen and sleepless eyes
Watch to see the morning rise;

Ye, by fiercer anguish torn,
Guilt, in strong remorse, who mourn,
15     Here repose your heavy care,
Troubled conscience[2] who can bear!

Sinner, come! for here is found
Balm that flows for every wound;
Peace, that ever shall endure,
20     Rest eternal, sacred, sure.

---

1   Matthew 11:28.
2   Troubled conscience: from 1810, replacing "A wounded spirit" in 1792.

[In September 1792 the newly-proclaimed French Republic was in grave danger from external foes and internal disorders. A royalist army led by the Duke of Brunswick threatened invasion; on 29 August an English spy in Paris reported the new government's frantic effort to raise troops, munitions and supplies to repel it. In London, on 13 September, a subscription in support of France was signed by a number of Barbauld's friends; the money was sent to Paris accompanied by addresses of sympathy. We speculate that this poem went with them; it might even have been the English song, "faite par une dame anglaise," which was sung by a gathering of English radicals in Paris on 19 November to celebrate the French defeat of the invaders at Jemappes (Woodward, *Hélène-Maria Williams*, p. 72; Woodward assumes, however, that the song was by Williams). In any case, it was published in *The Cambridge Intelligencer* (a newspaper), 2 November 1793, signed only "by a Lady."]

> Rise mighty nation! in thy strength,
> And deal thy dreadful vengeance round;
> Let thy great spirit rous'd at length,
> Strike hordes of Despots to the ground.
>
> Devoted[1] land! thy mangled breast,     5
> Eager the royal vultures tear:[2]
> By friends betray'd, by foes oppress'd,
> And virtue struggles with despair.
>
> The tocsin[3] sounds! arise, arise,
> Stern o'er each breast let country reign;     10

---

1 Three senses seem pertinent: "dedicated; consecrated"; "zealously attached ... to a ... cause; enthusiastically loyal or faithful"; "consigned to evil or destruction; doomed" (*OED*).

2 The Duke of Brunswick proclaimed (25 July 1792) that his Austrian and Prussian army would "restore Louis XVI to his rightful and legitimate authority" (Goodwin, *Friends of Liberty*, p. 240). In the 1793 printing, "royal" is printed as "r——l."

3 Alarm bell.

Nor virgin's plighted hand, nor sighs
Must now the ardent youth detain.

Nor must the hind[1] who tills thy soil,
The ripen'd vintage stay to press,
'Till rapture crown the flowing bowl,
And Freedom boast of full success.

*Briareus*-like,[2] extend thy hands,
That every hand may crush a foe;
In millions pour thy generous bands,
And end a warfare by a blow.

Then wash with sad repentant tears,
Each deed that clouds thy glory's page;
Each phrensied start impell'd by fears,
Each transient burst of headlong rage.[3]

Then fold in thy relenting arms,
Thy wretched outcasts where they roam;
From pining want and war's alarms,
O call the child of Misery home.[4]

Then build the tomb—O not alone,
Of him who bled in freedom's cause;
With equal eye the martyr own,
Of faith revered and antient laws.

Then be thy tide of glory stay'd,
Then be thy conquering banners furl'd,
Obey the laws thyself hast made,
And rise—the model of the world!

---

1  Farm worker.
2  "*Briareus* was a giant of ancient fable, represented with a hundred hands, and fifty heads" (note, 1793).
3  Lines 23-24 probably refer to the massacre of the King's guard by Parisians on 10 August and the massacres of prisoners in Paris on 2-3 September.
4  The "outcasts" are emigrés and exiles from the Revolution, of whom many had found asylum in England.

[The Birmingham Riots of 14-17 July 1791, in which Joseph Priestley lost home and goods, initiated a campaign of public reaction against pro-French and pro-reform sentiment in Britain. In May 1792 the government officially banned "Seditious Writings and Publications"; in November, John Reeves founded an Association for the Preservation of Liberty and Property against Republicans and Levellers, the aim of which was to bully people into signing loyalty oaths. Because Priestley was the most conspicuous and controversial Dissenter, Dissenters in general were targeted. Those who resisted intimidation were threatened or ostracized; when Rochemont Barbauld refused to sign a loyalty oath, he received hate mail. Priestley himself no longer felt physically safe even in London. Many Dissenters yielded to pressure and hastened to declare loyalty to "the Constitution of this kingdom, consisting of King, Lords, and Commons" (*Gentleman's Magazine* 62 [1792]: 1070). This poem, one of a number addressed to Priestley by sympathizers (including the young Samuel Taylor Coleridge), was published anonymously without Barbauld's consent in *The Morning Chronicle* on 8 January 1793.]

> Stirs not thy spirit, Priestley, as the train
> With low obeisance, and with servile phrase,
> File behind file, advance, with supple knee,
> And lay their necks beneath the foot of power?
> Burns not thy cheek indignant, when thy name,  5
> On which delighted science lov'd to dwell,
> Becomes the bandied theme of hooting crowds?[1]
> With timid caution, or with cool reserve,
> When e'en each reverend Brother[2] keeps aloof,
> Eyes the struck deer, and leaves thy naked side  10
> A mark for power to shoot at? Let it be.

---

1 Loyalist mobs sometimes burned Priestley in effigy.
2 Many of Priestley's fellow ministers protected themselves by pointedly proclaiming their loyalty to government.

"On evil days though fallen and evil tongues,"[1]
To thee, the slander of a passing age
Imports not. Scenes like these hold little space
15    In his large mind, whose ample stretch of thought
Grasps future periods.—Well can'st thou afford
To give large *credit* for that debt of fame
Thy country owes thee. Calm thou can'st consign it
To the slow payment of that distant day,
20    If distant, when thy name, to freedom's join'd,
Shall meet the thanks of a regenerate land.


# HYMN:
## "YE ARE THE SALT OF THE EARTH"[2]

[In this political hymn Barbauld responds to the Reign of Ter-
ror in Paris (lines 41-42), which ended in August 1794; to the
imprisonment at Olmütz in Austria (from May 1794) of the
Marquis de Lafayette, hero of the American Revolution and, in
its early years, of the French (lines 45-48); and to the Polish
national uprising led by Tadeusz Kosciuszko, in progress at the
time of writing (lines 43-44). She published the poem in *The
Monthly Magazine*, 4 (July 1797), signed "A. L. B."]

Salt of the earth, ye virtuous few,
     Who season human kind;
Light of the world, whose cheering ray
     Illumes the realms of mind;

5    Where Misery spreads her deepest shade,
     Your strong compassion glows;
From your blest lips the balm distils,
     That softens mortal woes.

---

1    Quoted from Milton, *Paradise Lost*, 7:26. Priestley's friend Theophilus Lindsey
     remarked of Barbauld's poem that "Milton himself might have been proud to own"
     it ("Preface" to *Answer*, p. xxiv).
2    Matthew 5:13.

By dying beds, in prison glooms,
    Your frequent steps are found;[1]
Angels of love! you hover near,
    To bind the stranger's wound.

You wash with tears the bloody page,
    Which human crimes deform;
When vengeance threats, your prayers ascend,
    And break the gathering storm.

As down the summer stream of vice
    The thoughtless many glide;
Upward you steer your steady bark,
    And stem the rushing tide.

Where guilt her foul contagion breathes,
    And golden spoils allure;
Unspotted still your garments shine—
    Your hands are ever pure.

Whene'er you touch the poet's lyre,
    A loftier strain is heard;
Each ardent thought is your's alone,
    And every burning word.

Your's is the large expansive thought,
    The high heroic deed;
Exile[2] and chains to you are dear;
    To you 'tis sweet to bleed.

You lift on high the warning voice,
    When public ills prevail;

---

1  A reference to John Howard (1726-90), philanthropist, who investigated conditions
   in hospitals and prisons throughout Europe.
2  The Scottish reformers Thomas Muir (1765-98) and Thomas Palmer (1747-1802)
   had been exiled to Australia in February 1794.

Your's is the writing on the wall,[1]
         That turns the tyrant pale.

    The dogs of hell your steps pursue,
         With scoff, and shame, and loss;
    The hemlock bowl[2] 'tis your's to drain,
To taste the bitter cross.

    E'en yet the steaming scaffolds smoke
         By Seine's polluted stream;
    With your rich blood the fields are drench'd
         Where Polish sabres gleam.

E'en now, through those accursed bars,
         In vain we send our sighs;
    Where, deep in Olmutz' dungeon glooms,
         The patriot martyr lies.

    Yet your's is all thro' hist'ry's rolls
The kindling bosom feels;
    And at your tomb, with throbbing heart,
         The fond enthusiast kneels.

    In every faith, thro' every clime,
         Your pilgrim steps we trace;
And shrines are drest, and temples rise,
         Each hallow'd spot to grace.

    And Paeans loud, in every tongue,
         And choral hymns resound;
    And length'ning honours hand your name
To time's remotest bound.

---

1   In Daniel 5:5ff, only the prophet Daniel is able to interpret the writing on the wall
    at Belshazzar's feast; the writing prophesies Belshazzar's downfall.
2   A bowl of hemlock (a poison) was the means by which the government of Athens
    executed Socrates.

Proceed! your race of glory run,
Your virtuous toils endure!
You come, commission'd from on high,
And your reward is sure.


## TO THE POOR

["These lines, written in 1795, were described by Mrs. B., on
sending them to a friend, as 'inspired by indignation on hearing
sermons in which the poor are addressed in a manner which
evidently shows the design of making religion an engine of
government'" (Lucy Aikin's note to this poem in *Works* [1825],
its first publication). 1794 had produced a bad harvest; its results
were felt most severely by the poor, who staged bread riots and
other protests to draw attention to their plight. Hester Thrale
Piozzi saw "Handbills ... posted on our Church Doors ...
*demanding*, not *requesting* Relief for the lower Orders"
(*Thraliana*, p. 909). A reviewer of *Works* in 1825 cited this poem
as evidence of "Mrs. Barbauld's fiery democracy" (*Literary
Gazette*, p. 611).]

Child of distress, who meet'st the bitter scorn
Of fellow men to happier prospects born,
Doomed art and nature's various stores to see
Flow in full cups of joy,—and not for thee,
Who seest the rich, to heaven and fate resign'd, 5
Bear *thy* afflictions with a patient mind;
Whose bursting heart disdains unjust controll,
Who feel'st oppression's iron in thy soul,
Who drag'st the load of faint and feeble years,
Whose bread is anguish and whose water tears—[1] 10
Bear, bear thy wrongs, fulfil thy destined hour,
Bend thy meek neck beneath the foot of power!
But when thou feel'st the great deliverer nigh,
And thy freed spirit mounting seeks the sky,

---

1 Cf. Isaiah 30:20.

Let no vain fears thy parting hour molest,
No whispered terrors shake thy quiet breast,
Think not their threats can work thy future woe,
Nor deem the Lord above, like Lords below.
Safe in the bosom of that love repose
20 By whom the sun gives light, the ocean flows,
Prepare to meet a father undismayed,
Nor fear the God whom priests and kings have made.

## INSCRIPTION FOR AN ICE-HOUSE[1]

[Ice-houses—architecturally imposing outdoor coolers stocked
with ice imported from Norway or even North America—
became a fashion among rich estate-owners in the late eigh-
teenth century. Barbauld wrote this inscription in 1795 for the
ice-house built by William Smith, MP, of Parndon in Essex,
whose family she visited regularly. A stimulating commentary
on the poem, relating it to Edmund Burke's idea of the "beauti-
ful" and to Thomas Malthus on population, is Armstrong, "The
Gush of the Feminine: How Can We Read Women's Poetry of
the Romantic Period?"]

Stranger, approach! within this iron door
Thrice locked and bolted, this rude arch beneath
That vaults with ponderous stone the cell; confined
By man, the great magician, who controuls
5 Fire, earth and air, and genii of the storm,
And bends the most remote and opposite things
To do him service and perform his will,—
A giant sits; stern Winter; here he piles,
While summer glows around, and southern gales
10 Dissolve the fainting world, his treasured snows
Within the rugged[2] cave.—Stranger, approach!

---

1 Published in *Works*. A manuscript copy by Elizabeth Bridget (Mrs. Charles James)
  Fox (Add. MS 51515, British Library) identifies the date and place and adds one
  line: see p.141, note 2.
2 rugged: "hollow" in Fox MS.

He will not cramp thy limbs with sudden age,
~~Nor wither with his touch the coyest flower~~
That decks thy scented hair. Indignant here,
Like fettered Sampson[1] when his might was spent            15
In puny feats to glad the festive halls
Of Gaza's wealthy sons; or he who sat[2]
Midst laughing girls submiss, and patient twirled
The slender spindle in his sinewy grasp;[3]
The rugged power, fair Pleasure's minister,                   20
Exerts his art to deck the genial board;[4]
Congeals the melting peach, the nectarine smooth,[5]
Burnished and glowing from the sunny wall:
Darts sudden frost into the crimson veins
Of the moist berry; moulds the sugared hail:[6]               25
Cools with his icy breath our flowing cups;
Or gives to the fresh dairy's nectared bowls
A quicker zest. Sullen he plies his task,
And on his shaking fingers counts the weeks
Of lingering Summer, mindful of his hour                      30
To rush in whirlwinds forth, and rule the year.

---

1   The Hebrew hero in Judges who, when shorn of his hair by his Philistine wife
    Delilah, was captured by the Philistines, blinded, and set to work at a mill in Gaza.
    As his hair grew back so did his strength, and the Philistines made him entertain
    them with feats of strength.
2   Between ll. 17 and 18, the Fox MS gives this line: "(Melted his strength by female
    blandishments)."
3   he who sat … grasp: from "Deianira to Hercules" in Ovid's *Heroides*. The preter-
    naturally strong Hercules held the wool-basket for the girls of Ionia as they spun;
    sometimes he accidentally crushed the spindle.
4   Dining table.
5   smooth: absent in the Fox MS. Its presence in 1825 upsets the meter of the line,
    unless "nectarine" is read as two syllables.
6   the sugared hail: here and in l. 10 above, Barbauld nearly quotes James Thomson,
    *The Seasons* (1746), "Winter," ll. 895-900: "Here winter holds his unrejoicing Court
    … Moulds his fierce Hail, and treasures up his Snows."

# TO MR. S. T. COLERIDGE

[Barbauld wrote this poem shortly after meeting Samuel Taylor Coleridge in Bristol, August 1797. The poem registers her impression that he was gifted but self-destructive. At the time of their meeting and for some years afterwards, Coleridge highly esteemed Barbauld and was inclined to admit her view of him: "The more I see of Mrs. Barbauld the more I admire her," he wrote to a friend in 1800. "She has great *acuteness* ... yet how steadily she keeps it within the bounds of practical Reason. This I almost envy as well as admire—My own Subtleties too often lead me into strange ... Out-of-the-waynesses" (*Letters*, 1:578). The poem was published, unsigned and titled "To Mr. C———ge," in *The Monthly Magazine*, 7 (April 1799).]

Midway the hill of Science,[1] after steep
And rugged paths that tire th' unpractised feet
A Grove extends, in tangled mazes wrought,
And fill'd with strange enchantment:—dubious shapes
5   Flit thro' dim glades, and lure the eager foot
Of youthful ardour to eternal chase.
Dreams hang on every leaf; unearthly forms
Glide thro' the gloom, and mystic visions swim
Before the cheated sense. Athwart the mists,
10   Far into vacant space, huge shadows stretch
And seem realities; while things of life,
Obvious to sight and touch, all glowing round
Fade to the hue of shadows. *Scruples* here
With filmy net, most like th' autumnal webs
15   Of floating Gossamer, arrest the foot
Of generous enterprize; and palsy hope
And fair ambition, with the chilling touch

---

1   Barbauld's figure of a tempting but dangerous resting-place on a hill glances at Coleridge's own poem, "The Eolian Harp" (1796): "as on the midway slope / Of yonder hill I stretch my limbs at noon" (Coleridge, *Poems*, 1:101), and alludes to the Hill Difficulty in John Bunyan's *Pilgrim's Progress*: "Now about the midway to the top of the Hill, was a pleasant *Arbour* ... for the refreshing of weary Travailers." Here Bunyan's hero, Christian, rests so well that he falls asleep and loses his scroll (p. 42).

Of sickly hesitation and blank fear.
Nor seldom *Indolence* these lawns among
Fixes her turf-built seat, and wears the garb                            20
Of deep philosophy, and museful sits,
In dreamy twilight of the vacant mind,
Soothed by the whispering shade; for soothing soft
The shades, and vistas lengthening into air,
With moon beam rainbows tinted. Here each mind                           25
Of finer mold, acute and delicate,
In its high progress to eternal truth
Rests for a space, in fairy bowers entranced;
And loves the softened light and tender gloom;
And, pampered with most unsubstantial food,                             30
Looks down indignant on the grosser world,
And matter's cumbrous shapings. Youth belov'd
Of Science—of the Muse belov'd, not here,
Not in the maze of metaphysic lore
Build thou thy place of resting; lightly tread                          35
The dangerous ground, on noble aims intent;
And be this Circe[1] of the studious cell
Enjoyed, but still subservient. Active scenes
Shall soon with healthful spirit brace thy mind,
And fair exertion, for bright fame sustained,                           40
For friends, for country, chase each spleen-fed fog
That blots the wide creation—
Now Heaven conduct thee with a Parent's love!


# WASHING-DAY

[Written after 1783 (see note to line 82); published in *The Monthly Magazine*, 4 (December 1797). In 1807 the critic Francis Jeffrey, reviewing Wordsworth's poems, ridiculed them along with "Washing-Day" and the poems of Robert Southey: "All the world laughs at Elegiac stanzas to a sucking-pig—a Hymn on Washing-day—Sonnets to one's grandmother—or

---

1   In *The Odyssey*, an enchantress who turns men into swine.

Pindarics on gooseberry-pye" (p. 218). From lines 1–3 of her poem, however, Barbauld could be inferred to be ridiculing Southey's poems of simple domestic scenes herself. At the same time, as Ann Messenger remarks, washing-day was truly a major event in the domestic schedule, and in some respects a feminist occasion: "Women had power on washing day." Hence "its importance gives a doubleness to the mock heroic treatment it gets in her poem" (*His and Hers*, p. 188). For a reading of the way the poem transcends gender categories to make a signifi-cant statement about the creative imagination, see Kraft, "Anna Letitia Barbauld's 'Washing Day' and the Montgolfier Bal-loon."]

> ............. and their voice,
> Turning again towards childish treble, pipes
> And whistles in its sound.———¹

The Muses are turned gossips; they have lost
The buskin'd² step, and clear high-sounding phrase,
Language of gods. Come, then, domestic Muse,
In slip-shod³ measure loosely prattling on
5   Of farm or orchard, pleasant curds and cream,
Or drowning flies, or shoe lost in the mire
By little whimpering boy, with rueful face;
Come, Muse, and sing the dreaded *Washing-Day*.
—Ye who beneath the yoke of wedlock bend,
10   With bowed soul, full well ye ken⁴ the day
Which week, smooth sliding after week, brings on
Too soon; for to that day nor peace belongs
Nor comfort; ere the first grey streak of dawn,
The red-arm'd washers come and chase repose.
15   Nor pleasant smile, nor quaint device of mirth,
E'er visited that day; the very cat,
From the wet kitchen scared, and reeking hearth,

---

1   Shakespeare, *As You Like It*, II.vii.161–63 (slightly altered).
2   Appropriate to tragedy.
3   Alluding to the "slip-shod Sybil" of Pope's *Dunciad*, 3:15.
4   Know.

Visits the parlour, an unwonted guest.
The silent breakfast-meal is soon dispatch'd
Uninterrupted, save by anxious looks                                    20
Cast at the lowering sky, if sky should lower.
From that last evil, oh preserve us, heavens!
For should the skies pour down, adieu to all
Remains of quiet; then expect to hear
Of sad disasters—dirt and gravel stains                                 25
Hard to efface, and loaded lines at once
Snapped short—and linen-horse by dog thrown down,
And all the petty miseries of life.
Saints have been calm while stretched upon the rack,
And Guatimozin[1] smil'd on burning coals;                              30
But never yet did housewife notable
Greet with a smile a rainy washing-day.
—But grant the welkin[2] fair, require not thou
Who call'st thyself perchance the master there,
Or study swept, or nicely dusted coat,                                  35
Or usual 'tendance; ask not, indiscreet,
Thy stockings mended, tho' the yawning rents
Gape wide as Erebus,[3] nor hope to find
Some snug recess impervious; should'st thou try
The 'customed garden walks, thine eye shall rue                         40
The budding fragrance of thy tender shrubs,
Myrtle or rose, all crushed beneath the weight
Of coarse check'd apron, with impatient hand
Twitch'd off when showers impend: or crossing lines
Shall mar thy musings, as the wet cold sheet                            45
Flaps in thy face abrupt. Woe to the friend
Whose evil stars have urged him forth to claim
On such a day the hospitable rites;
Looks, blank at best, and stinted courtesy,
Shall he receive. Vainly he feeds his hopes                             50

---

1   Guatimozin: so in *Works*; in *MM*, "Montezuma." Guatimozin, nephew and son-in-
    law of Montezuma, was the last Aztec emperor. Conquered by Spanish invaders, he
    endured torture stoically.
2   Poetic term for sky.
3   In Greek mythology, a place of darkness on the way to Hades.

With dinner of roast chicken, savoury pie,
Or tart or pudding:—pudding he nor tart
That day shall eat; nor, tho' the husband try,
Mending what can't be help'd, to kindle mirth
55  From cheer deficient, shall his consort's brow
Clear up propitious; the unlucky guest
In silence dines, and early slinks away.
       I well remember, when a child, the awe
This day struck into me; for then the maids,
60  I scarce knew why, looked cross, and drove me from them;
Nor soft caress could I obtain, nor hope
Usual indulgencies; jelly or creams,
Relique of costly suppers, and set by
For me their petted one; or butter'd toast,
65  When butter was forbid; or thrilling tale
Of ghost, or witch, or murder—so I went
And shelter'd me beside the parlour fire:
There my dear grandmother, eldest of forms,
Tended the little ones, and watched from harm,
70  Anxiously fond, tho' oft her spectacles
With elfin cunning hid, and oft the pins
Drawn from her ravell'd stocking, might have sour'd
One less indulgent.—
At intervals my mother's voice was heard,
75  Urging dispatch; briskly the work went on,
All hands employed to wash, to rinse, to wring,
To fold, and starch, and clap, and iron, and plait.[1]
Then would I sit me down, and ponder much
Why washings were. Sometimes thro' hollow bole
80  Of pipe amused we blew, and sent aloft
The floating bubbles, little dreaming then
To see, Mongolfier,[2] thy silken ball
Ride buoyant thro' the clouds—so near approach

---

1  clap: to flatten by striking with a flat surface; plait: to fold.
2  In 1783 Joseph Michel Montgolfier (1740-1810) and his brother Jacques Étienne
   (1745-99) launched the first hot-air balloon, initiating a number of ballooning
   experiments throughout Europe, including England. Barbauld attended a balloon
   exhibit in London in January 1784, writing enthusiastically about it: "nothing …

The sports of children and the toils of men.
Earth, air, and sky, and ocean, hath its bubbles,[1]
And verse is one of them—this most of all.


## TO A LITTLE INVISIBLE BEING WHO IS EXPECTED SOON TO BECOME VISIBLE

[Published in *Works* (1825). A newly-discovered manuscript text, "Miscellaneous Extracts in Prose and Poetry" (ca. 1828), identifies the expectant mother to whom Barbauld addresses these lines as Frances Carr, one of Barbauld's Hampstead neighbors; the invisible being is her first child, born in 1799 (Edgeworth, *Letters*, p. 621). The manuscript also gives an additional stanza, which we print as a note.]

Germ of new life, whose powers expanding[2] slow
For many a moon their full perfection wait,—
Haste, precious pledge of happy love, to go
Auspicious borne through life's mysterious gate.

What powers lie folded in thy curious frame,— 5
Senses from objects locked, and mind from thought!
How little canst thou guess thy lofty claim
To grasp at all the worlds the Almighty wrought!

And see, the genial season's warmth to share,
Fresh younglings shoot, and opening roses glow! 10
Swarms of new life exulting fill the air,—
Haste, infant bud of being, haste to blow!

---

has given us so much pleasure as the balloon which is now exhibiting in the Pantheon.... When set loose from the weight which keeps it to the ground, it mounts to the top of that magnificent dome with such an easy motion as put me in mind of Milton's line, 'rose like an exhalation'" (*Works*, 2:22-23).
1  Cf. Shakespeare, *Macbeth*, I.iii.79: "The earth hath bubbles, as the water has."
2  Germ ... expanding: In the MS, "Fruit of the swelling womb, which ripening."

For thee the nurse prepares her lulling songs,
The eager matrons count the lingering day;
But far the most thy anxious parent longs
On thy soft cheek a mother's kiss to lay.[1]

She only asks to lay her burden down,
That her glad arms that burden may resume;
And nature's sharpest pangs her wishes crown,
That free thee living from thy living tomb.

She longs to fold to her maternal breast
Part of herself, yet to herself unknown;
To see and to salute the stranger guest,
Fed with her life through many a tedious moon.

Come, reap thy rich inheritance of love!
Bask in the fondness of a Mother's eye!
Nor wit nor eloquence her heart shall move
Like the first accents of thy feeble cry.[2]

Haste, little captive, burst thy prison doors!
Launch on the living world, and spring to light!
Nature for thee displays her various stores,
Opens her thousand inlets of delight.

If charmed verse or muttered prayers had power,
With favouring spells to speed thee on thy way,
Anxious I'd bid my beads[3] each passing hour,
Till thy wished smile thy mother's pangs o'erpay.

---

1   Between this stanza and the next, the MS includes these lines:

   Oft have her conscious looks her joy betray'd,
   When thy life-throbs the sudden start reveal'd;
   And busy fancy oft the form pourtray'd
   So long beneath those sacred veils conceal'd.

2   Lines 25-28 are absent in the MS text.
3   Bid my beads: pray.

# ON THE DEATH OF MRS. MARTINEAU

[Barbauld's friend Sarah Meadows Martineau, matriarch of the Martineau family of Norwich, died 26 November 1800, age 75. "She was endowed with a strong mind and a well-cultivated understanding, and lived in the constant exercise of every moral and religious duty. Her loss will be severely felt by a numerous family, by many whom her charity daily relieved, and also by those who resorted to her judgment for advice" (her obituary, in Martineau, *Notes on the Pedigree of the Martineau Family*, p. 25). In August 1801 Lucy Aikin reported that Barbauld had written this poem and that copies were to be privately printed for the family. The copies bore the dedication, "To her honoured friends of the families of MARTINEAU and TAYLOR these lines are inscribed by their affectionate A. L. Barbauld." The poem was first published in the American edition of *Poems* (Boston, 1820); its first English publication was in *Works* (1825).]

Ye who around this venerated bier
In pious anguish pour the tender tear,
Mourn not!—'Tis Virtue's triumph, Nature's doom,
When honoured Age, slow bending to the tomb,
Earth's vain enjoyments past, her transient woes,          5
Tastes the long sabbath of well-earned repose.
No blossom here, in vernal beauty shed,
No lover lies, warm from the nuptial bed;
Here rests *the full of days*,[1]—each task fulfilled,
Each wish accomplished, and each passion stilled.          10
You raised her languid head, caught her last breath,
And cheered with looks of love the couch of death.
     Yet mourn!—for sweet the filial sorrows flow,
When fond affection prompts the gush of woe;
No bitter drop, 'midst Nature's kind relief,             15
Sheds gall into the fountain of your grief;
No tears you shed for patient love abused,

---

1  An Old Testament phrase (e.g., "When David was old and full of days," 1 Chronicles 23:1).

And counsel scorned, and kind restraints refused.
Not yours the pang the conscious bosom wrings,
20  When late remorse inflicts her fruitless stings.
Living you honoured her, you mourn for, dead;
Her God you worship, and her path you tread:
Your sighs shall aid reflection's serious hour,
And cherished virtues bless the kindly shower:
25  On the loved theme your lips unblamed shall dwell;
Your lives, more eloquent, her worth shall tell.
—Long may that worth, fair Virtue's heritage,
From race to race descend, from age to age!
Still purer with transmitted lustre shine
30  The treasured birthright of the spreading line!
        —For me, as o'er the frequent grave I bend,
And pensive down the vale of years descend;
Companions, Parents, Kindred called to mourn,
Dropt from my side, or from my bosom torn;
35  A boding voice, methinks, in Fancy's ear
Speaks from the tomb, and cries "Thy friends are here!"


## [LINES FOR ANNE WAKEFIELD ON HER WEDDING TO CHARLES ROCHEMONT AIKIN, WITH A PAIR OF CHIMNEY ORNAMENTS IN THE FIGURES OF TWO FEMALES SEATED WITH OPEN BOOKS]

[Anne Wakefield married Barbauld's nephew Charles in August 1806 (Aikin, *Memoirs, Miscellanies and Letters,* p. 136; Rodgers, *Georgian Chronicle,* p. 227). Their daughter recalled long afterwards "a pair of chimney ornaments in my mother's room—two beautiful little female figures [in Wedgwood ware] seated on cushions, each with an open book on her knees, and in one hand a gilt flower cup to hold a candle. They were sent as a wedding present to my mother from Mrs Barbauld, with the following lines" ([LeBreton], *Memories of Seventy Years,* p. 61; the poem follows, and is reprinted here for the first time).]

"Sister, who with me doth hold
~~The open book and lamp of gold,~~
Say whence the lamp, and what the book
On which thine eyes unwearied look?"

"Mine the lamp of Science bright,[1]                    5
Here I muse from morn till night,
The stores of Rome and Greece I spoil,[2]
And feed my lamp with Attic[3] oil;
While for my mistress I explore
The treasures deep of ancient lore,                    10
And from their blooms a garland bind
To deck her pure and polished mind."

"The golden lamp of Love I bear,
A brighter flame, a nobler care;
In critic learning all unskilled,                      15
My page with softer lines is filled;
Here in my tablet I record
Every fond and faithful word
That Love hath spoke, and Hymen[4] sworn,
To Heaven the words, the vows were borne.              20
I trim my lamp with duteous care,
And guard from blasts of ruder air,
And zealous feed its holy fires
With incense drawn from chaste desires,
From gentle deeds and rosy smiles,                     25
And honeyed speech that care beguiles;
And while I thus supply my urn,
Its constant torch shall ever burn."

---

1   Science: in reference to Charles, who had studied medicine and chemistry. "My
    father's lamp of Science burned long, my poor mother's lamp of Love [line 13] was
    soon extinguished by the hand of Death" ([LeBreton], p. 62). Anne Wakefield
    Aikin died 8 Oct. 1821.
2   Acquire by conquest.
3   Greek.
4   God of marriage.

"Then let our mingling flames unite,
30     The mingled flames shall burn more bright;
May never from this hearth remove
The lamp of Science or of Love!"


## WEST END FAIR

[To her young friend and pupil Sarah Taylor, Barbauld
described West End Fair in Hampstead as "the *Ladies* fair....
There were abundance of elegant things [for sale] from two
guineas to sixpence, they took seventy pounds, a considerable
sum.... A number of genteel people of course were there. The
whole struck me as very pretty, but as a sort of *playing* at Chari-
ty, which gave occasion to the lines I enclose for your amuse-
ment" (Barbauld to Taylor, 13 Aug. [1807]). The poem was first
published in *Works* (1825).]

Dame Charity one day was tired
With nursing of her children three,[1]—
     So might you be
If you had nursed and nursed so long
5          A little squalling throng;—
So she, like any earthly lady,
Resolved for once she'd have a play-day.

"I cannot always go about
To hospitals and prisons trudging,
10          Or fag[2] from morn to night
Teaching to spell and write
          A barefoot rout,
Swept from the streets by poor Lancaster,[3]
          My sub-master.

---

1   The three children of Charity are faith, hope, and love.
2   Work hard.
3   Joseph Lancaster (1778-1838), educator, whose approach to teaching the poor
    included the use of "submasters," older students who instructed younger ones. Bar-
    bauld visited Lancaster's school and admired his achievement.

"That Howard[1] ran me out of breath,                          15
And Thornton[2] and a hundred more
        Will be my death:
The air is sweet, the month is gay,
And I," said she, "must have a holiday."

So said, she doffed her robes of brown                         20
In which she commonly is seen,—
        Like French Beguine,[3]—
And sent for ornaments to town:
And Taste in Flavia's[4] form stood by,
Penciled her eyebrows, curled her hair,                         25
Disposed each ornament with care,
And hung her round with trinkets rare,—
She scarcely, looking in the glass,
        Knew her own face.

So forth she sallied blithe and gay,                           30
And met dame Fashion by the way;
And many a kind and friendly greeting
        Passed on their meeting:
Nor let the fact your wonder move,
Abroad, and on a gala-day,                                     35
Fashion and she are hand and glove.

        So on they walked together,
        Bright was the weather;
Dame Charity was frank and warm;                               40
But being rather apt to tire,
        She leant on Fashion's arm.

And now away for West End fair,
Where whiskey,[5] chariot, coach, and chair,

---

1  John Howard (1726-90), philanthropic reformer of prisons and hospitals.
2  Henry Thornton (1760-1815), founder of the British and Foreign Bible Society
   (1804), supporter of Hannah More's Sunday schools, financier, and philanthropist.
3  One of a French order of secular nuns devoted to charity work.
4  A generic name for a fashionable woman; perhaps from the character Flavia in
   William Law's *Serious Call to a Devout and Holy Life* (1729).
5  A small one-horse carriage with two wheels.

Are all in requisition.
45      In neat attire the Graces
Behind the counters take their places,
And humbly do petition
To dress the booths with flowers and sweets,
As fine as any May-day,
50      Where Charity with Fashion meets,
And keeps her play-day.


# THE PILGRIM

[This poem alludes in general to John Bunyan's *Pilgrim's Progress*
(1678). In particular, "the road to Zion's gates" (line 5) is the
road to Heaven which Bunyan's Christian always seeks; lines 7–
10 refer to the "straight and narrow" path to which Christian is
directed by Good Will and others; lines 11–17 suggest the easy
road that leads to Doubting Castle; and lines 19–20 imply the
river (death) which Christian must ford to reach the Celestial
City. Barbauld published the poem in *The Monthly Repository*, 2
(June 1807).]

Gentle Pilgrim, tell me why
Dost thou fold thine arms and sigh;
And wistful cast thine eyes around:
Whither, Pilgrim, art thou bound?

5       The road to Zion's gates I seek,
If thou canst inform me, speak.

Keep yon right-hand path with care,
Though crags obstruct and brambles tear;
You just discern a narrow track,
10      Enter there, and turn not back.

. Say where that pleasant path-way leads,
Winding down yon flowery meads;
Song and dance the way beguiles,

Every face is drest in smiles.

Shun with care that flowery way,                              15
'T will lead thee, Pilgrim, far astray.

Guide or counsel do I need?

Pilgrim, he who runs may read.[1]

Is the way that I must keep
Cross'd by waters wide and deep?                              20

Did it lead thro' floods and fire,
Thou must not stop—thou must not tire.

Till I have my journey past,
Tell me, will the day-light last?
Will the sky be bright and clear                              25
Till the evening shades appear?

Tho' the sun now rides so high,
Clouds may veil the evening sky:
Fast sinks the sun, fast wears the day,
Thou must not stop—thou must not stay,                        30
God speed thee, Pilgrim, on thy way.

---

1   An allusion to Habbakuk 2:2 ("Write the vision, and make it plain ... that he may
    run that readeth it"), mediated through William Cowper, *Tirocinium* (1785), ll. 78-
    79: "Shine by the side of every path we tread / With such a luster, he that runs may
    read."

# DIRGE: WRITTEN NOVEMBER 1808

[Rochemont Barbauld suffered from a mental disorder which became increasingly critical in the 1800s. Early in 1808 he threatened to kill Anna Letitia; she escaped only by jumping from a window. They were obliged to separate. On 11 November Rochemont drowned himself. In her "Memoir" of him, Barbauld speaks with evident sincerity of her grief at his death and of his "tender and delicate" affection for her during most of their marriage (p. 709). This poem was published in *Works* (1825).]

Pure spirit! O where art thou now!
    O whisper to my soul!
O let some soothing thought of thee,
    This bitter grief controul!

5  'Tis not for thee the tears I shed,
    Thy sufferings now are o'er;
The sea is calm, the tempest past,
    On that eternal shore.

No more the storms that wrecked thy peace
10     Shall tear that gentle breast;
Nor Summer's rage, nor Winter's cold,
    Thy poor, poor frame molest.

Thy peace is sealed, thy rest is sure,
    My sorrows are to come;
15  Awhile I weep and linger here,
    Then follow to the tomb.

And is the awful veil withdrawn,
    That shrouds from mortal eyes,
In deep impenetrable gloom,
20     The secrets of the skies?

O, in some dream of visioned bliss,
~~Some trance of rapture, show~~
Where, on the bosom of thy God,
Thou rest'st from human woe!

Thence may thy pure devotion's flame[1]                    25
On me, on me descend;
To me thy strong aspiring hopes,
Thy faith, thy fervours lend.

Let these my lonely path illume,
And teach my weakened mind                                  30
To welcome all that's left of good,
To all that's lost resigned.

Farewell! With honour, peace, and love,
Be thy dear memory blest!
Thou hast no tears for me to shed,                          35
When I too am at rest.

---

1   Rochemont's "religious sentiments were of the most pure and liberal cast, and his
    pulpit services ... were characterized by the rare union of a warm fervent spirit of
    devotion, with a pure, sublime philosophy" ("Memoir," p. 708).

# ON THE KING'S ILLNESS

[In the summer of 1811 George III suffered the final, perma-
nent onset of his lifelong illness, thought by contemporaries to
be insanity but now diagnosed as porphyria, a blood disorder.
He had also become totally blind. On 26 August, Barbauld read
this poem on George's illness to Henry Crabb Robinson
(Robinson, *On Books*, p. 45); she published it in *The Monthly
Repository*, 6 (October 1811). In Part Two of *The Rights of Man*
(1792), the radical republican Tom Paine had assailed as idolatry
the English attachment to monarchy. Barbauld's expression of
sympathy for George as a person is more subtle but not less
republican: she herself "did not think [the poem] quite calcu-
lated to please a courtly ear" (LeBreton, *Memoir*, p. 75).]

Rest, rest afflicted spirit, quickly pass
Thine hour of bitter suffering! Rest awaits thee,
There, where, the load of weary life laid down,
The peasant and the king repose together.
5    There peaceful sleep, thy quiet grave bedewed
With tears of those who loved thee. Not for thee,
In the dark chambers of the nether world,
Shall spectre kings rise from their burning thrones,
And point the vacant seat, and scoffing say
10   "Art thou become like us?" Oh not for thee:
For thou hadst human feelings, and hast liv'd
A man with men, and kindly charities,
Even such as warm the cottage hearth, were thine.[1]
And therefore falls the tear from eyes not used
15   To gaze on kings with admiration fond:
And thou hast knelt at meek Religion's shrine
With no mock homage, and hast owned her rights
Sacred in every breast:[2] and therefore rise,

---

1  George III was known affectionately as "Farmer George" for his reputed personal
    kindess to common people.

2  "He was conscientiously religious, and observed not only public but also domestic
    worship; but, at the same time, he was free from bigotry ... and on all occasions he
    was forward to protect ... the just liberties of the Protestant Dissenters" ("Death of
    His Majesty George the Third," p. 118).

Affectionate, for thee, the orisons
~~And mingled prayers, alike from vaulted domes~~                    20
Whence the loud organ peals, and raftered roofs
Of humbler worship.[1]—Still, remembering this,
A Nation's pity and a Nation's love
Linger beside thy couch, in this the day
Of thy sad visitation, veiling faults                              25
Of erring judgment and not will perverse.
Yet, Oh that thou hadst closed the wounds of war![2]
That had been praise to suit a higher strain.
　　　Farewell the years rolled down the gulph of time!
Thy name has chronicled a long bright page                          30
Of England's story,[3] and perhaps the babe
Who opens, as thou closest thine, his eyes
On this eventful world, when aged grown,
Musing on times gone by, shall sigh and say,
Shaking his thin grey hairs, whitened with grief,                  35
"Our fathers' days were happy."—Fare thee well!
My thread of life has even run with thine
For many a lustre,[4] and thy closing day
I contemplate, not mindless of my own,
Nor to its call reluctant.                                          40

---

1  domes: Anglican cathedrals; roofs: dissenting chapels.

2  In its obituary of George III *The Monthly Repository* attributed to his "principles of
   government" the wars with America and with revolutionary France: "Humanity
   shudders at the recollection of the awful effusion of blood in [those] contests"
   ("Death of His Majesty," p. 118).

3  George III ascended the throne in 1760; his reign witnessed not only the American
   and French Revolutions but also the industrialization of Britain and the abolition
   of the British slave trade in 1807.

4  Period of five years. King George's and Anna Barbauld's birthdays both fell in June,
   five years apart.

# EIGHTEEN HUNDRED AND ELEVEN,
## A POEM

[Since 1793, with one short interruption, Britain had been at war with France—first with the Republic, then with the Empire of Napoleon. The war was international and inter-continental, and carried on by economic as well as military means: mutual blockades of shipping imposed shortages and high prices on civilians. In 1807 Britain's chief ally, Russia, capitulated; two years later Austria did likewise, and almost the whole of Europe came under French control. At the end of 1810 the British economy was near collapse; then, in 1811, George III succumbed to permanent dementia. Antiwar senti-ment could show plenty of reasons for seeking peace, but the government would not do it.

Barbauld completed *Eighteen Hundred and Eleven* by Decem-ber of the year; it was published in January or February of 1812. John Aikin predicted that "its view of present & vatication of future evils will not please those *patriots* who think their coun-try just in all her projects" (John Aikin to James Montgomery, 29 Feb. 1812). Reviews, whether in liberal or conservative magazines, ranged from cautious to patronizingly negative to outrageously abusive (John Wilson Croker's, in the Tory *Quar-terly Review*). Private readers took sides warmly: the poet Eliza-beth Cobbold thought the poem "dangerous"—and the more so "on account of its poetical excellence"; her friend Sir James Edward Smith declared in reply that it "may take its stand amongst the most lofty productions of any poet, male or female" (Smith, *Memoir and Correspondence*, 2:177-78). To a friend, Barbauld defended her pessimistic view of Britain's future: "I acknowledge it to be gloomy & I am sure I do not wish to be a true prophet; yet when one sees the ... astonishing revolutions which have changed ... the political face of the globe, what nation has a right to say 'My mountain stands strong, I shall *never* be moved'?" (to Judith Beecroft, 19 March 1812).

Written in the tradition of Juvenalian satires such as Samuel Johnson's *London* (1738), *Eighteen Hundred and Eleven* elaborates a topical theme, the passing of empire from east to west. (Earlier treatments include George Berkeley's "On the Prospect of Planting Arts and Learning in America" [1752], Oliver Goldsmith's *The Deserted Village* [1770], and *Les Ruines; ou Méditations sur les Révolutions des Empires* [1791], by Constantin François, comte de Volney.) The poem engages with numerous other texts as well. Its catalogue of British cultural triumphs (lines 67ff) recalls a passage in James Thomson's *Summer* (1746) beginning "Happy Britannia! where, the Queen of Arts"; the lines on the transformation of ancient Britain into modern London (lines 275ff) remember Thomson's, in *Winter*, of Russia modernized by Peter the Great. Perhaps most of all, as William Richey has argued, Barbauld "systematically inverts" Alexander Pope's paean to British progress, *Windsor Forest* (1713): Pope's prophecy of a British "golden age" is unmasked by Barbauld as delusory, a "Midas dream" ("Anna Letitia Barbauld and the Myth of Progress").]

Still the loud death drum, thundering from afar,
O'er the vext nations pours the storm of war:
To the stern call still Britain bends her ear,
Feeds the fierce strife, the alternate hope and fear;
Bravely, though vainly, dares to strive with Fate,     5
And seeks by turns to prop each sinking state.[1]
Colossal Power[2] with overwhelming force
Bears down each fort of Freedom in its course;
Prostrate she lies beneath the Despot's sway,
While the hushed nations curse him—and obey.     10
    Bounteous in vain, with frantic man at strife,
Glad Nature pours the means—the joys of life;
In vain with orange blossoms scents the gale,
The hills with olives clothes, with corn the vale;
Man calls to Famine, nor invokes in vain,[3]     15

---

1   Despite Britain's efforts, Russia, Spain and Austria had all capitulated to France. Elizabeth Cobbold saw ll. 3-6 as accusing Britain of "voluntarily protracting ... the Horrors of War" (MS draft letter to Sir J.E. Smith, 31 May 1812).

2   Napoleon, often depicted in political cartoons as a giant.

3   Croker, in his review, attacked this line: "What does Mrs. Barbauld mean? Does she seriously accuse mankind of wishing for a famine, and interceding for starva-

Disease and Rapine follow in her train;
The tramp of marching hosts disturbs the plough,
The sword, not sickle, reaps the harvest now,
And where the Soldier gleans the scant supply,
20  The helpless Peasant but retires to die;
No laws his hut from licensed outrage shield,
And war's least horror is the ensanguined field.
  Fruitful in vain, the matron counts with pride
The blooming youths that grace her honoured side;
25  No son returns to press her widow'd hand,
Her fallen blossoms strew a foreign strand.
—Fruitful in vain, she boasts her virgin race,
Whom cultured arts adorn and gentlest grace;
Defrauded of its homage, Beauty mourns,
30  And the rose withers on its virgin thorns.[1]
Frequent, some stream obscure, some uncouth name
By deeds of blood is lifted into fame;
Oft o'er the daily page some soft-one bends
To learn the fate of husband, brothers, friends,
35  Or the spread map with anxious eye explores,
Its dotted boundaries and penciled shores,
Asks *where* the spot that wrecked her bliss is found,
And learns its name but to detest the sound.
  And think'st thou, Britain, still to sit at ease,
40  An island Queen amidst thy subject seas,
While the vext billows, in their distant roar,
But soothe thy slumbers, and but kiss thy shore?
To sport in wars, while danger keeps aloof,
Thy grassy turf unbruised by hostile hoof?[2]
45  So sing thy flatterers; but, Britain, know,
Thou who hast shared the guilt must share the woe.

---

tion?" (p. 310). "She means," William Keach has replied, "that the effects of the bad
harvest of 1811 were brutally intensified by government policies on food distribu-
tion and trade that were driven by the Tory war effort" ("A Regency Prophecy," p.
574). She means also the destruction of agriculture by troop movements and
seizures of crops to feed armies (ll. 17-20).

1  Young women are denied opportunity to marry because men are in military ser-
   vice.
2  Although threatened by invasion, Britain remained free of conflict on its own soil.

Nor distant is the hour; low murmurs spread,
~~And whispered fears, creating what they dread;~~
Ruin, as with an earthquake shock, is here,
There, the heart-witherings of unuttered fear, 50
And that sad death, whence most affection bleeds,
Which sickness, only of the soul, precedes.[1]
Thy baseless wealth dissolves in air away,
Like mists that melt before the morning ray:[2]
No more on crowded mart or busy street 55
Friends, meeting friends, with cheerful hurry greet;
Sad, on the ground thy princely merchants bend
Their altered looks, and evil days portend,
And fold their arms, and watch with anxious breast
The tempest blackening in the distant West.[3] 60
     Yes, thou must droop; thy Midas dream is o'er;
The golden tide of Commerce leaves thy shore,
Leaves thee to prove the alternate ills that haunt
Enfeebling Luxury and ghastly Want;
Leaves thee, perhaps, to visit distant lands, 65
And deal the gifts of Heaven with equal hands.
     Yet, O my Country, name beloved, revered,
By every tie that binds the soul endeared,
Whose image to my infant senses came
Mixt with Religion's light and Freedom's holy flame![4] 70
If prayers may not avert, if 'tis thy fate
To rank amongst the names that once were great,

---

1  An allusion, perhaps, to the suicide in 1810 of Abraham Goldsmid, financier and
philanthropist; more generally, to the sufferings of bankrupts in the fall of 1810.
"Thoroughly to understand and feel this passage [ll. 47-52] requires, perhaps, some
acquaintance with those silent miseries which have abounded during the last seven
years ... in ... the commercial world. They who have witnessed the dumb despair
of broken-hearted merchants, and the grief of their wives and daughters will be
able to appreciate the matchless beauty of [ll. 51-52]" (*New British Lady's Magazine*,
p. 320).

2  In January 1811 a Select Committee of the House of Commons reported that the
British government had issued paper currency in excess of its gold reserves and that
the currency therefore lacked credibility (*MM*, 30 [1811]:491-98).

3  The impending "tempest" is the threat of war with the United States. The war
began in June 1812.

4  Country, Religion, and Freedom invoke the Whig credo, "Protestantism, Liberty,
and England."

Not like the dim cold Crescent[1] shalt thou fade,
Thy debt to Science and the Muse unpaid;
75    Thine are the laws surrounding states revere,
Thine the full harvest of the mental year,
Thine the bright stars in Glory's sky that shine,
And arts that make it life to live are thine.
If westward streams the light that leaves thy shores,
80    Still from thy lamp the streaming radiance pours.
Wide spreads thy race from Ganges[2] to the pole,
O'er half the western world thy accents roll:
Nations beyond the Apalachian hills[3]
Thy hand has planted and thy spirit fills:
85    Soon as their gradual progress shall impart
The finer sense of morals and of art,
Thy stores of knowledge the new states shall know,
And think thy thoughts, and with thy fancy glow;[4]
Thy Lockes, thy Paleys[5] shall instruct their youth,
90    Thy leading star direct their search for truth;
Beneath the spreading Platan's[6] tent-like shade,
Or by Missouri's rushing waters laid,
"Old father Thames" shall be the Poet's theme,
Of Hagley's woods[7] the enamoured virgin dream,
95    And Milton's tones the raptured ear enthrall,
Mixt with the roar[8] of Niagara's fall;
In Thomson's glass the ingenuous youth shall learn
A fairer face of Nature to discern;

---

1    The Ottoman Empire.
2    A principal river of India.
3    The mountain range separating the Atlantic states of North America from the interior.
4    On ll. 85ff *The New British Lady's Magazine* commented, "On the supposition of the removal of the empire of commerce to the New World, the poet, in imagination, looks forward to those days when England will become to America what Greece and Rome are now to England" (p. 320).
5    John Locke (1632-1704), author of *An Essay concerning Human Understanding* (1690), and William Paley (1743-1805), author of polemics in defense of Christianity.
6    The plane tree or sycamore.
7    Lord Lyttelton's estate in Worcestershire, celebrated for its landscape gardens by James Thomson in *Spring* (1728). "Thomson's glass" (l. 97) is his poem *The Seasons*.
8    roar: In *Works*, "roaring." The change was made (by Lucy Aikin?) perhaps to correct the pronunciation of Niagara.

Nor of the Bards that swept the British lyre
Shall fade one laurel, or one note expire. 100
Then, loved Joanna,[1] to admiring eyes
Thy storied groups in scenic pomp shall rise;
Their high soul'd strains and Shakespear's noble rage
Shall with alternate passion shake the stage.
Some youthful Basil from thy moral lay 105
With stricter hand his fond desires shall sway;
Some Ethwald, as the fleeting shadows pass,
Start at his likeness in the mystic glass;
The tragic Muse resume her just controul,
With pity and with terror purge the soul, 110
While wide o'er transatlantic realms thy name
Shall live in light, and gather *all* its fame.
    Where wanders Fancy down the lapse of years
Shedding o'er imaged woes untimely tears?
Fond moody Power! as hopes—as fears prevail, 115
She longs, or dreads, to lift the awful veil,
On visions of delight now loves to dwell,
Now hears the shriek of woe or Freedom's knell:
Perhaps, she says, long ages past away,
And set in western waves our closing day, 120
Night, Gothic night, again may shade the plains
Where Power is seated, and where Science reigns;
England, the seat of arts, be only known
By the gray ruin and the mouldering stone;
That Time may tear the garland from her brow, 125
And Europe sit in dust, as Asia now.
    Yet then the ingenuous youth whom Fancy fires
With pictured glories of illustrious sires,
With duteous[2] zeal their pilgrimage shall take
From the Blue Mountains, or Ontario's lake,[3] 130

---

1  Joanna Baillie (1762-1851), dramatist, often compared by her contemporaries to
   Shakespeare. "Basil" (l. 105 below) is the title character in her tragedy, *Count Basil*
   (1798); Ethwald (ll. 107-08), in her tragedy of that name (1802), like Macbeth is
   shown a vision of himself as king by three "Mystic Sisters."
2  Dutiful.
3  The Blue Mountains in Pennsylvania, Lake Ontario, and Niagara Falls (l. 96) all are
   shown in William Winterbotham's *View of the American United States* (1795), 2:282;
   Barbauld owned a copy of this book.

With fond adoring steps to press the sod
By statesmen, sages, poets, heroes trod;
On Isis'[1] banks to draw inspiring air,
From Runnymede[2] to send the patriot's prayer;
135    In pensive thought, where Cam's[3] slow waters wind,
To meet those shades that ruled the realms of mind;
In silent halls to sculptured marbles bow,
And hang fresh wreaths round Newton's[4] awful brow.
Oft shall they seek some peasant's homely shed,
140    Who toils, unconscious of the mighty dead,
To ask where Avon's[5] winding waters stray,
And thence a knot of wild flowers bear away;
Anxious enquire where Clarkson,[6] friend of man,
Or all-accomplished Jones[7] his race began;
145    If of the modest mansion aught remains
Where Heaven and Nature prompted Cowper's strains;[8]
Where Roscoe,[9] to whose patriot breast belong
The Roman virtue and the Tuscan song,
Led Ceres to the black and barren moor
150    Where Ceres never gained a wreath before:
With curious search their pilgrim steps shall rove
By many a ruined tower and proud alcove,

---

1    The river Thames at Oxford.
2    Site of the signing of Magna Carta by King John.
3    The river that flows past the colleges of Cambridge University.
4    Sir Isaac Newton (1642-1727), physicist and mathematician, Lucasian Professor at
     Trinity College, Cambridge.
5    The river in Warwickshire that runs through Stratford, birthplace of William
     Shakespeare. "Wild flowers" in l. 142 signify Shakespeare's supposedly "natural"
     (uneducated) genius.
6    Thomas Clarkson (1760-1846), leading abolitionist.
7    Sir William Jones (1746-94), linguist and polymath who founded Asiatic studies.
8    William Cowper (1731-1800), poet, to whose *Olney Hymns* (1779) Barbauld
     alludes.
9    "The Historian of the age of Leo has brought into cultivation the extensive tract of
     Chatmoss" (Barbauld's note). William Roscoe (1753-1831), historian, poet, and
     agriculturalist, author of *The History of the Life and Pontificate of Leo the Tenth* (1805),
     demonstrated at Chat Moss in Lancashire that moors could yield good crops. He
     had also opposed the war from its start, and had written eloquently against it.
     Hence this praise of him enraged Croker, who ridiculed Barbauld for making
     Roscoe's "barns and piggeries ... objects not only of curiosity but even of rever-
     ence and enthusiasm" (p. 312).

Shall listen for those strains that soothed of yore
~~Thy rock, stern Skiddaw, and thy fall, Lodore;[1]~~
Feast with Dun Edin's[2] classic brow their sight,                155
And visit "Melross by the pale moonlight."[3]
    But who their mingled feelings shall pursue
When London's faded glories rise to view?
The mighty city, which by every road,
In floods of people poured itself abroad;                        160
Ungirt by walls, irregularly great,
No jealous drawbridge, and no closing gate;
Whose merchants (such the state which commerce brings)
Sent forth their mandates to dependant kings;
Streets, where the turban'd Moslem, bearded Jew,                 165
And woolly Afric, met the brown Hindu;[4]
Where through each vein spontaneous plenty flowed,
Where Wealth enjoyed, and Charity bestowed.
Pensive and thoughtful shall the wanderers greet
Each splendid square, and still, untrodden street;              170
Or of some crumbling turret, mined by time,
The broken stairs with perilous step shall climb,
Thence stretch their view the wide horizon round,
By scattered hamlets trace its antient bound,
And, choked no more with fleets, fair Thames survey            175
Through reeds and sedge pursue his idle way.[5]
    With throbbing bosoms shall the wanderers tread
The hallowed mansions of the silent dead,
Shall enter the long isle and vaulted dome
Where Genius and where Valour find a home;[6]                   180

---

1   Skiddaw (a mountain) and Lodore (site of a famous waterfall) are both in the Lake
    District.
2   A poetical name for Edinburgh.
3   Sir Walter Scott, *The Lay of the Last Minstrel* (1805): "If thou would'st view fair Mel-
    rose aright, / Go visit it by the pale moonlight" (II.i).
4   Barbauld perhaps remembers Voltaire's *Letters concerning the English Nation* (1733): at
    the Royal Exchange in London, "the Jew, the Mahometan, and the Christian trans-
    act together as tho' they all professed the same religion" (p. 30). We thank Andrew
    Ashfield for this suggestion.
5   Lines 171-76 suggest the Tower of London.
6   St. Paul's Cathedral, in which stand statues of Samuel Johnson (1709-84), lexicogra-
    pher, and John Howard (1726-90), philanthropist (ll. 185-86 below).

Awe-struck, midst chill sepulchral marbles breathe,
Where all above is still, as all beneath;
Bend at each antique shrine, and frequent turn
To clasp with fond delight some sculptured urn,
185   The ponderous mass of Johnson's form to greet,
Or breathe the prayer at Howard's sainted feet.
    Perhaps some Briton, in whose musing mind
Those ages live which Time has cast behind,
To every spot shall lead his wondering guests
190   On whose known site the beam of glory rests:
Here Chatham's[1] eloquence in thunder broke,
Here Fox persuaded, or here Garrick spoke;[2]
Shall boast how Nelson, fame and death in view,
To wonted victory led his ardent crew,
195   In England's name enforced, with loftiest tone,
Their duty,[3]—and too well fulfilled his own:
How gallant Moore, as ebbing life dissolved,
*But* hoped his country had his fame absolved.[4]
Or call up sages whose capacious mind
200   Left in its course a track of light behind;
Point where mute crowds on Davy's[5] lips reposed,
And Nature's coyest secrets were disclosed;
Join with their Franklin, Priestley's[6] injured name,

---

1   William Pitt, Earl of Chatham (1708-78), Prime Minister during the Seven Years' War, was famous for his oratory.

2   Charles James Fox (1749-1806), eloquent spokesman for liberal issues. David Garrick (1717-79), eminent actor.

3   "Every reader will recollect the sublime telegraphic dispatch, 'England expects every man to do his duty'" (Barbauld's note). She refers to the order issued by Admiral Horatio Nelson before the Battle of Trafalgar (21 October 1805), in which he lost his life.

4   "'I hope England will be satisfied' were the last words of General Moore" (Barbauld's note). General Sir John Moore failed to prevent Napoleon's capture of Madrid but evacuated his troops safely at the Battle of Corunna (January 1809), in which he died. Other poets followed Barbauld in celebrating Moore's sacrifice, most notably Anne Grant in *Eighteen Hundred and Thirteen* (1814) and Charles Wolfe in "The Burial of Sir John Moore" (1817).

5   Sir Humphrey Davy (1778-1829), lecturer on chemistry at the Royal Institution.

6   Benjamin Franklin (1706-90), American student of electricity. Joseph Priestley corresponded with Franklin. For his unorthodox opinions Priestley was attacked by a mob in 1791 and so harrassed thereafter that he emigrated to America in 1794. The

Whom, then, each continent shall proudly claim.
Oft shall the strangers turn their eager feet                    205
The rich remains of antient art to greet,
The pictured walls with critic eye explore,
And Reynolds be what Raphael was before.[1]
On spoils from every clime their eyes shall gaze,
Egyptian granites and the Etruscan vase;                         210
And when midst fallen London, they survey
The stone where Alexander's ashes lay,[2]
Shall own with humbled pride the lesson just
By Time's slow finger written in the dust.
There walks a Spirit[3] o'er the peopled earth,                  215
Secret his progress is, unknown his birth;
Moody and viewless[4] as the changing wind,
No force arrests his foot, no chains can bind;
Where'er he turns, the human brute awakes,
And, roused to better life, his sordid hut forsakes:             220
He thinks, he reasons, glows with purer fires,
Feels finer wants, and burns with new desires:
Obedient Nature follows where he leads;
The steaming marsh is changed to fruitful meads;
The beasts retire from man's asserted reign,                     225
And prove his kingdom was not given in vain.
Then from its bed is drawn the ponderous ore,
Then Commerce pours her gifts on every shore,

reviewer in *The Anti-Jacobin Review*, incensed by this line, declared that Priestley, "instead of being *proudly claimed* by *each* continent, is almost *disowned* by BOTH" (p. 208).

1 Sir Joshua Reynolds (1723-92), portrait painter who emulated the "grand manner" of the Renaissance master, Raphael.
2 Artifacts held in the British Museum. In Barbauld's day the stone was mistakenly believed to have held the remains of Alexander the Great.
3 Various interpretations of this Spirit were proposed by Barbauld's contemporaries. The *Anti-Jacobin Review* equated it with Liberty (p. 208). *The New British Lady's Magazine* regretted that Barbauld had not "entered into a fuller description of the power to whose presence and absence such effects are assigned as the growth and decay of nations and empires," and speculated that the Spirit was "some principle personated, analogous to Truth and Virtue, which includes liberty and knowledge" (p. 321). Sir James Edward Smith thought that the lines describe "a highly poetic personification of the power of civilization" (*Memoir and Correspondence*, 2:179).
4 Invisible.

Then Babel's towers and terrassed gardens rise,
230   And pointed obelisks invade the skies;
The prince commands, in Tyrian purple drest,
And Egypt's virgins weave the linen vest.
Then spans the graceful arch the roaring tide,
And stricter bounds the cultured fields divide.
235   Then kindles Fancy, then expands the heart,
Then blow the flowers of Genius and of Art;
Saints, Heroes, Sages, who the land adorn,
Seem rather to descend than to be born;
Whilst History, midst the rolls consigned to fame,
240   With pen of adamant inscribes their name.
        The Genius now forsakes the favoured shore,
And hates, capricious, what he loved before;
Then empires fall to dust, then arts decay,
And wasted realms enfeebled despots sway;
245   Even Nature's changed; without his fostering smile
Ophir[1] no gold, no plenty yields the Nile;
The thirsty sand absorbs the useless rill,
And spotted plagues from putrid fens distill.
In desert solitudes then Tadmor[2] sleeps,
250   Stern Marius then o'er fallen Carthage weeps;[3]
Then with enthusiast love the pilgrim roves
To seek his footsteps in forsaken groves,
Explores the fractured arch, the ruined tower,
Those limbs disjointed of gigantic power;
255   Still at each step he dreads the adder's sting,
The Arab's javelin, or the tiger's spring;
With doubtful caution treads the echoing ground,
And asks where Troy or Babylon[4] is found.

---

1   A Biblical land supposed to be rich in gold.
2   Or Tamar, Biblical names for Palmyra, an ancient desert city of Syria.
3   Caius Marius (2nd century BC), who, according to Plutarch, was "speechless" with
    "grief and indigation" when he was forbidden to enter Africa. Asked what message
    he wished to send to the governor, Marius replied, "Tell him … that thou has seen
    Marius a fugitive, seated amid the ruins of Carthage" (Plutarch, "Life of Caius Mar-
    ius.") Carthage was destroyed by Roman armies in 146 BC.
4   Troy: the great city in Asia Minor besieged by Greek armies for ten years, then
    conquered and destroyed. Babylon: an ancient city legendary for its luxury.

And now the vagrant Power no more detains
The vale of Tempe, or Ausonian[1] plains;
Northward he throws the animating ray,
O'er Celtic nations bursts the mental day:
And, as some playful child the mirror turns,
Now here now there the moving lustre burns;
Now o'er his changeful fancy more prevail
Batavia's[2] dykes than Arno's purple vale,
And stinted suns, and rivers bound with frost,
Than Enna's plains or Baia's[3] viny coast;
Venice the Adriatic weds in vain,
And Death sits brooding o'er Campania's plain;[4]
O'er Baltic shores and through Hercynian[5] groves,
Stirring the soul, the mighty impulse moves;
Art plies his tools, and Commerce spreads her sail,
And wealth is wafted in each shifting gale.
The sons of Odin[6] tread on Persian looms,
And Odin's daughters breathe distilled perfumes;
Loud minstrel Bards, in Gothic halls, rehearse
The Runic rhyme, and "build the lofty verse:"[7]
The Muse, whose liquid notes were wont to swell
To the soft breathings of the' Eolian shell,
Submits, reluctant, to the harsher tone,
And scarce believes the altered voice her own.
And now, where Caesar saw with proud disdain
The wattled hut and skin of azure stain,[8]

---

1  The Vale of Tempe is in Thessaly, and "Ausonian" is a Virgilian synonym for "Ital-
   ian"; together the names designate Greece and Rome.
2  Batavia: Holland. Arno (below): a river in Tuscany.
3  Enna: a valley in Sicily, compared to Eden by Milton in *Paradise Lost*, 4:268-70.
   Baia: a Roman resort on the Bay of Naples, known for its scenic beauty and mild
   climate.
4  An area in the region of Rome, notorious for unhealthy marshes.
5  Roman name for the Black Forest in Germany.
6  The chief god of Norse mythology. His "sons" and "daughters" are northern Euro-
   peans.
7  Milton, *Lycidas*, l. 11, slightly altered. Runic: referring to what Barbauld's contem-
   poraries took to be the Old Norse alphabet.
8  In his *Gallic War*, Julius Caesar tells of the ancient Scots who painted themselves
   blue before going into battle.

Corinthian columns rear their graceful forms,
And light varandas brave the wintry storms,
While British tongues the fading fame prolong
Of Tully's eloquence and Maro's song.[1]
Where once Bonduca[2] whirled the scythed car,
290 And the fierce matrons raised the shriek of war,
Light forms beneath transparent muslins float,
And tutored voices swell the artful note.
Light-leaved acacias and the shady plane
And spreading cedar grace the woodland reign;
295 While crystal walls the tenderer plants confine,
The fragrant orange and the nectared pine;[3]
The Syrian grape there hangs her rich festoons,
Nor asks for purer air, or brighter noons:
Science and Art urge on the useful toil,
300 New mould a climate and create the soil,
Subdue the rigour of the northern Bear,[4]
O'er polar climes shed aromatic air,
On yielding Nature urge their new demands,
And ask not gifts but tribute at her hands.

305     London exults:—on London Art bestows
Her summer ices and her winter rose;
Gems of the East her mural crown adorn,
And Plenty at her feet pours forth her horn;
While even the exiles her just laws disclaim,[5]
310 People a continent, and build a name:
August she sits, and with extended hands

---

1    Tully: the Roman rhetorician Cicero. Maro: the Roman poet Virgil. Both were staples of the British school curriculum.

2    Boadicea (d. AD 60), ancient British warrior queen.

3    Greenhouses, in which exotic plants such as the pineapple were grown. In 1811 eight-year-old Marjorie Fleming noted the luxurious character of pineapples: "the price of a pine-apple ... might have sustained a poor family a whole week and more perhaps" (*The Complete Marjory Fleming*, pp. 114-15).

4    The constellation Ursa Major or Ursa Minor; the latter contains the northern Pole Star.

5    Of this line, the *Anti-Jacobin Review* remarked, "We presume the writer means, the exiles, which the laws disclaim" (p. 208n). Barbauld refers perhaps to emigrants like Joseph Priestley, or to transported convicts like the Scottish reformers Thomas Muir and Thomas Palmer, sent to Australia in 1794.

Holds forth the book of life to distant lands.[1]
    But fairest flowers expand but to decay;
The worm is in thy core, thy glories pass away;
Arts, arms and wealth destroy the fruits they bring;       315
Commerce, like beauty, knows no second spring.
Crime walks thy streets, Fraud earns her unblest bread,
O'er want and woe thy gorgeous robe is spread,
And angel charities in vain oppose:
With grandeur's growth the mass of misery grows.[2]    320
For see,—to other climes the Genius soars,
He turns from Europe's desolated shores;
And lo, even now, midst mountains wrapt in storm,
On Andes' heights he shrouds his awful form;
On Chimborazo's[3] summits treads sublime,      325
Measuring in lofty thought the march of Time;
Sudden he calls:—"'Tis now the hour!" he cries,
Spreads his broad hand, and bids the nations rise.
La Plata hears amidst her torrents' roar,
Potosi hears it, as she digs the ore:      330
Ardent, the Genius fans the noble strife,
And pours through feeble souls a higher life,
Shouts to the mingled tribes from sea to sea,
And swears—Thy world, Columbus, shall be free.

---

1  Probably a reference to the work of the British and Foreign Bible Society, founded in 1804.

2  The growing gulf between the rich and the poor was a topic of much concern in the early nineteenth century: see headnote to Barbauld's essay "On the Inequality of Conditions."

3  Chimborazo: a mountain in Ecuador. La Plata (l. 329) and Potosi (l. 330) are cities in Argentina and Bolivia respectively. Barbauld chooses South America as the Spirit's new home probably in response to accounts of independence movements there. Venezuela declared independence from Spain in 1811; Barbauld would have read of these events in *The Monthly Repository*.

# LIFE

[Long the best known of Barbauld's writings, this poem—or, more often, only its last stanza—was widely anthologized during the century after her death. It was first published in *Works* (1825); Henry Crabb Robinson sent a copy to Dorothy Wordsworth, praising "the curious felicity of the language" (MS letter, 6 Jan. 1826). In his "Reminiscences," Robinson reports that he once overheard Dorothy's brother William mutter enviously about the poem's last stanza: "'I am not in the habit of grudging people their good things, but I wish I had written those lines'" (*On Books*, p. 8). The poet Samuel Rogers records Frances Burney d'Arblay's admiration: "Sitting with Madame d'Arblay some weeks before she died, I said to her, 'Do you remember those lines of Mrs. Barbauld's *Life* which I once repeated to you?' 'Remember them!' she replied; 'I repeat them to myself every night before I go to sleep'" (*Recollections of the Table-Talk*, p. 129).]

Animula, vagula, blandula.[1]

Life! I know not what thou art,
But know that thou and I must part;
And when, or how, or where we met,
I own to me's a secret yet.
5    But this I know, when thou art fled,
Where'er they lay these limbs, this head,
No clod so valueless shall be,
As all that then remains of me.
O whither, whither dost thou fly,
10    Where bend unseen thy trackless course,
        And in this strange divorce,
Ah tell where I must seek this compound I?

---

1 "Ah fleeting Spirit! wand'ring Fire" (Alexander Pope's translation of "To His Soul," attributed to the Emperor Hadrian [AD 76-138], a poem widely translated and imitated in the eighteenth century).

To the vast ocean of empyreal flame,
    ~~From whence thy essence came,~~
Dost thou thy flight pursue, when freed           15
From matter's base encumbering weed?
    Or dost thou, hid from sight,
    Wait, like some spell-bound knight,
Through blank oblivious years th' appointed hour,
To break thy trance and reassume thy power?[1]     20
Yet canst thou without thought or feeling be?
O say what art thou, when no more thou'rt thee?


    Life! we've been long together,
Through pleasant and through cloudy weather;
'Tis hard to part when friends are dear;         25
    Perhaps 'twill cost a sigh, a tear;
    Then steal away, give little warning,
        Choose thine own time;
Say not Good night, but in some brighter clime
        Bid me Good morning.[2]         30


## A THOUGHT ON DEATH

[One of the most popular of all Barbauld's poems during her life, "A Thought on Death" circulated in manuscript so far afield that it first saw print in Boston in 1821; Thomas Jefferson quoted it to John Adams while Barbauld was yet unaware of its publication. Once made aware, she sent a correct text to *The Monthly Repository* (November 1822). Lucy Aikin printed a different text, dated "November 1814," in *Works* (1825).]

---

1   Lines 13-20 present first the traditional view that the soul and body separate at death, and then Joseph Priestley's view that the spirit and flesh die and are resurrected together.
2   Perhaps an allusion to Sir Thomas Overbury, *A Wife* (1614): "No man goes to bed till he dies, nor wakes till he be dead. And therefore, / Good night to you here, / and good morrow hereafter."

When life, as opening buds, is sweet,
And golden hopes the spirit greet,
And youth prepares his joys to meet,
 Alas! how hard it is to die!

5 When scarce is seiz'd some valu'd prize,
And duties press, and tender ties
Forbid the soul from earth to rise,
 How awful then it is to die!

When, one by one, those ties are torn,
10 And friend from friend is snatched forlorn,
And man is left alone to mourn,
 Ah! then, how easy 'tis to die!

When faith is strong, and conscience clear,
And words of peace the spirit cheer,
15 And vision'd glories half appear,
 'Tis joy, 'tis triumph, then to die!

When trembling limbs refuse their weight,
And films, slow gathering, dim the sight,
And clouds obscure the mental light,
20 'Tis nature's precious boon to die!


## THE FIRST FIRE
### OCTOBER 1ST, 1815

[First published in *Works* (1825), "The First Fire" has been persuasively read as a "greater Romantic lyric" of the same kind as Coleridge's "Frost at Midnight" (1798), a poem to which in a number of ways it responds (Anderson, "'The First Fire': Barbauld Rewrites the Greater Romantic Lyric").]

Ha, old acquaintance! many a month has past
Since last I viewed thy ruddy face; and I,
Shame on me! had mean time well nigh forgot

That such a friend existed. Welcome now!—
When summer suns ride high, and tepid airs                         5
Dissolve in pleasing languor; then indeed
We think thee needless, and in wanton pride
Mock at thy grim attire and sooty jaws,
And breath sulphureous, generating spleen,—
As Frenchmen say;[1] Frenchmen, who never knew             10
The sober comforts of a good coal fire.
—Let me imbibe thy warmth, and spread myself
Before thy shrine adoring:—magnet thou
Of strong attraction, daily gathering in
Friends, brethren, kinsmen, variously dispersed,              15
All the dear charities of social life,
To thy close circle. Here a man might stand,
And say, This is my world! Who would not bleed
Rather than see thy violated hearth
Prest by a hostile foot?[2] The winds sing shrill;            20
Heap on the fuel! Not the costly board,
Nor sparkling glass, nor wit, nor music, cheer
Without thy aid. If thrifty thou dispense
Thy gladdening influence, in the chill saloon[3]
The silent shrug declares the'[4] unpleased guest.           25
—How grateful to belated traveller
Homeward returning, to behold the blaze
From cottage window, rendering visible
The cheerful scene within! There sits the sire,
Whose wicker chair, in sunniest nook enshrined,              30
His age's privilege,—a privilege for which
Age gladly yields up all precedence else
In gay and bustling scenes,—supports his limbs.

---

1   "At Dover I first burnt coal and found it very inconvenient. I regretted ... that we
    had no firewood.... Coal is much better for warming a room. But I found the
    smell of coal extremely disagreeable" (La Rochefoucauld, *A Frenchman's Year in
    Suffolk ... in 1784*, p. 4).
2   During the Napoleonic Wars, just ended, anti-French patriotism had been stirred
    up by appeals to the defense of the home and hearth.
3   Salon, the visiting room in an elegant house.
4   the': so in *Works*. Possibly Barbauld wrote "th'," intending elision with "unpleased,"
    which would then be three syllables. See l. 55 also.

Cherished by thee, he feels the grateful warmth
35  Creep through his feeble frame and thaw the ice
Of fourscore years, and thoughts of youth arise.
—Nor less the young ones press within, to see
Thy face delighted, and with husk of nuts,
Or crackling holly, or the gummy pine,
40  Feed thy immortal hunger: cheaply pleased
They gaze delighted, while the leaping flames
Dart like an adder's tongue upon their prey;
Or touch with lighted reed thy wreaths of smoke;
Or listen, while the matron sage remarks
45  Thy bright blue scorching flame and aspect clear,
Denoting frosty skies. Thus pass the hours,
While Winter spends without his idle rage.
        —Companion of the solitary man,
From gayer scenes withheld! With thee he sits,
50  Converses, moralizes; musing asks
How many eras of uncounted time
Have rolled away since thy black unctuous food
Was green with vegetative life,[1] and what
This planet then: or marks, in sprightlier mood,
55  Thy flickering smiles play round the' illumined room,
And fancies gay discourse, life, motion, mirth,
And half forgets he is a lonely creature.
        —Nor less the bashful poet loves to sit
Snug, at the midnight hour, with only thee
60  Of his lone musings conscious. Oft he writes,
And blots, and writes again; and oft, by fits,
Gazes intent with eyes of vacancy
On thy bright face;[2] and still at intervals,
Dreading the critic's scorn, to thee commits,
65  Sole confidant and safe, his fancies crude.
        —O wretched he, with bolts and massy bars
In narrow cell immured, whose green damp walls,

---

1   The vegetable origin of coal is mentioned by Barbauld's nephew, Arthur Aikin, in
    his *Manual of Mineralogy* (1814).
2   Lines 58-63 recall the opening of Coleridge's "Frost at Midnight," but with humor
    at the poet's expense.

That weep unwholesome dews, have never felt
Thy purifying influence! Sad he sits
Day after day, till in his youthful limbs                           70
Life stagnates, and the hue of hope is fled
From his wan cheek.—And scarce less wretched he—
When wintry winds blow loud and frosts bite keen,—
The dweller of the clay-built tenement,
Poverty-struck, who, heartless,[1] strives to raise                 75
From sullen turf, or stick plucked from the hedge,
The short-lived blaze; while chill around him spreads
The dreary fen, and Ague, sallow-faced,
Stares through the broken pane;—Assist him, ye
On whose warm roofs the sun of plenty shines,                       80
And feel a glow beyond material fire!


## THE CATERPILLAR

[Conjectural date of composition: c. 1816. First published in
*Works* (1825). Caterpillars appear in other poems of the period:
one, from 1804, argues against philosophical materialism by
asserting that the caterpillar has a soul (*Poems never before Pub-
lished*, p. 16).]

No, helpless thing, I cannot harm thee now;
Depart in peace, thy little life is safe,
For I have scanned thy form with curious eye,
Noted the silver line that streaks thy back,
The azure and the orange that divide                                5
Thy velvet sides; thee, houseless wanderer,
My garment has enfolded, and my arm
Felt the light pressure of thy hairy feet;
Thou hast curled round my finger; from its tip,
Precipitous descent! with stretched out neck,                       10
Bending thy head in airy vacancy,
This way and that, inquiring, thou hast seemed

---

1   heartless: so in *Works*. It seems likely that Barbauld's MS. read "heartless."

To ask protection; now, I cannot kill thee.
Yet I have sworn perdition to thy race,
And recent from the slaughter am I come
Of tribes and embryo nations: I have sought
With sharpened eye and persecuting zeal,[1]
Where, folded in their silken webs they lay
Thriving and happy; swept them from the tree
And crushed whole families beneath my foot;
Or, sudden, poured on their devoted heads
The vials of destruction.[2]—This I've done,
Nor felt the touch of pity: but when thou,—
A single wretch, escaped the general doom,
Making me feel and clearly recognise
Thine individual existence, life,
And fellowship of sense with all that breathes,—
Present'st thyself before me, I relent,
And cannot hurt thy weakness.—So the storm
Of horrid war, o'erwhelming cities, fields,
And peaceful villages, rolls dreadful on:
The victor shouts triumphant; he enjoys
The roar of cannon and the clang of arms,
And urges, by no soft relentings stopped,
The work of death and carnage. Yet should one,
A single sufferer from the field escaped,
Panting and pale, and bleeding at his feet,
Lift his imploring eyes,—the hero weeps;
He is grown human, and capricious Pity,
Which would not stir for thousands, melts for one
With sympathy spontaneous:—'Tis not Virtue,
Yet 'tis the weakness of a virtuous mind.

15
20
25
30
35
40

---

1  By using this phrase Barbauld likens herself to a religious persecutor such as Bishop
   Bonner (see "The Apology of the Bishops").
2  Pesticides, represented in Biblical idiom (cf. Jeremiah 7:20 and Romans 9:22).

# ON THE DEATH OF THE PRINCESS CHARLOTTE

[On 6 November 1817 Charlotte Augusta, daughter of George, the Prince Regent, died in childbirth at the age of twenty-one. Although she was intensely disliked by her father, the nation loved her and mourned her death deeply: "Spontaneously the streets of every city, town and village exhibited the outward signs of inward distress.... Universally the sable garbs of mourning were worn" (*Monthly Repository*, 12 [1817]:693). On the day of the funeral, people crowded the churches to hear sermons on the occasion. Maria Edgeworth wrote that "every human Creature seems to feel [the princess's death] as if it were a *private* misfortune!" (letter to C. S. Edgeworth, Nov. 1817). Barbauld's was one of many poems written on the event; it was published in the *Annual Register ... for the Year 1818* (1819), titled "Elegy" and signed "Mrs. B———d." This text was reprinted in *Works* (1825). But Barbauld revised the poem when she sent it to her friends, the Carrs, and that is the text we print.]

Yes Britain mourns, as with electric shock
For youth, for love, for happiness destroyed.
Her universal population wells[1]
In grief spontaneous; and hard hearts are moved,
And rough unpolished natures learn to feel          5
For those they envied, humbled[2] in the dust
By fate's impartial hand; and pulpits sound
With vanity and woe to earthly goods,
And urge, and dry the tear—Yet one[3] there is
Who midst this general burst of grief remains          10
In strange tranquillity; whom not the stir
And long drawn murmurs of the gathering crowd,
That by his very windows trail the pomp

---

1   wells: in *Works*, "melts."
2   humbled: in *Works*, "levelled."
3   The Prince Regent, her father. His dislike of his daughter arose from his hatred of her mother, Princess Caroline.

Of hearse, and blazoned arms, and long array
Of sad funereal rites, nor the loud groans
And deep felt anguish of a husband's[1] heart
Can move to mingle with this flood one tear.
In careless apathy—perhaps in mirth
He spends the day;[2] yet is he near in blood,
The very stem on which this blossom grew,
And at his knees she fondled, in the charm
And grace spontaneous, which alone belongs
To untaught infancy; yet—Oh forbear
Nor deem him hard of heart, for, awful, struck
By heaven's severest visitation, sad,
Like a scathed oak amidst the forest trees
Lonely he stands; leaves sprout, and fade,[3] and fall,
And seasons run their round, to him in vain,[4]
He holds no sympathy with living nature,
Or time's incessant change. Then, in this hour,
While pensive thought is busy with the woes
And restless cares of poor humanity,
Oh think of him, and set apart one sigh,[5]
From the full tide of sorrow spare one tear
For him who does not weep.

---

1   Leopold of Saxe-Coburg. He and Charlotte married in 1816 and were regarded as
a model couple.
2   spends: in *Works*, "wears." The Prince Regent sent a representative to the funeral
but did not attend it himself. When she died, he was on a hunting party in Norfolk
(*MM*, 44 [1817]:468).
3   sprout, and fade: in *Works*, "bud, and shoot."
4   Line 28 is absent in *Works*.
5   In *Works*, l. 33 reads, "Think then, oh think of him, and breathe one prayer"; in the
earliest autograph copy, ll. 32-33 read, "Of poor humanity, then think of him, / Liv-
ing shut out from life, and breathe one prayer."

# THE BABY-HOUSE

[Date of composition not known; published in *Works* (1825).
Nor have we identified Agatha, presumably the daughter of a
friend.]

Dear Agatha, I give you joy,
And much admire your pretty toy,
A mansion in itself complete
And fitted to give guests a treat;
With couch and table, chest and chair,     5
The bed or supper to prepare;
We almost wish to change ourselves
To fairy forms of tripping elves,
To press the velvet couch and eat
From tiny cups the sugared meat.     10
    I much suspect that many a sprite
Inhabits it at dead of night;
That, as they dance, the listening ear
The pat of fairy feet might hear;
That, just as you have said your prayers,     15
They hurry-scurry down the stairs:
And you'll do well to try to find
Tester[1] or ring they've left behind.
    But think not, Agatha, you own
That toy, a Baby-house, alone;     20
For many a sumptuous one is found
To press an ampler space of ground.
The broad-based Pyramid that stands
Casting its shade in distant lands,
Which asked some mighty nation's toil     25
With mountain-weight to press the soil,
And there has raised its head sublime
Through eras of uncounted time,—
Its use if asked, 'tis only said,
A Baby-house to lodge the dead.     30

---

1   A sixpence.

Nor less beneath more genial skies
The domes of pomp and folly rise,
Whose sun through diamond windows streams,
While gems and gold reflect his beams;
35 Where tapestry clothes the storied wall,
And fountains spout and waters fall;
The peasant faints beneath his load,
Nor tastes the grain his hands have sowed,
While scarce a nation's wealth avails
40 To raise thy Baby-house, Versailles.[1]
And Baby-houses oft appear
On British ground, of prince or peer;
Awhile their stately heads they raise,
The' admiring traveller stops to gaze;
45 He looks again—where are they now?
Gone to the hammer[2] or the plough:
Then trees, the pride of ages, fall,
And naked stands the pictured wall;
And treasured coins from distant lands
50 Must feel the touch of sordid hands;
And gems, of classic stores the boast,
Fall to the cry of—Who bids most?
Then do not, Agatha, repine
That cheaper Baby-house is thine.

---

1 The sumptuous palace of Louis XIV.
2 Auctioned off (to pay the owner's debts).

# LINES WRITTEN AT THE CLOSE OF THE YEAR

[A series of deaths in her family culminated in the death, on 7 December 1822, of Barbauld's beloved brother, John Aikin. Barbauld published these lines in *The Monthly Repository* in January 1823; they were reprinted in *Works* (1825) under the title, "Octogenary Reflections."]

Say, ye who thro' this round of eighty[1] years
Have proved its joys and sorrows, hopes and fears,
Say what is Life, ye veterans who have trod,
Step following step, its flow'ry, thorny road?
Enough of good to kindle strong desire,                    5
Enough of ill to damp the rising fire,
Enough of love and fancy, joy and hope,
To fan desire and give the passions scope,
Enough of disappointment, sorrow, pain,
To seal the wise man's sentence "All is vain,"[2]          10
And quench the wish to live those years again.
Science for man unlocks her various store,
And gives enough to urge the wish for more;
Systems and suns lie open to his gaze,
Nature invites his love and God his praise;                15
Yet doubt and ignorance with his feelings sport,
And Jacob's ladder[3] is some rounds[4] too short.
Yet still to humble hope enough is given
Of light from reason's lamp and light from heaven,
To teach us what to follow, what to shun,                  20
To bow the head, and say, "Thy will be done."

---

1   eighty: in *Monthly Repository*, fourscore.
2   Ecclesiastes 1:2.
3   "And [Jacob] dreamed, and behold a ladder set up on the earth, and the top of it reached to heaven: and behold the angels of God ascending and descending on it" (Genesis 28:12).
4   Rungs.

# AGAINST INCONSISTENCY IN OUR EXPECTATIONS

[Written in or after 1769 (the year of publication of William Shenstone's letters, to which it refers), first published in *Miscellaneous Pieces in Prose* (1773), and often reprinted thereafter, this essay was admired, both as English prose and as wisdom literature, for a full century. It was praised by William Hazlitt ("one of the most ingenious and sensible essays in the language" ["On the Living Poets," p. 147]); the poet Anna Seward ranked it with Samuel Johnson's *Rambler* essays (*Letters of Anna Seward*, 4:85), and Mary Wollstonecraft recommended it in *A Vindication of the Rights of Woman*. The kind of use made of the essay, perhaps especially by young people, is suggested by a divinity student's letter to his father in 1819: "We must always, as Mrs. Barbauld observes, pay the price of the article we purchase: with my talents, if I mean ... to unite two professions, I must be satisfied with respectability, and not look for eminence in both" (Tayler, *Letters*, 1:36).

The epigraph to the essay comes from Elizabeth Carter's translation of *All the Works of Epictetus* (1758). Epictetus was a Greek exponent of Stoicism, a philosophy that advocated acting in accordance with the laws of nature and developing self-knowledge and self-control as defenses against the sorrows of life. Elizabeth Carter (1717-1806), linguist and polymath, earned the respect of the learned world with her translation of Epictetus.]

What is more reasonable, than that they who take pains for any thing, should get most in that particular, for which they take pains? They have taken pains for power; you for right principles: they for riches; you for a proper use of the appearances of things: see whether they have the advantage of you in that, for which you have taken pains, and which they neglect: If they are in power, and you not; why will not you speak the truth to yourself; that you do nothing for the sake of power; but that they do every thing? No, but since I take care to have right principles, it is more reasonable that I should have power. Yes, in respect to what you take care about, your principles. But give up to others the things in which they have taken more care than you. Else it is just as if, because you have right principles, you should think it fit that when you shoot an arrow, you should hit the mark better than an archer, or that you should forge better than a smith.

Carter's Epictetus.[1]

As most of the unhappiness in the world arises rather from disappointed desires, than from positive evil, it is of the utmost consequence to attain just notions of the laws and order of the universe, that we may not vex ourselves with fruitless wishes, or give way to groundless and unreasonable discontent. The laws of natural philosophy, indeed, are tolerably understood and attended to; and though we may suffer inconveniences, we are seldom disappointed in consequence of them. No man expects to preserve orange-trees in the open air through an English winter;[2] or when he has planted an acorn, to see it become a large oak in a few months. The mind of man naturally yields to necessity; and our wishes soon subside when we see the impossibility of their being gratified. Now, upon an accurate inspection, we shall find, in the moral government of the world, and the order of the intellectual system, laws as determinate, fixed, and invariable as any in Newton's Principia.[3] The progress of vegetation is not more certain than the growth of habit; nor is the power of attraction more clearly proved than the force of affection, or the influence of example. The man, therefore, who has well studied the operations of nature in mind as well as matter, will acquire a certain moderation and equity in his claims upon Providence. He never will be disappointed either in himself or others. He will act with precision; and expect that effect, and that alone, from his efforts, which they are naturally

---

1   See Appendix A.
2   preserve orange-trees ... air through: In *MPP* eds. 1-2, "preserve oranges through."
3   *Philosophiae Naturalis Principia Mathematica* (1687), in which Sir Isaac Newton expounded his theory of the laws of motion and universal gravitation ("attraction," below).

adapted to produce. For want of this, men of merit and integri-
ty often censure the dispositions of Providence for suffering
characters they despise to run away with advantages which,
they yet know, are purchased by such means as a high and noble
spirit could never submit to. If you refuse to pay the price, why
expect the purchase? We should consider this world as a great
mart of commerce, where Fortune exposes to our view various
commodities, riches, ease, tranquility, fame, integrity, knowl-
edge. Every thing is marked at a settled price. Our time, our
labour, our ingenuity, is so much ready money which we are to
lay out to the best advantage. Examine, compare, chuse, reject;
but stand to your own judgment; and do not, like children,
when you have purchased one thing, repine that you do not
possess another which you did not purchase. Such is the force
of well-regulated industry, that a steady and vigorous exertion
of our faculties, directed to one end, will generally insure suc-
cess. Would you, for instance, be rich? Do you think that single
point worth the sacrificing every thing else to? You may then
be rich. Thousands have become so from the lowest beginnings
by toil, and patient diligence, and attention to the minutest arti-
cles of expence and profit. But you must give up the pleasures
of leisure, of a vacant mind, of a free unsuspicious temper. If
you preserve your integrity, it must be a coarse-spun and vulgar
honesty. Those high and lofty notions of morals which you
brought with you from the schools must be considerably low-
ered, and mixed with the baser alloy of a jealous and worldly-
minded prudence. You must learn to do hard,[1] if not unjust
things; and for the nice embarrassments of a delicate and ingen-
uous spirit, it is necessary for you to get rid of them as fast as
possible. You must shut your heart against the Muses, and be
content to feed your understanding with plain, houshold
truths. In short, you must not attempt to enlarge your ideas, or
polish your taste, or refine your sentiments; but must keep on in
one beaten track, without turning aside either to the right hand
or to the left. "But I cannot submit to drudgery like this—I feel
a spirit above it." 'Tis well: be above it then; only do not repine
that you are not rich.

---

1   Unfeeling.

Is knowledge the pearl of price?[1] That too may be purchased—by steady application and long solitary hours of study and reflection. Bestow these, and you shall be wise. "But (says the man of letters) what a hardship is it that many an illiterate fellow who cannot construe the motto of the arms on his coach shall raise a fortune and make a figure, while I have little more than the common conveniences of life." *Et tibi magna satis!*[2]—Was it in order to raise a fortune that you consumed the sprightly hours of youth in study and retirement? Was it to be rich that you grew pale over the midnight lamp, and distilled the sweetness from the Greek and Roman spring? You have then mistaken your path, and ill employed your industry. "What reward have I then for all my labours?" What reward! A large comprehensive soul, well purged from vulgar fears, and perturbations, and prejudices; able to comprehend and interpret the works of man—of God. A rich, flourishing, cultivated mind, pregnant with inexhaustible stores of entertainment and reflection. A perpetual spring of fresh ideas; and the conscious dignity of superior intelligence. Good heaven! and what reward can you ask besides?

"But is it not some reproach upon the economy of Providence that such a one, who is a mean dirty fellow, should have amassed wealth enough to buy half a nation?" Not in the least. He made himself a mean dirty fellow for that very end. He has paid his health, his conscience, his liberty for it; and will you envy him his bargain? Will you hang your head and blush in his presence because he outshines you in equipage and show? Lift up your brow with a noble confidence, and say to yourself, I have not these things, it is true; but it is because I have not sought, because I have not desired them; it is because I possess something better. I have chosen my lot. I am content and satisfied.

You are a modest man—You love quiet and independence, and have a delicacy and reserve in your temper which renders it impossible for you to elbow your way in the world, and be the herald of your own merits. Be content then with a modest

---

1  Cf. Matthew 13:46.
2  And large enough for you. Virgil, *Eclogue* I.47 (Loeb translation).

retirement, with the esteem of your intimate friends, with the praises of a blameless heart, and a delicate ingenuous spirit; but resign the splendid distinctions of the world to those who can better scramble for them.

The man whose tender sensibility of conscience and strict regard to the rules of morality makes him scrupulous and fearful of offending, is often heard to complain of the disadvantages he lies under in every path of honour and profit. "Could I but get over some nice points, and conform to the practice and opinion of those about me, I might stand as fair a chance as others for dignities and preferment." And why can you not? What hinders you from discarding this troublesome scrupulosity of yours which stands so grievously in your way? If it be a small thing to enjoy a healthful mind, sound at the very core, that does not shrink from the keenest inspection; inward freedom from remorse and perturbation; unsullied whiteness and simplicity of manners; a genuine integrity

Pure in the last recesses of the mind;[1]

if you think these advantages an inadequate recompense for what you resign, dismiss your scruples this instant, and be a slave-merchant, a parasite,[2] or—what you please.

If these be motives weak, break off betimes;[3]

and as you have not spirit to assert the dignity of virtue, be wise enough not to forego the emoluments of vice.

I much admire the spirit of the antient philosophers, in that they never attempted, as our moralists often do, to lower the tone of philosophy, and make it consistent with all the indulgences of indolence and sensuality. They never thought of having the bulk of mankind for their disciples; but kept themselves as distinct as possible from a worldly life. They plainly told men

---

1 John Dryden, translation of "Second Satire of Perseus," l. 133.
2 parasite: In *MPP* eds. 1-2, "director" (of a joint-stock company).
3 Shakespeare, *Julius Caesar*, II.i.116.

what sacrifices were required, and what advantages they were which might be expected.

> Si virtus hoc una potest dare, fortis omissis
> Hoc age deliciis——————————————————[1]

If you would be a philosopher these are the terms. You must do thus and thus: There is no other way. If not, go and be one of the vulgar.

There is no one quality gives so much dignity to a character as consistency of conduct. Even if a man's pursuits be wrong and unjustifiable, yet if they are prosecuted with steadiness and vigour, we cannot with-hold our admiration. The most characteristic mark of a great mind is to chuse some one important object, and pursue it through life. It was this made Caesar a great man.[2] His object was ambition; he pursued it steadily, and was always ready to sacrifice to it every interfering passion or inclination.

There is a pretty passage in one of Lucian's dialogues, where Jupiter complains to Cupid that though he has had so many intrigues he was never sincerely beloved. In order to be loved, says Cupid, you must lay aside your aegis and your thunderbolts, and you must curl and perfume your hair, and place a garland on your head, and walk with a soft step, and assume a winning obsequious deportment. But, replied Jupiter, I am not willing to resign so much of my dignity. Then, returns Cupid, leave off desiring to be loved[3]—He wanted to be Jupiter and Adonis at the same time.

It must be confessed, that men of genius are of all others most inclined to make these unreasonable claims. As their relish for enjoyment is strong, their views large and comprehensive, and they feel themselves lifted above the common bulk of

---

1  If then Virtue alone can confer this boon, boldly drop trifles and set to work! Horace, *Epistle* VI.30-31 (Loeb translation).
2  Barbauld's likely source is Plutarch, who portrays Caesar as single-mindedly pursuing power, honor and empire through the course of his life.
3  Barbauld summarizes "Eros and Zeus" from *Dialogues of the Gods* by Lucian (2nd century AD). "Aegis" (above) is the shield of Jupiter.

mankind, they are apt to slight that natural reward of praise and admiration which is ever largely paid to distinguished abilities; and to expect to be called forth to public notice and favour: without considering that their talents are commonly very unfit for active life; that their excentricity and turn for speculation disqualifies them for the business of the world, which is best carried on by men of moderate genius; and that society is not obliged to reward any one who is not useful to it. The Poets have been a very unreasonable race,[1] and have often complained loudly of the neglect of genius and the ingratitude of the age. The tender and pensive Cowley, and the elegant Shenstone, had their minds tinctured by this discontent; and even the sublime melancholy of Young was too much owing to the stings of disappointed ambition.[2]

The moderation we have been endeavouring to inculcate will likewise prevent much mortification and disgust in our commerce with mankind. As we ought not to wish in ourselves, so neither should we expect in our friends contrary qualifications. Young and sanguine, when we enter the world, and feel our affections drawn forth by any particular excellence in a character, we immediately give it credit for all others; and are beyond measure disgusted when we come to discover, as we soon must discover, the defects in the other side of the balance. But nature is much more frugal than to heap together all manner of shining qualities in one glaring mass.[3] Like a judicious painter she endeavours to preserve a certain unity of stile and

---

1   An echo of Alexander Pope's "Preface" to his *Works* (1717): "I am inclined to think that both the writers of books, and the readers of them, are generally not a little unreasonable in their expectations. The first seem to fancy that the world must approve whatever they produce ..." (Pope, *Poems*, p. xxv).

2   Abraham Cowley (1618-67) complains of neglect in the preface to his *Poems* (1656), and Samuel Johnson, in *Rambler* 6, criticizes Cowley's professed wish to retire to America. Likewise the poet William Shenstone (1714-63): "I am vain enough to imagine that the little merit I have, deserves somewhat more regard than I have met with from the world" (*Works, in Verse and Prose*, 3:132). The poet and dramatist Edward Young (1681-1765) was notorious for disappointed ambition and for claiming to despise the world: see the "Life of Young" in Johnson's *Lives of the Poets* (1781).

3   An allusion to Pope's *Essay on Criticism* (1711), l. 292: "One *glaring Chaos* and *wild Heap of Wit*" (*Poems*, p. 153).

colouring in her pieces. Models of absolute perfection are only to be met with in romance; where exquisite beauty, and brilliant wit, and profound judgment, and immaculate virtue are all blended together to adorn some favourite character. As an anatomist knows that the racer cannot have the strength and muscles of the draught-horse; and that winged men, gryffons, and mermaids must be mere creatures of the imagination; so the philosopher is sensible that there are combinations of moral qualities which never can take place but in idea. There is a different air and complexion in characters as well as in faces, though perhaps each equally beautiful; and the excellencies of one cannot be transferred to the other. Thus if one man possesses a stoical apathy of soul, acts independent of the opinion of the world, and fulfils every duty with mathematical exactness, you must not expect that man to be greatly influenced by the weakness of pity, or the partialities of friendship: you must not be offended that he does not fly to meet you after a short absence; or require from him the convivial spirit and honest effusions of a warm, open, susceptible heart. If another is remarkable for a lively active zeal, inflexible integrity, a strong indignation against vice, and freedom in reproving it, he will probably have some little bluntness in his address not altogether suitable to polished life; he will want the winning arts of conversation; he will disgust by a kind of haughtiness and negligence in his manner, and often hurt the delicacy of his acquaintance with harsh and disagreeable truths.

We usually say—that man is a genius, *but* he has some whims and oddities—such a one has a very general knowledge, *but* he is superficial; &c. Now in all such cases we should speak more rationally did we substitute *therefore* for *but*. He is a genius, *therefore* he is whimsical; and the like.

It is the fault of the present age, owing to the freer commerce that different ranks and professions now enjoy with each other, that characters are not marked with sufficient strength: the several classes run too much into one another. We have fewer pedants, it is true, but we have fewer striking originals. Every one is expected to have such a tincture of general knowledge as is incompatible with going deep into any science; and such a conformity to fashionable manners as checks the free workings of the ruling passion,[1] and gives an insipid sameness to the face of society, under the idea of polish and regularity.

There is a cast of manners peculiar and becoming to each age, sex and profession; one, therefore, should not throw out illiberal and common-place censures against another. Each is perfect in its kind. A woman as a woman; a tradesman as a tradesman. We are often hurt by the brutality and sluggish conceptions of the vulgar; not considering that some there must be to be hewers of wood and drawers of water,[2] and that cultivated genius, or even any great refinement and delicacy in their moral feelings would be a real misfortune to them.

Let us then study the philosophy of the human mind. The man who is master of this science will know what to expect from every one. From this man, wise advice; from that, cordial sympathy; from another, casual entertainment. The passions and inclinations of others are his tools, which he can use with as much precision as he would the mechanical powers; and he can as readily make allowance for the workings of vanity, or the bias of self-interest in his friends, as for the power of friction, or the irregularities of the needle.[3]

---

1   The "ruling Passion" is Pope's name, in *An Essay on Man* (1733-34), ii.131ff, for the dominant motive that impels each person's actions: love of power, of wealth, of glory, or whatever.
2   Joshua 9:21.
3   Needle of the compass, that is.

# AN ENQUIRY INTO THOSE KINDS OF DISTRESS WHICH EXCITE AGREEABLE SENSATIONS

[The subject of this essay—the fact that people enjoy fictional representations of pain and suffering—is as old as Aristotle's *Poetics*. It was made newly current in the mid-eighteenth century by the development of what G.J. Barker-Benfield has called "the Culture of Sensibility," a taste for intense emotional response to experience and for theorizing emotional response in quasi-scientific terms. A leading mid-century theorist of emotions arising from ideas of pain and pleasure was Edmund Burke, in *A Philosophical Enquiry into the Origin of our Ideas of the Sublime and Beautiful* (1757). Barbauld may be assumed to have read the *Enquiry* (see our headnote to her 1767 poem, "An Address to the Deity"), and in this essay she commences an ongoing, if intermittent, engagement with Burke. She imitates some of his discursive procedures, such as the description of the manifestations of emotion in the human body (see p. 197 n. 1). More, she follows him—and many other contemporaries—in assuming that, in Burke's words, "a consideration of the rationale of our passions seems ... very necessary for all who would affect them upon solid and sure principles" (*Sublime and Beautiful*, p. 48). Accepting Burke's distinction between power (the source of ideas of sublimity) and love (the source of ideas of beauty), Barbauld enquires into the "management" of pity, an emotion blended (as her allegory says) of love and sorrow. It is pre-eminently an emotion experienced by readers of recent fictions such as Samuel Richardson's *Clarissa* (1748); Barbauld suggests, too, that it is more often felt by women than by men.

She parts company with Burke, preferring instead the ethics of the Scottish philosopher Francis Hutcheson (see p. 206 n. 1), on the moral value of cultivating intense emotional response to imaginary distresses. If, as Barker-Benfield remarks, her essay "provided cultists of sensibility with a refreshed version of *The Spectator*'s rationale for the 'pleasures of the imagination'" (*The Culture of Sensibility*, p. 338), it also gave them a sharp reminder that cultivating imagination would not guarantee their ethical improvement: "we must not fancy ourselves charitable, when we are only pleasing our imagination."

Date of composition not known; the essay was first published in *Miscellaneous Pieces in Prose* (1773). "A Tale" enjoyed many reprintings by itself, including one in Mary Wollstonecraft's *The Female Reader* (1789).]

It is undoubtedly true, though a phenomenon of the human mind difficult to account for, that the representation of distress frequently gives pleasure; from which general observation many of our modern writers of tragedy and romance seem to have drawn this inference, that in order to please they have nothing more to do than to paint distress in natural and striking colours. With this view, they heap together all the afflicting events and dismal accidents their imagination can furnish; and when they have half broke the reader's heart, they expect he should thank them for his agreeable entertainment. An author of this class sits down, pretty much like an inquisitor,[1] to compute how much suffering he can inflict upon the hero of his tale before he makes an end of him: with this difference, indeed, that the inquisitor only tortures those who are at least reputed criminals; whereas the writer generally chooses the most excellent character in his piece for the subject of his persecution. The great criterion of excellence is placed in being able to draw tears plentifully; and concluding we shall weep the more, the more the picture is loaded with doleful events, they go on telling

——————————of sorrows upon sorrows
Even to a lamentable length of woe.[2]

A monarch once proposed a reward for the discovery of a new pleasure;[3] but if any one could find out a new torture, or

---

1   As in the Spanish Inquisition.
2   Nicholas Rowe, *Ulysses: A Tragedy* (1706), IV.i.200-01.
3   The monarch was Xerxes, king of Persia 485-465 BC. Barbauld perhaps recalls David Hume's essay, "The Epicurean": "Why did none of them claim the reward which XERXES promised to him who should invent a new pleasure?" (Hume, *Selected Essays*, p. 78)

non-descript calamity, he would be more entitled to the applause of those who fabricate books of entertainment.

But the springs of pity require to be touched with a more delicate hand; and it is far from being true that we are agreeably affected by every thing that excites our sympathy. It shall therefore be the business of this Essay to distinguish those kinds of distress which are pleasing in the representation, from those which are really painful and disgusting.

The view or relation of mere misery can never be pleasing. We have, indeed, a strong sympathy with all kinds of misery; but it is a feeling of pure unmixed pain, similar in kind, though not equal in degree to what we feel for ourselves on the like occasions; and never produces that melting sorrow, that thrill of tenderness, to which we give the name of pity. They are two distinct sensations, marked by very different external expression. One causes the nerves to tingle, the flesh to shudder, and the whole countenance to be thrown into strong contractions; the other relaxes the frame, opens the features, and produces tears.[1] When we crush a noxious or loathsome animal, we may sympathize strongly with the pain it suffers, but with far different emotions from the tender sentiment we feel for the dog of Ulysses, who crawled to meet his long-lost master, looked up, and died at his feet.[2] Extreme bodily pain is perhaps the most intense suffering we are capable of, and if the fellow-feeling with misery alone was grateful to the mind, the exhibition of a man in a fit of the tooth-ach, or under a chirurgical[3] operation, would have a fine effect in a tragedy. But there must be some other sentiment combined with this kind of instinctive sympathy, before it becomes in any degree pleasing, or produces the sweet emotion of pity. This sentiment is love, esteem, the complacency[4] we take in the contemplation of beauty, of mental or moral excellence, called forth and rendered more interesting, by circumstances of pain and danger. Tenderness is, much more

---

1 Barbauld emulates Burke's practice of describing bodily responses to emotional stimuli: cf. *Sublime and Beautiful*, pp. 119, 135.
2 In *The Odyssey*, Book 17, at Ulysses' arrival home after twenty years' absence.
3 Surgical.
4 "Tranquil pleasure or satisfaction" (*OED*).

properly than sorrow, the spring of tears; for it affects us in that manner whether combined with joy or grief; perhaps more in the former case than the latter. And I believe we may venture to assert that no distress which produces tears is wholly without a mixture of pleasure. When Joseph's brethren were sent to buy corn,[1] if they had perished in the desert by wild beasts, or been reduced (as in the horrid adventures of a Pierre de Vaud)[2] to eat one another, we might have shuddered, but we should not have wept for them. The gush of tears breaks forth[3] when Joseph made himself known to his brethren, and fell on their neck, and kissed them. When Hubert prepares to burn out prince Arthur's eyes,[4] the shocking circumstance, of itself, would only affect us with horror; it is the amiable simplicity of the young prince, and his innocent affection to his intended murderer that draws our tears, and excites that tender sorrow which we love to feel, and which refines the heart while we do feel it.

We see, therefore, from this view of our internal feelings, that no scenes of misery ought to be exhibited which are not connected with the display of some moral excellence or agreeable quality. If fortitude, power, and strength of mind are called forth, they produce the sublime feelings of wonder and admiration: if the softer qualities of gentleness, grace, and beauty, they inspire love and pity. The management of these latter emotions is our present object.

And let it be remembered, in the first place, that the misfortunes which excite pity must not be too horrid and overwhelming. The mind is rather stunned than softened by great calamities. They are little circumstances that work most sensibly upon the tender feelings. For this reason, a well written novel generally draws more tears than a tragedy. The distresses of tragedy are more calculated to amaze and terrify, than to

---

1   In Genesis 42; below, Barbauld refers to Joseph's reconciliation with his brothers in Genesis 45.
2   Pierre de Vaud, or Peter Walden, religious reformer of the twelfth century, founder of a sect persecuted through the seventeenth century as documented in Milton's "Sonnet 18: On the Late Massacre in Piemont." The anecdote involving the extremity Barbauld cites here remains unidentified.
3   breaks forth: In *MPP* eds. 1–2, "is."
4   Shakespeare, *King John*, IV.i.

move compassion. Battles, torture and death are in every page. The dignity of the characters, the importance of the events, the pomp of verse and imagery interest the grander passions, and raise the mind to an enthusiasm little favourable to the weak and languid notes of pity. The tragedies of Young are in a fine strain of poetry, and the situations are worked up with great energy, but the pictures are in too deep a shade: all his pieces are full of violent and gloomy passions, and so over-wrought with horror, that instead of awakening any pleasing sensibility, they leave on the mind an impression of sadness mixed with terror.[1] Shakespear is sometimes guilty of presenting scenes too shocking. Such is the trampling out of Gloster's eyes; and such is the whole play of Titus Andronicus.[2] But Lee,[3] beyond all others, abounds with this kind of images. He delighted in painting the most daring crimes, and cruel massacres; and though he has shewn himself extremely capable of raising tenderness, he continually checks its course by shocking and disagreeable expressions. His pieces are in the same taste with the pictures of Spagnolet,[4] and there are many scenes in his tragedies which no one can relish who would not look with pleasure on the flaying of St. Bartholomew.[5] The following speech of Marguerité, in the Massacre of Paris, was, I suppose, intended to express the utmost tenderness of affection.

> Die for him! that's too little; I could burn
> Piece-meal away, or bleed to death by drops,

---

1  Edward Young's tragedies, *Busiris* (1719), *The Revenge* (1721), and *The Brothers* (1753) are notable for violence; Samuel Johnson remarks that Young "seemed to have one favourite catastrophe, as his three plays all concluded with a lavish suicide" (*Lives of the Poets*, 3:396).

2  In *King Lear*, III.vii, the earl of Gloucester is shown having his eyes plucked out; *Titus Andronicus* has been characterized by a modern editor as a "gallimaufry of murders, rape, lopped limbs, and heads baked in a pie" (Gustav Cross, "Introduction" to *Titus Andronicus*, in Shakespeare, *Complete Works*, p. 823).

3  Nathaniel Lee (1653?-92), author of *The Massacre of Paris: A Tragedy* (1690) on the subject of the St. Bartholomew's Day slaughter of Protestants by a Catholic faction; below, Barbauld quotes the speech of Marguerite from III.i.22-27.

4  Jusepe de Ribera (1588-1656), called "Lo Spagnoletto," Spanish painter who specialized in gruesome depictions of martyrdoms.

5  St. Bartholomew, apostle (1st century AD), said to have been martyred by being flayed alive.

Be flay'd alive, then broke upon the wheel,
Yet with a smile endure it all for Guise:
And when let loose from torments, all one wound,
Run with my mangled arms, and crush him dead.

Images like these will never excite the softer passions. We
are less moved at the description of an Indian tortured with all
the dreadful ingenuity of that savage people, than with the fatal
mistake of the lover in the Spectator, who pierced an artery in
the arm of his mistress as he was letting her blood.[1] Tragedy
and romance-writers are likewise apt to make too free with the
more violent expressions of passion and distress, by which
means they lose their effect. Thus an ordinary author does not
know how to express any strong emotion otherwise than by
swoonings or death; so that a person experienced in this kind
of reading, when a girl faints away at parting with her lover, or
a hero kills himself for the loss of his mistress, considers it as the
established etiquette upon such occasions, and turns over the
pages with the utmost coolness and unconcern; whereas real
sensibility and a more intimate knowledge of human nature
would have suggested a thousand little touches of grief, which
though slight are irresistible. We are too gloomy a people.
Some of the French novels are remarkable for little affecting
incidents, imagined with delicacy and told with grace. Perhaps
they have a better turn than we have for this kind of writing.[2]

A judicious author will never attempt to raise pity by any
thing mean or disgusting. As we have already observed, there
must be a degree of complacence mixed with our sorrows to
produce an agreeable sympathy; nothing, therefore, must be
admitted which destroys the grace and dignity of suffering; the
imagination must have an amiable figure to dwell upon; there
are circumstances so ludicrous or disgusting, that no character

---

1 In *Spectator* No. 368, by Addison, a surgeon is summoned by his beloved to let
  blood for a minor ailment; but in his agitation he opens her artery and causes her
  death.
2 Likewise, the Scottish rhetorician Hugh Blair (1718–1800) considers the French
  writers superior "in expressing the nicer shades of character; especially those vari-
  eties of manner, temper, and behaviour, which are displayed in our social inter-
  course with one another" (*Lectures on Rhetoric and Belles Lettres*, 1:219).

can preserve a proper decorum under them, or appear in an agreeable light. Who can read the following description of Polypheme without finding his compassion entirely destroyed by aversion and loathing?

> ——————————————————His bloody hand
> Snatch'd two unhappy of my martial band,
> And dash'd like dogs against the stony floor,
> The pavement swims with brains and mingled gore;
> Torn limb from limb he spreads his horrid feast,
> And fierce devours it like a mountain beast,
> He sucks the marrow and the blood he drains,
> Nor entrails, flesh, nor solid bone remains.

Or that of Scylla,

> In the wide dungeon she devours her food,
> And the flesh trembles while she churns the blood.[1]

Deformity is always disgusting, and the imagination cannot reconcile it with the idea of a favourite character; therefore the poet and romance-writer are fully justified in giving a larger share of beauty to their principal figures than is usually met with in common life. A late genius indeed, in a whimsical mood, gave us a lady with her nose crushed for the heroine of his story;[2] but the circumstance spoils the picture; and though in the course of the story it is kept a good deal out of sight, whenever it does recur to the imagination we are hurt and disgusted. It was an heroic instance of virtue in the nuns of a certain abbey, who cut off their noses and lips to avoid violation;[3] yet this would make a very bad subject for a poem or a

---

1 Alexander Pope's translation of *The Odyssey*, 9:342–49 and 12:306–07.
2 In Henry Fielding's *Amelia* (1751), the heroine has had "her nose beat to pieces by the overturning of a chaise" (*London Magazine*, review of *Amelia*, quoted in Paulson and Lockwood, p. 289).
3 Versions of the story of voluntarily mutilated nuns circulated widely in Europe in the late Middle Ages and the sixteenth century. Versions survive in both Latin and German. (Thanks to Charles Doyle for this information.) We have not identified Barbauld's particular source.

play. Something akin to this is the representation of any thing unnatural; of which kind is the famous story of the Roman charity,[1] and for this reason I cannot but think it an unpleasing subject for either the pen or the pencil.[2]

Poverty, if truly represented, shocks our nicer feelings; therefore whenever it is made use of to awaken our compassion, the rags and dirt, the squalid appearance and mean employments incident to that state must be kept out of sight, and the distress must arise from the idea of depression, and the shock of falling from higher fortunes. We do not pity Belisarius as a poor blind beggar; and a painter would succeed very ill who should sink him to the meanness of that condition. He must let us still discover the conqueror of the Vandals, the general of the imperial armies, or we shall be little interested.[3] Let us look at the picture of the old woman in Otway:

> ——————————A wrinkled hag with age grown double,
> Picking dry sticks, and muttering to herself;
> Her eyes with scalding rheum were gall'd and red;
> Cold palsie shook her head; her hands seem'd wither'd;
> And on her crooked shoulder had she wrapt
> The tatter'd remnant of an old strip'd hanging,
> Which serv'd to keep her carcase from the cold;
> So there was nothing of a piece about her.[4]

Here is the extreme of wretchedness, and instead of melting into pity, we should turn away with disgust, if we were not

---

1  "The Roman charity" refers to the story of Pero and her aged father Cimon. When he was condemned to die in prison of starvation, she fed him with her breast milk. The story is from Valerius Maximus and was the subject for paintings by Peter Paul Rubens (1612) and Jean-Baptiste Greuze (1770).

2  Artist's brush.

3  Belisarius (505-565 AD), a general who defended the Byzantine Empire against numerous enemies but fell victim to court intrigue. The legend that he was reduced to beggary supplied a subject for several eighteenth-century fictions, of which the best-known was *Bélisaire* [1766] by Jean François Marmontel. In his preface Marmontel writes, "the idea of a blind old man reduced to beggary is now so associated with the name of Belisarius, that the latter never occurs without presenting to the imagination a picture of the former" (*Belisarius*, p. [vii]).

4  Thomas Otway, *The Orphan*, II.i.244-51.

pleased with it, as we are with a Dutch painting,[1] from its exact imitation of nature.[2] Indeed the author only intended it to strike horror. But how different are the sentiments we feel for the lovely Belvidera! We see none of those circumstances which render poverty an unamiable thing. When the goods are seized by an execution, our attention is turned to *the piles of massy plate, and all the antient most domestic ornaments,* which imply grandeur and consequence;[3] or to such instances of their hard fortune as will lead us to pity them as lovers: we are struck and affected with the general face of ruin, but we are not brought near enough to discern the ugliness of its features. Belvidera ruined, Belvidera deprived of friends, without a home, abandoned to the wide world—we can contemplate with all the pleasing sympathy of pity; but had she been represented as really sunk into low life, had we seen her employed in the most servile offices of poverty, our compassion would have given way to contempt and disgust. Indeed, we may observe in real life that poverty is only pitied so long as people can keep themselves from the effects of it. When in common language we say *a miserable object,* we mean an object of distress which, if we relieve, we turn away from at the same time. To make pity pleasing, the object of it must not in any view be disagreeable to the imagination. How admirably has the author of Clarissa managed this point?[4] Amidst scenes of suffering which rend the heart, in poverty, in a prison, under the most shocking outrages, the grace and delicacy of her character never suffers even for a moment: there seems to be a charm about her which prevents her receiving a stain from any thing which happens; and Clarissa, abandoned and undone, is the object not only of complacence but veneration.

I would likewise observe, that if an author would have us

---

1    The Dutch painters of the seventeenth century cultivated realistic representation of ordinary, "real-life" scenes.

2    we should turn ... nature: In *MPP* eds. 1–2, "we turn away with aversion."

3    Barbauld quotes Otway's *Venice Preserv'd* (1682), I.i; the hero, Jaffeir, has lost his and Belvidera's possessions to a seizure for debt by her father. They are separated, and she is cast out on her own.

4    For further commentary by Barbauld on Richardson's novel, *Clarissa* (1748), see our extracts from her "Life" of Richardson.

feel a strong degree of compassion, his characters must not be too perfect. The stern fortitude and inflexible resolution of a Cato[1] may command esteem, but does not excite tenderness; and faultless rectitude of conduct, though no rigour be mixed with it, is of too sublime a nature to inspire compassion. Virtue has a kind of self-sufficiency; it stands upon its own basis, and cannot be injured by any violence. It must therefore be mixed with something of helplessness and imperfection, with an excessive sensibility, or a simplicity bordering upon weakness, before it raises, in any great degree, either tenderness or familiar love. If there be a fault in the masterly performance just now mentioned, it is that the character of Clarissa is so inflexibly right, her passions are under such perfect command, and her prudence is so equal to every occasion, that she seems not to need that sympathy we should bestow upon one of a less elevated character: and perhaps we should feel a livelier emotion of tenderness for the innocent girl whom Lovelace calls his Rose-bud,[2] but that the story of Clarissa is so worked up by the strength of colouring[3] and the force of repeated impressions, as to command all our sorrow.

Pity seems too degrading a sentiment to be offered at the shrine of faultless excellence. The sufferings of martyrs are rather beheld with admiration and sympathetic triumph than with tears; and we never feel much for those whom we consider as themselves raised above common feelings.

The last rule I shall insist upon is, that scenes of distress should not be too long continued. All our finer feelings are in a manner momentary, and no art can carry them beyond a certain point, either in intenseness or duration. Constant suffering deadens the heart to tender impressions; as we may observe in sailors, and others who are grown callous by a life of continual hardships. It is therefore highly necessary in a long work to

---

1   Marcus Portius Cato (95-46 BC), who tried to save the Roman Republic from the dictatorship of Julius Caesar, was defeated in battle, and committed suicide; he was legendary as a model of severe civic virtue.

2   the innocent ... calls his: In *MPP* eds. 1-2, "Lovelace's." An innkeeper's daughter in *Clarissa* whom Robert Lovelace, the hero-villain of the novel, refrains from seducing.

3   A painterly metaphor for "vividness."

relieve the mind by scenes of pleasure and gaiety: and I cannot think it so absurd a practice as our modern delicacy has represented it, to intermix wit and fancy with the pathetic, provided care be taken not to check the passions while they are flowing.[1] The transition from a pleasurable state of mind to tender sorrow is not so difficult as we imagine. When the mind is opened by gay and agreeable scenes, every impression is felt more sensibly. Persons of a lively temper are much more susceptible of that sudden swell of sensibility which occasions tears, than those of a grave and saturnine cast: for this reason women are more easily moved to weeping than men. Those who have touched the springs of pity with the finest hand have mingled light strokes of pleasantry and mirth in their most pathetic passages. Very different is the conduct of many novel writers, who by plunging us into scenes of distress without end or limit, exhaust the powers, and before the conclusion either render us insensible to every thing, or fix a real sadness upon the mind. The uniform stile of tragedies is one reason why they affect so little. In our old plays all the force of language is reserved for the more interesting parts; and in the scenes of common life there is no attempt to rise above common language: whereas we, by that pompous manner and affected solemnity which we think it necessary to preserve through the whole piece, lose the force of an elevated or passionate expression where the occasion really suggests it.

Having thus considered the manner in which fictitious distress must be managed to render it pleasing, let us reflect a little upon the moral tendency of such representations. Much has been said in favour of them, and they are generally thought to improve the tender and humane feelings;[2] but this, I own, appears to me very dubious. That they exercise sensibility is true, but sensibility does not increase with exercise. By the

---

1  Barbauld here concurs with Samuel Johnson's defence, in the Preface to his edition of Shakespeare (1765), of Shakespeare's "mingled drama" against the demand for "unity of effect."

2  A common argument in behalf of Sensibility; thus Burke claims that "the pain we feel, prompts us to relieve ourselves in relieving those who suffer" (*Sublime and Beautiful*, p. 43).

constitution of our frame our habits increase, our emotions decrease, by repeated acts; and thus a wise provision is made, that as our compassion grows weaker, its place should be supplied by habitual benevolence. But in these writings our sensibility is strongly called forth without any possibility of exerting itself in virtuous action, and those emotions, which we shall never feel again with equal force, are wasted without advantage. Nothing is more dangerous than to let virtuous impressions of any kind pass through the mind without producing their proper effect. The awakenings of remorse, virtuous shame and indignation, the glow of moral approbation, if they do not lead to action, grow less and less vivid every time they recur, till at length the mind grows absolutely callous. The being affected with a pathetic story is undoubtedly a sign of an amiable disposition, but perhaps no means of increasing it. On the contrary, young people, by a course of this kind of reading, often acquire something of that apathy and indifference which the experience of real life would have given them, without its advantages.[1]

Another reason why plays and romances do not improve our humanity is, that they lead us to require a certain elegance of manners and delicacy of virtue which is not often found with poverty, ignorance, and meanness. The objects of pity in romance are as different from those in real life as our husbandmen from the shepherds of Arcadia;[2] and a girl who will sit

---

1  The reasoning in this paragraph agrees with Alexander Gerard's in *An Essay on Taste* (1759): "Sensibility ... [is] less than any other of the qualities of good taste *improvable* by use. The effect of *habit* on our *perceptions* is the very reverse of that, which it produces on our *active powers*. It *strengthens* the latter, but gradually *diminishes* the vivacity of the former" (p. 107). Concern for moral action rather than mere sentiment is also prominent in the thought of the Scottish philosopher Francis Hutcheson (1694-1746), with whose work Barbauld was acquainted: "But we must still remember, that mere kind affection without action, or slothful wishes, will never make us happy. Our chief joy consists in the exercise of our more honourable powers; and when kind affections are tolerably lively, they must be the spring of vigorous efforts to do good" (*Short Introduction to Moral Philosophy*, p. 68). Many years later, Barbauld reported reading the gritty realist poems of George Crabbe with actual pain: she hated to read about misery that she could do nothing to relieve (Scott, *Letters*, p. 75).

2  husbandmen: farmers; Arcadia: in poetry, a land of primitive innocence.

weeping the whole night at the delicate distresses of a lady Charlotte or lady Julia,[1] shall be little moved at the complaint of her neighbour, who, in a homely phrase and vulgar accent, laments to her that she is not able to get bread for her family. Romance-writers likewise make great misfortunes so familiar to our ears, that we have hardly any pity to spare for the common accidents of life: but we ought to remember, that misery has a claim to relief, however we may be disgusted with its appearance; and that we must not fancy ourselves charitable, when we are only pleasing our imagination.

It would perhaps be better, if our romances were more like those of the old stamp, which tended to raise human nature, and inspire a certain grace and dignity of manners of which we have hardly the idea. The high notions of honour, the wild and fanciful spirit of adventure and romantic love, elevated the mind;[2] our novels tend to depress and enfeeble it. Yet there is a species of this kind of writing which must ever afford an exquisite pleasure to persons of taste and sensibility; where noble sentiments are mixed with well fancied incidents, pathetic touches with dignity and grace, and invention with chaste correctness. Such will ever interest our sweetest passions. I shall conclude this paper[3] with the following tale.

## A Tale

In the happy period of the golden age, when all the celestial inhabitants descended to the earth, and conversed familiarly with mortals, among the most cherished of the heavenly powers were twins, the offspring of Jupiter, LOVE and JOY. Where they appeared, the flowers sprung up beneath their feet, the sun shone with a brighter radiance, and all nature seemed embellished by their presence. They were inseparable companions,

---

1 Characters in Samuel Richardson's *Sir Charles Grandison* (1753-54) and Frances Brooke's *History of Lady Julia Mandeville* (1763), respectively. Both novels are included in Barbauld's edition of *The British Novelists* (1810).

2 For Barbauld's later thoughts about romances "of the old stamp" (i.e., seventeenth-century French romances of courtly love), see "The Origin and Progress of Novel-Writing" later in this volume.

3 A locution frequently used by Joseph Addison in *The Spectator*.

and their growing attachment was favoured by Jupiter, who had decreed that a lasting union should be solemnized between them so soon as they were arrived at maturer years. But in the mean time the sons of men deviated from their native innocence; vice and ruin over-ran the earth with giant strides; and Astrea[1] with her train of celestial visitants forsook their polluted abodes. Love alone remained, having been stolen away by Hope, who was his nurse, and conveyed by her to the forests of Arcadia, where he was brought up among the shepherds. But Jupiter assigned him a different partner, and commanded him to espouse SORROW, the daughter of Até.[2] He complied with reluctance; for her features were harsh and disagreeable, her eyes sunk, her forehead contracted into perpetual wrinkles, and her temples were covered with a wreath of cypress and wormwood. From this union sprung a virgin, in whom might be traced a strong resemblance to both her parents; but the sullen and unamiable features of her mother were so mixed and blended with the sweetness of her father, that her countenance, though mournful, was highly pleasing. The maids and shepherds of the neighbouring plains gathered round and called her PITY. A red-breast was observed to build in the cabin where she was born; and while she was yet an infant, a dove pursued by a hawk flew into her bosom. This nymph had a dejected appearance, but so soft and gentle a mien that she was beloved to a degree of enthusiasm. Her voice was low and plaintive, but inexpressibly sweet; and she loved to lie for hours together on the banks of some wild and melancholy stream, singing to her lute. She taught men to weep, for she took a strange delight in tears; and often, when the virgins of the hamlet were assembled at their evening sports, she would steal in amongst them, and captivate their hearts by her tales full of a charming sadness. She wore on her head a garland composed of her father's myrtles twisted with her mother's cypress.[3]

---

1 Astrea: a goddess of justice.
2 Até is the Greek personification of "infatuation, mad impulse; ... the goddess of mischief and authoress of rash destructive deeds" (*OED*; cf. *Iliad* XIX.90ff which includes a long allegory concerning Ate).
3 Myrtle is associated with Venus and love; cypress is the tree of mourning or sorrow.

One day, as she sat musing by the waters of Helicon,[1] her tears by chance fell into the fountain; and ever since, the Muses' spring has retained a strong taste of the infusion. Pity was commanded by Jupiter to follow the steps of her mother through the world, dropping balm into the wounds she made, and binding up the hearts she had broken. She follows with her hair loose, her bosom bare and throbbing, her garments torn by the briars, and her feet bleeding with the roughness of the path. The nymph is mortal, for her mother is so; and when she has fulfilled her destined course upon the earth, they shall both expire together, and LOVE be again united to JOY, his immortal and long betrothed bride.

## THOUGHTS ON THE DEVOTIONAL TASTE, ON SECTS, AND ON ESTABLISHMENTS

[In 1775 Barbauld published a selection of psalms, prefacing it with this essay, which may or may not have been written for the occasion. The essay, in some ways the most remarkable of her early writings, carries on the project initiated in "An Enquiry into those Kinds of Distress which Excite Agreeable Sensations": in the manner of Burke and David Hume, it launches a "philosophical" (i.e., "scientific") "examination of the natural influence of religious principles and ideas on the human mind." Her friend William Enfield, a Warrington Academy tutor from whose review of *Devotional Pieces* we have just quoted, fully appreciated the boldness of Barbauld's attempt. "Devotion," he observed, "considered as the natural expression of religious emotions, is a subject which hath seldom been treated with philosophic precision," but Barbauld, "with her usual originality of conception and elegance of expression, ... has traced out the causes of the decay of [the] devotional taste" ([Enfield], pp. 419, 420). "Taste," a key word in later eighteenth-century aesthetics, may be defined, in the words of John

---

1   Helicon: Mt. Helicon, in Greek myth the seat of the Muses.

Gregory, as "the improvement of the powers of the Imagination" (*Comparative View*, p. 72).

In the second part of her essay Barbauld undertakes a startlingly "sociological" analysis of the rise and fall of religious sects and the psycho-social differences between sects and "established" (old, state-supported) religions. Here too Enfield appreciated her daring: "her Thoughts on Sects and Establishments ... are the thoughts ... of an enlarged and independent mind, capable of comprehending the most extensive views, and of tracing the past and present appearances in the moral and religious state of mankind to their true sources" (p. 421).

Barbauld does not simply analyze the devotional "taste"; she argues warmly in behalf of devotional feeling and against the intellectual and professional practices which, she believes, chill it. Here she concurs with Edmund Burke "that whilst we consider the Godhead merely as he is an object of the understanding ... the imagination and passions are little or nothing affected" (*Sublime and Beautiful*, p. 62). From living among theologians at Warrington she knew at first hand the habits and—as she experienced them—the effects of religious disputation, a distinctly male behavior. By demanding that room be made for the emotional experience of religion, Barbauld, as G. J. Barker-Benfield has perceived, "presents her God in that feminized version promoted by her forebears and contemporaries, personifying the traits women wished to see in reformed men." Thus "Barbauld became a kind of self-appointed theologian of the cult of sensibility" (*Culture of Sensibility*, pp. 274, 477).

Barbauld dedicated the essay to her father. What he thought of it is not known, but his colleagues (apart from Enfield) and other Dissenters took offense—none more so than Joseph Priestley, who disagreed with every part of it. (We give some of his criticisms in our notes.) He even insinuated that she had betrayed the cause of Dissent itself. But the reviewer in the *Gentleman's Magazine*, not a Dissenting journal, was only a little more favorable: "Her own sensibility and the warmth of her imagination seem to have betrayed her into the same error which formerly deluded the refined and elegant Fenelon" (p. 581). The comparison was apt: François de Salignac de la

Mothe Fénelon (1651-1715), an author whom Barbauld admired, was accused in his time of deviating into mysticism.

The essay was published in Barbauld's *Devotional Pieces* (1775); in 1792 she revised it for inclusion in the third edition of *Miscellaneous Pieces in Prose.*]

It is observed by a late most amiable and elegant writer, that Religion may be considered in three different views. As a system of opinions, its sole object is truth, and the only faculty that has any thing to do with it is Reason, exerted in the freest and most dispassionate inquiry. As a principle regulating our conduct, Religion is a habit, and like all other habits, of slow growth, and gaining strength only by repeated exertions. But it may likewise be considered as a taste, an affair of sentiment and feeling, and in this sense it is properly called Devotion. Its seat is in the imagination and the passions, and it has its source in that relish for the sublime, the vast, and the beautiful, by which we taste the charms of poetry and other compositions that address our finer feelings; rendered more lively and interesting by a sense of gratitude for personal benefits. It is in a great degree constitutional, and is by no means found in exact proportion to the virtue of a character.[1]

It is with relation to this last view of the subject that the observations in this essay are hazarded: for though as a rule of life, the authority and salutary effects of religion are pretty universally acknowledged, and though its tenets have been defended with sufficient zeal; its affections languish, the spirit of Devotion is certainly at a very low ebb amongst us, and what is surprising, it has fallen, I know not how, into a certain contempt, and is treated with great indifference, amongst many of

---

1    Barbauld summarizes John Gregory, *A Comparative View of the State and Faculties of Man with those of the Animal World* (1765), p. 174: "Religion may be considered in three different views. First, As containing doctrines relating to the being and perfections of God, his moral administration of the World, a future state of existence, and particular communications to Mankind by an immediate supernatural revelation.—Secondly, As a rule of life and manners.—Thirdly, As the source of certain peculiar Affections of the Mind, which either give pleasure or pain, according to the particular genius and spirit of the Religion that inspires them." She glances also at p. 196, "The devotional spirit is in a great measure constitutional."

those who value themselves on the purity of their faith, and who are distinguished by the sweetness of their morals.[1] As the religious affections in a great measure rise and fall with the pulse, and are affected by every thing which acts upon the imagination,[2] they are apt to run into strange excesses, and if directed by a melancholy or enthusiastic faith, their workings are often too strong for a weak head, or a delicate frame; and for this reason they have been almost excluded from religious worship by many persons of real piety. It is the character of the present age to allow little to sentiment, and all the warm and generous emotions are treated as romantic by the supercilious brow of a cold-hearted philosophy. The man of science, with an air of superiority, leaves them to some florid declaimer who professes to work upon the passions of the lower class, where they are so debased by noise and nonsense, that it is no wonder if they move disgust in those of elegant and better-informed minds.[3]

Yet there is a devotion generous, liberal, and humane, the child of more exalted feelings than base minds can enter into, which assimilates man to higher natures, and lifts him "above this visible diurnal sphere."[4] Its pleasures are ultimate, and when early cultivated continue vivid even in that uncomfortable season of life when some of the passions are extinct, when imagination is dead, and the heart begins to contract within itself. Those who want this taste, want a sense, a part of their nature, and should not presume to judge of feelings to which they must ever be strangers. No one pretends to be a judge in poetry or the fine arts, who has not both a natural and a cultivated

---

1  By "us" Barbauld may mean Dissenters specifically, but complaints of indifference to religion were general. John Gregory warned his daughters against "a levity and dissipation in the present manners, a coldness and listlessness in whatever relates to religion, which cannot fail to infect you, unless you purposely cultivate in your minds a contrary bias, and make the devotional taste habitual" (*A Father's Legacy*, p. 21).

2  Gregory also asserts the dependence of devotion upon the imagination: see p. 221, n. 5 below. Enthusiastic (below): emotionally high-strung.

3  Rodgers notes that Barbauld "disliked Methodism" and that by "florid declaimer" she probably meant the Methodist preachers John Wesley or George Whitefield (*Georgian Chronicle*, pp. 66–67).

4  Milton, *Paradise Lost*, 7:22 (misquoted).

relish for them; and shall the narrow-minded children of earth absorbed in low pursuits, dare to treat as visionary, objects which they have never made themselves acquainted with? Silence on such subjects will better become them.[1] But to vindicate the pleasures of devotion to those who have neither taste nor knowledge about them, is not the present object. It rather deserves our inquiry, what causes have contributed to check the operation of religious impressions amongst those who have steady principles, and are well disposed to virtue.

And, in the first place, there is nothing more prejudicial to the feelings of a devout heart, than a habit of disputing on religious subjects. Free inquiry is undoubtedly necessary to establish a rational belief; but a disputatious spirit, and fondness for controversy, give the mind a sceptical turn, with an aptness to call in question the most established truths. It is impossible to preserve that deep reverence for the Deity with which we ought to regard him, when all his attributes, and even his very existence become the subject of familiar debate.[2] Candor demands that a man should allow his opponent an unlimited freedom of speech, and it is not easy in the heat of discourse to avoid falling into an indecent or careless expression; hence those who think seldomer of religious subjects, often treat

---

1 John Gregory and Mary Wollstonecraft both share Barbauld's opinion, if not her haughty tone: "The devotional Taste, like all other Tastes, has had the fate to be condemned as a weakness by all who are strangers to its joys and its influence" (Gregory, *Comparative View*, p. 198); "The generality of people cannot see or feel poetically, they want fancy" (Wollstonecraft, *Rights of Woman*, p. 220). Priestley objected that treating devotion as a *taste* trivializes it: "being a thing so vague and so rare as taste in works of genius, it may be thought that the want of it is not much to be regretted" (*Works*, 1.i:280).

2 Likewise Gregory: "The very habit of frequent reasoning and disputing upon religious Subjects takes off from that reverence with which the Mind would otherwise consider them. This seems particularly to be the case, when Men presume to enter into an exact scrutiny of the views and economy of Providence in the administration of the World, why God Almighty made it as it is, the freedom of his actions, and many other such questions infinitely beyond our reach.... Accordingly we find amongst those Sectaries where such disquisitions have principally prevailed, that he has been spoke of and even addressed with the most indecent and shocking familiarity" (*Comparative View*, pp. 178-79). Priestley objected: "few persons now living have had more to do with religious controversy than myself," yet he lays claim to "fervour of mind" (*Works*, 1.i:284).

them with more respect than those whose profession keeps them constantly in their view. A plain man of a serious turn[1] would be shocked to hear questions of this nature treated with that ease and negligence with which they are generally discussed by the practised Theologian, or the young lively Academic ready primed from the schools of logic and metaphysics.[2] As the ear loses its delicacy by being obliged only to *hear* coarse and vulgar language, so the veneration for religion wears off by hearing it treated with disregard, though we ourselves are employed in defending it; and to this it is owing that many who have confirmed themselves in the belief of religion, have never been able to recover that strong and affectionate sense of it which they had before they began to inquire, and have wondered to find their devotion grown weaker when their faith was better grounded. Indeed, strong reasoning powers and quick feelings do not often unite in the same person. Men of a scientific turn seldom lay their hearts open to impression. Previously biassed by the love of system, they do indeed attend the offices of religion, but they dare not trust themselves with the preacher, and are continually upon the watch to observe whether every sentiment agrees with their own particular tenets.

The spirit of inquiry is easily distinguished from the spirit of disputation. A state of doubt is not a pleasant state. It is painful, anxious, and distressing beyond most others: it disposes the mind to dejection and modesty. Whoever therefore is so unfortunate as not to have settled his opinions in important points, will proceed in the search of truth with deep humility, unaffected earnestness, and a serious attention to every argu-

---

1 plain man ... turn: in 1775, "a sober Officer."
2 Between this and the next sentence, 1775 reads: "In general, I believe we may venture to assert, that no man, who has a proper veneration for the primary truths of religion, will be fond of making them the subjects of common discourse; any more than a person who loved with ardour and delicacy would chuse to introduce the name of his mistress amongst mixed companies in every light and trivial conversation. The regard in both cases would be deep and silent, and not apt to vent itself in words, unless called forth by some interesting occasion." This comparison offended both the *Gentleman's Magazine* and Priestley: "the very fault condemned seems here committed," wrote the former (p. 581).

ment that may be offered, which he will be much rather inclined to revolve in his own mind, than to use as materials for dispute. Even with these dispositions, it is happy for a man when he does not find much to alter in the religious system he has embraced; for if that undergoes a total revolution, his religious feelings are too generally so weakened by the shock, that they hardly recover again their original tone and vigour.

Shall we mention Philosophy as an enemy to Religion? God forbid! Philosophy,

> Daughter of Heaven, that slow ascending still
> Investigating sure the form of things
> With radiant finger points to heaven again.[1]

Yet there is a view in which she exerts an influence perhaps rather unfavourable to the fervor of simple piety. Philosophy does indeed enlarge our conceptions of the Deity, and gives us the sublimest ideas of his power and extent of dominion; but it raises him too high for our imaginations to take hold of, and in a great measure destroys that affectionate regard which is felt by the common class of pious christians.[2] When, after contemplating the numerous productions of this earth, the various forms of being, the laws, the mode of their existence, we rise yet higher, and turn our eyes to that magnificent profusion of suns and systems which astronomy pours upon the mind—When we grow acquainted with the majestic order of nature, and

---

1 Slightly misquoted from James Thomson, *The Seasons* (1746): "Summer," ll. 1548–50. "Philosophy" refers to the physical sciences, in which, despite the following paragraphs, Barbauld was keenly interested. Priestley complained that "if you mean a spurious and false philosophy, you should have specified it. At present, it will naturally be concluded ... that you have adopted the maxim ascribed to the Papists [Catholics] ... that 'ignorance is the mother of devotion'" (*Works*, 1.i:282). Explaining herself to another friend, Barbauld wrote, "I do not mean that such philosophical views should not be indulged, for they enlarge the mind ... & set religion upon a broad & firm basis. All I would say is, that we must correct what unfavorable tendency they may have, by often ... dwell[ing] on ... the more personal intercourse of a devout heart with its maker" (Letter to Nicholas Clayton).

2 Gregory again: "The Mind struck with the immensity of his being, and a sense of its own littleness and unworthiness, admires with that distant awe and veneration that rather excludes love" (*Comparative View*, p. 197).

those eternal laws which bind the material and intellectual worlds—When we trace the footsteps of creative energy through regions of unmeasured space, and still find new wonders disclosed and pressing upon the view—we grow giddy with the prospect;[1] the mind is astonished—confounded at its own insignificance; we think it almost impiety for a worm to lift its head from the dust, and address the Lord of so stupendous a universe; the idea of communion with our Maker shocks us as presumption,[2] and the only feeling the soul is capable of in such a moment is a deep and painful sense of its own abasement. It is true, the same philosophy teaches that the Deity is intimately present through every part of this complicated system, and neglects not any of his works: but this is a truth which is believed without being felt; our imagination cannot here keep pace with our reason, and the Sovereign of nature seems ever further removed from us in proportion as we enlarge the bounds of his creation.[3]

Philosophy represents the Deity in too abstracted a manner to engage our affections. A Being without hatred and without fondness, going on in one steady course of even benevolence, neither delighted with praises, nor moved by importunity, does not interest us so much as a character open to the feelings of indignation, the soft relentings of mercy, and the partialities of particular affections. We require some common nature, or at least the appearance of it, on which to build our intercourse. It is also a fault of which philosophers are often guilty, that they dwell too much in generals. Accustomed to reduce every thing to the operation of general laws, they turn our attention to larger views, attempt to grasp the whole order of the universe, and in the zeal of a systematic spirit seldom leave room for those particular and personal mercies which are the food of gratitude. They trace the great outline of nature, but neglect

---

1   Despite this disclaimer, Barbauld contemplated the suns and systems revealed by astronomy in her poem, "A Summer Evening's Meditation," and would do so again in one of the hymns added to *Hymns in Prose* in 1814. She included in her anthology *The Female Speaker* (1811) a devotional rhapsody on the planets by the earl of Shaftesbury.

2   shocks us as presumption: in 1775, "seems shocking."

3   we enlarge ... creation: in 1775, "the bounds of the creation are enlarged."

the colouring which gives warmth and beauty to the piece. As in poetry it is not vague and general description, but a few striking circumstances clearly related and strongly worked up—as in a landscape it is not such a vast extensive range of country as pains the eye to stretch to its limits, but a beautiful well-defined prospect, which gives the most pleasure—so neither are those unbounded views in which philosophy delights, so much calculated to touch the heart as home views and nearer objects. The philosopher offers up general praises on the altar of universal nature; the devout man, on the altar of his heart, presents his own sighs, his own thanksgivings, his own earnest desires: the former worship is more sublime,[1] the latter more personal and affecting.

We are likewise too scrupulous in our public exercises, and too studious of accuracy. A prayer strictly philosophical must ever be a cold and dry composition. From an over-anxious fear of admitting any expression that is not strictly proper, we are apt to reject all warm and pathetic imagery and in short, every thing that strikes upon the heart and the senses. But it may be said, "If the Deity be indeed so sublime a being, and if his designs and manner are so infinitely beyond our compre-hension, how can a thinking mind join in the addresses of the vulgar, or avoid being overwhelmed with the indistinct vastness of such an idea?" Far be it from me to deny that awe and veneration must ever make a principal part of our regards to the Master of the universe, or to defend that stile of indecent familiarity which is yet more shocking than indifference: but let it be considered that we cannot hope to avoid all impro-prieties in speaking of such a Being; that the most philoso-phical address we can frame is probably no more free from them than the devotions of the vulgar; that the scriptures set us an example of accommodating the language of prayer to com-mon conceptions, and making use of figures and modes of expression far from being strictly defensible; and that upon the whole it is safer to trust to our genuine feelings, feelings implanted in us by the God of nature, than to any metaphysical

---

1   sublime: in 1775, "grand."

subtleties. He has impressed me with the idea of trust and confidence, and my heart flies to him in danger; of mercy to forgive, and I melt before him in penitence; of bounty to bestow, and I ask of him all I want or wish for. I may make use of an inaccurate expression, I may paint him to my imagination too much in the fashion of humanity; but while my heart is pure, while I depart not from the line of moral duty, the error is not dangerous. Too critical a spirit is the bane of every thing great or pathetic. In our creeds let us be guarded, let us there weigh every syllable; but in compositions addressed to the heart, let us give freer scope to the language of the affections, and the overflowing of a warm and generous disposition.

Another cause which most effectually operates to check devotion, is Ridicule.[1] I speak not here of open derision of things sacred; but there is a certain ludicrous style in talking of such subjects, which without any ill design does much harm: and perhaps those whose studies or profession lead them to be chiefly conversant with the offices of religion, are most apt to fall into this impropriety; for their ideas being chiefly taken from that source, their common conversation is apt to be tinctured with fanciful allusions to scripture expressions, to prayers, &c. which have all the effect of a parody, and like parodies, destroy the force of the finest passage, by associating it with something trivial and ridiculous. Of this nature is Swift's well-known jest of "Dearly beloved Roger," which whoever has strong upon his memory, will find it impossible to attend with proper seriousness to that part of the service.[2] We should take great care to keep clear from all these trivial associations, in whatever we wish to be regarded as venerable.

Another species of ridicule to be avoided, is that kind of

---

1  So also Gregory: "Too frequent occasion has been given to turn this Subject [devotion] into ridicule" (p. 198).

2  Barbauld alludes to an anecdote in *Remarks on the Life and Writings of Dr. Jonathan Swift* by John, Earl of Orrery (1752): once, when Swift found his congregation "to consist only of himself, and his clerk Roger, he began with great composure and gravity, ... '*Dearly beloved ROGER, the scripture moveth you and me in sundry places.*' And then proceeded regularly through the whole service" (p. 32; we are grateful to Ann Kelly for this reference). In censuring this parody Barbauld admits to being amused by it.

sneer often thrown upon those whose hearts are giving way to honest emotion. There is an extreme delicacy in all the finer affections, which makes them shy of observation, and easily checked.[1] Love, Wonder, Pity, the enthusiasm of Poetry, shrink from the notice of even an indifferent eye, and never indulge themselves freely but in solitude, or when heightened by the powerful force of sympathy. Observe an ingenuous youth at a well-wrought tragedy. If all around him are moved, he suffers his tears to flow freely; but if a single eye meets him with a glance of contemptuous indifference, he can no longer enjoy his sorrow, he blushes at having wept, and in a moment his heart is shut up to every impression of tenderness. It is sometimes mentioned as a reproach to Protestants, that they are susceptible of a false shame when observed in the exercises of their religion, from which Papists are free. But I take this to proceed from the purer nature of our religion; for the less it is made to consist in outward pomp and mechanical worship, and the more it has to do with the finer affections of the heart, the greater will be the reserve and delicacy which attend the expression of its sentiments. Indeed, ridicule ought to be very sparingly used, for it is an enemy to every thing sublime or tender:[2] the least degree of it, whether well or ill founded, suddenly and instantaneously stops the workings of passion; and those who indulge a talent that way, would do well to consider, that they are rendering themselves for ever incapable of all the higher pleasures either of taste or morals. More especially do these cold pleasantries hurt the minds of youth, by checking that generous expansion of heart to which their open tempers are naturally prone, and producing a vicious shame, through which they are deprived of the enjoyment of heroic sentiments or generous action.

In the next place, let us not be superstitiously afraid of superstition. It shews great ignorance of the human heart, and

---

1  Gregory: "The feelings of a devout Heart should be mentioned with great reserve and delicacy ..." (p. 198).
2  Similarly Edmund Burke, considering the effects of different colors in producing sublimity, cautions "against any thing light and riant; as nothing so effectually deadens the whole taste of the sublime" (*Sublime and Beautiful*, p. 75).

the springs by which its passions are moved, to neglect taking advantage of the impression which particular circumstances, times and seasons, naturally make upon the mind. The root of all superstition is the principle of the association of ideas, by which, objects naturally indifferent become dear and venerable, through their connection with interesting ones. It is true, this principle has been much abused: it has given rise to pilgrimages innumerable, worship of relics, and priestly power.[1] But let us not carry our ideas of purity and simplicity so far, as to neglect it entirely. Superior natures, it is possible, may be equally affected with the same truths at all times, and in all places; but we are not so made. Half the pleasures of elegant minds are derived from this source. Even the enjoyments of sense without it would lose much of their attraction. Who does not enter into the sentiment of the Poet, in that passage so full of nature and truth:

> He that outlives this hour and comes safe home,
> Shall stand on tiptoe when this day is named,
> And rouse him at the name of Crispian:
> He that outlives this day and sees old age,
> Will yearly on the vigil feast his neighbours,
> And say, To morrow is St. Crispian.[2]

But were not the benefits of the victory equally apparent on any other day of the year? Why commemorate the anniversary with such distinguished regard? Those who can ask such a question, have never attended to some of the strongest instincts in our nature.[3] Yet it has lately been the fashion, amongst those who call themselves rational christians, to treat as puerile,

---

1 Perhaps a glance at David Hume's essay, "Of Superstition and Enthusiasm" (1748): "Superstition ... renders men tame and submissive ... till at last the priest ... becomes the tyrant and disturber of human society, by his endless contentions, persecutions, and religious wars.... [S]uperstition is an enemy to civil liberty" (Selected Essays, pp. 41-42). On this topic, Hume's position was that of Protestant Dissenters in general.

2 Shakespeare, Henry V, IV.iii.46.

3 Barbauld's defense of superstition as grounded in the laws of association may have influenced both Mary Wollstonecraft's Vindication of the Rights of Men and Burke's

all attentions of this nature when relative to religion. They would

> Kiss with pious lips the sacred earth
> Which gave a Hampden or a Russel birth.[1]

They will visit the banks of Avon[2] with all the devotion of enthusiastic zeal; celebrate the birth-day of the hero and the patriot; and yet pour contempt upon the Christian[3] who suffers himself to be warmed by similar circumstances relating to his Master,[4] or the connection of sentiments of peculiar reverence with times, places, and men which have been appropriated to the service of religion. A wise preacher will not, from a fastidious refinement, disdain to affect his hearers from the season of the year, the anniversary of a national blessing, a remarkable escape from danger, or, in short, any incident that is sufficiently guarded, and far enough removed from what is trivial, to be out of danger of becoming ludicrous.

It will not be amiss to mention here, a reproach which has been cast upon devotional writers, that they are apt to run into the language of love. Perhaps the charge would be full as just, had they said that Love borrows the language of Devotion;[5] for

---

*Reflections on the Revolution in France* (1790); her rebuke, "those who can ask such a question ... the strongest instincts in our nature" resembles Burke's appeals to "nature" and "her unerring and powerful instincts" (*Reflections*, p. 39).

1   George Lyttleton, "To the Reverend Dr. Ayscough at Oxford" (*Poems*, 1777), ll. 126-27. Lyttleton reads "a Burleigh, or a Russel." Barbauld replaces the first with a reference to John Hampden (1594-1643), who led Parliamentary opposition to Charles I's attempts to impose taxes. Lord William Russell opposed Charles II's pro-French and pro-Catholic policies, and was executed in 1683; both were regarded as heroes by English liberals.

2   the banks of Avon: Stratford-on-Avon, birthplace of Shakespeare.

3   Christian: in 1775, "man."

4   Jesus.

5   Cf. Gregory: "What shews the great dependence [the devotional spirit] has on the Imagination, is the remarkable attachment it has to Poetry and Music, which Shakespear calls the Food of Love, and which may with equal truth be called the Food of Devotion" (p. 197). Barbauld herself, in some of her Songs and Hymns, mixes the idioms of love and devotion; so did one of her favorite poets, Elizabeth Singer Rowe (see "Verses on Mrs. Rowe"). Priestley disapproved: "Many serious persons are ... offended, and I think justly, at your comparing devotion to the passion of love" (*Works*, 1.i:280).

the votaries of that passion are fond of using those exaggerated expressions, which can suit nothing below divinity; and you can hardly address the greatest of all Beings in a strain of more profound adoration, than the lover uses to the object of his attachment.[1] But the truth is, Devotion does in no small degree resemble that fanciful and elevated kind of love which depends not on the senses. Nor is the likeness to be wondered at, since both have their source in the love of beauty and excellence. Both are exceeding prone to superstition, and apt to run into romantic excesses. Both are nourished by poetry and music, and felt with the greatest fervour in the warmer climates.[2] Both carry the mind out of itself, and powerfully refine the affections from every thing gross, low, and selfish.

But it is time to retire; we are treading upon enchanted ground, and shall be suspected by many of travelling towards the regions of chivalry and old romance. And were it so, many a fair majestic idea might be gathered from those forgotten walks, which would well answer the trouble of transplanting. It must however be owned, that very improper language has formerly been used on these subjects; but there cannot be any great danger of such excesses, where the mind is guarded by a rational faith, and the social affections have full scope in the free commerce and legitimate connections of[3] society.

Having thus considered the various causes which contribute to deaden the feelings of devotion, it may not be foreign to the subject to inquire in what manner they are affected by the different modes of religion. I speak not of opinions; for these have much less influence upon the heart, than the circumstances which attend particular persuasions. A sect *may* only differ from an establishment, as one absurd opinion differs from another: but there is a character and cast of manners belonging to each, which will be perfectly distinct; and of a sect, the character will

---

1 Priestley singled out this sentence for severe censure: "Now if there be any persons who apply the language of 'profound adoration' to a human being, I consider it as a most abominable practice, as nothing less than direct impiety" (*Works*, 1.i:281).

2 "The devotional spirit ... prevails more in warmer climates than ours" (Gregory, pp. 196–97).

3 and legitimate connections: added in *MPP* ed. 3.

vary as it is a rising or a declining sect, persecuted or at ease. Yet while divines have wearied the world with canvassing contrary doctrines and jarring articles of faith, the philosopher has not considered as the subject deserved what situation was most favourable to virtue, sentiment, and pure manners. To a philosophic eye, free from prejudice, and accustomed to large views of the great polity carried on in the moral world, perhaps varying and opposite forms may appear proper, and well calculated for their respective ends; and he will neither wish entirely to destroy the old, nor wholly to crush the new.

The great line of division between different modes of religion, is formed by Establishments and Sects. In an infant sect, which is always in some degree a persecuted one, the strong union and entire affection of its followers, the sacrifices they make to principle, the force of novelty, and the amazing power of sympathy, all contribute to cherish devotion. It rises even to passion, and absorbs every other sentiment. Severity of manners imposes respect; and the earnestness of the new proselytes renders them insensible to injury, or even to ridicule. A strain of eloquence, often coarse indeed, but strong and persuasive, works like leaven in the heart of the people. In this state, all outward helps are superfluous, the living spirit of devotion is amongst them, the world sinks away to nothing before it, and every object but one is annihilated.[1] The social principle mixes with the flame, and renders it more intense; strong parties are formed, and friends or lovers are not more closely connected than the members of these little communities.

It is this kind of devotion, a devotion which those of more settled and peaceable times can only guess at, which made amends to the first Christians for all they resigned, and all they suffered: this draws the martyr to a willing death, and enables the confessor to endure a voluntary poverty. But this stage cannot last long; the heat of persecution abates, and the fervour of

---

1  Barbauld's description of the religious experience of new sects parallels Burke's of the Sublime: when it experiences the Sublime, "the mind is so entirely filled with its object, that it cannot entertain any other" (*Sublime and Beautiful*, p. 53). This is also the condition which Barbauld herself experiences in her poem, "An Address to the Deity": "One vast object fills my aching sight."

zeal feels a proportional decay. Now comes on the period of reasoning and examination. The principles which have produced such mighty effects on the minds of men, acquire an importance, and become objects of the public attention. Opinions are canvassed. Those who before bore testimony to their religion only by patient suffering, now defend it with argument; and all the keenness of polemical disquisition is awakened on either side. The fair and generous idea of religious liberty, which never originates in the breast of a triumphant party, now begins to unfold itself. To vindicate these rights, and explain these principles, learning, which in the former state was despised, is assiduously cultivated by the sectaries; their minds become enlightened, and a large portion of knowledge, especially religious knowledge, is diffused through their whole body. Their manners are less austere, without having as yet lost any thing of their original purity. Their ministers gain respect as writers, and their pulpit discourses are studied and judicious. The most unfavourable circumstance of this era is, that those who dissent, are very apt to acquire a critical and disputatious spirit; for, being continually called upon to defend doctrines in which they differ from the generality, their attention is early turned to the argumentative part of religion; and hence we see that sermons, which afford food for this taste, are with them thought of more importance than prayer and praise, though these latter are undoubtedly the more genuine and indispensible parts of public worship.[1]

This then is the second period; the third approaches fast: men grow tired of a controversy which becomes insipid from being exhausted; persecution has not only ceased, it begins to be forgotten; and from the absence of opposition in either kind, springs a fatal and spiritless indifference.[2] That sobriety, industry, and abstinence from fashionable pleasures, which dis-

---

1   public worship: in 1775, "devotion."

2   Barbauld's account of three "periods" from early zeal to "spiritless indifference" appears to enlarge on Hume's remark, "When the first fire of enthusiasm is spent, men naturally, in all fanatical sects, sink into the greatest remissness and coolness in sacred matters" ("Of Superstition and Enthusiasm," *Selected Essays*, p. 41). It is echoed, in turn, by John Stuart Mill in Chapter 2 of *On Liberty* (1859), in a paragraph tracing "the experience of almost all ethical doctrines and religious creeds."

tinguished the fathers, has made the sons wealthy; and eager to enjoy their riches, they long to mix with that world, a separation from which was the best guard to their virtues.[1] A secret shame creeps in upon them, when they acknowledge their relation to a disesteemed sect; they therefore endeavour to file off its peculiarities, but in so doing they destroy its very being. Connections with the establishment, whether of intimacy, business, or relationship, which formerly, from their superior zeal, turned to the advantage of the sect, now operate against it. Yet these connections are formed more frequently than ever; and those who a little before, soured by the memory of recent suffering, betrayed perhaps an aversion from having any thing in common with the Church, now affect to come as near it as possible; and, like a little boat that takes a large vessel in tow, the sure consequence is, the being drawn into its vortex. They aim at elegance and show in their places of worship, the appearance of their preachers, &c. and thus impoliticly awaken a taste it is impossible they should ever gratify. They have worn off many forbidding singularities, and are grown more amiable and pleasing. But those singularities were of use: they set a mark upon them,[2] they pointed them out to the world, and thus obliged persons so distinguished to exemplary strictness. No longer obnoxious to the world, they are open to all the seductions of it. Their minister, that respectable character which once inspired reverence and affectionate esteem, their teacher and their guide, is now dwindled into the mere leader of the public devotions; or lower yet, a person hired to entertain them every week with an elegant discourse. In proportion as his importance decreases, his salary sits heavy on the people; and he feels

---

1   On this topic Barbauld agrees with John Wesley (despite her distaste for Methodism): "I do not see how it is possible," Wesley wrote, "… for any revival of true religion to continue long. For religion must necessarily produce both industry and frugality, and these cannot but produce riches. But as riches increase, so will … love of the world in all its branches" (quoted in Barker-Benfield, *Culture of Sensibility*, pp. 74–75).

2   As in Ezekiel 9:4: "And the Lord said unto him, Go through the midst of … Jerusalem, and set a mark upon the foreheads of the men that sigh and that cry for all the abominations that be done in the midst thereof" (so that they will be spared when the Lord slays the others).

himself depressed, by that most cruel of all mortifications to a generous mind, the consciousness of being a burden upon those from whom he derives his scanty support.[1] Unhappily, amidst this change of manners, there are forms of strictness, and a set of phrases introduced in their first enthusiasm, which still subsist: these they are ashamed to use, and know not how to decline; and their behaviour, in consequence of them, is aukward and irresolute. Those who have set out with the largest share of mysticism and flighty zeal, find themselves particularly embarrassed by this circumstance.

When things are come to this crisis, their tendency is evident: and though the interest and name of a sect may be kept up for a time by the generosity of former ages, the abilities of particular men, or that reluctance which keeps a generous mind from breaking old connections; it must in a short course of years melt away into the establishment, the womb and the grave of all other modes of religion.

An *Establishment* affects the mind by splendid buildings, music, the mysterious pomp of antient ceremonies; by the sacredness of peculiar orders, habits, and titles; by its secular importance; and by connecting with religion, ideas of order, dignity, and antiquity.[2] It speaks to the heart, through the imagination and the senses; and though it never can raise devotion so high as we have described it in a beginning sect, it will preserve it from ever sinking into contempt.[3] As to a woman in the glow of health and beauty, the most careless dress is the most becoming; but when the freshness of youth is worn off, greater attention is necessary, and rich ornaments are required to throw an air of dignity round her person: so while a sect

---

1  Dissenting ministers were hired by their congregations and paid by contributions from them. The scantiness of ministerial salaries was a general complaint.

2  Priestley objected that this claim "only applies to some establishments, and does not belong to them as such." He instanced the Scottish Church, "which is as meagre in these respects as almost any sect" (*Works*, 1.i:283).

3  Barbauld's susceptibility to effects of pomp was shared by Mary Wollstonecraft: "The performance of high mass on the Continent must impress every mind, where a spark of fancy glows, with that awful melancholy, that sublime tenderness, so near akin to devotion…. [T]he theatrical pomp which gratifies our senses, is to be preferred to the cold parade that insults the understanding without reaching the heart" (*Rights of Woman*, p. 277).

retains its first plainness, simplicity, and affectionate zeal, it wants nothing an establishment could give; but that once declined, the latter becomes far more respectable. The faults of an establishment grow venerable from length of time; the improvements of a sect appear whimsical from their novelty. Antient families, fond of rank, and of that order which secures it to them, are on the side of the former. Traders incline to the latter; and so do generally men of genius, as it favours their originality of thinking. An establishment leans to superstition, a sect to enthusiasm; the one is a more dangerous and violent excess, the other more fatally debilitates the powers of the mind; the one is a deeper colouring, the other a more lasting dye: but the coldness and languor of a declining sect produces scepticism.[1] Indeed, a sect is never stationary, as it depends entirely on passions and opinions; though it often attains excellence, it never rests in it, but is always in danger of one extreme or the other: whereas an old establishment, whatever else it may want, possesses the grandeur arising from stability.

We learn to respect whatever respects itself; and are easily led to think that system requires no alteration, which never admits of any. It is this circumstance, more than any other, which gives a dignity to that accumulated mass of error, the Church of Rome. A fabric which has weathered many successive ages, though the architecture be rude, the parts disproportionate, and overloaded with ornament, strikes us with a sort of admiration, merely from its having held so long together.[2]

The *minister* of a sect, and of an establishment, is upon a very different footing. The former is like the popular leader of an army; he is obeyed with enthusiasm while he is obeyed at all; but his influence depends on opinion, and is entirely personal: the latter resembles a general appointed by the monarch; he has soldiers less warmly devoted to him, but more steady, and better disciplined. The dissenting teacher is nothing, if he have not the spirit of a martyr; and is the scorn of the world, if he be not

---

1 Here again Barbauld picks up David Hume's comparison between enthusiasm and superstition (*Selected Essays*, p. 41).

2 From this paragraph Andrew Kippis, a leading Dissenter, inferred that Barbauld in fact admired the Church of Rome (*Monthly Review*, 54 [1776]:72).

above the world. The clergyman, possessed of power and affluence, and for that reason chosen from among the better ranks of people, is respected as a gentleman, though not venerated as an apostle; and as his profession generally obliges him to decent manners, his order is considered as a more regular and civilized class of men than their fellow-subjects of the same rank. The dissenting teacher, separated from the people, but not raised above them, invested with no power, entitled to no emoluments, if he cannot acquire for himself authority, must feel the bitterness of dependance. The ministers of the former denomination cannot fall, but in some violent convulsion of the state: those of the latter, when indifference and mutual neglect begin to succeed to that close union which once subsisted between them and their followers, lose their former influence without resource; the dignity and weight of their office is gone for ever, they feel the insignificancy of their pretensions, their spirits sink, and, except they take refuge in some collateral pursuit, and stand candidates[1] for literary fame, they slide into an ambiguous and undecided character; their time is too often sacrificed to frivolous compliances; their manners lose their austerity, without having proportionally gained in elegance;[2] the world does not acknowledge them, for they are not of the world; it cannot esteem them, for they are not superior to the world.

Upon the whole, then, it should seem, that the strictness of a sect (and it can only be respectable by being strict) is calculated for a few finer spirits, who make Religion their chief object. As to the much larger number, on whom she has only an imperfect influence, making them decent if not virtuous, and meliorating the heart without greatly changing it, for all these the genius of an establishment is more eligible, and better fitted to cherish that moderate devotion of which alone they are capable. All those who have not strength of mind to think for themselves, who would live to virtue without denying the

---

1   stand candidates: in 1775, "push."

2   slide into an ... elegance: in 1775, "quickly degenerate into mere triflers. Their time is sacrificed to the most idle and frivolous compliances; their manners are effeminate, without being elegant:"

world, who wish much to be religious, but more to be genteel—naturally flow into the establishment. If it offered no motives to their minds, but such as are perfectly pure and spiritual, their devotion would not for that be more exalted, it would die away to nothing; and it is better their minds should receive only a tincture of religion, than be wholly without it. Those too, whose passions are regular and equable, and who do not aim at abstracted virtues, are commonly placed to most advantage within the pale of the national faith.

All the greater exertions of the mind, spirit to reform, fortitude and constancy to suffer, can be expected only from those who, forsaking the common road, are exercised in a peculiar course of moral discipline: but it should be remembered, that these exertions cannot be expected from every character, nor on every occasion. Indeed, religion is a sentiment which takes such strong hold on all the most powerful principles of our nature, that it may easily be carried to excess. The Deity never meant our regards to him should engross the mind: that indifference to sensible objects, which many moralists preach, is not perhaps desireable, except where the mind is raised above its natural tone, and extraordinary situations call forth extraordinary virtues.

If the peculiar advantages of a sect were well understood, its followers would not be impatient of those moderate restraints which do not rise to persecution, nor affect any of their more material interests: for, do they not bind them closer to each other, cherish zeal, and keep up the love of liberty? What is the language of such restraints? Do they not say, with a prevailing voice, Let the timorous and the worldly depart; no one shall be of this persuasion, who is not sincere, disinterested, conscientious. It is notwithstanding proper, that men should be sensible of all their rights, assert them boldly, and protest against every infringement; for it may be of advantage to bear what yet it is unjustifiable in others to inflict.

Neither would dissenters, if they attended to their real interests, be so ambitious as they generally are of rich converts. Such converts only accelerate their decline; they relax their discipline, and they acquire an influence very pernicious in societies which ought to breathe nothing but the spirit of equality.

Sects are always strict, in proportion to the corruption of establishments, and the licentiousness of the times; and they are useful in the same proportion. Thus the austere lives of the primitive Christians counterbalanced the vices of that abandoned period; and thus the Puritans in the reign of Charles the Second seasoned with a wholesome severity the profligacy of public manners.[1] They were less amiable than their descendants of the present day; but to be amiable was not the object: they were of public utility; and their scrupulous sanctity (carried to excess, themselves only considered) like a powerful antiseptic, opposed the contagion breathed from a most dissolute court. In like manner, that sect, one of whose most striking characteristics is a beautiful simplicity of dialect, served to check that strain of servile flattery and Gothic compliment so prevalent in the same period, and to keep up some idea of that manly plainness with which one human being ought to address another.[2]

Thus have we seen that different modes of religion, though they bear little good-will to each other, are nevertheless mutually useful. Perhaps there is not an establishment so corrupt, as not to make the gross of mankind better than they would be without it. Perhaps there is not a sect so eccentric, but that it has set some one truth in the strongest light, or carried some one virtue, before neglected, to its utmost height, or loosened some obstinate and long-rooted prejudice. They answer their end; they die away; others spring up, and take their place. So the purer part of the element, continually drawn off from the mighty mass of waters, forms rivers, which running in various directions, fertilize large countries; yet, always tending towards the ocean, every accession to their bulk or grandeur but precipitates their course, and hastens their re-union with the common reservoir from which they were separated.

---

1  To Puritans then, and posterity afterwards, the reign of Charles II (1660-85) appeared unusually given to sex, drink, and (on the stage) bawdy language.
2  The Quakers, who emerged in the later seventeenth century, were noted for their practice of addressing all persons, regardless of rank, as "thee."

In the mean time, the devout heart always finds associates suitable to its disposition, and the particular cast of its virtues; while the continual flux and reflux of opinions prevents the active principles from stagnating. There is an analogy between things material and immaterial. As from some late experiments in philosophy it has been found, that the process of vegetation restores and purifies vitiated air;[1] so does that moral and political ferment which accompanies the growth of new sects, communicate a kind of spirit and elasticity necessary to the vigour and health of the soul, but soon lost amidst the corrupted breath of an indiscriminate multitude.

There remains only to add, lest the preceding view of Sects and Establishments should in any degree be misapprehended, that it has nothing to do with the *truth* of opinions, and relates only to the influence which the adventitious circumstances attending them may have upon the manners and morals of their followers. It is therefore calculated to teach us candour, but not indifference. Large views of the moral polity of the world may serve to illustrate the providence of God in his different dispensations, but are not made to regulate our own individual conduct, which must conscientiously follow our own opinions and belief. We may see much good in an Establishment, the doctrines of which we cannot give our assent to without violating our integrity; we may respect the tendencies of a Sect, the tenets of which we utterly disapprove. We may think practices useful which we cannot adopt without hypocrisy. We may think all religions beneficial, and believe of one alone that it is true.[2]

---

1 In March 1772 Priestley reported to the Royal Society a series of experiments on air, some of which showed that bad air could be purified by growing plants in it (Schofield, *Joseph Priestley*, pp. 259, 266). See also headnote to "The Mouse's Petition."

2 In this paragraph added in 1792, Barbauld concurs with Burke's definition, in *Reflections on the Revolution in France*, of "the true spirit of toleration": "They think the dogmas of religion, though in different degrees, are all of moment; and that amongst them there is, as amongst all things of value, a just ground of preference.... They would ... protect all religions, because they love and venerate the great principle upon which they all agree, and the great object to which they are all directed" (p. 185).

[The final paragraph, from "There remains only to add," first appeared in 1792, replacing the original conclusion to the essay in 1775. Below, we print the original concluding paragraphs from the 1775 text.]

It remains now to say something of the following compilation. Unconnected as it seems with the preceding observations, the same turn of thought led to both. It was impossible to treat of the devotional spirit, without calling to mind the most beautiful compositions which that spirit ever inspired, the Psalms of David. In these, the boldest figures of the high Eastern poetry are united with a simplicity which makes them intelligible to the common ear. The sublimest ideas are given of the Deity; he is spoken of with the deepest reverence, and yet with all the warmth and pathos of personal gratitude and affection. Such pieces are certainly proper not only to be read as compositions, but to be used as acts of devotion, either in private, or in public and social worship. But unhappily, the very great mixture there is in these divine odes,[1] renders them unfit for either of these purposes. We cannot enter into all the situations, and it would not be safe to adopt all the sentiments of their author; for the royal Poet had strong passions, and was very sensible to resentment, as well as to gratitude. Nor is this inconvenience sufficiently obviated by using only chosen pieces; for it is not easy, on the sudden, to make a selection: and besides, there are in the finest psalms exceptionable passages, and in the most improper ones some verses too beautiful to be lost.

It was hoped, therefore, that it might be of service to the cause of religion, to make a collection of the kind now offered to the public. In this collection, all the Psalms which would bear it are given entire; others, where the connected sense could be preserved with such an omission, have only the exceptionable parts left out; and a third class is formed of separate passages scattered through several pieces, which are attempted to be formed into regular and distinct odes. With

---

1    For regarding psalms as odes Barbauld had the precedent of John Milton, who compared the Psalms to the odes of Pindar and Callimachus (*The Reason of Church Government*, 1642).

regard to their subjects, they may be divided into Moral, Devotional, and Occasional. Amongst the Occasional ones, but few have been admitted. The Devotional may be subdivided into Psalms of Praise, Penitence, and Prayer. Most of the Prophetic pieces are excluded, as not properly entering into the idea of worship. The book of Job, being so similar in style, has been taken into the scheme.

Some persons may perhaps expect, that in a plan like this, every phrase should be struck out that bore an allusion to the customs and worship of the Jews, or which contained idioms that in their literal sense we can no longer use. But this has not been thought necessary. These phrases are familiarized to the ear, and well understood by all Christians, who easily adapt them to their own ideas. Scripture expressions, and allusions to the scriptures, produce the same pleasing effect in a devotional piece, which allusions to the Greek and Roman authors do in a common poem; they form indeed the true classical style of these writings. The courts of Zion, and the walls of Jerusalem, are not more foreign to an English reader, than the hill of Parnassus, or the fountain of Hippocrene;[1] and it ought to be no more an objection to a religious ode, that we are called upon to praise God with the psaltery and timbrel, than it is to a pastoral writer that he sings to his pipe and his lyre, since both are equally disused. Poetry cannot subsist without ornament; these are the appropriated ornaments of religious poetry, and contribute to give a picturesque air to compositions in which every other species of embellishment would be improper and unbecoming.

After all, it is not reading alone these noble pieces that will give us their full force: they must be really used as acts of worship. It was not in so cold, so unaffecting a manner, that the Psalms of David were first exhibited. The living voice of the people, the animating accompanyments of music, the solemnity of public pomp, the reverent prostrations of deep humility, or the exulting movements of pious joy, all conspired to raise, to touch, to subdue the heart. Perhaps a time may come, when

---

1   Zion is another name for Jerusalem, the seat of Judaism; in Greek myth, Parnassus and Hippocrene are associated with the muses and poetic inspiration.

our worship (amongst those at least who are happy enough to be at liberty to make alterations)[1] shall be new modelled by some free and enlarged genius. Perhaps the time may come, when the spirit of philosophy, and the spirit of devotion, shall join to conduct our public assemblies; when to all that is graceful in order and well-regulated pomp, we shall add whatever is affecting in the warmth of zeal, and all that is delightful in the beauty of holiness.

## HYMNS IN PROSE FOR CHILDREN[2]

[Barbauld's most famous and influential work originated as a devotional exercise for her young pupils at Palgrave School. Following the publication of *Lessons for Children* (1778-79), her elementary reading book, she turned to the question of elementary religious instruction. By January 1780 she had written six of the original twelve hymns (Letter to John Aikin).

To move from reading instruction to religious instruction was logical, for reading primers conventionally progressed, between the covers of the same book, from alphabets and phonics directly to catechisms or Bible stories. Barbauld based her reading pedagogy on the principle that a child should be presented only ideas that it was ready to understand. She had therefore excluded religion from *Lessons*. *Hymns*, designed for children who had graduated from *Lessons* (children of four or older), was written to implant religious ideas, and to do so using the same appeals to the child's previous experience that *Lessons* had used. (We notice some examples on pp. 243 n.1, 246 n.3, and 247 n.3.)

---

1  That is, among Dissenters, whose congregations could alter their liturgy on their own initiative, unlike Church-of-England congregations.

2  At least 17 editions of *Hymns in Prose* were printed in Great Britain in Barbauld's lifetime; the latest (1824) calls itself the "twenty-fourth." The most important is the "sixteenth edition, much enlarged" (1814), for Barbauld augmented it with three new hymns. We have fully collated copies of the following editions: 1 (1781, our copytext), 3 (1784), "16" (1814, our copytext for the added hymns), an 1815 ed. printed by Barbauld's protegé Richard Taylor, and "23" (1820). We have also examined eds. 2 (1782), 5 (1791), and "24" (1824).

*Hymns* was innovative in more than its pedagogy, however. "Perhaps a time may come," Barbauld had written at the end of "Thoughts on the Devotional Taste," "when our worship ... shall be new modelled by some free and enlarged genius. Perhaps the time may come, when the spirit of philosophy, and the spirit of devotion, shall join to conduct our public assemblies...." In *Hymns*, Barbauld herself undertook that remodelling. Liturgically, *Hymns* was composed for alternate recitation by the "congregation" (her pupils). Even more important, *Hymns* presents a doctrinal reformation. It departs from its most popular predecessor, Isaac Watts's *Divine Songs* (1715), in encouraging a *benevolent* idea of religion derived ultimately from the benevolist ethics of Francis Hutcheson (1694-1746), the influential Scottish philosopher who urged an optimistic and uplifting view of human motivation and of God: humans, Hutcheson argued, are the fundamentally good creatures of a kind and loving creator. Hence, *Hymns* is entirely free of any suggestion of human sin or corruptibility. The child reader is invited to associate God with the beauties, pleasures, and goodness of the natural and human worlds; Barbauld attaches religion not just to science, but almost to hedonism itself.

Her associationist psychology descends ultimately from David Hartley (1705-57) but perhaps came to her through Hartley's disciple, her friend Joseph Priestley, whose sermon "On Habitual Devotion" (1767) had inspired her poem, "An Address to the Deity." Priestley advises cultivating devotion by association: "In the course of your usual employments, omit no proper opportunity of turning your thoughts towards God. Habitually regard him as *the ultimate cause*, and *proper author* of every thing you see" (Priestley, *Works*, 15:114). Early association is believed crucial to forging a person's habits of thought and feeling; hence Barbauld writes in her Preface, "a child, to feel the full force of the idea of God, ought never to remember the time when he had no such idea."

Published in 1781, *Hymns* made a deep impression on readers of all ages over several generations. "I do not wonder you were struck with Mrs. Barbauld's Hymns," wrote Elizabeth Carter to a friend. "They are all excellent, but there are some passages amazingly sublime" (Carter, *A Series of Letters*, 2:346). Mary Wollstonecraft recommended *Hymns* in her *Thoughts on the Education of Daughters* (1787): they "would contribute," she thought, "to … make the Deity obvious to the senses" (*Works*, 4:10). Thomas DeQuincey recalled as a grown man that *Hymns* "left upon my childish recollection a deep impression of solemn beauty and simplicity" (*Autobiography*, p. 127n). The Victorian writer Harriet Martineau had been greatly affected at age eight: "parts of [*Hymns*] … I dearly loved: but other parts made me shiver with awe" (*Autobiography*, p. 34). Another woman, known only by her initials, remembered how, "when a little girl … I used to retire to a quiet room … and read [*Hymns*] aloud, in a solemn voice, page after page…. The grave and well sustained rhythm had a charm for my ear; … and the elevated and reverent spirit of the compositions evoked similar feelings in my own breast" (S.A.A., "Notable North Londoners").

*Hymns* was reprinted in England for over 120 years, and in the United States, where it may have been initially even more popular, for over eighty. It was translated into French, Italian, Spanish, German, and Hungarian; in 1816 an English-language edition appeared in Calcutta. Its influence on nineteenth-century Anglo-American culture is incalculable. The American Unitarian William B.O. Peabody was confident in 1826 that "thousands look back [to *Hymns*] as the source of much happiness and devotion" (Review of Barbauld's *Works*, p. 310). Its literary influence has been traced in William Blake's *Songs of Innocence* (Summerfield, *Fantasy and Reason*, pp. 216-19) and Wordsworth's "Ode on Intimations of Immortality" (Zall, "Wordsworth's 'Ode'"); its theology of God teaching through Nature reappears in Coleridge's "Frost at Midnight." Less definably, the structure of feeling at the close of *Hymns*—a consolation blended of grief and joy—seems to carry forward to such places in Charles Dickens as the end of *Dombey and Son* (1846) and the reformation of Scrooge. Barbauld's measured prose has impressed even twentieth-century commentators: extracts from *Hymns in Prose* "might easily to-day be mistaken for simple passages from [the Symbolist poet Maurice] Maeterlinck," opined the *Cambridge History of English Literature* in 1914 (p. 426).

The doctrinal optimism of *Hymns* caused consternation in strict religious circles. When ten-year-old Mary Howitt was enrolled in a Quaker school in 1809 her copy of *Hymns* was confiscated (Feldman, *British Women Poets*, p. 325). In 1840, an unnamed clergyman's wife undertook to rescue *Hymns* for orthodoxy by adding materials about sin and salvation: "The divinity and incarnation of our Saviour, the fall and consequent depravity of man, are topics which are quite as well adapted to the capacities of children as many of those subjects of which Mrs. Barbauld has treated. The present edition is, therefore, undertaken to supply the deficiency which has been so long felt" (quoted in R., Review of *Hymns in Prose*, p. 39). Sarah Trimmer, who vetted children's books for the orthodox in *The Guardian of Education*, admired *Hymns* but criticized it for doctrinal errors; we quote her comments in our notes to the text.]

*Preface*

Among the number of Books composed for the use of Children; though there are many, and some on a very rational plan, which unfold the system, and give a summary of the doctrines of religion; it would be difficult to find *one* calculated to assist them in the devotional part of it, except indeed *Dr. Watts' Hymns for Children*.[1] These are in pretty general use, and the author is deservedly honoured for the condescension of his Muse, which was very able to take a loftier flight. But it may well be doubted, whether poetry *ought* to be lowered to the capacities of children, or whether they should not rather be kept from reading verse, till they are able to relish good verse: for the very essence of poetry is an elevation in thought and style above the common standard; and if it wants this character, it wants all that renders it valuable.

The Author of these Hymns has therefore chosen to give

---

1   Isaac Watts, *Divine Songs attempted in easy Language for the Use of Children* (1715), a popular and much-reprinted collection.

them in prose. They are intended to be committed to memory, and recited. And it will probably be found, that the measured prose in which such pieces are generally written, is nearly as agreeable to the ear as a more regular rhythmus.[1] Many of these Hymns are composed in alternate parts, which will give them something of the spirit of social worship.

The peculiar design of this publication is, to impress devotional feelings as early as possible on the infant mind; fully convinced as the author is, that they cannot be impressed too soon, and that a child, to feel the full force of the idea of God, ought never to remember the time when he had no such idea—to impress them by connecting religion with a variety of sensible objects; with all that he sees, all he hears, all that affects his young mind with wonder or delight; and thus by deep, strong, and permanent associations, to lay the best foundation for practical devotion in future life. For he who has early been accustomed to see the Creator in the visible appearances of all around him, to feel his continual presence, and lean upon his daily protection—though his religious ideas may be mixed with many improprieties, which his correcter reason will refine away—has made large advances towards that habitual piety, without which religion can scarcely regulate the conduct, and will never warm the heart.

A.L.B.

### Hymn I

Come, let us praise God, for he is exceeding great; let us bless God, for he is very good.

He made all things; the sun to rule the day, the moon to shine by night.[2]

He made the great whale, and the elephant; and the little worm that crawleth on the ground.

---

1  Rhythm (in prosody and music).
2  Alludes to Genesis 1:16 ("the greater light to rule the day, and the lesser light to rule the night"). The next verse alludes to Genesis 1:21 ("And God created great whales") and 26 ("And God made ... every thing that creepeth upon the earth").

The little birds sing praises to God, when they warble sweet-ly in the green shade.

The brooks and rivers praise God, when they murmur melodiously amongst the smooth pebbles.

I will praise God with my voice; for I may praise him, though I am but a little child.

A few years ago, and I was a little infant, and my tongue was dumb within my mouth:

And I did not know the great name of God, for my reason was not come unto me.

But now I can speak, and my tongue shall praise him; I can think of all his kindness, and my heart shall love him.

Let him call me, and I will come unto him: let him command, and I will obey him.

When I am older, I will praise him better; and I will never forget God, so long as my life remaineth in me.

### Hymn II

Come, let us go forth into the fields, let us see how the flowers spring, let us listen to the warbling of the birds, and sport ourselves upon the new grass.

The winter is over and gone, the buds come out upon the trees, the crimson blossoms of the peach and the nectarine are seen, and the green leaves sprout.

The hedges are bordered with tufts of primroses, and yellow cowslips that hang down their heads; and the blue violet lies hid beneath the shade.

The young goslings are running upon the green, they are just hatched, their bodies are covered with yellow down; the old ones hiss with anger if any one comes near.

The hen sits upon her nest of straw, she watches patiently the full time, then she carefully breaks the shell, and the young chickens come out.

The lambs just dropt are in the field, they totter by the side of their dams, their young limbs can hardly support their weight.

If you fall, little lambs, you will not be hurt; there is spread under you a carpet of soft grass, it is spread on purpose to receive you.[1]

The butterflies flutter from bush to bush, and open their wings to the warm sun.

The young animals of every kind are sporting about, they feel themselves happy, they are glad to be alive,—they thank him that has made them alive.

They may thank him in their hearts, but we can thank him with our tongues; we are better than they, and can praise him better.

The birds can warble, and the young lambs can bleat; but we can open our lips in his praise, we can speak of all his goodness.

Therefore we will thank him for ourselves, and we will thank him for those that cannot speak.

Trees that blossom, and little lambs that skip about, if you could, you would say how good he is; but you are dumb, we will say it for you.

We will not offer you in sacrifice, but we will offer sacrifice for you, on every hill, and in every green field, we will offer the sacrifice of thanksgiving, and the incense of praise.[2]

## Hymn III

Behold the Shepherd of the flock,[3] he taketh care for his sheep, he leadeth them among clear brooks, he guideth them to fresh pasture; if the young lambs are weary, he carrieth them in his arms; if they wander, he bringeth them back.

---

1   If you fall … you: Elizabeth Gaskell, the novelist, recalls that "my eldest girl used to quote that [passage] to her second sister when she could just walk" (Lewis, p. 55).

2   Sarah Trimmer objected to this paragraph: "May not children be led from this promise to the little lambs, to infer, when they read in the Bible an account of the sacrifices of Abel and of the Mosaic Law, that it was cruel in the Almighty to ordain the sacrifice of a Lamb as an offering of atonement; that an offering chosen by mankind will be as acceptable to the Deity as one expressly ordained by Himself; and that we may offer thanksgiving as a *sacrifice*, and praise as *incense*, in any place we please…. [N]or do we read in Scripture that human beings, who stand in constant need of a Mediator themselves, have ever been appointed to officiate as *Priests* for any of the brute creation" (Trimmer, p. 47).

3   Here and at its close, Hymn III alludes to Psalm 23 ("The Lord is my shepherd").

But who is the shepherd's shepherd? who taketh care for him? who guideth him in the path he should go? and if he wander, who shall bring him back?

God is the shepherd's shepherd. He is the Shepherd over all; he taketh care for all; the whole earth is his fold: we are all his flock; and every herb, and every green field is the pasture which he hath prepared for us.

The mother loveth her little child; she bringeth it up on her knees; she nourisheth its body with food; she feedeth its mind with knowledge: if it is sick, she nurseth it with tender love; she watcheth over it when asleep; she forgetteth it not for a moment; she teacheth it how to be good; she rejoiceth daily in its growth.

But who is the parent of the mother? who nourisheth her with good things, and watcheth over her with tender love, and remembereth her every moment? Whose arms are about her to guard her from harm? and if she is sick, who shall heal her?

God is the parent of the mother; he is the parent of all, for he created all. All the men, and all the women who are alive in the wide world, are his children; he loveth all, he is good to all.

The king governeth his people; he hath a golden crown upon his head, and the royal sceptre is in his hand; he sitteth upon a throne, and sendeth forth his demands;[1] his subjects fear before him; if they do well, he protecteth them from danger; and if they do evil, he punisheth them.

But who is the sovereign of the king? who commandeth him what he must do? whose hand is reached[2] out to protect him from danger? and if he doeth evil, who shall punish him?

God is the sovereign of the king; his crown is of rays of light, and his throne is amongst the stars. He is King of kings, and Lord of lords:[3] if he biddeth us live, we live; and if he biddeth us die, we die: his dominion is over all worlds, and the light of his countenance[4] is upon all his works.

---

1   demands: in eds. 1-3, 5, and 1815, "commands."
2   reached: in eds. 1-3, 5, and 1815, "stretched."
3   Revelations 17:14.
4   "Light of his countenance" is a phrase used often in Psalms: see 4:6, 44:3, 89:15, 90:8.

God is our Shepherd, therefore we will follow him: God is our Father, therefore we will love him: God is our King, therefore we will obey him.

## Hymn IV

Come, and I will shew you what is beautiful. It is a rose fully blown. See how she sits upon her mossy stem, like the queen of all the flowers! her leaves glow like fire; the air is filled with her sweet odour; she is the delight of every eye.

She is beautiful, but there is a fairer than she. He that made the rose, is more beautiful than the rose: he is all lovely; he is the delight of every heart.

I will shew you what is strong. The lion is strong; when he raiseth up himself from his lair, when he shaketh his mane, when the voice of his roaring is heard, the cattle of the field fly, and the wild beasts of the desart hide themselves, for he is very terrible.

The lion is strong, but he that made the lion is stronger than he: his anger is terrible; he could make us die in a moment, and no one could save us out of his hand.[1]

I will shew you what is glorious. The sun is glorious. When he shineth in the clear sky, when he sitteth on his bright throne in the heavens, and looketh abroad over all the earth, he is the most excellent and glorious creature the eye can behold.[2]

The sun is glorious, but he that made the sun is more glorious than he. The eye beholdeth him not, for his brightness is more dazzling than we could bear. He seeth in all dark places; by night as well as by day; and the light of his countenance is over all his works.

Who is this great name, and what is he called, that my lips may praise him?

---

1 Save us out of his hand: 2 Kings 19:19 (where the context is a prayer to save the Israelites from an earthly tyrant, Sennacherib).

2 This paragraph disturbed Sarah Trimmer: "We think that children from this description may be apt to form an idea of the sun as an *intelligent being*. Neither can this bright luminary be properly called 'the *most excellent creature the eye can behold*,' because this epithet, in respect to the visible creation, is appropriate to MAN" (Trimmer, p. 47).

This great name is GOD. He made all things, but he is himself more excellent than all which he hath made: they are beautiful, but he is beauty; they are strong, but he is strength; they are perfect, but he is perfection.

## Hymn V

The glorious sun is set in the west; the night-dews fall; and the air which was sultry, becomes cool.

The flowers fold up their coloured leaves; they fold themselves up, and hang their heads on the slender stalk.

The chickens are gathered under the wing of the hen, and are at rest: the hen herself is at rest also.

The little birds have ceased their warbling; they are asleep on the boughs, each one with his head behind his wing.

There is no murmur of bees around the hive, or amongst the honeyed woodbines; they have done their work, and lie close in their waxen cells.

The sheep rest upon their soft fleeces, and their loud bleating is no more heard amongst the hills.

There is no sound of a number of voices, or of children at play, or the trampling of busy feet, and of people hurrying to and fro.

The smith's hammer is not heard upon the anvil; nor the harsh saw of the carpenter.[1]

All men are stretched on their quiet beds; and the child sleeps upon the breast of its mother.

Darkness is spread over the skies, and darkness is upon the ground; every eye is shut, and every hand is still.

Who taketh care of all people when they are sunk in sleep; when they cannot defend themselves, nor see if danger approacheth?

There is an eye that never sleepeth; there is an eye that seeth

---

1  This sentence seems partly to echo, and partly to transpose into terms appropriate to an English village like Palgrave, Revelations 18:22 ("And the voice of harpers, and musicians, and of pipers, and trumpeters, shall be heard no more at all in thee; and no craftsman ... shall be found any more in thee; and the sound of a millstone shall be heard no more at all in thee").

in dark night, as well as in the bright sun-shine.[1]

When there is no light of the sun, nor of the moon; when there is no lamp in the house, nor any little star twinkling through the thick clouds; that eye seeth every where, in all places, and watcheth continually over all the families of the earth.

The eye that sleepeth not is God's; his hand is always stretched out over us.[2]

He made sleep to refresh us when we are weary: he made night, that we might sleep in quiet.

As the mother moveth about the house with her finger on her lips, and stilleth every little noise, that her infant be not disturbed; as she draweth the curtains around its bed, and shutteth out the light from its tender eyes; so God draweth the curtains of darkness around us; so he maketh all things to be hushed and still, that his large family may sleep in peace.

Labourers spent with toil, and young children, and every little humming insect, sleep quietly, for God watcheth over you.

You may sleep, for he never sleeps: you may close your eyes in safety, for his eye is always open to protect you.

When the darkness is passed away, and the beams of the morning-sun strike through your eye-lids, begin the day with praising God, who hath taken care of you through the night.

Flowers, when you open again, spread your leaves, and smell sweet to his praise.

Birds, when you awake, warble your thanks amongst the green boughs; sing to him, before you sing to your mates.

Let his praise be in our hearts, when we lie down; let his praise be on our lips, when we awake.[3]

---

1  Cf. Psalm 15:3: "The eyes of the Lord are in every place...."
2  His hand ... over us: Barbauld uses the phrase in a sense contrary to its Biblical sense, of God's wrath (e.g., in Isaiah 14:27: "For the Lord of hosts hath purposed [to destroy Assyria] ... and his hand is stretched out, and who shall turn it back?").
3  Comparable Biblical texts are Psalms 34:1, 35:28, 51:15, 119:171, and 138:1.

Child of reason,[1] whence comest thou? What has thine eye observed, and whither has thy foot been wandering?

I have been wandering along the meadows, in the thick grass; the cattle were feeding around me, or reposing in the cool shade; the corn sprung up in the furrows; the poppy and the hare-bell grew among the wheat; the fields were bright with summer, and glowing with beauty.

Didst thou see nothing more? Didst thou observe nothing besides? Return again, child of reason, for there are greater things than these.[2]—God was among the fields; and didst thou not perceive him? his beauty was upon the meadows; his smile enlivened the sun-shine.

I have walked through the thick forest; the wind whispered among the trees; the brook fell from the rocks with a pleasant murmur; the squirrel leapt from bough to bough: and the birds sung to each other amongst the branches.

Didst thou hear nothing, but the murmur of the brook? no whispers, but the whispers of the wind? Return again, child of reason, for there are greater things than these.—God was amongst the trees; his voice sounded in the murmur of the water; his music warbled in the shade; and didst thou not attend?

I saw the moon rising behind the trees: it was like a lamp of gold. The stars one after another appeared in the clear firmament. Presently I saw black clouds arise, and roll towards the south; the lightning streamed in thick flashes over the sky; the thunder growled at a distance; it came nearer, and I felt afraid, for it was loud and terrible.

Did thy heart feel no terror, but of the thunderbolt? Was there nothing bright and terrible, but the lightning? Return, O

---

1  Cruden's *Concordance to the Holy Scriptures* shows no Biblical phrase of the form "child of X," but it does show "children of X" (e.g., "Children of Judah," "children of light," "children of Israel").

2  Cruden lists a number of Biblical texts using "turn again" (often having the sense of reforming one's life); "greater things than these" is quoted from John 1:50 ("Jesus answered and said unto him, Because I said unto thee, I saw thee under the fig tree, believest thou? thou shalt see greater things than these").

child of reason, for there are greater things than these.—God was in the storm,[1] and didst thou not perceive him? His terrors were abroad, and did not thine heart acknowledge him?

God is in every place; he speaks in every sound we hear; he is seen in all that our eyes behold: nothing, O child of reason, is without God;—let God therefore be in all thy thoughts.[2]

## Hymn VII

Come, let us go into the thick shade, for it is the noon of day, and the summer sun beats hot upon our heads.

The shade is pleasant, and cool; the branches meet above our heads, and shut out the sun, as with a green curtain; the grass is soft to our feet, and a clear brook washes the roots of the trees.

The sloping bank is covered with flowers: let us lie down upon it; let us throw our limbs on the fresh grass, and sleep; for all things are still, and we are quite alone.

The cattle can lie down to sleep in the cool shade, but we can do what is better; we can raise our voices to heaven; we can praise the great God who made us. He made the warm sun, and the cool shade; the trees that grow upwards, and the brooks that run murmuring along. All the things that we see are his work.

Can we raise our voices up to the high heaven? can we make him hear who is above the stars? We need not raise our voices to the stars, for he heareth us when we only whisper; when we breathe out words softly with a low voice. He that filleth the heavens is here also.

May we that are so young, speak to him that always was? May we that can hardly speak plain, speak to God?

We that are so young, are but lately made alive;[3] therefore we

---

1 Cf. Nahum 1:3 ("the Lord hath his way in the whirlwind and in the storm, and the clouds are the dust of his feet").

2 Let ... thoughts: A positive version of Psalm 10:4, which condemns the wicked: "God is not in all his thoughts." The paragraph as a whole expresses the theme of the sermon "On Habitual Devotion" (1767) by Priestley that had inspired Barbauld's poem, "An Address to the Deity."

3 "Made alive" echoes a phrase used in 1 Samuel 2:6 to signify "created" ("The Lord killeth, and maketh alive"), and quotes 1 Corinthians 15:22 ("even so in Christ shall all be made alive"), where it signifies, metaphorically, "reborn." An example of

should not forget his forming hand, who hath made us alive. We that cannot speak plain, should lisp out praises to him who teacheth us how to speak, and hath opened our dumb lips.[1]

When we could not think of him, he thought of us; before we could ask him to bless us, he had already given us many blessings.

He fashioneth our tender limbs, and causeth them to grow; he maketh us strong, and tall, and nimble.

Every day we are more active than the former day, therefore every day we ought to praise him better than the former day.

The buds spread into leaves, and the blossoms swell to fruit; but they know not how they grow, nor who caused them to spring up from the bosom of the earth.

Ask them, if they will tell thee; bid them break forth into singing, and fill the air with pleasant sounds.[2]

They smell sweet; they look beautiful; but they are quite silent: no sound is in the still air; no murmur of voices amongst the green leaves.

The plants and the trees are made to give fruit to man; but man is made to praise God who made him.

We love to praise him, because he loveth to bless us; we thank him for life, because it is a pleasant thing to be alive.

We love God, who hath created all beings; we love all beings, because they are the creatures of God.

We cannot be good, as God is good, to all persons every where; but we can rejoice, that every where there is a God to do them good.

We will think of God when we play, and when we work; when we walk out, and when we come in;[3] when we sleep, and

---

Barbauld's method in *Hymns*, of introducing the child to Biblical metaphor by way of phrases whose literal meaning is available to the child's understanding.

1   "And hath ... lips" echoes Psalm 51:15 ("O Lord, open thou my lips") and Ezekiel 33:22 ("and my mouth was opened, and I was no more dumb").

2   This sentence suggests the mocking questions in Job, e.g., 12:7 ("But ask now the beasts, and they shall teach thee").

3   "Walk ... come in" in the literal sense available to a child, signifies daily comings and goings. In the Bible, however, *walk* is charged with metaphoric meaning, typically signifying the manner in which one lives ("walk[ing] in darkness" or "in the light" [1 John 1:6, 7]). Again, Barbauld prepares the child to learn a primary Biblical metaphor by way of the word's literal meaning.

when we wake; his praise shall dwell continually upon our lips.[1]

## Hymn VIII

See where stands the cottage of the labourer, covered with warm thatch; the mother is spinning at the door; the young children sport before her on the grass; the elder ones learn to labour, and are obedient; the father worketh to provide them food: either he tilleth the ground, or he gathereth in the corn, or shaketh his ripe apples from the tree: his children run to meet him when he cometh home, and his wife prepareth the wholesome meal.

The father, the mother, and the children, make a family; the father is the master thereof. If the family be numerous, and the grounds large, there are servants to help to do the work: all these dwell in one house; they sleep beneath one roof; they eat of the same bread; they kneel down together and praise God every night and every morning with one voice; they are very closely united, and are dearer to each other than any strangers. If one is sick, they mourn together; and if one is happy, they rejoice together.

Many houses are built together; many families live near one another; they meet together on the green, and in pleasant walks, and to buy and sell, and in the house of justice; and the sound of the bell calleth them to the house of God, in company. If one is poor, his neighbour helpeth him; if he is sad, he comforteth him. This is a village; see where it stands enclosed in a green shade, and the tall spire peeps above the trees. If there be very many houses, it is a town—it is governed by a magistrate.

Many towns, and a large extent of country, make a kingdom: it is enclosed by mountains; it is divided by rivers; it is washed by seas; the inhabitants thereof are countrymen; they speak the same language; they make war and peace together—a king is the ruler thereof.

Many kingdoms, and countries full of people, and islands,

---

1   See p. 244, n. 3.

and large continents, and different climates, make up this whole world—God governeth it. The people swarm upon the face of it like ants upon a hillock: some are black with the hot sun; some cover themselves with furs against the sharp cold; some drink of the fruit of the vine; some the pleasant milk of the cocoa-nut; and others quench their thirst with the running stream.

All are God's family; he knoweth every one of them, as a shepherd knoweth his flock: they pray to him in different languages, but he understandeth them all; he heareth them all; he taketh care of all; none are so great, that he cannot punish them; none are so mean, that he will not protect them.

Negro woman, who sittest pining in captivity, and weepest over thy sick child; though no one seeth thee, God seeth thee; though no one pitieth thee, God pitieth thee: raise thy voice, forlorn and abandoned one; call upon him from amidst thy bonds, for assuredly he will hear thee.[1]

Monarch, that rulest over an hundred states; whose frown is terrible as death, and whose armies cover the land, boast not thyself as though there were none above thee:—God is above thee; his powerful arm is always over thee; and if thou doest ill, assuredly he will punish thee.

Nations of the earth,[2] fear the Lord; families of men, call upon the name of your God.

Is there any one whom God hath not made? let him not worship him: is there any one whom he hath not blessed? let him not praise him.

---

1   This is Barbauld's first expression of abolitionist sentiment; Moira Ferguson has suggested that it was prompted by a much-publicized visit to London, in 1773, of the African-American poet and domestic servant, Phillis Wheatley: "Wheatley's impact on women's circles undoubtedly helped to prompt Anna Barbauld's hymn .... The African mother of *Hymn* emblemizes loss, sorrow, severed families, love, and a sense of community; she potently stands for domestic and spiritual values that women have come to represent" (*Subject to Others*, p. 132). Mary Wollstonecraft reprinted this passage in her 1789 anthology, *The Female Reader*.
2   A frequent Biblical phrase (e.g., Deuteronomy 28:1).

## Hymn IX[1]

Come, let us walk abroad; let us talk of the works of God.

Take up a handful of the sand; number the grains of it; tell them one by one into your lap.

Try if you can count the blades of grass in the field, or the leaves on the trees.

You cannot count them, they are innumerable; much more the things which God has made.

The fir groweth on the high mountain, and the grey willow bends above the stream.

The thistle is armed with sharp prickles; the mallow[2] is soft and woolly.

The hop layeth hold with her tendrils, and claspeth the tall pole; the oak hath firm root in the ground, and resisteth the winter storm.

The daisy enamelleth the meadows, and groweth beneath the foot of the passenger:[3] the tulip asketh a rich soil, and the careful hand of the gardener.

The iris and the reed spring up in the marsh; the rich grass covereth the meadows; and the purple heath-flower enliveneth the waste ground.

The water-lilies grow beneath the stream; their broad leaves float on the surface of the water: the wall-flower takes root in the hard stone, and spreads its fragrance amongst broken ruins.

Every leaf is of a different form; every plant hath a separate inhabitant.

Look at the thorns that are white with blossoms, and the flowers that cover the fields, and the plants that are trodden in the green path. The hand of man hath not planted them; the sower hath not scattered the seeds from his hand, nor the gardener digged a place for them with his spade.

---

1    Hymn IX uses a lesson in botany to inculcate reverence for the divine plan; like other Dissenting intellectuals, Barbauld regarded the physical sciences as means to the knowledge of God. Rhetorically, the questions throughout Hymn IX are roughly analogous to those in Job 38-41, where God humbles Job by convincing him how little he understands the natural world.

2    A trailing herb with downy leaves and pink flowers.

3    Passer-by.

Some grow on steep rocks, where no man can climb; in shaking bogs, and deep forests, and desert islands: they spring up every where, and cover the bosom of the whole earth.

Who causeth them to grow every where, and bloweth the seeds about in winds, and mixeth them with the mould, and watereth them with soft rains, and cherisheth them with dews? Who fanneth them with the pure breath of Heaven; and giveth them colours, and smells, and spreadeth our their thin transparent leaves?

How doth the rose draw its crimson from the dark brown earth, or the lily its shining white? How can a small seed contain a plant? How doth every plant know its season to put forth? They are marshalled in order: each one knoweth his place, and standeth up in his own rank.

The snow-drop,[1] and the primrose, make haste to lift their heads above the ground. When the spring cometh, they say, here we are! The carnation waiteth for the full strength of the year; and the hardy laurustinus[2] cheereth the winter months.

Every plant produceth its like. An ear of corn will not grow from an acorn; nor will a grape stone produce cherries; but every one springeth from its proper seed.

Who preserveth them alive through the cold of winter, when the snow is on the ground, and the sharp frost bites on the plain? Who soweth[3] a small seed, and a little warmth in the bosom of the earth, and causeth them to spring up afresh, and sap to rise through the hard fibres?

The trees are withered, naked, and bare; they are like dry bones.[4] Who breatheth on them with the breath of spring, and they are covered with verdure, and green leaves sprout from the dead wood?

Lo, these are a part of his works; and a little portion of his wonders.

There is little need that I should tell you of God, for every thing speaks of him.

---

1 See "The Invitation," ll. 41–46.
2 "An evergreen winter-flowering shrub" (OED).
3 soweth: in eds. 1–3 and 1815, "saveth."
4 An allusion to the valley full of dry bones in Ezekiel 37:1–10.

Every field is like an open book; every painted flower hath a lesson written on its leaves.

Every murmuring brook hath a tongue; a voice is in every whispering wind.

They all speak of him who made them; they all tell us, he is very good.

We cannot see God, for he is invisible; but we can see his works, and worship his foot-steps in the green sod.

They that know the most, will praise God the best; but which of us can number half his works?

## Hymn X[1]

Look at that spreading oak, the pride of the village green![2] its trunk is massy, its branches are strong. Its roots, like crooked fangs, strike deep into the soil, and support its huge bulk. The birds build among the boughs; the cattle repose beneath its shade; the neighbours form groups beneath the shelter of its green canopy. The old men point it out to their children, but they themselves remember not its growth: generations of men one after another have been born and died, and this son of the forest has remained the same, defying the storms of two hundred winters.

Yet this large tree was once a little acorn; small in size, insignificant in appearance; such as you are now picking up upon the grass beneath it. Such an acorn, whose cup can only contain a drop or two of dew, contained the whole oak. All its massy trunk, all its knotted branches, all its multitude of leaves were in that acorn; it grew, it spread, it unfolded itself by degrees, it received nourishment from the rain, and the dews, and the well adapted soil, but it was all there. Rain, and dews, and soil, could not raise an oak without the acorn; nor could they make the acorn any thing but an oak.

---

1  Hymns X-XII were added in 1814; the hymns originally numbered X-XII became XIII-XIV.

2  According to Edmund Burke, the oak is sublime: "the oak, the ash, [and] the elm ... are awful and majestic; they inspire a sort of reverence" (*Sublime and Beautiful*, p. 105).

The mind of a child is like the acorn; its powers are folded up, they do not yet appear, but they are all there. The memory, the judgment, the invention,[1] the feeling of right and wrong, are all in the mind of a child; of a little infant just born; but they are not expanded, you cannot perceive them.

Think of the wisest man you ever knew or heard of; think of the greatest man; think of the most learned man, who speaks a number of languages and can find out hidden things; think of a man who stands like that tree, sheltering and protecting a number of his fellow men, and then say to yourself, the mind of that man was once like mine, his thoughts were childish like my thoughts, nay, he was like the babe just born, which knows nothing, remembers nothing, which cannot distinguish good from evil, nor truth from falsehood.

If you had only seen an acorn you could never guess at the form and size of an oak: if you had never conversed with a wise man, you could form no idea of him from the mute and helpless infant.

Instruction is the food of the mind; it is like the dew and the rain and the rich soil. As the soil and the rain and the dew cause the tree to swell and put forth its tender shoots, so do books and study and discourse feed the mind, and make it unfold its hidden powers.

Reverence therefore your own mind; receive the nurture of instruction, that the man within you may grow and flourish. You cannot guess how excellent he may become.

It was long before this oak shewed its greatness; year after year passed away, and it had only shot a little way above the ground, a child might have plucked it up with his little hands; it was long before any one called it a tree; and it is long before the child becomes a man.

The acorn might have perished in the ground, the young tree might have been shorn of its graceful boughs, the twig might have bent, and the tree would have been crooked, but if it grew at all it could have been nothing but an oak, it would not have been grass or flowers, which live their season and then perish from the face of the earth.

---

1 Creative imagination.

The child may be a foolish man, he may be a wicked man, but he must be a man; his nature is not that of any inferior creature, his soul is not akin to the beasts which perish.

O cherish then this precious mind, feed it with truth, nourish it with knowledge; it comes from God, it is made in his image; the oak will last for centuries of years, but the mind of man is made for immortality.

Respect in the infant the future man. Destroy not in the man the rudiments of an angel.

## Hymn XI[1]

The golden orb of the sun is sunk behind the hills, the colours fade away from the western sky, and the shades of evening fall fast around me.

Deeper and deeper they stretch over the plain; I look at the grass, it is no longer green; the flowers are no more tinted with various hues; the houses, the trees, the cattle, are all lost in the distance. The dark curtain of night is let down over the works of God; they are blotted out from the view, as if they were no longer there.

Child of little observation! canst thou see nothing because thou canst not see grass and flowers, trees and cattle? Lift up thine eyes from the ground shaded with darkness, to the heavens that are stretched over thy head; see how the stars one by one appear and light up the vast concave.

There is the moon bending her bright horns like a silver bow, and shedding her mild light, like liquid silver over the blue firmament.

There is Venus, the evening and the morning star; and the Pleiades, and the Bear that never sets, and the Pole star that guides the mariner over the deep.

Now the mantle of darkness is over the earth; the last little gleam of twilight is faded away; the lights are extinguished in the cottage windows, but the firmament burns with innumer-

---

1   As Hymn IX used a botany lesson, so Hymn XI uses an astronomy lesson to inculcate reverence for God. Similar feelings arise from contemplation of the night sky in "A Summer Evening's Meditation."

able fires; every little star twinkles in its place. If you begin to count them they are more than you can number; they are like the sands of the sea shore.

The telescope shows you far more, and there are thousands and ten thousands of stars which no telescope has ever reached.

Now Orion heaves his bright shoulder above the horizon, and Sirius, the dog star, follows him, the brightest of the train.

Look at the milky way, it is a field of brightness; its pale light is composed of myriads of burning suns.

All these are God's families; he gives the sun to shine with a ray of his own glory; he marks the path of the planets, he guides their wanderings through the sky, and traces out their orbit with the finger of his power.

If you were to travel as swift as an arrow from a bow, and to travel on further and further still, for millions of years, you would not be out of the creation of God.

New suns in the depth of space would still be burning round you, and other planets fulfilling their appointed course.

Lift up thine eyes, child of earth, for God has given thee a glimpse of heaven.

The light of one sun is withdrawn, that thou mayest see ten thousand. Darkness is spread over the earth, that thou mayest behold, at a distance, the regions of eternal day.

This earth has a variety of inhabitants; the sea, the air, the surface of the ground, swarm with creatures of different natures, sizes, and powers; to know a very little of them is to be wise among the sons of men.

What then, thinkest thou, are the various forms and natures and senses and occupations of the peopled universe?

Who can tell the birth and generation of so many worlds? who can relate their histories? who can describe their inhabitants?

Canst thou measure infinity with a line? canst thou grasp the circle of infinite space?

Yet these all depend upon God, they hang upon him as a child upon the breast of its mother; he tempereth the heat to the inhabitant of Mercury; he provideth resources against the cold in the frozen orb of Saturn. Doubt not that he provideth for all beings that he has made.

Look at the moon when it walketh in brightness; gaze at the stars when they are marshalled in the firmament, and adore the Maker of so many worlds.

## Hymn XII

It is now Winter, dead Winter. Desolation and silence reign in the fields, no singing of birds is heard, no humming of insects. The streams murmur no longer; they are locked up in frost.

The trees lift their naked boughs like withered arms into the bleak sky; the green sap no longer rises in their veins; the flowers and the sweet smelling shrubs are decayed to their roots.

The sun himself looks cold and chearless; he gives light only enough to show the universal desolation.

Nature, child of God, mourns for her children. A little while ago, and she rejoiced in her offspring; the rose shed its perfume upon the gale; the vine gave its fruit; her children were springing and blooming around her, on every lawn and every green bank.

O Nature, beautiful Nature, beloved child of God, why dost thou sit mourning and desolate? Has thy father forsaken thee, has he left thee to perish? Art thou no longer the object of his care?

He has not forsaken thee, O Nature; thou art his beloved child, the eternal image of his perfections; his own beauty is spread over thee, the light of his countenance is shed upon thee.

Thy children shall live again, they shall spring up and bloom around thee; the rose shall again breathe its sweetness on the soft air, and from the bosom of the ground verdure shall spring forth.

And dost thou not mourn, O Nature, for thy human births; for thy sons and thy daughters that sleep under the sod; and shall they not also revive? Shall the rose and the myrtle bloom anew, and shall man perish? Shall goodness sleep in the ground, and the light of wisdom be quenched in the dust, and shall tears be shed over *them* in vain?

They also shall live; their winter shall pass away; they shall bloom again. The tears of thy children shall be dried up when the eternal year proceeds. Oh come that eternal year![1]

## Hymn XIII

Child of mortality, whence comest thou? why is thy countenance sad, and why are thine eyes red with weeping?

I have seen the rose in its beauty; it spread its leaves to the morning sun—I returned, it was dying upon its stalk; the grace of the form of it was gone; its loveliness was vanished away; the leaves thereof were scattered on the ground, and no one gathered them again.

A stately tree grew on the plain; its branches were covered with verdure; its boughs spread wide and made a goodly shadow; the trunk was like a strong pillar; the roots were like crooked fangs.—I returned, the verdure was nipt by the east wind; the branches were lopt away by the ax; the worm had made its way into the trunk, and the heart thereof was decayed; it mouldered away, and fell to the ground.

I have seen the insects sporting in the sun-shine, and darting along the streams; their wings glittered with gold and purple; their bodies shone like the green emerald: they were more numerous than I could count; their motions were quicker than my eye could glance—I returned, they were brushed into the pool; they were perishing with the evening breeze; the swallow had devoured them; the pike had seized them: there were none found of so great a multitude.[2]

I have seen man in the pride of his strength; his cheeks glowed with beauty; his limbs were full of activity; he leaped; he walked; he ran; he rejoiced in that he was more excellent than those—I returned, he lay stiff and cold on the bare ground; his feet could no longer move, nor his hands stretch

---

1  Cf. John Dryden, "To the Pious Memory of … Mrs. Anne Killigrew" (1685): "Thou wilt have time enough for hymns divine, / Since heav'n's eternal year is thine."

2  There were … multitude: As often in *Hymns*, the sentence resonates of the Bible without quoting any particular passage. It is a pastiche of Biblical phraseology; *multitude*, for example, is Biblical for "a large number" or "a crowd."

themselves out; his life was departed from him; and the breath out of his nostrils:—therefore do I weep, because DEATH is in the world; the spoiler is among the works of God: all that is made, must be destroyed; all that is born, must die: let me alone, for I will weep yet longer.[1]

## Hymn XIV

I have seen the flower withering on the stalk, and its bright leaves spread on the ground—I looked again, and it sprung forth afresh; the stem was crowned with new buds, and the sweetness thereof filled the air.

I have seen the sun set in the west, and the shades of night shut in the wide horizon: there was no colour, nor shape, nor beauty, nor music; gloom and darkness brooded around—I looked, the sun broke forth again from the east, he gilded the mountain tops; the lark rose to meet him from her low nest, and the shades of darkness fled away.

I have seen the insect, being come to its full size, languish, and refuse to eat: it spun itself a tomb, and was shrouded in the silken cone; it lay without feet, or shape, or power to move—I looked again, it had burst its tomb; it was full of life, and sailed on coloured wings through the soft air; it rejoiced in its new being.

Thus shall it be with thee, O man! and so shall thy life be renewed.

Beauty shall spring up out of ashes, and life out of the dust.

A little while shalt thou lie in the ground, as the seed lieth in the bosom of the earth: but thou shalt be raised again; and, if thou art good, thou shalt never die any more.[2]

---

1   die ... longer: In eds. 1–2, "die."

2   This paragraph occasioned an anecdote published in the *Christian Reformer* in 1819. A Unitarian minister "lost an infant about five weeks old. The child was placed in its coffin, & the father and mother were sitting pensively beside it. A little boy scarcely seven years old, was leaning over the coffin in mournful silence, with the tears running down his cheeks. He stood silent a considerable time, then ... broke out into the following quotation from ... Mrs Barbauld's Hymns. 'A little while shalt thou lie in the ground ... any more'" (quoted in Rodgers, *Georgian Chronicle*, pp. 73–74).

Who is he that cometh to burst open the prison doors of the tomb; to bid the dead awake, and to gather his redeemed from the four winds of heaven?[1]

He descendeth on a fiery cloud;[2] the sound of a trumpet goeth before him; thousands of angels are on his right hand.

It is Jesus, the Son of God; the saviour of men; the friend of the good.

He cometh in the glory of his Father; he hath received power from on high.[3]

Mourn not therefore, child of immortality!—for the spoiler, the cruel spoiler that laid waste the works of God, is subdued: Jesus hath conquered death:—child of immortality! mourn no longer.

## Hymn XV

The rose is sweet, but it is surrounded with thorns: the lily of the valley is fragrant, but it springeth up amongst the brambles.

The spring is pleasant, but it is soon past: the summer is bright, but the winter destroyeth the beauty thereof.

The rainbow is very glorious, but it soon vanisheth away: life is good, but it is quickly swallowed up in death.

There is a land, where the roses are without thorns, where the flowers are not mixed with brambles.

In that land, there is eternal spring, and light without any cloud.

The tree of life groweth in the midst thereof;[4] rivers of pleasures are there, and flowers that never fade.

Myriads of happy spirits are there, and surround the throne of God with a perpetual hymn.

---

1  In Acts 5:19 and 16:27 "prison doors" carries a literal meaning. "To gather ... heaven" nearly quotes Matthew 24:31, as do "trumpet" and "angels" in the following sentence.

2  Cloud (but not fire): Matthew 24:30 and Revelations 1:7.

3  He cometh ... Father: Mark 8:38. "Received power" echoes Revelations 4:11. This and the three preceding paragraphs were among the passages Elizabeth Carter found "amazingly sublime" (see headnote).

4  "The tree of life" grows in Genesis 2:9.

The angels with their golden harps sing praises continually, and the cherubim fly on wings of fire!

This country is Heaven: it is the country of those that are good; and nothing that is wicked must inhabit there.

The toad must not spit its venom amongst turtle doves; nor the poisonous hen-bane grow amongst sweet flowers.

Neither must any one that doeth ill enter into that good land.

This earth is pleasant, for it is God's earth, and it is filled with many delightful things.

But that country is far better: there we shall not grieve any more, nor be sick any more, nor do wrong any more; there the cold of winter shall not wither us, nor the heats of summer scorch us.[1]

In that country there are no wars nor quarrels, but all love one another with dear love.

When our parents and friends die, and are laid in the cold ground, we see them here no more; but there we shall embrace them again, and live with them, and be separated no more.

There we shall meet all good men, whom we read of in holy books.

There we shall see Abraham, the called of God, the father of the faithful; and Moses, after his long wanderings in the Arabian desart; and Elijah, the prophet of God; and Daniel, who escaped the lion's den; and there the son of Jesse, the shepherd king, the sweet singer of Israel.[2]

They loved God on earth; they praised him on earth; but in that country they will praise him better, and love him more.

There we shall see Jesus, who is gone before us to that happy place; and there we shall behold the glory of the high God.

We cannot see him here, but we will love him here: we must be now on earth, but we will often think on heaven.

That happy land is our home: we are to be here but for a little while, and there for ever, even for ages of eternal years.

---

1  Perhaps an allusion to Shakespeare's *Cymbeline*, IV.ii.258: "Fear no more the heat o' the sun, / Nor the furious winter's rages."

2  David, the supposed author of Psalms.

# AN ADDRESS TO THE OPPOSERS OF THE REPEAL OF THE CORPORATION AND TEST ACTS

[After nine years of silence, Barbauld surprised the public by returning to print as a political writer. Her occasion was the rejection of a motion in Parliament, on 2 March 1790, to repeal two laws which declared Dissenters ineligible to hold various public offices. (For details about the laws and excerpts from the debates, see Appendix B.) It was the third rebuff in four years to the efforts of Dissenters to achieve equal citizenship with Church-of-England members.

The repeal movement produced a huge pamphlet literature in which Dissenters contended for repeal on the ground that, as men and citizens, they were deprived of their natural rights. Their argument was similar to that being made simultaneously (and by many of the same people) for a reform of representation in Parliament. Conservatives resisted by calling up baleful memories of the Puritan overthrow of the Anglican Church 140 years earlier—and by claiming to see in the more politically insurgent Dissenters, such as Joseph Priestley, a reincarnation of militant Puritanism. The progress of revolution in France, which included bloodshed (the capture of the Bastille in July 1789, the forcible return of the king to Paris in October) and the nationalization of Church property, was cited melodramatically as evidence that reform at home would lead to anarchy (see Burke's speech, Appendix B.2). In this atmosphere, reform had no chance. The repeal motion lost by 189 votes.

Barbauld must have composed her *Address* at white heat; an excerpt from it was printed in a newspaper on 25 March, and its publication (signed only "A Dissenter") was announced on 27 March. A second, revised, edition followed, perhaps in April, and two more before the year's end. The *Address* was warmly received by liberals. "Of all the pamphlets which the press has brought forth, on this singularly prolific subject," wrote the *Monthly Review*, "the address now before us is, perhaps, the most spirited, and most agreeably written" (p. 460). Conservatives were stung by its irony: "taunting," the *Gentle-*

*man's Magazine* declared it (60:347). One clergyman, William Keate, commenting at some length on the *Address*, conceded that its author's "abilities certainly command respect; his conceptions are strong, and his language, in general, elegant and nervous. I could only wish that his sentiments were more moderate, and his charity less confined." When Keate learned who had written the *Address*, he added a postscript of slack-jawed astonishment: "Since the above was at the press, the author hears, with infinite surprize, not unmixed with concern, that the Address to the Opposers of the Repeal is from a female pen!" (*A Free Examination*, p. 64) Indeed, Barbauld probably was the only woman to enter the repeal debate. When the *Address* reappeared in her *Works*, an American reviewer admired "the sincerity and boldness with which she writes, the well bred sarcasm, often employed by powerful minds to express their deepest emotions,—and the hopelessness, resembling that of an ancient prophet, with which she reminds the nation that it is now too late to conciliate their injured brethren, if they would, as the spirit of liberty is abroad, and her reign is almost come" (Peabody, pp. 311-12).

Our text is that of the revised second edition, corrected in a few places from *Works*.]

A System of Toleration, attended with humiliating Distinctions, is so vicious in itself, that the Man who is forced to tolerate is as much dissatisfied with the Law as he that obtains such a Toleration.

Speech of Count Clermont Tonnere.[1]

Gentlemen,
Had the question of yesterday been decided in a manner more favourable to our wishes, which however the previous intimations of your temper in the business left us little room to expect, we should have addressed our thanks to you on the

---

1   *Translation of a Speech, Spoken by the Count Clermont Tonnere … on the Subject of admitting Non-Catholics, Comedians, and Jews, to all the Privileges of Citizens …* (London, 1790), p. 11. Barbauld added this quotation to the title-page of ed. 2. The speech was originally delivered in the French National Assembly.

occasion.[1] As it is, we address to you our thanks for much casu-al light thrown upon the subject, and for many incidental testi-monies of your esteem (whether voluntary or involuntary we will not stop to examine) which in the course of this discussion you have favoured us with. We thank you for the compliment paid the Dissenters, when you suppose that the moment they are eligible to places of power and profit, all such places will at once be filled with them.[2] Not content with confounding, by an artful sophism, the right of eligibility with the right to offices, you again confound that right with the probable fact, and then argue accordingly.[3] Is then the Test Act, your boasted bulwark, of equal necessity with the dykes in Holland; and do we wait, like an impetuous sea, to rush in and overwhelm the land? Our pretensions, Gentlemen, are far humbler. *We* had not the presumption to imagine that, inconsiderable as we are in numbers, compared to the established Church; inferior too in fortune and influence; labouring, as we do, under the frown of the Court, and the anathema of the orthodox; we should make our way so readily into the secret recesses of royal favour; and, of a sudden, like the frogs of Egypt, swarm about your barns, and under your canopies, and in your kneading troughs, and in the chamber of the King.[4] We rather wished this act as the removal of a stigma than the possession of a certain advantage, and we might have been cheaply pleased with the acknowledg-

---

1   The Address of Thanks was a known and practised genre, at least among Dissenters. Barbauld's cousin, the Rev. Thomas Belsham, delivered addresses of thanks to his pupils at Daventry Academy at the close of sessions (Williams, *Belsham*, pp. 387-88, 424-25).

2   Places are public offices. Priestley, with less suave irony, had made the same point in a 1787 pamphlet: "The consequence [of repeal] would not be the instantly filling of all the executive offices of government with Dissenters" (*Letter to … William Pitt*, p. 11).

3   The willful or panicky confusion of "right to be eligible" with "right to office" was a staple of conservative resistance; see, for an example, Appendix B.3. Proponents of repeal often reassured conservatives that "the repeal of the Test Laws would not exclude a single churchman, or put the Dissenters in possession of any one public office, but would only render them eligible to such as might be offered" (*Right of Protestant Dissenters*, p. 72).

4   In Exodus 8:1-3, Pharaoh's refusal to free the Israelites is punished by a plague of frogs.

ment of the right, though we had never been fortunate enough to enjoy the emolument.

Another compliment for which we offer our acknowledgements may be extracted from the great ferment, which has been raised by this business all over the country. What stir and movement has it occasioned among the different orders of men! How quick the alarm has been taken, and sounded from the Church to the Senate,[1] and from the press to the people; while fears and forebodings were communicated like an electric shock! The old cry of, *the Church is in danger,* has again been made to vibrate in our ears.[2] Here too if we gave way to impressions of vanity, we might suppose ourselves of much greater importance in the political scale than our numbers and situation seem to indicate. It shews at least we are feared, which to some minds would be the next grateful thing to being beloved. We, indeed, should only wish for the latter; nor should we have ventured to suppose, but from the information you have given us, that your Church *was* so weak. What! fenced and guarded as she is with her exclusive privileges and rich emoluments, stately with her learned halls and endowed colleges, with all the attraction of her wealth, and the thunder of her censures; all that the orator calls *the majesty of the Church* about her, and does she, resting in security under the broad buckler[3] of the State, does she tremble at the naked and unarmed sectary? him, whose early connections, and phrase uncouth, and unpopular opinions set him at a distance from the means of advancement; him, who in the intercourses of neighbourhood and common life, like new settlers, finds it necessary to clear the ground before him, and is ever obliged to root up a preju-

---

1  The House of Commons, that is.

2  "That *the Church is in danger,* is an alarm that [Dissenters] laugh at our allowing to disturb our repose; but sober, cautious people cannot help looking back to see what has endangered it, and looking forward to what again might do it" (*A Look to the Last Century,* pp. 127-28, voicing conservative fear). Arguing for repeal, Charles James Fox noted that the Church had a long history of thinking itself endangered without in fact being so; but in the same debate, Edmund Burke accused Dissenters of "asserting doctrines that threatened the most imminent danger to the future safety, and even the very being of the Church" (*Debate* [1790], pp. 9-10, 43).

3  Shield. The Church of England was state-supported as well as protected by legislation.

dice before he can plant affection. He is not of the world, Gen-
tlemen, and the world loveth her own.[1] All that distinguishes
him from other men to common observation, operates in his
disfavour. His very advocates, while they plead his cause, are
ready to blush for their client; and in justice to their own char-
acter think it necessary to disclaim all knowledge of his obscure
tenets.[2] And is it from his hand you expect the demolition of so
massy an edifice? Does the simple removal of the Test Act
involve its destruction? These were not *our* thoughts. *We* had
too much reverence for your establishment to imagine that the
structure was so loosely put together, or so much shaken by
years, as that the removal of so slight a pin should endanger the
whole fabric[3] —or is the Test Act the *talisman* which holds it
together, that, when it is broken, the whole must fall to pieces
like the magic palace of an enchanter? Surely no species of reg-
ular architecture can depend upon so slight a support.—After
all what is it we have asked?—to share in the rich benefices of
the established church? to have the gates of her schools and
universities thrown open to us? No, let her keep her golden
prebends, her scarfs, her lawn, her mitres.[4] Let her dignitaries be
still associated to the honours of legislation; and, in our courts
of executive justice, let her inquisitorial tribunals continue to
thwart the spirit of a free constitution by a heterogeneous mix-
ture of priestly jurisdiction.[5] Let her still gather into barns,
though she neither sows nor reaps.[6] We desire not to share in

---

1  John 8:23 and 15:19.
2  Perhaps an allusion to a remark by one proponent of repeal that "he had never any
   connection with Dissenters otherwise than with his Constituents" (*Debate* [1790],
   p. 53).
3  removal ... fabric: alluding to Jonathan Swift's "Argument against Abolishing
   Christianity" (1708), a defence of the Test Act: "And therefore, the Free-Thinkers
   consider it as a Sort of Edifice, wherein all the Parts have such a mutual Depen-
   dance on each other, that if you happen to pull out one single Nail, the whole Fab-
   rick must fall to the Ground" (*Writings*, p. 470).
4  A prebend is a stipend paid by a cathedral to a clergyman; a scarf, a sash indicating
   rank in a hierarchy; lawn, a fine linen (used in clerical garb); and a mitre, a headdress
   worn by bishops.
5  Anglican bishops sat ex officio (but with a vote) in the House of Lords, and the
   English legal system included an ecclesiastical court with jurisdiction over mar-
   riages, divorces, and wills.
6  Matthew 6:26.

her good things. We know it is the children's bread, which must not be given to dogs.[1] But *having* these good things, we *could* wish to hear her say with the generous spirit of Esau, *I have enough, my brother.*[2] We could wish to be considered as children of the State, though we are not so of the Church. She must excuse us if we look upon the alliance between her and the State as an ill sorted union, and herself as a mother-in-law[3] who, with the too frequent arts of that relation, is ever endeavouring to prejudice the State, the common parent of us all, against a part of his offspring, for the sake of appropriating a larger portion to her own children. We claim no share in the dowry of her who is not our mother, but we may be pardoned for thinking it hard to be deprived of the inheritance of our father.

But it is objected to us that we have sinned in the manner of making our request; we have brought it forward as a claim instead of asking it as a favour.[4] We should have sued, and crept, and humbled ourselves. Our preachers and our writers should not have dared to express the warm glow of honest sentiment, or, even in a foreign country glance at the downfall of a haughty aristocracy.[5] As we were suppliants, we should have behaved like suppliants, and then perhaps————No, Gentlemen, we wish to have it understood, that we *do* claim it as a right. It loses otherwise half its value. We claim it as men, we claim it as citizens, we claim it as good subjects.[6] We are not

---

1   Matthew 15:26. Moving for repeal in 1787, Henry Beaufoy made the same disclaimer (without irony): see Appendix B.1.

2   Genesis 33:9.

3   Stepmother.

4   In the 1787 debate Lord North wished that "the Dissenters had proceeded in a more regular manner, … by a petition to the House," and regretted that they had "chosen to adopt another mode" instead (*Debate* [1787], p. 45). In the 1790 debate, a Dissenting member said that "he joined in the present application, upon the ground of a claim of right"; an opponent referred angrily to "a *claim* made by the Dissenters; a pretty singular claim!" (*Debate* [1790], pp. 12, 36) A *petition* is a request; a *claim* is a demand.

5   As Richard Price had done in a sermon (4 Nov. 1789) congratulating the French on achieving liberty. Edmund Burke alluded darkly to Price in his speech on the Army budget (see Appendix B.2), and was to make Price the villain of his *Reflections on the Revolution in France.*

6   These were the grounds on which Henry Beaufoy had urged his motion in 1787. See Appendix B.1.

conscious of having brought the disqualification upon our-
selves by a failure in any of these characters.

But we already enjoy a complete toleration[1]—It is time, so
near the end of the eighteenth century, it is surely time to speak
with precision, and to call things by their proper names. What
you call toleration, we call the exercise of a natural and unalien-
able right.[2] We do not conceive it to be toleration, first to strip
a man of all his dearest rights, and then to give him back a part;
or even if it were the whole. You tolerate us in worshipping
God according to our consciences—and why not tolerate a
man in the use of his limbs, in the disposal of his private prop-
erty, the contracting his domestic engagements, or any other
the most acknowledged privileges of humanity? It is not to
these things that the word toleration is applied with propriety.
It is applied, where from lenity or prudence we forbear doing
all which in justice we might do. It is the bearing with what is
confessedly an evil, for the sake of some good with which it is
connected. It is the Christian virtue of long suffering; it is the
political virtue of adapting measures to times and seasons and
situations. *Abuses* are tolerated, when they are so interwoven
with the texture of the piece, that the operation of removing
them becomes too delicate and hazardous. *Unjust claims* are tol-
erated, when they are complied with for the sake of peace and
conscience. The failings and imperfections of those characters
in which there appears an evident preponderancy of virtue, are
tolerated. These are the proper objects of toleration, these
exercise the patience of the Christian and the prudence of the
Statesman; but if there be a power that advances pretensions
which we think unfounded in reason or scripture, that exercis-
es an empire within an empire, and claims submission from
those naturally her equals; and if we, from a spirit of brotherly

---

1   Opponents of repeal often claimed that Dissenters enjoyed full toleration of their
    religion. Thus Lord North in 1787 "allowed that a complete toleration, in the true
    meaning of the words, was proper," and then went on to oppose repeal (*Debate*
    [1787], p. 44).
2   "In the very idea of religious toleration, the state is supposed to concede that as a
    favour, which is due as a matter of right" (John Disney, quoted in *Right of Protestant
    Dissenters*, p. 94n). Other Dissenters also redefined the idea of toleration in terms of
    rights.

charity, and just deference to public opinion, and a salutary dread of innovation, acquiesce in these pretensions; let her at least be told that the virtue of forbearance should be transferred, and that it is we who tolerate her, not she who tolerates us.

*Complete Toleration*,[1] though an expression often adverted to by both parties, is in truth a solecism in terms; for all that is tolerated ought to be done away whenever it is found practicable and expedient. Complete Convalescence is no longer Convalescence, but Health; and complete Toleration is no longer Toleration, but Liberty. Let the term therefore be discarded, which, however softened, involves in it an insult with regard to us, and however extended, an absurdity with regard to yourselves. Sensible that a spirit of liberality requires the indulgence to be *complete*, and desirous at the same time to retain the idea of our holding it through sufferance and not of right, you have been betrayed into this incongruity of expression. Those are always liable to be betrayed into such, who have not the courage to embrace a system in its full extent, and to follow a principle wherever it may lead them. Hence the *progress* from Error to Truth, and from Bigotry to the most enlarged freedom of sentiment, is marked with greater *inconsistencies* than that state in which the mind quietly rests in the former position. It is only when we view objects by a dubious and uncertain twilight that we are apt to mistake their figure and distances, and to be disturbed by groundless terrors; in perfect darkness we form no judgment about them.—It has ever been the untoward fate of your Church to partake largely of these inconsistencies. Placed between the Catholics on one side, and the Dissenters on the other, she has not been able to defend either her resistance or her restraints, and lies equally open to censure for her persecution and her dissent. Pressed by the difficulties of her

---

1  This and the following paragraph (through "quit possession of the field") were added in ed. 2, possibly in response to reports of a speech in the French National Assembly by Jean-Paul Rabaut St. Étienne, 28 Aug. 1789, denouncing the very word *toleration* and demanding instead full liberty. Barbauld could perhaps have seen an extract from it in *A Letter to the Reverend John Martin* (London, [1790]), p. 16.

peculiar situation, she is continually obliged in the course of her polemic warfare to change her ground, and alter her mode of defence; and like the poor Bat in the fable, to tell a different story upon every new attack;[1] and thus it must be, till she shall have the magnanimity to make use of all her light, and follow her reason without reserve.

For Truth is of a nature strangely encroaching, and ought to be kept out entirely if we are not disposed to admit her with perfect freedom. You cannot say to her, Thus far shalt thou go, and no further. Give her the least entrance, and she will never be satisfied till she has gained entire possession. Allow her but a few plain axioms to work with, and step by step, syllogism after syllogism, she insensibly mines her way into the very heart of her enemy's entrenchments. Truth is of a very intolerant spirit. She will not make any compromise with Error, and if she be obliged to hold any fellowship with her, it is such fellowship as light has with darkness, a perpetual warfare and opposition. Every concession made by her antagonist is turned into a fresh weapon against her, and being herself invulnerable, she is sure to gain by each successive contest, till her adversary is driven from every shelter and lurking-hole, and fairly obliged to quit possession of the field.

But this, it is again imputed to us, is no contest for religious liberty, but a contest for power, and place, and influence. We want civil offices[2] —And why should citizens *not* aspire to civil offices? Why should not the fair field of generous competition be freely opened to every one!—A contention for power—It is not a contention for power between Churchmen and Dissenters, nor is it as Dissenters we wish to enter the lists; we

---

1   In the fable of the Bat and the Two Weasels (in Phaedrus and LaFontaine), a bat is attacked by a weasel who takes him for a bird. No, says the bat, I'm a mouse. Attacked by another weasel who takes him for a mouse, the bat declares himself a bird.

2   "What [the Dissenters] now ask is not religious liberty (for that they enjoy), but a participation of power" (*Observations upon the Case of the Protestant Dissenters*, p. 15); "to be admitted into places of power, honour, and profit, was their aim" (*A Look to the Last Century*, p. 8). And likewise William Pitt, in the 1787 debate: "The persons who make this application ... have *not* a participation of *offices: this* is what they desire" (*Debate* [1787], p. 53).

wish to bury every name of distinction in the common appella-
tion of Citizen. We wish not the name of Dissenter to be pro-
nounced, except in our theological researches and religious
assemblies. It is you, who by considering us as Aliens, make us
so. It is you who force us to make our dissent a prominent
feature in our character. It is you who give relief, and cause to
come out upon the canvas what we modestly wished to have
shaded over, and thrown into the back ground. If we are a
party, remember it is you who force us to be so.—We should
have sought places of trust—By no unfair, unconstitutional
methods should we have sought them, but in the open and
honourable rivalship of virtuous emulation; by trying to
deserve well of our King and our Country. Our attachment to
both is well known.[1]

Perhaps however we have all this while mistaken the matter,
and what we have taken for bigotry and a narrow-minded spir-
it is after all only an affair of calculation and arithmetic. Our
fellow-subjects remember the homely proverb, "the fewer the
better cheer,"[2] and, very naturally, are glad to see the number of
candidates lessened for the advantages they are themselves striv-
ing after. If so, we ask their excuse, their conduct is quite sim-
ple, and if, from the number of concurrents,[3] Government were
to strike out all above or under five feet high, or all whose
birth-days happened before the Summer Solstice, or, by any
other mode of distinction equally arbitrary and whimsical were
to reduce the number of their rivals, *they* would be equally
pleased, and equally unwilling to admit an alteration. We are a
mercantile people, accustomed to consider chances, and we can
easily perceive that in the lottery of life, if a certain proportion
are by some means or other excluded from a prize, the adven-
ture is exactly so much the better for the remainder. If this
indeed be the case, as I suspect it may, we have been accusing

---

1 The loyalty of modern Dissenters to the Crown was strongly emphasized by pro-
ponents of repeal.
2 "The fewer there are, the more there is for each to eat" (*OED*). Other writers
occasionally made the same observation: "the members of the church of England
thus secure to themselves a monopoly of all those [offices] accompanied with trust
or profit" (*Right of Protestant Dissenters*, p. 40).
3 Competitors.

you wrongfully. Your conduct is founded upon principles as sure and unvarying as mathematical truths; and all further discussion is needless. We drop the argument at once. Men have now and then been reasoned out of their prejudices, but it were a hopeless attempt to reason them out of their interest.[1]

We likewise beg leave to apologize to those of the clergy, whom we have unwittingly offended by endeavouring to include *them* as parties in our cause. "Pricked to it by foolish honesty and love,"[2] we thought that what appeared so grievous to us could not be very pleasant to them: but we are convinced of our mistake, and sorry for our officiousness. We own it, Sirs, it was a fond imagination that because *we* should have felt uneasy under the obligation imposed upon you, it should have the same effect upon yourselves. It was weak to impute to you an idle delicacy of conscience, which perhaps can only be preserved at a distance from the splendid scenes which you have continually in prospect. But you will pardon us. We did not consider the force of early discipline over the mind. *We* are not accustomed to those salvos, and glosses,[3] and accommodating modes of reasoning with which you have been long familiarized. You have the happy art of making easy to yourselves greater things than this. You are regularly disciplined troops, and understand every nice manoeuvre and dextrous evolution[4] which the nature of the ground may require. We are like an unbroken horse; hard mouthed, and apt to start at shadows. Our conduct towards you in this particular we acknowledge may fairly provoke a smile at our simplicity. Besides, upon reflection what should you startle at? The mixture of secular and religious concerns cannot to you appear extraordinary; and in truth nothing is more reasonable than that, as the State has been drawn in to the aggrandizement of your Church, your

---

1  Self-interest, that is.
2  *Othello*, III.iii.412. Proponents of repeal argued that the use of the Church-of-England rite as a political test must hurt the consciences of Anglican clergy: see, for example, Beaufoy in Appendix B.1.
3  A salvo is a mental reservation to preserve one's conscience; a gloss, an interpretation of a text.
4  The well-drilled movement of a body of troops into a formation.

Church should in return make itself subservient to the convenience of the State. If we are wise, we shall never again make ourselves uneasy about your share of the grievance.

But we were enumerating our obligations to you, Gentlemen, who have thwarted our request, and we must take the liberty to inform you that if it be any object of our ambition to exist and attract notice as a separate body, you have done us the greatest service in the world. What we desired, by blending us with the common mass of citizens, would have sunk our relative importance, and consigned our discussions to oblivion. You have refused us; and by so doing, you keep us under the eye of the public, in the interesting point of view of men who suffer under a deprivation of their rights. You have set a mark of separation upon us,[1] and it is not in our power to take it off, but it is in our power to determine whether it shall be a disgraceful stigma or an honourable distinction. If, by the continued peaceableness of our demeanour, and the superior sobriety of our conversation, a sobriety for which we have not yet quite ceased to be distinguished; if, by our attention to literature, and that ardent love of liberty which you are pretty ready to allow us, we deserve esteem, we shall enjoy it. If our rising seminaries should excel in wholesome discipline and regularity, if *they* should be schools of morality, and yours, unhappily, should be corrupted into schools of immorality, you will entrust us with the education of your youth, when the parent, trembling at the profligacy of the times, wishes to preserve the blooming and ingenuous child from the degrading taint of early licentiousness.[2] If our writers are solid, elegant, or nervous,[3] you will read our books and imbibe our sentiments, and even your Preachers will not disdain, occasionally, to *illustrate* our morality.[4] If we enlighten the world by philosophical discoveries, you will pay the involuntary homage due to genius, and boast of our names

---

1 See "On the Devotional Taste," p. 225, n. 2.

2 The Establishment schools, such as Eton, were notorious for cruelty, drinking and other vices, and general disorder. Many of the students at Warrington Academy and the pupils at Palgrave School were sent by Church-of-England parents.

3 Energetic.

4 To illustrate is to make clear by commentary. Barbauld seems to be quoting, but we have not traced the quotation.

when, amongst foreign societies, you are inclined to do credit to your country.[1] If your restraints operate towards keeping us in that middle rank of life where industry and virtue most abound, we shall have the honour to count ourselves among that class of the community which has ever been the source of manners, of population and of wealth. If we seek for fortune in that track which you have left most open to us, we shall increase your commercial importance.[2] If, in short, we render ourselves worthy of respect, you cannot hinder us from being respected—you cannot help respecting us—and in spite of all names of opprobrious separation, we shall be bound together by mutual esteem and the mutual reciprocation of good offices.

One good office we shall most probably do you is rather an invidious one, and seldom meets with thanks. By laying us under such a marked disqualification, you have rendered us— we hope not uncandid—we hope not disaffected—May the God of love and charity preserve us from all such acrimonious dispositions! But you certainly have, as far as in you lies, rendered us quick sighted to encroachment and abuses of all kinds. We have the feelings of men; and though we should be very blameable to suffer ourselves to be biassed by any private hardships, and hope that, as a body, we never shall, yet this you will consider, that we have at least no bias on the other side. We have no favours to blind us, no golden padlock on our tongues, and therefore it is probable enough, that, if cause is given, we shall cry aloud and spare not.[3] But in this you have done yourselves no disservice. It is perfectly agreeable to the jealous spirit of a free constitution that there should be some who will season the mass with the wholesome spirit of opposition. Without a little of that bitter leaven there is great danger of its being corrupted.

With regard to ourselves, you have by your late determination given perhaps a salutary, perhaps a seasonable check to that

---

1  A reference to Joseph Priestley, whose scientific work was by now internationally known.
2  The contributions of Dissenters to the British economy were emphasized also by Henry Beaufoy in the 1787 debate (*Substance of the Speech*, p. 11).
3  Isaiah 58:1.

spirit of worldliness, which of late has gained but too much ground amongst us. Before you—before the world—we have a right to bear the brow erect, to talk of rights and services; but there is a place and a presence where it will become us to make no boast. We, as well as you, are infected. We, as well as you, have breathed in the universal contagion—a contagion more noxious, and more difficult to escape, than that which on the plains of Cherson has just swept from the world the martyr of humanity.[1] The contagion of selfish indifference, and fashionable manners has seized us: and our languishing virtue feels the debilitating influence.—If you were more conversant in our assemblies than your prejudices will permit you to be, you would see indifference, where you fancy there is an over proportion of zeal: you would see principles giving way, and families melting into the bosom of the church under the warm influence of prosperity. You would see that establishments, without calling coercive measures to their aid, possess attraction enough severely to try the virtue and steadiness of those who separate from them. You need not strew thorns, or put bars across our path; your golden apples are sufficient to make us turn out of the way.[2] Believe me, Gentlemen, you do not *know* us sufficiently to aim your censure where we should be most vulnerable.

Nor need you apprehend from us the slightest danger to your own establishment. If you will needs have it that it *is* in danger, we wish you to be aware that the danger arises from among yourselves. If ever your creeds and formularies become as grievous to the generality of your Clergy as they already are to many delicate and thinking minds amongst them:[3] if ever any material articles of your professed belief should be generally

---

1   John Howard, philanthropist, who died in the Crimea doing hospital work during the Russian-Turkish War. His death was announced by one of the speakers during the 1790 debate.

2   In Ovid's *Metamorphoses*, Book X, Hippomenes beats Atalanta in a foot race by dropping golden apples in her way; she falls behind him when she stops to gather them.

3   Conspicuous among "delicate and thinking minds" was the Rev. Theophilus Lindsey, whose doctrinal doubts caused him to leave the Church of England. In 1773 a clergyman tried to comfort the doubts of young Gilbert Wakefield in these terms: "You have doubts on the subject of our Articles, and where is the Man who has

disbelieved, or that order which has been accustomed to supply faithful pastors and learned enquirers after truth should become a burden upon a generous public, and if her dignities and emoluments, instead of being graced by merit or genius, and thus in some measure balancing the weight of hereditary honour and influence, should be considered as appendages to them,[1] the cry for reformation would then be loud and prevailing. It *would* be heard. Doctrines which will not stand the test of argument and reason will not always be believed, and when they have ceased to be generally believed they will not long be articles of belief. If therefore there is any weak place in your system, any thing which you are obliged to gloss over, and touch with a tender hand, any thing which shrinks at investigation—Look ye to it, its extinction is not far off. Doubts and difficulties, that arise first among the learned, will not stop there; they inevitably spread downwards from class to class; and if the people should ever find that your articles are generally subscribed as articles of peace, they will be apt to remember that they articles of expence too.[2] If all the Dissenters in the kingdom, still believing as Dissenters do, were this moment, in order to avoid the reproach of schism, to enter the pale of your church, they would do you mischief; they would hasten its decline; and if all who in their hearts dissent from your professions of faith were to cease making them, and throw themselves amongst the Dissenters, you would stand the firmer for it. Your church is in no danger because we are of a different church; they might stand together to the end of time without interference; but it will be in great danger whenever it has within itself many who have thrown aside its doctrines, or even, who do not embrace them in the simple and obvious sense.[3] All the power and policy of

---

not; … the only difference between us is that you suppose no man in such circumstances can conscientiously subscribe to articles which he does not believe…. [I]t is certainly the case that they are, and must be subscribed in different senses by different Men" (Bennet, Letter). Wakefield left the Church.

1    and if her dignities … to them: added in ed. 2. Barbauld alludes to the practice of rich bishoprics being reserved for sons of aristocratic families.

2    The Church was supported in part by tithes (taxes) paid by the public—including Dissenters.

3    See p. 274, n. 3; the clergyman there quoted encourages sophisticated "relativist" interpretation of the Articles to fit each person's ideas.

man cannot continue a system *long* after its truth has ceased to be acknowledged, or an establishment *long* after it has ceased to contribute to utility.[1] It is equally vain, as to expect to preserve a tree, whose roots are cut away. It may look as green and flourishing as before for a short time, but its sentence is passed, its principle of life is gone, and death is already within it. If then you think the church in danger, be not backward to preserve the sound part by sacrificing the decayed.

To return to ourselves, and our feelings on the business lately in agitation—You will excuse us if we do not appear with the air of men baffled and disappointed. Neither do we blush at our defeat; we may blush, indeed, but it is for our country; but we lay hold on the consoling persuasion, that reason, truth and liberality must finally prevail.[2] We appeal from Philip intoxicated to Philip sober.[3] We know you will refuse us while you are narrow minded, but you will not always be narrow minded. You have too much light and candour not to have more. We will no more attempt to pluck the green unripe fruit. We see in you our future friends and brethren, eager to confound and blend with ours your interests and your affections. You will grant us all we ask. The only question between us is, whether you will do it to-day—To-morrow you certainly will. You will even intreat us, if need were, to allow you to remove from your country the stigma of illiberality. We appeal to the certain, sure operation of increasing light and knowledge, which it is no more in your power to stop, than to repel the tide with your naked hand, or to wither with your breath the genial influence of vegetation. The spread of that light is in general gradual and imperceptible; but there are periods when its progress is accelerated, when it seems with a sudden flash to open the firma-

---

1   Probably in the sense used by Francis Hutcheson, "the common good" of society (*Short Introduction to Moral Philosophy*, p. 120).

2   Barbauld's optimism agrees with Joseph Priestley's, almost in the same words: "The voice of *reason*, of *truth*, and of *right*, is sure to be heard, and to prevail in the end; and though prejudice, with which we have to contend, may overbear it, it can only be for a time" (*The Conduct to be observed by Dissenters*, p. 10).

3   Barbauld alludes to a story told by Roman historian Valerius Maximus (1st cent. AD): Philip, king of Macedon, when drunk unjustly sentenced a woman to punishment; she declared she would appeal to him when sober.

ment, and pour in day at once. Can ye not discern the signs of the times?[1] The minds of men are in movement from the Borysthenes to the Atlantic. Agitated with new and strong emotions, they swell and heave beneath oppression, as the seas within the Polar Circle, when, at the approach of Spring, they grow impatient to burst their icy chains; when what, but an instant before, seemed so firm, spread for many a dreary league like a floor of solid marble, at once with a tremendous noise gives way, long fissures spread in every direction, and the air resounds with the clash of floating fragments, which every hour are broken from the mass.[2] The genius of Philosophy is walking abroad, and with the touch of Ithuriel's spear is trying the establishments of the earth.[3] The various forms of Prejudice, Superstition and Servility start up in their true shapes, which had long imposed upon the world under the revered semblances of Honour, Faith, and Loyalty. Whatever is loose must be shaken, whatever is corrupted must be lopt away; whatever is not built on the broad basis of public utility must be thrown to the ground. Obscure murmurs gather, and swell into a tempest; the spirit of Enquiry, like a severe and searching wind, penetrates every part of the great body politic; and whatever is unsound, whatever is infirm, shrinks at the visitation.[4] Liberty, here with the lifted crosier in her hand, and the

---

1 Matthew 16:3. *Borysthenes* (below): classical name for the river Dnieper in Russia (an allusion to the government of empress Catherine the Great, perceived in the west as enlightened).

2 Barbauld remembers a description of the spring breakup of the ice on the St. Lawrence River in Frances Brooke's novel, *The History of Emily Montague* (1765), Letter 131. The passage deeply impressed her: She quotes it in her preface to Brooke in *British Novelists*, and again in *The Female Speaker* (1811), in the section of "Descriptive and Pathetic" pieces. In his *Reflections* (1790) Edmund Burke appears to respond to Barbauld's trope when he writes, "Many parts of Europe are in open disorder. In many others there is a hollow murmuring under ground; a confused movement is felt, that threatens a general earthquake in the political world" (pp. 191–92).

3 In *Paradise Lost*, 4:810–14, the angel Ithuriel discovers Satan in the shape of a toad: "Him ... *Ithuriel* with his Spear / Touch'd lightly; for no falshood can endure / Touch of Celestial temper, but returns / Of force to its own likeness" (Milton, *Complete Poetry*, p. 337).

4 Likewise the author of *The Right of Protestant Dissenters*: "for, whenever the spirit of inquiry goes forth, all ... usurpations are in danger" (p. 85).

crucifix conspicuous on her breast; there led by Philosophy, and crowned with the civic wreath, animates men to assert their long forgotten rights. With a policy, far more liberal and comprehensive than the boasted establishments of Greece and Rome, she diffuses her blessings to every class of men; and even extends a smile of hope and promise to the poor African, the victim of hard, impenetrable avarice.[1] Man, *as* man, becomes an object of respect. Tenets are transferred from theory to practice. The glowing sentiment and the lofty speculation no longer serve "but to adorn the pages of a book;"[2] they are brought home to men's business and bosoms; and, what some centuries ago it was daring but to think, and dangerous to express, is now realized, and carried into effect. Systems are analysed into their first principles, and principles are fairly pursued to their legitimate consequences. The enemies of reformation, who palliate what they cannot defend, and defer what they dare not refuse; who, with Festus,[3] put off to a more convenient season what, only because it is the present season is inconvenient, stand aghast; and find they have no power to put back the important hour, when nature is labouring with the birth of great events. Can ye not discern—But you do discern these signs; you discern them well, and your alarm is apparent.[4] You see a mighty empire breaking from bondage, and exerting the energies of recovered freedom: and England—which was used to glory in being the assertor of liberty, and refuge of the oppressed— England, who with generous and respectful sympathy, in times

---

1  Barbauld alludes to the movement to abolish the British slave trade. Liberty today is more liberal than the "boasted" democracies of Greece and Rome because they did not imagine extending freedom to slaves.

2  Perhaps a misquotation from Samuel Johnson's *The Vanity of Human Wishes* (1749), line 222 ("to point a moral, or adorn a tale"). Barbauld's next phrase, "brought home ... bosoms," quotes the "Dedication" to Francis Bacon's *Essays* (1625).

3  Actually Felix, Roman governor of Palestine who delayed releasing the apostle Paul (Acts 24:22–25).

4  From this point on, Barbauld responds to Edmund Burke's speech on the Army budget, 5 Feb. 1790 (see Appendix B.2). England was compared unfavorably to France by Priestley as well: "Is it to be believed that all remains of persecution shall now be banished from France, and continue much longer in England? ... [A]s we formerly took the lead in this respect, and set an example to others, it cannot surely be long before we follow the example they are now setting us" (*The Conduct to be observed by Dissenters*, pp. 12–13).

not far remote from our own memory, has afforded an asylum to so many of the subjects of that very empire, when crushed beneath the iron rod of persecution;[1] and, by so doing, circulated a livelier abhorrence of tyranny within her own veins— England, who has long reproached her with being a slave, now censures her for daring to be free. England, who has held the torch to her, is mortified to see it blaze brighter in her hands. England, for whom, and for whose manners and habits of thinking, that empire has, for some time past, felt even an enthusiastic predilection; and to whom, as a model of laws and government, she looks up with affectionate reverence— England, nursed at the breast of liberty, and breathing the purest spirit of enlightened philosophy, views a sister nation with affected scorn and real jealousy, and presumes to ask whether she yet exists—Yes, all of her exists that is worthy to do so. Her dungeons indeed exist no longer, the iron doors are forced, the massy walls are thrown down; and the liberated spectres, trembling between joy and horror, may now blazon the infernal secrets of their prison house.[2] Her cloistered Monks no longer exist, nor does the soft heart of sensibility beat behind the grate of a convent, but the best affections of the human mind permitted to flow in their natural channel, diffuse their friendly influence over the brightening prospect of domestic happiness. Nobles, the creatures of Kings, exist there no longer;[3] but Man, the creature of God, exists there. Millions of men exist there who, only now, truly begin to exist, and hail with shouts of grateful acclamation the better birth-day of their country. Go on, generous nation, set the world an example of virtues as you have of talents. Be our model, as we have been yours. May the spirit of wisdom, the spirit of moderation, the spirit of firm-

---

1   After the repeal of Protestant toleration in France (1685), French Protestants sought refuge abroad. Among those who settled in England were Rochemont Barbauld's ancestors.

2   The Bastille, captured and destroyed by the people of Paris, 14 July 1789. In the next sentence Barbauld refers to the abolition of cloistered religious orders by the National Assembly (13 Feb. 1790), which freed monks and nuns from vows of celibacy.

3   Titles of nobility were not abolished in France until June 1790, but decrees in August 1789 and February 1790 suppressed feudal privileges and tenures.

ness, guide and bless your counsels. With intelligence to discern the best possible, may you have prudence to be content with the best practicable.[1] Overcome our wayward perverseness by your steadiness and temper. Silence the scoff of your enemies, and the misgiving fears of your timorous well-wishers. Go on to destroy the empire of prejudices, that empire of gigantic shadows, which are only formidable while they are not attacked. Cause to succeed to the mad ambition of conquest the pacific industry of commerce, and the simple, useful toils of agriculture. While your corn springs up under the shade of your Olives, may bread and peace be the portion of the Husbandman; and when beneath your ardent sun, his brow is bathed in honest sweat, let no one dare any longer with hard and vexatious exactions to wring from him the bitter drop of anguish.[2] Instructed by the experience of past centuries, and by many a sad and sanguine page in your own histories, may you no more attempt to blend what God has made separate; but may religion and civil polity, like the two necessary but opposite elements of fire and water, each in its province do service to mankind, but never again be forced into discordant union. Let the wandering pilgrims of every tribe and complexion, who in other lands find only an asylum, find with you a country, and may you never seek other proof of the purity of your faith than the largeness of your charity. In your manners, your language, and habits of life, let a manly simplicity, becoming the intercourse of equals with equals, take the place of overstrained refinement and adulation.[3] Let public reformation prepare the way for private. May the abolition of domestic tyranny introduce the modest train of houshold virtues, and purer incense be burned upon the hallowed altar of conjugal fidelity.[4] Exhibit to the world the rare phenomenon of a patriot minister, of a philosophic senate. May a pure and perfect system of legislation proceed from their forming hands, free from those irregularities

---

1  With intelligence ... practicable: added in ed. 2.
2  While your corn ... anguish: added in ed. 2. "Hard and vexatious exactions" refers to a variety of taxes on peasants and farmers.
3  The French revolutionary term of address, "Citizen," replaced previous titles.
4  The laws governing marriage in France were not rewritten until 1792.

and abuses, the wear and tear of a constitution, which in a course of years are necessarily accumulated in the best formed States; and like the new creation in its first gloss and freshness, yet free from any taint of corruption, when its Maker blest and called it good.[1] May you never lose sight of the great principle you have held forth, the natural equality of men.[2] May you never forget that without public spirit there can be no liberty; that without virtue there may be a confederacy, but cannot be a community. May you, and may we, consigning to oblivion every less generous competition, only contest who shall set the brightest example to the nations, and may its healing influence be diffused, till the reign of Peace shall spread

————from shore to shore,
'Till *Wars* shall cease, and *Slavery* be no more.[3]

Amidst causes of such mighty operation, what are we, and what are our petty, peculiar interests! Triumph, or despondency, at the success or failure of our plans, would be treason to the large, expanded, comprehensive wish which embraces the general interests of humanity. Here then we fix our foot with undoubting confidence, sure that all events are in the hands of him, who from seeming evil

———— is still educing good;
And better thence again, and better still,
In infinite progression.[4]

In this hope we look forward to the period when the name of *Dissenter* shall no more be heard of, than that of *Romanist* or *Episcopalian*, when nothing shall be venerable but truth, and nothing valued but utility.

*March* 3, 1790.                    A DISSENTER.

---

1  Barbauld alludes to the creation story in Genesis 1.
2  Article I of the "Declaration of the Rights of Man and of Citizens" (1789) reads, "Men are born, and always continue, free, and equal in respect of their rights."
3  Pope, *Windsor Forest* (1713), ll. 407-08, slightly misquoted.
4  James Thomson, "A Hymn on the Seasons" (1746), ll. 114-16.

# FASHION, A VISION

[*"*The following letter was sent to a young lady, five or six years ago. If it will contribute to entertain the readers of your Magazine, it is much at your service." Barbauld thus introduced "Fashion" when she published it, unsigned, in *The Monthly Magazine* 3 (April 1797):254-56. The young lady for whom she wrote it was a pupil, Flora Wynch; and, as her opening paragraph makes clear, Barbauld considered it pertinent to the questions of human liberty that writers like Tom Paine and Mary Wollstonecraft were addressing in 1792. Connections between Revolutionary politics and women's dress were noted at the time (often, by conservatives, with horror); but Barbauld's niece Lucy Aikin, looking back from 1842, perceived their connection as good for women: "Down to ... fifty years ago, our ladies, tight-laced and 'propped on French heels,' had a short mincing step, pinched figures, pale faces, weak nerves, much affectation, a delicate helplessness, and miserable health.... Then came that event which is the beginning or end of everything—the French Revolution. The Parisian women ... emancipated themselves from their stays, and kicked off their *petits talons*. We followed the example.... We have now well-developed figures, blooming cheeks, active habits, firm nerves, natural and easy manners, a scorn of affectation, and vigorous constitutions" (*Memoirs, Miscellanies, and Letters*, p. 435).

Our text adopts a few of the corrections, but none of the changes in paragraphing, introduced when the piece was reprinted in *A Legacy for Young Ladies* (1826).]

Young as you are, my dear Flora, you cannot but have noticed the eagerness with which questions, relative to civil liberty, have been discussed in every society. To break the shackles of oppression, and assert the native rights of man, is esteemed by many, among the noblest efforts of heroic virtue; but vain is the possession of political liberty, if there exists a tyrant of our own creation; who, without law, or reason, or even external force, exercises over us the most despotic authority; whose jurisdiction is extended over every part of private and domestic life;

controuls our pleasures, fashions our garb, cramps our motions, fills our lives with vain cares and restless anxiety. The worst slavery is that which we voluntarily impose upon ourselves; and no chains are so cumbrous and galling, as those which we are pleased to wear by way of grace and ornament.—Musing upon this idea, gave rise to the following dream or vision:

Methought I was in a country, of the strangest and most singular appearance I had ever beheld: the rivers were forced into jet d'eaus,[1] and wasted in artificial water-works; the lakes were fashioned by the hand of art; the roads were sanded with spar and gold-dust; the trees all bore the marks of the shears, they were bent and twisted into the most whimsical forms, and connected together by festoons of ribband and silk fringe; the wild flowers were transplanted into vases of fine china, and painted with artificial white and red.—The disposition of the ground was full of fancy, but grotesque and unnatural, in the highest degree; it was all highly cultivated, and bore the marks of wonderful industry; but among its various productions, I could hardly discern one that was of any use. My attention, however, was soon called off from the scenes of inanimate life, by the view of the inhabitants, whose form and appearance was so very preposterous, and, indeed, so unlike any thing human, that I fancied myself transported to the country of the Anthropophagi, and men whose heads

——do grow beneath their shoulders:[2]

for the heads of many of these people were swelled to an astonishing size, and seemed to be placed in the middle of their bodies; of some, the ears were distended, till they hung upon the shoulders; and of others, the shoulders were raised, till they met the ears: there was not one free from some deformity, or monstrous swelling, in one part or other—either it was before, or behind, or about the hips, or the arms were puffed up to an unusual thickness, or the throat was increased to the same size with the poor objects lately exhibited under the name of the

---

1   Ornamental fountains.
2   *Othello*, I.iii.144.

Monstrous Craws;[1] some had no necks—others had necks that reached almost to their waists; the bodies of some were bloated up to such a size, that they could scarcely enter a pair of folding doors; and others had suddenly sprouted up to such a disproportionate height, that they could not sit upright in their loftiest carriages.[2]—Many shocked me with the appearance of being nearly cut in two, like a wasp; and I was alarmed at the sight of a few, in whose faces, otherwise very fair and healthy, I discovered an eruption of black spots,[3] which I feared was the fatal sign of some pestilential disorder. The sight of these various and uncouth deformities inspired me with much pity; which, however, was soon changed into disgust, when I perceived, with great surprize, that every one of these unfortunate men and women was exceedingly proud of his own peculiar deformity, and endeavoured to attract my notice to it as much as possible. A lady, in particular, who had a swelling under her throat, larger than any goitre in the Valais,[4] and which, I am sure, by its enormous projection, prevented her from seeing the path she walked in, brushed by me, with an air of the greatest self-complacency, and asked me, if she was not a charming creature?—But, by this time, I found myself surrounded by an immense crowd, who were all pressing along in one direction; and I perceived that I was drawn along with them, by an irresistible impulse, which grew stronger every moment: I asked, whither we were hurrying, with such eager steps? and was told, that we were going to the court of the Queen FASHION, the great Diana, whom all the world worshippeth.[5] I would have retired, but felt myself impelled to go on, though without being

---

1 The "Monstrous Craws" would have been an exhibit of people suffering from goitres (enlargements of the thyroid gland), but we have not traced it. Barbauld's comparison probably alludes to the starched ruffled collars worn in Queen Elizabeth's time.

2 "The head-dresses of the ladies, during my youth, were of a truly preposterous size. I have gone … in a coach with a lady who was obliged to sit upon a stool placed in the bottom of the coach, the height of her head-dress not allowing her to occupy the regular seat" (Rogers, *Table-Talk*, p. 12).

3 Beauty patches, fashionable in the late seventeenth century.

4 A poor district in Switzerland, many of whose inhabitants suffered from goitres.

5 Acts 19:27, in which silversmiths who profit from making shrines for the goddess Diana raise an uproar against the apostle Paul for endangering their trade.

sensible of any outward force.—When I came to the royal presence, I was astonished at the magnificence I saw around me! The queen was sitting on a throne, elegantly fashioned, in the form of a shell, and inlaid with gems and mother-of-pearl. It was supported by a cameleon, formed of a single emerald. She was dressed in a light robe of changeable silk, which fluttered about her in a profusion of fantastic folds, that imitated the form of clouds, and like them, were continually changing their appearance. In one hand, she held a rouge-box, and in the other, one of those optical glasses, which distort figures in length or in breadth, according to the position in which they are held. At the foot of the throne was displayed a profusion of the richest productions of every quarter of the globe—tributes from land and sea—from every animal, and plant[1] —perfumes, sparkling stones, drops of pearl, chains of gold, webs of the finest linen, wreaths of flowers, the produce of art, which vied with the most delicate productions of nature—forests of feathers, waving their brilliant colours in the air, and canopying the throne;—glossy silks, net-work of lace, silvery ermine, soft folds of vegetable wool, rustling paper, and shining spangles; the whole intermixed with pendants and streamers, of the gayest tinctured ribbon. All these, together, made so brilliant an appearance, that my eyes were at first dazzled; and it was some time before I recovered myself enough to observe the ceremonial of the court. Near the throne, and its chief supports, stood the queen's two prime ministers, CAPRICE on the one side, and VANITY on the other. Two officers seemed chiefly busy among the attendants. One of them was a man, with a pair of shears in his hand, and a goose by his side, a mysterious emblem, of which I could not fathom the meaning:[2] he sat cross-legged, like the great Lama of the Tartars;[3]—he was busily employed in cutting out coats and garments, not, however, like Dorcas, for

---

1    Reminiscent of Belinda's dressing-table in Pope's *The Rape of the Lock* (1714), Canto 1.

2    A glance at the tailor who is represented as an "idol" in Jonathan Swift's *Tale of a Tub* (1704): "This God had a *Goose* for his Ensign" (*Writings*, p. 303). A tailor's "goose" is an iron.

3    The Dali Lama, spiritual head of Tibetan Buddhism. Dorcas (below): A Christian woman who made clothing for the poor. Cf. Acts 9:39.

the poor—nor, indeed, did they seem intended for any mortal whatever, so ill were they adapted to the shape of the human body; some of the garments were extravagantly large, others as preposterously small; of others, it was difficult to guess to what part of the person they were meant to be applied. Here were coverings, which did not cover—ornaments, which disfigured—and defences against the weather, more slight and delicate than what they were meant to defend; but all were eagerly caught up, without distinction, by the crowd of votaries who were waiting to receive them. The other officer was dressed in a white succinct[1] linen garment, like a priest of the lower order. He moved in a cloud of incense, more highly scented than the breezes of Arabia; he carried a tuft of the whitest down of the swan in one hand, and in the other, a small iron instrument,[2] heated red-hot, which he brandished in the air. It was with infinite concern, I beheld the Graces bound at the foot of the throne, and obliged to officiate, as handmaids, under the direction of these two officers. I now began to enquire, by what laws this queen governed her subjects, but soon found her administration was that of the most arbitrary tyrant ever known. Her laws are exactly the reverse of those of the Medes and Persians;[3] for they are changed every day, and every hour; and what makes the matter still more perplexing, they are in no written code, nor even made public by proclamation; they are only promulgated by whispers, an obscure sign, or turn of the eye, which those only, who have the happiness to stand near the queen, can catch with any degree of precision: yet the smallest transgression of the laws is severely punished, not indeed by fines or imprisonment, but by a sort of interdict similar to that which, in superstitious times, was laid by the Pope on disobedient princes, and which operated in such a manner, that no one would eat, drink, or associate with the forlorn culprit; and he was almost deprived of the use of fire and water. This difficulty of discovering the will of the goddess occasioned so much

---

1 Close-fitting.
2 A curling-iron.
3 Daniel 6:12 ("according to the law of the Medes and Persians, which altereth not").

crowding to be near the throne, such jostling and elbowing one another, that I was glad to retire, and observe what I could among the scattered crowd: and the first thing I took notice of, was various instruments of torture which every where met my eyes. Torture has, in most other governments of Europe, been abolished by the mild spirit of the times;[1] but it reigns here in full force and terror. I saw officers of this cruel court employed in boring holes, with red-hot wires, in the ears, nose, and various parts of the body, and then distending them with the weight of metal chains, or stones, cut into a variety of shapes; some had invented a contrivance for cramping the feet in such a manner, that many are lamed by it for their whole lives. Others I saw, slender and delicate in their form, and naturally nimble as the young antelope, who were obliged to carry constantly about with them a cumbrous unwieldy machine, of a pyramidal form, several ells[2] in circumference. But the most common, and one of the worst instruments of torture, was a small machine, armed with fish-bone and ribs of steel, wide at top, but extremely small at bottom.[3] In this detestable invention, the queen orders the bodies of her female subjects to be inclosed: it is then, by means of silk cords, drawn closer and closer, at intervals, till the unhappy victim can scarcely breathe; and they have found the exact point that can be borne without fainting, which, however, not unfrequently happens. The flesh is often excoriated, and the very ribs bent, by this cruel process; yet, what astonished me more than all the rest, these sufferings are borne with a degree of fortitude, which, in a better cause, would immortalize a hero, or canonize a saint. The Spartan who suffered the fox to eat into his vitals, did not bear pain with greater resolution:[4] and as the Spartan mothers brought

---

1   Torture was abolished by law in France in 1789, in Tuscany in 1786, in Austria in 1776, and in the Netherlands in 1787.

2   An *ell* was a unit of measure equal to 45 inches. Elsewhere Barbauld notices "a very humorous account" of the hoop petticoat in Sir Richard Steele's *Tatler* ("Comparison of Manners," p. 2).

3   The corset.

4   Plutarch's life of Lycurgus includes the story of the Spartan youth who stole a fox and suffered as Barbauld describes rather than reveal his crime. The same paragraph in Plutarch refers (more elliptically) to the Lacedemonian custom of scourging in the temple of Diana to which Barbauld alludes below.

their children to be scourged at the altar of Diana, so do the mothers here bring their children,—and chiefly those whose tender sex, one would suppose, excused them from such exertions,—and early inure them to this cruel discipline. But neither Spartan, nor Dervise, nor Bonze, nor Carthusian monk,[1] ever exercised more unrelenting severities over their bodies, than these young zealots; indeed the first lesson they are taught, is a surrender of their own inclinations, and an implicit obedience to the commands of the goddess; but they have, besides a more solemn kind of dedication, something similar to the rite of confirmation. When a young woman approaches the marriageable age, she is led to the altar: her hair, which before fell loosely about her shoulders, is tied up in a tress, sweet oils, drawn from roses and spices, are poured upon it, she is involved in a cloud of scented dust, and invested with ornaments under which she can scarcely move. After this solemn ceremony, which is generally concluded by a dance round the altar, the damsel is obliged to a still stricter conformity than before to the laws and customs of the court, and any deviation from them is severely punished. The courtiers of Alexander, it is said, flattered him by carrying their heads on one side, because he had the misfortune to have a wry neck,[2] but all adulation is poor, compared to what is practised in this court. Sometimes the queen will lisp and stammer, and then none of her attendants can speak plain; sometimes she chooses to totter as she walks, and then they are seized with sudden lameness; accordingly as she appears half undressed, or veiled from head to foot, her subjects become a procession of nuns, or a troop of Bacchanalian nymphs[3]—I could not help observing, however, that those who stood at the greatest distance from the throne, were the most extravagant in their imitation. I was, by this time, thoroughly disgusted with the character of a sovereign, at once so light and so cruel, so fickle and so arbitrary, when one who stood next

---

1  A Dervish is a member of a Muslim religious order noted for its devotional discipline; a Bonze, a Buddhist monk; a Carthusian, a member of an austere Christian monastic order.

2  Alexander the Great (356-23 BC) is said to have had a malformed neck.

3  Female devotees of the god Bacchus, who held orgies half naked.

me, bade me attend to still greater contradictions in her charac-
ter, and such as might serve to soften the indignation I had
conceived: He took me to the back of the throne, and made me
take notice of a number of industrious poor, to whom the
queen was secretly distributing bread.[1] I saw the Genius of
Commerce doing her homage, and discovered the British cross
woven into the insignia of her dignity. While I was musing on
these things, a murmur arose among the crowd, and I was told
that a young votary was approaching; I turned my head, and
saw a light figure, the folds of whose garment showed the ele-
gant turn of the limbs they covered, tripping along with the
step of a nymph. I soon knew it to be yourself—I saw you led
up to the altar—I saw your beautiful hair tied in artificial tress-
es, and its bright gloss stained with coloured dust—I even fan-
cied I beheld produced the dreadful instruments of torture—
my emotions increased—I cried out, "Oh, spare her! spare my
Flora!" with so much vehemence, that I awaked.

---

1   Like the fashionable ladies who hold a charity sale in Barbauld's poem "West End
    Fair." Below, Commerce pays homage to Fashion because Fashion is a strong
    motive to trade; in this context, "the British cross" suggests the British Empire and
    its world-wide economic network.

[In 1792 Barbauld's brother, John Aikin, inspired by a recent French work, *Les Veillées du Chateau* ("Evenings at the Castle," 1784), a collection of stories and dialogues for children by Caroline-Stéphanie-Félicité de Genlis, gathered pieces he had written over the years for his own children into what became a six-volume collection, *Evenings at Home* (1792-96). Barbauld contributed 14 of its 99 pieces (Lucy Aikin, "Memoir," p. xxxvi n.). Some, such as "Things by their Right Names," she had probably written for her nephew and foster son, Charles; others were probably composed for pupils at Palgrave School. At least one, "The Four Sisters," was sent directly to John Aikin, probably for his children's amusement but also for his own.

Evenings was an immediate success, enjoying thirteen editions in Barbauld's lifetime and remaining more or less continually in print until the early twentieth century. Educational progressives such as Maria Edgeworth and her father admired it and learned from it; educational conservatives such as Sarah Trimmer, who monitored children's books for *The Guardian of Education*, thought it insufficiently Christian if not actually subversive of the Bible. Liberal politics were indeed integral to *Evenings*, and Lucy Aikin characterized it well: "the morality which [the pieces] inculcate is not that of children merely, but of men and of citizens; ... it engages the youthful feelings in the cause of truth, of freedom, and of virtue" (*Memoir of Dr. John Aikin*, 1:159). We draw our texts from the first editions: 1:18-20 ("The Young Mouse") and 150-52 ("Things by their Right Names"), and 6:30-38 ("The Four Sisters")]

*The Young Mouse*
*A Fable*

A young Mouse lived in a cupboard where sweetmeats were kept; she dined every day upon biscuit, marmalade, or fine sugar. Never any little Mouse had lived so well. She had often ventured to peep at the family while they sat at supper; nay, she had sometimes stole down on the carpet, and picked up the crumbs, and nobody had ever hurt her. She would have been quite happy, but that she was sometimes frightened by the cat, and then she ran trembling to her hole behind the wainscot. One day she came running to her mother in great joy; Mother! said she, the good people of this family have built me a house to live in; it is in the cupboard: I am sure it is for me, for it is just big enough: the bottom is of wood, and it is covered all over with wires; and I dare say they have made it on purpose to screen me from that terrible cat, which ran after me so often: there is an entrance just big enough for me, but puss cannot follow; and they have been so good as to put in some toasted cheese, which smells so deliciously, that I should have run in directly and taken possession of my new house, but I thought I would tell you first, that we might go in together, and both lodge there to-night, for it will hold us both.

My dear child, said the old Mouse, it is most happy that you did not go in, for this house is called a trap, and you would never have come out again, except to have been devoured, or put to death in some way or other. Though man has not so fierce a look as a cat, he is as much our enemy, and has still more cunning.

### Things by their Right Names

*Charles.* Papa, you grow very lazy. Last winter you used to tell us stories, and now you never tell us any; and we are all got round the fire quite ready to hear you. Pray, dear papa, let us have a very pretty one?

*Father.* With all my heart—What shall it be?

*C.* A bloody murder, papa!

*F.* A bloody murder! Well then—Once upon a time, some men, dressed all alike ....

*C.* With black crapes over their faces.

*F.* No; they had steel caps on:—having crossed a dark heath, wound cautiously along the skirts of a deep forest ...

*C.* They were ill-looking fellows, I dare say.

*F.* I cannot say so; on the contrary, they were tall personable men as most one shall see:—leaving on their right hand an old ruined tower on the hill …

*C.* At midnight, just as the clock struck twelve; was it not, papa?

*F.* No, really; it was on a fine balmy summer's morning:—and moved forwards, one behind another ….

*C.* As still as death, creeping along under the hedges.

*F.* On the contrary—they walked remarkably upright; and so far from endeavouring to be hushed and still, they made a loud noise as they came along, with several sorts of instruments.

*C.* But, papa, they would be found out immediately.

*F.* They did not seem to wish to conceal themselves: on the contrary, they gloried in what they were about.—They moved forwards, I say, to a large plain, where stood a neat pretty village, which they set on fire ….

*C.* Set a village on fire? wicked wretches!

*F.* And while it was burning, they murdered—twenty thousand men.

*C.* O fie! papa! You do not intend I should believe this! I thought all along you were making up a tale, as you often do; but you shall not catch me this time. What! they lay still, I suppose, and let these fellows cut their throats!

*F.* No, truly—they resisted as long as they could.

*C.* How should these men kill twenty thousand people, pray?

*F.* Why not? the *murderers* were thirty thousand.

*C.* O, now I have found you out! You mean a BATTLE.

*F.* Indeed I do. I do not know of any *murders* half so bloody.[1]

---

1   This story incurred strong censure from Sarah Trimmer in *The Guardian of Educa-tion*:"Evidently designed to impress children with the idea that all *warriors* are *mur-derers*. But to call a battle 'a *bloody murder*,' when the cause on one side or other is justifiable, is *not* 'calling things by their *right names*;' if it were, then the people of Israel, when they went against the idolatrous nations to extirpate them from the earth, were *bloody murderers*, though they acted by the express command of the LORD GOD" (p. 308).

# The Four Sisters[1]

I am one of four Sisters; and having some reason to think myself not well used either by them or by the world, I beg leave to lay before you a sketch of our history and characters. You will not wonder there should be frequent bickerings amongst us, when I tell you that in our infancy we were continually fighting; and so great was the noise, and din, and confusion, in our continual struggles to get uppermost, that it was impossible for any body to live amongst us in such a scene of tumult and disorder—These brawls, however, by a powerful interposition, were put an end to;[2] our proper place was assigned to each of us, and we had strict orders not to encroach on the limits of each other's property, but to join our common offices for the good of the whole family.

My first sister, (I call her the first, because we have generally allowed her the precedence in rank,) is, I must acknowledge, of a very active sprightly disposition; quick and lively, and has more brilliancy than any of us: but she is hot: every thing serves for fuel to her fury when it is once raised to a certain degree, and she is so mischievous whenever she gets the upper hand, that, notwithstanding her aspiring disposition, if I may freely speak my mind, she is calculated to make a good servant, but a very bad mistress.

I am almost ashamed to mention, that notwithstanding her seeming delicacy, she has a most voracious appetite,[3] and devours every thing that comes in her way; though, like other eager thin people, she does no credit to her keeping. Many a time has she consumed the product of my barns and store-

---

1   Two manuscript copies of this piece exist: Liverpool Record Office MS 920 NIC 22/2/6 (by Matthew Nicholson, a graduate of Warrington Academy); and an unidentified copy in the Beinecke Library, Yale University. In both, the piece is titled "To Doctor Aikin." The piece is designed to be a riddle. We recommend reading it and trying to solve it before reading our notes to it.

2   Barbauld draws her description of the primal chaos from Ovid, *Metamorphoses*, 1:1–31. All the elements were originally "at odds, for ... cold things strove with hot, and moist with dry," until "God—or kindlier Nature—composed this strife" (Loeb translation).

3   Conduct books for women strongly discouraged appetite: "the luxury of eating ... in *your* sex ... is beyond expression indelicate and disgusting" (Gregory, *A Father's Legacy*, p. 28).

houses, but it is all lost upon her. She has even been known to get into an oil-shop or tallow-chandler's[1] when every body was asleep, and lick up with the utmost greediness whatever she found there. Indeed, all prudent people are aware of her tricks, and though she is admitted into the best families, they take care to watch her very narrowly. I should not forget to mention, that my sister was once in a country where she was treated with uncommon respect; she was lodged in a sumptuous building, and had a number of young women of the best families to attend on her, and feed her, and watch over her health: in short, she was looked upon as something more than a common mortal.[2] But she always behaved with great severity to her maids, and if any of them were negligent of their duty, or made a slip in their own conduct, nothing would serve her but burying the poor girls alive. I have myself had some dark hints and intimations from the most respectable authority, that she will some time or other make an end of me.[3] You need not wonder, therefore, if I am jealous of her motions.

The next sister I shall mention to you, has so far the appearance of Modesty and Humility, that she generally seeks the lowest place. She is indeed of a very yielding easy temper, generally cool, and often wears a sweet placid smile upon her countenance; but she is easily ruffled, and when worked up, as she often is, by another sister, whom I shall mention to you by and by, she becomes a perfect fury. Indeed she is so apt to swell with sudden gusts of passion, that she is suspected at times to be a little lunatic.[4] Between her and my first mentioned sister, there is a more settled antipathy than between the Theban pair;[5] and they never meet without making efforts to destroy

---

1    A tallow-chandler is a maker of cheap candles. Chandlers' shops were frequent sites of fires.

2    The Roman goddess Vesta, a fire deity, had a temple consecrated to her and was attended by young virgins selected for their purity of character. The punishment of misconduct by a Vestal virgin was, as Barbauld states below, to be buried alive.

3    Barbauld alludes to 2 Peter 3:7: "the heavens and the earth ... are ... reserved unto fire against the day of judgment."

4    Besides "insane," a second (now obsolete) meaning of lunatic is "influenced by the moon" (OED), as tides are.

5    The Theban pair are Polyneices and Eteocles, sons of Oedipus, king of Thebes, who contended bitterly with each other for the throne of Thebes.

one another. With me she is always ready to form the most intimate union, but it is not always to my advantage. There goes a story in our family, that when we were all young, she once attempted to drown me. She actually kept me under a considerable time, and though at length I got my head above water, my constitution is generally thought to have been essentially injured by it ever since.[1] From that time she has made no such atrocious attempt, but she is continually making encroachments upon my property; and even when she appears most gentle, she is very insidious, and has such an undermining way with her, that her insinuating arts are as much to be dreaded as open violence. I might indeed remonstrate, but it is a known part of her character, that nothing makes any lasting impression upon her.

As to my third sister, I have already mentioned the ill offices she does me with my last mentioned one, who is entirely under her influence. She is besides of a very uncertain variable temper, sometimes hot, and sometimes cold, nobody knows where to have her. Her lightness is even proverbial, and she has nothing to give those who live with her more substantial than the smiles of courtiers. I must add, that she keeps in her service three or four rough blustering bullies with puffed cheeks,[2] who, when they are let loose, think they have nothing to do but to drive the world before them. She sometimes joins with my first sister, and their violence occasionally throws me into such a trembling, that, though naturally of a firm constitution, I shake as if I was in an ague fit.[3]

As to myself, I am of a steady solid temper; not shining indeed, but kind and liberal, quite a Lady Bountiful. Every one tastes of my beneficence, and I am of so grateful a disposition, that I have been known to return an hundred-fold for any present that has been made me. I feed and clothe all my children, and afford a welcome home to the wretch who has no other

---

1  A reference to the Biblical Flood, perhaps by way of Thomas Burnet's interpretation in *The Theory of the Earth* (1691): "this unshapen Earth we now inhabit, is the Form it was found in when the Waters had retir'd … " (p. 13).

2  The bullies are the Four Winds (North, East, South, and West), often represented in the corners of maps as faces.

3  In ancient Greek science, earthquakes were believed to result from movements of hot subterranean winds.

home. I bear with unrepining patience all manner of ill usage; I am trampled upon, I am torn and wounded with the most cutting strokes; I am pillaged of the treasures hidden in my most secret chambers; notwithstanding which, I am always ready to return good for evil, and am continually subservient to the pleasure or advantage of others; yet, so ungrateful is the world, that because I do not possess all the airiness and activity of my sisters, I am stigmatised as dull and heavy. Every sordid miserly fellow is called by way of derision one of *my* children; and if a person on entering a room does but turn his eyes upon me, he is thought stupid and mean, and not fit for good company. I have the satisfaction, however, of finding that people always incline towards me as they grow older; and that those who seemed proudly to disdain any affinity with me, are content to sink at last into my bosom. You will probably wish to have some account of my person. I am not a regular beauty; some of my features are rather harsh and prominent, when viewed separately; but my countenance has so much variety of expression, and so many different attitudes of elegance, that those who study my face with attention, find out continually new charms; and it may be truly said of me, what Titus says of his mistress, and for a much longer space,

> Pendant cinq ans entiers tous les jours je la vois,
> Et crois toujours la voir pour la premiere fois.[1]

> For five whole years each day she meets my view,
> Yet every day I seem to see her new.

Though I have been so long a mother, I have still a surprising air of youth and freshness, which is assisted by all the advantages of well chosen ornament, for I dress well, and according to the season.

This is what I have chiefly to say of myself and my sisters. To a person of your sagacity it will be unnecessary for me to sign my name. Indeed, one who becomes acquainted with any one

---

1  Slightly misquoted from *Bérénice* (1670), II.ii, by Jean Racine.

of the family, cannot be at a loss to discover the rest, notwith-
standing the difference in our features and characters.[1]


## SINS OF GOVERNMENT, SINS OF THE NATION; OR, A DISCOURSE FOR THE FAST, APPOINTED ON APRIL 19, 1793. BY A VOLUNTEER.

[During 1792 the British government issued decrees against
reformers at home (a Royal Proclamation against Seditious
Writings and Publications, 21 May) and made hostile gestures
against the Revolutionary government of France (the recall of
the British ambassador in August, efforts to stop private ship-
ments of grain to France in the autumn). When war broke out
(February 1793), the British government resumed a customary
wartime practice, the appointment of a day for obligatory
"Public Fast and Humiliation" in all places of worship through-
out the kingdom. Its purpose was to implore divine aid in car-
rying on the war. (We print the text of the Fast Proclamation, 2
March, as Appendix C.) Many Dissenting ministers pondered
what to do: obey the order and violate their consciences by
praying for success in a war they disapproved? observe the Fast,
but preach against the war? defy the Proclamation and refuse to
take any part in the Fast?

In the opening paragraphs of her Fast "discourse" (a Dissent-
ing term for "sermon"), Barbauld brilliantly addresses this
moral problem by observing the Fast but interpreting it as an
admission by King George and his ministers that the people
themselves are responsible for the good or ill done by the

---

1  In place of this paragraph, the manuscript copies read: "Of you Sir I have no com-
plaints to make. I know that you are one of my most constant admirers, & have
even attempted to delineate some striking lines of my countenance,—But what
most attaches me to you is your having sent from time to time so many of your
friends to lodge with me;—for this mark of your kindness I am Sir with an affec-
tion truly maternal Yours &c." The Nicholson MS adds the signature, "A.L. Bar-
bauld." John Aikin had "delineated" some of Earth's features in *The Calendar of
Nature* (1785); Barbauld's joke that he "sent so many ... friends to lodge with me"
refers to Aikin's medical practice.

nation; she makes the Fast into a democratic occasion. A conservative journal, *The British Critic*, perceived what she was doing, and was outraged: to make the public in general responsible "for the public transactions of the nation," it fumed, was a doctrine "*perfectly French*…. Here we have *organ*, and *national will*, and all the jargon of French republicanism" (p. 81). The liberal *Analytical Review*, on its side, ranked *Sins of Government* "as a literary performance, … in the first order of merit; … with a most happy union of energy and moderation, it inculcates sentiments of political and moral wisdom of the highest importance to the peace and prosperity of this country" (p. 186). A historian of the British antiwar movement calls *Sins* "the most famous" of all anti-war sermons (Cookson, *Friends of Peace*, p. 119). As an exercise in what Edward Said has called "speaking truth to power" (*The Independent* [London], 22 July 1993); as a condemnation of "war itself, the very quintessence [in Paul Fussell's words] of immoral activity" (*Doing Battle*, p. 291); as an unmasking of the hypocrisy by which, as late as 1991, an American head of state could still declare a "national day of prayer" for victory in a war against a weaker nation; and—not least—as a statement of the ethical principles that ought to govern democratic citizenship, *Sins of Government* remains powerfully relevant today.

Like her *Address to the Opposers*, *Sins of Government* was probably the only intervention by a woman in its debate. Denied a regular, physical pulpit from which to preach, Barbauld published *Sins of Government* as "a Volunteer." Its publication was announced in *The London Chronicle* for 25-28 May 1793, and it ran to four editions. Our copytext is ed. 1, occasionally corrected from later editions.]

My Brethren,

We are called upon by high authority to separate, for religious purposes, this portion of our common time. The shops are shut; the artisan is summoned from his loom; and the husbandman from his plough; the whole nation, in the midst of its business, its pleasures, and its pursuits, makes a sudden stop, and wears the semblance, at least, of seriousness and concern. It is natural for you to enquire, What is the purport of all this?—the answer is in the words of my text: "*Ye stand this day, all of you, before the face of the Lord.*"—Deuteronomy, xxix. 10. You stand all of you, that is, you stand here as a nation, and you stand for the declared purpose of confessing your sins, and humbling yourselves before the Supreme Being.

Every individual, my brethren, who has a sense of religion, and a desire of conforming his conduct to its precepts, will frequently retire into himself to discover his faults; and having discovered to repent of, and having repented of, to amend them. Nations have likewise *their* faults to repent of, *their* conduct to examine; and it is therefore no less becoming and salutary, that *they*, from time to time, should engage in the same duty. Those sins which we have to repent of as individuals, belong to such transactions as relate to our private concerns, and are executed by us in our private capacity, such as buying, selling, the management of our family economy, differences arising from jarring interests and interfering claims between us and our neighbours, &c. Those sins which, as a nation, we have to repent of, belong to national acts.

We act as a nation, when, through the organ of the legislative power, which speaks the will of the nation, and by means of the executive power which does the will of the nation, we enact laws, form alliances, make war or peace, dispose of the public money, or do any of those things which belong to us in our collective capacity. As, comparatively, few individuals have any immediate share in these public acts, we might be tempted to forget the responsibility which attaches to the nation at large with regard to them, did not the wisdom and piety of the governing powers, by thus calling us together on every public emergency, remind us that they are all *our own* acts; and that, for every violation of integrity, justice, or humanity in public affairs, it is incumbent upon every one of us, to humble himself personally before the tribunal of Almighty God.

That this is the true and only rational interpretation of the solemnities of this day, is evident from hence, that we are never enjoined to confess the sins of other people; but our own sins.

To take upon ourselves the faults of others, savours of presumption, rather than humility. There would be an absurd mockery in pretending to humble ourselves before God for misdeeds which we have neither committed, nor have any power to amend. Those evils which we could not help, and in which we have had no share, are subjects of grief indeed, but not of remorse. If an oppressive law, or a destructive war, were of the nature of a volcano or a hurricane, proceeding from causes totally independent of our operations, all we should have to do, would be to bow our heads in silent submission, and to bear their ravages with a manly patience. We do not *repent* of a dangerous disorder or a sickly constitution, because these are things which do not depend upon our own efforts. If, therefore, the nation at large had nothing to do in the affairs of the nation, the piety of our rulers would have led them to fast and pray by themselves alone, without inviting *us* to concur in this salutary work. But we are called upon to repent of national sins, because we *can* help them, and because we ought to help them. We are not fondly to imagine we can make of kings, or of lawgivers, the scape-goats to answer for our follies and our crimes: by the services of this day they call upon us to answer for them; they throw the blame where it ought ultimately to rest; that is, where the power ultimately rests. It were trifling with our consciences to endeavour to separate the acts of governors sanctioned by the nation, from the acts of the nation; for, in every transaction the principal is answerable for the conduct of the agents he employs to transact it. If the maxim that the king can do no wrong[1] throws upon ministers the responsibility, because without ministers no wrong could be done, the same reason throws it from them upon the people, without whom ministers could do no wrong.

The language of the Proclamation then may be thus interpreted—People! who in your individual capacities are rich and poor, high and low, governors and governed, assemble yourselves in the unity of your public existence; rest from your ordinary occupations, give a different direction to the exercises of

---

1   That "the king can do no wrong" was a principle of British law codified in William Blackstone's *Commentaries on the Laws of England* (1765-69).

your public worship, confess—not every man his own sins, but all the sins of all. We, your appointed rulers, before we allow ourselves to go on executing *your will* in a conjuncture so important, force you to make a pause, that you may be constrained to reflect, that you may bring this will, paramount [to] every thing else,[1] into the sacred presence of God; that you may there examine it, and see whether it be agreeable to his will, and to the eternal obligations of virtue and good morals. If not, the guilt be upon your own heads; we disclaim the awful responsibility.

Supposing that you are now prepared by proper views of the subject, I shall go on to investigate those sins which a nation is most apt to be betrayed into, leaving it to each of you to determine whether, and how far, any one of them ought to make a part of *our* humiliation on this day.

Societies being composed of individuals, the faults of societies proceed from the same bad passions, the same pride, selfishness and thirst of gain, by which individuals are led to transgress the rules of duty; they require therefore the same curb to restrain them, and hence the necessity of a national religion. You will probably assert, that most nations have one; but, by a national religion, I do not mean the burning a few wretches twice or thrice in a year in honour of God, nor yet the exacting subscription to some obscure tenets, believed by few, and understood by none;[2] nor yet the investing a certain order of men dressed in a particular habit, with civil privileges and secular emolument; by national religion I understand, the extending to those affairs in which we act in common and as a body, that regard to religion, by which, when we act singly, we all profess to be guided. Nothing seems more obvious; and yet there are men who appear not insensible to the rules of morality as they respect individuals, and who unaccountably disclaim them with respect to nations. They will not cheat their oppo-

---

1  paramount [to] every thing else: "paramount every else" in eds. 1–4; "paramount every thing else" in *Works*.

2  A reference to the 39 Articles of the Church of England, to which all candidates for University degrees were required to subscribe. *The British Critic* complained of this passage that "sarcasm is a figure which this lady, forgetting its impropriety in a sermon, is very fond of using" (p. 83).

site neighbour, but they will take a pride in over-reaching a neighbouring state; they would scorn to foment dissentions in the family of an acquaintance, but they will do so by a community without scruple; they would not join with a gang of house-breakers to plunder a private dwelling, but they have no principle which prevents them from joining with a confederacy of princes to plunder a province.[1] As private individuals, they think it right to pass by little injuries, but as a people they think they cannot carry too high a principle of proud defiance and sanguinary revenge.[2] This sufficiently shews, that whatever rule they may acknowledge for their private conduct, they have nothing that can be properly called *national religion*; and indeed, it is very much to be suspected, that their religion in the former case, is very much assisted by the contemplation of those pains and penalties which society has provided against the crimes of individuals. But the united will of a whole people cannot make wrong right, or sanction one act of rapacity, injustice, or breach of faith. The first principle, therefore, we must lay down, is, that we are to submit our public conduct to the same rules by which we are to regulate our private actions:[3] A nation that does this, is, as a nation, religious; a nation that does it not, though it should fast, and pray, and wear sackcloth, and pay tithes, and build churches, is, as a nation, profligate and unprincipled.

The vices of nations may be divided into those which relate to their own internal proceedings, or to their relations with other states. With regard to the first, the causes for humiliation are various. Many nations are guilty of the crime of permitting oppressive laws and bad governments to remain amongst them, by which the poor are crushed, and the lives of the innocent

---

1　The Kingdom of Poland, partitioned by Russia and Prussia in 1793.

2　Thus William Windham, Minister for War, in 1802 in a bellicose speech urged Parliament to reject peace with France: "while in private life points of honour are attended to with the most scrupulous exactitude, a slap upon the national face or a kick upon the public posterior goes for nothing" (quoted in Jewson, *Jacobin City*, p. 108).

3　Barbauld agrees with David Hume, in his essay "Of Public Credit": "For why should the case be so different between the public and an individual, as to make us establish different maxims of conduct for each?" (*Selected Essays*, p. 204).

are laid at the mercy of wicked and arbitrary men. This is a national sin of the deepest dye, as it involves in it most others. It is painful to reflect how many atrocious governments there are in the world; and how little even they who enjoy good ones, seem to understand their true nature. We are apt to speak of the *happiness* of living under a mild government, as if it were like the happiness of living under an indulgent climate; and when we thank God for it, we rank it with the blessings of the air and of the soil; whereas we ought to thank God for the *wisdom* and *virtue* of living under a good government; for a good government is the first of national duties. It is indeed a happiness, and one which demands our most grateful thanks, to be born under one which spares us the trouble and hazard of changing it; but a people born under a good government, will probably not die under one, if they conceive of it as an indolent and passive happiness, to be left for its preservation, to fortunate conjunctures, and the floating and variable chances of incalculable events;—our second duty is to keep it good.

We shall not be able to fulfil either of these duties, except we cultivate in our hearts the requisite dispositions. One of the most fruitful sources of evil in the transaction of national affairs, is a spirit of *insubordination*. Without a quiet subordination to lawful authority, peace, order, and the ends of good government, can never be attained. To fix this subordination on its proper basis, it is only necessary to establish in our minds this plain principle, that the will of the minority should ever yield to that of the majority. By this simple axiom, founded on those common principles of justice which all men understand, the largest society may be held together with equal ease as the smallest, provided only some well contrived and orderly method be established for ascertaining that will. It is the immediate extinction of all faction, sedition, and tyranny. It supersedes the necessity of governing by systems of blinding or terrifying the people. It puts an end equally to the cabinet cabal,[1] and the muffled conspiracy, and occasions every thing to go on smoothly, openly, and fairly; whereas, if the minority attempt to

---

1  Conspiracy by the king's ministers.

impose their will upon the majority, so unnatural a state of things will not be submitted to without constant struggles on the one side, and constant jealousies on the other. There are two descriptions of men who are in danger of forgetting this excellent rule; *public functionaries*, and *reformers*. Public functionaries, being entrusted with large powers for managing the affairs of their fellow-citizens, which management, from the nature of things, must necessarily be in the hands of a few, are very apt to confound the executive power with the governing will; they require, therefore, to be observed with a wholesome suspicion, and to be frequently reminded of the nature and limits of their office.—Reformers, conceiving of themselves, as of a more enlightened class than the bulk of mankind, are likewise apt to forget the deference due to them. Stimulated by newly discovered truths, of which they feel the full force, they are not willing to wait for the gradual spread of knowledge, the subsiding of passion, and the undermining of prejudices.[1] They too contemn a *swinish multitude*,[2] and aim at an aristocracy of talents. It is indeed their business to attack the prejudices, and to rectify, if they can, the systems[3] of their countrymen, but, in the mean time, to acquiesce in them. It is their business to sow the seed, and let it lie patiently in the bosom of the ground, perhaps for ages—to prepare, not to bring about revolutions. The public is not always in the wrong for not giving into their views, even where they have the appearance of reason; for their plans are often crude and premature, their ideas too refined for real

1 Barbauld perhaps recalls Priestley's *Letter to … William Pitt* (1787): "I do not say … that nothing should be done by the governors of a nation but what the body of it shall have previously considered and approved, … because many lesser changes may be made by way of *experiment*…. The minds of the higher ranks in any community may well be presumed to be more enlightened than those of the lower. It is therefore their proper business to speculate, to devise plans for the public good, and to make trials of such as promise the best" (pp. 8-9).

2 Barbauld quotes a notorious phrase from Edmund Burke, *Reflections on the late Revolution in France* (1790): "Along with its natural protectors and guardians, learning will be cast into the mire, and trodden down under the hoofs of a swinish multitude" (p. 95). She had been meditating a reply to Burke as early as February 1791 (Rodgers, *Georgian Chronicle*, p. 210); quite possibly, *Sins of Government* originated as that reply.

3 I.e., systems of thought and belief.

life, and influenced by their own particular cast of thinking; they want people to be happy their way; whereas every one must be happy his own way. Freedom is a good thing, but if a nation is not disposed to accept of it, it is not to be presented to them on the point of a bayonet. Freedom is a valuable blessing, but if even a nation that has enjoyed that blessing, evidently *chooses* to give it up, the voice of the people ought to prevail; men of more liberal minds should warn them indeed what they are about; but having done that, they should acquiesce. If the established religion, in any country, is absurd and superstitious in the eyes of thinking men, so long as it is the religion of the generality, it ought to prevail, and the minority should not even wish to supplant it. The endeavouring to overthrow any system *before* it is given up by the majority, is faction; the endeavouring to keep it *after* it is given up by them, is tyranny; both are equally wrong, and both proceed from the same cause, the want of a principle of due subordination.[1]

If we find reason to be satisfied with the general sketch and outline of government, and with that basis of subordination on which we have placed it, it becomes us next to examine, whether the filling up of the plan be equally unexceptionable. Our laws, are they mild, equal, and perspicuous; free from burdensome forms and unnecessary delays; not a succession of expedients growing out of temporary exigences, but a compact whole; not adapted to local prejudices, but founded on the broad basis of universal jurisprudence?—Are they accessible to rich and poor, sparing of human blood, calculated rather to check and set bounds to the inequality of fortunes than to increase them, rather to prevent and reform crimes than to punish them?—If good, are they well administered?—Is the lenity of the laws shewn in the moderation of the penalties, or in the facility of evasion and the frequency of escape?—Do we profit from greater degrees of instruction and longer experience, and from time to time clear away the trash and refuse of

---

1  Barbauld's forward-looking views on "subordination" have been enunciated more recently by the Russian democrat Roy Medvedev: "The minority cannot refuse to implement a majority decision. But it should not renounce its own views on controversial matters" (*On Socialist Democracy*, p. 46).

past ages? What all are bound to observe, are they so framed as that all may understand? Is there any provision for instructing the people in the various arbitrary obligations that are laid upon them, or are they supposed to understand them by intuition, *because* they are too intricate to be explained methodically?—Are punishments proportioned to crimes, and rewards to services, or have we two sets of officers, the one to do the work, the other to be paid without doing it?—Have we any locusts in the land, any who devour the labours of the husbandman without contributing any thing to the good of society by their labours of body or of mind?—Is the name of God, and the awfulness of religious sanctions, profaned among us by frequent, unnecessary, and ensnaring oaths, which lie like stumbling blocks in every path of business and preferment,[1] tending to corrupt the singleness of truth, and wear away the delicacy of conscience; entangling even the innocence and inexperience of children?—Have we calculated the false oaths which, in the space of one sun, the accusing angel has to carry up from our customs-houses, our various courts, our hustings, our offices of taxation, and—from our altars?—Are they such as a tear, if we do shed tears on a day such as this, will blot out?—Have we calculated the mischief which is done to the ingenuous mind, when the virgin dignity of his soul is first violated by a falsehood?—Have we calculated the wound which is given to the peace of a good man, the thorns that are strewed upon his pillow, when through hard necessity, he complies with what his soul abhors? Have we calculated the harm done to the morals of a nation, by the established *necessity* of perjury? We shall do well, being now by the command of our rulers before the Lord, to reflect on these things; and if we want food for our national penitence, perhaps we may here find it.

*Extravagance* is a fault, to which nations, as well as private persons, are very prone, and the consequences to both are

---

1 Barbauld alludes to the practices of (mis)using religious ritual as a test of fitness to hold public office, and of requiring sworn oaths on various public or official occasions. She may also allude to the current demand for "loyalty oaths"—statements swearing loyalty to the British Constitution—from Dissenters and others.

exactly similar. If a private man lives beyond his income, the consequence will be loss of independence, disgraceful perplexity, and in the end certain ruin. The catastrophes of states are slower in ripening, but like causes must in the end produce like effects.—If you are acquainted with any individual, who, from inattention to his affairs, misplaced confidence, foolish lawsuits, anticipation of his rents and profusion in his family expences, has involved himself in debts that eat away his income, what would you say to such a one? Would you not tell him, Contract your expences; look yourself into your affairs; insist upon exact accounts from your steward and bailiffs; keep no servants for mere show and parade; mind only your own affairs, and keep at peace with your neighbours; set religiously apart an annual sum for discharging the mortgages on your estate.—If this be good advice for one man, it is good advice for nine millions of men.—If this individual should persist in his course of unthrifty profusion, saying to himself, The ruin will not come in my time; the misery will not fall upon me; let posterity take care of itself! would you not pronounce him at once very weak and very selfish? My friends, a *nation* that should pursue the same conduct, would be equally reprehensible.

*Pride* is a vice in individuals; it cannot, therefore, be a virtue in that number of individuals called a Nation. A disposition to prefer to every other our own habits of life, our own management, our own systems, to suppose that we are admired and looked up to by others—something of this perhaps is natural, and may be pardoned as a weakness, but it can never be exalted into a duty; it is a disposition we ought to check, and not to cultivate; there is neither patriotism nor good sense in fostering an extravagant opinion of ourselves and our own institutions, in being attached even to our faults, because they are ours, and because they have been ours from generation to generation.[1]

---

1  Barbauld censures Edmund Burke's paean to British "prejudice": "instead of casting away all our old prejudices, we cherish them to a very considerable degree, ... and the longer they have lasted, and the more generally they have prevailed, the more we cherish them" (*Reflections on the late Revolution*, p. 105).

An exclusive admiration of ourselves is generally founded on extreme ignorance, and it is not likely to produce any thing of a more liberal or better stamp.

Amongst our national faults, have we any instances of *cruelty* or *oppression* to repent of? Can we look round from sea to sea, and from east to west, and say, *that our brother hath not aught against us?*[1] If such instances do not exist under our immediate eye, do they exist any where under our influence and jurisdiction? There are some, whose nerves, rather than whose principles, cannot bear cruelty—like other nuisances, they would not chuse it in sight, but they can be well content to know it exists, and that they are indebted to it for[2] the increase of their income, and the luxuries of their table. Are there not some *darker-coloured* children of the same family, over whom we assume a hard and unjust controul?[3] And have not these our brethren *aught against us?* If we *suspect* they have, would it not become us anxiously to enquire into the truth, that we may deliver our souls; but if we know it, and cannot help knowing it, if such enormities have been pressed and forced upon our notice, till they are become flat and stale in the public ear, from fulness and repetition, and satiety of proof; and if they are still sanctioned by our legislature, defended by our princes—deep indeed is the colour of our guilt.—And do we appoint fasts, and make pretences to religion? Do we pretend to be shocked at the principles or the practices of neighbouring nations, and start with affected horror at the name of Atheist?[4] Are our consciences so tender, and our hearts so hard? Is it possible we should meet as a nation, and knowing ourselves to be guilty of these things, have the confidence to implore the blessing of

---

1  "Therefore if thou bring thy gift to the altar, and there rememberest that thy brother hath aught against thee; ... first be reconciled to thy brother, and then come and offer thy gift" (Matthew 5:23-24).

2  to it for: all texts read "for it to," an apparent error.

3  Barbauld alludes to slavery in the British West Indies; slave labor produced most of the sugar used in Britain. Below, she alludes to the speech of William Wilberforce in his 1791 motion in Parliament to end British participation in the slave trade: see headnote to *An Epistle to William Wilberforce*.

4  Barbauld rebukes Edmund Burke's attack on the French "literary cabal" (Voltaire, Diderot, and others) for supposedly planning the overthrow of Christianity; "these Atheistical fathers," he at one point calls them (*Reflections*, p. 135).

God upon our commerce and our colonies: preface with prayer our legislative meetings, and then deliberate *how long* we shall continue human sacrifices? Rather let us

> Never pray more, abandon all remorse.[1]

Let us lay aside the grimace of hypocrisy, stand up for what we are, and boldly profess, like the emperor of old, that every thing is sweet from which money is extracted, and that we know better than to deprive ourselves of a gain for the sake of a fellow-creature.[2]

I next invite you, my friends, to consider your conduct with regard to other states. Different communities are neighbours, living together in a state of nature;[3] that is, without any common tribunal, to which they may carry their differences; but they are not the less bound to all the duties of neighbours; to mutual sincerity, justice, and kind offices.

First to sincerity. It is imagined, I know not why, that transactions between states cannot be carried on without a great deal of intrigue and dissimulation. But I am apt to think the nation that should venture to disclaim this narrow and crooked policy, and should act and speak with a noble frankness, would lose nothing by the proceeding; honest intentions will bear to be told in plain language; if our views upon each other are for our mutual advantage, the whole mystery of them may be unfolded without danger; and if they are not, they will soon be detected by practitioners as cunning and dextrous as ourselves.

Secondly, we are bound to justice—Not only in executing our engagements, but in cultivating a spirit of moderation in our very wishes. Most contrary to this is a species of patriotism, which consists in inverting the natural course of our feel-

---

1  *Othello*, III.iii.369.

2  Barbauld perhaps alludes to the Roman Emperor Caligula (reigned AD 37-41), notorious for his avarice and the ingeniously cruel means by which he raised money.

3  The state of nature is the condition of human beings prior to their forming governments (according to prevailing eighteenth-century theory). Barbauld regards it as Francis Hutcheson did: "[T]he state of nature is that of peace and good-will, of innocence and beneficence, and not of violence, war, and rapine" (Hutcheson, *Short Introduction to Moral Philosophy*, p. 116).

ings, in being afraid of our neighbour's prosperity, and rejoicing at his misfortunes. We should be ashamed to say, My neighbour's house was burnt down last night, I am glad of it, I shall have more custom to my shop. My neighbour, thank God, has broken his arm, I shall be sent for to attend the families in which he was employed; but we are not ashamed to say, Our neighbours are weakening themselves by a cruel war, we shall rise upon their ruins. We must act in opposition to the peacemakers; we must hinder them from being reconciled, and blow the coals of discord, otherwise their commerce will revive, and goods may remain in our crammed warehouses. Our neighbours have bad laws and a weak government; Heaven forbid they should change them, for then they might be more flourishing than ourselves. We have tracts of territory which we cannot people for ages, but we must take great care that our neighbour does not get any footing there, for he would soon make them very useful to him.—Thus do we extend our grasping hands from east to west, from pole to pole, and in our selfish monopolizing spirit are almost angry that the sun should ripen any productions but for our markets, or the ocean bear any vessels but our own upon its broad bosom. We are not ashamed to use that solecism in terms *natural enemies*;[1] as if nature, and not our own bad passions, made us enemies; as if that relation, from which, in private life, flows confidence, affection, endearing intercourse, were in nations only a signal for mutual slaughter; and we were like animals of prey, solitarily ferocious, who look with a jealous eye on every rival that intrudes within their range of devastation—and yet this language is heard in a Christian country, and these detestable maxims veil themselves under the semblance of virtue and public spirit.—We have a golden rule, if we will but apply it; it will measure great things as well as small; it will measure as true at the Antipodes, or on the coast of Guinea,[2] as in our native

1  A member of Parliament in December 1792 referred to France as "our natural enemy"; and an address to the National Convention in Paris from the London Revolution Society declared that it was time to abandon the traditional "falsehood" that France was the "natural enemy" of England (*Moniteur Universel* [Paris], 27 Dec. and 23 Nov. 1792).
2  On the west coast of Africa. Barbauld alludes again to the slave trade.

fields. It is that universal standard of weights and measures which alone will simplify all business:[1] Do to others, as ye would that others should do unto you.

There is a notion which has a direct tendency to make us unjust, because it tends to make us think God so; I mean the idea which most nations have entertained, that they are the peculiar favourites of Heaven. We nourish our pride by fondly fancying that we are the only nation for whom the providence of God exerts itself; the only nation whose form of worship is agreeable to him, the only nation whom he has endowed with a competent share of wisdom to frame wise laws and rational governments. Each nation is to itself the fleece of Gideon,[2] and drinks exclusively the dew of science; but as God is no respecter of persons,[3] so neither is he of nations; he has not, like earthly monarchs, his favourites. There is a great deal even in our thanksgivings, which is exceptionable on this account; "God, we thank thee, that we are not like other nations;"[4]—yet we freely load ourselves with every degree of guilt; but then we like to consider *ourselves* as a child that is chidden, and others as outcasts.

When the workings of these bad passions are swelled to their height by mutual animosity and opposition, *war* ensues. War is a state in which all our feelings and our duties suffer a total and strange inversion; a state, in which

> Life dies, Death lives, and Nature breeds
> Perverse, all monstrous, all prodigious things.[5]

A state in which it becomes our business to hurt and annoy our

---

1  A universal standard of weights and measures (now called the metric system) was introduced by the revolutionary French government. Barbauld's standard (below) is the "Golden Rule."

2  In Judges 6:36-40, Gideon asks the Lord to prove to skeptics that he will save Israel by Gideon's hand. The proof is that a fleece of wool becomes wet on a dry night, and remains dry on a wet night.

3  Acts 10:34.

4  Alluding to the Pharisee who "stood and prayed thus with himself, God, I thank thee, that I am not as other men are" (Luke 18:11).

5  Milton, *Paradise Lost*, 2:624.

neighbour by every possible means; instead of cultivating, to destroy; instead of building, to pull down; instead of peopling, to depopulate; a state in which we drink the tears, and feed upon the misery of our fellow-creatures; such a state, therefore, requires the extremest necessity to justify it; it ought not to be the common and usual state of society. As both parties *cannot* be in the right, there is always an equal chance, at least, to either of them, of being in the wrong; but as both parties *may* be to blame, and most commonly are, the chance is very great indeed against its being entered into from any adequate cause; yet war may be said to be, with regard to nations, the sin which most easily besets them. We, my friends, in common with other nations, have much guilt to repent of from this cause, and it ought to make a large part of our humiliations on this day. When we carry our eyes back through the long records of our history, we see wars of plunder, wars of conquest, wars of religion, wars of pride, wars of succession, wars of idle speculation, wars of unjust interference, and hardly among them one war of necessary self-defence in any of our essential or very important interests. Of late years, indeed, we have known none of the calamities of war in our own country but the wasteful expence of it; and sitting aloof from those circumstances of personal provocation, which in some measure might excuse its fury, we have calmly voted slaughter and merchandized destruction—so much blood and tears for so many rupees,[1] or dollars, or ingots. Our wars have been wars of cool calculating interest, as free from hatred as from love of mankind; the passions which stir the blood have had no share in them. We devote a certain number of men to perish on land and sea, and the rest of us sleep sound, and, protected in our usual occupations, talk of the events of war as what diversifies the flat uniformity of life.

We should, therefore, do well to *translate* this word war into language more intelligible to us. When we pay our army and our navy estimates, let us set down—so much for killing, so much for maiming, so much for making widows and orphans, so much for bringing famine upon a district, so much for cor-

---

1  An Indian unit of money. Barbauld thus alludes to British conquests in India.

rupting citizens and subjects into spies and traitors, so much for ruining industrious tradesmen and making bankrupts,[1] (of that species of distress at least, we *can* form an idea,) so much for letting loose the demons of fury, rapine, and lust, within the fold of cultivated society, and giving to the brutal ferocity of the most ferocious, its full scope and range of invention. We shall by this means know what we have paid our money for, whether we have made a good bargain, and whether the account is likely to pass—elsewhere. We must take in too, all those concomitant circumstances which make war, considered as battle, the least part of itself, *pars minima sui*.[2] We must fix our eyes, not on the hero returning with conquest, nor yet on the gallant officer dying in the bed of honour, the subject of picture and of song, but on the private soldier, forced into the service, exhausted by camp-sickness and fatigue; pale, emaciated, crawling to an hospital with the prospect of life, perhaps a long life, blasted, useless and suffering. We must think of the uncounted tears of her who weeps alone, because the only being who shared her sentiments is taken from her; no martial music sounds in unison with her feelings; the long day passes and he returns not. She does not shed her sorrows over his grave, for she has never learnt whether he ever had one. If he had returned, his exertions would not have been remembered individually, for he only made a small imperceptible part of a human machine, called a Regiment. We must take in the long sickness which no glory soothes, occasioned by distress of mind, anxiety and ruined fortunes.—These are not fancy-pictures, and if you please to heighten them, you can every one of you do it for yourselves. We must take in the consequences, felt perhaps for ages, before a country which has been compleatly desolated, lifts its head again; like a torrent of lava, its worst mischief is not the first overwhelming ruin of towns and palaces, but the long sterility to which it condemns the track it

---

1  "[O]ne of the first belligerent acts of the British government in 1793 was to prohibit exports of corn to France, and this was followed by an attempt to induce a monetary crisis and the overthrow of the Paris regime by seeding the currency with counterfeit notes" (Cookson, *Friends of Peace*, p. 43).
2  Barbauld translates this phrase in her text.

has covered with its stream. Add the danger to regular govern-
ments which are changed by war, sometimes to anarchy, and
sometimes to despotism. Add all these, and then let us think
when a General performing these exploits, is saluted with, "well
done good and faithful servant",[1] whether the plaudit is likely
to be echoed in another place.

In this guilty business there is a circumstance which greatly
aggravates its guilt, and that is the impiety of calling upon the
Divine Being to assist us in it. Almost all nations have been in
the habit of mixing with their bad passions a shew of religion,
and of prefacing these their murders with prayers, and the
solemnities of worship. When they send out their armies to
desolate a country, and destroy the fair face of nature, they have
the presumption to hope that the sovereign of the universe will
condescend to be their auxiliary, and to enter into their petty
and despicable contests. Their prayer, if put into plain language,
would run thus: God of love, father of all the families of the
earth, we are going to tear in pieces our brethren of mankind,
but our strength is not equal to our fury, we beseech thee to
assist us in the work of slaughter. Go out we pray thee with our
fleets and armies; we call them christian, and we have interwo-
ven in our banners and the decorations of our arms the sym-
bols of a suffering religion, that we may fight under the cross
upon which our Saviour died. Whatever mischief we do, we
shall do it in thy name; we hope, therefore, thou wilt protect us
in it. Thou, who hast made of one blood all the dwellers upon
the earth, we trust thou wilt view us alone with partial favour,
and enable us to bring misery upon every other quarter of the
globe—Now if we really expect such prayers to be answered,
we are the weakest, if not, we are the most hypocritical of
beings.

Formerly, this business was managed better, and had in it
more shew of reason and probability. When mankind con-
ceived of their Gods as partaking of like passions with them-
selves, they made a fair bargain with them on these occasions.
Their chieftains, they knew, were influenced by such motives,

---

1  Matthew 25:21.

and they thought their Gods might well be so too. Go out with us, and you shall have a share of the spoil. Your altars shall stream with the blood of so many noble captives, or you shall have a hecatomb of fat oxen, or a golden tripod. Have we any thing of this kind to propose? Can we make any thing like a *handsome offer*[1] to the Almighty, to tempt him to enlist himself on our side? Such things have been done before now in the christian world. Churches have been promised, and church lands, aye, and honestly paid too; at other times silver shrines, incense, vestments, tapers, according to the occasion.—Oh how justly may the awful text be here applied! He that sitteth in the heavens shall laugh, the Lord shall have them in derision.[2]— Christians! I shudder, lest in the earnestness of my heart I may have sinned, in suffering such impious propositions to escape my lips. In short, while we must be perfectly conscious in our own minds, that the generality of our wars are the offspring of mere worldly ambition and interest, let us, if we must have wars, carry them on as other such things are carried on, and not think of making a prayer to be used before murder, any more than of composing prayers to be used before we enter a gambling house, or a place of licentious entertainment.[3] Bad actions are made worse by hypocrisy; an unjust war is in itself so bad a thing, that there is only one way of making it worse, and that is, by mixing religion with it.

These, my friends, are some of the topics on which, standing as a nation this day before the Lord, it will be proper that we should examine ourselves. There yet remains a serious question: How far, as individuals, are we really answerable for the guilt of national sins? For his own sins, it is evident, every man is wholly answerable; for those of an aggregate body, it is as evident he can be only answerable in part; and that portion and measure of iniquity, which falls to his share, will be more or less, according as he has been more or less deeply engaged in those transactions which are polluted with it. There is an active and a passive concurrence. We give our active concurrence to

---

1   A commercial phrase, as in "handsome price" (*OED*, s.v. "handsome," sense 4.b.).
2   Psalm 2:4.
3   A house of prostitution.

any measure, when we support it by any voluntary exertion, or bestow on it any mark of approbation; when, especially, we are the persons, for *whose sake*, and for whose emolument, systems of injustice or cruelty are carried on. The man of wealth and influence, who feeds and fattens upon the miseries of his fellow-creatures; the man in power, who plans abuses, or prevents their being swept away, is the very Jonas of the ship,[1] and ought this day to stand foremost in the rank of national penitents. But there is also a passive concurrence, and this, in common cases, the community appears to have a right to expect from us. Society could not exist, if every individual took it upon himself not only to judge, but to act from his own judgment in those things in which a nation acts collectively. The law, therefore, which is the expression of the general will, seems to be a sufficient sanction for us, when, in obedience to its authority, we pay taxes, and comply with injunctions, in support of measures which we believe to be hurtful, and even iniquitous; and this, not because the guilt of a bad action, as some fondly imagine, is diluted and washed away in the guilt of multitudes; but because it is a necessary condition of political union, that private will should be yielded up to the will of the public. We shall do well, however, to bear in mind the principle on which we comply, that we may not go a step beyond it.

There are, indeed, cases of such atrocity, that even this concurrence would be criminal. What these are, it is impossible to specify; every man must draw the line for himself.—I suppose no one will pretend, that any maxims of military subordination could justify the officers of Herod in the slaughter of the children of Bethlehem; and certainly the orders of Louvois, in the Palatinate, and of Catherine de Medicis, on the day of St. Bartholomew, were not less cruel.[2] In our own country, it has been the official duty of magistrates to burn alive quiet and

---

1 In the Old Testament, Jonah seeks to escape the Lord by taking passage in a ship; when the ship is beset by a storm, its crew beseech the Lord, "let us not perish for this man's life, and lay not upon us innocent blood" (Jonah 1:14).

2 The slaughter of the children of Bethlehem on orders from king Herod is told in Matthew 2:16. François Michel le Tellier, marquis de Louvois, Minister of War to Louis XIV, ordered the destruction of the German state of the Palatinate in winter

innocent subjects, who differed from them in opinion.[1] Rather than fulfil such *duties*, a man of integrity will prepare himself to suffer, and a Christian knows where such sufferings will be rewarded.—The honourable delinquency of those who have submitted to be the victims, rather than the instruments of injustice, has ever been held worthy of praise and admiration.[2]

But though, for the sake of peace and order, we ought, in general cases, to give our passive concurrence to measures which we may think wrong, peace and order do not require us to give them the sanction of our approbation. On the contrary, the more strictly we are bound to acquiesce, the more it is incumbent on us to remonstrate. Every good man owes it to his country and to his own character, to lift his voice against a ruinous war, an unequal tax, or an edict of persecution: and to oppose them, temperately, but firmly, by all the means in his power; and indeed this is the only way reformations can ever be brought about, or that government can enjoy the advantage of general opinion.

This general opinion has, on a recent occasion, been sedulously called for,[3] and most of you have complied with the requisition. You, who have, on this occasion, given warm and unqualified declarations of attachment to the existing system, you have done well—You, who have denounced abuses, and declared your wishes for reform, you have done well likewise, provided each of you has acted from the sincere, unbiassed con-

---

1689, with such devastating effect that the French officers who executed his order were ashamed of it (says Voltaire, in whose *Age of Louis XIV* [Chap. 16] Barbauld probably read this story). Catherine de Medici (1519-89), de facto ruler of France in 1572, instigated a massacre of French Protestants throughout the country on 24 August 1572, the festival of St. Bartholomew.

1  Most conspicuously, the Anglican bishops Hugh Latimer and Nicholas Ridley were burned at the stake (1555) by magistrates carrying out the attempted restoration of English Catholicism by Queen Mary.

2  Barbauld anticipates the so-called "Nuremburg Defence," the plea by Nazi officials at their trials that they were "only following orders."

3  The "recent occasion" is probably the campaign by adherents of John Reeves's Association for the Preservation of Liberty and Property against Republicans and Levellers to induce their neighbors throughout Britain to sign oaths of loyalty to the Constitution. When signed, the oaths were published in the newspapers with the names of their signers. Those who refused to sign were harrassed and threatened.

viction of his own mind.[1] But if you have done it lightly, and without judgment, you have done ill; if against judgment, worse: if, by any improper influence, you have interfered with the liberty of your neighbour, or your dependant, and caused him to act against his judgment and his conscience—worse still. If the ferment of party has stirred up a spirit of rancour and animosity among friends and townsmen, or introduced the poison of distrust amidst the freedom and security of social life, we stand this day before the Lord; and if our brother hath aught against us, "let us go first, and be reconciled to our brother, and then come and offer our gift."[2]

If any of us have disturbed or misled weaker minds by exaggerated danger and affected alarm, and practising on their credulity or their ignorance, have raised passions which it would have better become us to have moderated—or if, on the other hand, we have cried, peace, peace, where there is no peace:[3]—we are this day before the Lord, let shame and remorse for these practices make a distinguished part of our national humiliation.

Repent this day, not only of the actual evil you have done, but of the evil of which your actions have been the cause.—If you slander a good man, you are answerable for all the violence of which that slander may be the remote cause;[4] if you raise undue prejudices against any particular class or description of citizens, and they suffer through the bad passions your misrepresentations have worked up against them, you are answerable

---

1 I.e., each person on each side of the issue. The atmosphere of intimidation produced much insincere signing, as one Dissenting minister noted: "We have had meetings of all ye Parishes in Exeter in order to declare their Loyalty & attachment to ye constitution. most of our people have joined with ye establishment upon these occasions, & have hereby been induced to set their signatures to things wch I fear they did not in their Hearts approve" (Kenrick, *Chronicles of a Nonconformist Family*, p. 68).

2 See p. 308, n.1.

3 Ezekiel 13:10.

4 The "good man" is Joseph Priestley, who was slandered frequently in the press (as "Gunpowder Priestley," as if he were another Guy Fawkes) until at last, on 14 July 1791, a "Church-and-King" mob ransacked and destroyed his house at Birmingham. Dissenters in general were represented at this period as subversives, and others besides Priestley suffered from violence.

for the injury, though you have not wielded the bludgeon, or applied the firebrand; if you place power in improper hands, you are answerable for the abuse of that power; if you oppose conciliatory measures, you are answerable for the distress which more violent ones may produce. If you use intemperate invectives and inflammatory declamation, you are answerable if others shed blood. It is not sufficient, even if our intentions are pure; we must weigh the tendencies of our actions, for we are answerable, in a degree at least, for those remote consequences, which, though we did not intend, we might have foreseen. If we inculcate the plausible doctrine of unlimited confidence,[1] we draw upon ourselves the responsibility of all the future measures which that confidence may sanction. If we introduce tenets leaning towards arbitrary power, the generations to come will have a right to curse the folly of their forefathers, when they are reaping the bitter fruits of them in future star-chambers, and courts of inquisitorial jurisdiction. If the precious sands of our liberty are, perhaps, of themselves running out, how shall we be justified to ourselves, or to posterity, if, with a rash hand, we shake the glass.

If, on the other hand, through vanity, a childish love of novelty, a spirit of perverse opposition, or any motive still more sordidly selfish, we are precipitated into measures which ought to be the result of the most serious consideration—if by "foolish talking or jestings, which are not convenient,"[2] we have lessened the reverence due to constituted authorities, or slackened the bonds which hold society together; ours is the blame, when the hurricane is abroad in the world, and doing its work of mischief.

The course of events in this country has now, for a number of generations, for a long reach, as it were, of the stream of time, run smooth, and our political duties have been proportionally easy; but it may not always be so. A sudden bend may change the direction of the current, and open scenes less calm.

---

1   Unlimited confidence: in the government (a demand often made in wartime). Star chambers (below) are arbitrary and oppressive courts, proverbial types of tyrannical government.
2   Ephesians 5:4.

It becomes every man, therefore, to examine his principles, whether they are of that firmness and texture, as suits the occasion he may have for them. If we want a light gondola to float upon a summer lake, we look at the form and gilding; but if a vessel to steer through storms, we examine the strength of the timbers, and the soundness of the bottom. We want principles, not to figure in a book of ethics, or to delight us with "grand and swelling sentiments;"[1] but principles by which we may act, and by which we may suffer. Principles of benevolence, to dispose us to real sacrifices; political principles, of practical utility; principles of religion, to comfort and support us under all the trying vicissitudes we see around us, and which we have no security that we shall be long exempt from. How many are there now suffering under such overwhelming distresses, as, a short time ago, we should have thought it was hardly within the verge of possibility that they should experience! Above all, let us keep our hearts pure, and our hands clean. Whatever part we take in public affairs, much will undoubtedly happen which we could by no means foresee, and much which we shall not be able to justify; the only way, therefore, by which we can avoid deep remorse, is to act with simplicity and singleness of intention, and not to suffer ourselves to be warped, though by ever so little, from the path which honour and conscience approve.

Principles, such as I have been recommending, are not the work of a day; they are not to be acquired by any formal act of worship, or manual of devotion adapted to the exigency; and it will little avail us, that we have stood here, as a nation, *before the Lord*, if, individually, we do not remember that we are always so.

---

1    Not identified.

# WHAT IS EDUCATION?

[This essay, published in *The Monthly Magazine* 5 (March 1798): 167-71, and "On Prejudice," published two years later, present Barbauld's thoughts on leading issues in Enlightenment education theory. "What Is Education?" comments on the pedagogic schemes of Jean-Jacques Rousseau and Stéphanie-Félicité du Crest, Countess de Genlis. Like almost everyone else writing on education in the later eighteenth century, Barbauld responds to Rousseau's fiction, in *Émile* (1762), of an education derived entirely from the pupil's actual lived experience and complete-ly uninfluenced by society's existing body of knowledge and belief. This major premise of Rousseau's education theory was adopted in *Adèle et Théodore* (1784) by the Countess de Genlis, a writer whom Barbauld and her brother read with interest (see headnote to *Evenings at Home*). Barbauld herself, the daughter and grand-daughter of teachers, was a pedagogic innovator in *Lessons for Children* and *Hymns in Prose for Children* and had taught pupils aged three to seventeen at Palgrave School; she could comment as a full equal on Rousseau's and Genlis's projects.

Her essay accepts Rousseau's main premise only to show how it defeats his enterprise. Yes, we *are* educated by the totali-ty of our lived experience—and that totality includes the very beliefs and practices which Rousseau and Genlis seek to excise from it. Against their project for a selected experience, always controlled (indeed, manipulated) by the parent or teacher, Bar-bauld sets the unruly facts of living which overwhelm theory or render it pointless. She agrees with Mary Wollstonecraft (another practised teacher) in doubting that "a private educa-tion [i.e., one carried out in seclusion from the world] can work the wonders which some sanguine writers have attrib-uted to it. Men and women must be educated, in a great degree, by the opinions and manners of the society they live in" (*Rights of Woman*, p. 102).

According to Lucy Aikin, "What Is Education?" earned the gratitude of parents who felt intimidated by "the numerous conflicting systems of education then fashionable" ("Memoir,"

p. lxvii). A mid-nineteenth-century commentator admired its "originality of thought and vigour of expression," and declared it perpetually relevant: "Its sentiments will never become obsolete, nor its truths lose their value" (Hale, *Woman's Record*, p. 198).]

The other day I paid a visit to a gentleman with whom, though greatly my superior in fortune, I have long been in habits of an easy intimacy. He rose in the world by honourable industry; and married, rather late in life, a lady to whom he had been long attached, and in whom centered the wealth of several expiring families. Their earnest wish for children was not immediately gratified. At length they were made happy by a son, who, from the moment he was born, engrossed all their care and attention. My friend received me in his library, where I found him busied in turning over books of education, of which he had collected all that were worthy notice, from Xenophon to Locke, and from Locke to Catharine Macauley.[1] As he knows I have been engaged in the business of instruction, he did me the honour to consult me on the subject of his researches, hoping, he said, that, out of all the systems before him, we should be able to form a plan equally complete and comprehensive; it being the determination of both himself and his lady to chuse the best that could be had, and to spare neither pains nor expence in making their child all that was great and good. I gave him my thoughts with the utmost freedom, and after I returned home, threw upon paper the observations which had occurred to me.

The first thing to be considered, with respect to education, is the object of it. This appears to me to have been generally misunderstood. Education, in its largest sense, is a thing of great scope and extent. It includes the whole process by which a human being is formed to be what he is, in habits, principles, and cultivation of every kind. But of this a very small part is in the power even of the parent himself; a smaller still can be

---

1  Xenophon (ca. 435-354 BC), *The Cyropedia* (The Education of Cyrus); John Locke (1632-1704), *On Education* (1693); Macaulay, *Letters on Education* (1790).

directed by purchased tuition of any kind.[1] You engage for your child masters and tutors at large salaries, and you do well, for they are competent to instruct him; they will give him the means, at least, of acquiring science and accomplishments; but in the business of education, properly so called, they can do little for you. Do you ask then, what will educate your son? Your example will educate him; your conversation with your friends; the business he sees you transact; the likings and dislikings you express; these will educate him—the society you live in will educate him; your domestics will educate him; above all, your rank and situation in life, your house, your table, your pleasure-grounds, your hounds and your stables will educate him. It is not in your power to withdraw him from the continual influence of these things, except you were to withdraw yourself from them also. You speak of *beginning* the education of your son. The moment he was able to form an idea his education was already begun; the education of circumstances—insensible education—which, like insensible perspiration, is of more constant and powerful effect, and of infinitely more consequence to the habit than that which is direct and apparent.[2] This education goes on at every instant of time; it goes on *like* time; you can neither stop it nor turn its course. What these have a tendency to make your child, that he will be. Maxims and documents are good precisely till they are tried, and no longer; they will teach him to talk, and nothing more. The *circumstances* in which your son is placed will be even more prevalent than your example; and you have no right to expect *him* to become what you yourself are, but by the same means. You, that have toiled during youth, to set your son upon higher ground, and to enable him to begin where you left off, do not expect that son to be what you were, diligent, modest, active, simple in his

---

1   William Wordsworth, who read this essay attentively, remembers this passage in an 1829 letter: education, he says, is "everything that *draws out* the human being, of which *tuition*, the teaching of schools especially, however important, is comparatively an insignificant part" (*Letters of William and Dorothy Wordsworth*, p. 19).

2   According to Robert Hooper's *Lexicon Medicum; or Medical Dictionary* (1798), "insensible perspiration" has important beneficial effects on the body, whereas "sensible perspiration"(i.e., sweat) is less evidently helpful (s.v. "Perspiration"; we are grateful to Dr. David Zuck for this reference).

tastes, fertile in resources. You have put him under quite a different master. Poverty educated you; wealth will educate him. You cannot suppose the result will be the same. You must not even expect that he will be what you now are; for though relaxed perhaps from the severity of your frugal habits, you still derive advantage from having formed them; and, in your heart, you like plain dinners, and early hours, and old friends, whenever your fortune will permit you to enjoy them. But it will not be so with your son: his tastes will be formed by your present situation, and in no degree by your former one. But I take great care, you will say, to counteract these tendencies, and to bring him up in hardy and simple manners. I know their value, and am resolved that he shall acquire no other. Yes, you make him hardy; that is to say, you take a country-house in a good air, and make him run, well clothed and carefully attended, for, it may be, an hour in a clear frosty winter's day upon your gravelled terrace; or perhaps you take the puny shivering infant from his warm bed, and dip him in an icy cold bath, and you think you have done great matters. And so you have; you have done all you can. But *you* were suffered to run abroad half the day on a bleak heath, in weather fit and unfit, wading barefoot through dirty ponds, sometimes losing your way benighted, scrambling over hedges, climbing trees, in perils every hour both of life and limb. Your life was of very little consequence to any one; even your parents, encumbered with a numerous family, had little time to indulge the softnesses of affection, or the solicitude of anxiety; and to every one else it was of no consequence at all. It is not possible for you, it would not even be right for you, in your present situation, to pay no more attention to your child than was paid to you. In these mimic experiments of education, there is always something which distinguishes them from reality; some weak part left unfortified, for the arrows of misfortune to find their way into. Achilles was a young nobleman, *dios Achilleus*, and therefore, though he had Chiron for his tutor, there was one foot left undipped.[1] You

---

1  Barbauld alludes pointedly to Rousseau, who in *Émile* uses the story of the education of the Greek hero Achilles as a metaphor. Achilles was dipped by his mother in a river that made him invulnerable to injury—but the part by which she held

may throw by Rousseau; your parents practiced without having read it;[1] and you may read, but *imperious circumstances*[2] forbid you the practice of it.

You are sensible of the advantages of simplicity of diet, and you make a point of restricting that of your child to the plainest food, for you are resolved that he shall not be nice.[3] But this plain food is of the choicest quality, prepared by your own cook; his fruit is ripened from your walls; his cloth, his glasses, all the accompaniments of the table, are such as are only met with in families of opulence; the very servants who attend him are neat, well dressed, and have a certain air of fashion. You may call this simplicity, but I say he will be nice, for it is a kind of simplicity which only wealth can attain to, and which will subject him to be disgusted at all common tables. Besides, he will from time to time partake of those delicacies which your table abounds with; you yourself will give him of them occasionally; you would be unkind if you did not; your servants, if good natured, will do the same. Do you think you can keep the full stream of luxury running by his lips, and he not taste of it? Vain imagination!

I would not be understood to inveigh against wealth, or against the enjoyments of it; they are real enjoyments, and allied to many elegancies in manners and in taste; I only wish to prevent unprofitable pains and inconsistent expectations.[4]

You are sensible of the benefit of early rising, and you may, if you please, make it a point that your daughter shall retire with her governess, and your son with his tutor, at the hour when you are preparing to see company. But their sleep, in the first place, will not be so sweet and undisturbed amidst the rattle of

---

him, his heel, remained undipped. Rousseau urges that the child be hardened to pain, and refers to the dipping of Achilles as if it had succeeded (p. 47). At the end of the book, Rousseau admits that his "dipping" of Émile has failed in one respect: it has left Émile vulnerable to his own passions (p. 443). Barbauld treats the dipping failure as the failure (inevitable) of "mimic experiments" like Rousseau's. Chiron, tutor to Achilles, taught him how to run.

1  Rousseau counsels subjecting the small child to a severe regimen (cold baths, light clothing in all weathers, plain food) to toughen it.

2  Apparently a quotation, but we have not traced it.

3  Fastidious, demanding.

4  See Barbauld's early essay, "Against Inconsistency in our Expectations."

carriages, and the glare of tapers glancing through the rooms, as that of the village child in his quiet cottage, protected by silence and darkness; and, moreover, you may depend upon it, that as the coercive power of education is laid aside, they will in a few months slide into the habitudes of the rest of the family, whose hours are determined by their company and situation in life. You have, however, done good as far as it goes; it is something gained to defer pernicious habits, if we cannot prevent them.

There is nothing which has so little share in education as direct precept.[1] To be convinced of this, we need only reflect, that there is no one point we labour more to establish with children than that of their speaking truth, and there is not any in which we succeed worse. And why? Because children readily see we have an interest in it. Their speaking truth is used by us as an engine of government.[2] "Tell me, my dear child, when you have broken any thing, and I will not be angry with you." "Thank you for nothing, says the child. If I prevent you from finding it out, I am *sure* you will not be angry;" and nine times out of ten he *can* prevent it. He knows that, in the common intercourses of life, *you* tell a thousand falsehoods. But these are necessary lies on important occasions.

Your child is the best judge how much occasion he has to tell a lie; he may have as great occasion for it, as you have to conceal a bad piece of news from a sick friend, or to hide your vexation from an unwelcome visitor. That authority which extends its claims over every action, and even every thought, which insists upon an answer to every interrogation, however indiscreet or oppressive to the feelings, will, in young or old, produce falsehood; or, if in some few instances, the deeply

---

1 A point urged repeatedly by both Rousseau and Genlis.

2 Among the precepts which Barbauld, like Rousseau, Genlis, and other educational reformers, regarded as useless were those in reading primers which urged children to "Speak the Truth and lie not" (quoted in McCarthy, "Mother of All Discourses," p. 203). Barbauld agrees with Rousseau that demanding truthfulness from children is a means of controlling them (*Émile*, p. 102). Her example, below ("'Tell me, my dear child …'"), may allude to Maria Edgeworth's tale, "The Little Dog Trusty," in *The Parent's Assistant* (1796), in which a mother encourages her son to "tell me the truth [when he has broken anything]—I shall not be angry with you, child" (quoted in McCarthy, "Celebrated Academy," p. 381 n. 30).

imbibed fear of future and unknown punishment should restrain from direct falsehood, it will produce a habit of dissimulation, which is still worse.[1] The child, the slave, or the subject, who, on proper occasions may not say, "I do not chuse to tell," will certainly, by the circumstances in which you place him, be driven to have recourse to deceit, even should he not be countenanced by your example.

I do not mean to assert, that sentiments inculcated in education have no influence; they have much, though not the most: but it is the sentiments we let drop occasionally, the conversation they overhear when playing unnoticed in a corner of the room, which has an effect upon children, and not what is addressed directly to them in the tone of exhortation. If you would know precisely the effect these set discourses have upon your child, be pleased to reflect upon that which a discourse from the pulpit, which you have reason to think merely professional, has upon you. Children have almost an intuitive discernment between the maxims you bring forward for their use, and those by which you direct your own conduct. Be as cunning as you will, they are always more cunning than you. Every child knows whom his father and mother love, and see with pleasure, and whom they dislike; for whom they think themselves obliged to set out their best plate and china; whom they think it an honour to visit, and upon whom they confer honour by admitting them to their company. "Respect nothing so much as virtue, (says Eugenio to his son) virtue and talents are the only grounds of distinction." The child presently has occasion to enquire why his father pulls off his hat to some people and not to others; he is told, that outward respect must be proportioned to different stations in life. This is a little difficult of comprehension; however, by dint of explanation, he gets over it tolerably well. But he sees his father's house in the bustle and hurry of preparation; common business laid aside, every body

---

1 Barbauld's criticism of indiscreet and oppressive questioning may derive from her father's practice of never questioning his son (her brother) about his schoolmates' activities (Aikin, *Memoir of John Aikin*, 1:3). One of Barbauld's friends regretted that her own upbringing was so strict that it encouraged "concealment, which is always dangerous" (Ross, *Three Generations*, p. 51).

in movement, an unusual anxiety to please and to shine. Nobody is at leisure to receive his caresses, or attend to his questions; his lessons are interrupted, his hours deranged. At length a guest arrives—It is my Lord —— whom he has heard you speak of, twenty times, as one of the most worthless characters upon earth. Your child, Eugenio, has received a lesson of education. Resume, if you will, your systems of morality on the morrow, you will in vain attempt to eradicate it. "You expect company, Mamma, must I be dressed to-day?" "No, it is only good Mrs. such a one." Your child has received a lesson of education, one which she well understands, and will long remember. You have sent your child to a public school, but to secure his morals against the vice which you too justly apprehend abounds there,[1] you have given him a private tutor, a man of strict morals and religion. He may help him to prepare his tasks, but do you imagine it will be in his power to form his mind? His schoolfellows, the allowance you give him, the manners of the age, and of the place, will do that, and not the lectures which he is obliged to hear. If these are different from what you yourself experienced, you must not be surprised to see him gradually recede from the principles, civil and religious, which you hold, and break off from your connections, and adopt manners different from your own. This is remarkably exemplified amongst those of the Dissenters who have risen to wealth and consequence. I believe it would be difficult to find an instance of families, who, for three generations, have kept their carriage and continued Dissenters.[2]

Education, it is often observed, is an expensive thing. It is so, but the paying for lessons is the smallest part of the cost. If you would go to the price of having your son a worthy man, you must be so yourself;[3] your friends, your servants, your company

---

1  Cf. *An Address to the Opposers*, p. 272 above.

2  That is, families rich enough to own a carriage for three generations are likely to have gone over to the more "respectable" Anglican Church. In an 1834 letter Wordsworth quoted this passage in justification of his prejudice against Dissenters (*Letters*, p. 699).

3  Rousseau and Genlis likewise emphasize the importance of parental example. As Genlis puts it, "if *you* cannot suffer pain or illness without complaining every moment, all you can say about fortitude and courage will make little impression" (*Adelaide and Theodore*, 1:91-92).

must be all of that stamp. Suppose this to be the case, much is done; but there will remain circumstances which perhaps you cannot alter, that will still have their effect. Do you wish him to love simplicity? Would you be content to lay down your coach, to drop your title? Where is the parent who would do this to educate his son? You carry him to the workshops of artisans, and show him different machines and fabrics, to awaken his ingenuity. The necessity of getting his bread would awaken it much more effectually. The single circumstance of having a fortune to get, or a fortune to spend, will probably operate more strongly upon his mind, not only than your precepts, but even than your example. You wish your child to be modest and unassuming; you are so, perhaps, yourself, and you pay liberally a preceptor for giving him lessons of humility. You do not perceive, that the very circumstance of having a man of letters and accomplishments retained about his person, for his sole advantage, tends more forcibly to inspire him with an idea of self-consequence, than all the lessons he can give him to repress it. *Why do not you look sad, you rascal?* says the Undertaker to his man, in the play of the Funeral, *I give you I know not how much money for looking sad, and the more I give you, the gladder I think you are.*[1] So will it be with the wealthy heir. The lectures that are given him on condescension and affability, only prove to him upon how much higher ground he stands than those about him; and the very pains that are taken with his moral character will make him proud, by shewing him how much he is the object of attention. You cannot help these things. Your servants, out of respect to you, will bear with his petulance; your company, out of respect to you, will forbear to check his impatience; and you yourself, if he is clever, will repeat his observations.

In the exploded doctrine of sympathies,[2] you are directed, if you have cut your finger, to let that alone, and put your plaister upon the knife. This is very bad doctrine, I must confess, in

---

1   Barbauld quotes (very approximately) the speech of Sable to his assistants in Sir Richard Steele's *The Funeral* (1701), I.i.
2   The obsolete ("exploded") belief that whatever affects a thing will also affect another thing associated with it.

philosophy, but very good in morals. Is a man luxurious, self-indulgent? do not apply your *physic of the soul* to him, but cure his fortune. Is he haughty? cure his rank, his title. Is he vulgar? cure his company. Is he diffident, or mean-spirited? cure his poverty, give him consequence—but these prescriptions go far beyond the family recipes of education.

What then is the result? In the first place, that we should contract our ideas of education, and expect no more from it than it is able to perform. It can give *instruction*. There will always be an essential difference between a human being culti-vated and uncultivated. Education can provide proper instruc-tors in the various arts and sciences, and portion out to the best advantage, those precious hours of youth which never will return. It can likewise give, in a great degree, personal habits; and even if these should afterwards give way, under the infl-uence of contrary circumstances, your child will feel the good effects of them, for the later and the less will he go into what is wrong. Let us also be assured, that the business of education, properly so called, is not transferrable. You may engage masters to instruct your child in this or the other accomplishment, but you must *educate* him yourself. You not only ought to do it, but you *must* do it, whether you intend it or no. As education is a thing necessary for all; for the poor and for the rich, for the illiterate as well as for the learned; providence has not made it dependent upon systems uncertain, operose,[1] and difficult of investigation. It is not necessary with Rousseau or Madame Genlis, to devote to the education of one child, the talents and the time of a number of grown men;[2] to surround him with an artificial world; and to counteract, by maxims, the natural ten-dencies of the situation he is placed in by society. Every one has time to educate his child;—the poor man educates him while working in his cottage—the man of business while employed in his counting-house.

---

1  Tedious.

2  Rousseau's narrator devotes his entire time to educating Émile from young child-hood until his marriage. The mother in *Adèle et Théodore* retires from the world to educate her children, and brings with her "two persons well qualified to instruct children, who will remain here till their education is compleated" (1:18).

Do we see a father who is diligent in his profession, domestic in his habits, whose house is the resort of well-informed intelligent people—a mother, whose time is usefully filled, whose attention to her duties secures esteem, and whose amiable manners attract affection? Do not be solicitous, respectable couple, about the moral education of your offspring! do not be uneasy because you cannot surround them with the apparatus of books and systems; or fancy you must retire from the world to devote yourselves to their improvement. In *your* world they are brought up much better than they could be under any plan of factitious education which you could provide for them; they will imbibe affection from your caresses; taste from your conversation; urbanity from the commerce of your society; and mutual love from your example. Do not regret that you are not rich enough to provide tutors and governors, to watch his steps with sedulous and servile anxiety, and furnish him with maxims it is morally impossible he should act upon when grown up. Do not you see how seldom this over culture produces its effect, and many shining and excellent characters start up every day, from the bosom of obscurity, with scarcely any care at all?

Are children then to be neglected? surely not; but having given them the instruction and accomplishments which their situation in life requires, let us reject superfluous solicitude, and trust that their characters will form themselves from the spontaneous influence of good examples, and circumstances which impel them to useful action.

But the education of your house, important as it is, is only a part of a more comprehensive system. Providence takes your child, where you leave him. Providence continues his education upon a larger scale, and by a process which includes means far more efficacious. Has your son entered the world at eighteen, opinionated, haughty, rash, inclined to dissipation? Do not despair, he may yet be cured of these faults, if it pleases heaven. There are remedies which you could not persuade yourself to use, if they were in your power, and which are specific in cases of this kind. How often do we see the presumptuous, giddy youth, changed into the wise counsellor, the considerate, steady friend! How often the thoughtless, gay girl, into the sober wife, the affectionate mother! Faded beauty, humbled self-consequence, disappointed ambition, loss of fortune, this is the rough physic provided by Providence, to meliorate the temper, to correct the offensive petulancies of youth, and bring out all the energies of the finished character. Afflictions soften the proud; difficulties push forward the ingenious; successful industry gives consequence and credit, and developes a thousand latent good qualities. There is no malady of the mind so inveterate, which this education of events is not calculated to cure, if life were long enough; and shall we not hope, that he, in whose hand are all the remedial processes of nature, will renew the discipline in another state, and finish the imperfect man?

States are educated as individuals, by circumstances; the prophet may cry aloud, and spare not;[1] the philosopher may descant on morals; eloquence may exhaust itself in invective against the vices of the age: these vices will certainly follow certain states of poverty or riches, ignorance or high civilization. But what these gentle alteratives[2] fail of doing, may be accomplished by an unsuccessful war, a loss of trade, or any of those great calamities, by which it pleases Providence to speak to a nation in such language as will be heard. If, as a nation, we would be cured of pride, it must be by mortification; if of luxury, by a national bankruptcy, perhaps; if of injustice, or the spirit of domination, by a loss of national consequence. In comparison of these strong remedies, a *fast*, or a *sermon*, are prescriptions of very little efficacy.[3]

---

1   Isaiah 58:1.
2   Drugs used to change the course of an illness.
3   On fasts, see the headnote to *Sins of Government*.

[Perhaps the most important issue in Enlightenment culture was its ideal of human understanding grounded entirely in the subject's direct, conscious experience. From John Locke through Jean-Jacques Rousseau, people are held to "know" only what they have actually sensed, or what they have inferred—without suggestion or outside influence—from their sensations. All the rest, the totality of practices and beliefs by which the subject is surrounded from birth to death, is regarded with deep suspicion as "prejudice," the detritus of society's history. Rousseau put the case at its most extreme: "All our wisdom consists in servile prejudices. All our practices are only subjection, impediment, and constraint" (*Émile*, p. 42). More moderate views, like David Hume's, treated prejudice as a threat to intellectual integrity: "It is well known, that, in all questions submitted to the understanding, prejudice is destructive of sound judgment, and perverts all operations of the intellectual faculties" (*Selected Essays*, p. 146). Only an Enlightenment person could have uttered this prayer by the Rev. Thomas Belsham in 1787: "How numerous are the prejudices to which I am exposed; how difficult is it to be aware of them, and to fortify myself against them! Do thou deliver me, I beseech thee, from the prejudices of education, of fashion, of novelty, of pride and vanity, of self-interest, and from every other improper bias of mind, however unknown and unsuspected" (Williams, *Memoirs*, pp. 342-43).

The implications for pedagogy and politics were immense. Rousseau sets out to "protect" his pupil "from men's opinions": "the first education ought to be purely negative" (*Émile*, pp. 443, 93). The countess de Genlis proudly claims that her pupil Adèle at age twelve "will have but few ideas, but they will be rational ones" (*Adelaide and Theodore*, 1:51). In politics, Tom Paine declares that "the prejudices which men have from education and habit, in favor of any particular form or system of government ... have yet to stand the test of reason and reflection" (*The Rights of Man*, p. 393). Conservatives, apparently led by Edmund Burke in his *Reflections on the late Revolution in*

*France* (1790), accordingly set out to rehabilitate prejudice as the embodiment of "natural"—and therefore traditional—feeling. "[A] kind of fashion now prevails," Mary Wollstonecraft noticed in 1792, "of respecting prejudices; and when anyone dares to face them ... he is superciliously asked whether his ancestors were fools" (*Rights of Woman*, p. 216).

These are the issues Barbauld addresses in "On Prejudice," published in *The Monthly Magazine*, 9 (March 1800): 139-44. Negotiating, with customary independence of mind, between Enlightened and conservative dogmas, she argues that all learning is situated, and that to be situated is—inescapably—to be "prejudiced." Her argument prefigures developments in modern philosophy and finds an echo in the nineteenth-century American philosopher Charles Sanders Peirce: "We cannot begin with complete doubt. We must begin with all the prejudices which we actually have when we enter upon the study of philosophy. These prejudices are not to be dispelled by a maxim, for they are things which it does not occur to us *can* be questioned. Hence this initial skepticism will be a mere self-deception..." (*Values*, p. 40).]

It is to speculative people, fond of novel doctrines, and who, by accustoming themselves to make the most fundamental truths the subject of discussion, have divested their minds of that reverence which is generally felt for opinions and practices of long standing, that the world is ever to look for its improvement or reformation.[1] But it is also these speculatists who introduce into it absurdities and errors more gross than any which have been established by that common consent of numerous individuals, which opinions long acted upon must have required for their basis. For systems of the latter class must at least possess one property,—that of being practicable: and there is likewise a presumption that they are, or at least originally were, useful; whereas the opinions of the speculatist may turn out to be

---

1 Barbauld might well be thinking of her friend Joseph Priestley, who argued that it is the "proper business" of the "more enlightened" minds in a community "to speculate, to devise plans for the public good, and to make trials of such as promise the best" (*Letter to ... William Pitt*, p. 9).

utterly incongruous and eccentric. The speculatist may invent machines which it is impossible to put in action, or which, when put in action, may possess the tremendous power of tearing up society by the roots. Like the chemist, he is not sure in the moment of projection whether he shall blow up his own dwelling and that of his neighbour, or whether he shall be rewarded with a discovery which will secure the health and prolong the existence of future generations. It becomes us therefore to examine with peculiar care those maxims, which, under the appearance of following a closer train of reasoning, militate against the usual practices or genuine feelings of mankind. No subject has been more canvassed than education. With regard to that important object, there is a maxim avowed by many sensible people, which seems to me to deserve particular investigation: "Give your child," it is said, "no *prejudices*: let reason be the only foundation of his opinions; where he cannot reason, let him suspend his belief. Let your great care be, that, as he grows up, he has nothing to unlearn; and never make use of authority in matters of opinion, for authority is no test of truth." The maxim sounds well, and flatters perhaps the secret pride of man, in supposing him more the creature of reason than he really is; but, I suspect, on examination we shall find it exceedingly fallacious. We must first consider what a *prejudice* is. A prejudice is a sentiment in favour or disfavour of any person, practice or opinion, previous to and independent of examining their merits by reason and investigation. Prejudice is prejudging; that is, judging previously to evidence. It is therefore sufficiently apparent, that no *philosophical belief* can be founded on mere prejudice; because it is the business of philosophy to go deep into the nature and properties of things;[1] nor can it be

---

1   philosophy: includes science. In asserting that philosophical investigations must be carried on in strict neutrality (below), Barbauld accepts what historians Joyce Appleby, Lynn Hunt, and Margaret Jacob have called "the heroic model of science": "the rationality of science [as understood in the Enlightenment] derived from the disinterested posture of its practitioners, their openness to all criticism (if based upon experimentation), and from their refusal to countenance belief, opinion, self-interest, or passion in the search for truth about nature" (*Telling the Truth about History*, pp. 29-30). "Audacious boldness" (below) characterizes Priestley's positions in religion and politics.

allowable for *those* to indulge prejudice who aspire to lead the public opinion, those to whom the high office is appointed of sifting truth from error, of canvassing the claims of different systems, of exploding old and introducing new tenets. These must investigate with a kind of audacious boldness every subject that comes before them; these, neither imprest with awe for all that mankind have been taught to reverence, nor swayed by affection for whatever the sympathies of our nature incline us to love,[1] must hold the balance with a severe and steady hand while they are weighing the doubtful scale of probabilities; and, with a stoical apathy of mind, yield their assent to nothing but a preponderancy of evidence. But is this an office for a child? Is it an office for more than one or two men in a century? And is it desirable that a child should grow up without opinions to regulate his conduct, till he is able to form them fairly by the exercise of his own abilities? Such an exercise requires at least the sober period of matured reason: reason not only sharpened by argumentative discussion, but informed by experience. The most sprightly child can only possess the former; for let it be remembered, that though the reasoning powers put forth pretty early in life, the faculty of using them to effect does not come till much later. The first efforts of a child in reasoning resemble those quick and desultory motions by which he gains the play of his limbs; they show agility and grace, they are pleasing to look at, and necessary for the gradual acquirement of his bodily powers; but his joints must be knit into more firmness, and his movements regulated with more precision, before he is capable of useful labour and manly exertion. A reasoning child is not yet a reasonable being. There is great propriety in the legal phraseology which expresses maturity, not by having arrived at the possession of reason, but of that power, the late result of information, thought, and experience—*discretion*, which alone teaches with regard to *reason*, its powers, its limits, and its use. This the child of the most sprightly parts cannot have, and therefore his attempts at reasoning, whatever acuteness they may show, and how much soever they may please a parent with

---

1  the sympathies of our nature: alludes to Edmund Burke's frequent appeals to "natural feeling" in his *Reflections*.

the early promise of future excellence, are of no account whatever in the sober search after truth.—Besides, taking it for granted (which however is utterly impossible) that a youth could be brought up to the age of fifteen or sixteen without prejudice in favour of any opinions whatever,[1] and that he is then set to examine for himself some important proposition, how is he to set about it? Who is to recommend books to him? Who is to give him the previous information necessary to comprehend the question? Who is to tell him whether or no it is important? Whoever does these will infallibly lay a bias upon his mind according to the ideas he himself has received upon the subject. Let us suppose the point in debate was the preference between the Roman Catholic and Protestant modes of religion. Can a youth in a Protestant country, born of Protestant parents, with access, probably, to hardly a single controversial book on the Roman Catholic side of the question, can such a one study the subject without prejudice? His knowledge of history, if he has such knowledge, must, according to the books he has read, have already given him a prejudice on the one side or the other; so must the occasional conversation he has been witness to, the appellations he has heard used, the tone of voice with which he has heard the words monk or priest pronounced, and a thousand other evanescent circumstances. It is likewise to be observed, that every question of any weight and importance has numerous dependencies and points of connexion with other subjects, which make it impossible to enter upon the consideration of it without a great variety of previous knowledge. There is no object of investigation perfectly insulated; we must not conceive therefore of a man's sitting down to it with a mind perfectly new and untutored; he must have passed more or less through a course of studies, and, according to the colour of those studies, his mind will have received a tincture, that is, a prejudice.—But it is, in truth, the most absurd of all suppositions that a human being can be educated, or even nourished and brought up, without imbibing numberless pre-

---

1  At this age, Rousseau's Émile "refuses his attention to everything beyond his reach and listens to things he does not understand with the most profound indifference" (p. 259).

judices from every thing which passes around him. A child cannot learn the signification of words without receiving ideas along with them; he cannot be impressed with affection to his parents and those about him, without conceiving a predilection for their tastes, opinions, and practices. He forms numberless associations of pain or pleasure, and every association begets a prejudice; he sees objects from a particular spot, and his views of things are contracted or extended according to his position in society; as no two individuals can have the same horizon, so neither can any two have the same associations; and different associations will produce different opinions, as necessarily as, by the laws of perspective, different distances will produce different appearances of visible objects. Let us confess a truth, humiliating perhaps to human pride: a very small part only of the opinions of the coolest philosopher are the result of fair reasoning; the rest are formed by his education, his temperament, by the age in which he lives, by trains of thought directed to a particular track through some accidental association—in short, by *prejudice.*—But why after all should we wish to bring up children without prejudices? A child has occasion to act long before he can reason. Shall we leave him destitute of all the principles that should regulate his conduct till he can discover them by the strength of his own genius? If it were possible that one whole generation could be brought up without prejudices, the world must return to the infancy of knowledge, and all the beautiful fabric which has been built up by successive generations must be begun again from the very foundation. Your child has a claim to the advantage of your experience, which it would be cruel and unjust to deprive him of. Will any father say to his son, "My dear child, you are entering upon a world full of intricate and perplexed paths, in which many miss their way, to their final misery and ruin. Amidst many false systems, and much vain science, there is also some true knowledge; there is a right path; I believe I know it, for I have the advantage of years and experience; but I will instil no prejudices into your mind; I shall therefore leave you to find it out as you can; whether your abilities be great or small, you must take the chance of them. There are various systems in morals; I have examined and found some of a good, others of a bad tendency. There is such a thing as religion; many people think it the most important concern of life; perhaps I am one of them: perhaps I have chosen from amidst the various systems of belief, many of which are extremely absurd, and some even pernicious, that which I cherish as the guide of my life, my comfort in all my sorrows, and the foundation of my dearest hopes: but far be it from me to influence you in any manner to receive it; when you are grown up, you must read all the books upon these subjects on which you can lay your hands, for neither in the choice of these would I presume to prejudice your mind; converse with all who pretend to any opinions upon the subject; and whatever happens to be the result, you must abide by it. In the mean time, concerning these important objects you must keep your mind in a perfect equilibrium. It is true that you want these principles more now than you can do at any other period of your life, but I had rather you never had them at all, than that you should not come fairly by them." Should we commend the wisdom or the kindness of such a parent? The parent will perhaps plead in his behalf, that it is by no means his intention to leave the mind of his child in the uncultivated state I have supposed. As soon as his understanding begins to open, he means to discuss with him those propositions on which he wishes him to form an opinion. He will make him read the best books on the subject, and, by free conversation and explaining the arguments on both sides, he does not doubt but the youth will soon be enabled to judge satisfactorily for himself. I have no objection to make against this mode of proceeding: as a mode of *instruction*, it is certainly a very good one; but he must know little of human nature, who thinks that after this process the youth will be really in a capacity of judging for himself, or that he is less under the dominion of prejudice than if he had received the same truths from the mere authority of his parent; for most assuredly the arguments on either side will not have been set before him with equal strength, or with equal warmth. The persuasive tone, the glowing language, the triumphant retort, will all be reserved for the side on which the parent has formed his own conclusions. It cannot be otherwise:

he cannot be convinced himself of what he thinks a truth without wishing to convey that conviction, nor without thinking all that can be urged on the other side weak and futile. He cannot in a matter of importance neutralize his feelings: perfect impartiality can be the result only of indifference. He does not perhaps seem to dictate, but he wishes gently to guide his pupil, and that wish is seldom disappointed. The child adopts the opinion of his parent, and seems to himself to have adopted it from the decisions of his own judgment: but all these reasonings must be gone over again, and these opinions undergo a fiery ordeal, if ever he comes really to think and determine for himself.

The fact is, that no man, whatever his system may be, refrains from instilling prejudices into his child in any matter he has much at heart. Take a disciple of Rousseau, who contends that it would be very pernicious to give his son any ideas of a Deity, till he is of an age to read Clarke or Leibnitz,[1] and ask him if he waits so long to impress on his mind the sentiments of patriotism—the civic affection.[2] O no; you will find his little heart is early taught to beat at the very name of liberty, and that, long before he is capable of forming a single political idea, he has entered with warmth into all the party sentiments and connections of his parent. He learns to love and hate, to venerate or despise, by rote, and he soon acquires decided opinions, of the real ground of which he can know absolutely nothing. Are not ideas of female honour and decorum imprest first as prejudices; and would any parent wish they should be so much as canvassed till the most settled habits of propriety have rendered it safe to do it? In teaching first by prejudice that which is afterwards to be proved, we do but follow Nature. Instincts are the

---

1 At 15, Émile has not yet heard of God and does not know whether he has a soul; Rousseau derides teaching catechisms to children (*Émile*, pp. 254, 257). However, Rousseau admired Samuel Clarke (1675-1729), an English theologian who corresponded with the German philosopher Gottfried Leibniz and wrote in defence of the Christian religion.

2 Rousseau exhorts Émile to love his country, but only when Émile is grown (p. 473). Perhaps Barbauld is thinking of actual parents she knew. At Palgrave School, she herself had inculcated a civic spirit in her pupils.

prejudices she gives us:[1] we follow them implicitly, and they lead us right; but it is not till long afterwards that reason comes and justifies them. Why should we scruple to lead a child to right opinions in the same way by which Nature leads him to right practices.

Still it will be urged that man is a rational being, and therefore reason is the only true ground of belief, and authority is not reason. This point requires a little discussion. That he who receives a truth upon authority has not a reasonable belief, is in one sense true, since he has not drawn it from the result of his own inquiries; but in another it is certainly false, since the authority itself may be to him the best of all reasons for believing it. There are few men, who from the exercise of the best powers of their minds could derive so good a *reason* for believing a mathematical truth as the *authority* of Sir Isaac Newton.[2] There are two[3] principles deeply implanted in the mind of man, without which he could never attain knowledge,—curiosity, and credulity; the former to lead him to make discoveries himself, the latter to dispose him to receive knowledge from others. The credulity of a child to those who cherish him is in early life unbounded. This is one of the most useful instincts he has, and is in fact a precious advantage put into the hands of the parent for storing his mind with ideas of all kinds. Without this principle of assent he could never gain even the rudiments of knowledge. He receives it, it is true, in the shape of prejudice, but the prejudice itself is founded upon sound reasoning, and conclusive though imperfect experiment. He finds himself weak, helpless, and ignorant; he sees in his parent a being of knowledge and powers more than his utmost capacity can fathom; almost a god to him. He has often done him good, therefore he believes he loves him; he finds him capable of giv-

---

1   Barbauld agrees with Edmund Burke in regarding prejudices as effects of nature (*Reflections*, p. 105); but she stops short of giving them the political content that he does (fear of God, awe of kings, affection for parliaments, respect for nobility, p. 104).

2   Celebrated English physicist and mathematician, author of *Principia Mathematica* (1687).

3   two: thus in *Works*; "too" in 1798.

ing him information upon all the subjects he has applied to him about; his knowledge seems unbounded, and his information has led him right, whenever he has had occasion to try it by actual experiment; the child does not draw out his little reasonings into a logical form, but this is to him a ground of belief, that his parent knows every thing, and is infallible. Though the proposition is not exactly true, it is sufficiently so for him to act upon; and when he believes in his parent with implicit faith, he believes upon grounds as truly rational as when in after life he follows the deductions of his own reason.

But you will say, I wish my son may have nothing to *unlearn*, and therefore I would have him wait to form an opinion till he is able to do it on solid grounds. And why do you suppose he will have less to unlearn if he follows his own reason than if he followed yours? If he thinks, if he inquires, he will no doubt have a great deal to unlearn, whichever course you take with him; but it is better to have some things to unlearn, than to have nothing learnt. Do you hold your own opinions so loosely, so hesitatingly, as not to think them safer to abide by than the first results of his stammering reason? Are there no truths to learn so indubitable as to be without fear of their not approving themselves to his mature and well-directed judgment? Are there none you esteem so useful as to feel anxious that he be put in possession of them? We are solicitous not only to put our children in a capacity of acquiring their daily bread, but to bequeath to them riches which they may receive as an inheritance. Have you no mental wealth you wish to transmit, no stock of ideas he may begin with, instead of drawing them all from the labour of his own brain? If, moreover your son should not adopt your prejudices, he will certainly adopt those of other people; or, if on subjects of high interest he *could* be kept totally indifferent, the consequence would be, that he would conceive either that such matters were not worth the trouble of inquiry, or that nothing satisfactory was to be learnt about them: for there are negative prejudices as well as positive.

Let parents therefore not scruple to use the power which God and nature have put into their hands for the advantage of their offspring. Let them not fear to impress them with prejudices for whatever is fair and honourable in action—whatever is useful and important in systematic truth. Let such prejudices be wrought into the very texture of the soul. Such truths let them appear to know by intuition. Let the child never remember the period when he did not know them.[1] Instead of sending him to that cold and hesitating belief which is founded on the painful and uncertain consequences of late investigation, let his conviction of all the truths you deem important be mixed up with every warm affection of his nature, and identified with his most cherished recollections—the time will come soon enough when his confidence in you will have received a check. The growth of his own reason and the developement of his powers will lead him with a sudden impetus to examine every thing, to canvass every thing, to suspect every thing. If he find, as he certainly will find, the results of his reasoning different in some respects from those you have given him, far from being now disposed to receive your assertions as proofs, he will rather feel disinclined to any opinion you profess, and struggle to free himself from the net which you have wove about him.

The calm repose of his mind is broken, the placid lake is become turbid, and reflects distorted and broken images of things; but be not you alarmed at the new workings of his thoughts, it is the angel of reason which descends and troubles the waters. To endeavour to influence by authority would be as useless now as it was salutary before. Lie by in silence and wait the result. Do not expect the mind of your son to resemble yours, as your figure is reflected by the image in the glass; he was formed, like you, to use his own judgment, and he claims the high privilege of his nature. His reason is mature, his mind must now form itself. Happy must you esteem yourself, if amidst all lesser differences of opinion, and the wreck of many of your favourite ideas, he still preserve those radical[2] and primary truths which are essential to his happiness, and which different trains of thought and opposite modes of investigation will often equally lead to.

---

1  Barbauld uses almost the same words in the "Advertisement" to *Hymns in Prose*.
2  Fundamental.

Let it be well remembered that we have only been recommending those prejudices which go before reason, not those which are contrary to it. To endeavour to make children, or others over whom we have influence, receive systems which we do not believe, merely because it is convenient to ourselves that they should believe them, though a very fashionable practice, makes no part of the discipline we plead for. These are not prejudices but impositions. We may also grant that nothing should be received as a prejudice which can be easily made the subject of experiment. A child may be allowed to find out for himself that boiling water will scald his fingers, and mustard bite his tongue; but he must be *prejudiced* against rats-bane,[1] because the experiment would be too costly. In like manner it may do him good to have experienced that little instances of inattention or perverseness draw upon him the displeasure of his parent; but that profligacy is attended with loss of character,[2] is a truth one would rather wish him to take upon trust.

There is no occasion to inculcate by prejudices those truths which it is of no importance for us to know till our powers are able to investigate them. Thus the metaphysical questions of space and time, necessity and free-will, and a thousand others, may safely be left for that age which delights in such discussions. They have no connection with conduct, and none have any business with them at all but those who are able by such studies to exercise and sharpen their mental powers: but it is not so with those truths on which our well-being depends; these must be taught to all, not only before they can reason upon them, but independently of the consideration whether they will ever be able to reason upon them as long as they live.—What has hitherto been said relates only to instilling prejudices into *others;* how far a man is to allow them in himself, or, as a celebrated writer expresses it, to *cherish* them,[3] is a

---

1 Rat poison.

2 Reputation.

3 Edmund Burke, who in *Reflections* declares that the English, "instead of casting away all our old prejudices, ... cherish them to a very considerable degree, and ... cherish them because they are prejudices; and the longer they have lasted, and the more generally they have prevailed, the more we cherish them" (p. 105).

different question, on which perhaps I may some time offer my thoughts.[1] ~~In the mean time I cannot help concluding, that to~~ reject the influence of prejudice in education, is itself one of the most unreasonable of prejudices.

## THOUGHTS ON THE INEQUALITY OF CONDITIONS

[This essay appears to have been provoked by Barbauld's encounter with *A Treatise on the Police of the Metropolis* by Patrick Colquhoun (1796, and later editions through 1806). Colquhoun's subject was "the various Crimes and Misdemeanors By which Public and Private Property and Security are, at present, injured and endangered," particularly in and around London; his aim was to suggest "Remedies for their Prevention." The *Treatise* achieved prominence in a growing discussion of the working class, poverty, and the poor. Conducted by middle-class intellectuals, that discussion was moved in part by shocked humanitarianism: the working class was visibly ill-housed, ragged, malnourished, and diseased, conditions aggravated by the declining relative wages and crowded factories characteristic of the Industrial Revolution. To many, like John Aikin in 1794, society seemed to be splitting into two species: "Between the inhabitant of the splendid square, and the tenant of the gloomy alley, the apparent difference is such, that if we take our ideas of the nature and destination of man from the one, they seem no more applicable to the other, than if they were beings of different orders" ("On the Inequality of Conditions," pp. 207-08). The discussion was moved also by fear: of working-class "combinations" (concerted demands for better wages and working conditions, which seemed like insurrection), and also of a moral "contagion" that many believed would be spread by the "ignorance" and "irresponsible" behavior associated in public discourse with the working class. Hence, proposed solutions generally took the form of man-

---

1   "It is to be regretted that Mrs. Barbauld never fulfilled the intention here intimated" (Lucy Aikin's note, *Works*).

aging or controlling the poor: by laws forbidding combinations (the Combination Acts of 1799-1800) or by education, as in the Sunday-School Movement. A brave few suggested that raising wages might help.

In her essay Barbauld argues, heretically, that the combination of the poor against the rich is inevitable in an unequal society, and even that crimes against property are one of the means of holding together a society unequally divided between rich and poor. A respondent whom that idea deeply troubled nevertheless thought the essay "highly laudable in the attempt to prove to the rich, that they themselves are the causes of much that they complain of in the poor" ("Demophilus," p. 241).

Written in or after 1800, the year of the Combination Acts, this essay was published in John Aikin's short-lived magazine *The Athenaeum*, 2 (July 1807):14-19, signed "A.L.B." Ours is its first reprinting.]

There is nothing which a humane and considerate mind contemplates with more pain, than the great inequality with which the advantages and enjoyments of life are dealt out to different classes of men. I mean to take these terms in their common acceptation, and to understand by the enjoyments of life, a plentiful table, lightsome and well-furnished apartments, apparel of delicate manufacture, power to command the attendance of others, and freedom from any obligation to coarse or disgusting employments; to labour that exhausts life, or privations that render it of little value. To these may be added a share of deference, respect, a facility of access to objects of taste and curiosity, with all those other circumstances through which the rich feel their superiority over the poor. I know very well that with philosophers these advantages are of little or no account; they can prove by many learned and logical arguments that external goods have nothing to do with happiness, which resides exclusively in the mind. We are therefore bound to believe that these gentlemen, though they appear to enjoy a good table, or an elegant carriage as well as their neighbours, in fact regard them with perfect indifference; for which reason I beg to be considered as only addressing those who share in the common feelings of mankind, and who are therefore apt, at times, to repine that in the common blessings of it there should exist so striking a disproportion.

The honourable origin of this disproportion is *industry*. By the order of Providence the advantages of life are made the reward of diligence, active exertion, and superior talent. According as a man is distinguished by these, his share will of course encrease at the expence of his weaker or more indolent neighbour. But this alone would not account for the prodigious accumulation which by degrees takes place, were it not that this larger share generates *power*;[1] and here begins the mischief, for power embanks and confines the riches which otherwise would disperse and flow back in various channels to the community at large. Power enables the indolent and the useless not only to retain, but to add to their possessions, by taking from the industrious the natural reward of *their* labour, and applying it to their own use. It enables them to limit the profits and exact the services of the rest of the community, and to make such an unnatural separation between the enjoyment of a thing and the power of producing it, that where we see the one, we are habitually led to infer the privation of the other.[2] The sinews of industry become relaxed by the plenty it produces, but the gripe[3] of power is firm, and can only be unloosed by power. All the fences of law are provided, all the watchfulness of suspicion is awakened, all the salutary prejudices are cherished which may serve to keep down those who are already undermost, and to secure to those who have once acquired them the enjoyments and advantages of life.[4]

---

1    Up to this point, this paragraph summarizes standard economic doctrine; see Adam Smith, *The Wealth of Nations* (1776) Book I, Chap. 5, on individual labor as the source of wealth, and wealth as the power to command labor.

2    Barbauld here states an idea which would become famous in Karl Marx's thought as the concept of "alienated labor." Below, her phrase "tendency to accumulation" prefigures Marx's account of the tendency of capital to accumulate in ever fewer hands: see *Capital* (1867), Chap. 25.

3    I.e., grip.

4    In this single sentence Barbauld prefigures Marx's critique of bourgeois law and culture as devices for perpetuating bourgeois hegemony over the working class: its

Since things are so, how is it, it may be asked, that they are not worse? How is it that this continual tendency to accumulation has not long ago centered in a few hands all that is valuable in life? To solve this difficulty we must recollect, that as in the material, so in the moral world, there are opposite laws and tendencies which counteract each other, so that the weaker, though it never can subdue the stronger, yet acts as a continual check upon it, and serves to prevent it from ever passing a certain point. In this light I have often considered with pleasure those levelling principles[1] which are constantly at work, and prevent the accumulating principle, not indeed from preponderating to a degree that often shocks humanity, but at least from entirely destroying the balance of society.

The first of these levelling principles is, the number of adventitious wants and infirmities which take possession of a rich man, and make him dependent on those who administer to them. The enjoyments of sense are limited, those of fancy are infinite. If the rich had no fantastic wants, it is probable no more poor would be suffered to subsist in a country than would suffice to procure a plentiful subsistence for the owners of the soil; just as we maintain no more oxen than will serve for food, or horses than are wanted for the draft or the saddle; the rest of the land would lie uncultivated, as indeed it does, whenever those who possess the property of it are not stimulated by some advantage to themselves to make it productive. In conformity with this idea, we always use the phrase of *a numerous poor, a burdensome poor, a country overstocked with poor*, whenever, from any accidental overflow, they happen to exist in greater numbers than we can conveniently *use*.[2] But in general, where taste

---

classic expression is *The Communist Manifesto* (1848), Sect. II. Her phrase, "salutary prejudices" glances at Edmund Burke's conservative defence of prejudice in *Reflections on the Late Revolution in France* (1790).

1   "Levelling" was a term charged with revolutionary import and detested by conservatives; in 1792 Barbauld and other liberals had been targets of an anti-revolutionary "Association for the Preservation of Liberty and Property against Republicans and Levellers."

2   Middle-class fear that the poor were increasing dangerously in number was most famously expressed by Thomas Malthus in *An Essay on the Principle of Population* (1798); Barbauld criticizes Malthus explicitly in "Dialogue in the Shades." One of

and fashion exist, their various demands are drawing off, by numberless little channels, that wealth which its possessor would not otherwise be induced to part with. Nor is mere subsistence all that is thus gained; those tastes, to supply which talent is required, require also education, they require a certain degree of affluence, they bring the different ranks into contact with each other. The rude hind[1] from his mud-walled cottage may raise corn for the table of the nobleman; but if the latter chuses to have an artist, he must occasionally admit him to that table. Leonardo da Vinci died in the arms of Francis the first.[2] The wants of taste, and they alone, supply a gradation of ranks; for the man who is able to administer to the more refined pleasures of life, himself requires to be placed several rounds above the foot of the ladder.

Another levelling principle, akin to the former, is that *personal consequence* which is the result of personal capacity and experience. Of this no artificial state of society, no station of inferiority, not even a state of slavery itself, can entirely divest its possessor. Skill is power. The owner of a large house and domain may call himself, if he pleases, the master of them, and in a certain sense he is so, for all his dependants are labouring for him; but he cannot deprive his steward, his butler, his gardener, his cook, even his dairy maid, of that importance which arises from their understanding what he does not understand. He may give general orders, but if he attempts to interfere in the management of their departments, he will find himself become the object of their contempt instead of their reverence. If he talks with his gardener about fruit walls,[3] or with his housekeeper about setting out an entertainment, he will find they are the

---

Patrick Colquhoun's other books addressed "the Means of Affording Profitable Employment to the Redundant Population of Great Britain and Ireland through … an improved … System of Colonization in the British Territories in Southern Africa"—i.e., ship the poor abroad.

1  Farmworker.

2  King Francis I of France, who had invited Leonardo to his Court. Barbauld perhaps found this story in Giorgio Vasari's *Lives of the Artists* (1550; several Italian-language editions were printed in London during her lifetime, and in the later 1780s she studied Italian).

3  Walls against which fruit trees were planted.

people of consequence, and that the wages he pays them will not prevent their telling him with an air of authority, "Sir, you must do so and so." So well is this understood, that workmen of all kinds are the acknowledged masters of those who employ them; and the man who directs the affairs of a kingdom, if he wants to repair his house, is obliged to submit with the conscious littleness of ignorance to the impositions of his bricklayer, mason, and carpenter. Some kinds of authority may be usurped, but the authority which arises from technical skill never can.

Another circumstance which serves to lessen the superiority of the rich is, the *number of restraints* which they themselves, as rich people, lie under. A rich man has a kind of enchanted circle drawn about him, out of which he can no more move than the poor man out of his sphere. He is forbidden, by the custom of the community, from making use of his talents and activity, except in his own department. He is interdicted the use of fire and water, except by the ministration of others. He is as really prohibited, and under as severe penalties (the penalties of disgrace and universal odium) from carrying a parcel, or cleaning his own shoes, or currying his own horse, as the poor man is forbidden any office for which he is incapacitated by his indigence. With regard to women, particularly, the restraints laid upon them in what is called civilized society by the despot *Qu'en dirat'on?* (What will people say?) make their whole lives a series of constraint and sacrifices. "I should be glad to walk in the fields," says the poor sempstress, "but I cannot, for I have not finished my task;" "I should be glad to walk in the fields," says the young lady, "but I cannot possibly go, for the footman who should walk behind me is not at leisure." The poor woman, whose thin and scanty garment is not sufficient to defend her from the blasts of winter, suffers, no doubt, from the cold; and so does the young lady of fashion, who is also obliged, by that fashion from whence she derives her importance, to shiver in a thin and scanty garment, and to expose her health by encountering without sufficient covering the noxious damp of the midnight air. A man who is born rich, consequently in a certain rank of society, finds the greatest part of his income appropriated to expences which he is not the master to indulge or to restrain, and is forced, in spite of himself, to diffuse largely around him the bounties of Providence which, perhaps, if not thus constrained, he would be willing to confine to the narrow circle of his own enjoyments. He must not only support those who work for him, but all who approach his person must share the affluence and luxury in which he lives; if he eats white bread, his servants will not eat brown;[1] though, perhaps, his tenants may. His own pride, his own comfort, require that all who are within the circle of contact should have an air of neatness, decorous manners, and harmonize by their appearance with the principal object in the piece; as the approaches to a nobleman's mansion must indicate from afar the grandeur of the place. Neither will the sensibilities of cultured life bear to have misery intrude too near the eye; the distress which might languish at a distance, will be amply relieved if it comes near enough to affect the nerves. There is a happy contagion in wealth, which spreads itself to the remotest circle of its influence. "No man liveth to himself,"[2] is exemplified by the rich man, whether he intend it or not.

It is true, this tendency is very much strengthened by another principle, *the secret combination of the poor against the rich*.[3] There is in man an obscure sense of natural equality, which, without much reasoning, impresses on the mind a tacit conviction that some can spare a great deal, and that others want a great deal. Every body, therefore, who is not a party concerned, is rather glad than otherwise when the stores of the rich are lessened by overcharges, extravagant bills, and a number of little impositions, which he is continually exposed to. "He can well

---

1  By 1790 the majority of English regarded white bread "as a symbol of their status," but as the Industrial Revolution developed, they were increasingly degraded (in status terms) to a brown-bread or even potato diet (Thompson, *The Making of the English Working Class*, p. 315).

2  Romans 14:7.

3  A phrase calculated to terrify middle- and upper-class readers. Even those sympathetic to the misery of the working class recoiled from the possibility of combinations, or united action by workers: "combinations are extremely dangerous things, and therefore great care should be taken to prevent them," wrote one person, "Philanthropos," in 1801 ("On Regulating Wages of Workmen").

afford it, the expence is nothing to him," is the common language on such occasions. The inferior classes are quick in seizing this advantage, and it is well understood that a rich or a titled man pays more than another for whatever he has. The best thing he can do is to submit with a good grace, for if he is strict in insisting upon his right, he loses his character as a gentleman. Laws are continually made against combinations, but the secret combination of the low against the high can never be prevented, because it is founded on the interest of the many, and the moral sense of all.

These various causes are thus continually at work, draining off, as it were, the superfluous moisture, and dewing with it the parched and barren field; still, much more misery would be suffered than is suffered, if it were not for another corrective which Providence has caused to exist, in the vices of mankind. That private vices are public benefits, may be thought a dangerous doctrine;[1] but as vice exists, the fact surely tends to vindicate the divine government in permitting it; and I think it must be clear to a reflecting mind, that *caeteris manentibus*,[2] so strong a sense of principle as would entirely prevent the lower orders from preying upon the property of the higher, would be a curse and not a blessing. When, with these sentiments, I read such a book as Colquhoun's history of the police, and see the various tribes of *mud-larks, lumpers*,[3] &c. exercising their depredations, instead of indulging the melancholy with which such scenes of depravity inspire us at first view, I rather wish to consider them as usefully employed in lessening the enormous

---

1   It was the doctrine of Bernard Mandeville's *Fable of the Bees: or, Private Vices, Publick Benefits* (1714), which scandalized English society by its argument that the "elegant Comforts of Life ... in an industrious, wealthy and powerful Nation" are incompatible with "the Virtue and Innocence" to which people pretend.

2   Other things being equal.

3   "*Mud-Larks*, so called from their being accustomed to prowl about ... under the quarters of West India ships ... under pretence of grubbing in the mud for *old ropes, iron,* and *coals*, &c., but whose chief object ... was to receive and conceal small bags of sugar, coffee, pimiento, ginger and other articles, and sometimes bladders containing rum, which they conveyed to such houses as they were directed, and for which services they generally received a share of the booty" (Colquhoun, pp. 230-31). Lumpers were longshoremen who unloaded ships' cargoes by day and returned to plunder them by night (ibid., pp. 224-25).

inequality between the miserable beings who engage in them, and the great commercial speculators, in their way equally rapacious, against whom their frauds are exercised. It is the intent of Nature that all her children should live, yet she has not made specific provision for them all. The larger cattle graze the meadows, and strong animals subdue their prey, but she has likewise formed a countless number of smaller tribes who have no pasture but the field of other's labours. These watch their time, and pick up the superfluous crumbs of our plenty; they annoy us, we are in a constant state of warfare with them; and when their audacity arrives at a certain height, we provide effectual checks; in the mean time they live upon our abundance, they admonish us not to let things waste and mould in our barns and storehouses; they are for ever nibbling at our property, living upon the scraps and parings of our festival dainties, hovering about and sipping in our cup, some with insidious stealth, others with bolder warfare; some make us sensible of their sting; the defence of others is their minuteness and insignificance; many tribes of them are got rid of by order and cleanliness; others we keep within certain bounds, but we cannot destroy, without giving up the things which allure them. So it is in human polity. We send the cat after the rat, and the bailiffs after the rogue, but nature intended all should live. When a rich West India fleet has sailed into the docks, and wealth is flowing in full tides into the crammed coffers of the merchant, can we greatly lament that a small portion of his immense property is by these means diverted from its course, and finds its way to the habitations of penury?[1] Instead, therefore, of feeling strong indignation at these mal-practices, I am apt to say with Burns to the little Mouse,

---

1 Barbauld responds to Colquhoun's lament over "the immense depredations committed on every species of Commercial Property in the River Thames, but particularly on West India produce, ... exceedingly hurtful to the Commerce and Revenue of the port of London, and deeply affecting the interest of the Colonial Planters, as well as every description of Merchants and Ship-Owners concerned in the Trade of the River Thames" (p. 214). West Indian goods were produced by slave labor, and Barbauld would therefore have an additional reason to feel little sympathy for the losses suffered by West Indian planters.

> I doubt na, whiles, but thou mayest thieve;
> What then, poor Beastie! thou must live.[1]

The sanctity of oaths and promises is another very essential branch of morality; yet if it were invariably observed by those on whose necks the foot of power is planted, and there were no proportional amelioration in the dispositions of those who possess power, a more complete and hopeless tyranny would be exercised, than it is now possible for any despot to maintain. Arbitrary power could never be resisted; for it would begin with imposing sanctions which could not be broken without crime. As taxes and prohibitions could never be evaded, an unprincipled government would feel no limit to its exactions; and that party in society which once happened to be undermost, would be in the situation of a man who has an oath imposed upon him with a pistol at his breast, which he thinks himself bound to observe, however ruinous to his fortune.[2]

At the same time that we acknowledge the wisdom of Providence in this system of checks, which by evil preserves the race from greater evil, this ought not to shake our principles or alter our ideas of individual morality. Fraud and robbery are not right because other things are worse. A reflecting mind, contemplating the picture from a distance, may feel satisfaction that, by the various channels of imposition and peculation, that property is drawn off and dispersed, which would otherwise stagnate; but if any one among the classes by which such practices are exercised, has by any means formed higher notions of virtue, and a more delicate moral sense, to him they are forbidden; he must starve rather than steal, and trust for his recompence to the conscious purity of his own mind, and to an order of things not found in the present state. An individual cannot do better than by giving a high example of virtue; and if he conceives it, if he is capable of it, it is his duty at whatever per-

---

1 Robert Burns, "To a Mouse, On turning her up in her Nest, with the Plough, November 1785."

2 Like other principled Dissenters, Barbauld perceived oaths as means of social control at the expense of the individual's conscience; see her criticism of them in *Sins of Government.*

sonal risk. At the same time the rich may be told, that it is in their own power to get rid of many of these grievances whenever they please. It is not sufficiently considered how many virtues depend upon comfort, and cleanliness, and decent apparel. Destroy dirt and misery, and you will destroy at once a great many vices. Provide those accomodations which favour decorum and self respect, and you have done much to promote female chastity. Let every man know what it is to have property, and you will soon awaken in him a sense of honesty. Make him a citizen, and he will love the constitution to which he belongs, and obey the laws he has helped to make. Educate the poor, inform their minds, and they will have a sense of religion; but if we will not, or cannot do this; if our commerce, or the defence of our territories, or the distinction of ranks require that large classes shall be sacrificed in these respects; if we must have fleets and armies and crowded work-rooms, the steaming hot-beds of infant depravity;[1] then Nature has said that their vices shall in part repair to them the privations we impose, and soften their state of degradation by rendering them insensible to shame or honour. It is good that in the hovels of the poor there does not exist a nice taste of food, a nice regard to delicacy; it is also, and for the same reason, good, that his moral sense should be in some degree adapted to his circumstances. These considerations may perhaps suggest an additional motive for charitable exertions. I am apt to suspect that the greatest good done by the numerous societies for the reformation of manners[2] is, by bringing the poor in contact with the rich, by which, as a necessary consequence, many are drawn out of the state of destitute misery in which they were plunged, and placed in more respectable situations. The rich cannot seek the poor without beneficial effects to both parties. The best levelling principle is that philanthropy which is continually at work to smooth and soften the too great inequalities of life, and

---

1   Factories (work-rooms) employed children as young as four, and were widely believed to corrupt their morals as well as injuring their bodies.
2   Societies for the reformation of the manners of the working class, or for their religious instruction, were founded and staffed generally by Evangelical Christians such as William Wilberforce and Hannah More.

to present the eye, instead of proud summits and abrupt precipices, with the gentler undulations of hill and vale, with eminences of gradual ascent, and humble but happy vallies.

## LETTER FROM GRIMALKIN TO SELIMA

[In this letter from an old mother cat to her adolescent daughter Barbauld parodies a prevalent genre, the conduct book for young ladies—especially those books written as from a parent to a daughter, such as John Gregory's *A Father's Legacy to His Daughters* (1774) and Sarah Pennington's *An Unfortunate Mother's Advice to Her Absent Daughters* (1761). Besides signifying "an old female cat," "Grimalkin" pejoratively signified an elderly woman. "Selima" is the name of the greedy cat drowned in a goldfish bowl in Thomas Gray's "Ode on the Death of a Favorite Cat" (1753).

The piece was written in or after 1802, the year of publication of Elizabeth Hamilton's *Letters on the Elementary Principles of Education*, which it mentions. Lucy Aikin published it in *A Legacy for Young Ladies* (1826), pp. 198–204, from which we reprint it.]

My dear Selima,

As you are now going to quit the fostering cares of a mother, to enter, young as you are, into the wide world, and conduct yourself by your own prudence, I cannot forbear giving you some parting advice in this important era of your life.

Your extreme youth, and permit me to add, the giddiness incident to that period, make me particularly anxious for your welfare. In the first place then, let me beg you to remember that life is not to be spent in running after your own tail. Remember you were sent into the world to catch rats and mice. It is for this you are furnished with sharp claws, whiskers to improve your scent,[1] and with such an elasticity and spring

---

1    I.e., sense of smell.

in your limbs. Never lose sight of this great end of your exis-
tence. When you and your sister are jumping over my back,
and kicking and scratching one another's noses, you are
indulging the propensities of your nature, and perfecting your-
selves in agility and dexterity. But remember that these frolics
are only preparatory to the grand scene of action. Life is long,
but youth is short. The gaiety of the kitten will most assuredly
go off. In a few months, nay even weeks, those spirits and that
playfulness, which now exhilarate all who behold you, will sub-
side; and I beg you to reflect how contemptible you will be, if
you should have the gravity of an old cat without that useful-
ness which alone can ensure respect and protection for your
maturer years.

In the first place, my dear child, obtain a command over
your appetites,[1] and take care that no tempting opportunity
ever induces you to make free with the pantry or larder of your
mistress. You may possibly slip in and out without observation;
you may lap a little cream, or run away with a chop without its
being missed: but depend upon it, such practices sooner or later
will be found out; and if in a single instance you are discovered,
every thing which is missing will be charged upon you. If
Mrs. Betty or Mrs. Susan[2] chooses to regale herself with a cold
breast of chicken which was set by for supper,—you will have
clawed it; or a raspberry cream,—you will have lapped it. Nor
is this all. If you have once thrown down a single cup in your
eagerness to get out of the storeroom, every china plate and
dish that is ever broken in the house, you will have broken it;
and though your back promises to be pretty broad, it will not
be broad enough for all the mischief that will be laid upon it.
Honesty you will find is the best policy.

Remember that the true pleasures of life consist in the exer-
tion of our own powers. If you were to feast every day upon
roasted partridges from off Dresden china,[3] and dip your

---

1  Advice typically urged on young women, as G.J. Barker-Benfield notices, quoting
   John Gregory against "the luxury of eating" (*Culture of Sensibility*, pp. 289–90; Gre-
   gory, *Father's Legacy*, p. 28).
2  Generic names for female servants.
3  A particularly fine china from Dresden in Germany. Syllabubs (below) are milk
   drinks sweetened with wine.

whiskers in syllabubs and creams, it could never give you such true enjoyment as the commonest food procured by the labour of your own paws. When you have once tasted the exquisite pleasure of catching and playing with a mouse, you will despise the gratification of artificial dainties.[1]

I do not with some moralists call cleanliness a half virtue only. Remember it is one of the most essential to your sex and station; and if ever you should fail in it, I sincerely hope Mrs. Susan will bestow upon you a good whipping.[2]

Pray do not spit at strangers who do you the honour to take notice of you. It is very uncivil behaviour, and I have often wondered that kittens of any breeding should be guilty of it.

Avoid thrusting your nose into every closet and cupboard,—unless indeed you smell mice; in which case it is very becoming.

Should you live, as I hope you will, to see the children of your patroness, you must prepare yourself to exercise that branch of fortitude which consists in patient endurance: for you must expect to be lugged about, pinched and pulled by the tail, and played a thousand tricks with; all which you must bear without putting out a claw: for you may depend upon it, if you attempt the least retaliation you will for ever lose the favour of your mistress.

Should there be favourites in the house, such as tame birds, dormice, or a squirrel, great will be your temptations. In such a circumstance, if the cage hangs low and the door happens to be left open,—to govern your appetite I know will be a difficult task. But remember that nothing is impossible to the governing mind; and that there are instances upon record of cats who, in the exercise of self-government, have overcome the strongest propensities of their nature.

If you would make yourself agreeable to your mistress, you

---

1 A glance at Rousseau's praise in *Emile* (1762), of simple food simply prepared.

2 "Cleanliness was another sign of the tendency toward 'civilization' with which women were particularly identified" (Barker-Benfield, p. 290; he quotes James Fordyce, whose *Sermons to Young Women* [1766] Barbauld particularly disliked: "A dirty woman—I turn from the shocking idea").

must observe times and seasons. You must not startle her by
~~jumping upon her in a rude manner: and above all, be sure to~~
sheathe your claws when you lay your paw upon her lap.

You have like myself been brought up in the country, and I
fear you may regret the amusements it affords; such as catching
butterflies, climbing trees, and watching birds from the win-
dows, which I have done with great delight for a whole morn-
ing together. But these pleasures are not essential. A town life
has also its gratifications. You may make many pleasant
acquaintances in the neighbouring courts and alleys. A concert
upon the tiles[1] in a fine moonlight summer's evening may at
once gratify your ear and your social feelings. Rats and mice
are to be met with everywhere: and at any rate you have reason
to be thankful that so creditable a situation[2] has been found for
you; without which you must have followed the fate of your
poor brothers, and with a stone about your neck have been
drowned in the next pond.

It is only when you have kittens yourself, that you will be
able to appretiate the cares of a mother. How unruly have you
been when I wanted to wash your face! how undutiful in gal-
loping about the room instead of coming immediately when I
called you! But nothing can subdue the affections of a parent.
Being grave and thoughtful in my nature, and having the
advantage of residing in a literary family, I have mused deeply
on the subject of education; I have pored by moonlight over
Locke, and Edgeworth, and Mrs. Hamilton, and the laws of
association:[3] but after much cogitation I am only convinced of
this, that kittens will be kittens, and old cats old cats. May you,
my dear child, be an honour to all your relations and to the
whole feline race. May you see your descendants of the fiftieth

---

1   On the rooftop.
2   Position in an office or household (as for a servant).
3   John Locke, *Some Thoughts Concerning Education* (1693), a foundation of eighteenth-
   century ideas about education; Maria and Richard Lovell Edgeworth, *Practical Edu-
   cation* (1798), an advanced and controversial new theory; and Elizabeth Hamilton,
   *Letters on the Elementary Principles of Education* (1802), a conservative counter-theory.
   "The laws of association" refers to the best current theory of psychological func-
   tion, which Barbauld accepted.

generation. And when you depart this life, may the lamentations of your kindred exceed in pathos the melody of an Irish howl.[1]

> Signed by the paw of your affectionate mother,
> Grimalkin.

## FROM "LIFE OF SAMUEL RICHARDSON, WITH REMARKS ON HIS WRITINGS" (IN *THE CORRESPONDENCE OF SAMUEL RICHARDSON*)

[Samuel Richardson (1689-1761), author of *Pamela* (1741), *Clarissa* (1748-49) and *Sir Charles Grandison* (1753-54), figured importantly in the development and reception of the eighteenth-century novel because his fictions claimed, and were awarded, popular approbation for moral respectability and seriousness of purpose. Phenomenally successful both in England and Europe, his novels exerted immense influence on the novelists who followed him, including most importantly Henry Fielding and Jane Austen.

Early in 1804, the bookseller Richard Phillips acquired a large collection of letters to and from Richardson and engaged Barbauld to prepare an edition of it. Long an admirer of *Clarissa*, Barbauld not only edited five and a half volumes of Richardson's correspondence but also composed a 212-page essay on his life and works, the first substantial Richardson biography. Reviewers thought her biography the most valuable part of the edition, and it retains its importance: "no evidence discovered since her time has basically changed the picture she gave," write Richardson's modern biographers (Eaves and Kimpel, p. viii).

---

1 "The present Irish cry, or howl, cannot boast of such melody, nor is the funeral procession conducted with much dignity. The crowd of people ... at these funerals sometimes amounts to a thousand.... They gather as the bearers of the hearse proceed on their way, and when they pass through any village ... they begin to cry— Oh! Oh! Oh! Oh! Oh! Agh! Agh! raising their notes ... in a kind of mournful howl" (Edgeworth, *Castle Rackrent* [1800], p. 125; we are grateful to Mitzi Myers for this reference).

When Barbauld included *Clarissa* and *Sir Charles Grandison* in *The British Novelists* (1810), she quarried her preface to them (1.i-xlvi) out of her 1804 biography; the commentary on *Clarissa* that appears there is verbally unchanged from its 1804 original (1.lxxx-ciii), which we print below. (For clarity we sometimes adopt 1810 punctuation in preference to that of 1804.) Found only in 1804 (1. xx-xxviii) is our first excerpt, in which Barbauld—apparently for the first time in English commentary on fiction—discriminates different methods of telling a story.]

Richardson was the man who was to introduce a new kind of moral painting; he drew equally from nature and from his own ideas. From the world about him he took the incidents, manners, and general character, of the times in which he lived, and from his own beautiful ideas he copied that sublime of virtue which charms us in his Clarissa, and that sublime of passion which interests us in his Clementina.[1] That kind of fictitious writing of which he has set the example, disclaims all assistance from giants or genii. The moated castle is changed to a modern parlour; the princess and her pages to a lady and her domestics, or even to a simple maiden, without birth or fortune; we are not called on to wonder at improbable events, but to be moved by natural passions, and impressed by salutary maxims. The pathos of the story, and the dignity of the sentiments, interest and charm us; simplicity is warned, vice rebuked, and, from the perusal of a novel, we rise better prepared to meet the ills of life with firmness, and to perform our respective parts on the great theatre of life. It was the high and just praise given by our great critic, Dr. Johnson, to the author of Clarissa, that "he had enlarged the knowledge of human nature, and taught the passions to move at the command of virtue."[2] The novelist has,

---

1 Clarissa Harlowe, exemplary female protagonist of Richardson's second novel, who preserves her virtue and integrity despite, first, parental tyranny, then abduction and rape by Lovelace, and *Sir Charles Grandison*'s Clementina della Poretta, whose response to thwarted desire (her marriage to Sir Charles is forbidden due to his refusal to convert to Roman Catholicism) is stoical acceptance of filial duty.

2 From Samuel Johnson's introduction to Richardson's essay on marriage in *Rambler* 97 (19 February 1751).

indeed, all the advantage of the preacher in introducing useful maxims and sentiments of virtue; an advantage which Richardson made large use of, and he has besides the power of impressing them upon the heart through the best sensibilities of our nature. Richardson prided himself on being a moral and religious writer; and, as Addison did before him, he professed to take under his particular protection that sex which is supposed to be most open to good or evil impressions; whose inexperience most requires cautionary precepts, and whose sensibilities it is most important to secure against a wrong direction.[1] The manner of this captivating writer was also new.

There are three modes of carrying on a story: the narrative or epic as it may be called; in this the author relates himself the whole adventure; this is the manner of Cervantes in his Don Quixote, and of Fielding in his Tom Jones. It is the most common way. The author, like the muse, is supposed to know every thing; he can reveal the secret springs of actions, and let us into events in his own time and manner. He can be concise, or diffuse, according as the different parts of his story require it. He can indulge, as Fielding has done, in digressions, and thus deliver sentiments and display knowledge which would not properly belong to any of the characters.[2] But his narration will not be lively, except he frequently drops himself, and runs into dialogue: all good writers therefore have thrown as much as possible of the dramatic into their narrative. Mad. D'Arblay[3] has done this so successfully, that we have as clear an idea, not only of the sentiments, but the manner of expression of her different personages, as if we took it from the scenes in a play.

Another mode is that of memoirs; where the subject of the adventures relates his own story. Smollet, in his Roderic Random, and Goldsmith, in his Vicar of Wakefield, have adopted

---

1    In *Spectator* 10, Joseph Addison writes "there are none to whom this Paper will be more useful, than to the female world." Both by its contemporaries and by later readers, *The Spectator* was considered proper reading for ladies; in her "Preliminary Essay" to an 1804 selection from it, Barbauld remarked that it "has ever been the favourite of the toilette and the dressing-room" (p. xviii).

2    A reference to the initial chapters in each book of Fielding's *Tom Jones* and *Joseph Andrews*, in which the narrator speaks to us in his own voice.

3    I.e., Frances Burney.

this mode; it confines the author's stile, which should be suited, though it is not always, to the supposed talents and capacity of the imaginary narrator. It has the advantage of the warmth and interest a person may be supposed to feel in his own affairs; and he can more gracefully dwell upon minute circumstances which have affected him. It has a greater air of truth, as it seems to account for the communication to the public. The author, it is true, knows every thing, but when the secret recesses of the heart are to be laid open, we can hear no one with so much pleasure as the person himself. Marivaux, whose productions partly followed, and partly were cotemporary with those of Richardson, has put the history of Marianne into her own mouth, and we are amused to hear her dwell on little touches which are almost too trivial to be noticed by any body but herself.

But what the hero cannot say, the author cannot tell, nor can it be rendered probable, that a very circumstantial narrative should be given by a person, perhaps at the close of a long life, of conversations that have happened at the beginning of it. The author has all along two characters to support, for he has to consider how his hero felt at the time [of] the events to be related, and how it is natural he should feel them at the time he is relating them; at a period, perhaps, when curiosity is extinguished, passion cooled, and when, at any rate, the suspense which rendered them interesting is over. This seems, therefore, the least perfect mode of any.

A third way remains, that of *epistolary correspondence*, carried on between the characters of the novel. This is the form made use of by Richardson and many others after, none, I believe, before him.[1] He seems to have been led to it by circumstances in his early youth, which will be hereafter related. This method unites, in a good measure, the advantages of the other two; it

---

1 Previous histories of the novel by James Beattie ("On Fable and Romance," 1783) and John Moore (1797) had also declared Richardson the innovator of (in Moore's words) "a new species of romance, wherein the persons concerned are supposed to be the relaters of what passes" ("View of the Commencement and Progress of Romance," p. 67). But they and Barbauld were wrong in this surmise. Aphra Behn's *Love Letters Between a Nobleman and his Sister* (1684-87) is one notable earlier example of epistolary fiction. For others, see Day, *Told in Letters*.

gives the feelings of the moment as the writers felt them *at* the moment. It allows a pleasing variety of stile, if the author has sufficient command of pen to assume it. It makes the whole work dramatic, since all the characters speak in their own persons. It accounts for breaks in the story, by the omission or loss of letters. It is incompatible with a rapid stile, but gives room for the graceful introduction of remark and sentiment, or any kind, almost, of digressive matter. But, on the other hand, it is highly fictitious; it is the most natural and the least probable way of telling a story. That letters should be written at all times, and upon every occasion in life, that those letters should be preserved, and altogether form a connected story, it requires much art to render specious. It introduces the inconvenience so much felt in dramatic writing, for want of a narrator; the necessity of having an insipid confidant to tell the circumstances [to] that an author cannot relate in any other way. It obliges a man to tell of himself, what perhaps no man would tell; and sometimes to repeat compliments which modesty would lead him to suppress: and when a long conversation is repeated, supposes a memory more exact than is generally found. Artificial as it therefore is, still as it enables an author to assume, in a lively manner, the hopes and fears, and passions, and to imitate the peculiar way of thinking of his characters, it became fashionable, and has been adopted by many both at home and abroad, especially by the French writers; their language, perhaps, being particularly suited to the epistolary stile, and Rousseau himself, in his Nouvelle Heloise, has followed the steps of our countryman.[1]

...

The production upon which the fame of Richardson is principally founded, that which will transmit his name to posterity, as one of the first geniuses of the age in which he lived, is undoubtedly his *Clarissa*. Nothing can be more simple than the story, —A young lady, pressed by her parents to marry a man

---

1   *Julie ou la nouvelle Héloïse* (1761) by Jean-Jacques Rousseau was, like Richardson's epistolary novels, a great success; 72 editions were published before 1800.

every way disagreeable to her, and placed under the most cruel restraint, leaves her father's house, and throws herself upon the protection of her lover, a man of sense and spirit, but a libertine. When he finds her in his power he artfully declines marriage, and conveys her to a house kept for the worst of purposes. There, after many fruitless attempts to ensnare her virtue, he at length violates her person. She escapes from further outrage: he finds her out in her retreat; offers her marriage, which she rejects. Her friends are obdurate. She retires to solitary lodgings; grief and shame overwhelm her, and she dies broken-hearted: her friends lament their severity when too late. Her violator is transiently stung with remorse, but not reformed; he leaves the kingdom in order to dissipate his chagrin, and is killed in a duel by a relation of the lady's.

On this slight foundation, and on a story not very agreeable or promising in its rude outline, has our author founded a most pathetic tale, and raised a noble temple to female virtue. The first volumes are somewhat tedious, from the prolixity incident to letter-writing, and require a persevering reader to get through them: but the circumstantial manner of writing which Richardson practised, has the advantage of making the reader thoroughly acquainted with those in whose fate he is to be interested. In consequence of this, our feelings are not transient, elicited here and there by a pathetic stroke; but we regard his characters as real personages, whom we know and converse with, and whose fate remains to be decided in the course of events. The characters, much more numerous than in *Pamela*, are all distinctly drawn and well preserved, and there is a proper contrast and variety in the casting of the parts. The plot, as we have seen, is simple, and no under-plots interfere with the main design. No digressions, no episodes. It is wonderful that without these helps of common writers, he could support a work of such length. With Clarissa it begins,—with Clarissa it ends. We do not come upon unexpected adventures and wonderful recognitions, by quick turns and surprises: we see her fate from afar, as it were through a long avenue, the gradual approach to which, without ever losing sight of the object, has more of simplicity and grandeur than the most cunning labyrinth that can be contrived by art. In the approach to the modern country seat, we are made to catch transiently a side-view of it through an opening of the trees, or to burst upon it from a sudden turning in the road; but the old mansion stood full in the eye of the traveller, as he drew near it, contemplating its turrets, which grew larger and more distinct every step that he advanced; and leisurely filling his eye and his imagination with still increasing ideas of its magnificence. As the work advances, the character rises; the distress is deepened; our hearts are torn with pity and indignation; bursts of grief succeed one another, till at length the mind is composed and harmonized with emotions of milder sorrow; we are calmed into resignation, elevated with pious hope, and dismissed glowing with the conscious triumphs of virtue.

The first group which presents itself is that of the Harlowe family. They are sufficiently discriminated, yet preserve a family likeness. The stern father, the passionate and dark-souled brother, the envious and ill-natured sister, the money-loving uncles, the gentle, but weak-spirited mother, are all assimilated by that stiffness, love of parade, and solemnity, which is thrown over the whole, and by the interested family views in which they all concur. Miss Howe is a young lady of great generosity and ardent feelings, with a high spirit and some love of teazing, which she exercises on her mother, a managing and notable widow lady, and on her humble servant Mr. Hickman, a man deserving of her esteem, but prim and formal in his manner. Miss Howe is a character of strong lights and shades, but her warmest affections are all along directed to her friend, and the correspondence between them is made the great vehicle of Clarissa's narrative of events, as that between Lovelace and his friend Belford is of *his* schemes and designs. The character of Clarissa herself is very highly wrought: she has all the grace, and dignity, and delicacy, of a finished model of female excellence. Her duty to her parents is implicit, except in the article of sacrificing herself to a man utterly disgustful to her; and she bears, with the greatest meekness, the ill usage she receives from the other branches of the family. Duty, indeed, is the great principle of her conduct. Her affections are always compleatly under command; and her going off with Lovelace appears a step she was betrayed, not persuaded, into. His persuasions she had withstood, and it was fear, not love, that at last precipitated her into his protection. If, therefore, the author meant to represent her subsequent misfortunes as a punishment, he has scarcely made her faulty enough. That a young lady has eloped from her father's house with a libertine, sounds, indeed, like a grave offence; but the fault, when it is examined into, is softened, and shaded off by such a variety of circumstances, that it becomes almost evanescent. Who that reads the treatment she experienced, does not wonder at her long-suffering? After Clarissa finds herself, against her will and intention, in the power of her lover, the story becomes, for a while, a game at chess, in which both parties exert great skill and presence of mind, and quick observation of each other's motions. Not a moment of weakness does Clarissa betray, and she only loses the game because she plays fairly, and with integrity, while he is guilty of the basest frauds.

During this part of the story, the generality of readers are perhaps inclined to wish, that Lovelace should give up his wicked intentions, reform, and make Clarissa happy in the marriage state. This was the conclusion which Lady Bradshaw[1] so vehemently and passionately urged the author to adopt. But when the unfeeling character of Lovelace proceeds to deeper and darker wickedness, when his unrelenting cruelty meditates, and actually perpetrates, the last unmanly outrage upon unprotected innocence and virtue; the heart surely cannot have right feelings that does not cordially detest so black a villain, notwithstanding the agreeable qualities which are thrown into his character, and that woman must have little delicacy, who does not feel that his crime has raised an eternal wall of separation between him and the victim of his treachery, whatever affection she might have previously entertained for him. Yet it

---

1 Dorothy Bradshaigh, one of Richardson's best correspondents, argued that he should end *Clarissa* in the way that Barbauld describes. Parts of her letters to him are printed in Barbauld's edition.

is said by some, that the author has made Lovelace too agree-
able, and his character has been much the object of criticism.[1]
But a little reflection will shew us, that the author had a more
difficult part to manage, in drawing his character, than that of
any other in the work, and that he could not well have made
him different from what he is. If he had drawn a mean-spirited
dark villain, without any specious qualities, his Clarissa would
have been degraded. Lovelace, as he is to win the affections of
the heroine, is necessarily, in some sort, the hero of the piece,
and no one in it must be permitted to outshine him. The
author, therefore, gives him wit and spirit, and courage, and
generosity, and manly genteel address, and also transient gleams
of feeling, and transient stings of remorse; so that we are often
led to hope he may follow his better angel, and give up his
atrocious designs. This the author has done, and less he could
not do, for the man whom Clarissa was inclined to favour.
Besides, if it was part of his intention to warn young women
against placing their affections upon libertines, it was certainly
only against the agreeable ones of that class, that he had any
occasion to warn them.[2] He tells us in one of his letters, that
finding he had made him too much a favourite, he had thrown
in some darker shades to obviate the objection; and surely the
shades are dark enough.[3] In one particular, however, the author
might perhaps have improved the moral effect of the work; he
might have given more of horror to the last scene of Lovelace's
life. When Clarissa and he were finally separated, there was no
occasion to keep measures with him; and why should Belton
die a death of so much horror, and Lovelace of calm composure
and self-possession? Lovelace dies in a duel, admirably well

---

1   Richardson himself was led by reader responses to darken Lovelace's character in
    editions after the first. Even so, it became a regular part of commentary on *Clarissa*
    to deplore the dangerous attractiveness of Lovelace's character: "The brilliant
    colours in which Lovelace is painted are too apt to fascinate the imagination, and
    may have secured him a corner in the hearts even of some young women of char-
    acter, in spite of his crimes" (Moore, "View," p. 68).
2   Richardson's stated purpose in writing *Clarissa* was to disprove the adage that "a
    reformed rake makes the best husband."
3   Letter to Lady Bradshaigh, 10 October 1748, *Correspondence of Samuel Richardson*, 4:
    177-82.

described, in which he behaves with the cool intrepidity of a gentleman and a man of spirit. Colonel Morden could not behave better. Some tender strokes are thrown in on his parting with Belford, and on other occasions, tending to interest the reader in his favour; and his last words, "Let this expiate," are manifestly intended to do away our resentment, and leave a favourable impression on our minds with regard to his future prospects. Something, indeed, is mentioned of impatience, and a desire of life; but Richardson *could* have drawn a scene which would have made us turn with horror from the features of the gay, the agreeable seducer, when changed into the agonizing countenance of the despairing self-accuser.

But, if the author might have improved, in this respect, the character of Lovelace, that of Clarissa comes up to all the ideas we can form of female loveliness and dignified suffering. The first scenes with her hard-hearted family, shew the severe struggles she had with herself, before she could withdraw her obedience from her parents. The measure of that obedience, in Richardson's mind, was very high; and, therefore, Clarissa seems all along, rather to lament the cruelty, than to resent the injustice, of imposing a husband upon her without her own consent. It is easy to see she would have thought it her duty to comply, if he had not been quite so disagreeable. The mother is a very mean character; she gives a tacit permission to Clarissa, to correspond with Lovelace, to prevent mischief, and yet consents to be the tool of the family in persecuting her innocent and generous daughter;—but, this was her duty to her husband!—Yet, distressing as Clarissa's situation is in her father's house, the author has had the address to make the reader feel, the moment she has got out of it, that he would give the world to have her safe back again. Nothing takes place of that pleasure and endearment which might naturally be expected on the meeting of two lovers; we feel that she has been hunted into the toils, and that every avenue is closed against her escape. No young person, on reading *Clarissa*, even at this period of the story, can think of putting herself into the power of a lover, without annexing to it the strongest sense of degradation and anxiety. A great deal of contrivance is expended by the author, in the various plots set on foot by Lovelace, to keep his victim tolerably easy in her ambiguous situation; and, though some of these are tedious, it was necessary, for Clarissa's honour, to make the reader sensible that she had an inextricable net wound around her, and that it was not owing to her want of prudence or vigilance, that she did not escape. In the mean time the wit of Lovelace, and the sprightliness of Miss Howe, prevent monotony. In one instance, however, Clarissa certainly sins against the delicacy of her character, that is, in allowing herself to be made a show of to the loose companions of Lovelace:— But, how does her character rise, when we come to the more distressful scenes; the view of her horror, when, deluded by the pretended relations, she re-enters the fatal house, her temporary insanity after the outrage, in which she so affectingly holds up to Lovelace the licence he had procured, and her dignified behaviour when she first sees her ravisher, after the perpetration of his crime. What finer subject could be presented to the painter, than that in which Clarissa grasps the pen-knife in her hand, "her eyes lifted up to heaven, the whites of them only visible,"[1] ready to plunge it in her breast, to preserve herself from further outrage: Lovelace, aghast with terror, and speechless, thrown back to the further end of the room? Or, the prison scene, where she is represented kneeling amidst the gloom and horror of the dismal abode; illuminating, as it were, the dark chamber, her face reclined on her crossed arms, her white garments floating round her in the negligence of woe; Belford contemplating her with respectful commiseration; or, the scene of calmer, but heart-piercing sorrow, in the interview Colonel Morden has with her in her dying moments: She is represented "fallen into a slumber, in her elbow-chair, leaning on the widow Lovick, whose left arm is around her neck; one faded cheek resting on the good woman's bosom, the kindly warmth of which had overspread it with a faintish flush, the other pale and hollow, as if already iced over by death; her hands, the blueness of the veins contrasting their whiteness, hanging lifelessly

---

1    Letter 281. The passage in quotation marks is a paraphrase of Richardson's text, not quoted verbatim.

before her, the widow's tears dropping unfelt upon her face—
Colonel Morden, with his arms folded, gazing on her in
silence, her coffin just appearing behind a screen."[1] What admi-
ration, what reverence does the author inspire us with for the
innocent sufferer, the sufferings too of such a peculiar nature.

There is something in virgin purity, to which the imagina-
tion willingly pays homage. In all ages, something saintly has
been attached to the idea of unblemished chastity. Hence the
dignity of the lady in *Comus*; hence the interest we take in
those whose holy vows have shrowded them from even the
wanton glances of an assailer; hence the supposed virtue of
prayers

> From fasting maids whose minds are dedicate,
> ————————To nothing earthly.[2]

Beauty is a flower which was meant in due time to be gath-
ered, but it attracts the fondest admiration whilst still on the
stalk, before it has felt the touch of any rude hand.

> *Sic virgo, dum intacta manet, dum cara suis est.*[3]

It was reserved for Richardson to overcome all circum-
stances of dishonour and disgrace, and to throw a splendour
round the *violated virgin*, more radiant than she possessed in her
first bloom. He has made the flower, which grew

> ————————Sweet to sense and lovely to the eye,[4]

throw out a richer fragrance *after* "the cruel spoiler has *cropped
the fair rose, and rifled its sweetness.*"[5] He has drawn the triumph
of mental chastity; he has drawn it uncontaminated, untar-

---

1   Letter 474; again, a loose quotation.
2   Not Milton's *Comus*, but Shakespeare's *Measure for Measure* II.ii.154.
3   Catullus. Poem LXII, l.45. "So a maiden, whilst she remains untouched, so long is
    she dear to her own." (Loeb translation)
4   Mary Robinson, "Monody to the Memory of Marie Antoinette, Queen of
    France," l.68, slightly altered (*Works*, 1806).
5   Thomas Otway, *The Orphan* IV.i.302-303.

nished, and incapable of mingling with pollution.—The scenes which follow the death of the heroine, exhibit grief in an affecting variety of forms, as it is modified by the characters of different survivors. They run into considerable length, but we have been so deeply interested, that we feel it a relief to have our grief drawn off, as it were, by a variety of sluices, and we are glad not to be dismissed till we have shed tears, even to satiety. We enjoy, besides, the punishment of the Harlowes, in the contemplation of their merited anguish. Sentiments of piety pervade the whole work; but the death-bed of Clarissa, her Christian forgiveness, and her meek resignation, are particularly edifying. Richardson loved to draw death-beds: He seems to have imbibed, from his friend Dr. Young, an opinion of their being a touch-stone of merit or demerit.[1] There are three described in this work, besides that of Lovelace; that, it has already been mentioned, would have had a more moral effect, if it had been fuller of horror. Lovelace is made to declare, that he cannot be totally unhappy, whatever be his own lot in a future state, if he is allowed to contemplate the happiness of Clarissa: He exclaims,

> Can I be at worst? avert that worst,
> O thou Supreme, who only canst avert it!
> So much a wretch, so very far abandoned,
> But that I must, even in the horrid'st gloom,
> Reap intervenient joy; at least, some respite
> From pain and anguish in her bliss.[2]

This is a sentiment much too generous for a Lovelace.—The author has shewn himself embarrassed with regard to the duel, by his principles, which forbade duelling. Yet, it was necessary to dispatch Lovelace; for what family could sit down with such an injury unpunished? or which of his readers could be satisfied

---

1   In "Conjectures on Original Composition in a Letter to the Author of Sir Charles Grandison" (1759), Edward Young devotes a few paragraphs to the death of Joseph Addison, whose pious and peaceful death illustrated, according to Addison himself, the way a Christian should die.
2   Lovelace to Colonel Morden after Clarissa's death. (*Clarissa*, Letter 535).

to see the perpetrator of so much mischief escape vengeance? Colonel Morden was a man of the world, acted upon the maxims of it, and, therefore, it seemed hardly necessary to make *him* express regret at having precipitated Lovelace into a future state; Richardson was not then drawing his perfect character, and did not seem called upon to blame a duel, which, in our hearts we cannot, from Colonel Morden, but approve of.

That *Clarissa* is a highly moral work, has been always allowed; but what is the moral? Is it that a young lady who places her affections upon a libertine, will be deceived and ruined? Though the author, no doubt, intended this as one of the conclusions to be drawn, such a maxim has not dignity or force enough in it, to be the chief moral of this interesting tale. And, it has been already mentioned, that Clarissa can hardly stand as an example of such a choice, as she never fairly made the choice. On the contrary, she is always ready, both before her elopement and after it, to resign the moderate, the almost insensible predilection she feels for Lovelace, to the will of her parents; if she might only be permitted to refuse the object of her aversion. Is she, then, exhibited as a rare pattern of chastity? Surely this is an idea very degrading to the sex. Lovelace, indeed, who has a very bad opinion of women, and thinks that hardly any woman can resist him, talks of trying her virtue, and speaks as if he expected her to fail in the trial. But, surely, the virtue of Clarissa could never have been in the smallest danger. The virtue of Pamela was tried, because the pecuniary offers were a temptation which many, in her station of life, would have yielded to; and, because their different situations in life opposed a bar to their legitimate union, which she might well believe would be insuperable.[1] The virtue of Werter's Charlotte was tried, and the virtue of the wife of Zeluco was tried, because the previous marriage of one of the parties made a virtuous union impossible.—But Clarissa! a young lady of birth and fortune, marriage completely in her lover's power—she

---

1  A reference to Richardson's first novel wherein a servant, Pamela, is pursued and tempted to yield by her master. She withstands his advances and eventually they are married. The following examples of tested virtue are from Goethe's *Sorrows of Young Werter* (1774) and John Moore's *Zeluco* (1789) respectively.

could have felt nothing but indignation at the first idea which entered her mind, that he meant to degrade her into a mistress. Was it likely that she, who had shewn that her affections were so much under her command, while the object of his addresses appeared to be honourable marriage, should not guard against every freedom with the most cautious vigilance, as soon as she experienced a behaviour in him, which must at once destroy her esteem for him, and be offensive to her just pride, as well as to her modesty? It is absurd, therefore, in Lovelace to speak of trying her chastity; and the author is not free from blame in favouring the idea that such resistance had any thing in it uncommon, or peculiarly meritorious. But the real moral of *Clarissa* is, that virtue is triumphant in every situation; that in circumstances the most painful and degrading, in a prison, in a brothel, in grief, in distraction, in despair, it is still lovely, still commanding, still the object of our veneration, of our fondest affections; that if it is seated on the ground it can still say with Constance,

Here is my throne; kings, come and bow to it![1]

The Novelist that has produced this effect, has performed his office well, and it is immaterial what particular maxim is selected under the name of a moral, while such are the reader's feelings. If our feelings are in favour of virtue, the novel is virtuous; if of vice, the novel is vicious. The greatness of Clarissa is shewn by her separating herself from her lover, as soon as she perceives his dishonourable views; in her chusing death rather than a repetition of the outrage; in her rejection of those overtures of marriage, which a common mind might have accepted of, as a refuge against worldly dishonour; in her firm indignant carriage, mixed with calm patience and christian resignation, and in the greatness of mind with which she views and enjoys the approaches of death, and her meek forgiveness of her unfeeling relations.

---

1  Shakespeare, *King John,* III.i.74, slightly altered.

[Late in 1807 a consortium of thirty-seven booksellers—thirty-five from London, one from Edinburgh and one from York—undertook to print "a selection of English Novels, with biographical notices and critical remarks, by Mrs. Barbauld" (*Athenaeum*, 2: 513). Published in 1810 in fifty volumes, *The British Novelists* soon became known as "Mrs. Barbauld's Novelists," just as, thirty years earlier, the set of *English Poets* for which Samuel Johnson wrote prefaces came to be called "Johnson's Poets."

Earlier multi-volume editions of novels had been published in England. Elizabeth Griffith "collected and revised" a three-volume edition of English and English translations of French novels in 1777. From 1780-88, bookseller James Harrison published *The Novelist's Magazine*, a collection that came to twenty-three volumes in the end. Charles Cook, another bookseller, printed individual titles in a series called *Select British Novels* in the 1790s. *The British Novelists*, however, was the first English edition to make comprehensive critical and historical claims. Barbauld's participation in this project represents the exercise of the cultural authority she had accrued over the thirty-five years prior to its appearance. Educator, intellectual, and, most recently, editor of Samuel Richardson, she was well-positioned to preside over a large a canon-making enterprise.

The novel had been a recognizable genre in Britain since the 1740s. Before that, there were prose narratives—generally termed romances—stories of love and intrigue that enjoyed a devoted, largely female, readership. The writers were mostly female too: Aphra Behn, Penelope Aubin, Delarivier Manley, Jane Barker, Eliza Haywood, and others published their often salacious tales from the 1680s to the 1740s. There were also other popular narrative forms: confessions of thieves, highwaymen, and murderers, stories of spiritual conversion, tales of strange and surprising adventures in remote lands. Daniel Defoe's realistic narratives published in the 1720s transformed the conventions of these genres into something quite new. It was not until the 1740s, however, that novels gained sufficient moral respectability and generic stability to make it possible to describe them as a distinct form. Even so, among serious critics novels remained controversial: condemned as trivial or (at worst) destructive of their readers' moral character, and defended by appeal to the relatively narrow terms of traditional literary ethics (the argument that novels support moral ideas by presenting them in the attractive guise of fiction). In her wide-ranging preface to the edition, "The Origin and Progress of Novel-Writing," Barbauld enters an ongoing discourse about the history and social value of the novel. In our notes we indicate some of the points of contact between her and her predecessors. But *The British Novelists* differs from all of them by being an encyclopedic venture that implies both historical perspective and enduring value. The definition of the novel, its evolution from the narrative forms that preceded it, the writers—from the ancients to Barbauld's contemporaries, in Europe and elsewhere—who contributed most significantly to its development and definition: these are the concerns of Barbauld's preface.

Our selections include the full text of Barbauld's introductory essay, a long extract from her preface to Fielding, and the prefaces to Samuel Johnson, Elizabeth Inchbald, Charlotte Smith, Frances Burney, and Ann Radcliffe. We reprint the 1810 texts (1:1-62, 18:xii-xxxii, 26:i-viii, 28:i-iv, 36:i-viii, 38:i-xi, 43:i-viii), corrected by the few verbal revisions Barbauld made for an 1820 edition. (For her commentary on Samuel Richardson, see the extracts from her 1804 "Life" of Richardson; the discussion of *Clarissa* was reprinted verbatim in 1810.) In Appendix D we list the full contents of *The British Novelists*, and, to avoid swelling the already significant number of footnotes to "The Origin and Progress of Novel-Writing," we identify the authors and titles mentioned there.]

A Collection of Novels has a better chance of giving pleasure than of commanding respect. Books of this description are condemned by the grave, and despised by the fastidious; but their leaves are seldom found unopened, and they occupy the parlour and the dressing-room while productions of higher name are often gathering dust upon the shelf. It might not perhaps be difficult to show that this species of composition is entitled to a higher rank than has been generally assigned it. Fictitious adventures, in one form or other, have made a part of the polite literature of every age and nation. These have been grafted upon the actions of their heroes; they have been interwoven with their mythology; they have been moulded upon the manners of the age,—and, in return, have influenced the manners of the succeeding generation by the sentiments they have infused and the sensibilities they have excited.

Adorned with the embellishments of Poetry, they produce the epic; more concentrated in the story, and exchanging narrative for action, they become dramatic. When allied with some great moral end, as in the *Telemaque* of Fenelon, and Marmontel's *Belisaire*, they may be termed didactic. They are often made the vehicles of satire, as in Swift's *Gulliver's Travels*, and the *Candide* and *Babouc* of Voltaire. They take a tincture from the learning and politics of the times, and are made use of successfully to attack or recommend the prevailing systems of the day. When the range of this kind of writing is so extensive, and its effects so great, it seems evident that it ought to hold a respectable place among the productions of genius; nor is it easy to say, why the poet, who deals in one kind of fiction, should have so high a place allotted him in the temple of fame; and the romance-writer so low a one as in the general estimation he is confined to. To measure the dignity of a writer by the pleasure he affords his readers is not perhaps using an accurate criterion; but the invention of a story, the choice of proper incidents, the ordonnance of the plan, occasional beauties of description, and above all, the power exercised over the reader's heart by filling it with the successive emotions of love, pity, joy, anguish, transport, or indignation, together with the grave impressive moral resulting from the whole, imply talents of the highest order, and ought to be appretiated accordingly. A good novel is an epic in prose, with more of character and less (indeed in modern novels nothing) of the supernatural machinery.[1]

If we look for the origin of fictitious tales and adventures, we shall be obliged to go to the earliest accounts of the literature of every age and country.[2] The Eastern nations have always been fond of this species of mental gratification. The East is emphatically the country of invention. The Persians, Arabians, and other nations in that vicinity have been, and still are, in the habit of employing people whose business it is to compose and to relate entertaining stories; and it is surprising how many stories (as Parnell's Hermit[3] for instance) which have passed current in verse and prose through a variety of forms, may be traced up to this source. From Persia the taste passed into the soft and luxurious Ionia.[4] The *Milesian Tales*, written by Aristides of Miletus, at what time is not exactly known, seem to have been a kind of novels. They were translated into Latin during the civil wars of Marius and Sylla.[5] They consisted of loose love stories, but were very popular among the Romans;

---

1 Barbauld echoes Henry Fielding who, in the Preface to his novel *Joseph Andrews* (1742), defines the kind of narrative he writes (which he calls a "comic romance") as "a comic Epic-Poem in Prose." "Supernatural machinery" refers to the gods and goddesses who participate in the action of epic narrative in particular.

2 For the broad outlines of the history of the ancient novel or romance, Barbauld is indebted to Pierre-Daniel Huet's *Treatise of Romances and their Original* (1668).

3 Poem by Thomas Parnell, first published by Alexander Pope in *Poems on Several Occasions* (1722), frequently reprinted throughout the eighteenth century. Parnell's immediate source was Henry More's *Divine Dialogues* (1668) which was based on a narrative in the Koran. Other versions appear in *Spectator* no. 237 and Voltaire's *Zadig*. See *Collected Poems of Thomas Parnell*, pp. 527-30.

4 Ancient Hellenic nation comprised of Attica, the Aegean islands and the coast of Asia Minor. Huet notes that the romances of the east spread to Greece and Italy by way of Ionia (*Treatise*, pp. 26-29).

5 That is, around 88 BC when Roman generals Gaius Marius (157-86 BC) and Lucius Cornelius Sylla or Sulla (138-79 BC) vied for power in the Roman republic. . Huet notes of Aristides of Miletus: "he lived before the Wars of *Marius* and *Sylla*, for *Sisenna* a *Roman* Historian of that time translated his *Milesian* Fables" (p. 32). This dating of the translation seems about a decade early, according to the *Oxford Classical Dictionary*, s.v. Aristides (2).

and the Parthian general who beat Crassus took occasion, from his finding a copy of them amongst the camp equipage, to reproach that nation with effeminacy, in not being able, even in time of danger, to dispense with such an amusement.[1] From Ionia the taste of romances passed over to the Greeks about the time of Alexander the Great. The *Golden Ass* of Lucian, which is exactly in the manner of the Arabian Tales, is one of the few extant.

In the time of the Greek emperors these compositions were numerous, and had attained a form and a polish which assimilates them to the most regular and sentimental of modern productions. The most perfect of those which are come down to our time is *Theagenes and Chariclea*, a romance or novel, written by Heliodorus bishop of Tricca in Thessaly, who flourished under Arcadius and Honorius.[2] Though his production was perfectly chaste and virtuous, he was called to account for it by a provincial synod, and ordered to burn his book or resign his bishopric; upon which, with the heroism of an author, he chose the latter. Of this work a new translation was given in 1789; and had this Selection admitted translations, it would have found a place here.[3] It is not so much read as it ought to be; and it may not be amiss to inform the customers to circulating libraries,[4] that they may have the pleasure of reading a genuine novel, and at the same time enjoy the satisfaction of knowing how people wrote in Greek about love, above a thousand years ago. The scene of this work is chiefly laid in Egypt. It opens in

---

1  Huet recounts an anecdote drawn, no doubt, from Plutarch's "Life of Crassus" concerning Surena, the commander of the Parthians, who, after the defeat of the Roman army under Marcus Licinius Crassus (115?-53 BC), found the *Milesian Tales* "among the Baggage of *Bosetus*, [and] took occasion ... to insult over and rail at the weakness and effeminate disposition of the *Romans*, who even during the War could not be without such like diversions" (*Treatise*, p. 32).

2  Roman emperor of the east Arcadius (AD 383-408) and emperor of the west Honorius (AD 395-423). Heliodorus's dates are still a matter of scholarly dispute. Barbauld here seems to be following Huet, who asserts "that he was contemporary of *Arcadius* and *Honorius*" (*Treatise*, p. 38).

3  This anonymous translation was published in two volumes in London.

4  From the mid-eighteenth century on, the number of circulating libraries in England increased, with novels being the most popular literature borrowed and women readers the most usual patrons.

a striking and picturesque manner. A band of pirates, from a hill that overlooks the Heracleotic mouth of the Nile, see a ship lying at anchor, deserted by its crew; a feast spread on the shore; a number of dead bodies scattered round, indicating a recent skirmish or quarrel at an entertainment: the only living creatures, a most beautiful virgin seated on a rock, weeping over and supporting a young man of an equally distinguished figure, who is wounded and apparently lifeless. These are the hero and the heroine of the piece, and being thus let into the middle of the story, the preceding events are given in narration. The description of the manner of life of the pirates at the mouth of the Nile is curious, and no doubt historical. It shows that, as well then as in Homer's time, piracy was looked upon as a mode of honourable war, and that a captain who treated the women with respect, and took a regular ransom for his captives, and behaved well to his men, did not scruple to rank himself with other military heroes. Indeed it might be difficult to say why he should not. It is a circumstance worth observing, that Tasso has in all probability borrowed a striking circumstance from the Greek romance. *Chariclea* is the daughter of a queen of Ethiopia, exposed by her mother to save her reputation, as, in consequence of the queen, while pregnant, having gazed at a picture of Perseus and Andromeda, her infant was born with a fair complexion. This is the counterpart of the story of Clorinda, in the Gierusalemme Liberata, whose mother is surprised with the same phenomenon, occasioned by having had in her chamber a picture of St. George.[1] The discovery is kept back to the end of the piece, and is managed in a striking manner. There is much beautiful description, of which the pomp of heathen sacrifices and processions makes a great part; and the love is at once passionate and chaste.

The pastoral romance of Longus is also extant in the Greek language. It is esteemed elegant, but it would be impossible to chastise it into decency. The Latins, who had less invention, had no writings of this kind, except the *Golden Ass* of Apuleius may be reckoned such. In it is found the beautiful episode of Cupid

---

1   Barbauld refers to Tasso, *Gerusalemme Liberata* (1581), XII.xxiii-iv; Clorinda, a
    white-skinned warrior, is the daughter of a black king and queen of Ethiopia.

and Psyche, which has been elegantly modernized by La Fontaine.[1] ~~But romance writing was destined to revive with~~ greater splendour under the Gothic powers,[2] and it sprung out of the histories of the times, enlarged and exaggerated into fable. Indeed all fictions have probably grown out of real adventures. The actions of heroes would be the most natural subject for recital in a warlike age; a little flattery and a little love of the marvellous would overstep the modesty of truth in the narration. A champion of extraordinary size would be easily magnified into a giant. Tales of magic and enchantment probably took their rise from the awe and wonder with which the vulgar looked upon any instance of superior skill in mechanics or medicine, or acquaintance with any of the hidden properties of nature. The Arabian tales, so well known and so delightful, bear testimony to this. At a fair in Tartary a *magician* appears, who brings various curiosities, the idea of which was probably suggested by inventions they had heard of, which to people totally ignorant of the mechanical powers would appear the effect of enchantment. How easily might the exhibition at Merlin's, or the tricks of Jonas, be made to pass for magic in New Holland or Otaheite![3] Letters and figures were easily turned into talismans by illiterate men, who saw that a great deal was effected by them, and intelligence conveyed from place to place in a manner they could not account for. Medicine has always, in rude ages and countries, been accompanied with charms and superstitious practices, and the charming of serpents in the East is still performed in a way which the Europeans cannot discover. The total separation of scholastic characters from men of the world favoured the belief of magic; and when to these causes are added the religious superstitions

---

1   "Fontenelle" in 1810. Although Bernard le Bovier de Fontenelle (1657-1757) wrote a play, *Psyché* (1678), Barbauld's 1820 revision indicates that she meant *Les Amours de Psiche et de Cupidon* (1669) by Jean de la Fontaine.

2   The kingdoms established in Italy by the Goths after their conquest of Rome.

3   Merlin's Mechanical Museum in London's Hanover Square (established in the 1770s, closed 1808) housed a collection of mechanical devices and toys invented by John Joseph Merlin (d. 1803). The eastern coast of Australia was known as New Holland in the seventeenth and eighteenth centuries; Otaheite is another name for Tahiti; Jonas remains unidentified.

of the times, we shall be able to account for much of the marvellous in the first instance. These stories, as well as the historical ones, would be continually embellished, as they passed from hand to hand, till the small mixture of truth in them was scarcely discoverable.

The first Gothic romances appeared under the venerable guise of history. Arthur and the knights of the round table, Charlemagne[1] and his peers, were their favourite heroes. The extended empire of Charlemagne and his conquests naturally offered themselves as subjects for recital; but it seems extraordinary that Arthur, a British prince, the scene of whose exploits was in Wales, a country little known to the rest of Europe, and who was continually struggling against ill-fortune, should have been so great a favourite upon the continent. Perhaps, however, the comparative obscurity of his situation might favour the genius of the composition, and the intercourse between Wales and Brittany would contribute to diffuse and exaggerate the stories of his exploits. In fact, every song and record relating to this hero was kept with the greatest care in Brittany, and, together with a chronicle deducing Prince Arthur from Priam king of Troy, was brought to England about the year 1100, by Walter Mapes archdeacon of Oxford, when he returned from the continent through that province.[2] This medley of historical songs, traditions, and invention, was put into Latin by Geoffry of Monmouth, with many additions of his own, and from Latin translated into French in the year 1115, under the title of *Brut d'Angleterre*. It is full of the grossest anachronisms. *Merlin*, the enchanter, is a principal character in it. He opposes his Christian magic to the Arabian sorcerers. About the same time appeared a similar history of *Charlemagne*. Two expeditions of his were particularly celebrated; his conversion of the Saxons by force of arms, and his expedition into Spain against the Sara-

---

1 Charles I or Charles the Great, Frankish King (768-814) and Emperor of the West (800-814).

2 Walter Mapes or Map (fl. 1200). His authorship of Arthurian materials is a persistent tradition, a probable truth, but an undocumented and probably undocumentable fact (*DNB*, s.v. Map, Walter). Barbauld's sentence follows almost verbatim John Moore's account of Arthurian legend in his 1797 "View of the Commencement and Progress of Romance."

cens; in returning from which he met with the defeat of Ron-
cevaux, in which was slain the celebrated *Roland*. This was
written in Latin by a monk, who published it under the name
of Archbishop Turpin, a cotemporary of Charlemagne, in order
to give it credit. These two works were translated into most of
the languages of Europe, and became the groundwork of num-
berless others, each more wonderful than the former, and each
containing a sufficient number of giants, castles and dragons,
beautiful damsels and valiant princes, with a great deal of reli-
gious zeal, and very little morality. *Amadis de Gaul* was one of
the most famous of this class. Its origin is disputed between
France and Spain. There is a great deal of fighting in it, much
of the marvellous, and very little of sentiment. It has been
given lately to the public in an elegant English dress by Mr.
Southey;[1] but notwithstanding he has considerably abridged its
tediousness, a sufficiency of that ingredient remains to make it
rather a task to go through a work which was once so great a
favourite. *Palmerin of England*, *Don Belianis of Greece*, and the
others which make up the catalogue of Don Quixote's library,
are of this stamp.[2]

Richard Coeur de Lion and his exploits were greatly to the
taste of the early romance writers. The Crusades kindled a taste
for romantic adventure; the establishment of the Saracens in
Spain had occasioned a large importation of genii and enchant-
ments, and Moorish magnificence was grafted upon the tales of
the Gothic chivalry. Of these heroic romances, the Trouba-
dours were in France the chief composers: they began to flour-
ish about the end of the tenth century. They by degrees min-
gled a taste for gallantry and romantic love with the adventures
of heroes, and they gave to that passion an importance and a
refinement which it had never possessed among the ancients. It
was a compound of devotion, metaphysics, Platonism, and

---

1   Robert Southey's translation of *Amadis of Gaul* was published in four volumes in
    1803. It was reviewed with great enthusiasm in the *Monthly Mirror* (16 November
    1803) and favorably by Walter Scott in the *Edinburgh Review* (3 October 1803).
2   Other romances in the library of the gentleman of La Mancha include *Olivante de
    Laura* (1564), *Amadís de Grecia* (1530), and the *Jardin de Flores* (1570). The library
    from which Don Quixote fashioned his sense of reality is inventoried by a priest
    and a barber in chapter 6 of part 1 of Cervantes's novel.

chivalry, making altogether such a mixture as the world had never seen before. There is something extremely mysterious in the manner in which ladies of rank allowed themselves to be addressed by these poetical lovers; sometimes no doubt a real passion was produced, and some instances there are of its having had tragical consequences: but in general it may be suspected that the addresses of the Troubadours and other poets were rather a tribute paid to rank than to beauty; and that it was customary for young men of parts, who had their fortune to make, to attach themselves to a patroness, of whom they made a kind of idol, sometimes in the hopes of rising by her means, sometimes merely as a subject for their wit.[1] The manner in which Queen Elizabeth allowed herself to be addressed by her courtiers, the dedications which were in fashion in Dryden's time, the letters of Voiture, and the general strain of poetry of Waller and Cowley, may serve to prove that there may be a great deal of gallantry without any passion.[2] It is evident that, while these romance writers worshipped their mistress as a distant star, they did not disdain to warm themselves by meaner and nearer fires; for the species of love or rather adoration they professed did not at all prevent them from forming connexions with more accessible fair ones. Of all the countries on the continent, France and Spain had the greatest number of these chivalrous romances. In Italy the genius of the nation and the facility of versification led them to make poetry the vehicle of this kind of entertainment. The Cantos of Boiardo and Ariosto are romances in verse.

---

1  Barbauld refers here to the conventions of courtly love—a late medieval conventionalized code of address and behavior between a man and a lady whom he idealized to the point of worship.
2  References to sixteenth and seventeenth-century echoes of the courtly love tradition. Queen Elizabeth I (1533-1603) was celebrated and idealized by Edmund Spenser, Sir Walter Ralegh and William Shakespeare, among others. Dedications to printed poems and plays in John Dryden's time (the late seventeenth century) often contained fulsome praise of noblewomen. The letters of Vincent Voiture (1597-1648) published after his death, contained many sophisticated, eloquent passages on female beauty. Edmund Waller (1606-87) praised in verse his "Sacharissa" (Lady Dorothy Sidney) and others. Abraham Cowley (1618-67) published a collection of love poems under the title *The Mistress* in 1647.

In the mean time Europe settled into a state of comparative
tranquillity: castles and knights and adventures of distressed
damsels ceased to be the topics of the day, and romances found-
ed upon them had begun to be insipid when the immortal
satire of Cervantes drove them off the field, and they have
never since been able to rally their forces.[1] The first work of
entertainment of a different kind which was published in
France (for the *Pantagruel* of Rabelais is rather a piece of licen-
tious satire than a romance) was the *Astrea* of M. d'Urfé. It is a
pastoral romance, and became so exceedingly popular, that the
belles and beaux of that country assumed the airs and language
of shepherds and shepherdesses. A Celadon (the hero of the
piece) became a familiar appellation for a languishing lover, and
men of gallantry were seen with a crook in their hands, leading
a tame lamb about the streets of Paris. The celebrity of this
work was in great measure owing to its being strongly seasoned
with allusions to the intrigues of the court of Henry the
Fourth, in whose reign it was written. The volumes of *Astrea*
are never opened in the present day but as a curiosity; to read
them through would be a heavy task indeed. There is in the
machinery a strange mixture of wood nymphs and druids. The
work is full of anachronisms, but the time is supposed to be in
the reign of Pharamond or his successors.[2] The tale begins with
the lover, who is under the displeasure of his mistress, throwing
himself into the water, where he narrowly escapes drowning at
the very outset of the piece. We find here the *fountain of love*, in
which if a man looks, he sees, if he is beloved, the face of his
mistress; but if not, he is presented with the countenance of his
rival: long languishing speeches and little adventures of intrigue
fill up the story. It is interspersed with little pieces of poetry,
very tolerable for the time, but highly complimentary. One of
them turns upon the incident of the poet's mistress having

---

1  This view of the impact of *Don Quixote* on literary taste was traditional in
   "progress" histories of literature; James Beattie, for example, claims that Cervantes
   "brought about a great revolution in the manners and literature of Europe, by ban-
   ishing the wild dreams of chivalry, and reviving a taste for the simplicity of nature"
   ("On Fable," p. 94).
2  According to Arthurian legend, Pharamond, a knight of the Round Table, was the
   first king of France, reigning in the early fifth century.

burnt her cheek with her curling-iron; on which he takes occasion to say, "*that the fire of her eyes caused the mischief*." This work was however found so interesting by M. Huet, the grave bishop of Avranches, that when he read it along with his sisters, he was often obliged (as he tells us) to lay the book down, that he and they might give free vent to their tears.[1]

Though Cervantes had laid to rest the giants and enchanters, a new style of fictitious writing was introduced, not less remote from nature, in the romances *de longue haleine*,[2] which originated in France, and of which Calprénede and Mad. Scudery were the most distinguished authors. The principle of these was high honour, impregnable chastity, a constancy unshaken by time or accident, and a species of love so exalted and refined, that it bore little resemblance to a natural passion. These, in the construction of the story, came nearer to real life than the former had done. The adventures were marvellous, but not impossible. The heroes and heroines were taken from ancient history, but without any resemblance to the personages whose names they bore. The manners therefore and passions referred to an ideal world, the creation of the writer; but the situations were often striking, and the sentiments always noble. It is a curious circumstance that Rousseau, who tells us that his childhood was conversant in these romances, (a course of reading which no doubt fed and inflamed his fine imagination) has borrowed from them an affecting incident in his *Nouvelle Heloise*.[3] *St. Preux*, when his mistress lies ill of the small-pox, glides into the room, approaches the bed in order to imbibe the danger, and retires without speaking. *Julie*, when recovered, is impressed with a confused idea of having seen him, but whether in a dream, a vision, or a reality, she cannot determine. This striking circumstance is taken from the now almost forgotten *Cassandra* of Scudery. The complimentary language of these productions seems to have influenced the

---

1    Huet, *Memoirs* (1718, translated by John Aikin, 1810), 2:53.
2    Literally, "of long wind or breath."
3    Rousseau notes in Book 1 of his *Confessions* (1781-88) that his earliest reading consisted of novels from his father's library. The following incident, adapted from Madame Scudery, occurs in volume 2 of *Julie, ou la nouvelle Héloïse* (1761).

intercourse of common life, at least in the provinces, for Boileau introduces in his satires—

> *Deux nobles campagnards, grands lecteurs de romans,*
> *Qui m'ont dit tout Cyrus dans leurs longs compliments.*[1]

The same author made a more direct attack upon these productions in a dialogue entitled *Les Héros de Roman*, a humorous little piece, in which he ridiculed these as Cervantes had done the others, and drove them off the stage.[2]

Heroic sentiment and refined feeling, as expressed in romances and plays, were at their height about this time in France; and while the story and adventures were taken from the really chivalrous ages, it is amusing to observe how the rough manners of those times are softened and polished to meet the ideas of a more refined age. A curious instance of this occurs in Corneille's well-known play of the *Cid*.[3] *Chimene*, having lost her father by the hand of her lover, not only breaks off the connexion, but throws herself at the feet of the king to entreat him to avenge her by putting *Rodrigues* to death: "*Sire, vengeance!*" But in the genuine chronicle of the *Cid*, with which curious and entertaining work Mr. Southey has lately obliged the public, the previous incidents of the combat are nearly the same, and *Ximena* in like manner throws herself at the feet of the king; but to beg what?—not vengeance upon the murderer of her father, but that the king would be pleased to give her *Rodrigues* for a husband, to whom moreover she is not supposed to have had any previous attachment; her request seems to proceed from the simple idea that *Rodrigues*, by killing her father, having deprived her of one protector, it was but reasonable that he should give her another.

---

1  Boileau, "Satire III," ll. 43-44. Two country gentlemen, avid readers of novels, who recited to me the whole of the *Cyrus* in their drawn-out compliments. (tr. Francis Assaf). Boileau was adamantly against the reading of novels, including Mme. de Scudery's *Le Grand Cyrus*. We suspect that Barbauld picked up this reference from her brother's note 24 to his translation (1810) of Huet's *Memoirs*.

2  The full title is *Dialogue des héros de roman*, composed c. 1666.

3  *Le Cid* (1637) by Pierre Corneille (1606-84), a tragicomedy set in medieval Spain. The action described takes place in Act 4 scene 5.

Rude times are fruitful of striking adventures; polished times must render them pleasing.—The ponderous volumes of the romance writers being laid upon the shelf, a closer imitation of nature began to be called for; not but that, from the earliest times, there had been stories taken from, or imitating, real life. The *Decameron* of Boccacio (a storehouse of tales, and a standard of the language in which it is written), the *Cent Nouvelles* of the Queen of Navarre, *Contes et Fabliaux*[1] without number, may be considered as novels of a lighter texture: they abounded with adventure, generally of the humorous, often of the licentious kind, and indeed were mostly founded on intrigue, but the nobler passions were seldom touched. The *Roman Comique* of Scarron is a regular piece of its kind. Its subject is the adventures of a set of strolling players. Comic humour it certainly possesses, but the humour is very coarse and the incidents mostly low. Smollet seems to have formed himself very much upon this model.—But the *Zaide* and the *Princesse de Cleves* of Madame de la Fayette are esteemed to be the first which approach the modern novel of the serious kind, the latter especially. Voltaire says of them, that they were "*les premiers romans ou l'on vit les moeurs des honnêtes gens, et des avantures naturelles décrites avec grace. Avant elle on écrivoit d'un stile empoulé des choses peu vraisemblables.*"[2] "They were the first novels which gave the manners of cultivated life and natural incidents related with elegance. Before the time of this lady, the style of these productions was affectedly turgid, and the adventures out of nature." The modesty of Mad. de la Fayette led her to shelter her productions, on their first publication, under the name of Segrais, her friend, under whose revision they had passed.[3] Le Sage in his *Gil Blas*, a work of infinite entertainment though of dubi-

---

1  We believe Barbauld refers to no specific work here, just stories and fables in general, though the reference could allude to La Fontaine's often expanded *Contes et Nouvelles* (1664-74), poetic versions of stories by Boccaccio, Rabelais and Ariosto.

2  *Le Siécle de Louis XIV*, "Catalogue des Écrivains." s.v. LaFayette (in Voltaire's *Oeuvres Complètes*, 1785-89).

3  Jean Regnauld de Segrais (1624-1701) enjoyed a 20-year collaboration with the Duchesse de Montpensier. Their works are published under his name. Segrais had a similar relationship with Madame de Lafayette; *Zayde* (1670) was published under his name, though her authorship is assumed.

ous morality, has given us pictures of more familiar life, abounding in character and incident. The scene is laid in Spain, in which country he had travelled, and great part of it is imitated from the adventures of *Don Gusman d'Alvarache*; for Spain, though her energies have so long lain torpid, was earlier visited by polite literature than any country of Europe, Italy excepted. Her authors abounded in invention, so that the plots of plays and groundwork of novels were very frequently drawn from their productions. Cervantes himself, besides his Don Quixote, which has been translated and imitated in every country, wrote several little tales and novels, some of which he introduced into that work, for he only banished one species of fiction to introduce another. The French improved upon their masters. There is not perhaps a more amusing book than *Gil Blas*; it abounds in traits of exquisite humour and lessons of life, which, though not always pure, are many of them useful.[1] In this work of Le Sage, like some of Smollet's, the hero of the piece excites little interest, and it rather exhibits a series of separate adventures, slightly linked together, than a chain of events concurring in one plan to the production of the catastrophe, like the *Tom Jones* of Fielding. The scenes of his *Diable Boiteux* are still more slightly linked together. That, and his *Bachelier de Salamanque*, are of the same stamp with *Gil Blas*, though inferior to it.

Marivaux excelled in a different style. His *Marianne* and *Paisan Parvenu* give a picture of French manners with all their refinement and delicacy of sentiment. He lays open the heart, particularly the female heart, in its inmost folds and recesses; its little vanities and affectations as well as its finer feelings. He abounds in wit, but it is of a refined kind, and requires thought in the reader to enter into it. He has also much humour, and describes comic scenes and characters amongst the lower and middle ranks with a great deal of the comic effect, but without the coarseness, of Fielding. He eluded the difficulty of winding up a story by leaving both his pieces unfinished. Marivaux was

---

1   On *Gil Blas*, Barbauld agrees with James Beattie's assessment ("On Fable," p. 107), and on Marivaux (below), she concurs with John Moore's ("View of the Commencement and Progress of Romance," pp. 63-64).

contemporary with our Richardson: his style is found fault with by some French critics.[1] From his time, novels of all kinds have made a large and attractive portion of French literature.

At the head of writers of this class stands the seductive, the passionate Rousseau,—the most eloquent writer in the most eloquent modern language: whether his glowing pencil paints the strong emotions of passion, or the enchanting scenery of nature in his own romantic country, or his peculiar cast of moral sentiment,—a charm is spread over every part of the work, which scarcely leaves the judgement free to condemn what in it is dangerous or reprehensible. His are truly the "Thoughts that breathe and words that burn."[2] He has hardly any thing of story; he has but few figures upon his canvass; he wants them not; his characters are drawn more from a creative imagination than from real life, and we wonder that what has so little to do with nature should have so much to do with the heart. Our censure of the tendency of this work will be soft-ened, if we reflect that Rousseau's aim, as far as he had a moral aim, seems to have been to give a striking example of fidelity in the *married* state, which, it is well known, is little thought of by the French; though they would judge with greatest severity the more pardonable failure of an unmarried woman. But Rousseau has not reflected that *Julie* ought to have considered herself as indissolubly united to *St. Preux*; her marriage with another was the infidelity.[3] Rousseau's great rival in fame, Voltaire, has written many light pieces of fiction which can scarcely be called novels. They abound in wit and shrewdness, but they are all composed to subserve his particular views, and to attack systems which he assailed in every kind of way. His *Candide* has much strong painting of the miseries and vices which abound in this world, and is levelled against the only sys-tem which can console the mind under the view of them. In *L'Ingénu*, beside the wit, he has shown that he could also be

---

1   Voltaire, among others, found his style abstract, affected and unnatural (*Oxford Com-panion to French Literature*, s.v. Marivaux).

2   Thomas Gray, "The Progress of Poesy: A Pindaric Ode" (1757), l. 110.

3   Julie promised to marry St. Preux but broke the engagement in compliance with her father's opposition to the union. Barbauld's objection to this "infidelity" agrees with Clara Reeve's in *The Progress of Romance* (1785), 2: 17-18.

pathetic. *Les Lettres Peruviennes*, by Mad. Grafigny, is a most ingenious and charming little piece. *Paul et Virginie*, by that friend of humanity St. Pierre, with the purest sentiment and most beautiful description, is pathetic to a degree that even distresses the feelings. *La Chaumiere Indienne*, also his, breathes the spirit of universal philanthropy. *Caroline de Lichtfeld* is justly a favourite; but it were impossible to enumerate all the elegant compositions of this class which later times have poured forth. For the expression of sentiment in all its various shades, for the most delicate tact, and a refinement and polish, the fruit of high cultivation, the French writers are superior to those of every other nation.

There is one species of this composition which may be called the *Didactic Romance*, which they have particularly made use of as a vehicle for moral sentiment, and philosophical or political systems and opinions.—Of this nature is the beautiful fiction of *Telémaque*, if it be not rather an Epic in prose; the high merit of which cannot be sufficiently appretiated, unless the reader bears in mind when and to whom it was written; that it dared to attack the fondness for war and the disposition to ostentatious profusion, under a monarch the most vain and ambitious of his age, and to draw, expressly as a pattern for his successor, the picture of a prince, the reverse of him in almost every thing.[1] *Les Voyages de Cyrus*, by Ramsay, and *Sethos*, by the Abbé Terrasson, are of the same kind; the former is rather dry and somewhat mystical: it enters pretty deeply into the mythology of the ancients, and aims at showing that the leading truths of religion,—an original state of happiness, a fall from that state, and the final recovery and happiness of all sentient beings,—are to be found in the mythological systems of all nations. Ramsay was a Scotchman by birth, but had lived long enough in France to write the language like a native; a rare acquisition! The latter, *Sethos*, contains, interwoven in its story, all that we know concerning the customs and manners of the ancient Egyptians; the trial of the dead before they are received

---

1   A reference to King Louis XIV, who eventually banished from Versailles the author of *Telémaque*, François de Salignac de la Mothe-Fenelon (1651-1715)—though their disagreement stemmed from religious, not political, differences.

to the honours of sepulture, and the various ordeals of the initiation, are very striking. A high and severe tone of morals reigns through the whole, and indeed both this and the last mentioned composition are much too grave for the readers of romance in general. That is not the case with the *Belisaire*, and *Les Incas*, of Marmontel, in which the incidents meant to strike the feelings and the fancy are executed with equal happiness with the preceptive part. Writings like these cooperated powerfully with the graver labours of the encyclopedists in diffusing sentiments of toleration, a spirit of free inquiry, and a desire for equal laws and good government over Europe.[1] Happy, if the mighty impulse had permitted them to stop within the bounds of justice and moderation![2] The French language is well calculated for eloquence. The harmony and elegance of French prose, the taste of their writers, and the grace and amenity which they know how to diffuse over every subject, give great effect to compositions of this kind. When *we* aim at eloquence in prose, we are apt to become turgid. Florian, though a feeble writer, is not void of merit. His *Galatée* is from Cervantes; his *Gonsalve de Cordoue* is built upon the history of that hero.

There is one objection to be made to these romances founded on history, which is, that if the personages are not judiciously selected, they are apt to impress false ideas on the mind. *Sethos* is well chosen for a hero in this respect. His name scarcely emerges from the obscurity of half fabulous times, and of a country whose records are wrapped in mystery; for all that is recorded of *Sethos* is, merely that there was such a prince, and that, for some reason or other, he entered into the priesthood. *Cyrus*, though so conspicuous a character, was probably thought a fair one for the purpose, as Xenophon has evidently made use

---

1   *L'Encyclopédie* (published between 1751 and 1772) offered a survey of the arts and sciences of Europe based on Enlightenment principles that opposed religious and political bigotry by emphasizing philosophy over theology and supporting a reformist social agenda from a rationalist intellectual point of view.

2   A reference to the Reign of Terror. Works such as *L'Encyclopédie* were understood to have provided the intellectual basis of the Revolution, which began with the storming of the Bastille in 1789 and which culminated in the Reign of Terror and the guillotining of the King and Queen in 1793.

of him in the same manner; but it may admit a doubt whether *Belisarius* is equally so; still less, many in more modern times that have been selected for writings of this kind. *Telemachus* is a character already within the precincts of poetry and fable, and may illustrate without any objection the graceful fictions of Fenelon.[1] Our own Prince *Arthur* offers himself with equal advantage for poetry or romance. Where history says little, fiction may say much: events and men that are dimly seen through the obscurity of remote periods and countries, may be illuminated with these false lights; but where history throws her light steady and strong, no artificial colouring should be permitted. Impressions of historical characters very remote from the truth, often remain on the mind from dramatic compositions. If we examine into our ideas of the Henries and Richards of English history, we shall perhaps find that they are as much drawn from Shakespear as from Hume or Rapin.[2] Some of our English romances are very faulty in this respect. A lady confessed that she could never get over a prejudice against the character of our Elizabeth, arising from her cruelty to two imaginary daughters of Mary Queen of Scots, who never existed but in the pages of a novel. The more art is shown, and much is often shown, in weaving the fictitious circumstances into the texture of the history, the worse is the tendency. A romance of which *Edward the Black Prince* is the hero, by Clara Reeve, has many curious particulars of the customs of that age; but the manners of his court are drawn with such a splendid colouring of heroic virtue, as certainly neither that court nor any other ever deserved.

Among the authors of preceptive novels, Mad. Genlis stands very high. Her *Adele et Théodore* is a system of education, the whole of which is given in action; there is infinite ingenuity in the various illustrative incidents: the whole has an air of the world and of good company; to an English reader it is also

---

1 Cyrus was King of Persia (ca. 585-529 BC); Belisarius, a Byzantine general (ca. 505-565); and Telemachus, the son of Odysseus.

2 David Hume and Paul de Rapin Thoyras, authors of histories of England, Hume's published 1754-63, Rapin's 1724-36 in French and translated into English shortly thereafter.

interesting as exhibiting traits of Parisian manners, and modern manners, from one who was admitted into the first societies. A number of characters are delineated and sustained with truth and spirit, and the stories of *Cecile* and the *Duchesse de C.* are uncommonly interesting and well told, while the sublime benevolence of M. and Mad. Lagaraye presents a cure for sorrow worthy of a Howard.[1] From the system of Mad. Genlis many useful hints may be gathered, though the English reader will probably find much that differs from his own ideas. A good bishop, as Huet relates, conceiving of love as a most formidable enemy to virtue, entertained the singular project of writing, or procuring to be written, a number of novels framed in such a manner as to inspire an antipathy to this profane passion.[2] Madame Genlis seems to have had the same idea; and in this manual of education, love is represented as a passion totally unfit to enter the breast of a young female; and in this, and in all her other works, she invariably represents as ending in misery, every connexion which is begun by a mutual inclination. The parent, the mother rather, must dispose of her daughter; the daughter must be passive; and the great happiness of her life, is to be the having in her turn a daughter, in whose affections *she* is to be the prime object. Filial affection is no doubt much exaggerated by this writer. It is not natural that a young woman should make it an indispensable condition of marrying an amiable young man, that he will not separate her from her mother.[3] We know in England what filial affection is, and we know it does not rise so high, and we know too that it ought not. There is another objection to Mad. Genlis' system of education, which applies also to Rousseau's *Emile*, which is, that it is

---

1 Caroline-Stéphanie-Félicité de Genlis (1746-1830), governess to the children of the Duke d'Orleans, educational writer, and novelist. Her novel *Adèle et Théodore, ou Lettres sur l'Éducation* (1782) includes the interpolated tales of Cecile, a young woman who is forced to enter a nunnery and dies of grief; the Duchess of C, imprisoned by a jealous husband; and M. and Mme. de Lagaraye, rich society people who are made serious by the death of their only child, and thereupon—in the spirit of John Howard the philanthropist—turn their castle into a charity hospital.

2 We have not identified this passage in either Huet's *Treatise* or his *Memoirs.*

3 Adele "confessed that she preferred this match to any other," especially because her fiancé promised never to separate her from her mother (*Adelaide and Theodore*, 3: 241).

too much founded upon deception. The pupil never sees the real appearance of life and manners: the whole of his education is a series of contrived artificial scenery, produced, as occasion demands, to serve a particular purpose. Few of these scenes would succeed at all; a number of them certainly never would. Indeed Mad. Genlis is not very strict in the point of veracity. A little fibbing is even enjoined to Adele occasionally on particular emergencies.[1] *Les Veillées du Chateau*, by the same author, has great merit.[2] A number of other productions which have flowed from her pen witness her fertility of invention and astonishing rapidity of execution: their merit is various; all have great elegance of style: but it is observable, that in some of her later novels, she has endeavoured to favour the old order of things, to make almost an object of worship of Louis the Fourteenth, and to revive the reverence for monastic seclusion, which, with so much pathos, she had attacked in her charming story of *Cecile*.[3] The *Attala* of M. Chateau Briand is in like manner directed to prop the falling fabric of Romish faith.[4]

The celebrated daughter of Necker is one whose name cannot be passed over in this connexion. Her *Delphine* exhibits great powers: some of the situations are very striking; and the passion of love is expressed in such a variety of turns and changes, and with so many refined delicacies of sentiment, that it is surprising how any language could, and surely no language could but the French, find a sufficient variety of phrases in which to dress her ideas.—Yet this novel cannot be called a pleasing one. One monotonous colour of sadness prevails through the whole, varied indeed with deeper or lighter

---

1  Many incidents in *Adèle et Théodore* are contrived by the mother to test the children's fortitude or obedience. The mother also counsels lying in order to protect a friend (3: 82).
2  A 1784 collection of instructive tales for children and young persons; the model for John Aikin's *Evenings at Home*.
3  The same criticism is made in reviews of Genlis's novels *The Dutchess of La Valliere* and *Madame de Maintenon* in the *Annual Review* in 1805 and 1807; it is probable that Barbauld wrote these reviews.
4  François-René Chateaubriand (1768-1848), whose novel *Attala* was published as part of his *Génie du Christianisme* (1802). Barbauld reviewed *Génie* in the *Annual Review* (1803), criticizing it for encouraging a purely emotional and sentimental faith in Roman Catholicism.

shades, but no where presenting the cheerful hues of content-ment and pleasure. A heavier accusation lies against this work from its tendency, on which account it has been said that the author was desired by the present sovereign of France to leave Paris; but we may well suspect that a scrupulous regard to morality had less share than political motives in such a prohibi-tion. *Corinne*, by the same author, is less exceptionable, and has less force. It has some charming descriptions, and a picture of English country manners which may interest our curiosity, though it will not greatly flatter our vanity. Elegant literature has sustained a loss in the recent death of Mad. Cotin. Her *Elizabeth* and *Matilde* have given her a deserved celebrity. The latter is however very enthusiastic[1] and gloomy.

A number of other French writers of this class might have been mentioned, as Mad. Riccoboni, Mad. Elie de Beaumont, the Abbé Prévost, whose *Chevalier de Grieux* though otherwise not commendable, has some very pathetic parts. To these may be added Crebillon, and a number of writers of his class; for it must not be disguised, that besides the more respectable French novels, there are a number of others, which having passed no license of press, were said to be sold *sous le manteau*,[2] and were not therefore the less read. These are not merely exceptionable, they are totally unfit to enter a house where the morals of young people are esteemed an object. They are generally not coarse in language, less so perhaps than many English ones which aim at humour; but gross sensual pleasure is the very soul of them. The awful frown with which the better part of the English public seem disposed to receive any approaches, either in verse or prose, to the French voluptuousness, does honour to the national character.

The Germans, formerly remarkable for the laborious heavi-ness and patient research of their literary labours, have, within this last century, cultivated with great success the field of polite literature. Plays, tales, and novels of all kinds, many of them by their most celebrated authors, were at first received with avidity

---

1 Superstitious.
2 Secretly, clandestinely.

in this country, and even made the study of their language popular. The tide has turned, and they are now as much depreciated. The *Sorrows of Werter*, by Goethe, was the first of these with which we were familiarized in this country: we received it through the medium of a French translation. It is highly pathetic, but its tendency has been severely, perhaps justly, censured; yet the author might plead that he has given warning of the probable consequences of illicit and uncontrolled passions by the awful catastrophe.[1] It is certain, however, that the impression made is of more importance than the moral deduced; and if Schiller's fine play of *The Robbers*[2] has had, as we are assured was the case, the effect of leading some well-educated young gentlemen to commit depredations on the public, allured by the splendour of the principal character, we may well suppose that Werter's delirium of passion will not be less seducing. Goethe has written another novel, much esteemed, it is said, by the Germans, which contains, amongst other things, criticisms on the drama. The celebrated Wieland has composed a great number of works of fiction; the scene of most of them is laid in ancient Greece. His powers are great, his invention fertile, but his designs insidious. He and some others of the German writers of philosophical romances have used them as a frame to attack received opinions, both in religion and in morals. Two at least of his performances have been translated, *Agathon* and *Peregrine Proteus*. The former is beautifully written, but its tendency is seductive. The latter has taken for its basis a historical character; its tendency is also obvious. Klinger is an author who deals in the horrid. He subsists on murders and atrocities of all sorts, and introduces devils and evil spirits among his personages; he is said to have powers, but to labour under a total want of taste. In contrast to this writer and those of his class, may be mentioned *The Ghost Seer*, by Schiller, and *The Sorcerer* by another hand. These were written to expose the artifices of the Italian adepts of the school of

---

1   *Werter* ends with its hero's suicide.
2   Johann Christoph Friedrich von Schiller's sensationally popular first play, produced in 1781.

Cagliostro.[1] It is well known that these were spreading supersti-
tion and enthusiasm on the German part of the continent to an
alarming degree, and had so worked upon the mind of the late
king of Prussia, that he was made to believe he possessed the
power of rendering himself invisible, and was wonderfully
pleased when one of his courtiers (who, by the way, understood
his trade) ran against and jostled him, pretending not to see his
Majesty. These have been translated; as also a pleasant and lively
satire on Lavater's system of physiognomy,[2] written by Museus,
author of *Popular Tales of the Germans.* The Germans abound in
materials for works of the imagination; for they are rich in tales
and legends of an impressive kind, which have perhaps amused
generation after generation as nursery stories, and lain like ore
in the mine, ready for the hand of taste to separate the dross and
polish the material: for it is infinitely easier, when a nation has
gained cultivation, to polish and methodize than to invent. A
very pleasing writer of novels, in the more common accepta-
tion of the term, is Augustus la Fontaine;[3] at least he has writ-
ten some for which he merits that character, though perhaps
more that are but indifferent. His *Tableaux de Famille* contains
many sweet domestic pictures and touches of nature. It is imi-
tated from *The Vicar of Wakefield.*—The Germans are a very
book-making people. It is calculated that twenty thousand
authors of that nation live by the exercise of the pen; and in the
article of novels it is computed that seven thousand, either orig-
inal or translated, have been printed by them within the last
five-and-twenty years.[4]

One Chinese novel has been translated. It is called *The Pleas-*

---

1   Count Alessandro di Cagliostro (1743-95), an Italian adventurer, alchemist, propa-
    gandist and self-promoter. His "miracle cures" and marvelous experiments made
    him a sensation throughout Europe. Works by Schiller and Goethe in his own time
    and Strauss later attest to his popularity and influence in Germany.
2   Johann Kaspar Lavater (1741-1801), founder of the "science" of phrenology where-
    in character and intelligence are said to be indicated by the shape of the skull and
    the expressions of the face.
3   In the *Monthly Review* Barbauld had reviewed Fontaine's *Les Querelles de Famille*
    (1809); later she would review several more of his books.
4   "Germany ... contains above 20,000 authors who live by writing. More than seven
    thousand novels have been published in that country within the last twenty-five
    years" (*MM*, 8 [Sept. 1799]: 636).

*ing History, or the Adventures of Hau Kiou Choan.* It is said to be much esteemed, but can only be interesting to an European, as exhibiting something of the manners of that remote and singular country. It chiefly turns upon the stratagems used by the heroine to elude the ardour of her lover, and retard his approaches, till every circumstance of form and ceremony had been complied with. In their most tender assignations the lady is hid behind a curtain, as he is not permitted to see her face; and a female attendant conveys the tender speeches from one to the other; by which, according to our ideas, they would lose much of their pathos. The chief quality the heroine exhibits is cunning, and the adventures are a kind of hide-and-seek between the lovers. In short, *Shuy Ping Sin* to a Chinese may possibly be as great an object of admiration as *Clarissa*, but her accomplishments are not calculated for the meridian of this country.

In England, most of the earlier romances, from the days of Chaucer to James the First,[1] were translations from the Spanish or French. One of the most celebrated of our own growth is Sir Philip Sidney's *Arcadia*, dedicated to his sister the Countess of Pembroke. It is a kind of pastoral romance, mingled with adventures of the heroic and chivalrous kind. It has great beauties, particularly in poetic imagery. It is a book which all have heard of, which some few possess, but which nobody reads. The taste of the times seems to have been for ponderous performances. The Duchess of Newcastle was an indefatigable writer in this way. Roger Boyle, earl of Orrery, published, in 1664, a romance called *Parthenissa*. It was in three volumes folio, and unfinished, to which circumstance alone his biographer, Mr. Walpole, attributes its being but little read.[2] He must have had a capacious idea of the appetite of the readers of those days. There is a romance of later date, in one small volume, by

---

1  From the mid-fourteenth to the mid-seventeenth centuries, that is. In this sentence, and in the characterization of Sidney's *Arcadia* below, Barbauld follows verbatim John Moore's "View of the Commencement," p. 59.

2  Exactly the same comment on Boyle's *Parthenissa*, with the same reference to Horace Walpole's life of Boyle, is made by Clara Reeve (*Progress of Romance*, 1: 74) and John Moore ("View of the Commencement," p. 59).

the Hon. Robert Boyle—*The Martyrdom of Didymus and Theodora*, a Christian heroic tale. We had pretty early some celebrated political romances. Sir Thomas More's *Utopia*, Barclay's *Argenis*, and Harrington's *Oceana*, are of this kind: the two former are written in Latin.[1] The *Utopia*, which is meant as a model of a perfect form of civil polity, is chiefly preserved in remembrance at present by having had the same singular fortune with the *Quixote* of Cervantes, of furnishing a new word, which has been adopted into the language as a permanent part of it; for we speak familiarly of an Utopian scheme and a Quixotish expedition. Barclay was a Scotchman by birth; he was introduced at the court of James the First, and was afterwards professor of civil law at Angers; he died at Rome. His *Argenis* is a political allegory, which displays the revolutions and vices of courts; it is not destitute of imagery and elevated sentiment, and displays much learning; and while the allusions it is full of were understood, it was much read, and was translated into various languages, but is at present sunk into oblivion, though a new translation was made not many years since by Mrs. Clara Reeve.[2] Harrington's *Oceana* is meant as a model of a perfect republic, the constant idol of his imagination. All these, though works of fiction, would greatly disappoint those who should look into them for amusement. Of the lighter species of this kind of writing, *the Novel*, till within half a century we had scarcely any. *The Atalantis* of Mrs. Manley lives only in that line of Pope which seems to promise it immortality:

As long as *Atalantis* shall be read.[3]

It was, like *Astrea*, filled with fashionable scandal. Mrs. Behn's Novels were licentious; they are also fallen; but it ought not to be forgotten that Southern borrowed from her his affecting

---

1    Here Barbauld extends Huet's definition of romance.   To Huet, "Romances ... have Love for their principal Theme, and meddle not with War or Politicks but by accident" (*Treatise*, p. 6).
2    Reeve's translation of *Argenis* was published under the title of *The Phoenix* in 1772.
3    *The Rape of the Lock*, 3: 164.

story of *Oroonoko*.[1] Mrs. Haywood was a very prolific genius; her earlier novels are in the style of Mrs. Behn's, and Pope has chastised her in his *Dunciad* without mercy or delicacy, but her later works are by no means void of merit.[2] She wrote *The Invisible Spy*, and *Betsy Thoughtless*, and was the author of *The Female Spectator*.

But till the middle of the last century, theatrical productions and poetry made a far greater part of polite reading than novels, which had attained neither to elegance nor discrimination of character. Some adventures and a love story were all they aimed at. The ladies' library, described in the Spectator, contains "*The grand Cyrus*, with a pin stuck in one of the leaves," and "*Clelia*, which opened of itself in the place that describes two lovers in a bower:" but there does not occur either there, or, I believe, in any other part of the work, the name of one English novel, the *Atalantis* only excepted; though plays are often mentioned as a favourite and dangerous part of ladies' reading, and certainly the plays of those times were worse than any novels of the present.[3] The first author amongst us who distinguished himself by natural painting, was that truly original genius De Foe. His *Robinson Crusoe* is to this day an *unique* in its kind, and he has made it very interesting without applying to the common resource of love. At length, in the reign of George the Second, Richardson, Fielding, and Smollet, appeared in quick succession; and their success raised such a demand for this kind of entertainment, that it has ever since been furnished from the press, rather as a regular and necessary supply, than as an occasional gratification. Novels have indeed been numerous "as leaves in Vallombrosa."[4] The indiscriminate

---

1   Barbauld refers to Thomas Southerne's popular play, *Oroonoko* (1695), the plot of which is adapted from Behn's novel of the same name (1688).
2   Pope's derisive lines are in 2: 157-64. Haywood is the "prize" in the urinating contest between booksellers Osborne and Curl. In her respectful mention of Haywood, Barbauld agrees with Clara Reeve (*Progress of Romance*, 1:121).
3   *Spectator* no. 37 (1711). The list includes "A Book of Novels" by unspecified authors, philosophy, romances and sermons, but, as Barbauld suggests, no English novels besides *The New Atalantis*.
4   Milton, *Paradise Lost*, 1: 302-303: "Thick as autumnal leaves that strow the brooks / In Vallombrosa."

passion for them, and their bad effects on the female mind, became the object of the satire of Garrick, in a sprightly piece entitled *Polly Honeycomb*.[1] A few deserve to be mentioned, either for their excellence or the singularity of their plan.

The history of *Gaudentio di Lucca*, published in 1725, is the effusion of a fine fancy and a refined understanding; it is attributed to Bishop Berkeley. It gives an account of an imaginary people in the heart of Africa, their manners and customs. They are supposed to be descended from the ancient Egyptians, and to be concealed from all the world by impenetrable deserts. The description of crossing the sands is very striking, and shows much information as well as fancy. It is not written to favour any particular system; the whole is the play of a fine imagination delighting itself with images of perfection and happiness, which it cannot find in any existing form of things. The frame is very well managed; the whole is supposed to be read in manuscript to the fathers of the Inquisition,[2] and the remarks of the holy office are very much in character. A highly romantic air runs through the whole, but the language is far from elegant.

Another singular publication which appeared in 1756, was *The Memoirs of several Ladies*, by John Buncle, followed the next year by the *Life of Buncle*. These volumes are very whimsical, but contain entertainment. The ladies, whose memoirs he professes to give, are all highly beautiful and deeply learned; good Hebrew scholars; and, above all, zealous Unitarians. The author generally finds them in some sequestered dell, among the fells and mountains of Westmoreland, where, after a narrow escape of breaking his neck amongst rocks and precipices, he meets, like a true knight-errant, with one of these adventures. He marries in succession four or five of these prodigies, and the intervals between description and adventure are filled up with learned conversations on abstruse points of divinity. Many of

---

1 Not by Garrick but George Colman, the elder. This play begins with the title character reading a novel aloud to herself and ends with her imprudent marriage and her father's lament: "a man might as well turn his Daughter loose in Covent-garden, as trust the cultivation of her mind to a circulating library" (*Polly Honeycombe, a Dramatick Novel of One Act*, p. 44).

2 The Roman Catholic judicial body that sought out and banned works containing heretical religious doctrine or ideas.

the descriptions are taken from nature; and, as the book was much read, have possibly contributed to spread that taste for lake and mountain scenery which has since been so prevalent. The author was a clergyman.

A novel universally read at the time was *Chrysal, or The Adventures of a Guinea*. It described real characters and transactions, mostly in high life, under fictitious names; and certainly if a knowledge of the vicious part of the world be a desirable acquisition, *Chrysal* will amply supply it; but many of the scenes are too coarse not to offend a delicate mind, and the generation it describes is past away. *Pompey the Little*, with a similar frame, has less of personality, and is a lively pleasant satire. Its author is unknown.

About fifty years ago a very singular work appeared, somewhat in the guise of a novel, which gave a new impulse to writings of this stamp; namely, *The Life and Opinions of Tristram Shandy*, followed by *The Sentimental Journey*, by the Rev. Mr. Sterne, a clergyman of York. They exhibit much originality, wit, and beautiful strokes of pathos, but a total want of plan or adventure, being made up of conversations and detached incidents. It is the peculiar characteristic of this writer, that he affects the heart, not by long drawn tales of distress, but by light electric touches which thrill the nerves of the reader who possesses a correspondent sensibility of frame. His characters, in like manner, are struck out by a few masterly touches. He resembles those painters who can give expression to a figure by two or three strokes of bold outline, leaving the imagination to fill up the sketch; the feelings are awakened as really by the story of *Le Fevre*, as by the narrative of *Clarissa*. The indelicacies of these volumes are very reprehensible, and indeed in a clergyman scandalous, particularly in the first publication, which however has the richest vein of humour. The two *Shandys*, *Trim*, *Dr. Slop*, are all drawn with a masterly hand. It is one of the merits of Sterne that he has awakened the attention of his readers to the wrongs of the poor negroes, and certainly a great spirit of tenderness and humanity breathes throughout the work. It is rather mortifying to reflect how little the power of expressing these feelings is connected with moral worth; for

Sterne was a man by no means attentive to the happiness of those connected with him; and we are forced to confess that an author may conceive the idea of "brushing away flies without killing them," and yet behave ill in every relation of life.[1]

It has lately been said that Sterne has been indebted for much of his wit to *Burton's Anatomy of Melancholy*.[2] He certainly exhibits a good deal of reading in that and many other books out of the common way, but the wit is in the application, and that is his own. This work gave rise to the vapid effusions of a crowd of sentimentalists, many of whom thought they had seized the spirit of Sterne, because they could copy him in his breaks and asterisks. The taste spread, and for a while, from the pulpit to the playhouse, the reign of sentiment was established. Among the more respectable imitators of Sterne may be reckoned Mr. Mackenzie in his *Man of Feeling* and his *Julia de Roubigné*, and Mr. Pratt in his *Emma Corbett*.

An interesting and singular novel, *The Fool of Quality*, was written by Henry Brooke, a man of genius, the author of *Gustavus Vasa* and many other productions. Many beautiful and pathetic episodical stories might be selected from it, but the story runs out into a strain romantic and improbable beyond the common allowed measure of this kind of writing; so that as a whole it cannot be greatly recommended: but it ought not to be forgotten that the very popular work of *Sandford and Merton* is taken from it. It has not merely given the hint for that publication; but the plan, the contrasted character of the two boys, and many particular incidents are so closely copied, that it will hardly be thought by one who peruses them both together, that Mr. Day has made *quite* sufficient acknowledgement in his

---

1  Barbauld probably refers to the estrangement between Sterne and his mother; she may also be alluding to domestic difficulties between Sterne and his wife that led to their separation. See Arthur Cash, *Laurence Sterne: The Early and Middle Years*, pp. 224–26, and *Laurence Sterne: The Later Years*, pp. 172–73. The quotation is not verbatim from *Tristram Shandy* but refers to an incident in vol. II where Uncle Toby releases a fly instead of killing it, for, he says, "this world is surely wide enough to hold both thee and me" (*The Life and Opinions of Tristram Shandy, Gentleman*, I: 131).

2  John Ferriar (1761–1815), a physician, read a paper before the Literary and Philosophical Society of Manchester on 21 January 1791 in which he asserted that "all the singularities" of Walter Shandy's character were derived from Burton's *Anatomy of Melancholy* (1651) (*Sterne: The Critical Heritage*, p. 285).

preface. Rousseau had about this time awakened the public attention to the preference of natural manners in children, in opposition to the artificial usages of fashionable life; and much of the spirit of *Emile* is seen in this part of the work.[1] The present generation have been much obliged to Mr. Day for separating this portion of the novel from the mass of improbable adventure in which it is involved, clothing it in more elegant language, and giving those additions which have made it so deservedly a favourite in the juvenile library. The religious feelings are often awakened in *The Fool of Quality*, not, however, without a strong tincture of enthusiasm, to which the author was inclined. Indeed, his imagination had at times prevailed over his reason before he wrote it.

A number of novels might be mentioned, which are, or have been, popular, though not of high celebrity. Sarah Fielding, sister to the author of *Tom Jones*, composed several; among which *David Simple* is the most esteemed: she was a woman of good sense and cultivation; and if she did not equal her brother in talent, she did not, like him, lay herself open to moral censure. She translated Xenophon's *Socrates*[2] and wrote a very pretty book for children, *The Governess, or Female Academy*.

Many tears have been shed by the young and tender-hearted over *Sidney Biddulph*, the production of Mrs. Sheridan, the wife of Mr. Thomas Sheridan the lecturer,[3] an ingenious and amiable woman: the sentiments of this work are pure and virtuous, but the author seems to have taken pleasure in heaping distress upon virtue and innocence, merely to prove, what no one will deny, that the best dispositions are not always sufficient to ward off the evils of life. Why is it that women when they write are apt to give a melancholy tinge to their compositions? Is it that they suffer more, and have fewer resources against melancholy? Is it that men, mixing at large in society, have a brisker flow of

---

1   *Émile* (1762) concerns the education of a natural man for life in society. His education is conducted through experience and reflection, not books.

2   Specifically, Xenophon's (c. 430-352 BC) *Memorabilia* and *Apologia* of Socrates.

3   Thomas Sheridan (1719-88) was an actor and theater manager before becoming a renowned lecturer on the art of elocution. In addition to being the husband of novelist Frances Sheridan, he was the father of playwright Richard Brinsley Sheridan (1751-1816).

ideas, and, seeing a greater variety of characters, introduce more of the business and pleasures of life into their productions? Is it that humour is a scarcer product of the mind than sentiment, and more congenial to the stronger powers of man? Is it that women nurse those feelings in secrecy and silence and diversify the expression of them with endless shades of sentiment, which are more transiently felt, and with fewer modifications of delicacy, by the other sex? The remark, if true, has no doubt many exceptions; but the productions of several ladies, both French and English, seem to countenance it.

*Callistus, or The Man of Fashion,* by Mr. Mulso,[1] is a pathetic story; but it is written entirely for moral effect, and affords little of entertainment. Mr. Graves, an author of a very different cast, is known in this walk by *Columella* and his *Spiritual Quixote.* The latter is a popular work, and possesses some humour; but the humour is coarse, and the satire much too indiscriminately levelled against a society whose doctrines, operating with strong effect upon a large body of the most ignorant and vicious class, must necessarily include in their sweeping net much vice and folly, as well as much of sincere piety and corresponding morals. The design of his *Columella* is less exceptionable. It presents a man educated in polite learning and manners, who, from a fastidious rejection of the common active pursuits of life, rusticates in a country solitude, grows morose and peevish, and concludes with marrying his maid; no unusual consequence of a whimsical and morose singularity, the secret springs of which are, more commonly, a tincture of indolence and pride than superiority of genius. Mr. Graves was brought up originally for physic, but took orders and became rector of Claverton near Bath. He was the author of several publications, both translations and original; he was fond of writing, and published what he entitled his *Senilities* when at the age of near ninety. He died in 1804.—But it is time to retire from the enumeration of these works of fancy, or the reader might be as much startled with the number of heroes and heroines called up around him, as Ulysses was

1    Thomas Mulso (1721-99), brother of Hester Mulso Chapone and an acquaintance of Barbauld.

with the troops of shades that came flocking about him in the infernal regions.[1]

If the end and object of this species of writing be asked, many no doubt will be ready to tell us that its object is,—to call in fancy to the aid of reason, to deceive the mind into embracing truth under the guise of fiction:

> Cosi a l'egro fanciul porgiamo aspersi
> Di soave licor gli orli del vaso,
> Succhi amari, ingannato in tanto ei beve,
> E da l'inganno suo vita riceve:[2]

with such-like reasons equally grave and dignified. For my own part, I scruple not to confess that, when I take up a novel, my end and object is entertainment; and as I suspect that to be the case with most readers, I hesitate not to say that entertainment is their legitimate end and object. To read the productions of wit and genius is a very high pleasure to all persons of taste, and the avidity with which they are read by all such shows sufficiently that they are calculated to answer this end. Reading is the cheapest of pleasures: it is a domestic pleasure. Dramatic exhibitions give a more poignant delight, but they are seldom enjoyed in perfection, and never without expense and trouble. Poetry requires in the reader a certain elevation of mind and a practised ear. It is seldom relished unless a taste be formed for it pretty early. But the humble novel is always ready to enliven the gloom of solitude, to soothe the languor of debility and disease, to win the attention from pain or vexatious occurrences, to take man from himself, (at many seasons the worst company he can be in) and, while the moving picture of life passes before

---

1    *Odyssey*, Book XI.

2    From Tasso, *Gerusalemme Liberata* (1575), I.iii: "So we, if children young diseas'd we find, / Anoint with sweets the vessel's foremost parts, / To make them taste the potions sharp we give; / They drink deceiv'd; and so deceiv'd they live" (Fairfax translation). The usual defence of fiction in the Renaissance and eighteenth century was that it imparts moral ideas in attractive guise (like Tasso's sweetened medicine). Barbauld's phrase, "to call in fancy to the aid of reason" echoes Samuel Johnson's in his "Life of Milton" (1779): "Poetry is the art of uniting pleasure with truth, by calling imagination to the help of reason" (*Lives of the Poets*, 1:170).

him, to make him forget the subject of his own complaints. It is pleasant to the mind to sport in the boundless regions of possibility;[1] to find relief from the sameness of every-day occurrences by expatiating amidst brighter skies and fairer fields; to exhibit love that is always happy, valour that is always successful; to feed the appetite for wonder by a quick succession of marvellous events; and to distribute, like a ruling providence, rewards and punishments which fall just where they ought to fall.

It is sufficient therefore as an end, that these writings add to the innocent pleasures of life; and if they do no harm, the entertainment they give is a sufficient good. We cut down the tree that bears no fruit, but we ask nothing of a flower beyond its scent and its colour. The unpardonable sin in a novel is dullness: however grave or wise it may be, if its author possesses no powers of amusing, he has no business to write novels; he should employ his pen in some more serious part of literature.

But it is not necessary to rest the credit of these works on amusement alone, since it is certain they have had a very strong effect in infusing principles and moral feelings. It is impossible to deny that the most glowing and impressive sentiments of virtue are to be found in many of these compositions, and have been deeply imbibed by their youthful readers. They awaken a sense of finer feelings than the commerce of ordinary life inspires. Many a young woman has caught from such works as *Clarissa* or *Cecilia*, ideas of delicacy and refinement which were not, perhaps, to be gained in any society she could have access to. Many a maxim of prudence is laid up in the memory from these stores, ready to operate when occasion offers.

The passion of love, the most seductive of all the passions, they certainly paint too high, and represent its influence beyond what it will be found to be in real life; but if they soften the heart they also refine it. They mix with the common[2] passions of our nature all that is tender in virtuous affection; all

---

1   Barbauld recalls Johnson's remark on Milton's imagination in *Paradise Lost*: "Milton's delight was to sport in the wide regions of possibility" (*Lives of the Poets*, 1:177-78).
2   common: in 1810, "natural."

that is estimable in high principle and unshaken constancy; all
that grace, delicacy, and sentiment can bestow of touching and
attractive. Benevolence and sensibility to distress are almost
always insisted on in modern works of this kind; and perhaps it
is not exaggeration[1] to say, that much of the softness of our pre-
sent manners, much of that tincture of humanity so conspicu-
ous amidst all our vices, is owing to the bias given by our dra-
matic writings and fictitious stories. A high regard to female
honour, generosity, and a spirit of self-sacrifice, are strongly
inculcated. It costs nothing, it is true, to an author to make his
hero generous, and very often he is extravagantly so; still, senti-
ments of this kind serve in some measure to counteract the
spirit of the world, where selfish considerations have always
more than their due weight. In what discourse from the pulpit
are religious feelings more strongly raised than in the prison
sermon of *The Vicar of Wakefield*, or some parts of *The Fool of
Quality*?

But not only those splendid sentiments with which, when
properly presented, our feelings readily take part, and kindle as
we read; the more severe and homely virtues of prudence and
economy have been enforced in the writings of a Burney and
an Edgeworth. Writers of their good sense have observed, that
while these compositions cherished even a romantic degree of
sensibility, the duties that have less brilliancy to recommend
them were neglected. Where can be found a more striking les-
son against unfeeling dissipation than the story of the *Harrels*?[2]
Where have order, neatness, industry, sobriety, been recom-
mended with more strength than in the agreeable tales of Miss
Edgeworth? If a parent wishes his child to avoid caprice, irreg-
ularities of temper, procrastination, coquetry, affectation,—all
those faults and blemishes which undermine family happiness,
and destroy the every-day comforts of common life,—whence
can he derive more impressive morality than from the same
source? When works of fancy are thus made subservient to the

---

1  exaggeration: in 1810, "too much."
2  In Burney's *Cecilia*, the Harrels' fiscal irresponsibility leads Mr. Harrel to commit
   suicide at Vauxhall Gardens. The grim episode is recounted in chapters 12 and 13
   of Book V.

improvement of the rising generation, they certainly stand on a higher ground than mere entertainment, and we revere while we admire.

Some knowledge of the world is also gained by these writings, imperfect indeed, but attained with more ease, and attended with less danger, than by mixing in real life. If the stage is a mirror of life, so is the novel, and perhaps a more accurate one, as less is sacrificed to effect and representation. There are many descriptions of characters in the busy world, which a young woman in the retired scenes of life hardly meets with at all, and many whom it is safer to read of than to meet; and to either sex it must be desirable that the first impressions of fraud, selfishness, profligacy and perfidy should be connected, as in good novels they always will be, with infamy and ruin. At any rate, it is safer to meet with a bad character in the pages of a fictitious story, than in the polluted walks of life; but an author solicitous for the morals of his readers will be sparing in the introduction of such characters.—It is an aphorism of Pope,

> Vice is a monster of such frightful mien
> As to be hated, needs but to be seen.

But he adds,

> But seen too oft, familiar with her face,
> We first endure, then pity, then embrace.[1]

Indeed the former assertion is not true without considerable modifications. If presented in its naked deformity, vice will indeed give disgust; but it may be so surrounded with splendid and engaging qualities, that the disgust is lost in admiration. Besides, though the selfish and mean propensities are radically unlovely, it is not the same with those passions which all have felt, and few are even desirous to resist. To present these to the young mind in the glowing colours of a Rousseau or a Madame de Stael is to awaken and increase sensibilities, which

---

1 *Essay on Man*, 2: 217-20.

it is the office of wise restraint to calm and to moderate. Humour covers the disgust which the grosser vices would occasion; passion veils the danger of the more seducing ones.

After all, the effect of novel-reading must depend, as in every other kind of reading, on the choice which is made. If the looser compositions of this sort are excluded, and the sentimental ones chiefly perused, perhaps the danger lies more in fixing the standard of virtue and delicacy too high for real use, than in debasing it. Generosity is carried to such excess as would soon dissipate even a princely fortune; a weak compassion often allows vice to escape with impunity; an overstrained delicacy, or regard to a rash vow, is allowed to mar all the prospects of a long life: dangers are despised, and self is annihilated, to a degree that prudence does not warrant, and virtue is far from requiring. The most generous man living, the most affectionate friend, the most dutiful child, would find his character fall far short of the perfections exhibited in a highly-wrought novel.

Love is a passion particularly exaggerated in novels. It forms the chief interest of, by far, the greater part of them. In order to increase this interest, a false idea is given of the importance of the passion. It occupies the serious hours of life; events all hinge upon it; every thing gives way to its influence, and no length of time wears it out.[1] When a young lady, having imbibed these notions, comes into the world, she finds that this formidable passion acts a very subordinate part on the great theatre of the world; that its vivid sensations are mostly limited to a very early period; and that it is by no means, as the poet sings,

All the colour of remaining life.[2]

She will find but few minds susceptible of its more delicate

---

1 Barbauld argues as Samuel Johnson did in the "Preface" to his edition of Shakespeare (1765): "But love is only one of many passions, and ... has no great influence upon the sum of life" (*Johnson on Shakespeare*, p. 63).

2 Matthew Prior, "Solomon or the Vanity of the World. Pleasure, the 2nd Book," l. 235.

influences. Where it is really felt, she will see it continually overcome by duty, by prudence, or merely by a regard for the show and splendour of life; and that in fact it has a very small share in the transactions of the busy world, and is often little consulted even in choosing a partner for life. In civilized life both men and women acquire so early a command over their passions, that the strongest of them are taught to give way to circumstances, and a moderate liking will appear apathy itself, to one accustomed to see the passion painted in its most glowing colours.[1] Least of all will a course of novels prepare a young lady for the neglect and tedium of life which she is perhaps doomed to encounter. If the novels she reads are virtuous, she has learned how to arm herself with proper reserve against the ardour of her lover; she has been instructed how to behave with the utmost propriety when run away with, like *Miss Byron*, or locked up by a cruel parent, like *Clarissa*; but she is not prepared for indifference and neglect. Though young and beautiful, she may see her youth and beauty pass away without conquests, and the monotony of her life will be apt to appear more insipid when contrasted with scenes of perpetual courtship and passion.

It may be added with regard to the knowledge of the world, which, it is allowed, these writings are calculated in some degree to give, that, let them be as well written and with as much attention to real life and manners as they can possibly be, they will in some respects give false ideas, from the very nature of fictitious writing. Every such work is a *whole*, in which the fates and fortunes of the personages are brought to a conclusion, agreeably to the author's own preconceived idea. Every incident in a well written composition is introduced for a certain purpose, and made to forward a certain plan. A sagacious reader is never disappointed in his forebodings. If a prominent circumstance is presented to him, he lays hold on it, and may be

---

1  Cf. Clara Reeve: "false expectations are raised.—A young woman is taught to expect adventures and intrigues,—she expects to be addressed in the style of these books, with the language of flattery and adulation.—If a plain man addresses her in rational terms and pays her the greatest of compliments,—that of desiring to spend his life with her,—that is not sufficient, her vanity is disappointed, she expects to meet a Hero in Romance" (*Progress of Romance*, 2:78).

very sure it will introduce some striking event; and if a charac-
ter has strongly engaged his affections, he need not fear being
obliged to withdraw them: the personages never turn out dif-
ferently from what their first appearance gave him a right to
expect; they gradually open, indeed; they may surprise, but they
never disappoint him. Even from the elegance of a name he
may give a guess at the amenity of the character. But real life is
a kind of chance-medley, consisting of many unconnected
scenes. The great author of the drama of life has not finished
his piece; but the author must finish his; and vice must be pun-
ished and virtue rewarded in the compass of a few volumes; and
it is a fault in *his* composition if every circumstance does not
answer the reasonable expectations of the reader. But in real life
our reasonable expectations are often disappointed; many inci-
dents occur which are like "passages that lead to nothing,"[1] and
characters occasionally turn out quite different from what our
fond expectations have led us to expect.

In short, the reader of a novel forms his expectations from
what he supposes passes in the mind of the author, and guesses
rightly at his intentions, but would often guess wrong if he
were considering the real course of nature. It was very proba-
ble, at some periods of his history, that *Gil Blas*, if a real char-
acter, would come to be hanged; but the practised novel-reader
knows well that no such event can await the hero of the tale.
Let us suppose a person speculating on the character of *Tom
Jones* as the production of an author, whose business it is pleas-
ingly to interest his readers. He has no doubt but that, in spite
of his irregularities and distresses, his history will come to an
agreeable termination. He has no doubt but that his parents
will be discovered in due time; he has no doubt but that his
love for *Sophia* will be rewarded sooner or later with her hand;
he has no doubt of the constancy of that young lady, or of their
entire happiness after marriage. And why does he foresee all
this? Not from the real tendencies of things, but from what he
has discovered of the author's intentions. But what would have
been the probability in real life? Why, that the parents would

---

1   Thomas Gray, "A Long Story," line 8.

either never have been found, or have proved to be persons of no consequence—that *Jones* would pass from one vicious indulgence to another, till his natural good disposition was quite smothered under his irregularities—that *Sophia* would either have married her lover clandestinely, and have been poor and unhappy, or she would have conquered her passion and married some country gentleman with whom she would have lived in moderate happiness, according to the usual routine of married life. But the author would have done very ill so to have constructed his story. If *Booth* had been a real character, it is probable his *Amelia* and her family would not only have been brought to poverty, but left in it; but to the reader it is much more probable that by some means or other they will be rescued from it, and left in possession of all the comforts of life. It is *probable* in *Zeluco* that the detestable husband will some way or other be got rid of; but woe to the young lady, who, when married, should be led, by contemplating the possibility of such an event, to cherish a passion which ought to be entirely relinquished!

Though a great deal of trash is every season poured out upon the public from the English presses, yet in general our novels are not vicious; the food has neither flavour nor nourishment, but at least it is not poisoned. Our national taste and habits are still turned towards domestic life and matrimonial happiness, and the chief harm done by a circulating library is occasioned by the frivolity of its furniture, and the loss of time incurred. Now and then a girl perhaps may be led by them to elope with a coxcomb; or if she is handsome, to expect the homage of a *Sir Harry* or *My lord*, instead of the plain tradesman suitable to her situation in life; but she will not have her mind contaminated with such scenes and ideas as Crebillon, Louvet, and others of that class have published in France.[1]

---

1   Claude-Prosper Jolyot de Crébillon or Crébillon *fils* (1707-77) wrote a number of novels with a variety of themes, but Barbauld here refers to his licentious fiction such as *Lettres de la duchesse de* \*\*\* (1768) and *Lettres athéniennes* (1771). Jean-Baptiste Louvet de Courvay (1760-97) was the author of *Les amours du chevalier de Faublas* (1787-90) which contained early scenes that Barbauld would consider objectionable, though the ending (wherein Faublas goes mad) is certainly sober enough.

And indeed, notwithstanding the many paltry books of this kind published in the course of every year, it may safely be affirmed that we have more good writers in this walk living at the present time, than at any period since the days of Richardson and Fielding. A very great proportion of these are ladies: and surely it will not be said that either taste or morals have been losers by their taking the pen in hand. The names of D'Arblay, Edgeworth, Inchbald, Radcliffe, and a number more, will vindicate this assertion.

No small proportion of modern novels have been devoted to recommend, or to mark with reprobation, those systems of philosophy or politics which have raised so much ferment of late years. Mr. Holcroft's *Anna St. Ives* is of this number: its beauties, and beauties it certainly has, do not make amends for its absurdities. What can be more absurd than to represent a young lady gravely considering, in the disposal of her hand, how she shall promote the greatest possible good of the system? Mr. Holcroft was a man of strong powers, and his novels are by no means without merit, but his satire is often partial, and his representations of life unfair. On the other side may be reckoned *The modern Philosophers*, and the novels of Mrs. West. In the war of systems these light skirmishing troops have been often employed with great effect; and, so long as they are content with fair, general warfare, without taking aim at individuals, are perfectly allowable. We have lately seen the gravest theological discussions presented to the world under the attractive form of a novel, and with a success which seems to show that the interest, even of the generality of readers, is most strongly excited when some serious end is kept in view.[1]

It is not the intention in these slight remarks to enumerate those of the present day who have successfully entertained the public; otherwise Mr. Cumberland might be mentioned, that veteran in every field of literature; otherwise a tribute ought to be paid to the peculiarly pathetic powers of Mrs. Opie; nor would it be possible to forget the very striking and original novel of *Caleb Williams*, in which the author, without the assis-

---

1   Probably Hannah More's *Coelebs in Search of a Wife* (1809), in which morals and doctrines are discussed at length.

tance of any of the common events or feelings on which these stories generally turn, has kept up the curiosity and interest of the reader in the most lively manner; nor his *St. Leon*, the ingenious speculation of a philosophical mind, which is also much out of the common track. It will bear an advantageous comparison with Swift's picture of the *Strulbrugs* in his *Voyage to Laputa*,[1] the tendency of which seems to be to repress the wish of never-ending life in this world: but in fact it does not bear at all upon the question, for no one ever did wish for immortal life without immortal youth to accompany it, the one wish being as easily formed as the other; but *St. Leon* shows, from a variety of striking circumstances, that both together would pall, and that an immortal *human* creature would grow an insulated unhappy being.

With regard to this particular selection, it presents a series of some of the most approved novels, from the first regular productions of the kind to the present time: they are of very different degrees of merit; but none, it is hoped, so destitute of it as not to afford entertainment. Variety in manner has been attended to. As to the rest, no two people probably would make the same choice, nor indeed the same person at any distance of time. A few of superior merit were chosen without difficulty, but the list was not completed without frequent hesitation. Some regard it has been thought proper to pay to the taste and preference of the public, as was but reasonable in an undertaking in which their preference was to indemnify those who are at the expense and risk of the publication. Copyright also was not to be intruded on,[2] and the number of volumes was determined by the booksellers. Some perhaps may think that too much importance has been already given to a subject so frivolous, but a discriminating taste is no where more called for than with regard to a species of books which every body reads. It was said by Fletcher of Saltoun, "Let me make the ballads of a nation, and I care not who makes the laws."[3] Might it not be

---

1   In Book III of *Gulliver's Travels*.

2   In 1810, the author retained the right to benefits from his or her work until 28 years after publication, at which time the work passed into public domain.

3   Andrew Fletcher of Saltoun (1655-1716) makes this observation in *Conversation Concerning a Right Regulation of Government for the Common Good of Mankind* (1704).

said with as much propriety, Let me make the novels of a coun-
try, and let who will make the systems?

## From *Fielding*

[Along with Samuel Richardson, Henry Fielding (1707-54)
dominated the novel-writing world of the 1740s. He had
begun his writing career as a satirical playwright. When the
1737 Licensing Act limited the venues for political satire on the
stage, Fielding turned to journalism, first, and then prose fiction
to exercise his comic wit. With the publication of Richardson's
*Pamela* in 1740, Fielding found a new satiric target. His *Shamela*
(1741) was the most popular of the "anti-*Pamelas*," and his
*Joseph Andrews*, (1742), the story of Pamela's "brother," a
paragon of *male* chastity, likewise owes its genesis to ridicule
inspired by Richardson's fiction. *Tom Jones* (1749) is Fielding's
masterpiece, featuring a wry, self-conscious narrator, a cast of
characters ranging from poachers and soldiers to country gen-
tlemen and the titled denizens of London. From the begin-
ning, reaction to *Tom Jones* combined admiration for its careful-
ly contrived plot and its variety of characters with reservations
about its morality. In her comments, Barbauld reflects this dual
response, entering the existing discourse begun by Samuel
Richardson (Letter to Astraea and Minerva Hill [4 August
1749]), Arthur Murphy (*The Works of Henry Fielding* [1762]),
James Beattie (*Dissertations Moral and Critical* [1783]), Clara
Reeve (*Progress of Romance* [1785 ]), Samuel Johnson (com-
ments recorded in Boswell's *Life of Johnson* [1791]), and others.
Fielding's final novel, *Amelia* (1752), is more somber in tone
than his earlier fiction, and (perhaps as a consequence) it was
less well received in his own time. Barbauld includes both
*Joseph Andrews* and *Tom Jones* in *The British Novelists*, and in her
preface she comments on all the fiction. We reprint her
remarks on *Tom Jones*.]

Henry Fielding was in his person tall, and of a robust make
with an originally strong constitution, qualities which, perhaps
for that reason, he seems fond of attributing to his heroes. He

was social, hospitable, fond of pleasure, and apt to be impatient under disappointment or ill usage. Though he might not be a very faithful, he was a very affectionate husband, as well as a very fond father; all the sympathies of a feeling heart were alive in him.[1] By seeing much of the vicious part of mankind, professionally in his latter years[2] and by choice in his earlier, his mind received a taint which spread itself in his works, but was powerfully counteracted by the better sensibilities of his nature. Notwithstanding his irregularities, he was not without a sense of religion, and had collected materials for an Answer to Lord Bolingbroke's posthumous works, in which he would probably have been much out of his depth.[3] No portrait was taken of him during his life. Hogarth, with whom he had an intimate friendship, executed one after his death, partly from recollection and partly from a profile cut by a lady with a pair of scissars. An engraving of it is prefixed to the edition of his works in ten volumes, with his Life, published by Mr. Murphy.[4]

...

*Joseph Andrews* was followed by *Tom Jones*, a novel produced when the author was in the meridian of his faculties, and after he had joined to his natural talents experience of the world, mature judgement, and practice in the art of writing. From these advantages a finished work may be expected; and such,

---

1  Fielding married Charlotte Craddock in 1734; she died in 1744. In 1747, he married Mary Daniel who was then pregnant with his child. Fielding's affection for his first wife was given legendary status by his tribute to her in the character of Sophia in *Tom Jones*. Barbauld's sense of Fielding's infidelity may derive from the fact that his second wife was a member of his household staff, or she may be following Fielding's first biographer, Arthur Murphy, who refers more generally to Fielding's youthful dissipations.

2  From 1748 on Fielding served as a justice of the peace for Westminster.

3  Barbauld's information comes from Murphy, who reviewed the eighty-one "fragments" Fielding compiled in response to the collection of Bolingbroke's posthumous works published by David Mallet in 1754. According to Martin Battestin, Fielding planned to satirize Bolingbroke's free-thinking approach to scripture (*Henry Fielding: A Life* pp. 582-83).

4  Martin Battestin has argued that three likenesses of Fielding were drawn from the life ("Pictures of Fielding," 1-13, and *Henry Fielding: A Life*, ix); but in 1810 the received opinion was that only the portrait by William Hogarth (1697-1764), completed after Fielding's death, existed.

considered as a composition, *Tom Jones* undoubtedly is. There is perhaps no novel in the English language so artfully conducted, or so rich in humour and character. Nor is it without scenes that interest the heart. The story of the highwayman, the distress of Mrs. Miller and her daughter in the affair with Nightingale, and many little incidents relating to Jones in his childhood, are highly affecting, and calculated to awaken our best feelings. Touches of the pathetic thus starting out in a work of humour, do not lose, they rather gain, from the contrast of sensations, and have a greater air of nature from being mixed with adventures drawn from common life. The conduct of the piece is as masterly as the details are interesting. It contains a story involving a number of adventures, and a variety of characters, all of which are strictly connected with the main design, and tend to the development of the plot; which yet is so artfully concealed, that it may be doubted whether it was ever anticipated by the most practised and suspicious reader. The story contains all that we require in a regular epopea[1] or drama; strict unity of design, a change of fortune, a discovery, punishment and reward distributed according to poetical or rather moral justice. The clearing up the character of Jones to Alworthy, the discovery of his relationship to him, and his union with Sophia, are all brought about at the end of the piece, and all obscurities satisfactorily cleared up; so that the reader can never doubt, as in some novels he may, whether the work should have ended a volume before, or have been carried on a volume after, the author's conclusion. The peculiar beauty of the plot consists in this; that though the author's secret is impenetrable, the discovery is artfully prepared by a number of circumstances, not attended to at the time, and by obscure hints thrown out, which, when the reader looks back upon them, are found to agree exactly with the concealed event. Of this nature is the cool unabashed behaviour of Jenny, the supposed delinquent, when she acknowledges herself the mother of the child; the flitting appearance from time to time of the attorney Dowling; and especially the behaviour of Mrs. Blifil to her son, which is

---

1   Epic.

wonderfully well managed in this respect.[1] She appears at first to notice him only in compliance, and an ungracious compliance too, with her brother's request; yet many touches of the mother are recollected when the secret is known; and the more open affection she shows him afterwards, when a youth of eighteen, has a turn given it which effectually misleads the reader. If he is very sagacious, he may perhaps suspect some mystery from the frequent appearance of Dowling; but he has no clue to find out what the mystery is, nor can he anticipate the very moment of discovery.[2]

But intricacy of plot, admirable as this is, is still of secondary merit compared with the exhibition of character, of which there is in this work a rich variety. Of the humorous ones Squire Western and his sister are the most prominent. They are admirably contrasted. He, rough, blunt, and boorish; a country squire of the last century; fond of his dogs and horses; a bitter Jacobite, as almost all the country squires at that time were; and from both causes averse to lords, and London, and every circumstance belonging to a court.[3] She a staunch whig, a politician in petticoats, valuing herself upon court breeding, finesse, and management, and not disposed, as Young says in one of his satires, "to take her tea without a stratagem."[4] Their opposite though both wrong modes of managing Sophia, their mutual quarrels, and the cordial contempt shown for female pretensions on the one side, and country ignorance on the other, are highly amusing. The character of Western is particularly well drawn: he is quite a worldly man, and strongly attached to money, notwithstanding an appearance of jollity and heartiness, which might seem to indicate a propensity to the social feelings. His extreme fondness for Jones, and his total blindness to the passion between him and his daughter, though he had

---

1    Bridget Allworthy, later Blifil, is the mother of Tom Jones, but to avoid the shame of unwed motherhood, she persuades Jenny Jones to claim maternity and suffer the punishment meted out by Squire Allworthy, Bridget's brother and Tom's adoptive father.

2    Lawyer Dowling is privy to Bridget's secret.

3    A Jacobite was one who supported the restoration of the Stuart line, deposed in 1688, to the throne of England.

4    Young, *Love of Fame, The Universal Passion* (1728): *Satire VI*, "On Women," l. 188.

thrown them continually in each other's way, are very natural, and what we see every day exemplified in real life, as well as the astonishment he expresses that a young lady of fortune should think of falling in love with a young fellow without any. Many parents seem by their conduct to think this as impossible as if the two parties were beings of a different species, and they deservedly suffer the consequences of their incautious folly. His fondness for Sophia too, like that of many parents, is very consistent with the most tyrannical behaviour to her in points essential to her happiness. His leaving the pursuit of his daughter when he hears the cry of the hounds, in order to join a fox-chase, is very characteristic and diverting.

It must be admitted that the language and manners of Western have a coarseness which in the present day may be thought exaggerated; and it is to be hoped it would be difficult now to find a breed of country squires quite so unpolished. Perhaps the improvement may be partly owing to their not being so independent as formerly. When they lived insulated, each in his own little domain, and their estates sufficed them to reside among their tenants and dependants in rustic consequence, they supplied such characters as a Western, a Sir Francis Wronghead, the Jacobite esquire in *The Freeholder*; and, of the more amiable sort, a Sir Roger de Coverley; for the drama and the novel;[1] which are now nearly extinct, from the necessity the increasing demands of luxury have occasioned of seeking an increase of fortune in the busy and active scenes of life. Estates are purchased by moneyed men; they bring down the habits of mercantile life from the brewery or the warehouse; a library and a drawing-room take the place of the hall hung with stags' horns and brushes[2] of foxes; the hounds are sold; the mansion is deserted during half the year for London or a watering-place.[3] It is probable there are more of his majesty's subjects at this moment hunting the tiger or the wild boar in India, than there are hunting foxes at home.

---

1   *The Freeholder* was a political newspaper written by Joseph Addison (1715-16); Sir Roger de Coverley is the country squire from Addison's *The Spectator* (1711-12).

2   Tails.

3   Health resorts, such as Bath.

Partridge is the Sancho Pancha[1] of the piece; like him, he deals in proverbs and scraps of wisdom; like him, he is cowardly, and puts his master in mind of bodily necessities. The author has taken occasion through this character to pay a delicate compliment to the acting of Garrick in the part of Hamlet.[2] Jones himself, the hero of the piece, for whom, notwithstanding his faults, the reader cannot help being interested, is contrasted with Blifil, the legitimate son of his mother. The two youths are brought up together under the same roof and the same discipline. Jones is a youth of true feeling, honour, and generosity; open and affectionate in his disposition, but very accessible to the temptations of pleasure. Blifil, with great apparent sobriety and decorum of manners, is a mean selfish hypocrite, possessing a mind of thorough baseness and depravity. In characters so contrasted, it is not doubtful to which of them the reader will, or ought to give the preference. To the faults of Blifil the reader has no inclination to be partial. They revolt the mind, particularly the minds of youth. The case is not the same with those more pardonable deviations from morals which are incident to youths of a warm temperament and an impressible heart: these are contagious in their very nature, and therefore the objections which have been made to the moral tendency of this novel are no doubt in some measure just. It is said to have been forbidden in France on its first publication. The faults of Jones are less than those of almost every other person who is brought upon the stage; yet they are of more dangerous example, because they are mixed with so many qualities which excite our affections.[3] Still, his character is of a totally different stamp

---

1 Don Quixote's companion.
2 In Book XVI, chapter v, Tom Jones, his landlady Mrs. Miller and the guileless Partridge see a production of *Hamlet*. Garrick's natural, believable style is deemed "the best" by Mrs. Miller who quotes the opinion of the town; Partridge disagrees because the actor did not seem to be acting at all!
3 A frequent objection to *Tom Jones*, raised obliquely (without naming the book) by Samuel Johnson in *Rambler* 4 (1750). Barbauld seems to respond to the version in Clara Reeve's *Progress of Romance* (1785): "Young men of warm passions and not strict principles, are always desirous to shelter themselves under the sanction of mixed characters, wherein virtue is allowed to be predominant.—In this light the character of *Tom Jones* is capable of doing much mischief; and for this reason a translation of this book was prohibited in France" (1:139).

from the heroes of Smollet's novels. He has an excellent heart and a refined sensibility, though he has also passions of a lower order. In every instance where he transgresses the rules of virtue, he is the seduced, and not the seducer; his youth, his constitution, his unprotected situation after he left Alworthy's, palliate his faults, and in honourable love he is tender and constant. His refusal of the young widow who makes him an offer of her hand does him honour. In one instance only is he *degraded*,—his affair with Lady Bellaston.

The character of Sophia was probably formed according to the author's ideas of female perfection: she is very beautiful, very sweet-tempered, very fond and constant to her lover; but her behaviour will scarcely satisfy one who has conceived high ideas of the delicacy of the female character. A young woman just come from reading *Clarissa* must be strangely shocked at seeing the heroine of the tale riding about the country on post-horses after her lover; and the incidents at Upton are highly indelicate.[1] It is observable that Fielding uniformly keeps down the characters of his women, as much as Richardson elevates his. A yielding easiness of disposition is what he seems to lay the greatest stress upon. Alworthy is made to tell Sophia, that what had chiefly charmed him in her behaviour was the great deference he had observed in her for the opinions of men. Yet Sophia, methinks, had not been extraordinarily well situated for imbibing such reverence. Any portion of learning in women is constantly united in this author with something disagreeable. It is given to Jenny, the supposed mother of Jones. It is given in a higher degree to that very disgusting character Mrs. Bennet in *Amelia*; Mrs. Western, too, is a woman of reading. A man of licentious manners, and such was Fielding, seldom respects the sex. Of the other characters, Lady Bellaston displays the ease, good-breeding, and impudence of a town-bred lady of fashion, who has laid aside her virtue. The scene where Jones meets Sophia at her house unexpectedly, the confusion of the lovers, and the civil, sly teasings of Lady Bellaston, are very diverting. Mrs. Miller is a specimen of a

---

1 Richardson was one of the first to make this point in the letter cited in the head-note.

natural character given without any exaggeration. She is warm-hearted, overflowing with gratitude, sanguine, and very loquacious. The behaviour of Jones in the affair between Nightingale and her daughter does him honour, and he manages the uncle and the father with much finesse. All the characters concerned are well drawn. The family of Black George exhibits natural but coarse painting; they would not be undeserving of a place in Mr. Crabb's parish register.[1] The character of Alworthy is not a shining one; he is imposed upon by every body: this may be consistent with goodness, but it is not consistent with that dignity in which an eminently virtuous character, meant to be exhibited as a pattern of excellence, ought to appear. But Fielding could not draw such a character. Traits of humanity and kindness he is able to give in all their beauty; but a religious and strictly moral character was probably connected in his mind with a want of sagacity, which those who have been conversant with the vicious part of the world are very apt to imagine must be the consequence of keeping aloof from it. Besides, it was necessary for the plot that Alworthy should be imposed upon. The character of Alworthy, it is said, was meant for Mr. Allen of Prior-park, a friend and patron of the author's, characterized by Pope in these well known lines,

> Let humble Allen, with an awkward shame,
> Do good by stealth, and blush to find it fame.[2]

The discovery of Jones's birth, and his restoration to the favour of Alworthy, wind up the whole, and give an animation to the concluding part, which is apt to become flat in the works of common authors. It is some drawback, however, upon the satisfaction of the reader, that poetic justice cannot be done without giving the good Alworthy the pain of being acquainted with the shame of his sister. It is not natural, when he does know it, that he should needlessly publish a circumstance of that kind, or consider Jones as having the same claims upon

---

1  A reference to George Crabbe's *The Parish Register* (1807), a realistic poem about village life and people.
2  "Epilogue to the Satires: Dialogue I," 135-36.

him as a legitimate child of his sister's; yet this is what he is made to do.

Upon the whole, *Tom Jones* is certainly for humour, wit, character, and plot, one of the most entertaining and perfect novels we possess. With regard to its moral tendency we must content ourselves with more qualified praise. A young man may imbibe from it sentiments of humanity, generosity, and all the more amiable virtues; a detestation of meanness, hypocrisy, and treachery: but he is not likely to gain from it firmness to resist temptation, or to have his ideas of moral purity heightened or refined by the perusal. More men would be apt to imitate Jones than would copy Lovelace; and it is to be feared there are few women who would not like him better than Sir Charles Grandison.[1] The greater refinement also and delicacy of the present age, a sure test of national civilization, though a very equivocal one of national virtue, has almost proscribed much of that broad humour which appears in the works of Fielding's times, and we should scarcely bear, in a new novel, the indelicate pictures which are occasionally presented to the imagination. The scenes at inns also are coarse, and too often repeated. The introductory chapters ought not to be passed over; they have much wit and grave Cervantic[2] humour, and occasionally display the author's familiarity with the classics.

### Johnson

[Samuel Johnson (1709-84) was the dominant literary figure of the latter half of the eighteenth century. Poet, essayist, lexicographer, critic, editor and novelist, Johnson embodied the profession of literature and letters. Generations of academics and public intellectuals have adopted his methods, improved on his conclusions, imitated his style, striven for his cultural clout, but few have so embodied the fullness of the literary life as the man who first defined it. Johnson's contemporaries recognized his intellectual prowess and responded to his humane authority—and his human quirkiness—as did Anna Barbauld, in several

---

1  The hero of Samuel Richardson's third novel, a paragon of male virtue.
2  In the manner of Cervantes, author of *Don Quixote*.

significant ways. The shape of her career owes much to Johnson's example. Poet, essayist, critic and editor, she, like Johnson, played a significant role in establishing a canon, defining and defying literary convention, addressing the political and social issues of the day. Barbauld won Johnson's praise for her style and intellect; she provoked his disdain by devoting her energies to the education of children. Her view of him is similarly balanced between admiration and reservation. Acknowledging his unparalleled public achievement, she faults his personal weaknesses, particularly his religious doubts.

Author of the *Dictionary of the English Language* (1755), the *Rambler* (1750-52), the *Lives of the Poets* (1779-81), the poems "London" (1738) and "The Vanity of Human Wishes" (1749), and many other works, Johnson also wrote a significant work of prose fiction, *Rasselas* (1759), which Barbauld included in *The British Novelists*].

Hercules, it is said, once wielded the distaff; and the Hercules of literature, Dr. Johnson, has not disdained to be the author of a novel.[1] To say the truth, nothing which he has written has more the touch of genius than *Rasselas, Prince of Abyssinia*: nor do any of his performances bear stronger marks of his peculiar character. It is solemn, melancholy and philosophical. The frame of the story is an elegant and happy exertion of fancy. It was probably suggested to his mind from recollections of the impression made upon his fancy by a book which he translated when he first entered on his literary career, namely, *Father Lobo's Account of a Voyage to Abyssinia*.[2]

In that country, it is said, the younger branches of the royal family, instead of being sacrificed, as in some of the Eastern monarchies, to the jealousy of the reigning sovereign, are secluded from the world in a romantic and beautiful valley, where they are liberally provided with every thing that can gratify their tastes or amuse their solitude. This recess, which Dr. Johnson calls *the happy valley*, he has described with much

---

1  One of the labors of Hercules involved his spinning (wielding the distaff—an instrument used for holding the flax as it is spun).
2  Johnson published this translation in 1735.

richness of imagination. It is represented as being shut in by inaccessible mountains, and only to be entered through a cavern closed up with massy gates of iron, which were thrown open only once a year, on the annual visit of the emperor. At that time artists and teachers of every kind, capable of contributing to the amusement or solace of the princes, were admitted; but once admitted, they were immured for life with the royal captives. Every charm of nature and every decoration of art is supposed to be collected in this charming spot, and that its inhabitants had been, in general, content with the round of amusements provided for them, till at length Rasselas, a young prince of a sprightly and active genius, grows weary of an existence so monotonous, and is seized with a strong desire of seeing the world at large. In pursuance of this project, he contrives to dig a passage through the mountain, and to escape from this paradise with his favourite sister Nekayah and her attendant, and the philosopher who had assisted them in their enterprise, and who, being previously acquainted with the world, is to assist their inexperience. They are all equally disgusted with the languor of sated desires and the inactivity of unvaried quiet, and agree to range the world in order to make their *choice of life*.

The author, having thus stretched his canvass, proceeds to exhibit and to criticize the various situations and modes of human existence; public life and private; marriage and celibacy; commerce, rustic employments, religious retirement, &c., and finds that in all there is something good and something bad— that marriage has many pains, but celibacy has no pleasures; that the hermit cannot secure himself from vice, but by retiring from the exercise of virtue; that shepherds are boors, and philosophers—only men.[1] Unable to decide amidst such various appearances of good and evil, and having seen enough of the world to be disgusted with it, they end their search by resolving to return with the first opportunity in order to end their days in the happy valley; and this, to use the author's

---

1  In chapters 26, 21, 19, and 22, respectively. "Marriage has many pains, but celibacy has no pleasures," and "secure himself from vice, but by retiring from the exercise of virtue" are direct quotations from *Rasselas*.

words in the title of his last chapter, is "the conclusion, in which nothing is concluded."

Such is the philosophic view which Dr. Johnson and many others have taken of life; and such indecision would probably be the consequence of thus narrowly sifting the advantages and disadvantages of every station in this mixt state, if done without that feeling reference to each man's particular position, and particular inclinations, which is necessary to incline the balance. If we choose to imagine an insulated being, detached from all connexions and all duties, it may be difficult for mere reason to direct his choice; but no man is so insulated: we are woven into the web of society, and to each individual it is seldom dubious what *he* shall do. Very different is the search after abstract good, and the pursuit of what a being born and nurtured amidst innumerable ties of kindred and companionship, feeling his own wants, impelled by his own passions, and influenced by his own peculiar associations, finds best for *him*. Except he is indolent or fastidious, he will seldom hesitate upon his choice of life. The same position holds good with regard to duty. We may bewilder ourselves in abstract questions of general good, or puzzle our moral sense with imaginary cases of conscience; but it is generally obvious enough to every man what duty dictates to him, in each particular case, as it comes before him.

The proper moral to be drawn from *Rasselas* is, therefore, not that goods and evils are so balanced against each other that no unmixed happiness is to be found in life,—a deduction equally trite and obvious; nor yet that a reasoning man can make no choice,—but rather that a *merely* reasoning man will be likely to make no choice,—and therefore that it becomes every man to make early that choice to which his particular position, his honest partialities, his individual propensities, his early associations impel him. Often does it happen that, while the over-refined and speculative are hesitating and doubting, the plain honest youth has secured happiness. Without this conclusion, the moral effect of the piece, loaded as it is with the miseries of life, and pointing out no path of action as more eligible than another, would resemble that of *Candide*,[1] where the party, after all their adventures, agree to plant cabbages in their own garden: but the gloomy ideas of the English philosopher are softened and guarded by sound principles of religion.

Along with Voltaire, he strongly paints and perhaps exaggerates the miseries of life; but instead of evading their force by laughing at them, or drawing from them a satire against Providence, which *Candide* may be truly said to be, our author turns the mind to the solid consolations of a future state: "All," says he, "that virtue can afford is quietness of conscience, and a steady prospect of a future state: this may enable us to endure calamity with patience, but remember that patience must suppose pain."

Such is the plan of this philosophical romance, in the progress of which the author makes many just strictures on human life, and many acute remarks on the springs of human passions; but they are the passions of the species, not of the individual. It is life, as viewed at a distance by a speculative man, in a kind of bird's-eye view; not painted with the glow and colouring of an actor in the busy scene: we are not led to say, "This man is painted naturally," but, "Such is the nature of man." The most striking of his pictures is that of the philosopher, who imagined himself to have the command of the weather, and who had fallen into that species of insanity by indulging in the luxury of solitary musing, or what is familiarly called castle-building. His state is strikingly and feelingly described, and no doubt with the peculiar interest arising from what the author had felt and feared in his own mind; for it is well known that at times he suffered under a morbid melancholy near akin to derangement, which occasionally clouded his mighty powers; and no doubt he had often indulged in these unprofitable abstractions of thought, these seducing excursions of fancy.

The following remark ought to startle those who have permitted their mind to feed itself in solitude with its own

---

1 Voltaire's tale, also about the search for happiness ("the best of all possible worlds"), was published in the same year as *Rasselas*.

creations and wishes. "All power of fancy over reason is a degree of insanity; but while this power is such as we can control or repress, it is not visible to others, nor considered as any depravation of the mental faculties. In time, some particular train of ideas fixes the attention, all other intellectual gratifications are rejected. By degrees the reign of fancy is confirmed; she grows first imperious, and in time despotic; then fictions begin to operate as realities, false opinions fasten upon the mind, and life passes away in dreams of rapture or of anguish."[1]

*Rasselas* is, perhaps, of all its author's works, that in which his peculiar style best harmonizes with the subject. That pompous flow of diction, that measured harmony of periods, that cadenced prose which Dr. Johnson introduced, though it would appear stiff and cumbrous in the frame of a common novel, is sanctioned by the imitation, or what our authors have agreed to call imitation, of the Eastern style, a style which has been commonly adopted in *Almoran and Hamet, Tales of the Genii*,[2] and other works, in which the costume is taken from nations whose remoteness destroys the idea of colloquial familiarity. We silence our reason by the laws we have imposed upon our fancy, and are content that both Nekayah and her female attendant, at the sources of the Nile, or the foot of the Pyramid, should express themselves in language which would appear unnaturally inflated in the mouths of a young lady and her waiting-maid conversing together in London or in Paris. It has been remarked, however, that Nekayah, it is difficult to say why, is more philosophical than her brother.

It has been already mentioned that the frame of this piece was probably suggested by the author's having some years before translated an account of Abyssinia. It may be remarked by the way, how different an idea of the country and its inhabitants seems to have been entertained at that time from that which is suggested by the accounts of Bruce and Lord Valentia.[3]

---

1  Quoted loosely from *Rasselas*, Ch. 44.
2  *Almoran and Hamet* (1761) by John Hawkesworth. James Ridley's *Tales of the Genii* (1764) was another popular oriental fiction.
3  James Bruce's *Interesting Narrative of the Travels of James Bruce, Esq. into Abyssinia, to Discover the Source of the Nile* (1790) and George Annesley [later Lord Valentia], *Voyages and Travels to India, Ceylon, the Red Sea, Abyssinia, and Egypt* (1809).

Thomson, who probably took his ideas from the voyage-writers of the time, represents the country of "jealous Abyssinia" as a perfect paradise, "a world within itself; disdaining all assault;" and mentions the "palaces, and fanes, and villas, and gardens, and cultured fields" of this innocent and amiable people with poetic rapture.[1] We must suppose that Father Lobo never had the honour of dancing with them on a gala-day.

*Rasselas* was published in 1759, and was then composed for the purpose of enabling the author to visit his mother in her last illness, and for defraying the expenses of her funeral. It was written with great rapidity; for the author himself has told us that it was composed in the evenings of one week, sent to the press in portions as it was written, and never reperused when finished. It was much read, and has been translated into several languages. Rich indeed must be the stores of that mind which could pour out its treasures with such rapidity, and clothe its thoughts, almost spontaneously, in language so correct and ornamented.

Perhaps the genius of Dr. Johnson has been in some measure mistaken. The ponderosity of his manner has led the world to give him more credit for science, and less for fancy, than the character of his works will justify. His remarks on life and manners are just and weighty, and show a philosophical mind, but not an original turn of thinking. The novelty is in the style; but originality of style belongs to that dress and colouring of our thoughts in which imagination is chiefly concerned.

In fact, imagination had great influence over him. His ideas of religion were awful and grand, and he had those feelings of devotion which seldom subsist in a strong degree in a cold and phlegmatic mind; but his religion was tinctured with superstition, his philosophy was clouded with partialities and prejudices, his mind was inclined to melancholy.

In the work before us he has given testimony to his belief in apparitions, and has shown a leaning towards monastic institutions. Of his discoveries in any region of science posterity will be able to speak but little; but in his *Ramblers* he will be consid-

---

1  James Thomson, *The Seasons: Summer*, ll. 752, 772–73, 769–70.

ered as having formed a new style, and his *Rasselas*, and *Vision of Theodore*,[1] must give him an honourable place among those writers who deck philosophy with the ornamented diction and the flowers of fancy.

It should not be forgotten to be noticed in praise of *Rasselas*, that it is, as well as all the other works of its author, perfectly pure. In describing the happy valley, he has not, as many authors would have done, painted a luxurious bower of bliss, nor once throughout the work awakened any ideas which might be at variance with the moral truths which all his writings are meant to inculcate.

### Mrs. Inchbald

[Elizabeth Inchbald (1753-1821) was a playwright and critic as well as a novelist. In fact, her output as a writer for the stage far exceeded her published work as a novelist, which consisted of *A Simple Story* (1791) and *Nature and Art* (1796). Still, in these two novels, Inchbald advanced the genre in significant ways. *A Simple Story* features an original plot structure spanning two generations and focusing on contrastive female protagonists. The novel relies on parallel incidents and thematic resonance rather than plot to establish narrative coherence, and the effect is one of deliberate moral complexity rather than the didactic clarity often claimed (however problematically) by eighteenth-century fiction. *Nature and Art* is similarly complex, refusing to shy away from the moral difficulties posed by such issues as prostitution and poverty. Barbauld's admiration for the works of Inchbald was perhaps abetted by the fact that the two were acquaintances, but the fact remains that slender though her output was Elizabeth Inchbald was a novelist of substance and vision whose works deserve the serious attention they are beginning to receive.]

---

1  Fable written by Johnson in 1748, published by Robert Dodsley in a miscellany for which Johnson also wrote the preface. Johnson himself considered "The Vision of Theodore" his best work (Wain, *Samuel Johnson*, p. 149).

To readers of taste it would be superfluous to point out the beauties of Mrs Inchbald's novels. The *Simple Story* has obtained the decided approbation of the best judges. There is an originality both in the characters and the situations which is not often found in similar productions. To call it a *simple story* is perhaps a misnomer, since the first and second parts are in fact two distinct stories, connected indeed by the character of Dorriforth, which they successively serve to illustrate.

Dorriforth is introduced as a Romish priest of a lofty mind, generous, and endued with strong sensibilities, but having in his disposition much of sternness and inflexibility. His being in priest's orders presents an apparently insurmountable obstacle to his marriage; but it is got over, without violating probability, by his becoming heir to a title and estate, and on that account receiving a dispensation from his vows. Though slow to entertain thoughts of love, as soon as he perceives the partiality of his ward, it enters his breast like a torrent when the flood-gates are opened. The perplexities in which he is involved by Miss Milner's gay unthinking conduct bring them to the very brink of separating for ever; and very few scenes in any novel have a finer effect than the intended parting of the lovers, and their sudden, immediate, unexpected marriage.

It is impossible not to sympathize with the feelings of Miss Milner, when she sees the corded trunks standing in the passage; or again, when after their reconciliation she sees the carriage, which was to take away her lover, drive empty from the door. The character of the ward of Dorriforth is so drawn as to excite an interest such as we seldom feel for more faultless characters. Young, sprightly, full of sensibility, gay and thoughtless, we feel such a tenderness for her as we should for a child who is playing on the brink of a precipice. The break between the first and second parts of the story has a singularly fine effect. We pass over in a moment a large space of years, and find every thing changed: scenes of love and conjugal happiness are vanished; and for the young, gay, thoughtless, youthful beauty, we see a broken-hearted penitent on her death-bed.

This sudden shifting of the scene has an effect which no continued narrative could produce; an effect which even the scenes of real life could not produce; for the curtain of futurity is lifted up only by degrees, and we must wait the slow succession of months and years to bring about events which are here presented close together. The death-bed letter of Lady Milner is very solemn, and cannot be perused without tears.

Dorriforth in these latter volumes is become, from the contemplation of his injuries, morose, unrelenting, and tyrannical. How far it was possible for a man to resist the strong impulse of nature, and deny himself the sight of his child residing in the same house with him, the reader will determine; but the situation is new and striking.

It is a particular beauty in Mrs. Inchbald's compositions, that they are thrown so much into the dramatic form. There is little of mere narrative, and in what there is of it, the style is careless; but all the interesting parts are carried on in dialogue:—we see and hear the persons themselves; we are but little led to think of the author, and it is only when we have done feeling that we begin to admire.

The only other novel which Mrs. Inchbald has given to the public is *Nature and Art*. It is of a slighter texture than the former, and put together without much attention to probability; the author's object being less to give a regular story, than to suggest reflections on the political and moral state of society. For this purpose two youths are introduced, one of whom is educated in all the ideas and usages of civilized life; the other (the child of Nature) without any knowledge of or regard to them. This is the frame which has been used by Mr. Day[1] and others for the same purpose, and naturally tends to introduce remarks more lively than solid, and strictures more epigrammatic than logical, on the differences between rich and poor, the regard paid to rank, and such topics, on which it is easy to dilate with an appearance of reason and humanity; while it requires a much profounder philosophy to suggest any alteration in the social system, which would not be rather Utopian than beneficial.

There is a beautiful stroke in this part of the work, where

---

1  Thomas Day (1748–89), author of *The History of Sandford and Merton* (1783–89).

Henry, who, according to Rousseau's plan, had not been taught to pray till he was of an age to know what he was doing,[1] kneels down for the first time with great emotion; and on being asked if he was not afraid to speak to God, says, "To be sure I trembled very much when I first knelt, but when I came to the words 'Our Father who art in heaven,' they gave me courage, for I know how kind a father is."

But by far the finest passage in this novel is the meeting between Hannah and her seducer, when he is seated as judge upon the bench, and, without recollecting the former object of his affection, pronounces sentence of death upon her. The shriek she gives, and her exclamation, "Oh, not from you!" electrifies the reader, and cannot but stir the coldest feelings.

Judgement and observation may sketch characters, and often put together a good story; but strokes of pathos, such as the one just mentioned, or the dying-scene in Mrs. Opie's *Father and Daughter*,[2] can only be attained by those whom nature has endowed with her choicest gifts.

One cannot help wishing the author had been a little more liberal of happiness to poor Henry, who sits down contented with poverty and his half-withered Rebecca.

There is another wish the public has often formed, namely, that these two productions were not the *only* novels of such a writer as Mrs. Inchbald.[3]

---

1 In Book 2 of his *Émile, or On Education* (1762), Rousseau criticizes the typical early religious training of children: "They are taken to church to be bored. Constantly made to mumble prayers, they are driven to aspire to the happiness of no longer praying to God" (*Émile*, p. 103).

2 Amelia Opie (1769-1853) was the author of several novels, including *Father and Daughter* (1801).

3 A contemporary reader, Sir James Mackintosh, remarked of this preface, "Female genius always revives Mrs. Barbauld's generous mind. Her remarks on Mrs. Inchbald are excellent" (*Life of Mackintosh*, 2:105).

[Charlotte Smith (1749-1807) was one of the most prolific novelists of the eighteenth century, writing a total of nine works that, strictly speaking, can be classified as novels, in addition to other narratives, natural history books for children, translations and one play. Her fame (which was instant and lasting) came as the author of poetry, specifically the sorrowful sonnets that she published under the title *Elegiac Sonnets* in 1784. This collection of poems (ever expanding in Smith's lifetime) was popular well into the nineteenth century; the eleventh edition was published in 1851. Smith's domestic troubles included an irresponsible and abusive husband from whom she separated in 1786 and a protracted legal battle for her children's inheritance that was not finally resolved until after her death. These difficulties fueled her writing career and provided much of the material (filtered through her imagination) for the plots of her novels and the emotion of her poems. Best known in our time for her contribution to the gothic (*Emmeline* and *The Old Manor House*, in particular), Smith was also avidly political, reflecting in other works (*Desmond, The Banished Man, The Young Philosopher*, for example) an abiding commitment to the aims and ideals of the French Revolution.]

Among those writers who have distinguished themselves in the polite literature of the present day, the late Mrs. CHARLOTTE SMITH well deserves a place, both from the number and elegance of her publications. She was the eldest daughter of Nicholas Turner, esq. a gentleman of fortune, who possessed estates in Surrey and Sussex; a man, it is said, of an improved mind and brilliant conversation. She lost her mother when very young, and was brought up under the care of an aunt, whose ideas of female education were less favourable to mental accomplishments than those of her father. She received, therefore, rather a fashionable than a literary education, and she was left to gratify her taste for books by desultory reading, and almost by stealth. Her genius, indeed, early showed itself in a propensity to poetry; but she was introduced while very young

to the gaieties and dissipation of London, and, becoming a wife
before she was sixteen, was plunged into the cares of a married
life before her fine genius had received all the advantages it
might have gained by a culture more regular and persevering.

Her husband, Mr. Smith, was the younger son of a rich
West-Indian merchant, and associated with him in the business.
The marriage had been brought about by parents, and did not
prove a happy one; it had probably been hastened on her side
by the dread of a mother-in-law,[1] as her father was on the point
of marrying a second wife. The married pair lived at first in
London, in the busy part of the town, but soon after took a
house at Southgate. The husband had little application to busi-
ness; and probably, of the young couple, neither party had
much notion of economy. The management of the concern
was soon resigned to the father of Mr. Smith, who purchased
for them an estate in Hampshire called Lys Farm. Here Mrs.
Smith found her tastes for rural scenery and for elegant society
gratified; but building and expensive improvements, joined to
an increasing family, soon brought them into difficulties, which
were not lessened by the death of her husband's grandfather, to
whom Mr. Smith acted as executor, in the discharge of which
office a litigation arose with the other branches of the family,
which plunged them into lawsuits for life.[2] The vexation
attending these perplexities, together with the pecuniary
embarrassments she was continually involved in, clouded the
serenity of Mrs. Smith's mind, and gave to her writings that
bitter and querulous tone of complaint which is discernible in
so many of them.

Possessed of a fine imagination, an ear and a taste for harmo-
ny, an elegant and correct style, the natural bent of Mrs. Smith's
genius seems to have been more to poetry than to any other
walk of literature. Her *Sonnets*, which was the first publication

---

1  I.e., a step-mother.
2  The "life-long" lawsuit was in fact over Benjamin Smith's father's will. Richard
   Smith died in 1776, leaving a legacy complicated by codicils over which family
   members and attorneys argued until a few years before Charlotte Smith's death.
   Indeed, though an initial settlement was reached in 1798, the will was not finally
   resolved until 1813.

she gave to the world, were universally admired. That species of verse, which in this country may be reckoned rather an exotic, had at that time been but little cultivated. For plaintive, tender, and polished sentiment the Sonnet forms a proper vehicle, and Mrs. Smith's success fixed at once her reputation as a poet of no mean class. They were published while her husband was in the King's Bench,[1] where she attended him with laudable assiduity, and exerted herself to further his liberation; her feelings upon which event she thus describes in a letter to a friend: "For more than a month I had shared the restraint of my husband amidst scenes of misery, of vice, and even of terror. Two attempts had, since my last residence among them, been made by the prisoners to procure their liberation by blowing up the walls of the house. Throughout the night appointed for this enterprise I remained dressed, watching at the window. After such scenes and such apprehensions, how deliciously soothing to my wearied spirits was the soft, pure air of the summer's morning, breathing over the dewy grass, as, having slept one night upon the road, we passed over the heaths of Surrey!"[2]

Their difficulties, however, were far from being terminated; and the increasing derangement of Mr. Smith's affairs soon afterwards obliged them to leave England, and they were settled some time in a large gloomy chateau in Normandy, where Mrs. Smith gave birth to her youngest child. Here also she translated *Manon l'Escaut*, a novel of the Abbé Prevôt, a work of affecting pathos, though exceptionable with regard to its moral tendency.[3]

Returning to England, they occupied for some time an ancient mansion belonging to the Mills' family, at Woodlading, in Sussex, where Mrs. Smith wrote several of her poems.

An entire separation afterwards taking place between her and her husband, she removed with most of her children to a

---

1  London prison where Benjamin Smith was held for debt and embezzlement in 1783.

2  Barbauld quotes from a letter reprinted in the biographical essay on Smith included in *Public Characters of 1800-1801*.

3  Smith, however, withdrew this translation from further printings after its initial publication due to (unfounded) charges of plagiarism.

small cottage near Chichester, where she wrote her novel of ~~Emmeline in the course of a few months.~~ She afterwards resided in various places, mostly on the coast of Sussex; for she was particularly fond of the neighbourhood of the sea. The frequent changes of scene which, either from necessity or inclination, she experienced, were no doubt favourable to that descriptive talent which forms a striking feature of her genius. Her frequent removals may be traced in her poems and other works. The name of the Arun is consecrated in poetry, and is often mentioned by her:

> Farewell, Aruna! on whose varied shore
> My early vows were paid to Nature's shrine,
> And whose lorn stream has heard me since deplore
> Too many sorrows....[1]

In another sonnet she addresses the South Downs:

> Ah hills beloved, where once, a happy child,
> Your beechen shades, your turf, your flowers among,
> I wove your blue-bells into garlands wild,
> And woke your echoes with my artless song;
> Ah hills beloved! your turf, your flowers remain,
> But can they peace to this sad breast restore;
> For one poor moment soothe the sense of pain,
> And teach a breaking heart to throb no more?[2]

Poets are apt to complain, and often take a pleasure in it; yet they should remember that the pleasure of their readers is only derived from the elegance and harmony with which they do it. The reader is a selfish being, and seeks only his own gratification. But for the language of complaint in plain prose, or the exasperations of personal resentment, he has seldom much sympathy. It is certain, however, that the life of this lady was a very chequered one.

---

1 "On leaving a part of Sussex," ll. 1-2, 4-5.
2 "To the South Downs," ll. 1-8.

Mrs. Smith had a family of twelve children, six only of whom survived her. Her third son lost a limb in the service of his country, and afterwards fell a sacrifice to the yellow fever at Barbadoes, whither he had gone to look after the family property. The severest stroke she met with was the loss of a favourite daughter, who died at Bath, where Mrs. Smith also was for the recovery of her health. The young lady had been married to the Chevalier de Faville, a French emigrant. Her mother is said never entirely to have recovered from this affliction.

Her last removal was to Stoke, a village in Surrey, endeared to her by her having spent there many years of her childhood; and there she died Oct. 28th, 1806, in her 57th year, after a tedious and painful illness. She was a widow at the time of her death, and, being in possession of her own fortune, had a prospect of greater ease in her pecuniary circumstances than she had for some time enjoyed. Her youngest son, who was advancing in the military career, fell a victim to the pestiferous climate of Surinam before her death, but the news had not reached her.

Though she was worn by illness, the powers of her mind retained their full vigour, and her last volume of poems, entitled *Beachy Head*, was in the press at the time of her decease; an elegant work, which no ways discredits her former performances.

She was the author of several publications for children and young people, which are executed with great taste and elegance, and communicate, in a pleasing way, much knowledge of botany and natural history, of which two studies she was very fond. That entitled *Conversations* is interspersed with beautiful little descriptive poems on natural objects.[1]

Mrs. Smith is most known to readers in general by her novels; yet they seem to have been less the spontaneous offspring of her mind than her poems. She herself represents them as being written to supply money for those emergencies which, from the perplexed state of her affairs, she was often thrown into;

---

1   The full title is *Conversations Introducing Poetry* (1804).

but, though not of the first order, they hold a respectable rank among that class of publications. They are written in a style correct and elegant; they show a knowledge of life, and of genteel life; and there is much beauty in the descriptive scenery, which Mrs. Smith was one of the first to introduce. Descriptions, of whatever beauty, are but little attended to in a novel of high interest, particularly if introduced, as they often are, during a period of anxious suspense for the hero or heroine; but are very properly placed, at judicious intervals, in compositions of which variety rather than deep pathos, and elegance rather than strength, are the characteristics.

The two most finished novels of Mrs. Smith are *Emmeline* and *Celestina*. In the first she is supposed to have drawn her own character, (with what degree of impartiality others must judge,) in that of Mrs. Stafford.

*Celestina* is not inferior to *Emmeline* in the conduct of the piece, and possesses still more beauties of description. The romantic scenes in the south of France are rich and picturesque. The story of Jesse and her lover is interesting, as well as that of Jaquelina.

The *Old Manor-House* is said to be the most popular of the author's productions. The best drawn character in it is that of a wealthy old lady who keeps all her relations in constant dependence, and will not be persuaded to name her heir. This was written during the war with America; and the author takes occasion, as also in many other of her publications, to show the strain of her politics.

She also wrote *Desmond*, *The Wanderings of Warwick*, *Montalbert*, and many others, to the number of thirty-eight volumes. They all show a knowledge of life, and facility of execution, without having any very strong features, or particularly aiming to illustrate any moral truth. The situations and the scenery are often romantic; the characters and the conversations are from common life.

Her later publications would have been more pleasing, if the author, in the exertions of fancy, could have forgotten herself; but the asperity of invective and the querulousness of complaint too frequently cloud the happier exertions of her imagination.

Another publication of this lady's ought to have been mentioned, *The Romance of real Life*, a very entertaining work, consisting of a selection of remarkable trials from the *Causes Célèbres*.[1] The title, though a happy and a just one, had the inconvenience of misleading many readers, who really thought it a novel. Their mistake was pardonable; for few novels present incidents so wonderful as are to be found in these surprising stories, which rest upon the sanction of judicial records.

## Miss Burney

[Frances Burney (1752–1840) achieved fame at the age of 26 with the publication of her first novel, *Evelina* (1778). Although the work was published anonymously, with cloak-and-dagger secrecy, its success guaranteed the revelation of the author and her subsequent elevation into the literary beau monde. Burney's father, musicologist Charles Burney, saw to it that his talented daughter come to the attention of Hester Thrale, who entertained writers and other artists at her home in Streatham Place where reigning literary lion Samuel Johnson was a frequent houseguest. For several years, Frances Burney enjoyed the intimacy of this group, but with the publication of her second novel, *Cecilia* (1782), her father's aspirations for her rose even higher, and she found herself an appointee of the court— Second Keeper of the Robes to Queen Charlotte, an employment that Burney found stressful and distasteful. She resigned from this post, ill, and, in 1793, married French émigré General Alexandre d'Arblay. After her marriage she published two more novels—*Camilla* (1796) and *The Wanderer* (1814), the latter unmentioned by Barbauld as it appeared after the first edition of *The British Novelists*.]

---

1   This translation, published in 1787, is a collection of French legal case histories, written by Guyot de Pitaval. His accounts were full of legal jargon and tedious detail. Smith rewrote the stories in elegant prose with streamlined plot sequences. The collection includes the original rendition of the story of Martin Guerre.

Scarcely any name, if any, stands higher in the list of novel-writers than that of Miss BURNEY, now Mrs. D'ARBLAY, daughter of the ingenious Dr. Burney.[1] She has given to the world three productions of this kind; *Evelina*, in three vols., *Cecilia*, in five vols., and, after a long interval, in which, however honourable her employment might be deemed, she was completely lost to the literary world,[2] *Camilla*, also in five vols.This latter was published by subscription in 1796.

It is necessary to speak of living authors with that temperance of praise which may not offend their delicacy; and though this lady by marriage with a foreigner, and her residence abroad, is in a manner lost to this her native country, the writer of these remarks does not feel herself at liberty to search for anecdotes which might gratify curiosity, or endeavour to detail the events of a life which every admirer of genius will wish prolonged to many succeeding years.[3] One anecdote, however, may be mentioned, which is current, and she believes has never been contradicted. Miss Burney composed her *Evelina* when she was in the early bloom of youth, about seventeen. She wrote it without the knowledge of any of her friends.[4] With the modesty of a young woman, and the diffidence of a young author, she contrived to throw it into the press anonymously, and, when published, laid the volumes in the way of her friends, whose impartial plaudits soon encouraged her to confess to whom they were obliged for their entertainment. There is perhaps no purer or higher pleasure than the young mind enjoys in the first burst of praise and admiration which attends a successful performance. To be lifted up at once into the favourite of the public; to be sensible that the name, hitherto pronounced only in the circle of family connexions, is become familiar to all that read, through every province of a large kingdom; to feel in the glow of genius and freshness of invention powers to continue that admiration to future years;—to feel all this, and at the same time to be happily ignorant of all the chills

---

1   Charles Burney (1726-1814), author of *The History of Music* (1776-89).
2   A reference to Burney's position at court as Second Keeper of the Robes.
3   Burney and her husband lived in France from 1802 to 1812.
4   I.e., relations.

and mortifications, the impossibility not to flag in a long work, the ridicule and censure which fasten on vulnerable parts, and the apathy or diffidence which generally seizes an author before his literary race is run;—this is happiness for youth, and youth alone.

*Evelina* became at once a fashionable novel: there are even those who still prefer it to *Cecilia*, though that preference is probably owing to the partiality inspired by a first performance. Evelina is a young lady, amiable and inexperienced, who is continually getting into difficulties from not knowing or not observing the established etiquettes of society, and from being unluckily connected with a number of vulgar characters, by whom she is involved in a series of adventures both ludicrous and mortifying. Some of these are certainly carried to a very extravagant excess, particularly the tricks played upon the poor Frenchwoman;[1] but the fondness for humour, and low humour, which Miss Burney discovered in this piece, runs through all her subsequent works, and strongly characterizes, sometimes perhaps blemishes, her genius. Lord Orville is a generous and pleasing lover; and the conclusion is so wrought, as to leave upon the mind that glow of happiness which is not found in her subsequent works. The meeting between Evelina and her father is pathetic. The agonizing remorse and perturbation of the man who is about to see, for the first time, his child whom he had deserted, and whose mother had fallen a sacrifice to his unkindness; the struggles between the affection which impels him towards her, and the dread he feels of seeing in her the image of his injured wife; are described with many touches of nature and strong effect.—Other characters in the piece are, Mrs. Selwyn, a wit and an oddity; a gay insolent baronet; a group of vulgar cits;[2] a number of young bucks, whose coldness, carelessness, rudeness, and impertinent gallantry, serve as a foil to the delicate attentions of Lord Orville.

Upon the whole, *Evelina* greatly pleased; and the interest the

---

1 Evelina's French grandmother, Madame Duval, is the butt of several practical jokes executed by Captain Mirvan and Sir Clement Willoughby. See volume 2, letter 2, especially.

2 Residents of the City of London; hence, lower middle-class.

public took in the young writer was rewarded with fresh plea-
sure by the publication of *Cecilia*, than which it would be diffi-
cult to find a novel with more various and striking beauties.
Among these may be reckoned the style, which is so varied,
according to the characters introduced, that, without any infor-
mation from the names, the reader would readily distinguish
the witty loquacity of Lady Honoria Pemberton, the unmean-
ing volubility of Miss Larolles, the jargon of the captain, the
affected indifference of Meadows, the stiff pomposity of
Delville senior, the flighty heroics of Albany, the innocent sim-
plicity of Miss Belfield, the coarse vulgarity of her mother, the
familiar address and low comic of Briggs, and the cool finesse
of the artful attorney, with many others,—all expressed in lan-
guage appropriate to the character, and all pointedly distin-
guished from the elegant and dignified style of the author her-
self. The character of the miser Briggs is pushed, perhaps, to a
degree of extravagance, though certainly not more so than
Moliere's Harpagon;[1] but it is highly comic, and it is not the
common idea of a miser half-starved, sullen and morose; an
originality is given to it by making him jocose, good-
humoured, and not averse to enjoyment when he can have it
for nothing. All the characters are well discriminated, from the
skipping Morrice, to the artful Monckton, and the high-toned
feeling of Mrs. Delville. The least natural character is Albany.
An idea prevailed at the time, but probably without the least
foundation, that Dr. Johnson had supplied the part.

Cecilia herself is an amiable and dignified character. She is
brought into situations distressful and humiliating, by the pecu-
liarity of her circumstances, and a flexibility and easiness readily
pardoned in a young female. The restriction she is laid under
of not marrying any one who will not submit to assume her
name is a new circumstance, and forms, very happily, the plot
of the piece. Love appears with dignity in Cecilia; with fervour,
but strongly combated by pride as well as duty, in young
Delville; with all the helplessness of unrestrained affection in
Miss Belfield, whose character of simplicity and tenderness

---

1    In his *Miser* (1668).

much resembles that of Emily in *Sir Charles Grandison*. If resemblances are sought for, it may also be observed that the situation of Cecilia with Mrs. Delville is similar to that of Marivaux's Marianne with the mother of Valville.[1]

Miss Burney possesses equal powers of pathos and of humour. The terrifying voice of the unknown person who forbids the banns[2] has an electrifying effect upon the reader; and the distress of Cecilia seeking her husband about the streets, in agony for his life, till her reason suddenly fails, is almost too much to bear. Indeed we lay down the volumes with rather a melancholy impression upon our minds; there has been so much of distress that the heart feels exhausted, and there are so many deductions from the happiness of the lovers, that the reader is scarcely able to say whether the story ends happily or unhappily. It is true that in human life things are generally so balanced; but in fictitious writings it is more agreeable, if they are not meant to end tragically, to leave on the mind the rainbow colours of delight in their full glow and beauty.

But the finest part of these volumes is the very moral and instructive story of the *Harrels*. It is the high praise of Miss Burney, that she has not contented herself with fostering the delicacies of sentiment, and painting in vivid colours those passions which nature has made sufficiently strong. She has shown the value of economy, the hard-heartedness of gaiety, the mean rapacity of the fashionable spendthrift. She has exhibited a couple, not naturally bad, with no other inlet to vice, that appears on the face of the story, than the inordinate desire of show and splendour, withholding his hard-earned pittance from the poor labourer, and lavishing it on every expensive trifle. She has shown the wife trifling and helpless, vain, incapable of serious thought or strong feeling; and has beautifully delineated the gradual extinction of an early friendship between two young women whom youth and cheerfulness alone had assimilated, as the two characters diverged in afterlife,—a circumstance that

---

1  Characters in Pierre Carlet de Chamblain de Marivaux's *Vie de Marianne* (1731-42).
2  At Cecilia's and young Delvile's attempt to marry clandestinely, a stranger declares them ineligible to marry at all.

frequently happens. She has shown the husband fleecing his guest and his ward by working on the virtuous feelings of a young mind, and has conducted him by natural steps to the awful catastrophe. The last scene at Vauxhall[1] is uncommonly animated; every thing seems to pass before the reader's eyes. The forced gaiety, the starts of remorse, the despair, the bustle and glare of the place, the situation of the unprotected females in such a scene of horror, are all most forcibly described. We almost hear and feel the report of the pistol.—In the uncommon variety of characters which this novel affords, there are many others deserving of notice; that, for instance, of the high-minded romantic Belfield may give a salutary lesson to many a youth who fancies his part in life *ill cast*, who wastes life in projects, and does nothing because he thinks every thing beneath his ambition and his talents.

Such are the various merits of *Cecilia*, through the whole of which it is evident that the author draws from life, and exhibits not only the passions of human nature, but the manners of the age and the affectation of the day.

The celebrity which Miss Burney had now attained awakened the idea of extending that patronage to her which, in most countries, it has been usual in one way or other to hold out to literary merit; and it was thought, we must presume, the most appropriate reward of her exertions, and the happiest method of fostering her genius, that she was made *dresser* to Her Majesty. She held this post for several years, during which the duties of her situation seem to have engrossed her whole time. Her state of health at length obliged her to resign it, and she was soon after married to M. D'Arblay, a French emigrant.

She now again resumed her pen, and gave to the world her third publication, entitled *Camilla*. This work is somewhat too much protracted, and is inferior to *Cecilia* as a whole, but it certainly exhibits beauties of as high an order. The character of Sir Hugh is new and striking. There is such an unconscious shrewdness in his remarks, that they have all the effect of the sharpest satire without his intending any malice; while, at the

---

1   In Book 5, chapters 12 and 13 of *Cecilia*, Mr. Harrell commits suicide at Vauxhall, a popular pleasure garden featuring musical entertainments and walks.

same time, his complaints are so meek, his self-humiliation so touching, his benevolence so genuine and overflowing, that the reader must have a bad heart who does not love while he laughs at him. The incidents of the piece show much invention, particularly that which induces Sir Hugh to adopt Eugenia instead of his favourite. How charmingly is Camilla described! "Every look was a smile, every step was a spring, every thought was a hope, and the early felicity of her mind was without alloy."

Camilla, in the course of the work, falls, like Cecilia, into pecuniary difficulties. They are brought on partly by milliners' bills, which unawares and through the persuasion of others she has suffered to run up, but chiefly from being drawn in to assist an extravagant and unprincipled brother. The character of the brother, Lionel, is drawn with great truth and spirit, and presents but too just a picture of the manner in which many deserving females have been sacrificed to the worthless part of the family. The author appears to have viewed with a very discerning eye the manners of those young men who aspire to lead the fashion; and in all three of her novels has bestowed a good deal of her satire upon the affected apathy, studied negligence, coarse slang, avowed selfishness, or mischievous frolic, by which they often distinguish themselves, and through which they contrive to be vulgar with the advantages of rank, mean with those of fortune, and disagreeable with those of youth.

A very original character in this work is that of Eugenia.[1] Her surprise and sorrow when, at the age of fifteen, she first discovers her deformity, and her deep, gentle, dignified sorrow for the irremediable misfortune, it is impossible to peruse without sympathy; and in the incident which follows, when her father, after a discourse the most rational and soothing, brings her to the sight of a beautiful idiot, the scene is one of the most striking and sublimely moral any where to be met with.

---

1 Eugenia is dwarfish and deformed, something she comes to realize in her fifteenth year. See Book 4, chapters 3–7, for her enlightenment and her reconciliation to her fate. Chapter 6 includes the scene mentioned below in which Eugenia observes the "beautiful idiot."

As well as great beauties there are great faults in *Camilla*. It is blemished by the propensity which the author has shown in all her novels, betrayed into it by her love of humour, to involve her heroines not only in difficult but in degrading adventures. The mind may recover from distress, but not from disgrace; and the situations Camilla is continually placed in with the Dubsters and Mrs. Mittin are of a nature to degrade. Still more, the overwhelming circumstance of her father's being sent to prison for her debts seems to preclude the possibility of her ever raising her head again. It conveys a striking lesson; and no doubt Mrs. D'Arblay, in her large acquaintance with life, must have often seen the necessity of inculcating, even upon *young* ladies, the danger of running up bills on credit; but the distress becomes too deep, too humiliating, to admit of a happy conclusion. The mind has been harassed and worn with excess of painful feeling. At the conclusion of *Clarissa*, we are dismissed in calm and not unpleasing sorrow; but on the winding up of *Cecilia* and *Camilla* we are somewhat tantalized with imperfect happiness. It must be added, that the interest is more divided in *Camilla* than in the author's former work, and the adventures of Eugenia become at length too improbable.

Among the new characters in this piece is Mrs. Arlberry, a woman of fashion, with good sense and taste, but fond of frivolity through *désoeuvrement*,[1] and amusing herself with a little court about her of fashionable young men, whom she at the same time entertains and despises.

In short, Mrs. D'Arblay has observed human nature, both in high and low life, with the quick and penetrating eye of genius. Equally happy in seizing the ridiculous, and in entering into the finer feelings, her pictures of manners are just and interesting, and the highest value is given to them by the moral feelings they exercise, and the excellent principles they inculcate.

Mrs. D'Arblay lived some years after her marriage at a sweet retirement in the shade of Norbury park, in a house built under Mr. D'Arblay's direction, which went by the name of Camilla

---

1   Idleness.

Lodge; but at the time when the greatest part of the emigrants returned to their native country, she followed her husband to France, in which country she now resides.[1]

A writer who has published three novels of so much merit may be allowed to repose her pen; yet the English public cannot but regret an expatriation which so much lessens the chance of their being again entertained by her.

### Mrs. Radcliffe

[Ann Ward Radcliffe (1764-1823) was best known for initiating the vogue for gothic novels, the most popular of which was her 1794 *Mysteries of Udolpho*. In this work as in others she united the thrill of the unknown with an astute understanding of the sublime as theorized by Edmund Burke in his *Philosophical Enquiry into the Sublime and Beautiful* (1757). While aficionados of the gothic genre would later fault her for always providing rational explanations for the phenomena experienced by her unusually sensitive female protagonists, Radcliffe's grasp of the psychological experience of confronting the great and the uncommon (to borrow Addison's terminology in *Spectator* 412) resonated with readers in the late eighteenth century to an unprecedented degree. The popularity of her fiction with a female readership is attested by Jane Austen's satiric response to the Radcliffian mode in *Northanger Abbey* (1818).]

Though every production which is good in its kind entitles its author to praise, a greater distinction is due to those which stand at the head of a class; and such are undoubtedly the novels of Mrs. Radcliffe,—which exhibit a genius of no common stamp. She seems to scorn to move those passions which form the interest of common novels: she alarms the soul with terror; agitates it with suspense, prolonged and wrought up to the most intense feeling, by mysterious hints and obscure intimations of unseen danger. The scenery of her tales is in "time-

---

1 Burney used part of the profit on *Camilla* to build "Camilla Lodge," which she sold in 1814 at a loss.

shook towers,"[1] vast uninhabited castles, winding stair-cases, long echoing aisles; or, if abroad, lonely heaths, gloomy forests, and abrupt precipices, the haunt of banditti;—the canvass and the figures of Salvator Rosa.[2] Her living characters correspond to the scenery:—their wicked projects are dark, singular, atrocious. They are not of English growth; their guilt is tinged with a darker hue than that of the bad and profligate characters we see in the world about us; they seem almost to belong to an unearthly sphere of powerful mischief. But to the terror produced by the machinations of guilt, and the perception of danger, this writer has had the art to unite another, and possibly a stronger feeling. There is, perhaps, in every breast at all susceptible of the influence of imagination, the germ of a certain superstitious dread of the world unknown, which easily suggests the ideas of commerce with it. Solitude, darkness, low-whispered sounds, obscure glimpses of objects, flitting forms, tend to raise in the mind that thrilling, mysterious terror, which has for its object the "powers unseen and mightier far than we."[3] But these ideas are suggested only; for it is the peculiar management of this author, that, though she gives, as it were, a glimpse of the world of terrible shadows, she yet stops short of any thing really supernatural: for all the strange and alarming circumstances brought forward in the narrative are explained in the winding up of the story by natural causes; but in the mean time the reader has felt their full impression.

The first production of this lady, in which her peculiar genius was strikingly developed, is *The Romance of the Forest*, and in some respects it is perhaps the best. It turns upon the machinations of a profligate villain and his agent against an amiable and unprotected girl, whose birth and fortunes have been involved in obscurity by crime and perfidy. The character of La Motte, the agent, is drawn with spirit. He is represented as weak and timid, gloomy and arbitrary in his family, drawn by

---

1   Elizabeth Carter, "Ode to Wisdom" (1747), l. 3.
2   Italian painter (1615-73), known for eerie, desolate landscapes and supernatural, gothic subjects associated with the sublime.
3   Pope, *Essay on Man*, 3.252, slightly altered.

extravagance into vice and atrocious actions; capable of remorse, but not capable of withstanding temptation. There is a scene between him and the more hardened marquis, who is tempting him to commit murder, which has far more nature and truth than the admired scene between King John and Hubert, in which the writer's imagination has led him rather to represent the action to which the king is endeavouring to work his instrument, as it would be seen by a person who had a great horror of its guilt, than in the manner in which he ought to represent it in order to win him to his purpose:

> ————If the midnight bell
> Did with his iron tongue and brazen mouth
> Sound one unto the drowsy ear of night,
> If this same were a churchyard where we stand,
> And thou possessed with a thousand wrongs,
> ————————if thou couldst see me without eyes,
> Hear me without thine ears, and make reply
> Without a tongue, &c.[1]

What must be the effect of such imagery, but to infuse into the mind of Hubert that horror of the crime with which the spectator views the deed, and which it was the business, indeed, of Shakespear to impress upon the mind of the spectator, but not of King John to impress upon Hubert? In the scene referred to, on the other hand, the marquis, whose aim is to tempt La Motte to the commission of murder, begins by attempting to lower his sense of virtue, by representing it as the effect of prejudices imbibed in early youth; reminds him that in many countries the stiletto is resorted to without scruple; treats as trivial his former deviations from integrity; and, by lulling his conscience and awakening his cupidity, draws him to his purpose.

There are many situations in this novel which strike strongly upon the imagination. Who can read without a shudder, that Adeline in her lonely chamber at the abbey hardly dared to lift her eyes to the glass, lest she should see another face than her

---

1 Shakespeare, *King John*, III.iii. 37-41, 48-50.

own reflected from it? or who does not sympathize with her feelings, when, thinking she has effected her escape with Peter, she hears a strange voice, and finds herself on horseback in a dark night carried away by an unknown ruffian?

The next work which proceeded from Mrs. Radcliffe's pen was *The Mysteries of Udolpho*. Similar to the former in the turn of its incidents, and the nature of the feelings it is meant to excite, it abounds still more with instances of mysterious and terrific appearances, but has perhaps less of character, and a more imperfect story. It has been the aim in this work to assemble appearances of the most impressive kind, which continually present the idea of supernatural agency, but which are at length accounted for by natural means. They are not always, however, *well* accounted for; and the mind experiences a sort of disappointment and shame at having felt so much from appearances which had nothing in them beyond "this visible diurnal sphere."[1] The moving of the pall in the funereal chamber is of this nature. The curtain, which no one dares to undraw, interests us strongly; we feel the utmost stings and throbs of curiosity; but we have been affected so repeatedly, the suspense has been so long protracted, and expectation raised so high, that no explanation can satisfy, no imagery of horrors can equal the vague shapings of our imagination.

The story of *Udolpho* is more complicated and perplexed than that of *The Romance of the Forest*; but it turns, like that, on the terrors and dangers of a young lady confined in a castle. The character of her oppressor, Montoni, is less distinctly marked than that of La Motte; and it is a fault in the story, that its unravelling depends but little on the circumstances that have previously engaged our attention. Another castle is introduced; wonders are multiplied upon us; and the interest we had felt in the castle of Udolpho in the Appenines, is suddenly transferred to Chateau le Blanc among the Pyrenees.[2]

*The Mysteries of Udolpho* is the most popular of this author's performances, and as such has been chosen for this Selection;

---

1  Milton, *Paradise Lost*, VII.22.
2  Appenines: an Italian mountain range. Pyrenees: mountains on the border of France and Spain.

but perhaps it is exceeded in strength by her next publication, *The Sicilian*.[1] Nothing can be finer than the opening of this story. An Englishman on his travels, walking through a church, sees a dark figure stealing along the aisles. He is informed that he is an assassin. On expressing his astonishment that he should find shelter there, he is told that such adventures are common in Italy. His companion then points to a confessional in an obscure aisle of the church. "There," says he, "in that cell, such a tale of horror was once poured into the ear of a priest as overwhelmed him with astonishment, nor was the secret ever disclosed."[2] This prelude, like the tuning of an instrument by a skilful hand, has the effect of producing at once in the mind a tone of feeling correspondent to the future story. In this, as in the former productions, the curiosity of the reader is kept upon the stretch by mystery and wonder. The author seems perfectly to understand that obscurity, as Burke has asserted, is a strong ingredient in the sublime:—a face shrowded in a cowl; a narrative suddenly suspended; deep guilt half revealed; the untold secrets of a prison-house; the terrific shape, "if shape it might be called, that shape had none distinguishable;"—all these affect the mind more powerfully than any regular or distinct images of danger or of woe.[3]

But this novel has also high merit in the character of Schedoni, which is strikingly drawn, as is his personal appearance. "His figure," says the author, "was striking, but not so from grace. It was tall, and though extremely thin, his limbs were large and uncouth; and as he stalked along, wrapped in the black garments of his order, there was something terrible in his air, something almost superhuman. His cowl too, as it threw a shade over the livid paleness of his face, increased its severe character, and gave an effect to his large melancholy eye which approached to horror. His physiognomy bore the trace of many passions, which seemed to have fixed the features they no

---

1  Barbauld confuses Radcliffe's second novel, *A Sicilian Romance*, with her last novel, *The Italian* (1797).

2  Barbauld loosely summarizes the opening pages of *The Italian*.

3  See Burke's *Sublime and Beautiful*, pp. 54-55; he quotes the passage Barbauld cites from Milton's *Paradise Lost* 2.667-68.

longer animated. His eyes were so piercing that they seemed to penetrate with a single glance into the hearts of men, and to read their most secret thoughts; few persons could support their scrutiny, or even endure to meet them twice." A striking figure for the painter to transfer to the canvass; perhaps some picture might originally have suggested it. The scene where this singular character is on the point of murdering his own daughter, as she then appears to be, is truly tragical, and wrought up with great strength and pathos. It is impossible not to be interested in the situation of Ellen, in the convent, when her lamp goes out while she is reading a paper on which her fate depends; and again when, in making her escape, she has just got to the end of the long vaulted passage, and finds the door locked, and herself betrayed. The scenes of the Inquisition are too much protracted, and awaken more curiosity than they fully gratify; perhaps than any story can gratify.

In novels of this kind, where the strong charm of suspense and mystery is employed, we hurry through with suspended breath, and in a kind of agony of expectation; but when we are come to the end of the story, the charm is dissolved, we have no wish to read it again; we do not recur to it as we do to the characters of Western in *Tom Jones*, or the Harrels in *Cecilia*; the interest is painfully strong while we read, and when once we have read it, it is nothing; we are ashamed of our feelings, and do not wish to recall them.

There are beauties in Mrs. Radcliffe's volumes, which would perhaps have more effect if our curiosity were less excited,— for her descriptions are rich and picturesque. Switzerland, the south of France, Venice, the valleys of Piedmont, the bridge, the cataract, and especially the charming bay of Naples, the dances of the peasants, with the vine-dressers and the fishermen, have employed her pencil. Though love is but of a secondary interest in her story, there is a good deal of tenderness in the parting scenes between Emily and Valancourt in *The Mysteries of Udolpho*, when she dismisses him, who is still the object of her tenderness, on account of his irregularities.

It ought not to be forgotten that there are many elegant pieces of poetry interspersed through the volumes of Mrs.

Radcliffe; among which are to be distinguished as exquisitely sweet and fanciful, the *Song to a Spirit*, and *The Sea Nymph*, "Down down a hundred fathom deep!" They might be sung by Shakespear's Ariel.[1] The true lovers of poetry are almost apt to regret its being brought in as an accompaniment to narrative, where it is generally neglected; for not one in a hundred, of those who read and can judge of novels, are at all able to appreciate the merits of a copy of verses, and the common reader is always impatient to get on with the story.

*The Sicilian* is the last of Mrs. Radcliffe's performances. Some have said that, if she wishes to rise in the horrors of her next, she must place her scene in the infernal regions. She would not have many steps to descend thither from the courts of the Inquisition.

Mrs. Radcliffe has also published, jointly with her husband, *Travels in Germany and Holland*.[2]

## LETTER TO THE
## *GENTLEMAN'S MAGAZINE*
## IN DEFENSE OF MARIA EDGEWORTH'S
## TALE, "THE DUN"

[Barbauld met Maria Edgeworth (1768–1849) in 1799 and corresponded with her intermittently for the rest of her life. She followed Edgeworth's publishing career almost from its beginning and greatly admired her work. "I know the homage paid you," she wrote to Edgeworth in 1816, "and I exulted in it for your sake and for my sex's sake" (LeBreton, *Memoir*, p. 162). Her preface to Edgeworth in *British Novelists* is self-effacingly short: "the editor feels it would be superfluous to indulge her feelings in dwelling on the excellencies of an author so fully in possession of the esteem and admiration of the public"

---

1   The airy spirit of Shakespeare's *Tempest* who sings "Full fathom five thy father lies / Of his bones are coral made" in Act I.ii.397–98.
2   Radcliffe's husband, William, was a journalist. The couple traveled in Holland and Germany, publishing in 1795 the account of their journey Barbauld mentions.

(49:[iii]). Thus, this letter seems to be her longest public state-
ment on Edgeworth.

By her own account, her letter was provoked by the conser-
vative *Quarterly Review*'s treatment of Edgeworth's *Tales of Fash-
ionable Life* (1809), from which her letter quotes the offending
passage. "I had not seen the Quarterly before you mentioned
it. I then read it with great indignation indeed, nor could I help
venting a little of it, as much as I thought would do good, in a
paper, which perhaps you saw in the Gentleman's Magazine.
Write on, shine out, and defy them" (letter to Edgeworth, [nd]
1810, in LeBreton, *Memoir*, pp. 144-45). Besides venting indig-
nation at the *Quarterly*'s tasteless innuendo about Edgeworth's
meaning, Barbauld expresses impatience with the conservative
demand not merely that fiction be "moral," but that it propa-
gate specific religious views. Her letter appeared in *The Gentle-
man's Magazine*, 80 (March, 1810):210-12, signed "Y.Z."; we
reprint that text.]

Mr. Urban,[1]                                              Feb. 20.


Independently of any high opinion of the taste or impartiality
of those self-erected tribunals, which assume the right of
directing the taste of the publick, I am entirely of opinion, that,
in general, it is very idle to appeal from their decision; never-
theless, the manner in which the "*Tales of Fashionable Life*," late-
ly published by Miss Edgeworth, have been criticised by one of
them, cannot be passed over by those who admire her virtues
equally with her genius; and I therefore beg permission to offer
a few remarks on it. The Review professes to think some of
the stories dull: of that every one will easily judge for himself;
for, whatever they may be, they are pretty universally *read*, and
few probably have waited for the sanction of the Criticks to
give them a perusal. The Critick's judgment may be right, or it
may be wrong; his taste good or bad: there is no greater proba-
bility, that an unknown person, who gives his opinion upon
books once a month, or once a quarter, should be right, than

---

1   The pseudonym under which *The Gentleman's Magazine* was edited was "Sylvanus
    Urban."

that any other unknown person should be so, who delivers his in a parlour or a coffee-house. I am also very ready to allow, that the Tales are of unequal merit, and open in many places to just criticism, as what productions are not? The matter of taste, therefore, I lay entirely out of the question; but imputations of a moral nature, delivered with as little decorum in the language as candour in the sentiment, ought not to be so easily passed over. I refer to the following critique on the story of the *Dun*.

> On the Tales contained in the two last volumes, we cannot bestow much praise. If it were required to make a choice between them, we should prefer *The Dun*; which, in the example of a Colonel Pembroke, who by his thoughtless neglect to pay his Tailor, brings a whole family into deplorable want and misery, gives a just and severe rebuke to hard-hearted fashionable debtors. The Colonel is reformed; and it may be useful to other gentlemen who labour under the same infirmity, to learn where a cure is to be had. He meets the daughter of his Creditor in a brothel, and, being shocked to find that she has been driven thither by his neglect to discharge his debts, becomes thenceforward a very accurate paymaster. Miss Edgeworth's morality is of a reasonable kind, and does not require too much. We therefore do not find that the Colonel's reformation extended any farther.
>
> Quarterly Review, No. III.[1]

Now, Sir, is it possible to read without indignation imputations so gross, conveyed in language so illiberal, upon a lady whose pen has been uniformly employed in the service of virtue and good morals? What is the story they thus censure? A gay young man of fortune, from an extravagant disposition, and inattention to the just claims of others upon him, ruins an industrious poor Weaver, by neglecting to pay his bill; and the daughter, an innocent and well-disposed young woman, is driven by distress, after many struggles, to enter a house where

---

1  *Quarterly Review*, 2 (Aug. 1809):153. The review, together with Barbauld's own account, below, accurately summarizes Edgeworth's tale.

her honour was to be sacrificed, in order to procure bread for herself and her father. Their Creditor happens to be the person to whom she is introduced; he is witness to her tears, her reluctance, and repentance, and, struck with the mischief he has occasioned, he relinquishes his victim, discharges his debt, and becomes thenceforward (according to the phrase of the Critick) "an accurate paymaster;" that is to say, he is reformed, precisely in that particular which the story was meant to bear upon. But, say the Reviewers, "Miss Edgeworth's morality is of a *reasonable* kind, it does not require too much; we hear nothing more of the gentleman's reformation." Would to Heaven that reasonable Morality, and reasonable Religion too, were a little more common than they are! It is true that Miss Edgeworth has not transformed this gay Colonel into a character totally opposite to the one he had so long borne. He does not immediately upon this incident become a new man; a grave, religious, thoroughly-moral character. Some Authors, I doubt not, would have worked this transformation; and very likely some would have been kind enough to marry him to the girl, in a fit of sentiment, and would have left them a very happy and virtuous couple. But Miss Edgeworth, I confess, has not done so. She has an inveterate habit of following human nature; and has probably thought that so complete a change could not be worked upon such a man, in any portion of time that she could afford to bestow upon him; but she has made him reform *that vice*, of the bad consequences of which he had received so striking a lesson, and which required only a little common sensibility, a little human feeling, to reform. In other respects, I must acknowledge, she does not seem to have cared much about this Colonel, for the good of whose soul the Reviewers are so kindly interested. He had served her purpose, and she had done with him. Perhaps sudden conversions are not among the articles of her creed; and she does not seem to have had sufficient regard for this gentleman, to draw out a slight story into half a volume more; which would have been necessary to work such a metamorphosis with any regard to probability. The poor girl too is no heroine, for her virtue has given way; but she is an innocent well-disposed girl, and has principles quite as strong, and stronger than the generality of women in her station. But what is the moral, if the gentleman is not reformed? Is it not easy to see, that the moral does not any way depend upon his reformation? He is not held up as a pattern. The impression meant to be given is, that the rich and thoughtless, by withholding a just debt, plunge those who depend upon them not only into poverty, but into vice. Perhaps the frailty of the young woman may give offence to some; but if she had been a Clarissa,[1] half the moral would have been lost. The story says to the licentious spendthrift, "You are driving the poor not only to want, to distress, but, what is infinitely worse, into temptations that will overcome their virtue; for we have no right to expect that, in such perilous circumstances, the virtue of the lower classes will not give way;" we know it does, in fact, from such causes, and yet they may have principle to a certain degree, nay, to a great degree; there is a great deal of good practical virtue which is assailable by temptation, and whoever will paint human nature must paint it as it is, or it becomes romance, which is not what Miss Edgeworth means to write. So much as to the moral of the story. Another question may arise, whether it is delicately told. To this we must suppose the words of the Reviewer allude, that "she has told those who labour under the same infirmity, *where* a cure is to be had;" for, though they will bear another interpretation, it is utterly impossible to suppose the Writers so void of common sense as to imagine that Miss Edgeworth recommends going to Brothels (to use their broad language), in order to cure people of vicious habits. They must mean, therefore, that there is a coarseness in the tale, which renders it unfit for the public ear. Let us compare it then with other stories from approved Authors, who have incurred no blame on this account. Hardly any of our periodical papers are without a story of this sort, more or less detailed; but I would particularly point out one from Hawkesworth's Adventurer, a work constantly put into the hands of young persons, and particularly commended for its moral purity. The History of a Parish Girl, given in Nos. 86 and 134, is of the same nature with

---

1    The heroine of Samuel Richardson's novel; for Barbauld's interpretation of her, see "Enquiry into ... Distress" and the excerpt from her "Life" of Richardson.

the story of the Dun;[1] it is much more detailed; the girl for
whom we are interested is completely ruined, and lives for
some time in a state of prostitution: and there are circumstances
in the tale peculiarly calculated to shock our feelings, for she
narrowly escapes an intercourse with her own father; yet
Hawkesworth was not, that I ever heard of, blamed by a single
person for a violation of either delicacy or morality. The
admired story of Fidelia, by Mrs. Chapone, in the same work,[2]
turns upon seduction; *that* has never been found fault with.
Pictures of vice which are so detailed as to sully the imagina-
tion, or stimulate the passions, are indeed highly immoral; but
the mind must be most peculiarly formed, that can feel or fear
any such effects from the story of the Dun; and little reason had
Miss Edgeworth to expect, that any story she could write
would, in a respectable Review, be censured in phrases only fit
to be used towards a novel of Crebillon.[3]

One word more on the reproach which a certain set are so
fond of throwing out against this Author, that there is no Reli-
gion in her works.[4] It is true she does not often advert to those
principles and motives which no doubt, where they are well

---

1 John Hawkesworth's *The Adventurer* (1752-54) was a well-regarded and often-
reprinted series of essays; Samuel Johnson wrote many of them. Nos. 86 and 134-
36, signed "Agamus," tell a story of a libertine who seduces a woman and abandons
their illegitimate daughter to the charity of the parish; years later he encounters the
girl in a brothel and almost sleeps with her.
2 Hester Mulso Chapone (1727-1802), eminent Bluestocking; her story of Fidelia
appeared as Nos. 77-79.
3 Claude Prosper Jolyot de Crébillon (1707-77), author of novels widely regarded as
lewd; for one of them he was banished from Paris on orders from the King.
4 A common criticism of Edgeworth, especially among conservative Christians. "It is
a striking fact," the *Quarterly* complained, "that in a treatise in which she professed
to give a summary of the duties of tuition [*Practical Education*, 1798], she purposely
excluded from her system all reference to the subject of religious instruction....
[T]he morality of Miss Edgeworth ... is accordingly a system of manners regulated
by prudence and a sense of propriety, having little connection with the heart ..."
(p. 148). Barbauld herself had been criticized by Evangelicals for ignoring Church
doctrine in her children's books, and she in turn had criticized the Evangelical
demand that authors be Christian: "It is not necessary to stigmatize a man for his
want of faith, who writes a book of science or general information; a practice
which, I observe with pain, is gaining ground amongst us, and which, if it becomes
prevalent, will be the destruction of all sound literature" ("Opprobrious Appella-
tions Reprobated," p. 482).

understood and strongly felt, are the highest of all. But there is nothing inimical to Religion, no insidious sophism, no concealed sneer; there is nothing which leads us to suppose her estimable characters are without Religion, though it is not brought forward on every occasion. Moreover, there is no want of Writers on religious subjects; there *is* a want of good moral writers. Why then cannot these people accept of the good she does, without throwing blame on her for not doing that good which she does not attempt to do; and which also if she were to attempt in any way but their own, she knows would draw upon her blame tenfold heavier. Let them remember who it was that said, "Forbid him not; for he that is not against us is for us."[1] Let them recollect that there is a large, a very large class in this kingdom called Christian, upon whom religious motives do not operate, because they are not religious; but they are accessible to motives drawn from worldly prudence, from the common feelings of humanity, from a sense of honour. In insisting upon these, you speak a language they understand; and however Theologians may dispose of the individual in another world, in this, society is much obliged to any one who will teach them to pay their debts, and be kind to their neighbours, though their virtue should rise no higher than that of poor Mr. Flam, in the story of Coelebs.[2] There are devils that are only cast out by fasting and prayer; but there are also devils that are cast out by ridicule, by sound logick, by conjuring up all the forms of worldly ruin and distress that wait upon improvidence and vice. While, therefore, it is allowed that the highest characters are formed by Religion, let Miss Edgeworth go on to do good with inferior motives; like a charitable country lady, who dispenses to her sick neighbours food and gentle alteratives, and a little common physick,[3] though she forbears to meddle with a few powerful medicines, of the operation of

---

1  Jesus says it to a disciple who reports that "we saw one casting out devils in thy name; and we forbad him, because he followeth not with us" (Luke 9:49-50).

2  *Coelebs in Search of a Wife* by Hannah More (1809). Mr. Flam is an old-fashioned country squire who says that personal integrity and benevolence towards others "are the sum and substance of religion" (More, *Works*, 7:214).

3  Alteratives: drugs used to alter the course of an ailment; physick is medicine.

which, and of the proper dose, she may not feel herself suf-
ficiently assured, and therefore modestly leaves them to the
regular practitioners.

## DIALOGUE IN THE SHADES

[Lucy Aikin reports ("Memoir," p. lxix) that Barbauld "early
read with great delight" the satirical Dialogues of Lucian of
Samosata (2nd century AD), a writer noted for his urbane tone
and skeptical views. Barbauld wrote several Lucianic dialogues.
In this one, between Clio, Muse of History, and Mercury, Bar-
bauld casts a skeptical eye over the canon of Western history
from antiquity to her own time. In a trope similar to that in
*Eighteen Hundred and Eleven* by which ancient grandeur yields
to modern in places the Ancients never heard of, she poses the
modern world, with its vast technologies of power and death,
against previous history, and asks whether previous history mat-
ters any more. Not that the modern is better: writing in early
1813, hard upon news of the catastrophic French retreat from
Moscow, Barbauld regards the modern as more of the same, but
bigger, meaner, and uglier. Gone, or at least deeply muted, is
the faith in the progress of reason that animated her *Address to
the Opposers* 23 years before. She does, however, see one excep-
tion in this gloomy survey: modern literary women, who both
in number and quality surpass their predecessors. The "Dia-
logue" was first published in *Works* (1825), 2:338-49; we reprint
that text.]

Clio.—There is no help for it,—they must go. The river
Lethe[1] is here at hand; I shall tear them off and throw them into
the stream.

Mercury.—Illustrious daughter of Mnemosyne, Clio! the
most respected of the Muses,—you seem disturbed. What is it
that brings us the honour of a visit from you in these infernal
regions?

---

1   The river of Forgetfulness in Hades ("the Shades"). Mnemosyne (below): Memory.

*Clio.*—You are a god of expedients, Mercury; I want to consult you. I am oppressed with the continually increasing demands upon me: I have had more business for these last twenty years[1] than I have often had for two centuries; and if I had, as old Homer says, "a throat of brass and adamantine lungs,"[2] I could never get through it. And what did he want this throat of brass for? for a paltry list of ships, canoes rather, which would be laughed at in the Admiralty Office of London. But I must inform you, Mercury, that my roll is so full, and I have so many applications which cannot in decency be refused, that I see no other way than striking off some hundreds of names in order to make room; and I am come to inform the shades of my determination.

*Mercury.*—I believe, Clio, you will do right: and as one end of your roll is a little mouldy, no doubt you will begin with that; but the ghosts will raise a great clamour.

*Clio.*—I expect no less; but necessity has no law. All the parchment in Pergamus[3] is used up,—my roll is long enough to reach from earth to heaven; it is grown quite cumbrous; it takes a life, as mortals reckon lives, to unroll it.

*Mercury.*—Yet consider, Clio, how many of these have passed a restless life, and encountered all manner of dangers, and bled and died only to be placed upon your list,—and now to be struck off!

*Clio.*—And committed all manner of crimes, you might have added;—but go they must. Besides, they have been sufficiently recompensed. Have they not been praised, and sung, and admired for some thousands of years? Let them give place to others: What! have they no conscience? no modesty? Would Xerxes, think you, have reason to complain, when his parading expeditions have already procured him above two thousand years of fame, though a Solyman or a Zingis Khan should fill

---

1   Since February 1793, when the war between England and France began.

2   *The Iliad* (Pope's translation), 2:581, introducing "The Catalogue of the [Greek] Ships." Ancient ships were small and technologically primitive compared to a modern man-of-war. The Admiralty Office (below) is the headquarters of the British Navy.

3   Pergamum, ancient Greek city in Asia Minor (now Turkey), where parchment was manufactured.

up his place?[1]

*Mercury.*—~~Surely you are not going to blot out Xerxes from~~ your list of names?

*Clio.*—I do not say that I am: but that I keep him is more for the sake of his antagonists than his own. And yet their places might be well supplied by the Swiss heroes of Morgarten, or the brave though unsuccessful patriot Aloys Reding.[2]—But pray what noise is that at the gate?

*Mercury.*—A number of the shades, who have received an intimation of your purpose, and are come to remonstrate against it.

*Clio.*—In the name of all the gods whom have we here?— Hercules, Theseus, Jason, Oedipus, Bacchus, Cadmus with a bag of dragon's teeth, and a whole tribe of strange shadowy figures! I shall expect to see the Centaurs and Lapithae, or Perseus on his flying courser.[3] Away with them; they belong to my sisters, not to me; Melpomene will receive them gladly.

*Mercury.*—You forget, Clio, that Bacchus conquered India.

*Clio.*—And had horns like Moses, as Vossius is pleased to say.[4] No, Mercury, I will have nothing to do with these; if ever I received them, it was when I was young and credulous.—As I have said, let my sisters take them; or let them be celebrated in tales for children.

*Mercury.*—That will not do, Clio; children in this age read none but wise books: stories of giants and dragons are all written for grown-up children now.[5]

---

1    Xerxes, King of Persia 485-465 BC, led a huge army against Greece and was bravely opposed by a small Greek force under Leonidas at the Battle of Thermopylae (480 BC). Solyman: Suleiman I, the Magnificent, Ottoman emperor 1520-66, conquered parts of southern Europe and North Africa. Zingis [Genghis] Khan: Mongol invader of Europe, c. 1162-1227.

2    Like the Greek Leonidas (note 1), the Swiss hero Aloys Reding led a small patriotic band against invasion (by France); he was defeated at Morgarten (1798). Reding was compared to Leonidas by the reviewer of a history of the invasion in *The Annual Review* (1 [1803]:340), edited by Barbauld's nephew Arthur Aikin.

3    Hercules … courser: All figures in Greek myth and tragedy, once thought to be historical. Melpomene (below) will receive them because she is the Muse of Tragedy.

4    Gerardus Joannes Vossius, Dutch humanist, in *De Theologia Gentili* (1641), Bk. I, Chap. 30.

5    Barbauld expressed the same sentiment some years earlier: "It is … a singular incongruity in our manners, that whilst mathematics, astronomy, chemistry, and

*Clio.*—Be that as it may, I shall clear my hands of them, and of a great many more, I do assure you.

*Mercury.*—I hope "the tale of Troy divine—!"[1]

*Clio.*—Divine let it be, but my share in it is very small; I recollect furnishing the catalogue.—Mercury, I will tell you the truth. When I was young, my mother (as arrant a gossip as ever breathed) related to me a great number of stories: and as in those days people could not read or write, I had no better authority for what I recorded: but after letters were found out, and now since the noble invention of printing,—why do you think, Mercury, any one would dare to tell lies in print?

*Mercury.*—Sometimes perhaps. I have seen a splendid victory in the gazette[2] of one country dwindle into an honourable retreat in that of another.

*Clio.*—In newspapers, very possibly: but with regard to myself, when I have time to consider and lay things together, I assure you you may depend upon me.—Whom have we in that group which I see indistinctly in a sort of twilight?

*Mercury.*—Very renowned personages; Ninus, Sesostris, Semiramis, Cheops who built the largest pyramid.[3]

*Clio.*—If Cheops built the largest pyramid, people are welcome to inquire about him at the spot,—room must be made. As to Semiramis, tell her her place shall be filled up by an empress and a conqueror from the shores of the wintry Baltic.[4]

*Mercury.*—The renowned Cyrus is approaching with a look of confidence, for he is introduced by a favourite of yours, the elegant Xenophon.

*Clio.*—Is that Cyrus? Pray desire him to take off that dress which Xenophon has given him; truly I took him for a Greek

---

natural history are occupying the nursery, the grown children with their parents should be going to see Blue-beard and Cinderella at the theatres-royal, and the young ladies should be warbling Cock Robin and Gaffer Grey-beard at their piano-fortes" ("Comparison of Manners," pp. 120-21).

1 Milton, "Il Penseroso," l. 100, referring to Homer's *Iliad*. The catalogue (below): of Greek ships in the *Iliad*.

2 An official government newspaper.

3 Ninus, Sesostris, Semiramis, Cheops: Ancient Egyptian or Assyrian monarchs legendary for large conquests.

4 The empress Catherine the Great of Russia (1729-96), on the Baltic Sea, who warred successfully against Sweden, Poland, and Turkey.

philosopher. I fancy queen Tomyris would scarcely recognise him.[1]

*Mercury.*—Aspasia[2] hopes, for the honour of her sex, that she shall continue to occupy a place among those you celebrate.

*Clio.*—Tell the mistress of Pericles we can spare her without inconvenience: many ladies are to be found in modern times who possess her eloquence and her talents, with the modesty of a vestal; and should a more perfect likeness be required, modern times may furnish that also.[3]

*Mercury.*—Here are two figures who approach you with a very dignified air.

*Solon and Lycurgus.*—We present ourselves, divine Clio, with confidence. We have no fear that you should strike from your roll the lawgivers of Athens and Sparta.

*Clio.*—Most assuredly not. Yet I must inform you that a name higher than either of yours, and a constitution more perfect, is to be found in a vast continent, of the very existence of which you had not the least suspicion.[4]

*Mercury.*—I see approaching a person of a noble and spirited air, if he did not hold his head a little on one side as if his neck were awry.

*Alexander.*—Clio, I need not introduce myself; I am, as you well know, the son of Jupiter Ammon, and my arms have reached even to the remote shore of the Indus.[5]

---

1  Cyrus the Great (d. 529 BC), founder of the Persian empire and hero of a philo-sophical fiction, the *Cyropedia*, by Xenophon (435-354 BC), who also wrote a famous work of history. Clio implies that Xenophon so glamorized the historical Cyrus that his enemy Tomyris, queen of the Massagetae, would not know him from the description.

2  Aspasia (fifth century BC) was the consort of Pericles, prince of Athens; she was leg-endary both as a wit and also, less kindly, as a courtesan.

3  In May 1813 Barbauld wrote to her pupil Lydia Rickards in praise of the eminent women Maria Edgeworth, Germaine de Stael, and Sarah Siddons; and some years earlier she had reported with satisfaction that "more women than men" were awarded prizes by the Society for the Encouragement of Arts (Rickards, "Mrs. Bar-bauld and her Pupil," pp. 723, 713).

4  Solon (c. 640-c. 559 BC) and Lycurgus (ninth century BC) were traditionally esteemed as the authors of wise laws. Clio informs them that they have been out-done by the framers of the United States Constitution.

5  Alexander the Great (356-323 BC), conqueror of western Asia as far as the border of India (the river Indus), invented a divine genealogy for himself and was said to have a crooked neck.

*Clio.*—Pray burn your genealogy; and for the rest, suffer me to inform you that the river Indus and the whole peninsula which you scarcely discovered, with sixty millions of inhabitants, is at this moment subject to the dominion of a few merchants in a remote island of the Northern Ocean, the very name of which never reached your ears.[1]

*Mercury.*—Here is Empedocles, who threw himself into Aetna merely to be placed upon your roll; and Calanus, who mounted his funeral pile before Alexander, from the same motive.[2]

*Clio.*—They have been remembered long enough in all reason: their places may be supplied by the two next madmen who shall throw themselves under the wheels of the chariot of Jaggernaut,[3]—fanatics are the growth of every age.

*Mercury.*—Here is a ghost preparing to address you with a very self-sufficient air: his robe is embroidered with flower-de-luces.[4]

*Louis XIV.*—I am persuaded, Clio, you will recognise *the immortal man*. I have always been a friend and patron of the Muses; my actions are well known; all Europe has resounded with my name,—the terror of other countries, the glory of my own: I am well assured you are not going to strike me off.

*Clio.*—To strike you off? certainly not; but to place you many degrees lower in the list; to reduce you from a sun, your

---

1 The British East India Company, headquartered in London, managed the British holdings in India. "Alexander disappears because his discovery of India is irrelevant to the current colonial exploitation of it" (Armstrong, "The Gush of the Feminine," p. 20).

2 The Greek philosopher Empedocles (d. c. 430 BC) died, according to legend, by leaping into the cone of the volcano, Mt. Aetna. Calanus or Kalanos was an Indian philosopher who followed Alexander to Persia where, becoming ill, he ordered his own funeral pyre which he ascended, predicting Alexander's death would soon follow. Barbauld's source for this tale is Plutarch's "Life of Alexander."

3 Barbauld perhaps alludes to Claudius Buchanan, *Christian Researches in Asia* (1811), in which the worshippers of the Hindu deity Vishnu are described as lying down to be crushed by the wheels of his chariot, called "Juggernaut."

4 flower-de-luces: fleur-de-lis (lily), the emblem of the Bourbon kings of France, of whom Louis XIV ("The Sun King," reigned 1643-1715) was the most ambitious, warlike, lavish, and powerful. "*The immortal man*" (below) translates the inscription on a statue to Louis XIV in Paris (Voltaire, *Age of Louis XIV*, p. 318).

favourite emblem, to a star in the galaxy. My sisters have cer-
tainly been partial to you: you bought their favour with—how
many livres a year? not much more than a London bookseller
will give for a quarto poem.[1] But me you cannot bribe.

*Louis.*—But, Clio, you have yourself recorded my
exploits;—the passage of the Rhine, Namur, Flanders, Franche
Comté.[2]

*Clio.*—O Louis, if you could but guess the extent of the pre-
sent French empire;—but no, it could never enter into your
imagination.

*Louis.*—I rejoice at what you say; I rejoice that my posterity
have followed my steps, and improved upon my glory.

*Clio.*—Your posterity have had nothing to do with it.[3]

*Louis.*—Remember too the urbanity of my character, how
hospitably I received the unfortunate James of England,[4]—
England, the natural enemy of France.[5]

*Clio.*—Your hospitality has been well returned. Your
descendants, driven from their thrones, are at this moment sup-
ported by the bounty of the nation and king of England.

*Louis.*—O Clio, what is it that you tell me! let me hide my
diminished head[6] in the deepest umbrage of the grove; let me
seek out my dear Maintenon, and tell my beads with her till I
forget that I have been either praised or feared.[7]

---

1 Louis conferred upon the poet Nicholas Boileau (1636-1711) a pension of 2000
   livres for writing flattering poems about him. In 1813 that would have equaled
   about £90, perhaps the sum Barbauld had received for her quarto poem, *Eighteen
   Hundred and Eleven*.

2 The military campaigns of Louis XIV, which astonished his contemporaries by
   their rapidity and boldness, were recorded by Voltaire in his history, *Le Siècle de
   Louis XIV* (1751), a book well known to Barbauld.

3 The French Empire under Napoleon Bonaparte (1769-1821), who was by birth
   Corsican, embraced almost all of Europe, whereas the conquests of Louis XIV were
   confined to lands neighboring France.

4 James II, dethroned in the Revolution of 1689, fled to France and was welcomed by
   Louis XIV. England returned the favor (below) during the French Revolution,
   when the surviving French royal family settled in London as guests of the nation.

5 For Barbauld's contempt for the geopolitical concept of "natural enemies," see *Sins
   of Government, Sins of the Nation*.

6 hide ... head: Milton, *Paradise Lost*, 4:35.

7 Françoise d'Aubigné, Madame de Maintenon (1635-1719), Louis' last mistress,
   turned him to Catholic piety. To "tell beads" is to say the Rosary, which consists of
   a prayer for every bead in the rosary chain.

*Clio.*—Comfort yourself, however; your name, like the red letter which marks the holiday, though insignificant in itself, shall still enjoy the honour of designating the age of taste and literature.[1]

*Mercury.*—Here is a whole crowd coming, Clio, I can scarcely keep them off with my wand: they have all got notice of your intentions, and the infernal regions are quite in an uproar,—what is to be done?

*Clio.*—I cannot tell; the numbers distract me: to examine their pretensions one by one is impossible; I must strike off half of them at a venture: the rest must make room,—they must crowd, they must fall into the back-ground; and where I used to write a name all in capitals with letters of gold illuminated, I must put it in *small pica.*[2] I do assure you, Mercury, I cannot stand the fatigue I undergo, much longer. I am not provided, as you very well know, with either chariot or wings, and I am expected to be in all parts of the globe at once. In the good old times my business lay almost entirely between the Hellespont and the Pillars of Hercules, with sometimes an excursion to the mouths (then seven) of the Nile, or the banks of the Euphrates.[3] But now I am required to be in a hundred places at once; I am called from Jena to Austerlitz, from Cape Trafalgar to Aboukir, and from the Thames to the Ganges and Burampooter; besides a whole continent, a world by itself, fresh and vigorous, which I foresee will find me abundance of employment.[4]

*Mercury.*—Truly I believe so; I am afraid the old leaven is working in the new world.

---

1    *The Age of Louis XIV* is the title in English of Voltaire's history; Voltaire considers it one of the four greatest ages of human civilization. The red letter (above) marks holidays in the Church calendar.

2    The print used in newspapers.

3    The world known to Greek and Roman historians was the Mediterranean Sea and its neighboring lands in southern Europe and North Africa, extending east to modern-day Iraq.

4    Jena and Austerlitz, in Germany and Austria, were sites of major Napoleonic victories (1806 and 1805), Trafalgar (off Spain) and Aboukir (Egypt) of British naval victories (1805, 1798). The river Thames is in England, the Ganges in India, the Brahmaputra in Tibet. The "whole continent" is North America, in which the War of 1812 was currently being fought.

*Clio.*—I am puzzled at this moment how to give the account, which always is expected of me, of the august sovereigns of Europe.

*Mercury.*—How so?

*Clio.*—I do not know where to find them; they are most of them upon their *travels.*[1]

*Mercury.*—You must have been very much employed in the French revolution.

*Clio.*—Continually; the actors in the scene succeeded one another with such rapidity, that the hero of today was forgotten on the morrow. Necker, Mirabeau, Dumourier, La Fayette, appeared successively like pictures in a magic lanthern—shown for a moment and then withdrawn: and now the space is filled by one tremendous gigantic figure, that throws his broad shadow over half the globe.[2]

*Mercury.*—The ambition of Napoleon has indeed procured you much employment.

*Clio.*—Employment! There is not a goddess so harrassed as I am; my sisters lead quite idle lives in comparison. Melpomene has in a manner slept through the last half-century, except when now and then she dictated to a certain favourite nymph.[3] Urania, indeed, has employed herself with Herschel in counting the stars;[4] but her task is less than mine. Here am I expected to calculate how many hundred thousands of rational beings cut one another's throats at Austerlitz, and to take the tale of two hundred and thirteen thousand human bodies and ninety-five thousand horses, that lie stiff, frozen and unburied on the

---

1 Traditional histories dealt at length with the acts of monarchs; Clio is unable to do that because most European monarchs have been overthrown and sent into exile by French invasion or domestic revolution.

2 Jacques Necker, Minister of Finance at the start of the Revolution, was dismissed after one year; Honoré-Gabriel Riquetti, comte de Mirabeau, orator and leader in the National Assembly, died suddenly in 1791; Charles-François Dumouriez, Minister of Foreign Affairs and then General of the French army in 1792, defected in April 1793; the gigantic figure is Napoleon Bonaparte. For the marquis de LaFayette, see Barbauld's "Hymn: 'Ye are the Salt of the Earth,'" ll. 47-48.

3 Melpomene is the Muse of Tragedy; her favorite nymph is Joanna Baillie (1762-1851), author of admired tragedies.

4 Sir William Herschel (1738-1822) and his sister Caroline, astronomers, undertook to count all the visible stars. Urania is the Muse of Astronomy.

banks of the Berecina;[1]—and do you think, Mercury, this can be a pleasant employment?

*Mercury.*—I have had a great increase of employment myself lately, on account of the multitude of shades I have been obliged to convey; and poor old Charon is almost laid up with the rheumatism: we used to have a holiday comparatively during the winter months; but of late, winter and summer I have observed are much alike to heroes.[2]

*Clio.*—I wish to Jupiter I could resign my office! Son of Maia,[3] I declare to you I am sick of the horrors I record; I am sick of mankind. For above these three thousand years have I been warning them and reading lessons to them, and they will not mend: Robespierre was as cruel as Sylla, and Napoleon has no more moderation than Pyrrhus.[4] The human frame, of curious texture, delicately formed, feeling, and irritable by the least annoyance, with face erect and animated with Promethean fire, they wound, they lacerate, they mutilate with most perverted ingenuity.—I will go and record the actions of the tigers of Africa; in them such fierceness is natural—Nay, the human race will be exterminated if this work of destruction goes on much longer.

*Mercury.*—With regard to that matter, Clio, I can set your heart at rest. A great philosopher has lately discovered that the world is in imminent danger of being over-peopled, and that if twenty or forty thousand men could not be persuaded every now and then to stand and be shot at, we should be forced to

1  For Austerlitz see p. 470, n. 4. The most horrific episode in Napoleon's catastrophic retreat from Moscow occurred when his army had to cross the freezing river Berezina (25-29 Nov. 1812) under fire from the Russian army. We have not traced Barbauld's source for the number of casualties.

2  Charon: In classical myth, the oarsman who ferries the souls of the dead across the river Lethe into Hades. He and Mercury used to have a winter holiday because military campaigns were conducted only during the summer, but modern war is a year-round thing. This discussion of current causes of death alludes to Lucian's dialogue, "Hermes and Charon," in his *Dialogues of the Dead.*

3  Mercury's mother, Maia, in Roman religion is a goddess of all living things.

4  Maximilien Robespierre (1758-94) presided over the Reign of Terror in the French Revolution; Lucius Cornelius Sulla (miscalled "Sylla," 138-78 BC), as dictator of Rome, purged his opponents. Pyrrhus (c. 318-272 BC) won victories at great expense of human life.

eat one another. This discovery has had a wonderful effect in quieting tender consciences.[1] The calculation is very simple, any schoolboy will explain it to you.

*Clio.*—O what a number of fertile plains and green savannahs, and tracts covered with trees of beautiful foliage, have never yet been pressed by human footsteps! My friend Swift's project of eating children[2] was not so cruel as these bloody and lavish sacrifices to Mars, the most savage of all the gods.

*Mercury.*—You forget yourself, Clio; Mars is not worshiped now in Christian Europe.

*Clio.*—By Jupiter but he is! Have I not seen the bloody and torn banners, with martial music and military procession, brought into the temple,—and whose temple, thinkest thou? and to whom have thanks been given on both sides, amidst smoking towns and wasted fields, after the destruction of man and devastation of the fair face of nature![3]—And Mercury, god of wealth and frauds, you have your temple too, though your name is not inscribed there.[4]

*Mercury.*—I am afraid men will always love wealth.

*Clio.*—O if I had to record only such pure names as a Washington or a Howard![5]

---

1  The philosopher is Thomas Malthus (1766-1834), whose *Essay on the Principle of Population* (1798) argued that population, if allowed to multiply unchecked, inevitably outstrips its food supply. The book was ill-received by liberals because it undercut their optimism about human progress and seemed to legitimize the atrocities of war. Isobel Armstrong remarks that the premise of "Dialogue in the Shades" parodies Malthus: the multiplying facts of history, like an unchecked population, have outstripped Clio's resources ("The Gush of the Feminine," p. 20).

2  Jonathan Swift's "A Modest Proposal" (1729) ironically proposes that the Irish poor solve their own population problem by eating their children. Swift is Clio's friend because he also wrote a work of history.

3  Mars: Roman god of war. The practice of bringing captured enemy banners with martial fanfare into the Cathedral of Notre Dame in Paris was noticed by Voltaire in *The Age of Louis XIV*, Chap. 16; Voltaire also remarks on "those indecisive battles for which each side sings the *Te Deum*, but whose only result is the slaughter of men" (*Age of Louis XIV*, p. 209). Barbauld's indignation at the hypocrisy of mixing religion with war is memorably expressed in *Sins of Government, Sins of the Nation*.

4  Mercury is associated in mythology with commerce; his modern temple is the Stock Exchange.

5  George Washington, General of the American army and first President of the United States, perceived by English liberals as a model of wise and patriotic statesmanship; John Howard (1723-90), philanthropist and prison reformer, one of Barbauld's heroes.

*Mercury.*—It would be very gratifying, certainly; but then, Clio, you would have very little to do, and might almost as well burn your roll.


## ON FEMALE STUDIES

[In 1787 Barbauld began to take female pupils. Some were daughters of neighbors and friends, others came from a distance and boarded with her for weeks or months at a time. Much of her instruction took the form of correspondence with her pupils. The pupil—or prospective pupil—to whom these two letters were written is not identified, and we are unable to date the letters. They were published by Lucy Aikin in *Legacy* (1826), pp. 41-56; the title is probably hers.

"On Female Studies" has been received as Barbauld's considered pronouncement on women's education, and cited as evidence of her supposed conservatism on that subject. A more nuanced reading would suggest that Barbauld was simply being cautious: she does not yet know the young lady with whom she is opening correspondence, so she sticks to general and widely-received ideas. Her statements are mostly factual rather than prescriptive: it was, for example, a fact that women were not called on to practice professions such as law or medicine. Barbauld registers the fact with a certain tight-lipped dryness that does not suggest approval. At the same time, in asserting the primacy of motherhood as women's social role she concurs with Mary Wollstonecraft. And she aligns herself with the older feminism of Mary Astell when she counsels her pupil to use intellectual attainments to create a sphere of inner autonomy from which to judge men.]

My Dear Young Friend,

If I had not been afraid you would feel some little reluctance in addressing me first, I should have asked you to begin the correspondence between us; for I am at present ignorant of your particular pursuits: I cannot guess whether you are climbing the hill of science, or wandering among the flowers of fancy; whether you are stretching your powers to embrace the planetary system, or examining with a curious eye the delicate veinings of a green leaf, and the minute ramifications of a sea-weed; or whether you are toiling through the intricate and thorny mazes of grammar.[1] Whichever of these is at present your employment, your general aim no doubt is the improvement of your mind; and we will therefore spend some time in considering what kind and degree of literary attainments sit gracefully upon the female character.

Every woman should consider herself as sustaining the general character of a rational being, as well as the more confined one belonging to the female sex;[2] and therefore the motives for acquiring general knowledge and cultivating the taste are nearly the same to both sexes. The line of separation between the studies of a young man and a young woman appears to me to be chiefly fixed by this,—that a woman is excused from all professional knowledge. Professional knowledge means all that is necessary to fit a man for a peculiar[3] profession or business. Thus men study in order to qualify themselves for the law, for physic, for various departments in political life, for instructing others from the pulpit or the professor's chair. These all require a great deal of severe study and technical knowledge; much of

---

1 Barbauld assumes that a young lady may study astronomy or botany. Astronomy was recommended by Hester Chapone in her 1773 *Letters on the Improvement of the Mind*; botany, however, was regarded by real conservatives as too sexually suggestive for a young lady to study.

2 Cf. Mary Wollstonecraft: "… [T]heir first duty is to themselves as rational creatures, and the next, in point of importance, as citizens, is that, which includes so many, of a mother" (*Rights of Woman*, p. 257).

3 I.e., particular.

which is nowise valuable in itself, but as a means to that particular profession. Now as a woman can never be called to any of these professions, it is evident you have nothing to do with such studies. A woman is not expected to understand the mysteries of politics, because she is not called to govern; she is not required to know anatomy, because she is not to perform surgical operations; she need not embarrass herself with theological disputes, because she will neither be called upon to make nor to explain creeds.

Men have various departments in active life; women have but one, and all women have the same, differently modified indeed by their rank in life and other incidental circumstances. It is, to be a wife, a mother, a mistress of a family. The knowledge belonging to these duties is your professional knowledge, the want of which nothing will excuse. Literary knowledge therefore, in men, is often an indispensable duty; in women it can be only a desirable accomplishment. In women it is more immediately applied to the purposes of adorning and improving the mind, of refining the sentiments, and supplying proper stores for conversation. For general knowledge women have in some respects more advantages than men. Their avocations often allow them more leisure; their sedentary way of life disposes them to the domestic quiet amusement of reading; the share they take in the education of their children throws them in the way of books. The uniform tenor and confined circle of their lives makes them eager to diversify the scene by descriptions which open to them a new world; and they are eager to gain an idea of scenes on the busy stage of life from which they are shut out by their sex. It is likewise particularly desirable for women to be able to give spirit and variety to conversation by topics drawn from the stores of literature, as the broader mirth and more boisterous gaiety of the other sex are to them prohibited. As their parties must be innocent, care should be taken that they do not stagnate into insipidity. I will venture to add, that the purity and simplicity of heart which a woman ought never, in her freest commerce with the world, to wear off; her very seclusion from the jarring interests and coarser amusements of society,—fit her in a peculiar manner for the worlds of fancy and sentiment, and dispose her to the quickest relish of what is pathetic, sublime, or tender. To you, therefore, the beauties of poetry, of moral painting, and all in general that is comprised under the term of polite literature, lie particularly open, and you cannot neglect them without neglecting a very copious source of enjoyment.

Languages are on some accounts particularly adapted to female study, as they may be learnt at home without experiments or apparatus, and without interfering with the habits of domestic life; as they form the style, and as they are the immediate inlet to works of taste. But the learned languages, the Greek especially, require a great deal more time than a young woman can conveniently spare. To the Latin there is not an equal objection; and if a young person has leisure, has an opportunity of learning it at home by being connected with literary people, and is placed in a circle of society sufficiently liberal to allow her such an accomplishment, I do not see, if she has a strong inclination, why she should not make herself mistress of so rich a store of original entertainment:—it will not in the present state of things excite either a smile or a stare in fashionable company.[1] To those who do not intend to learn the language, I would strongly recommend the learning so much of the grammar of it as will explain the name and nature of cases, genders, inflexion of verbs, &c.; of which, having only the imperfect rudiments in our own language, a mere English scholar can with difficulty form a clear idea. This is the more necessary, as all our grammars, being written by men whose early studies had given them a partiality for the learned languages, are formed more upon those than upon the real genius of our own tongue.

I was going now to mention French, but perceive I have written a letter long enough to frighten a young correspondent, and for the present I bid you adieu.

---

1   Barbauld recalls with very dry irony the time in her youth when a young lady's knowing Latin would have excited a smile or a stare. She had with difficulty prevailed on her father to teach her Latin, and had gained a slight acquaintance with Greek (Aikin, "Memoir," p. vii).

## Letter II

French you are not only permitted to learn, but you are laid under the same necessity of acquiring it as your brother is of acquiring Latin. Custom has made the one as much expected from an accomplished woman, as the other from a man who has had a liberal education. The learning French, or indeed any language completely, includes reading, writing, and speaking it. But here I must take the liberty to offer my ideas, which differ something from those generally entertained, and you will give them what weight you think they deserve.[1] It seems to me that the efforts of young ladies in learning French are generally directed to what is unattainable; and if attained, not very useful,—the speaking it. It is utterly impossible, without such advantages as few enjoy, to speak a foreign language with fluency and a proper accent; and if even by being in a French family some degree of both is attained, it is soon lost by mixing with the world at large. As to the French which girls are obliged to speak at boarding-schools, it does very well to speak in England, but at Paris it would probably be less understood than English itself.

I do not mean by this to say that the speaking of French is not a very elegant accomplishment; and to those who mean to spend some time in France, or who being in very high life often see foreigners of distinction, it may be necessary; but in common life it is very little so: and for English people to meet together to talk a foreign language is truly absurd. There is a sarcasm against this practice as old as Chaucer's time—

> .... Frenche she spake ful fayre and fetisely,
> After the schole of Stratford atte Bowe,
> For Frenche of Paris was to her unknowe.[2]

---

1  Barbauld will reject the customary boarding-school teaching of French, which emphasized speaking it as an "accomplishment," in favor of the utilitarian, and traditional Dissenting, practice of learning a language in order to read it.
2  *Canterbury Tales*: "General Prologue," ll. 124-26.

But with regard to reading French, the many charming publications in that language, particularly in polite literature, of which you can have no adequate idea by translation, render it a very desirable acquisition. Writing it is not more useful in itself than speaking, except a person has foreign letters to write; but it is necessary for understanding the language grammatically and fixing the rules in the mind. A young person who reads French with ease and is so well grounded as to write it grammatically, and has what I should call a good English pronunciation of it, will by a short residence in France gain fluency and the accent;[1] whereas one not grounded would soon forget all she had learned, though she had acquired some fluency in speaking. For speaking, therefore, love and cultivate your own: know all its elegancies, its force, its happy turns of expression, and possess yourself of all its riches. In foreign languages you have only to learn; but with regard to your own, you have probably to unlearn, and to avoid vulgarisms and provincial barbarisms.[2]

If after you have learned French you should wish to add Italian, the acquisition will not be difficult. It is valuable on account of its poetry, in which it far excels the French,—and its music. The other modern languages you will hardly attempt, except led to them by some peculiar bent.

History affords a wide field of entertaining and useful reading. The chief thing to be attended to in studying it, is to gain a clear well-arranged idea of facts in chronological order, and illustrated by a knowledge of the places where such facts happened. Never read without tables[3] and maps: make abstracts of

---

1 Barbauld presumably wrote from experience, having resided in France for nine months herself.

2 Provincial barbarisms: regional turns of phrase regarded as unfashionable in polished society. The regional dialects of England were much more marked then than now, and their respectability was debated: James Boswell, a Scot, prided himself on having purged his speech of "Scotticisms," and Barbauld's niece Lucy Aikin was taught strictly not to learn "Norfolk" (Lucy Aikin, *Memoirs, Miscellanies, and Letters*, p. xiv). Barbauld herself, however, once urged a friend to let her child speak Norfolk (*Works*, 2:80–81).

3 Such as Joseph Priestley's popular *Chart of Biography* (1765) and *New Chart of History* (1769).

what you read. Before you embarrass yourself in the detail of this, endeavour to fix well in your mind the arrangement of some leading facts, which may serve as landmarks to which to refer the rest. Connect the history of different countries together. In the study of history the different genius of a woman I imagine will show itself. The detail of battles, the art of sieges, will not interest her so much as manners and sentiment; this is the food she assimilates to herself.[1]

The great laws of the universe, the nature and properties of those objects which surround us, it is unpardonable not to know: it is more unpardonable to know, and not to feel the mind struck with lively gratitude.[2] Under this head are comprehended natural history, astronomy, botany, experimental philosophy, chemistry, physics. In these you will rather take what belongs to sentiment and utility than abstract calculations or difficult problems. You must often be content to know a thing is so, without understanding the proof. It belongs to a Newton to prove his sublime problems, but we may all be made acquainted with the result.[3] You cannot investigate; you may remember. This will teach you not to despise common things, will give you an interest in every thing you see. If you are feeding your poultry, or tending your bees, or extracting the juice of herbs, with an intelligent mind you are gaining real knowledge; it will open to you an inexhaustible fund of wonder and delight, and effectually prevent you from depending for your entertainment on the poor novelties of fashion and expense.

But of all reading, what most ought to engage your attention are works of sentiment and morals. Morals is that study in which alone both sexes have an equal interest; and in sentiment yours has even the advantage. The works of this kind often

---

1   Barbauld's deprecation of war as a subject of interest for women is consistent with her other antiwar writings, from "Written on a Marble" through "Dialogue in the Shades."

2   Gratitude for God's providential arrangement of the world. Like many Dissenters, Barbauld regarded science as a means to the knowledge and worship of God.

3   Sir Isaac Newton (1642-1727), founder of modern physics. Barbauld's view is identical with that of Lady Mary Wortley Montagu (in a letter to her daughter, 28 Jan. 1753); perhaps Barbauld read the 1803 edition of Montagu's letters in which it was published.

appear under the seducing form of novel and romance: here great care, and the advice of your older friends is requisite in the selection. Whatever is true, however uncouth in the manner or dry in the subject, has a value from being true: but fiction in order to recommend itself must give us *la belle Nature*.[1] You will find fewer plays fit for your perusal than novels, and fewer comedies than tragedies.[2]

What particular share any one of the studies I have mentioned may engage of your attention will be determined by your peculiar turn and bent of mind. But I shall conclude with observing, that a woman ought to have that general tincture of them all which marks the cultivated mind. She ought to have enough of them to engage gracefully in general conversation. In no subject is she required to be deep,—of none ought she to be ignorant. If she knows not enough to speak well, she should know enough to keep her from speaking at all; enough to feel her ground and prevent her from exposing her ignorance; enough to hear with intelligence, to ask questions with propriety, and to receive information where she is not qualified to give it. A woman who to a cultivated mind joins that quickness of intelligence and delicacy of taste which such a woman often possesses in a superior degree, with that nice sense of propriety which results from the whole, will have a kind of *tact* by which she will be able on all occasions to discern between pretenders to science and men of real merit. On subjects upon which she cannot talk herself, she will know whether a man talks with knowledge of his subject. She will not judge of systems, but by their systems[3] she will be able to judge of men. She will distinguish the modest, the dogmatical, the affected, the over-refined, and give her esteem and confidence accordingly. She will know with whom to confide the education of her children, and how to judge of their progress and the methods used to

---

1  Idealized Nature.

2  Cf. Barbauld's comment on Sheridan's comedy, *The School for Scandal* (1777): "one of the wittiest plays I remember to have seen; and I am sorry to add, one of the most immoral and licentious;—in principle I mean, for in language it is very decent" (*Works*, 2:19).

3  Philosophies.

improve them. From books, from conversation, from learned instructors, she will gather the flower of every science;[1] and her mind, in assimilating every thing to itself, will adorn it with new graces. She will give the tone to the conversation even when she chooses to bear but an inconsiderable part in it. The modesty which prevents her from an unnecessary display of what she knows, will cause it to be supposed that her knowledge is deeper than in reality it is:—as when the landscape is seen through the veil of a mist, the bounds of the horizon are hid. As she will never obtrude her knowledge, none will ever be sensible of any deficiency in it, and her silence will seem to proceed from discretion rather than a want of information. She will seem to know every thing by leading every one to speak of what he knows; and when she is with those to whom she can give no real information, she will yet delight them by the original turns of thought and sprightly elegance which will attend her manner of speaking on any subject. Such is the character to whom profest scholars will delight to give information, from whom others will equally delight to receive it:—the character I wish you to become, and to form which your application must be directed.

---

1  Barbauld here describes her own education—as well as the training of most educated women of her generation.

of Epictetus *(London: Millar, Rivington, and*
*Dodsley, 1758), Book IV, Chapter 6 ("Concerning*
*Those who grieve at being pitied")*

[Barbauld drew the motto to her essay "Against Inconsistency in our Expectations" from this famous work by the admired Bluestocking writer Elizabeth Carter. Her essay may be seen as an homage to Carter; in it Barbauld aligns herself with a British tradition of feminist stoicism practised by Carter and by her precursor, Mary Astell.]

"What says *Antisthenes* then? Have you never heard? It is Kingly, O *Cyrus,* to do well, and to be ill spoken of." My Head is well, and all around me think it akes. What is that to *me*? I am free from a Fever; and they compassionate me, as if I had one. "Poor Soul, what a long while have you had this Fever!" I say too, with a dismal Countenance, Ay, indeed, it is now a long time that I have been ill.— "What can be the Consequence then?"—What pleases God. And at the same time I secretly laugh at them, who pity me. What forbids then, but that the same may be done in the other Case? I am poor: but I have right Principles concerning Poverty. What is it to me then, if People pity me for my Poverty? I am not in Power, and others are: but I have such Opinions as I ought to have concerning Power, and the Want of Power. Let them see to it, who pity me. But I am neither hungry, nor thirsty, nor cold. But, because they are hungry and thirsty, they suppose me to be so too. What can I do for them then? Am I to go about, making Proclamation, and saying, Do not deceive yourselves, good People, I am very well: I regard neither Poverty, nor Want of Power, nor any thing else, but right Principles. These I possess unrestrained. I care for nothing farther.—But what Trifling is this? How have I right Principles, when I am not contented to be what I am; but am out of my Wits, how I shall appear?—But others will get more, and be preferred to me.—Why, what is more reasonable, than that they who take Pains for any thing, should get most in that Particular, in which they take Pains? They have taken Pains for Power; you, for right Principles: they, for Riches; you, for a proper Use of the Appearances of Things. See whether they have the Advantage of you in that, for which you have taken Pains, and which they neglect: if they assent better, concerning the natural Bounds and Limits of Things; if their Desires are less disappointed than yours, their Aversions less incurred; if they take a better Aim in their Intention, in their Purposes, in their Pursuits: whether they preserve a becoming Behaviour, as Men, as Sons, as Parents, and so on in respect of the other Relations of Life. But, if they are in Power, and you not: why will you not speak the Truth to yourself; that *you* do nothing for the Sake of Power; but that *they* do every thing? And it is very unreasonable, that he who carefully seeks any thing, should be less successful than he who neglects it.— "No: but, since I take Care to have right Principles, it is more reasonable, that I should have Power."—Yes, in respect to what you take Care about, your Principles. But give up to others the Things, in which they have taken more Care than you. Else it is just as if, because you have right Principles, you should think it fit, that, when you shoot an Arrow, you should hit the Mark better than an Archer, or that you should forge better than a Smith. Therefore let alone taking Pains about Principles, and apply yourself to the Things which you wish to possess, and then fall a crying, if you do not succeed; for you deserve to cry. But now you say, that you are engaged in other Things; intent upon other Things: and it is a true Saying, that one Business doth not suit with another. One Man, as soon as he rise and goes out, seeks to whom he may pay his Compliments; whom he may flatter; to whom he may send a Present; how he may please the Dancer [in Vogue]; how, by doing ill-natured Offices to one, he may oblige another. When-ever he prays, he prays for Things like these: when-ever he sacrifices, he sacrifices for Things like these….

But on the other hand, if you have in reality been careful about nothing else, but to make a right Use of the Appearance of Things; as soon as you are up in a Morning, consider, what do I want in order to be free from Passion? What, to enjoy Tranquillity? What am I? Am I mere worthless Body? Am I Estate? Am I Reputation? None of these. What then? I am a reasonable Creature. What then is required of me? Recollect your Actions. *Where have I failed*, in any Requisite for Prosperity? *What have I done*, either unfriendly, or unsociable? *What have I omitted*, that was necessary in these Points?

Since there is so much Difference then in your Desires, your Actions, your Wishes, would you yet have an equal Share with others in those Things, about which you have not taken Pains, and they have? And do you wonder, after all, and are you out of Humour, if they pity you? But they are not out of Humour, if you pity them. Why? Because they are convinced, that they are in Possession of their proper Good; but you are not convinced that you are. Hence you are not contented with your own Condition; but desire theirs: whereas they are contented with theirs, and do not desire yours. For, if you were really convinced, that it is *you* who are in Possession of what is good, and that *they* are mistaken, you would not so much as think what they say about you (pp. 390-93).

## Appendix B: The Debate on Repeal of the Test and Corporation Acts, 1787-1790

[The Corporation Act (1661) and the Test Act (1673) were enacted for the purpose of excluding avowed non-members of the Church of England (i.e., Dissenters, whether Protestant or Catholic) from elective offices in towns (corporations) and appointive offices under the Crown. (The Acts are described in Item 1 below.) Although the Toleration Act of 1689 permitted public worship to Protestant Dissenters, it did not set aside these two Acts; and although, after the Hanoverian succession to the throne in 1714 the Acts were seldom enforced against Protestants, they remained law until 1828. In 1787, 1789, and 1790 motions were offered in Parliament to repeal the Acts. As background to Barbauld's *Address to the Opposers of the Repeal*, we offer three selections from pertinent debates. Henry Beaufoy's 1787 speech, of which we give excerpts, describes the Acts and presents the case for their repeal. Edmund Burke's speech during a debate on the Army budget inaugurates his long and influential hostility to domestic reform, premised on fear that English reformers would follow the "evil" example of France. William Pitt's speech against repeal in the 1790 debate exemplifies the fears of conservatives that repeal would undermine the Established Church.]

1. From *The Substance of the Speech delivered by Henry Beaufoy, Esq. in the House of Commons, Upon the 28th of March, 1787, on his Motion for the Repeal of the Test and Corporation Acts ...* **(London: Cadell and Robinsons, 1787).**

Three different classes of our fellow-subjects are aggrieved by those provisions in our laws of which I shall propose the repeal.

The first is composed of all those Englishmen who are Dissenters from the Church of England.

The second is composed of all the members of the established Church of Scotland.

The third consists of all those respectable clergymen of the Church of England, who think that the prostitution of the most solemn ordinance of their faith to the purposes of a Civil Test, is little less than a sacrilegious abuse.

Of these several descriptions of my fellow citizens, entitled as they all are to particular regard, the Dissenters have the first claim to my attention; for they have publicly requested,—a request which they confined to their own case, lest they should be thought presumptuous in expressing the complaints of others—they have publicly requested that I would submit to the consideration of parliament, the propriety of relieving, from penalties of disqualification and reproach, so many hundred thousands of his Majesty's ardently loyal and affectionate subjects... (pp. 2-3).

They humbly solicit a restoration of their *Civil Rights*, not an enlargement of their *Ecclesiastical Privileges*. It is of consequence that this fact should be distinctly stated, and clearly understood; for the very word Dissenter leads, so naturally, to the supposition that their complaints are of an ecclesiastical kind; and their acknowledged merit as citizens, so naturally excludes the idea of its being possible that the law should have deprived them of any of their civil rights, that I feel myself under a necessity of stating ... that their prayer has nothing ecclesiastical for its object. They wish not to diminish the provision which the legislature has made for the established church, nor do they envy her the revenue she enjoys, or the ecclesiastical privileges of dignity and honour with which she is invested... (p. 6).

The disabilities which the law has imposed on the Dissenters, are contained in the provisions of two Acts of Parliament, that were passed in the reign of King Charles the Second, and which are generally known by the name of the Test and Corporation Acts....

The Corporation Act declares, that no person shall be elected into any corporation office [i.e. public office in a town], who shall not, within one year before such election, have taken the sacrament of the Lord's Supper, according to the usage of the Church of England.

The Test Act declares, that every person who accepts a civil office or a commission in the army or navy, and who does not within the time prescribed by the Act, take the Sacrament of the Lord's Supper, according to the usage of the Church of England, shall be disabled in law ... from occupying any such civil office, or from holding any such military commission; and if, without taking the sacramental qualification within the time prescribed by the Act, he does continue to occupy a civil office, or to hold a military commission, and is lawfully convicted, then, Sir, (and I beg leave to intreat the attention of the House to this most extraordinary punishment) then, he not only incurs a large pecuniary penalty, but is disabled from thenceforth, for ever, from bringing any action in course of law, from prosecuting any suit in any court of equity, from being guardian of any child, or executor or administrator of any person, as well as from receiving any legacy... (pp. 8-9).

Am I told that the Dissenters may avoid the penalties of the law merely by taking the Sacrament? What is this but to say, that they may avoid the disabilities imposed upon Dissenters by ceasing to be Dissenters; that they may escape the disadvantages annexed to their religion by renouncing their religion; that they may relieve themselves from the punishment imposed upon their Faith, by becoming apostates to that Faith. They do not deserve the insult of such a reply... (p. 12).

"But," I am asked, "Does not the Act of Indemnity, an Act which, for the most part, is annually passed, protect from the penalties of the Test and Corporation Laws, all such persons as have offended against them?"—Sir, if the Indemnity Act *does* protect from the dreadful penalties of those statutes, all such persons as have executed civil offices, or have held commissions in the army or the navy, without the sacramental qualification, then, what inconvenience can arise from a repeal of the statutes themselves? If, by the annual Indemnity Act, the execution of the law is relinquished, where is the objection to a repeal of the law itself?—To preserve the claim of a Test from the Dissenters, when the exercise of the claim is abandoned, may answer the purposes of *irritation*, but cannot answer the purposes of *power*. The claim, in that case, operates merely as a corrosive to a wound that otherwise would heal; it stimulates jealousies that otherwise would sleep; it agitates passions that otherwise would be at rest ... (pp. 26-27).

Since then the Dissenters have a right, as *men*, to think for themselves in matters of religion; and since they have a right, as *citizens*, to a common chance with their fellow-subjects for office[s] of civil and military trust, if their Sovereign should deem them worthy of his confidence, the only remaining question is, does the public good require, do the ends of civil society require that these rights should be superseded, and that the Dissenters should be excluded from the service of the state?

That a regard to the general good controuls all other considerations is readily admitted; and therefore all arguments to prove this point, if any such should be urged, will be very superfluous. But then it is equally certain that considerations of general good can never justify any invasion of civil rights that is not essential to that good: the ends of civil society can never justify any abridgement of natural rights that is not essential to these ends. If then I shall be able clearly to demonstrate that the continuance of those Acts which invade the rights of the Dissenters, is not necessary to the general good of the kingdom; is not necessary to the well being of the state; is not necessary to the establishment of the national church, then it will follow, as a certain conclusion, that they ought to be repealed....

To shew how unnecessary, how very useless the exclusion of the Dissenters from the offices of executive power demonstrably is, it will be sufficient to remark that to the higher trust of legislative authority, the Dissenters are admitted without hesitation or reserve. Of that power which controuls the executive, they have, equally with their fellow-citizens, a full and free participation. From the Members of this House, from the Members of the House of Peers, no religious test is required. Is then the taking the sacrament unnecessary in the legislators of the kingdom, who hold in their hands the lives and fortunes of their countrymen, and can it be requisite from the commissioners of the common sewers? Is the profession of a particular faith of more consequence in an exciseman than in a member of the House of Commons? Or must the office of a land-waiter be guarded by other proofs of attachment to the church than those which are deemed sufficient from a peer. Are oaths without the sacrament, an adequate security from innovation, when administered to those who may change the established religion if they will; and are not the same oaths equally sufficient when administered to those who have no power to introduce the smallest alteration?

The advocates for the continuance of the Test Act are reduced to this obvious dilemma. If they say that the state can never be secure unless the test of the sacrament be demanded from the legislators of the country, experience refutes their assertion. If they say that the security of the state requires from *executive officers* a stronger pledge than is requisite from *legislators*; that it requires a stronger pledge from those who *cannot* change the established religion, than it does from those who *can*, the assertion refutes itself.

I have heard of an idle opinion, that there is something of a republican tendency, something of an antimonarchical bias in the very doctrines of the Presbyterian church. In reply to that opinion, if indeed it deserves a reply, I appeal to the principles and practice of the inhabitants of that part of the island in which the Presbyterian church is established by law. Are the Scots suspected of an indifference to monarchy? Are they accused of an unwillingness to support the dignity and power of the sovereign? Is the prerogative of the crown that part of the constitution which they are the least anxious to uphold? I have heard them taxed with a predilection for those maxims of policy which are the most favourable to *power*; but of *levelling* principles, of *republican* attachments, I have never heard them accused.

Or if we speak of the English Dissenters, who will deny that, from the time that the establishment of William the Third on the throne of England [1689], gave her a constitution, ... the Dissenters have uniformly acted on principles the most constitutional, and have constantly proved themselves the ardent friends, the active supporters, the firm and faithful adherents of that system of monarchy which was then established by law? Or who will deny that from the accession of his Majesty's family to the crown [1714], no class of his subjects have shewn themselves more fervently attached to the person of the sovereign?... (pp. 28-31).

Whoever then shall be of opinion, that the general voice of all the enlightened nations of Europe is deserving of regard—Whoever shall admit that the exertions of the *whole* kingdom will have greater avail than its *mutilated* strength—whoever is convinced that *union* is better than *separation*; that *power* is preferable to *weakness*, and that national *justice* is the surest ground of national *prosperity*, will agree with me in thinking that the law which excludes the Dissenters from civil and military employments ought to be repealed... (p. 49).

**2. From the report of Edmund Burke's speech in Parliament during the Debate on the Army Estimates, 5 February 1790 (*The Parliamentary History of England* ... [London: Longman et al., 1816], 28:351-71).**

... France had hitherto been our first object, in all considerations concerning the balance of power. The presence or absence of France totally varied every sort of speculation relative to that balance.

... France is, at this time, in a political light to be considered as expunged out of the system of Europe. Whether she could ever appear in it again, as a leading power, was not easy to determine: but at present he considered France as not politically existing ... (col. 353).

Since the House had been prorogued in the summer, much work was done in France. The French had shown themselves the ablest architects of ruin that had hitherto existed in the world. In that very short space of time, they had completely pulled down to the ground their monarchy, their church, their nobility, their law, their revenue, their army, their navy, their commerce, their arts, and their manufactures....

France, by the mere circumstance of its vicinity, had been, and in a degree always must be, an object of our vigilance, either with regard to her actual power, or to her influence and example.... [A]s to the latter (her example), he should say a few words: for by this example, our friendship and our intercourse with that nation had once been, and might again become, more dangerous to us than their worst hostility... (col. 354).

In the last age, we were in danger of being entangled by the example of France in the net of a relentless despotism. It is not necessary to say any thing upon that example; it exists no longer. Our present danger from the example of a people, whose character knows no medium, is, with regard to government, a danger from anarchy; a danger of being led through an admiration of successful fraud and violence, to an imitation of the excesses of an irrational, unprincipled, proscribing, confiscating, plundering, ferocious, bloody, and tyrannical democracy. On the side of religion, the danger of their example is no longer from intolerance, but from atheism; a foul, unnatural vice, foe to all the dignity and consolation of mankind; which seems in France, for a long time, to have been embodied into a faction, accredited, and almost avowed... (col. 355).

... [H]e thought the French nation very unwise. What they valued themselves on, was a disgrace to them. They had gloried (and some people in England had thought fit to take share in that glory) in making a revolution: as if revolutions were good things in themselves. All the horrors, and all the crimes of the anarchy which led to their revolution, which attend its progress, and which may virtually attend it in its establishment, pass for nothing with the lovers of revolutions... (col. 357).

[The French,] with the most atrocious perfidy and breach of all faith among men, laid the axe to the root of all property, and consequently of all national prosperity, by the principles they established, and the example they set, in confiscating all the possessions of the church. They made and recorded a sort of institute and digest of anarchy, call the rights of man, in such a pedantic abuse of elementary principles as would have disgraced boys at school; but this declaration of rights was worse than trifling and pedantic in them; as by their name and authority they systematically destroyed every hold of authority by opinion, religious or civil, on the minds of the people....

... [I]f they should perfectly succeed in what they propose, as they are likely enough to do, and establish a democracy, or a mob of democracies, in a country circumstanced like France, they will establish a very bad government; a very bad species of tyranny... (col. 358).

He felt some concern that this strange thing, called a revolution in France, should be compared with the glorious event, commonly called the revolution in England (col. 361). [Burke refers to a sermon delivered by the eminent Dissenting minister Richard Price on 4 November 1789, the anniversary of the "Glorious Revolution" of 1689 which banished James II, in which Price had congratulated the French on achieving their liberty and prophesied an end to monarchical absolutism in Europe.].

... [H]e was concerned to find that there were persons in this country, who entertained theories of government, incompatible with the safety of the state, and who were, perhaps, ready to transfer a part, at least, of that anarchy which prevailed in France, to this kingdom, for the purpose of effectuating their designs (cols. 370-71).

### 3. From the speech of William Pitt in *The Debate in the House of Commons, on the Repeal of the Corporation and Test Acts, March 2d, 1790* .... (London: John Stockdale, 1790), pp. 14-22.

... [T]he point at issue between them, simply and plainly was, whether the House should or should not, at once relinquish those Acts which had, by the wisdom of our ancestors, served as a bulwark to the Church, the Constitution of which was so connected and interwoven with the interests and preservation of the Constitution of the State, that the former could not be endangered without hazarding the safety of the latter.

... Toleration by no means could be considered as equality; it differed from persecution, and it differed from an establishment: to avoid and abstain no man could be more ready to consent, and he was equally willing to grant every protection of the laws in support of the religion and property of individuals; but the necessity of a certain, permanent, and specifick Church Establishment, rendered it essential, that Toleration should not go to an equality which would endanger the establishment, and thence no longer be Toleration (p. 15).

... [I]n a country like this, where the Monarchy was limited, it was particularly necessary that the Executive Power should be admitted to exercise a right of discrimination into the fitness of individuals to fill those stations for which the Executive Power was responsible: the necessity of public offices for the benefit of the public at large justified a distinction in the distribution for the same reason, namely, the benefit of the publick; the idea of a right in any then to fill those offices, was ridiculous, no such thing could exist ... (p. 16).

It was not ... necessary ... to prove, that there ought to be an Established Church, as that was admitted on all sides the House .... He need not ... prove that the Dissenters would exercise power if put in possession of it, since the possession of power always produced the inclination to exercise it; and, without meaning to throw any stigma on the Dissenters, he could not hesitate a moment in supposing it probable that they might feel inclined to exercise their power to the subversion of the Established Church; it would be so far from reprehensible in them, that, possessing the principles they profess, and acting conscientiously upon those principles, it would become their duty, as honest men, to make the endeavour ... (p. 18).

He did not think ... that were Dissenters successful in this application, they would be desirous of proceeding no further; for ... some among them hav[e] openly declared their disaffection to the Constitution of the Church. There was sufficient ground, then, for alarm from such declarations, and it was the duty of the House to stand against the danger; in so doing, however, he would not refuse the Dissenters any right that belonged to them, nor refuse them any harmless regulation they might request, or any regulation which clearly led not to dangerous consequences (p. 19).

## Appendix C: The Royal Proclamation of a Fast in April 1793 (from London Chronicle, 2-5 March 1793)

[Soon after the outbreak of war with France, the British government announced a compulsory national day of prayer and fasting to implore divine aid for success in the war. Barbauld responded to this announcement with *Sins of Government, Sins of the Nation*, in which she refers several times to the proclamation. Its text follows.]

> From *the* LONDON GAZETTE *of March 2.*
> By the KING.
> A PROCLAMATION
> *For a* GENERAL FAST.

GEORGE R.

We, taking into our most serious consideration the just and necessary war in which we are engaged with France, and putting our trust in Almighty God that he will vouchsafe a special blessing on our arms both by sea and land, have resolved, and do, by and with the advice of our Privy Council, hereby command, that a Public Fast and Humiliation be observed throughout that part of our kingdom of Great Britain called England, our dominion of Wales, and town of Berwick upon Tweed, on Friday the 19th day of April next; that so both we and our people may humble ourselves before Almighty God, in order to obtain pardon of our sins; and may, in the most devout and solemn manner, send up our prayers and supplications to the Divine Majesty, for averting those heavy judgments, which our manifold sins and provocations have most justly deserved, and imploring his blessing and assistance on our arms, and for restoring and perpetuating peace, safety and prosperity to us, and our kingdoms: And we do strictly charge and command, that the said Public Fast be reverently and devoutly observed by all our loving subjects in England, our dominion of Wales, and town of Berwick upon Tweed, as they tender the favour of Almighty God, and would avoid his wrath and indignation; and upon pain of such punishment as we may justly inflict on all such as contemn and neglect the performance of so religious and necessary a duty. And for the better and more orderly solemnizing the same, we have given directions to the Most Reverend the Archbishops, and the Right Reverend the Bishops of England, to compose a Form of Prayer suitable to this occasion, to be used in all Churches, Chapels, and places of public worship, and to take care the same be timely dispersed throughout their respective dioceses.

Given at our Court at St. James's, the 1st day of March 1793, in the 33d year of our reign.

GOD save the KING.

# Appendix D: The British Novelists: Predecessors, Contents, Allusions

[To suggest the context of *The British Novelists* in its time, we have assembled in the first part of this three-part appendix a list of previous collections of novels. Most important among them was James Harrison's *The Novelist's Magazine*, a phenomenally successful series that established for the first time a "canon" of the genre. In the second part, we list the contents of *The British Novelists* so that its canon can be compared with its predecessors.

Finally, in the third part, we list authors and works mentioned by Barbauld in "The Origin and Progress of Novel-Writing." The reader will find here those names and titles to which she refers casually in ways that require (in our judgment) no further explanation. The list is alphabetical.]

## 1. Previous Collections of Novels

I. *A Collection of Novels selected and revised by Mrs. Griffith.* 3 vols. London, 1777.

*Zayde, Oroonoko, Princess of Cleves, The Fruitless Enquiry, The History of Agnes de Castro, The Noble Slaves, The History of the Count de Belflor, Leonora de Cespedes*

II. *The Novelist's Magazine,* 1780-1789

Volume 1: *Almoran and Hamet, Joseph Andrews, Amelia*
Volume 2: *Solyman and Almena, Vicar of Wakefield, Roderick Random, Zadig, The Devil upon Two Sticks*
Volume 3: *Tales of the Genii, Tom Jones*
Volume 4: *Gil Blas, Robinson Crusoe*
Volume 5: *Tristram Shandy, Chinese Tales, The Sisters*
Volume 6: *Peregrine Pickle, Moral Tales*

Volume 7: *Fortunate Country Maid, Memoirs of a Magdalen, Letters between Theodosius and Constantia, Ferdinand Count Fathom*

Volume 8: *Don Quixote*

Volume 9: *Sentimental Journey, Gulliver's Travels, David Simple, Sir Launcelot Greaves, Letters of a Peruvian Princess, Jonathan Wild the Great*

Volume 10: *Sir Charles Grandison*

Volume 11: *Sir Charles Grandison*

Volume 12: *Female Quixote, Journey from this World to the Next, Joe Thompson, Peter Wilkins*

Volume 13: *Betsy Thoughtless, Thousand and One Days*

Volume 14: *Clarissa*

Volume 15: *Clarissa*

Volume 16: *Don Quixote* (Avellaneda's "Continuation"), *Virtuous Orphan*

Volume 17: *Adventures of Telemachus, Henrietta, Countess Osenvor, Jemmy and Jenny Jessamy*

Volume 18: *Arabian Nights Entertainments*

Volume 19: *Humphry Clinker, Pompey the Little, Ophelia, Tartarian Tales*

Volume 20: *Pamela*

Volume 21: *Peruvian Tales, Gaudentio di Lucca, Adventures of an Atom, Sincere Huron, English Hermit*

Volume 22: *Lydia, Sidney Bidulph*

Volume 23: *Rasselas, Henrietta, Nourjahad, Letters from Felicia to Charlotte, Adventures of Mr. George Edwards a Creole, Invisible Spy*

III. An advertisement in the *Morning Chronicle* (London), 26 August 1808, for "Cooke's Elegant Editions of the most esteemed and popular Works, Superbly Embellished; with numerous Engravings" lists these "Select Novels":

*Solyman and Almena, Nourjahad, Almoran and Hamet, Zadig, Sentimental Journey, Castle of Otranto, Rasselas, Theodosius and Constantia, Belisarius, Journey to the next World, Pompey the Little, Candide, Jonathan Wild, Peruvian Princess, Louisa Mildmay, Adventures of an Atom, Vicar of Wakefield, Chinese*

Tales, Tale of a Tub, Launcelot Greaves, Devil on Two Sticks, Gulliver's Travels, Sisters, Henrietta, Joseph Andrews, Female Quixote, Telemachus, Humphrey Clinker, Moral Tales, Count Fathom, Tales of the Genii, Roderic Random, Tristram Shandy, Amelia, Robinson Crusoe, Adventures of a Guinea, Gil Blas, Peregrine Pickle, Tom Jones, Arabian Nights, Don Quixote, Pamela

## 2. Anna Barbauld's *The British Novelists* (50 vols., 1810): Contents

Volumes 1-8: Samuel Richardson, *Clarissa*
Volumes 9-15: Samuel Richardson, *Sir Charles Grandison*
Volumes 16-17: Daniel Defoe, *Robinson Crusoe*
Volume 18: Henry Fielding, *Joseph Andrews*
Volumes 19-21: Henry Fielding, *Tom Jones*
Volume 22: Clara Reeve, *Old English Baron*; Horace Walpole, *Castle of Otranto*
Volume 23: Francis Coventry, *History of Pompey the Little*; Oliver Goldsmith, *Vicar of Wakefield*
Volumes 24-25: Charlotte Lennox, *Female Quixote*
Volume 26: Samuel Johnson, *Rasselas*; John Hawkesworth, *Almoran and Hamet*
Volume 27: Frances Brooke, *Julia Mandeville*; Elizabeth Inchbald, *Nature and Art*
Volume 28: Elizabeth Inchbald, *A Simple Story*
Volume 29: Henry Mackenzie, *Man of Feeling*, *Julia de Roubigné*
Volumes 30-31: Tobias Smollett, *Humphry Clinker*
Volumes 32-33: Richard Graves, *Spiritual Quixote*
Volumes 34-35: John Moore, *Zeluco*
Volumes 36-37: Charlotte Smith, *The Old Manor House*
Volumes 38-39: Frances Burney, *Evelina*
Volumes 40-41: Frances Burney, *Cecilia*
Volumes 43-44: Ann Radcliffe, *Romance of the Forest*
Volumes 45-47: Ann Radcliffe, *Mysteries of Udolpho*
Volume 48: Robert Bage, *Hermsprong*
Volumes 49-50: Maria Edgeworth, *Belinda*
Volume 50: Maria Edgeworth, *Modern Griselda*

### 3. Authors and titles mentioned in "The Origin and Progress of Novel-Writing"

*Amadis de Gaul* (fifteenth-, sixteenth-century chivalric romance [first French version by Herberay des Essarts 1540])

Apuleius (*fl.* c. AD 155): *The Golden Ass*

Ariosto, Lodovico (1474-1535): [*Orlando Furioso* (1532)]

Aristides of Miletus (second century BC): *The Milesian Tales*

Barclay, John (1582-1621): *Argenis* (1621)

Beaumont, Anne Louise Elie de: [*Letters of the Marquis de Roselle* (1764)]

Behn, Aphra (1640-89): *Oroonoko* (1688)

Berkeley, George (1685-1753): Anglo-Irish bishop; philosopher; putative author of *Gaudentio di Lucca* (1725) [actually by Simon Berington (1737)]

Boccaccio, Giovanni (1313-75): *The Decameron* (1349-51)

Boiardo, Matteo Maria (1434?-94): [*Orlando Innamorato*]

Boyle, Robert (1627-91): *The Martyrdom of Didymus and Theodora* (1687)

Boyle, Roger, Earl of Orrery (1621-79): *Parthenissa* (1654-65)

Brooke, Henry (1703-83): *Gustavus Vasa* (1739); *The Fool of Quality* (1765-70)

Buncle, John [Thomas Amory (1691-1788)]: *Memoirs containing the Lives of Several Ladies of Great Britain* (1755); *Life and Opinions of John Buncle, Esq.* (1756; 1766)

*Caleb Williams.* See Godwin.

Calprénede, Gauthier de Costes de la (1614-63): [*Cassandra* (1644-50); *Cléopâtre* (1647-56); *Pharamond* (1661-70)]

*Caroline de Litchfield* (1786): [Jeanne Isabelle Bottens, Baroness de Montolieu]

*Cent nouvelles* (1464-67): from the court of Philip, Duke of Burgundy, recorded by several hands

Cervantes, Miguel de (1547-1616): *Don Quixote* (1605; 1615); [*Novelas ejemplares* (1613)]

Chateaubriand, François-René, vicomte de (1768-1848): *Atala* (1801)

*Chrysal; or the Adventures of a Guinea* (1760-65): [Charles Johnstone (?1719-1800)]

Cotin, [Cottin], Sophie (1770-1807): *Elizabeth* (1806); *Matilde* (1805)

Crébillon *(fils)*, Claude-Prosper Jolyot de (1707-77): [*Les Égarements de coeur et de l'esprit* (1736)]

Cumberland, Richard (1732-1811): [*Arundel* (1789); *Henry* (1795)]

Day, Thomas (1748-89): *Sandford and Merton* (1783-89)

Defoe, Daniel (1660-1731): *Robinson Crusoe* (1719)

*Don Belianis of Greece*

*Don Gusman d'Alvarache* (1599): [Mateo Alemán (1547-1615)]

D'Urfé, Honoré (1567-1625): *Astrea* [*L'Astrée*] (1607-27)

Edgeworth, Maria (1768-1849): [*Castle Rackrent* (1800); *Belinda* (1801); *Leonora* (1806)]

Fénelon, François de Salignac de la Mothe (1651-1715): *Télémaque* (1699)

Fielding, Sarah (1710-68): *The Adventures of David Simple* (1744); translation of Xenophon (1762); *The Governess* (1749)

Florian, Jean-Pierre-Claris de (1755-94): *Galatée* (1783); *Gonsalve de Cordoue* (1791)

Genlis, Stéphanie Félicité Ducrest de Saint-Aubin (1746-1830): *Adele et Théodore* (1782); *Les Veillées du Chateau* (1784)

Geoffrey of Monmouth (d. 1155). *Historia Regum Britanniae* (c. 1136), translated into Fr. as *Brut d'Angleterre*.

Godwin, William (1756-1836). *Adventures of Caleb Williams* (1794); *St. Leon* (1799)

Goethe, Johann Wolfgang von (1749-1832): *Sorrows of Young Werter* (1774); [*Wilhelm Meister's Apprenticeship* (1795-96), which contains criticism on the drama.]

Graffigny, Françoise d'Issembourg d'Aponcourt de (1695-1758): *Lettres d'une Péruvienne* (1747)

Graves, Richard (1715-1804): *The Spiritual Quixote* (1773); *Columella* (1779); *Senilities, or Solitary Amusements* (1801)

Harrington, James (1611-77): *The Commonwealth of Oceana* (1656)

Haywood, Eliza (?1693-1756): *The Invisible Spy* (1755); *Betsy Thoughtless* (1751); *The Female Spectator* (1744-46)

Heliodorus (third century AD?): *Theagenes and Chariclea*

Holcroft, Thomas (1745-1809): *Anna St. Ives* (1792)

Klinger, Friedrich Maximilian von (1752-1831): [Novels on Faust legend, 1790s]

La Fayette, Marie-Madeleine de la Vergue, comtesse de (1634-93): *La Princesse de Clèves* (1678); *Zaide* (1670)

La Fontaine, August (1758-1831): *Tableaux de Famille* (1802)

Le Sage, Alain-René (1668-1747): *Gil Blas* (1715-35); *Le Diable boiteux* (1707); *Bachelier de Salamanque* (1736)

Longus (third century AD?): *Daphnis and Chloe*

Lucian (*fl.* AD 115-c. 200): to whom Barbauld mistakenly attributes authorship of *The Golden Ass*. Lucian was commonly but doubtfully identified as the author of *Lucius or the Ass*, a source of Apuleius's later work.

Mackenzie, Henry (1745-1831): *The Man of Feeling* (1771); *Julia de Roubigné* (1777)

Manley, Delarivière (1663-1774): *The New Atalantis* (1709)

Marivaux, Pierre Carlet de Chamblain de (1688-1763): *La Vie de Marianne* (1731-41); *Paisan Parvenu* (1734-35)

Marmontel, Jean-François (1723-99): *Bélisaire* (1766); *Les Incas* (1767-77)

*Modern Philosophers* [*Memoirs of Modern Philosophers* (1800)]: [Elizabeth Hamilton (1758-1816)]

More, Thomas (1477-1535): *Utopia* (1516)

Mulso, Thomas (1721-99): *Callistus, or The Man of Fashion* (1768)

Museus [Musäus] Johann Karl August (1735-87): *Popular Tales of the Germans* [*Volksmärchen der Deutschen*] (1782-86); [*Physiognomische Reisen*], satire on Lavater (1778-79)

Necker, daughter of: see Staël.

Newcastle, Margaret, duchess of (1623-73): [*Poems and Fancies* (1653)]

Opie, Amelia (1769-1853): [*Adeline Mowbray* (1804); *Simple Tales* (1806)]

*Palmerin of England* (sixteenth century): attr. Francisco de Moraes

*Pleasing History, or the Adventures of Hau Kiou Choan*, Chinese novel, tr. from the Portuguese by Thomas Percy (1761)

*Pompey the Little* [*The History of Pompey the Little: or the Life and Adventures of a Lap-Dog*] (1751). [Francis Coventry (1725–54)]

Pratt, Samuel Jackson [a.k.a. Courtney Melmoth] (1749–1814): *Emma Corbett*

Prévost, Antoine-François, l'Abbé (1696–1763): *Chevalier de Grieux et Manon Lescaut* (1753)

Rabelais, François (1494?–1553): *Gargantua and Pantagruel* (1533–34)

Ramsay, Andrew (1686–1743): *Le Voyages de Cyrus* (1727)

Reeve, Clara (1729–1807): *Edward the Black Prince*; i.e., *Memoirs of Sir Roger de Clarendon, the Natural Son of Edward Prince of Wales* (1793)

Riccoboni, Marie-Jeanne Laboras de Mézières (1713–92): [*Marquis de Cressy* (1758); *Ernestine* (1770–98); *Letters of Sophie de Vallière* (1772)]

Rousseau, Jean-Jacques (1712–78): *Julie, ou la Nouvelle Héloïse* (1761); *Émile* (1762)

*St. Leon.* See Godwin.

St. Pierre, Jacques-Henri Bernardin de (1737–1814): *Paul et Virginie* (1787); *La Chaumiere Indienne* (1791)

Scarron, Paul (1610–60): *Le Roman Comique* (1651; 1657)

Schiller, Johann Christoph Friedrich von (1759–1805): *The Ghost Seer* (1786–89)

Scudéry, Madeleine de (1607–91): [*The Grand Cyrus* (1649–53); *Cassandra*]

Sheridan, Frances (1724–66): *The Memoirs of Miss Sidney Bidulph* (1761)

Sidney, Sir Philip (1554–86): *Arcadia* (1581; 1583–84)

Smollett, Tobias (1721–71): [*Roderick Random* (1748); *Peregrine Pickle* (1751); *The Expedition of Humphry Clinker* (1771)]

*Sorcerer.* [Georg Leonhard Wächter]

Staël, Anne-Louise-Germaine Necker, Mme de (1766–1817): *Delphine* (1802); *Corinne* (1807)

Sterne, Laurence (1713–68): *Life and Opinions of Tristram Shandy* (1759–67); *A Sentimental Journey* (1768)

Swift, Jonathan (1667–1745): *Gulliver's Travels* (1726)

Tasso, Torquato (1594–95): *Gerusalemme Liberata* (1581)

Terrasson, Jean (1670-1750): *Sethos* (1731)

[Turpin, Bishop of]: *Song of Roland* (c. 1110)

*Vicar of Wakefield* (1764): [Oliver Goldsmith (?1730-74)]

Voltaire [Arouet, François-Marie] (1694-1778): *Candide* (1759); *Babouc* (1754); *L'Ingenu* (1767)

West, Jane (1758-1852): [*The Advantages of Education* (1793); *A Gossip's Story* (1796); *A Tale of the Times* (1799)]

Wieland, Christoph Martin (1733-1813): [*Oberon* (1780) and others]; *Agathon* [*Geschichte des Agathon*](1766-67); *Peregrine Proteus* (1796; English translation)]

Xenophon (b. 430 BC-c. 355): [*Cyropedia* (*The Education of Cyrus*, tr. into English 1632)]

*Zeluco* (1786): John Moore (1729-1802)

## Sources of the Texts

### Manuscripts

Barbauld, Anna Letitia. "Inscription for an Ice-House." Copy by Elizabeth Bridget Fox, in Add. MS 51,515, fols. 32-33. British Library. Quoted by permission.

———. "To a Little Invisible Being...." "Miscellaneous Extracts in Prose and Poetry." Bound MS book, ca. 1828, copyist unknown. Private collection.

———. "To Doctor Aikin." MS 920 NIC 22/2/6, fols. 7-10. Liverpool Record Office, Liverpool Libraries and Information Services. (Copy of "The Four Sisters" by Matthew Nicholson. Quoted by permission.)

### Books

Aikin, John. *Evenings at Home; or, The Juvenile Budget Opened. Consisting of a Variety of Miscellaneous Pieces, for the Instruction and Amusement of Young Persons.* Vol. I. London: J. Johnson, 1792. ("The Young Mouse" and "Things by their Right Names.")

———. *Evenings at Home....* Vol. VI. London: J. Johnson, 1796. ("The Four Sisters.")

Aikin, John, and Anna Letitia. *Miscellaneous Pieces, in Prose.* London: J. Johnson, 1773. ("Against Inconsistency in our Expectations" and "An Enquiry into those Kinds of Distress which Excite Agreeable Sensations.") Second edition, 1775; third edition, 1792 ("Thoughts on the Devotional Taste ...," revised text).

Barbauld, Anna Letitia. *An Address to the Opposers of the Repeal of the Corporation and Test Acts.* London: J. Johnson, 1790. Revised in second edition, 1790; third and fourth editions, 1790.

———. *The British Novelists: with an Essay; and Prefaces, Biographical and Critical, by Mrs. Barbauld.* 50 vols. London: F.C. and J. Rivington *et al.*, 1810. Second edition, 1820.

———. *The Correspondence of Samuel Richardson, author of Pamela, Clarissa, and Sir Charles Grandison, selected from the Original Manuscripts, bequeathed by him to his family. To which are prefixed a Biographical Account of that author, and observations on his writings.* 6 vols. London: Richard Phillips, 1804.

———. *Devotional Pieces, compiled from the Psalms and the Book of Job: to which are prefixed, Thoughts on the Devotional Taste, on Sects, and on Establishments.* London: J. Johnson, 1775.

———: *Hymns in Prose for Children.* London: J. Johnson, 1781. Revised in "sixteenth" edition, 1814.

———. *A Legacy for Young Ladies, consisting of Miscellaneous Pieces, in prose and verse, by the late Mrs. Barbauld.* London: Longman, Hurst, Rees, Orme, Brown, and Green, 1826. ("On Female Studies" and "Letter from Grimalkin to Selima.")

———. *Poems.* London: J. Johnson, 1773. Second and third (revised) editions, 1773; fourth edition, 1774; fifth edition, 1776-77; revised edition, 1792.

———. *The Poems of Anna Letitia Barbauld.* Ed. William McCarthy and Elizabeth Kraft. Athens: The University of Georgia Press, 1994.

———. *Sins of Government, Sins of the Nation; or, a Discourse for the Fast, appointed on April 19, 1793. By a Volunteer.* London: J. Johnson, 1793. Second, third, and fourth editions, 1793.

———. *The Works of Anna Laetitia Barbauld. With a Memoir by Lucy Aikin.* 2 vols. London: Longman, Hurst, Rees, Orme, Brown, and Green, 1825. ("Dialogue in the Shades.")

[LeBreton, Anna Letitia.] *Memories of Seventy Years by one of a literary family.* Ed. Mrs Herbert Martin. London: Griffith & Farran, 1883. ("[Lines to Anne Wakefield ... ].")

Aikin, John. *A Description of the Country from Thirty to Forty Miles round Manchester*. 1795. Reprint. New York: Augustus M. Kelley, 1968.

——. Letter to James Montgomery, 29 Feb. 1812. Manuscript from Sheffield Literary and Philosophical Society Collection (Correspondence of James Montgomery) SLPS 36/245. Sheffield Archives, 52 Shoreham Street, Sheffield S1 4SP. Quoted by permission.

——. "On the Inequality of Conditions." *Letters from a Father to his Son, on various Topics*. 2nd ed. London: J. Johnson, 1794. 207–19.

Aikin, Lucy. "Memoir." In *The Works of Anna Laetitia Barbauld*. 1: [v]–lxxii.

——. *Memoir of John Aikin, M.D. With a Selection of his Miscellaneous Pieces*. 2 vols. London: Baldwin, Cradock and Joy, 1823.

——. *Memoirs, Miscellanies and Letters*. Ed. Philip Hemery LeBreton. London: Longman, 1864.

*Analytical Review*, 16 (1793):182–86. Review of *Sins of Government*.

Anderson, John. "'The First Fire': Barbauld Rewrites the Greater Romantic Lyric." *Studies in English Literature*, 34 (1994):719–38.

*Anti-Jacobin Review*, 42 (1812):203–09. Review of *Eighteen Hundred and Eleven*.

Appleby, Joyce, *et al. Telling the Truth about History*. New York: Norton, 1994.

Armstrong, Isobel. "The Gush of the Feminine: How Can We Read Women's Poetry of the Romantic Period?" In *Romantic Women Writers: Voices and Countervoices*, ed. Paula R. Feldman and Theresa M. Kelley. Hanover, N.H.: University Press of New England, 1995. 13–32.

*The Athenaeum*, 2 (1807): 512–13.

Balfour, Clara. *Working Women of the last Half Century: The Lesson of their Lives*. London: Cash, 1854.

[Barbauld, Anna Letitia]. "Comparison of Manners." *Athenaeum*, 1 (1807):111-21. Signed "Balance."

———. *Lessons for Children of Three Years Old*. 2 vols. London: J. Johnson, 1778.

———. Letter to John Aikin, 19 Jan. 1780. MS 15/21, fol. 31. The Hornel Library, Kirkcudbright, Scotland.

———. Letter to Judith Beecroft, 19 March 1812. MS, The Hyde Collection, Somerville, NJ. Quoted by permission.

———. Letter to Nicholas Clayton, 21 Feb. [1776]. MS 920 NIC 9/8/1. Liverpool Record Office, Liverpool Libraries and Information Services. Quoted by permission.

———. Letter to Sarah Taylor, 13 Aug. [1807]. MS. Waidner-Spahr Library, Dickinson College, Carlisle, PA. Quoted by permission.

[———]. "Memoir of the Rev. R. Barbauld." *Monthly Repository*, 3 (1808):706-09.

[———]. [Obituary of Thomas Mulso.] *Monthly Magazine*, 7 (1799):163.

———. "Opprobrious Appellations Reprobated." *Monthly Magazine*, 14 (1802):480-82.

———. "Preliminary Essay to the Selection from the Spectator, &c." *Selections from the Spectator, Tatler, Guardian, and Freeholder*. Vol. 1. London: Johnson, 1804.

———. *Remarks on Mr. Gilbert Wakefield's Enquiry into the Expediency and Propriety of Public or Social Worship*. London: Johnson, 1792.

Barker-Benfield, G.J. *The Culture of Sensibility: Sex and Society in Eighteenth-Century England*. Chicago: University of Chicago Press, 1992.

Battestin, Martin C. with Ruthe R. Battestin. *Henry Fielding: A Life*. London and New York: Routledge 1989.

Battestin, Martin C. "Pictures of Fielding," *Eighteenth-Century Studies* 17 (1983): 1-13.

Beattie, James. "On Fable and Romance." *Dissertations Moral and Critical*. Vol. 3. 1783. Reprint. Philadelphia, 1809.

Bennet, William. Letter to Gilbert Wakefield, 10 Sept. 1773. MS 15/21, fol. 6a. The Hornel Library, Kirkcudbright, Scotland. Quoted by permission.

Blair, Hugh. *Lectures on Rhetoric and Belles Lettres*. 2nd ed. London: Strahan, 1785.

Boswell, James. *An Account of Corsica, the Journal of a Tour to that Island, and Memoirs of Pascal Paoli*. 3rd ed. London: Dilly, 1769.

Bright, Henry A. *A Historical Sketch of Warrington Academy*. Liverpool: Brakell, 1859.

*British Critic*, 2 (1793):81–85. Review of *Sins of Government*.

Brooke, Frances. *The History of Emily Montague*. Ed. Mary Jane Edwards. Ottawa: Carleton University Press, 1985.

Bunyan, John. *The Pilgrim's Progress from this World to That which is to Come*. Ed. James Blanton Wharey. 2nd ed., rev. Roger Sharrock. Oxford: Clarendon Press, 1960.

Burke, Edmund. *A Philosophical Enquiry into the Origin of our Ideas of the Sublime and Beautiful*. Ed. Adam Phillips. Oxford: Oxford University Press, 1990.

——. *Reflections on the Revolution in France*. Ed. William B. Todd. New York: Rinehart, 1959.

Burnet, Thomas. *The Theory of the Earth*. Books 1–2. 1691. Reprint. London: Centaur Press, 1965.

Burney, Frances. *Journals and Letters*. Vol. 4. Ed. Joyce Hemlow. Oxford: Clarendon Press, 1973.

*Cambridge History of English Literature*, ed. Sir A.W. Ward and A.R. Waller. Vol. 11. New York: G.P. Putnam's Sons, 1914.

Carter, Elizabeth. *A Series of Letters between Mrs. Elizabeth Carter and Miss Catherine Talbot*. Ed. Montagu Pennington. 2 vols. London: Rivington, 1808.

Cash, Arthur. *Laurence Sterne: The Early and Middle Years*. London: Routledge, 1975.

——. *Laurence Sterne: The Later Years*. London: Routledge, 1986.

Castle, Terry. *The Female Thermometer: Eighteenth-Century Culture and the Invention of the Uncanny*. New York: Oxford University Press, 1995.

——. "Unruly and Unresigned." *Times Literary Supplement*, 10–16 Nov. 1989: 1228.

Chandler, David. "Wordsworth's 'Night-Piece' and Mrs. Barbauld." *Notes and Queries*, 238 (1993):40–41.

Chapone, Hester Mulso. *Letters on the Improvement of the Mind.* 3rd ed. 2 vols. London, 1774.

Cobbold, Elizabeth. Draft letter to Sir James Edward Smith, 31 May 1812. MS HA 231/3/2/38. Suffolk Record Office, Ipswich, England. Quoted by permission.

Coleridge, Samuel Taylor. *Collected Letters.* Ed. Earl Leslie Griggs. Vol. 1. Oxford: Clarendon Press, 1966.

———. *Complete Poetical Works.* Ed. Ernest Hartley Coleridge. Vol. 1. Oxford: Clarendon Press, 1912.

Colley, Linda. *Britons: Forging the Nation, 1707-1837.* New Haven: Yale University Press, 1992.

Colman, George, the Elder. *Polly Honeycomb, a Dramatick Novel in One Act.* London, 1760.

Colquhoun, Patrick. *A Treatise on the Police of the Metropolis.* 7th ed. London: Mawman et al., 1806.

Cookson, J.E. *The Friends of Peace: Anti-War Liberalism in England, 1793-1815.* Cambridge: Cambridge University Press, 1982.

*Critical Review,* 35 (1773):192-95. Review of Aikin's *Poems.*

[Croker, John Wilson.] Review of *Eighteen Hundred and Eleven.* *Quarterly Review,* 7 (1812):309-13.

Crook, Ronald E. *A Bibliography of Joseph Priestley.* London: The Library Association, 1966.

Cruden, Alexander. *A Complete Concordance to the Holy Scriptures.* [1737] New ed., ed. Alfred Jones. Chicago: Fleming H. Revell Co., n.d.

Davies, D.W. "'A Tongue in Every Star': Wordsworth and Mrs. Barbauld's 'A Summer Evening's Meditation.'" *Notes and Queries,* ns 43 (1996): 29-30.

Day, Robert Adams. *Told in Letters: Epistolary Fiction before Richardson.* Ann Arbor: University of Michigan Press, 1966.

"Death of His Majesty George the Third." *Monthly Repository,* 15 (1820): 117-18.

*The Debate on a Motion for the Abolition of the Slave-Trade, in the House of Commons, ... on April 18 and 19, 1791.* London: Woodfall, 1791.

*Debate on the Repeal of the Test and Corporation Act, In the House of Commons, March 28th, 1787*. London: Stockdale, 1787.

"Demophilus." "Remarks on the Letter on Inequality of Conditions," *Athenaeum*, 2 (1807): 240-41.

DeQuincey, Thomas. *Autobiography*. In *Collected Writings*, ed. David Masson. Vol. 11. London: Black, 1897.

Eaves, T.C. Duncan, and Kimpel, Ben D. *Samuel Richardson: A Biography*. Oxford: Clarendon Press, 1971.

Edgeworth, Maria. *Castle Rackrent and Ennui*. Ed. Marilyn Butler. London: Penguin, 1992.

———. Letter to C.S. Edgeworth, Nov. 1817. MS 10,166, item 1386. National Library of Ireland. Quoted by permission.

———. *Letters from England, 1813-1844*, ed. Christina Colvin. Oxford: Clarendon Press, 1971.

Edgeworth, Richard Lovell. Commentary on "Ode to Spring." MS Eng. misc. c. 894. Bodleian Library, University of Oxford. Quoted by permission.

Ellis, Grace A. *Memoir, Letters, and a Selection from the Poems and Prose Writings of Anna Letitia Barbauld*. 2 vols. Boston: Osgood, 1874.

[Enfield, William.] Review of *Devotional Pieces*. *Monthly Review*, 53 (1775):419-23.

Feldman, Paula R., ed. *British Women Poets of the Romantic Era*. Baltimore: Johns Hopkins University Press, 1997.

Ferguson, Moira. *Subject to Others: British Women Writers and Colonial Slavery, 1670-1834*. New York: Routledge, 1992.

Fleming, Marjory. *The Complete Marjory Fleming: Her Journals, Letters, and Verse*. Ed. Frank Sidgwick. London: Sidgwick and Jackson, 1934.

Fussell, Paul. *Doing Battle: The Making of a Skeptic*. Boston: Little, Brown, 1996.

Genlis, Stéphanie Félicité de. *Adelaide and Theodore; or, Letters on Education*. 3rd ed. 3 vols. London: Cadell, 1788.

*Gentleman's Magazine*, 45 (1775):581-83. Review of *Devotional Pieces*.

———, 60 (1790):347-48. Review of *An Address to the Opposers of the Repeal of the Corporation and Test Acts*.

Gerard, Alexander. *An Essay on Taste*. London: Millar, 1759.

Goodwin, Albert. *The Friends of Liberty: The English Democratic Movement in the Age of the French Revolution.* London: Hutchinson, 1979.

Gregory, John. *A Comparative View of the State and Faculties of Man, with those of the Animal World.* London: Dodsley, 1765.

———. *A Father's Legacy to His Daughters.* 1774. Reprint Boston, 1834.

Hale, Sarah Josepha. *Woman's Record: or, Sketches of all Distinguished Women ... to A.D. 1854.* New York: Harper, 1855.

Hazlitt, William. "On the Living Poets." In *Complete Works*, ed. P. P. Howe. Vol. 5. New York: AMS Press, 1967.

Holmes, Richard. *Coleridge: Early Visions.* New York: Viking, 1990.

Howes, Alan B., ed. *Sterne: The Critical Heritage.* London: Routledge and Kegan Paul, 1974.

Huet, Pierre-Daniel. *Memoirs of the Life of Peter Daniel Huet, Bishop of Avranches*, tr. John Aikin. 2 vols. London: Longman *et al.*, 1810.

———. *Treatise of Romances and their Original*, tr. Roger L'Estrange. London, 1672.

Hume, David. *Enquiries Concerning the Human Understanding and Concerning the Principles of Morals.* Ed. L. A. Selby-Bigge. 2nd ed. Oxford: Clarendon Press, 1902.

———. *Selected Essays.* Ed. Stephen Copley and Andrew Edgar. Oxford: Oxford University Press, 1993.

Hutcheson, Francis. *A Short Introduction to Moral Philosophy.* 1747. Reprint. Philadelphia: Crukshank, 1788.

[Jeffrey, Francis.] Review of *Poems in Two Volumes* by Wordsworth. *Edinburgh Review*, 11 (1807):214-31.

Jewson, C.B. *The Jacobin City: A Portrait of Norwich in its Reaction to the French Revolution, 1788-1802.* Glasgow: Blackie, 1975.

Johnson, Samuel. *Johnson on Shakespeare.* Ed. Arthur Sherbo. New Haven: Yale University Press, 1968.

———. *Lives of the English Poets.* Ed. George Birkbeck Hill. 3 vols. Oxford: Clarendon Press, 1905.

Keach, William. "A Regency Prophecy and the End of Anna Barbauld's Career." *Studies in Romanticism*, 33 (1994):569–77.

Keate, William. *A Free Examination of Dr. Price's and Dr. Priestley's Sermons*. London: Dodsley, 1790.

Kenrick, Norah, ed. *Chronicles of a Nonconformist Family: The Kenricks of Wynne Hall, Exeter and Birmingham*. Birmingham: Cornish, 1932.

Kenrick, Samuel. Letter to Timothy Kenrick, 7 June 1795. MS Sharpe 178/48, University College London, Library. Quoted by permission.

Kraft, Elizabeth. "Anna Letitia Barbauld's 'Washing Day' and the Montgolfier Balloon," *Literature and History* 4.2 (1995): 25–41.

*Lady's Monthly Museum*, 1 (1798):169–79. "Mrs. Anna Letitia Barbauld."

La Rochefoucauld, François de. *A Frenchman's Year in Suffolk: French Impressions of Suffolk Life in 1784*. Trans. and ed. Norman Scarfe. Suffolk Records Society, vol. 30. N.p.: Boydell Press, [1988].

LeBreton, Anna Letitia. *Memoir of Mrs. Barbauld*. London: Bell, 1874.

Lewis, Andrea. "A New Letter by Elizabeth Gaskell." *English Language Notes*, 30.3 (March 1993), 53–58.

Lindsey, Theophilus. "Preface." *An Answer to Mr. Paine's Age of Reason* by Joseph Priestley. London: Johnson, 1795.

*Literary Gazette*, 453 (24 Sept. 1825), 611–12. Review of *Works*.

Lonsdale, Roger, ed. *Eighteenth-Century Women Poets: An Oxford Anthology*. Oxford: Oxford University Press, 1989.

*A Look to the Last Century: or, the Dissenters weighed in their own Scales*. London: White and Faulder, 1790.

McCarthy, William. "The Celebrated Academy at Palgrave: A Documentary History of Anna Letitia Barbauld's School." *The Age of Johnson*, 8 (1997): 279–392.

———. "Mother of All Discourses: Anna Barbauld's *Lessons for Children*." *Princeton University Library Chronicle*, 60 (1998–99): 196–219.

———. "'We Hoped the *Woman* Was Going to Appear': Desire, Repression, and Gender in Anna Barbauld's Early Poems." *Romantic Women Writers: Voices and Counter-Voices*, ed. Paula Feldman and Theresa Kelley. Hanover, NH: University Press of New England, 1995. 113-37.

Mackintosh, Robert James, ed. *Memoirs of the Life of ... Sir James Mackintosh*. 2nd ed. 2 vols. London, 1836.

Mallet, David. *The Works of David Mallet*. New ed. London, 1759.

Marmontel, Jean-François. *Belisarius*. London: Vaillant, 1767.

Martineau, David. *Notes on the Pedigree of the Martineau Family*. London: privately printed, 1907.

Martineau, Harriet. *Autobiography*. Vol. 1. 1877. Reprint. London: Virago, 1983.

Mautner, Thomas. "Introduction." *On Human Nature*, by Francis Hutcheson. Ed. Thomas Mautner. Cambridge: Cambridge University Press, 1993.

Medvedev, Roy A. *On Socialist Democracy*. Trans. Ellen de Kadt. New York: Norton, 1977.

Merians, Maria Sybilla. *Dissertatio de Generatione et Metamorphosibus Insectorum Surinamensium*. The Hague: Gosse, 1726.

Messenger, Ann. *His and Hers: Essays in Restoration and Eighteenth-Century Literature*. Lexington: University Press of Kentucky, 1986.

Milton, John. *Complete Poetry*. Rev ed. Ed. John T. Shawcross. Garden City, NY: Doubleday, 1971.

*Monthly Review*, ns 1 (1790):460-62. Review of *Address to the Opposers of the Repeal of the Corporation and Test Acts*.

———, ns 6 (1791):226-27. Review of *An Epistle to William Wilberforce*.

Moore, John. "A View of the Commencement and Progress of Romance." *The Works of Tobias Smollett, M.D.* 1797; New ed., ed. James P. Browne. Vol. 1. London, 1872.

More, Hannah. *Works of Hannah More*. Vol. 7. London: Fisher, 1837.